W9-CCB-801

DEN

OF

VIPERS

K.A. KNIGHT

CONTENTS

CHAPTER ONE

"Y ou understand what that means, don't you, Rob?" Ryder murmurs as he straightens his suit, not that it was even wrinkled in the first place. Fuckeralways dresses like he's ready to walk a runway. Though the cold calculation in his gaze lets you know he's not just a pretty face.

I told him once I could scar his face for him, it might make others take him more seriously. I don't know why he said no.

I, on the other hand, am covered in Rob's blood, so is Garrett for that matter. His scarred, tatted up knuckles bleed from the punches he delivered to our unhappy host. Munching on the guy's crisps, I watch in glee as Garrett delivers another brutal blow before stepping back. There's a reason they call him Mad Dog in the ring—you don't even see the big bastard coming. I'd know, I've fought him a couple of times. They were good times, even if I did break some bones.

Blinking, I look back at the man in the chair opposite Ryder. Rob's eye is ballooned shut, his lip split and cheek already bruising. And those are only the wounds you can see. I know there are a few blisters forming under his shirt from where Ryder let me have some fun.

Kenzo is leaning against the wall opposite me, his dice rolling between his fingers like always. His face, similar to Ryder's, is locked in a death stare with the man, waiting for something interesting to happen. It was Kenzo who brought this man to our attention, after all. But Rob looks only to Ryder—good. Let him think Ryder is the only one in charge, we like to keep it that way. To have him as the face of our...company.

I snort at that, fucking company. We do have a few legit businesses, not that I have anything to do with them. I was deemed too insane to deal with employees after I burned one of their eyes out for calling me scum.

"Rob, pay attention, I don't like to repeat myself," Ryder snaps, so Garrett grabs Rob's greying, short hair and yanks his head back, a blade appearing in his hand, which he presses to the shaking man's throat. Sweat drips down his face as he cries out, and I wonder if Ryder will let me kill him.

It's been a whole two days since I got to kill someone, and I'm getting restless.

"Yes, yes, I understand, take her!" he screams.

What a prick. The loser would sell his own daughter to cover his debt to us. I suppose when you don't have the money to pay, and the only other option is to take it from your flesh...you become real easy on what you're willing to do.

This city is ours, he would never escape us. He knows that, it's written in the defeat in his brown eyes. I wonder if his daughter is better looking than him, either way, she'll be ours now. We normally don't deal in flesh, well, not live flesh, but beggars can't be choosers.

A debt is a debt, and it has to be paid or others will start to think we're going soft.

Ryder leans back, a smirk curling up his pretty boy lips. Rolling my eyes, I step forward from the dark, and that's when Rob starts to cry. He knows what I am—death. Ryder might be the face,

Garret might be the enforcer, the muscle, and Kenzo the dealer...but me?

I'm the fucking Grim Reaper.

"Have her!" he screams, thrashing in Garrett's grip, whose face tightens in disgust. Me? I laugh.

Leaning down, I get into his face, letting him see the madness in my gaze. My fingers itch to grab my lighter, to burn his house down with him in it until I hear his screams. Fuck, I can almost taste the fear, feel the flames licking me—my cock hardens in my trousers at the image.

"Tell me, when I burn her, will you care or not?" I laugh.

Garrett grins, flashing perfectly white teeth. The bastard is almost as crazy as I am, probably from one too many blows to his massive head. I smirk at him. "I wonder if she bleeds as pretty?"

"Enough," Ryder snaps, so I move away, doing as I'm told. "Where is she?"

"She-she owns a bar on the south side of the city, Roxers." He quivers, crying like a pussy. Big, fat tears drip down his face.

I wonder if she'll cry. It makes it sweeter when they do. I realise then I'm rubbing my cock through my jeans, and Kenzo is glaring at me, so I stop with a wink.

"Rob, if we aren't satisfied with her as payment, we'll be back, you can bet on that," Kenzo adds decisively, ending this deal. He knows the look on my face.

I want blood.

"Will you kill her?" Rob sobs pathetically.

"Do you care?" Ryder counters, arching an eyebrow at the man. "You just sold your daughter to cover your debt without even trying to stop us."

"I-I'm a shit father, but she deserves better than you monsters," he snarls, showing the first bit of balls I've seen from him.

"Hear that, Ry? We're monsters," I boom, laughing so hard I smack my jeans. "I told you that suit ain't fooling anyone, man."

Like usual, Ryder ignores my manic outbursts. "We'll do whatever we want to her. Fuck her. Torture her. Beat her. Kill her. I just wanted you to know that," Ryder remarks as he stands, buttoning his blue suit as he does so. Habitually, he swipes back his perfect hair and aims a business-like smile at Rob.

"We will be in touch." He turns and starts to walk away.

Kenzo pushes off the wall, pocketing his dice. "Don't be a stranger at the tables."

I laugh harder as Garrett releases Rob's neck, tapping his cheek with the blade, all friendly like. Me? I get in the man's face again, wanting him to look into the eyes of the man who's going to wreck his daughter. When I'm done with her, there won't even be enough to bury. "I'm going to make her scream, I might even record it for you."

"Diesel," Ryder calls from the doorway of the shitty little two-story house we're in.

Leaning forward, I press my lips near the man's ear. "I'll let you know if she comes before or after I slice her neck," I whisper, before lunging forward and biting off his earlobe.

He screams as I howl with laughter, spitting the flesh and blood across his chest as I turn to leave, whistling to myself as the copper tang fills my mouth and drips down my chin.

"You're a crazy bastard," Garrett grumbles.

"You too, brother, now let's go get our new toy!" I declare, suddenly in a good mood with the prospect of torture on the horizon.

Rob should have known better, the whole city should...

When you fuck with Vipers, you get fangs.

That poor little girl has no idea what's coming her way...

CHAPTER TWO

ROXY

"Alright, alright, I get it. You're the prettiest butterfly in the butterfly farm." I nod seriously as I grip Henry's shoulder and press him down, helping him into the cab. "See you tomorrow, Henry. Try not to choke on your own vomit." I chuckle as I slam the door shut. Heading to the front, I pass the driver some money and tell him Henry's address.

As a regular, he's here every night. I asked him once why he drank. Honestly, I didn't expect an answer. The poor bastard's daughter died a few years back. Murdered. Ever since, he drowns his sorrows, and I make sure he gets home okay. He might be a drunk, but I have a soft spot for him. I can see the pain in his eyes, and any father who cares that much about his daughter is a good man. But maybe that's my own daddy complex talking.

Turning back to my bar, I grin at the exterior. She ain't much to look at, but she's all mine. "Roxers," written in bright red LED letters, hangs above the door which has seen better days. She's rundown for sure, a dive, but she's one hell of a place to drink. The outside looks like an old cabin of some kind. Made from wood and mismatched brick. She has a porch wrapped all the way around where the patrons all smoke, with bike spaces in front of her. The two swinging doors are unlocked at the moment, and the filthy windows leave you unable to look inside.

We get all types here—truckers, bikers, criminals. Everyone is welcome. There's only one rule—don't break the fucking furniture. It's an old rule, put into place before I even owned it, I just carried on the tradition. The sandy parking lot is empty, apart from my beat-up muscle car that I won in a bet, so I head back inside, flicking off the sign as I go so everyone knows we're closed.

It's early, almost time for the sun to come up. I guess owning a bar makes me a nocturnal creature, I did always prefer the night and all the fun that comes with it. Sighing, I brush back my silver hair and put it in a quick ponytail as I start to close up. I sent Travis home earlier, his grandma is sick and needed his help, so clean up is on me now. Picking up one of the mismatched chairs, I lay it on the table before collecting the glasses, as many as I can.

I head towards the back, past the pool tables and dartboards, and march up the stairs to the left. I push open the kitchen door with my hip and rinse the glasses before running them through the washer. Flicking off the kitchen light, I walk back into the bar area to mop the floor, not that it stops it from being a sticky mess you wouldn't want to walk on with bare feet, but it's a habit.

To my left is the old bar, the top made from beer tops set in resin, a gift. It's clear of bottles at the moment, the differing stools empty before it. The old, wooden shelves hold every type of liquor you can imagine and the kegs waiting to be filled.

I already sorted the bar and cash register while Henry was pretending to be a butterfly, so not much more to do now before I can collapse into bed. Fuck, I need to find a new bartender. It's hard finding one with experience who will last here though. They either speak too freely or fall in with the bad crowd. Yeah, you can't look on a job website for this one, folks.

The last one we had was sent to jail for murder. Yeah, that's the kind of place it is. Although, I gotta say, I miss the old bastard, he played a mean hand of poker. I stop when I pass the door, and it swings shut behind me.

There, in my bar, are four massive men. Tattoos cover their knuckles and necks, one even has his head shaved. Unsavoury sorts, of course, but that ain't different from the usual around here. Their clothing is all black, and I narrow my eyes, assessing them quickly. "We're closed," I tell them, hoping they will take a hint.

Fucking sloppy, I didn't lock the door. That's what pulling pints and breaking up fights for fourteen days straight will do to you. I'm in desperate need of a day off, and now these assholes waltz in here like they own the joint.

One cracks his knuckles as they all smirk at me. If they think that will scare me, they should think again. I drink beer with men who would make these guys piss themselves, and I usually drink them under the table.

Everyone knows Roxers, and everyone knows me...and not to fuck with me. There's a reason they all call me Swinger, and it ain't 'cause I go to sex parties. Sliding closer to the bar, I slip my hand behind it, connecting with the smooth wood of my trusty bat, the bitch smacker. "I said we're closed. Better get out, boys."

"Or what?" one of them challenges as he steps forward. The fucker has a scar right across his eyelid. "Going to cry for help?" He laughs, and the others join in.

Rolling my eyes, I pull out my bat and rest it on my shoulder. "No, I'll break your fucking kneecaps and toss you outside like the garbage you are. Now, one more warning—we're closed."

They share looks again. "Is this broad serious?"

"Broad?" I snap, low and deadly as I step closer. "Did you just call me a broad?"

They ignore me, of course, so I palm my bat. That prick gets it first. Ain't nobody insulting me in my own bar, that's just plain rude.

Heading their way while they're still arguing about how best to grab me, I swing, letting the full force of the bat hit the asshole's knees. He crumples to the floor, a scream erupting from his throat as I smirk down at him from my five foot six frame—well, five foot nine with my biker boots. "Want to call me a broad again?"

"Fucking get her!" he wheezes, so I kick him in the balls, making him fall back with a cry as I turn to face the others, ducking their grabbing hands.

Swinging my bat, I hit one of them right in the junk, and he goes down hard, so I bring up my knee and smash it into his nose, hearing the crack as it bursts like a peach. Fuck, now there's blood on my floor. I just mopped!

Angry now, I swing like a woman possessed as the other two duck and dive, trying to stay out of my path. One of them falls onto a stool, smashing it beneath his gigantic frame. I freeze, my eyes narrowing dangerously, and he scampers backwards.

"Did you just break my stool?" I seethe.

He gulps as I fling myself at him with a *Braveheart* worthy war cry. I smack him with the bat, making him grunt. He punches his fist out as I kneel down to get his face. It connects with my jaw, and my head jerks to the side, blood filling my mouth.

Deadly fury fills me.

Turning back slowly, I glare down at him and he knows he fucked up. Just then, arms come around me from behind, hoisting me to my feet. Smashing my head back, I connect with the guy's chin, stomping on his foot as I elbow his junk and slip out of his hold while he grunts in pain.

Thank you very much, *Miss Congeniality*.

Lining up my bat, I swing, hitting him square in the face. He actually flies backwards from the force, landing hard on the floor and almost shaking the building. He stays down. One to go. I turn back to the guy who broke my stool. He's just getting to his feet, so I kick them out from under him, sweeping my leg as I bring my bat down across his spine.

He slumps forward, so I smash it down on the back of his head.

Whistling, I look around to see the first guy struggling to his feet, so I throw my bat at him, and it does as its name suggests—hits the bitch. He's out cold.

Stomping through the mess and their bodies, I pick up my bat and wipe it on his shirt before putting it on a nearby table. Propping my hands on my hips, I sigh at the sight before me. Now how the hell do I get them out?

Resigned, I grab one of their collars and start to tug, but he's a big bastard, so I pick one of the smaller guys first. Bending, I hoist my hands under his shoulders and grunt as I yank him towards the door.

The door that's swinging open.

I lift my head, blowing my hair from my face, and drop the guy I'm trying to drag to the door. Travis stands there, open-mouthed. He's still in this black Roxers shirt, which is tucked into blue jeans, and boots, his deceptively thin frame shivering from the cold. He flips his blue hair from his face, his green eyes peering at me. "Jesus, Roxy, what the fuck happened?"

"That one called me a broad, that one broke the furniture, I didn't like the other two's faces." I shrug, wiping away the sweat on my brow with my arm. "Whatcha doing here?"

"Forgot my key," he murmurs, looking at my handiwork.

"Good, you can help me toss these assholes outside." I grin, and he shakes his head.

"Never a dull day with you, babe." He drops his bag, though, and heads my way. With his help, it only takes me five minutes to toss them into the alley out back. Dusting off my hands, I head back inside, making sure to lock the door this time as I dial the local police. I'm going to tell them what happened and where the guys are, no doubt they will get spooked at the sirens and run...if they wake up.

Travis lifts his finger, showing me his keys as I lean against the bar. "You going to be okay?" he mouths.

I nod and wave him away as someone finally answers, then I relay the information before hanging up, ignoring the questions they sputter at me. "Sure thing, tell your grandma I said hi. I'm going to shower and sleep."

"See you tomorrow, babe." He snorts as he leaves.

I lock up behind him, putting the deadbolts and chains in place before heading past the bar and turning off the lights. I activate the alarm and head down the corridor, past the office and toilets, and up the stairs at the back to my place above the bar, where I have lived since I was seventeen.

I really need a day off.

CHAPTER THREE

RYDER

I'm going over tomorrow's calendar when I get the call. Placing the phone back on my desk, I lift my head and narrow my eyes at Garrett, who's prodding his split knuckles in the seat across from me. "Your guys are in lock up."

That gets his attention. He drops his dirty boots from my desk, leaving mud behind, making me frown. "What?" he snarls.

Leaning back in my chair, I steeple my hands. "It seems Rob's daughter managed to get the drop on them, beat them pretty good, and got them arrested."

He blinks, just staring for a moment. "You're fucking kidding? A tiny girl beat up my guys? Four of my guys, for fuck's sake?"

"Yes," I retort, raising my eyebrow.

"Fuck."

"Exactly." I nod. "If you want things done right, you gotta do them yourself. Go get your men free, tomorrow afternoon, we'll

Garrett nods, swearing as he stomps off to do just that. Leaning over, I brush off the dirt he left and go back to my calendar, but my thoughts are distracted by that call. She must have had help. No matter, we'll get her ourselves. No one escapes our clutches.

My office door slams open again, making me sigh as I lean back. Why doesn't anyone knock? Kenzo prowls my way, his thumbs gliding deftly across his phone for such a big man. "Just sent you the info on the girl, I gathered as much as I could. Also asked around a bit," he murmurs as he looks up.

My phone dings, but I ignore it for now. "And?"

"It seems Rob's daughter is quite the legend. Name's Roxy, owns that dive joint across town like he said. Lot of bastards even seem scared of the girl, others respect her. She ain't going to be an easy take."

"Nothing worth having ever is." I sigh as I pick up my phone and scroll through the information. Twenty-four, five foot six. Grey hair, brown eyes. Credit history is shocking, and there are some sealed documents from when she was seventeen. I'll have to ask Garrett about them. I look over her bank information and everything else he's gathered, thumbing through until I hit the end where her picture is.

My heart slams in my chest, my blood roaring straight to my cock, which twitches in my slacks. "Exactly." Kenzo snorts. "Why do you think I didn't just text it? I wanted to see your face. I'm betting you weren't expecting Rob's daughter to be so hot."

"Not at all," I mutter distractedly. Hot is an understatement. She's fucking breathtaking. Dark eyes lined and smoky. Big, plump, red lips. High, arched cheekbones and eyebrows. Short, shoulder-length, unnatural silver hair, which suits her pale complexion. Her cleavage catches my eye in the AC/DC tank top she's wearing when this was taken.

Stunning.

I actually can't speak as I stare at the picture, but then I push it away. This makes it easier, since she's easy to look at. Blinking, I meet

12

Kenzo's laughing eyes to see him discreetly rearranging himself. "I know, bro, first dibs."

I narrow my gaze on him. "Eyes on the prize, baby brother."

"Oh, they are, don't you fucking worry, and Roxy is that prize," he snaps, making me sigh. Whenever Kenzo sets his mind to something, he gets it. No need to bet on the odds on what he plans to do to Roxxane.

But she's a means to an end, a message not to fuck with us. Some of us have to remain smart about this, and as usual, it's me. "Tomorrow, Kenzo. Think with your head, not your dick, until we have her back here."

"And then?" He snorts.

"Then you can do whatever you want with her. She's ours, after all. Though I would suggest you try to keep her away from Diesel." I laugh.

He grins too, not a nice one. "For sure, she's exactly his type. Poor girl would be burnt to a crisp before she stepped through the door."

I nod. "He would, though I suspect he might have his fun with her first."

"I wonder if Garrett will," Kenzo muses, darkening the mood.

"Maybe, if she has that damsel in distress act down. He's a fool for them. Only this time, he might not let her almost ruin him." I sigh.

Kenzo nods, his fists clenching at the reminder of how we had nearly lost our brother. It won't happen again, that's why I'll remain smart even while the others think with their dicks. She might be attractive, but it's not worth losing my family over. I can get pretty pussy anywhere, and I don't have to buy it to get it in my bed.

"I'll keep my eye on him," I offer to mollify my brother. "Now, we have a meeting with the Triad in the morning about the treaty issues. I need you and Garrett with me."

"Not Diesel?" Kenzo questions seriously.

"Not yet, I want to scare them, not kill them. I'm hoping we can resolve this quickly. They're stopping our shipments at the moment, and it's causing a ripple through the business. One I don't like."

"Got it, boss man." Kenzo nods. "Don't forget to try and get some sleep. You're starting to look your age, old man," he teases as he turns to leave.

"Watch your mouth, baby brother. I can still kick your ass," I warn, only making him laugh.

Shaking my head, I turn back to the picture on my phone, my thumb caught just below her mouth. She's going to be trouble, I can feel it. But a Viper never goes back on a deal, Roxxane is ours now. Let's just hope she doesn't cause too many issues, it would be a shame to kill such a beautiful woman.

Dropping my phone to my desk, I get up and stretch. Kenzo is right. I need sleep. It's been two days, and I want to be sharp for tomorrow's meeting. With business plans whirring in my head, I pocket my phone and leave my office. The pounding of Diesel's music hits me out in the hallway, so I head to my bedroom instead of the living area.

Tomorrow is a new day. We're coming for you, Roxxane.

CHAPTER FOUR

ROXY

It's too fucking early. My head pounds as my alarm goes off again. Flinging the stupid old clock across the room, I bury my face in the pillow, seeing the smudges of my makeup there that I couldn't be bothered to take off last night when I crawled into bed after a shot of Jack.

But the alarm goes off again, and thanks to my half-asleep brain, it's now across the room. Sliding from the bed, I crawl over to it and smash it into the floor, groaning when it shatters. But at least the noise stops. I flop to my back in nothing but my panties and a tank top, then I debate calling Travis in to set up today and cover the dinner shift.

But he struggles by himself, so me it is. Defeated, I climb to my feet and flick on the radio, rock pounding out as I head to the shower. Stripping as I go, I turn on the spray and wait for it to warm up. I frown and look at the tangled mess which is my hair, shrugging before throwing it up in a bun. No way am I washing that rat's nest, it takes too long. That's why dry shampoo is a girl's best friend.

I have a quick shower, scrubbing my tattoo-covered skin. That reminds me, I've got another one booked next week with Zeke to finish off the roses across my thigh and the mandala pattern. The sleeve on my left arm is done and took four whole, eight hour sittings. But it was worth it, not that the pain bothers me. In fact, I can admit to myself I even like it. Especially at the hands of the hunk who's doing it.

Flicking off the water, I climb from the shower and wrap a fluffy towel around my body before brushing my teeth and moisturizing. I manage to get a brush through my hair, and it decides to lie nicely for once and hang straight after I dry shampoo it to hell. I take more time with my makeup, applying my signature red lipstick, dark liner, and eyeshadow, making my brown eyes pop. Some call me a typical rocker chick, fuck, I even have the piercings to go along with the tats and makeup.

It started out as a form of rebellion, a way to piss off my asshole father before I ran away. Then I grew to love this look and, well, now? Now it's just me. But that's enough dredging up ghosts from my past before breakfast. Letting the towel drop to the floor, I head into my bedroom again and get dressed. I slip into matching red, front closing bra and panties. My one vice...well, that and band merch.

I add a signed tour shirt from The Killers and tie it at the side before slipping into some tattered black shorts and my trusty high-heeled biker boots. Checking myself out in the mirror once more, I grab my keys and head out, locking up behind me. I trudge down the stairs and flick on the lights in the bar.

I saunter through the kitchen and check the alley, but it seems the assholes from last night got picked up. It makes me wonder who they were, but it wouldn't be the first time someone has jumped me. Nor the last, I'm betting. I leave the back door unlocked for Cook and return to the front.

I turn on the jukebox and get to restocking and tidying up, mad as hell when I have to throw the broken stool out back. One goddamn

16

rule. Jumping me I can understand, but breaking my furniture? Not fucking cool.

Right on time, I hear the telltale rumble of Cook's bike as he pulls up out back, and it makes me smile, least I know he'll feed me...unlike Truck, who works weekends, bastard is colder than a snake, even to me, who pays his bills and employs his ex-con ass.

I meet Cook at the back door, smiling sweetly at him as he swings off his Harley. He groans. "Let me guess, sausage with ketchup?"

"You're a doll." I blow him a kiss, but he stops dead when he sees the broken stool lying on the ground.

His head comes up slowly, his eyes widening. "Fuck, is he dead?"

"What?" I ask, way too tired for this.

"The man who broke the stool?" he queries seriously, making me laugh.

"He wishes he was, don't worry."

Cook chuckles and claps me on the shoulder. "Rich would be proud, kid. Go on, get started out front, I'll make you some food."

My heart cracks at the mention of Rich, but I brush it off, and with a now cheery smile at Cook, I head to the front. By the time the smell of sizzling meat wafts to me, I'm set up and ready, so when Cook pushes through the door, juggling two plates, I almost fall to my knees and worship him.

That's the way to my heart right there, food...or maybe just into my panties. We sit at one of the tables, my elbows sticking to the wood as I scarf down my breakfast, just as there's a knock at the door.

"Uh-oh, that's all you, kid," Cook murmurs with his mouth full, as he grabs both plates and heads back to the kitchen. Sighing, I march over to the door and yank it open.

"Sign says shut, asshole," I snarl, and then roll my eyes when I see who's on the other side. "Fred."

"You really shouldn't talk to cops like that." He smiles and looks behind me. "Going to let me in, Rox?"

"No," I snap, crossing my arms. "What's a matter? I heard or saw nothing before you even ask."

He raises his eyebrow, his fingers going to his trouser buckle. "I didn't even say anything."

"Yeah, well, I know the routine. I ain't pissing off my customers, so no. I don't know them, I don't know where they live, and I sure as shit don't know if they did it."

He shakes his head. "Not why I'm here this time, it's about the guys last night."

"Oh, you got them?" I ask, taking down the defensive attitude just a notch.

"We did, but within two hours, they were bailed out. High friends, if you get my meaning. I don't know who you're messing with, but when the chief tells me to stay clear of them, I do as I'm told. So should you."

"Wait, they got bailed? Who the fuck are those guys? I thought they were just lowlifes."

He winces. "Definitely not. You've pissed someone off, Rox. Better figure out who before I'm cleaning your remains up off the street. Or better yet, get gone. On a plane as far as I'm concerned. Have a good day." He nods, looking around before scurrying back to his car.

Fuck. Gazing around like the paranoid copper, I slam the door and lock it, putting my back to it. *Calm down, Rox, you've had worse. Whoever it is, is just trying to scare you...but to have the cops spooked and in your pocket?*

He's right, high places.

Maybe it would be best to leave, but fuck, this is my home! My goddamn bar. No. Shaking my head, I push away from the door. Ain't nobody scaring me away from here, high places or not.

Prowling to the bar, I pour myself a shot and neck it before slamming the glass to the wood. *Get it together, Rox, ain't no man making me run.* I did it once, never again. This is my life now, I either stand and fight or die. No other options.

Decision made, I throw another shot back before turning on the speakers, letting the music pump through the bar before unlocking

18

the door. It's opening time, and threat hanging over my head or not, I gotta work.

I'll ask around later, though, see what I can hear. If anybody knows something, it's the people who come here to drink away the darkness.

I'm busy after that, the place filling up, and I have no time to think on what someone wants me for. It's mainly food orders with beer, so I'm just pulling a pint when the door swings open, revealing four newcomers.

Four people who definitely don't belong here.

CHAPTER FIVE

GARRETT

The Triad sits before us, well, one of the Triad. They never keep all three leaders in one place at once. A smart move. Keeping my fists behind my back, I play the good little bodyguard, a scare tactic. I'm a big bastard, so I use it. My reputation as a fighter precedes me, even if they don't know I'm one of the Vipers.

Just how I like it.

I want to fly under the radar, it gets me into places and lets me learn things I might not otherwise. "Are you here to hand everything over?" The cocky bastard smirks, his chunky cheeks pulling up in a sickening way, tugging on a scar across his face.

Ryder chuckles, looking comfortable as he leans back in the opposite chair. We're the only people in the restaurant, a neutral place to meet. No blood will be spilled today...especially with D being absent.

"No, I'm here to give you a chance to give us back our shipments and go our separate ways as acquaintances," he rumbles.

The man loses his smile, and I feel Kenzo grinning next to me where we stand behind Ry's chair. He has that effect on people.

"You will all die. We rule this city," the Triad snarls.

Ryder casually sips his wine before looking back at the man. "You own a patch of land outside city limits, you were once rich and powerful. Not anymore. I will squash you like a bug. But remember that when you're torched with your people. Remember the olive branch I offered." He sighs and gets to his feet, buttoning up his suit jacket. To add insult to injury, he throws down the money to cover the bill. "It's on me. I know you're going through financial hardships, wouldn't want you to go bust long before I destroy you."

Without another word, Ryder turns to us, his eyes dark and triumphant. I wait, any moment now...

Boom.

The Triad stands, a snarl on his face. "You're children! You know nothing of this game! My family ran this city before you came along!" he roars.

Ryder glances at him over his shoulder. "You did, not anymore. Get with the times, or die."

Kenzo and I part for him. I go last, letting Kenzo protect Ryder's back. The man twitches, so I part my leather jacket and flash my piece at him. "I wouldn't," I growl, and when I'm sure he won't shoot I turn my back.

It's a risk, he could stab me or shoot me, but this way, I'm showing him exactly how scared of him we are. He swears, and I hear the smashing of glasses, making me smile. Before the month is through, they will be ours. Nothing gets in our way, not when Ryder sets his mind to it.

And the man just insulted Ryder and our family. They're dead men walking, they just don't know it yet. The man doesn't attack, though, he knows better. He threw down the gauntlet, and now he has to live with the consequences.

Exiting the restaurant, I pull on my shades and swing onto my bike as Kenzo shuts Ryder's door and climbs into the driver's seat. I nod and yank on my helmet. It's time. We have a debt to collect.

We race through the city back to the Viper Industries skyscraper. Roaring through the streets, I disregard the speed limit—this is the only time I feel alive—and pull into the underground garage before Ryder and Kenzo. I scan my hand and eyes in the security panel—you can never be too cautious—then pull into my spot before climbing off. Storing my helmet, I decide to go grab D before they get here.

I head to the elevator, riding it all the way down to the basement that most people don't even know exists. That's where he'll be, I know it.

I was right. I find Diesel in the basement, which he calls 'the fire cave.' Seriously, if this guy wasn't like a brother to me, I would be terrified. I'm pretty sure he's certifiable, but he always has our backs, and he's family.

I hear the screams from the elevator, the smell of smoke wafting to me. One of these days, he's going to burn the whole damn building down. Striding through the corridor, I follow the sound of heavy metal music and step into the room he's occupying. I lean against the wall, watching as he bends down and lights a cigarette before going back to burning the man's balls who he's strung up.

Smirking, I flick off the music, and he whirls with a glare, but when he sees it's me, he relaxes. "How'd the meeting go?" he asks, ignoring the blubbering man behind him. He has burn marks all over his body and missing fingers, so he's been down here for a while.

"Fine, no need to kill them just yet. Who's that?" I inquire, nodding my head to the guy.

Diesel shrugs. "Some fucker who bad-mouthed us."

"Well, he won't do that again." I laugh, and Diesel smirks around his cigarette. "Finish up, we're going to pick up Rob's daughter."

His eyes light up even more. Poor girl, when he gets his hands on her, she'll be toast. "Sure, one sec." He turns back to the guy and slaps him around the face to silence him. "Sorry, love, our time is up. I wish I could stay, but I have a date, you understand?"

He grabs the cloth next to him, the smell of petrol burning my nose as he sets it alight. Laughing, Diesel smashes it into the guy's mouth, breaking his teeth and covering his mouth with his hand, forcing him to keep it there. "Brother…" I warn, not wanting to interrupt, since that tends to lead to us fighting. We have a deal. When people are brought to him, he can do whatever he wants, but we need to get moving.

"Fine," he snaps and, grabbing the gun from the small of his back, shoots the man straight in the head before turning to me. He starts my way as I shake my head.

"Might wanna clean up, we don't want to scare her to death…just yet." I smirk.

He laughs, grabbing a rag and wiping away the blood on his face before puffing on his fag. "Let's go," he murmurs with a sigh, draping an arm around my shoulders which I shake off. "Hear anything about the girl?"

"Only that Kenzo, and I quote, jacked off four times last night since seeing a picture of her."

Diesel whistles, and I nod. To get Kenzo in such a tizzy, she must be something to look at. Ryder is the ladies' man, while Kenzo prefers a good bet or a dare over a pussy any day. "I wonder if they'll let me have her first…"

"Doubt it, you'd kill her, so you'll probably be last," I mutter, as we hit the elevator and ride it up to where Ryder and Garrett are waiting.

"Fuck, fine." He perks up then as he drops his fag to the floor. I stamp it out so it doesn't set the place ablaze. "I bet I can still make her scream."

"I don't doubt it, especially if you play with her like you do your toys," I offer as the door opens, emitting us to the parking garage.

Kenzo and Ryder are there, and when they spot me with D, they smirk. "D, you drive with Garrett, we need room for her."

D rubs his hands together and Ryder narrows his eyes. "No crazy stunts, I don't want to pull you two from a fucking wreck off the bridge again because you thought you could jump it."

D rolls his eyes, even as I laugh. "I'll drive."

"Like fucking hell you will!" D screams, before socking me right in the gut.

Wheezing, I manage to thrust out a fist, hitting him straight in the side. He slams into the wall, making us both laugh.

"Gentlemen, come, there is a lady waiting for us." Ryder smiles, the evil one. He has something up his sleeve, that's for sure.

The girl is safe from me. Not that I won't kill her, 'cause I will. I hate to do women like that, but sometimes I have to. Just because they have a pussy doesn't mean they won't try to kill you. But she won't have to worry about me touching her, taking her. That ship sailed years ago, even the thought of a woman touching me makes me angry.

Makes me want to hit something.

It's the others she should be worried about, because from the look in Ryder's eyes...he wants her too. And badly. Whatever Ryder wants, he gets. That's why we're as rich and as feared as we are now. Clearly Kenzo wants her, and Diesel? Well, he's due a new plaything.

The girl would be lucky to survive through the first night.

CHAPTER SIX

ROXY

I stare at the four men in my doorway. They're not my normal customers. One is wearing a suit that's tailored perfectly to fit him and is probably worth more than the whole bar. The other three look like mean sons of a bitches. I'm pretty sure the one in the back is an actual giant, as he ducks his head to get through the door.

And they're all packing, I catch glimpses of the guns. So do my customers.

The whole place clears, chairs scraping and falling to the floor in their rush to escape the newcomers. Cook pokes his head out, and I sigh. So this is them, the people hunting me. "Cook, go home," I order, knowing I won't be opening tonight.

"Smart." The one in the suit nods. His way too slick black hair is pushed back, styled flawlessly, long on top and short on the sides, so I have the insane urge to mess it up. But his eyes? They are black, cold, and calculating. They scan the room and me, noting everything. I bet if I asked, he could relay every single detail.

His cheekbones are high and sharp, his jaw chiselled with stubble covering it, only framing his lush, plump lips. He's tall, around six foot three, and his suit hugs his thick thighs and arms in the most tempting way. He's just too perfect to look at, like a model.

"Is this her?" One of them grins, strolling forward. His long blond hair is pushed behind pierced ears. Tattoos peek out of the top of his white shirt, which is partially tucked into ripped, faded jeans and black boots. His arms are huge and dotted with tattoos here and there, his skin golden and glistening, but he seems like the type to be covered in grease and dirt. His eyes are a bright blue and locked on me, but there's something not quite right about them.

His face is more angular than the first guy's, but no less striking, and he prowls around as he stares at me like a hungry panther.

"It is," another one confirms. This guy's facial structure is similar to the first one, but no stubble. He's clean shaven with a slightly squarer jaw. His hair is longer on top and shaved on the sides, shoved back carelessly. He's taller than the first and more stacked, not as put together, but hot as hell.

The last one doesn't speak, just stares at me from dark eyes. I spot his long eyelashes from here, the type girls would be envious of, but that's the only girly thing about him. He's massive, his arms are thicker than my whole body, and his white shirt clings to his bulging biceps and veiny forearms, indenting at his pecs and chiselled abs.

His jeans are tight, like he can't find the right size, and his hair is brown with blond streaks, styled casually to the side. Every single inch of him is covered in tattoos, and a black lip ring glistens in the light.

I look back over them as the blond-haired guy flicks open the top of a lighter again and again as he stares at me. "Who are you?" I snap, refusing to be intimidated.

"Won't you take a seat?" the first one offers, and I laugh.

"Why don't you fuck off? Now tell me why the hell you're in my bar or get the fuck out," I snarl.

The blond one chuckles. "Ooh, feisty, she's so little though. Too easy to break." He pouts, sighing like I've put him out.

"I ain't easy to break, asshole. I'll smash in your pretty boy face before you can blink, so answer my goddamn question."

These aren't the thugs from last night, no, these men are dangerous, and I'm clearly their target. I swallow hard as fear winds through my body. The man in the suit notices, since he's watching me carefully, and his lips tip up slightly in one corner at my show of panic.

"I like her," the blond declares, and the big guy finally talks.

"Poor her," he scoffs.

"Roxxane, please sit," the first one suggests again, but I know it's a demand.

So I yank out a stool and do as I'm told as far away from them as I can be. I lean my arms back on the bar so I can reach the blade at my waist. "Why are you here?" I repeat.

The first one looks around before selecting the closest table. The fucking bastard wipes down the chair and still frowns as he perches on the edge of it. I hope he stains his suit.

"Roxxane, I'm Ryder Viper," he introduces himself. I ignore his use of Roxxane, no one calls me that.

A shiver goes through me.

Viper.

As in the fucking nut jobs that run the city? The goddamn mafia who controls everything? No wonder the police freaked, they're in their pocket. So are the judges and the mayor.

Shit, this is serious.

"That's Diesel." He nods to the blond who's licking the flames from a lighter. "Kenzo." He gestures to the one who looks like him. "And Garrett."

"Well, nice to fucking meet you. Want to tell me why you had goons come here and attack me last night?" I snarl. When I get scared, I get defensive, sue me.

His eyebrow arches as he leans forward, his hands dangling

between his parted legs. Fuck, why is that hot? "As they explained it to me, you attacked them first."

I think back. Shit, maybe he's right. "They tried to grab me."

"They did." He nods. "But for engaging you in a brawl, they have been dealt with. That was not their orders. I understand one of them hit you?"

I reach up to my still sore lip but drop my hand—it's too late, he noticed. His eyes narrow. "That's not on, they're awaiting judgement for that."

"What does that even mean?" I yell.

"It means, pretty bird, they're going to die." The blond laughs, the sound a bit crazy.

"Why do you want me?" I question, holding my breath.

"Your father owed us a debt," Ryder starts, and I swear he arches an eyebrow again. "Yes, I understand your relationship is...rocky?"

"Rocky? I'd kill the bastard if I could. Fine." I slip from the chair. "How much does he owe you? I'll pay it if I can."

The blond, Diesel, slides in front of me, his blue eyes locked on me as he licks his lips. "No, we made a deal with your daddy, pretty bird. Tell me, love, are you a screamer? Me and your dad have a little bet," he queries.

I react without thinking, yanking back my fist and punching him in the face.

Shaking it off, I watch him lurch backwards. His hand comes up and prods his mouth and nose as blood gushes from the wound. He starts to laugh, making me jolt back myself. Lifting his head, he grins, his teeth covered in blood. "That was hot, want to do it again?"

My eyes widen, but Ryder's voice comes from behind him. "Enough, D."

Diesel sighs but winks as he backs away, only then do I notice the bulge in the front of his jeans...is he erect? Holy fuck. I jerk my eyes up, but it's too late, he noticed and is laughing again.

The crazy fucking bastard.

"What kind of deal?" I snap, growing tired of this game as a sick feeling rises in my stomach. They don't want my money, they made a deal...

"For you." Ryder shrugs.

Oh, for me he says, casual as you fucking may.

"He. Sold. Me. To. You?" I snarl.

"She's hot when she's angry," Diesel whispers to the big guy, Garrett, who rolls his eyes.

"Yes, he did. To cover his debt, and we always collect, Roxxane. Now, would you like to pack a bag, or shall we do it for you?" Ryder asks calmly.

Like I'll just agree to go with them. Fuck that. They might be the Vipers, the scariest fucking assholes in the city, but that doesn't mean I'll go willingly. Leaping over the bar, I grab my bat. "Get the fuck out! I ain't going anywhere with you crazy bastards. You want his debt? Take it from him, I don't care."

"I can't do that, love, a deal is a deal. You're ours." Ryder shrugs as he stands.

"Can I?" Diesel grins, stepping forward, but Ryder puts out his hand to block him.

"Go with Garrett and pack her bag," he orders, and Diesel deflates for a moment before wiggling his eyebrows at me.

"I'm going to jerk off into your panties. See you later, pretty bird."

The big guy steps forward and claps him on the shoulder. "Upstairs, they said."

Wait...they know where I live?

I step into their path, and the big guy stares down at me, his face hard. "Move, little one."

"Fucking make me," I snarl, and swing my bat at him.

He catches it mid-air like a fly and rips it from my hand before frowning at me. "That wasn't nice."

"Oh, well ex-fucking-scuse me," I taunt, then I dart my knee forward. He's too busy to notice, and it connects with his junk.

He grabs his cock with a wheeze, his face turning red as he falls to his knees. I lift my fist, but the blond catches it mid-flight, tutting at me. "Sorry, pretty bird, we can play later," he purrs, and then I see his fist coming towards me.

I don't have time to duck. It smashes right into my face, and I'm out cold.

CHAPTER SEVEN

KENZO

"You could have at least caught her." I laugh as I stare down at the beautiful girl out cold on the floor. Diesel punched her hard, her eye is already swelling, and I'm betting her head will hurt tomorrow.

Better than what Garrett would have done to her for that cheap shot, but when I actually look over at the guy, he's icing his cock and has a strangely impressed expression on his face as her bat leans next to him.

Who is this girl?

Definitely not the meek little good girl I was expecting, that's for sure. Hell, she didn't even seem scared when we told her everything. She tried to fight. I like that. It might keep her alive for a while. At least long enough for me to get my dick wet and see if she fights like that in bed.

I bet she does.

She's a wild one.

"Kenzo, go with Diesel and pack her a bag...more than just

panties." Ryder sighs, staring down at the girl. "Garrett, pick her up, will you?"

The big guy grumbles, pulling the ice from his dick, but he lifts her up and cradles her to his chest without looking down at her, his teeth clenched. Nodding, I follow Diesel upstairs. "Shit, I'll get the key," I tell him when he tries the handle and it doesn't budge.

I'm turning to do just that when I hear a smash. Glancing over my shoulder, I see he's kicked down the door. He grins back at me. "No need, it's open now."

Shaking my head, I grab my dice, a habit, as we step inside. My eyebrows rise, it's a fucking mess. Clothes and beer bottles are everywhere. Ryder would have a shit fit if he saw this place. Diesel, uncaring, heads straight for the half open wooden drawers on the back wall under a window. He starts grabbing handfuls of panties, I even catch him sniffing some.

I snatch a bag from the built-in wardrobe next to the bathroom door and fill it with her toiletries and makeup. I take some clothes that are hanging up and other articles from the room, as well as some bits and bobs she might need. We can always buy her whatever else she wants, but her having her own stuff might calm her somewhat.

I almost laugh out loud as I remember how she took down Garrett. It's not often someone gets a drop on him. Hardly ever, in fact. This is going to be fun. A noise drags my head up to see Diesel bouncing on her bed, his arms under his head.

"You going to help or jack off into her knickers?" I ask seriously, noticing a stringy pink piece clutched in his hand. "Remember what we said about touching yourself in public?"

He frowns, tucks the panties into his pocket, and fluffs up the pillow under his head but freezes. With a slow move, he reaches under the pillow and pulls out a gun—a small revolver. Well, well, well, where did our little one get that?

Diesel's face splits with a grin. "I think I'm in love. Do you think she would shoot me if I ask?"

"Probably, want to bet on it?"

"Hell no, you cheat!" he snaps, making me laugh. I do, sometimes. Other times, I just read people, it's a talent of mine I've honed. It makes me a bad person to bet against, and also the best bookie in the city.

Peering above the mini fridge, I spot a photograph, the only one I've seen up here. It's of a younger Roxy without as many tattoos, and her hair is longer and blonde. She has a nose stud, but it's definitely her, and next to her is a large man. Huge actually, with a bald head and greying beard, scars at the corner of his chin, and a nose that's been broken. Who is he?

It's not her dad, but it has to be someone important to her. So I take it, fold it away, and pocket it just in case we need to find him and use him as leverage. Looking around, I nod at Diesel. "I think that's everything. Let's go before she wakes up and starts punching people again."

"Do you think she would?" he questions wistfully.

"Crazy fucker," I mutter, as I hoist her tattered bag higher and head downstairs.

Garrett is still holding her, looking like he would rather be anywhere else, and Ryder is wandering around the bar. No doubt learning everything he can. I know how to read people, but Ryder? He's made it a fucking game, a sport, to find people's weaknesses and exploit them, destroy them with what he learned.

Little miss Roxy will be no different.

"All packed, she doesn't have much." I shrug.

Ryder nods. "I don't think Roxy cares about things other than this bar."

Garrett growls, "Fucking great, can we leave now?"

"Scared she's going to take a shot at your junk again?" I taunt, and he narrows his gaze at me.

"I'll carry her," Diesel offers. I step in his path as Garrett turns her away from him.

"That's okay, man, he's got it," I say to the man who frowns and peeks around me to try and see her. Fuck, I look over at Ryder and he nods, he's noticed it too. The last person Diesel became obsessed with ended up being burned to death. We want her to suffer, but not that much...not yet.

That means we need to stay between him and her, at least for now.

"Come on, we'll head back." I clap him on the shoulder, dragging him away as Ryder steps between him and Garrett to further block his view.

Diesel moans but perks up when I tell him he can drive.

"We'll meet you back here, get the guest room ready so she can stay there for now," Ryder calls, and I nod.

Guest room? Like she'll be staying in there for the long haul. It seems Roxy is going to live with us. And from just the moment I spent with her, I'm betting she's going to try her best to kill us for that.

I can't wait.

It's been awhile since we last did something fun, this one just happens to come in a delectable package which I plan to open. Yes, I'll have Roxy before we kill her. I'll make her beg for it, crave it until she caves...then I'll finally fuck her.

She's now lost the biggest bet of all—her freedom and her life.

CHAPTER EIGHT

ROXY

My head is killing me, almost like I've had one too many drinks. My face is aching, and my whole body is stiff from being in one position too long. Groaning, I keep my eyes shut to try and let the pain fade away as I rack my brain for what happened. But it's all a blur, and the more I try, the more the hammers dig into my brain.

Feeling around with my hand for my gun, I freeze. This isn't my usual crappy bedding...this is fucking silk. Who the hell has silk bedding?

No one I know, that's for sure.

That's when it all comes rushing back. The goons. The Vipers. The punch...

Snapping my eyes open, I stare up at the white ceiling, and right above me is a goddamn crystal chandelier. My heart slams in my chest as I shuffle up to the headboard, leaning against it as I prod my aching face, that bastard. I don't think anything is broken though. Breathing heavily, I panic as I look around at my surroundings.

They stole me.

Took me from my bar and left me in what looks like a fucking hotel room.

It's so...clean. Way too clean. All white walls and a deep grey carpeted floor. On the wall opposite the huge, king-sized bed I'm in is a flat screen TV bigger than my bathroom. To the right, the wall gives way to floor-to-ceiling windows which, when I slide from the bed and stumble over to them, allow me to see the city.

It's spread out beneath me like a goddamn poster. We're so high up and right smack bam in the middle of it. Turning away, I spot two doors on either side of the TV. I peek my head in one to see a built-in wardrobe. And by that, I mean a room with shelves upon shelves, mirrors with lights between them, and a sofa in the middle. Shutting the door with a disgusted sneer of my lips, I try the other one.

It's a bathroom. The left wall is taken up by an all glass shower cubicle with four shower heads aimed down, and a grey tiled seat in the back corner. To the back is a huge tub, big enough to hold at least six people. To the right are two sinks with a framed mirror above it. The toilet is tucked away next to me. It looks like someone spared no expense, the fucking rich bastards.

Heading back into the room, I scan the space looking for anything I can use as a weapon. Next to the bed are two antique, grey bedside tables. With lamps on both. Perfect. I race across the room on bare feet, since some bastard took my boots. Ripping the lamp from the wall, I hold it like a bat as I head to the white door to the left which clearly leads out of the room.

Trying the handle, I find it locked, of fucking course. I drop the lamp to my side and glare around at the room. These fuckers, they think they can own me? That I'm someone they can buy?

They're going to learn that money can't buy obedience. I'm no man's object. They are going to regret the day they took me.

Vipers? Bitch, please, I bite too.

I wait for over half an hour to see if they will come and unlock the door, but they don't and I get bored. Pissed and bored isn't a good combination for me. I have the insane urge to mess the place up, it's too perfect, too clean. So I do. Grinning, I head to the bathroom and decide to take my anger out on their precious bedroom.

Smashing the lamp into the mirror, I watch it shatter into pieces. I grin, picking up a piece, accidentally cutting myself. Hissing, I stare at the blood coating the glass and dripping to the pristine floor. Eh, fuck it.

Sauntering back into the bedroom, I let my blood drip behind me as I walk to the bed and start slashing. I get it all out. My fury at them, my rage at my father.

I should have known better by now, but every goddamn time I think I'm free of him, he does something. But this? Selling me? Even I didn't think he would be so low.

With a scream, I stab and slash until my arm aches and I'm panting. Feathers from the pillows cover me and the floor, the mattress has gaping holes in it, and the bedding is covered in blood and ripped to shreds.

It looks like I feel and makes me smile.

I'm laughing when the door opens. Hiding the glass in the back pocket of my shorts, I step away, my eyes narrowed. Ryder strolls inside. He looks around at the mess, and his arched eyebrow and the slight dipping of his perfect lips are the only signs of his displeasure.

I'm a panting, sweaty mess, and he's standing there in a suit like a goddamn model. I hate him, and not just because he kidnapped me and locked me in his creepy clean apartment.

"Well, I see you're making yourself comfortable," he comments, his voice smooth and low. Like a good shot of Jack. Does anything ruffle this man? I want to run over there and wipe my blood all over his perfect suit just to see what he would do.

"Let me go," I demand, but he ignores me. Bending down, he picks up a pillowcase and holds it in the air with one finger, showing off the material that's cut to ribbons.

"Your father sold you, you are ours now." His tone is so matter-of-fact that I want to explode again.

"I'm a human! You can't just sell another person!" I scream.

"It seems we can." He shrugs, dropping the pillowcase. "Your anger at the situation or disbelief will not make it any less real, I assure you. Your father did sell you to us, and you're now ours. I suggest you find a way to deal with that."

Deal with that?

Oh, this motherfucker.

Gripping the glass in my back pocket, I storm closer, getting in this face. "Let me go or I swear I'll—"

"You'll what?" He smirks, those ice-filled eyes finally thawing a bit to show a challenge there.

A dare.

The glass digs into my skin, cutting it anew as I whip out my hand and slice it towards his unprotected face. He blinks, his hand grabbing mine before the glass is an inch away from his cheek. He tightens his grip, making me gasp as it grinds my bones together, pain sparking through me. "You are ours, Roxxane. If we want to lock you up, we will. If we want to punish you for being a brat, we will. If we want to fuck you..." He leans closer, pressing into the glass, and a bead of blood bubbles on his cheek as he lowers his voice. "We will. If we want to kill you...we will, and there is nothing you can do about it. Deal with it, love, or you might find yourself in a worse place than this."

Leaning back, he snaps my wrist to the side, making my fingers spasm and release the glass which he pockets. I stare at him as fear and something I don't want to name fills me, watching that drop of blood racing down his cheek. He pulls out a handkerchief and stops it before it can reach his suit, wiping it away like he didn't just lean into glass to make a point.

"I can see you're in a bad mood, so I'll leave you to think on what I said." He turns, and I race forward, but I'm too slow. The door slams shut, and the deafening click of a lock slamming into place has me screaming at the wood as I batter my injured hand against it.

When no one comes back, I cut up more of the pillow and bind my hand to stop the bleeding before looking around. It was petty, but I seriously do feel better. Sighing, I lie near the window, staring out at the city as the sky starts to darken.

I used to live in this town, loved exploring it and seeing it grow. That was before I realised the darkness that hides beneath all the glass and glamour. And the Vipers? They are one of the worst.

When you're a kid, they tell you stories of monsters hiding under your bed or in the dark. They don't tell you of the very real human ones. Those who prey on people weaker than them, or even the monsters that hide within ourselves.

Rich or poor, it doesn't matter, humans are still monsters. They hide behind pretty faces, loved ones, blood. Yet they are all the same. They all want you for something, the difference is...how far they're willing to go to get it.

It seems the Vipers will go all the way.

And it's all because of my piece of shit father. Is it not enough he ruined my childhood? That I've spent every day of my life paying for his mistakes? No, now my future is taken away too.

Feeling sorry for myself, I close my eyes and try to rest my aching head. I'm a fighter, a survivor, always have been and always will be. I can get through this, I've survived worse before. Just because I'm locked up in a penthouse doesn't mean I'm not locked up...

The door slams open, waking me. It's late, really late, and dark. My stomach is hurting from not eating for almost two days, aside from those leftover bits of bread I found.

It's late.

That only means one thing.

I cover my mouth, trying to slow my breathing so he won't hear. My heart pounds so loudly, I want to cry. I hear his dragging footsteps as he stumbles up the stairs. Please, please let him forget I'm here.

Let this night be the night he carries on walking.

It's not. He stops outside my door. I watch from my bed as his shadow blocks the light at the crack in the bottom before his big hand turns the handle and swings it open. He stands there for a moment, peering in at me. His silhouette is all I can see, so I can't see his face or his expression. I know my mum's passed out, she injected herself before I went to bed, so she'll be out until morning. It's just me and him. And he knows it.

I can smell the whiskey on his breath from here, see the anger vibrating through his body. It's always the same. He gets drunk, he loses money, he takes it out on me. It's a vicious cycle. Every night, I expect it to be different, and every night, it's the same.

If you've never had a parent let you down, hurt you, and break your heart, then you don't know how it feels. They're supposed to protect you, love you, yet my parents are the reason I'm scared. I learned from a young age that they're the ones who hurt me, no one else. They don't care if I live or die, I'm just an object to them.

To vent to, to take for granted.

When I watch other kids at school talking about their parents, I get angry, the same anger my daddy has. I hate them for it, for being happy. For enjoying their life. Their parents love them, treasure them, shower them with gifts and happiness. Why can't I have that?

Yet even if my dad or mum ever tried to, I would flinch, expecting the punch that would come right after it. Because the truth is, I know at the base of all people, at their very core...all they care about is themselves. What something can bring them, do for them, and when push comes to shove, they will always choose themselves.

Some people are born with a rage, a need to hurt.

Some are born greedy, an addictive personality. Others hide it well, but in the end, we're all the same. We all bleed the same colour, and we are all just searching for something to make the truth of our souls disappear so we feel like good people.

I'm not fooling him, he knows I'm awake, so I sit up and face him. I refuse to cry, I refuse to beg. Not anymore. I did once, and I thought he might actually stop. I know better now. He won't stop until he kills me one day, but until then, I'm just surviving from one day to the next with that truth hanging over me.

"Get up," he slurs. I purse my lips, but do as I'm told, knowing that will get this over more quickly.

But every time this happens, something grows inside me, that anger morphing until I have to bite my tongue to stop from hitting back, from lashing out. I refuse to be like him.

He stumbles my way, swearing when he almost falls over. "I lost two thousand tonight, you know whose fault that is?" he yells.

I should say nothing, just nod and take the hit like a good girl.

But maybe I'm not a good girl, maybe I'm just as messed up as he is. "I'm guessing mine," I drawl.

Dumb, real dumb.

For a drunk man, the punch comes fast, he's big, and it shows in the power behind his fists. It smacks into my gut, bending me over as I struggle to breathe. My stomach aches even more now than just hunger pains.

He grabs my hair, making me cry out as he jerks up my head. His crooked teeth flash in the dark, his face blurry from my tears. He snarls at me, his rancid breath wafting into my face and making me gag. "Yours, you fucking little shit."

I'm so busy trying not to vomit—the last time I did, he broke my arm—that I don't see it coming. He throws me into the wall, and my head hits it with a sickening thud. My body goes limp as I slide down it, pain fracturing through my skull until I can't see.

I can't hear.

Then it all goes dark.

Gasping, I jerk upright. Sweat covers my entire body as adrenaline rushes through me. I lift my hand and press it to the back of my head where the dent still rests from that night. Fuck, that's why I drink before bed, to keep the nightmares away.

Blowing out a breath, I blink my blurry eyes to clear the sleep from them, knowing I won't be going back anytime soon. Not with my memories so dark tonight. Instead, I stare out at the city, it's still bright. All the light illuminating its angles and streets, even in the dark. Like a beacon.

Another lie.

That's when a wispy, dark voice comes from behind me, sending fear surging through me.

I'm not alone.

"Can't sleep, Little Bird? I wonder what you dream of..."

CHAPTER

NINE

DIESEL

She's having a bad dream, I can tell. Her limbs are jolting like she's trying to escape someone. Whimpers leave her lips, which does something strange to my brain. Just as I'm about to reach for her, she jerks away, breathing heavily. Sitting up abruptly, she places her hand on her racing heart, and it's so loud I can hear it.

I wonder if it would pound harder if she knew I was behind her? Reaching out, I brush my hand gently along her hair, so softly she doesn't feel it. Such a small, little creature, yet it houses such pain... such anger.

"Can't sleep, Little Bird? I wonder what you dream of," I murmur behind her.

Her head whips around, her dark eyes widening as they find me sitting right behind her. I can see the panic fluttering through her gaze as she looks around for a weapon. Laughing, I leap at her. She lets out a scream that goes right to my already hard cock as I pin her hands above her, pressing my lower body to hers to keep her there, letting her feel how hard I am.

The others thought locking her away from me would keep her safe. How foolish. This little bird is going to be fun, I can tell. And she's ours now. I can do whatever I want with her.

She thrashes beneath me, not freezing like most do when confronted with me. She fights, bucking and kicking. All it does is make my already hard cock twitch in my jeans as I imagine her doing that while I fuck her. I bet she fucks like she fights—hard, fast, and wild.

She might not survive it, but I *will* have her.

She spends herself, though, and stops, her eyes narrowing and flashing with anger and hatred as she pants. Her chest heaves, pushing her breasts against me. I lean down, and she turns her head away from me as I trail my tongue across her cheek. "Do you like pain?"

An image of her chained up in my den has me rocking against her, trailing my fingers across her bloody, beaten skin. My knife marks bright and pink across her body, like a lover's touch. Would she quake then too? Fight? Scream? I can't wait to find out. I wonder if she would beg...

"Fuck. You," she snarls.

"No, Little Bird, but I will fuck you." I chuckle against her cheek.

She freezes beneath me, turning rock-solid, and I lift my head. "But not tonight. When I fuck you, I want my toys there. I want to mark that pretty skin within an inch of your life." I trace my hand across her tattoos. "When you got these done, did you get wet from the pain? Or did you cry and suffer through it?"

Her head whips back around to glare at me, but I see a glint of truth in her eyes before she masks it. Ah, my little bird is scared of just how much she liked the pain. And I thought breaking her, killing her, would be fun. But this? Smashing those barriers until she comes while I torture her? That will be all the sweeter.

I'm going to burn down everything this little bird holds dear, and reform her into my own little plaything.

"You smell like smoke and petrol," she murmurs, and then blinks as if she didn't mean to say that, her lips rolling inwards, dragging my eyes to the plump redness. Does she taste like the tears she was shedding in her sleep?

"Eyes up here, asshole," she snaps, making me smirk. This girl really does like playing with fire.

Fuck, I've even had men pee themselves just from a glance from me. Yet, here she is, staring me down, even as I pin her to the floor. I bet she would fight this hard as she died...

I drag my eyes back up, but they catch on a stained, bloody white piece of fabric tied around one of her hands. Well, well, well, did the pretty bird hurt herself? Grabbing that hand, I slam it down on the floor next to her, making her gasp as she starts to struggle again.

Peeling back the blood-stained material, I thumb the edges of the cut, making her cry out before she bites down on her lower lip, an instinct from years of hiding her pain. One I recognise. Eyes on her, I press my thumb right into the center of the cut, testing her.

Blood forms on her lip, she's biting it that hard, her eyes dilating with fear and desire, one she's trying to hide. Her chest heaves, her nipples pebbling against the shirt she wears. Oh, my little bird likes it when it hurts...

"Little Bird, dirty Little Bird, look how sweetly you bleed," I murmur, leaning down and licking the blood from her lip before digging my teeth into it as I smash my thumb into her cut. She screams, lurching beneath me. I swallow her sound of pain and fear, feeding on it.

I hear the door open, but she doesn't. Lifting my head, I meet Garrett's eyes. He takes in our position and sighs. "Leave her be, D."

"But she's fun to play with." I pout, digging my thumb in deeper, making her whimper. The sound makes my cock jerk again as I grind it into her.

"D," Garrett warns, crossing his arms and giving me his best don't fuck with me face. "Go find someone else to play with, I heard Ryder was meeting with some new security people…"

I debate my options. Scaring the new guards or playing with the dirty bird? Sighing, I look back down at her. "Sorry, pretty bird, next time." Kissing her nose, I leap to my feet and stroll towards Garrett, who watches me with a worried expression.

"This isn't going to be a problem, is it?" he asks me, and I shake my head.

"Nope, I didn't kill her, did I?" I laugh as I clap him on the shoulder, but he doesn't even budge, the big bastard.

Sighing, he sweeps his hair back from his face. "Go on, I'll clean up."

Whistling, I stroll away as I hear him step farther into the room. "Are you okay?"

"Fuck you!" she screams, making me laugh. Oh yes, my dirty little bird will be playing with me again. I can't wait. Until then, I'll have to appease myself with others.

CHAPTER

TEN

ROXY

The big guy, Garrett, steps into the room, but doesn't seem to want to come near me. "Are you okay?"

"Fuck you," I shout, as I sit up and press my non-injured hand to my bloody one to try and stop the bleeding. It's not the worst I've had, but shit, it hurt...yeah, hurt. I cross my legs to stop myself from thinking about that other confusing...no, fuck that.

Dropping my eyes to my hands to avoid his too bright, all-seeing gaze, I prod at the cut. The crazy bastard opened it up again. It's not too deep, it doesn't need stitches—I got good at realising what does and doesn't need sutures after getting hurt every day. This one will heal, probably leaving another scar to add to my collection.

I jerk back when I raise my eyes and realise the big guy is crouched before me, his dark gaze locked on me, his black hair falling across his forehead in an oddly endearing way as he reaches for my hand. "May I?" he murmurs, but I keep it clutched to my chest, and he sighs. "I won't hurt you. I'm used to fixing cuts, bruises, and breaks."

"I bet you are," I snap, and his eyebrow rises.

"Not in that way, you should really avoid D though. He isn't like...us. He'll hurt you for fun," he warns softly, his tattooed knuckles clenching. He's so big, his hands must be bigger than my head. He could snap me in two and hurt me so easily. Yet he doesn't...why?

"Oh, avoid him? That didn't fucking occur to me, and how would you like me to avoid him when I'm in a locked room, and the crazy bastard breaks in and stares at me while I sleep?" I huff.

His lips twitch, and he nods at my cut again. "Let me at least clean it and wrap it. How's your lip?" he questions, his big thumb coming up and prodding at my sore lip. I freeze as he strokes his thumb across it, his eyes scrutinising and clinical. Cold. Like he isn't affected, like his touch isn't doing strange fucking things to me.

Things I have no business feeling when I'm his prisoner.

He nods. "It's not busted too badly, it will heal." He releases my lips and takes my hand gently, turning it to regard the cut before standing so quickly I jolt back—a habit, a habit I thought I'd broken. He sees it, of course he does, but doesn't comment. "Let me get a kit."

He leaves the room for a moment, and I scramble to my feet to run after him and escape, but he shuts the door and locks it. The bastard. Pacing, snarling, and swearing under my breath, I wait for him to return. There is no way I can take this big guy. I'm good, but I'm not that good. Plus, I've seen his scarred knuckles and crooked nose, which has been broken too many times, so I know he's a fighter. By the fluid way he moves for such a big guy, I would guess a boxer.

The door unlocks, and he comes back in with a first aid kit. He gestures for me to sit on the bed, so I do, hoping if I'm good, I can lull them into a false sense of security. He kneels down and cleans the cut, ignoring me completely.

"What will happen to my bar?" I demand. I love that place. It's my home, the only place I ever belonged, and I worked my ass off to keep it alive after...

"We locked it up, it will stay closed for now," he offers, uncaring about my questions or anger as he wraps my hand back up and stands. "You should get some sleep."

He turns then and starts to leave, so I leap into his path. "Why? Why are you doing this?" I whisper, tears finally filling my eyes. "I'm a person, a person! Not an object, please just let me go."

He sighs, scrubbing at his face. "No. Get some sleep."

Then he leaves, the click of the door signalling it's locked again. I wipe my tears away, angry with myself for letting him see that weakness. All of a sudden, everything closes in on me. I'm theirs, they are never letting me go.

I know that, I can feel it. I know too much, have seen too much... this is my life now. The question is, how long will I survive? Between the crazy bastard and the mean one...I'm betting not long.

My father gave me a death sentence at the hands of these Vipers, and I'm betting he doesn't even care. All my life, he's been taking it out on me. I always thought he would kill me. Turns out I was right, but not in the way I thought.

I DON'T SLEEP, NOT REALLY. I LIE ON THE FLOOR, WATCHING THE city come to life as the sun rises. All the while, thinking of a plan. I refuse to lie here and let these bastards do whatever they want to me and possibly kill me.

I have a life.

They picked the wrong fucking girl. I've been fighting longer than I've been walking. They want an easy slave? Tough fucking luck, 'cause I'm going to make them regret the day they took me. I need to gain their trust, make them think they're breaking my spirit. Then I'll escape.

If they try to kill me, I'll kill them. It's that simple.

This isn't a normal day anymore, this is a dog-eat-dog world...or more accurately, a Viper world. And right now, I'm the prey...

It should horrify me that I'm even contemplating killing them,

51

but I've seen shit most people would never even be able to dream of, and if I have to kill four, corrupt mafia assholes to get my freedom, I will.

I'll never stop fighting them.

I'll be free again, and then my dad is going to pay for this.

Feeling calmer with a plan in place, I get to my feet as I hear booted feet heading my way. Kenzo opens the door and peeks in, smiling at me. He always seems to do that, but it can't mask the calculation in his eyes, or the way he watches me and everyone. Waiting, observing.

His hair is shaved at the sides and slicked back today as he steps into the room. He's got on a white shirt, with two buttons undone at the top to show his chiselled chest and glimpses of chest hair. It's tucked into black trousers and shoes shinier than my life.

He's so put together, so perfect, and screams money and power. It flows from him. He's used to being the center of attention, the most powerful man in the room. What they don't realise? When you hit bottom, you only have one way to go, and that's up.

They took everything, including me.

I have nothing left to lose.

They have everything.

"You must be hungry. Come on, we're having breakfast and thought you might like to join us," he offers, his hands tucking into his pockets as he tries to make himself seem friendly. It might work on others, but not on me. I see behind that mask to the monster hiding beneath.

"Will I be chained like a dog?" I snarl, and he smirks.

"Do you want to be? It can be arranged, I'm sure," he retorts smugly, and I narrow my eyes. "Come, eat."

"And if I say no?"

He loses his smirk, his face going cold. "You better realise now that you have no power here, love. It will make it easier for you. If I wanted you chained like a dog, you would be. I'm being polite, so do not throw it in my face, or we might not be so polite in the future."

Then, he goes back to grinning. "Come." He nods his head and leaves the room.

I struggle for a moment before following after him. He's waiting right outside, giving me no time to try and escape. Like he can hear my thoughts, he chuckles, his hand going to the base of my spine, warming the skin there. He leans down, murmuring in my ear, "I wouldn't. D is looking for an excuse to rough you up. Don't tempt him to chase you, because when he gets you...well, you will have wished he was as nice as us."

"Do you always threaten people with death and torture over breakfast?" I snap, moving away from his hand.

He laughs behind me. "Of course, it isn't a good morning without at least one death threat or fight."

I stomp down the hallway, noting the other doors for later. It cuts off, opening up into the rest of the apartment, and I stop, gawking. "You're all crazy," I mutter distractedly.

He presses against my back, his heat and hard body making me freeze. I feel his lips at my ear, his breath wafting through my hair. "You have no idea."

I ignore him, too busy staring at the grandeur around me. If I thought that bedroom looked like something out of a showroom, I had no idea...fuck, I didn't even know places could look like this.

To the right are floor-to-ceiling windows, which cover two stories, and there are doors leading out onto what looks like a terrace with a pool and a bar. To the left is the front door with a scanner next to it, and behind that is a floating glass staircase leading up to another level.

Stepping into the room, I stare around further. The whole place is done in gold, white, and black. Marble floor with black accents squeak under my feet, leading to a living area. Sunk into the floor is a huge sofa, and when I say huge, I mean large enough to hold a full rugby team. It's in a square and looks like expensive leather, and, I shit you not, a fucking open fire is in front of it. There's a TV, which covers the whole wall next to me. Behind the sofa is a glass table that runs the length of an entire wall, with flowers and decorations across it and a grand piano.

Next to it is an open kitchen, with a white and grey marble island and black stools with gold legs in front of it. The kitchen is bigger than my whole apartment, equipped with every gadget and gizmo you could imagine. Large, chandelier pendant lights hang down from the ceiling, and the fridge and oven are a shiny black. Gold flowers sit perfectly in a vase. Ryder is moving around it. "Bin open," he orders, and the bin opens, letting him drop something inside.

Of course they have fucking talking appliances.

There are crystal chandeliers hanging low from the ceiling and art covering the white walls. It's all so clean, spotless, and perfect—and screams money. Every gilded edge, every vase and feature meant to impress.

Fuck, they even have stepping stones into what looks like a pond in a corner. How the other half lives. I shake my head as Kenzo pushes me forward, and I stumble before whipping my head around to glare at him. He's grinning, flashing straight white teeth at me. "Asshole," I sneer, and turn back to see all of them looking at me now.

I'm so out of place, I feel tiny and insignificant. My clothes are cheap, but fuck it. They stole me, they knew who I was. I tip my head back and give them a haughty look as I stroll over to the table where Garrett is nursing a mug of what smells like coffee. Diesel is there too, his booted feet propped up on the glass table as he flips a lighter around in his hand.

Ryder heads over, placing a platter on the table and sitting down in the head chair, setting a napkin delicately in his lap. He's in another suit today—a grey, pinstriped one with a fucking waistcoat, the material tightening around his impressive thighs as he leans back, sipping from a goddamn teacup.

He makes the thing look tiny, yet it seems to fit him somehow. His eyes watch me, analysing my every move as I stand there awkwardly before deciding to pick a chair and plop into it, very ungracefully.

Slamming my own bare feet on the table, I cross my arms and narrow my eyes at him. "I want my boots back."

Those boots cost me a small fortune and are one of the only things I've ever splurged on and bought for myself.

He sips from the cup and places it on a saucer on the table. It's weirdly fascinating and kind of arousing, watching the man wrap his lips around such a dainty cup. Not that I'll ever tell him that, asshole.

Diesel leans forward, his dark eyes watching me as he pushes his long, blond hair behind his ears. Like usual, Garrett ignores me.

Diesel is a fucking mad dog, Ryder is an arrogant asshole, and Kenzo is a charming psychopath...I can't figure Garrett out. He seems to want to ignore my presence altogether. He doesn't even look up at me. Kenzo sits next to me and grabs two mugs. "Coffee?"

"Dark," I reply, and he pours it for me. I wrap my hands around the mug, wincing as my injured one aches.

Ryder notices, of course. I don't think there is anything this man doesn't notice. He has eyes like a hawk. "That serves you right for acting like a child and destroying your room."

Did he just reprimand me...like a fucking kid? I have the urge to throw my coffee in his face, and he narrows his cold eyes like he knows my thoughts. "Do not test me. Because of your outburst, I have some people coming to fix the room today. You can't be left alone, so you will stay with Kenzo."

"A prison guard?" I laugh bitterly as I sip the coffee, which, annoyingly, is very fucking good.

"For your protection, and yes, to stop you from hurting yourself or trying to leave," Ryder replies matter-of-factly, as he picks up his cutlery and starts to slice into his food. "Eat, you must be hungry."

Then he ignores me like I'm nothing more than an annoyance. If that's true, then why did he grab me? Is it because it was business to cover a debt? A warning to others? I don't know, and honestly, I don't care.

Kenzo places food on my plate, a full English, but I feel too sick to eat. What do they think, that a fancy apartment and good food will make me stop trying to escape? Do they really just expect me to accept it?

Yes, I can tell they do. They are used to being obeyed, to people doing as they're told.

"Is your hand still bleeding, pretty bird?" Diesel inquires, propping his chin on his hand as he watches me. It doesn't escape me that Kenzo is between him and me.

They did it on purpose, but why? Why do they care what Diesel does to me? After all, they said I'm theirs to do with as they please. Ignoring him, I turn to Ryder, knowing he's the one who has answers.

"My bar—" I start.

He lifts those cold eyes, freezing me in place. Most people watch you, but they don't give you their full attention. Not Ryder, he locks you in place, analysing everything until I'm sure he knows there's a bead of sweat dripping down my spine and my hands are shaking slightly in fear despite my bravado. He notes it all, watching me, using it against me. This is a man who likes complete control.

"What of it?" he challenges, his voice smooth and cultured. There is nothing rough about this man, everything is so perfect, but underneath all that...there is still a viper. A deadly, accurate snake.

"What will happen to it?" I ask.

"We'll probably sell it or destroy it," he answers unemotionally. Curling my fingers into my injured palm, I stop myself from lunging at him and trying to choke the bastard. That's my bar.

Mine.

God, if Rich could see it now—it's that thought that stops me. I promised to look after the place, to keep it running for him. I have to, even if it kills me.

"Please, please don't." I grit my teeth over the words, the only hint of weakness I will allow.

He sits back, his lips tilting up at the corner ever so slightly. "Fine, until we have decided what to do with it, I'll allow your... associates to carry on business."

I snort at his use of the word 'associates.' He means Cook and Travis. "Do they know what happened to me?"

He raises his eyebrow. "No, they think you had a family emergency and had to leave."

I laugh, outright laugh, and he watches me. "Something funny?"

I can sense the others glancing between us, all sounds of eating stopping. Oh, Ryder doesn't like not knowing something, at being the butt of a joke. "I have no family, they know that." I snort.

"You have a father," he replies in confusion.

"I disowned him years ago." I shrug. "Everyone knows that."

He nods, wiping his mouth with his napkin before folding it perfectly and placing it on the table. "I saw you were emancipated at seventeen."

I lift my head then, wondering how. "How—"

He smiles then, and it's so cold and evil, I actually shudder. Fuck. "We have our ways, love. I could find out anything about anyone. Give me a moment, and I'll know the basics. An hour, I'll know your life..." He leans close, his minty breath wafting across me, he smells like mint and wood. "Give me a day, and I can destroy you with everything I know."

Tilting my head away, I keep my eyes locked on his, refusing to back down. "Fine, you know shit about me, who doesn't? That doesn't mean you know me."

"No?" he counters, arching a brow as he sits back. Surprise enters his eyes at my refusal to concede, to be scared or intimidated, and I can imagine it's a first. "Then let me enlighten you. You have broken nearly every bone in your body since you were three years old. Your father, probably, since he's a drunk. Your mother was a drug addict who finally killed herself when you were fourteen. You walk like someone who can hold her own, you know how to fight. Most likely took some lessons. You own a gun which shows you have some... unsavoury friends. You aren't afraid to run a dive bar, which shows you're brave and slightly stupid. You don't have a boyfriend, probably because of your glaring daddy issues—in fact, it seems you just have passing lovers. None who even know your full name, just the way you like it, keeping you in charge. How am I doing?"

"All right, apart from one," I snarl, standing. "My mother didn't kill herself. My father did that when he stuck the needle in her vein and pushed the plunger."

I turn away and Diesel blocks my path. "Where are you going, Little Bird?"

"I did not dismiss you," Ryder snaps behind me. "Sit down."

Grinding my teeth, I take a deep breath, balling my hands into fists, and spin back around and sit. He nods and carries on eating, ignoring me. "Today, I'm going to be in meetings until after lunch. Tonight, I expect you all here. Tomorrow, Garrett and I are away most of the day," he informs them.

"Where are you going, bro?" Kenzo inquires as he eats.

"We have some matters to deal with up north, a disagreement on pay." Ryder rolls his eyes. "It will be sorted quickly. In the meantime, I want your ears to the ground, Kenzo. Keep your eyes open for retribution from the Triad. They won't give up that easily."

I sit there soaking it all in, noting as much about them as I can. They are talking freely in front of me. Why?

Because they expect I'll never tell anyone.

It sends a bolt of fear through me, which burns away to anger. They plan to snuff me out like I'm nothing, just another business deal for them. It infuriates me, fuck fear. I'm angry, livid.

These bastards need to pay. I spend the rest of breakfast silently fuming, refusing to eat. I'm going to make them pay.

CHAPTER ELEVEN

RYDER

I watch Roxy out of the corner of my eye, or Roxxane, as her birth certificate read. Not that she goes by it. Overnight, I learned a lot about our new house guest.

It seems I was right, her father abused her. Something she cemented when she told us about her mother a moment ago. I knew he was a bastard, but I didn't know how much. It's a surprise she's even alive right now, the ER records made my blood boil. Even as a kid, she suffered. It all seemed very familiar and too close to home as I read back on the broken bones and internal injuries. Yet not one person tried to stop him nor cared enough to intervene.

Another child lost in the system.

Forgotten, unloved, left in the dark to suffer alone.

Yet here she is, fighting even now. I expect her to be dainty afraid, and like so many survivors. I expect her to flinch and wither away, but if anything, she seems to have used that to harden herself to the world. Her scars cover her body, only highlighted by her tattoos, a way to draw attention to her. Her story is written across her skin.

I read the judge ordered emancipation, but I'm still having it fully unsealed to see where she went after that. To destroy someone fully, you need to know everything about them, and I don't yet, though she clearly thinks I do. It keeps her on edge, guessing. The way I like it.

Her fists are clenched on the table, her lips taut and eyes flashing in anger. She sits bolt upright in her chair, not touching the food on her plate, even though I can hear her stomach rumbling. I'm betting she's used to going hungry. Kenzo is scarfing food next to her, a habit he's never broken. One ingrained into him from not knowing when he would next eat.

It hurts me for a moment to see that, but I push those memories away, resealing that behind a wall of ice as I sip my tea. I watch Roxxane, my eyes roving over her appreciatively. Even behind all that makeup and anger, she's beautiful. In fact, it only highlights her beauty. The colour of her hair is the shade of ice...the colour of my soul. Her eyes are dark rimmed and draw your gaze, and her lips are plump and red, even without lipstick and the puffiness to it.

She truly is gorgeous, a natural beauty that's clear to see. I've dated models, princesses, and some of the most beautiful women in the world, but Roxxane? She blows them away. She has an unadulterated loveliness and gracefulness they all strive for. Her curves are mouth-watering, not surgically enhanced like so many. Crossing my legs, I adjust my hard-on, trying to ignore it. I will never act on it.

She might be beautiful, and her fight, her willingness to not back down is a massive turn-on, but she's too wild. Too unpredictable to bed. I like my women meek, I like them there and gone when I order it. Never interrupting my life, just a primal urge that I have to let out.

Roxxane wouldn't be that, she would fight me the whole way. She would be memorable. I don't have time for distractions, and she's a massive one. I have a city to run and brothers to protect, and I won't let a woman destroy us again.

Not even one wrapped up in such a beautiful, tragic package like Roxxane.

She catches me looking and narrows her eyes, unafraid of me, even though I hold her life in my hands. It almost makes me smile —almost.

I can see why Diesel is so entranced by her and why Kenzo wants her. My phone vibrates, bringing me from my thoughts, and I check it to see it's my alarm. I'm almost late.

Unheard of.

Standing, I glance at the others, who nod, knowing the drill. "Let's go."

I look to her then. "Behave," I order, and I see anger flare in her eyes again, that same need to push her washing through me. She sure is fun to annoy.

I turn away, leaving Roxxane with Kenzo. I have an empire to run, and it's time to remind a few unruly businesses who think they can fight back of that fact. Slicking back my hair, I straighten my suit and stride from the apartment, my brothers on my heels.

Roxxane is nothing more than a disruption, one I will be rid of soon.

Honestly, I don't know what we are going to do with her. We took her as a lesson, a warning. The unknown aspect of it all is annoying me, leaving me unable to relax enough to sleep. A person is unpredictable, I have come to know that, but if you know them, how to control them, just where to push, just where to kick or hit—with both fists and information—you can get them to do what you want.

Roxxane will not be like that, I can tell. She doesn't react like a normal person, she's wild. Uncontrolled. A nightmare for me. Not that I will let her see that. No, she will come to heel, or we'll kill her.

Either works. For now, I'll ignore her the best I can. I have far more important matters to deal with than one trashy little girl from the southside with anger in her eyes and pain in her heart.

CHAPTER TWELVE

ROXY

Garrett and Diesel leave with Ryder, following behind him like little pets, only after Diesel blows me a kiss. Psycho. It leaves me with Kenzo, who I can feel staring at the side of my face. "You can explore the apartment if you wish."

"What? Not going to lock me back up?" I snap.

"Only if you're good." He leans closer then. "So be good."

His phone rings, and he picks it up, standing from the table and walking outside. He leans against the balcony as he talks, and I watch him, wondering if this is a trap. Who fucking cares? Even though I know it's pointless, I leap up and try the front door. But it's locked. Sighing, I look around at the rest of the apartment before deciding to explore like he said. I have nothing else to do, and I might find some-thing handy.

I head upstairs first, my bare feet slapping against the glass. At the top is what looks like a library with a fur carpet in the middle and huge, floor-to-ceiling antique bookcases. It's quite impressive actually. There's a corridor to the left and one to the right. I choose left. The first door is locked, but I can hear the hum of computers behind it. Maybe a security room?

The door next is also locked, but this one has a scanner on it, so I back away, knowing they don't want anyone getting at whatever's in there. The very next door is unlocked, so I slip inside and look around.

It's double the size of my room, but just as neat. A large, metal, low riding bed sits against the right wall. There are more floor-to-ceiling windows opposite me again. There's no TV or even much furniture. Just a desk with nothing on it but a pen and a pad, but the drawers are locked—I tried them. The floor is a super soft carpet, which my feet sink into as I wander around.

The bedding is so straight and perfect, I jump on it just to mess it up a bit. The silky grey material wrinkles under me as I roll around before getting up and smiling down at my handiwork.

Like my room, there are two doors, one leads to a bathroom and the first signs of life with toiletries and a half filled hamper. The other door is a wardrobe, which is filled with suits on the left, and shining shoes on the back with two pairs of trainers underneath. Hard to imagine Ryder in for sure. To the right is what looks like grey joggers and shirts, pajama pants, and boxers. I run my hand across the perfectly ironed and hung clothing before an evil thought comes to my mind.

It's petty, but honestly, they didn't just expect me to sit and wait for them like a dog, did they? I have this need to push them, to find out what they are willing to do. I head back to the bathroom, searching the cupboards until I find what I'm looking for then, giggling, head back to his closet. Picking the first suit, I drag the scissors through the material, slashing and hacking until it's ruined.

I leave only one untouched, grinning. I stare at the thousands upon thousands of pounds of perfectly tailored suits, which now lay in tatters. Proud of myself, I leave the scissors behind and exit his room. Now, what can I do to the other ones?

Heading back past the library, I travel down the other corridor to three more doors. I poke my head in the first two. The first one is certainly Diesel's room, it's painted black with leather cuts and jackets thrown everywhere. His bed is unmade, his room messy. There are lighters across his side table and cigarettes, and I frown when I spot some panties on his pillow which look suspiciously like mine.

Shaking my head, I leave his room alone. Who knows what he's keeping in there. The next is neater, cleaner, but more lived in. There is a pack of cards on the side table, so it must be Kenzo's. Not wanting to be caught snooping, I slip into the last room.

This must be Garrett's.

The big guy is scary, really fucking scary. As in he could rip me apart without blinking, *but* he also doesn't seem to know I exist, and that makes me curious. He isn't like the others, why?

He has a punching bag hung in one corner, and it looks well worn. A king-sized bed is pushed up in the other corner with dark sheets. His whole back wall is painted black with industrial style lights hanging above. The other wall is exposed brick. There's a TV opposite the bed with stacks and stacks of DVDs under it. I spot some old-school horror movies, seems he's a horror junkie.

There isn't much else here apart from clothing and toiletries. It's like they barely live here, this place is so...empty. Is it new? Or do they just really not spend that much time here? Sighing, I sit on his bed and look at the side table. Pulling it open curiously, I root through the junk in there before hitting a velvet box.

Pulling it out, I open it, and my eyes widen. It's a ring, a fucking huge ring. What the—

"You shouldn't be in here," Kenzo drawls from the door.

Looking up, I meet his eyes unapologetically. "You told me to look around, so I am."

Clicking the box shut, I carefully put it back in the drawer. Is Garrett married?

"I did." He smirks. "I'll have to be more careful of what I say in the future, but what I meant, Rox, is that you can't be in *here*."

"Why?" I ask, tilting my head.

"If Garrett finds you in here...well, it won't be pretty. He might seem calm and in control, but he hates women, so just stay away, okay?" He sighs.

"Hates women? Why?" I press, and he shakes his head.

"You ask a lot of questions for a captive," Kenzo mutters, not like it's a bad thing. His eyes light up. "Do you want to play a game?"

"Against you? No thanks." I snort.

"Why not? Scared?" he taunts.

"I saw the dice you keep in your pocket, the way your eyes track, things and the cards in your room...it's not hard to deduce that you like to play games. Probably win a lot." I shrug, standing up.

"That's true. What if I told you I owned every casino, backstreet dealing, and bookie in the city?" he questions, blocking the door, his arm outstretched.

"Then I would tell you that you have a gambling problem."

"Or maybe I just like to win," he murmurs, his eyes darkening as they run down my body. I swallow hard but don't back down.

"Or you just like money, greedy bastard," I snap, crossing my arms to block his eyes, but they drop to my exposed cleavage, and he licks his lips.

"That too," he agrees.

"Are you going to move?" I growl.

He watches me, seeming to deliberate my question. "Why aren't you more scared of us?"

My heartbeat triples at that. If only they knew that I *am* scared of them, but I get it. Why aren't I a sobbing, catatonic mess? "I've been scared nearly every day of my life, eventually, you stop letting it control you and get so used to it that it's just another day."

He blinks, probably not expecting that. "I can understand that."

"You can?" I counter, tilting my head. Shit, why am I talking to this bastard instead of smashing his head in and trying to escape?

Because he's too calm, way too calm, like he knows even if I do get past him somehow, I will never get free. Which tells me more than anything that this building won't be easy to escape from. Which makes sense if it's the Vipers HQ.

"We're not so different, Rox. You should remember that." He drops his arm. "Your room is still being repaired, and before you go to beg them for help, they are ours and don't care. Instead, let's go relax."

"Relax?" I yell after him, as he starts to walk away.

"Relax! It's my day off, after all!" He laughs as I stand there, but I don't want to be caught in Garrett's room if what he said is true.

Hates women...why?

Fuck, why do I care?

And why am I following Kenzo? Because, honestly, what else would I do? I might as well enjoy this lux penthouse before I escape.

I was expecting torture, or at least one of them to try and fuck me before now, yet they haven't, and that's throwing me off. They say I'm their prisoner, theirs to do with what they want. They watch me with cruel eyes, yet they don't touch me...well, apart from Diesel, but he's crazy.

I MUST HAVE BEEN EXHAUSTED. KENZO HAD FLICKED ON THE TV and put on some random chick flick. I didn't want to tell him that I hate them, even as I curled up as far away from him on the sofa as I could. My excuse? I needed to rest, to keep strong, but it sounded like a lie, even to me.

When I wake up, I'm still in the same position, but there's a blanket over me and the sun is lower in the sky. Kenzo is there, next to me, closer than before. His leg is crossed, his foot propped on his other knee, with an open tablet on his lap, the screen split between what looks like CCTV cameras of the inside of clubs.

"I thought today was your day off?" I murmur, my voice rough with sleep.

He blinks and looks over at me. "Darling, Vipers never take a day off—too many people to kill, too much money to earn."

Yawning, I sit up and stretch, reaching my arms out and cracking my back. When I blink and look over, Kenzo is watching me with hungry eyes. They run across my body like orbs of fire, and I shrink away, wondering if this will be the moment he attacks, but all he does is look back at his tablet.

Licking my lips, I cross my legs and turn to face him so I can see any of the blows that come—an old habit. He notices, of course, and turns slightly towards me, typing on his tablet. "Are the others still out?"

"Why? Anxious to see them?"

"Definitely not, just wondering if I need to hide yet." I sigh.

That has him lifting his head. "Hide?"

"Yes. From the crazy dude and, well, the one that's going to be pissed," I reply, wondering if Ryder will kill me when he sees his clothes, but I don't regret it. The perfect bastard deserved it after this morning.

"Diesel is harmless...okay, that's a lie. He's harmless to us. If he ever killed us, it would be because there was no other choice." Kenzo shrugs.

"And you're calm about that? What about everyone else?" I challenge.

"They are fair game," he retorts.

"Christ, he's literally insane, you can see that, right?" I almost yell.

Kenzo looks up, and I see that same darkness in his eyes the others have, the one he hides behind a charming persona. He might be calmer, he might talk sweeter and be more of a ladies' man, but underneath it all still lives a monster. "Do not talk about what you don't know, Roxy. That man has been through hell and back. It's bound to leave damage, and he's our brother. We'll protect him from anyone, understood?"

I nod, a little bit scared. Just as soon as it was there, he blinks, and is back to smiling again. It's fucking scary how quickly he can change. "Your room is done, I put your bag in there as well."

"My bag?" I repeat with a frown.

"Yes, you might want to shower and change. You're starting to smell." He smirks.

That rat fucking bastard.

He has the audacity to tell me that I smell after I was punched, knocked out, locked up, and became a prisoner? I should have cut his clothes up as well. Throwing him a glare, I storm back to my room, sniffing my armpit as I go.

Fucking Vipers.

CHAPTER THIRTEEN

GARRETT

We get back mid-afternoon. Kenzo is on the sofa, monitoring his clubs like normal, but Roxy is nowhere in sight. Not that I care. Not one bit.

Ryder, on the other hand, brushes his hair back before unbuttoning his jacket, the only sign he's as annoyed as I am with today's meetings. It seems the Triad has taken to threatening some of the businesses in the city, demanding they pay them for protection. Not us.

It's a challenge, one we need to rise to. Ryder's eyes are tight, even as he looks around. "Where is she?"

Kenzo doesn't even look up. "Hiding from you."

"Why?" Ryder questions, seeming confused. Roxy doesn't seem like the type to hide...

"She was snooping upstairs earlier when I caught her." He shrugs, tapping on his screen.

Ryder sighs and looks over at me. "I'm going to wash today's stink off, I've instructed Diesel to...have a talk with some of the other businesses to ensure they don't think they have to pay as well."

I nod as he heads upstairs and to his room. Deciding I could go for a shower myself, I head to my room, kicking my door closed and pressing my back against it as I suck in a deep breath.

But with it comes a scent, an unmistakable scent. Like whiskey and sex.

She's been in here.

Fury pounds through me. I snarl as I rip off my shirt and storm to my bag, throwing some punches and getting all my aggression out. How dare she. This is my room! My space! The only place I'm safe and now—now it smells like her!

Not that my body cares, the stupid bastard is hot and heavy, the fragrance wrapping around me and jerking my cock awake in my jeans. Of course the only woman it's reacted to since that cunt would be the one we're keeping prisoner. I don't need another woman, I don't need another fucking complication.

But my cock doesn't care, it twitches in my jeans, pressing uncomfortably against my zipper, so I yank them off and head to the shower, a cold one. But as the freezing spray pounds down on my back, it doesn't even dent the desire surging through me.

Glancing down, I spot the bead of pre-cum at my cock's tip, my vein throbbing on the side. Fuck. It's been way too long, but all of my need was taken away that night. I didn't know if it was because every time I'd even thought about fucking someone that night flashes through my head, dampening my need, or if my cock was just broken.

I didn't care...much.

But now, of all the fucking time, now it's decided to wake up and with a fury. Desire streams through me at every hour of the day. I swear I've fucked my hand more often this last twenty-four hours than I did even as a teenager. Last night, when I went to lie down to sleep, all I could see were those flashing, angry eyes. Her body spinning as she tried to attack me.

I imagined a different ending though, me throwing her over the bar, ripping up those tiny shorts, and pounding into her tight little cunt until she stopped fighting and started screaming.

Shit.

Reaching down, I can't help but squeeze my cock as I imagine her on her knees before me. Those dark eyes blinking up at me, those red lips wrapped around my cock. She would be angry, her nails digging into my skin, her eyes narrowed dangerously. Fuck. Leaning against the wall, I stroke my length as I imagine it, visualising how beautiful she would look naked and tied up, unable to do anything but suck me down. That silver hair soaking and stuck to her head from my hands as I slam into her mouth. Again and again.

With a grunt, my hips stutter as my release crashes through me, spraying across my stomach and the wall. Sighing, I turn the heat up in the shower and wash myself off, disgusted with where my mind is taking me. She's no one, she's just another gold-digging bitch. So what if she had no choice? She will be exactly like the others.

I've learned my lesson, no, Roxy is a distraction. One we need to get rid of before she destroys everything we have worked so hard to save.

Just then a yell comes from down the hall. Turning off the water, I grab a towel, wrap it around my waist, and head into my room, wrenching open the door. Frowning, I watch a scared-looking Roxy race down the hall right towards me. She doesn't even look where she's going, just slams into my wet chest. I peer down at her in confusion, and she glares back. We stare each other down.

Her chest is heaving as she glances over her shoulder, so I do the same, spotting Ryder coming out of his room holding scraps of material in his hand. His eyes are deadly as they lock on to the little woman pressed against me.

She yelps and slips past me, pressing to my back as if I'll protect her. I don't know why, but that makes me puff up, and I glare at Ryder as I slam the door. Crossing my arms, I turn around and look down at the woman in my room. Right where I didn't want her.

Shit, she's our enemy's daughter. A fucking debt. Nothing else...

73

so why does my heart pound as her eyes run across my destroyed chest? Why do I look away in disgust? She must feel sick looking at me.

Why do I care?

I don't.

"What did you do?" I snap.

She smiles sweetly at me, but it looks wrong on her face. I prefer the scowl, the anger...the heat. "Nothing."

"Don't fucking lie to me. I'll throw you back out there to deal with his wrath," I snarl.

She sighs, losing the innocent façade. Her eyes darken as her hands prop on her hips, her lips curling up in a sneer. "Nothing he didn't deserve."

"And what makes you think I'll save you?" I snap.

Her eyes drag across my chest again, and I stop myself from shrinking away. Fuck her and her opinions. "What happened to your chest?"

I growl, grabbing her throat and slamming her into the wall next to the door. Not cutting off her air supply, just applying pressure, but it's so hard not to squeeze. Especially when her eyes change to those blue mocking ones, her hair turning blonde and long, her lips thinning out. Shaking my head, I push back the vision, my chest heaving as I struggle to stay in the present. To not kill Roxy.

It's not her.

I repeat it over and over.

Roxy swallows against my grip, but doesn't fight me, just hangs there, her eyes watching me closely. I lean down and get right in her face, no doubt mine is transformed into a snarl. "I will not save you, little girl, if anything, I will be your death. Ryder might get annoyed and have it ordered, Kenzo might even help. Fuck, even Diesel would be kinder, he'd make sure you enjoyed it...me? I will make it hurt. I will make you suffer, because you mean nothing to me. I won't even care when you beg. You. Are. Nothing. Just another fucking debt. Another fucking whore through those doors."

She tips her head back, her eyes flashing. "Is that so? Then do it. Kill me. I'm tired of the uncertainty, just fucking do it. Stop threatening, just kill me," she taunts.

I snarl and slam her back again, she *oomphs* as the wind is knocked out of her, but still laughs, even though I can feel the rapid beat of her pulse against my hand, betraying her. She's scared of me. It's what brings me back. "Fucking do it! I'm sick of the threats, of waiting for it to happen! Just kill me and get it over with, it's better than this not knowing!" she screams right in my face.

I was so lost, I didn't even hear the door open until a hand touches my arm. Jerking my head around with a snarl, I look right into Ryder's calm eyes. "Garrett, it's not her. Look, see? It's not her. It's Roxxane. Let her go."

Breathing heavily, I swing around to look at the woman held in my arms. My heart stutters, fuck. Releasing her, I stumble back—fuck, fuck, fuck. Horror washes through me. Is this really what I have turned into? My hand shakes as I stare at Roxy, who falls to her knees, gasping for air. Ryder tries to help her up, but she smacks his hands away and gets to her feet, her angry eyes locked on me.

She looks between us then, so fucking angry. "If you're going to kill me, just do it. I'm sick of this shit. Sick of looking over my shoulder, of being scared to sleep. I know I'm nothing to you, just another debt, but I didn't ask for this. I'm asking you now, kill me. Make it quick."

Ryder narrows his eyes as she stands there and waits, so brave, this little one. "We won't, and you do not order us, Roxxane."

"Then fuck you!" she yells, lashing out in fear. I know because I do the same thing. I see it in her gaze, the same ghosts that haunt me. "You think I'm going to sit here like another one of your fucking-fucking women? I am a person! I have a life." She looks to Ryder then, staring straight into his eyes. "You will regret the day you took me, I guarantee it. I'm going to destroy you." She strides right up to me, despite the fact I almost just killed her, and goes chest to chest with me.

"And you? You touch me again, and I will slit your throat in your sleep. Den of vipers or not, even if it means I won't make it out alive." She pulls back her fist, I see it coming, habit of a fighter, but I don't try to block it as it connects with my face. I hear my nose crack a little, pain flaring through me. But I'm used to it, I live in that pain.

Live for it, the only time I feel alive, feel normal. Not this scarred up monster hiding behind gloves and suits.

She shakes out her hand, and I know she hurt it, but she doesn't let it show as she turns and, with her head held high, leaves the room. I stand there, staring after her. She hit me. Again. That woman—she's a fucking hurricane.

Even when faced with death, she fights. It reminds me so much of some other men I know—my brothers—who never stop, never give up, even when the odds seem extreme.

I deserved her hit. Shit, I knew I shouldn't have let her in here. Let her get close enough to crawl under my skin, to poke and prod. It will be her death, that's all I can offer anyone. There is nothing else left of me but anger.

Hate.

"She sure is something," Ryder mutters, watching me. As always, his eyes sadden when they spot my chest. He blames himself, I know it. Always does when one of us gets hurt, always thinking he has to protect us. Save us. He doesn't, but he won't listen to me, not that we ever spoke about what happened. "Maybe you shouldn't be around her, I'm sorry, I didn't think about what it would do to bring her here..." He scrubs his hand through his hair, mussing it slightly.

That, in Ryder standards, is a meltdown.

"No, it's fine," I snap, turning away, not letting him see how close I came to losing myself to those emotions. To that darkness...those demons, the ones I fight every day. The ones I beat down with pain, fists, and kicks.

"I can kill her, she wouldn't be a problem then," he muses, so calmly, but when I drop the towel, yanking on my grey shorts, I look over to see his lips tilting down. He doesn't want to kill her. She's under his skin as well—interesting.

"No, it's fine. I wasn't prepared, I will be now. I'll stay away from her until we decide what we're doing with her," I reply, as I tug on a shirt and grab my bag, tucking my gun into my waistband.

"You going to the pits?" he asks, letting out a long breath as he slicks his hair back.

"I need to." I sigh, looking at my back, and his hand lands on my arm again.

"I know, go, do what you need to do to beat this. But then come back to us," he orders before leaving.

Sucking in a breath, I let his words guide me. *Come back to us.* How does he know I'm so close to being lost? So close to dropping my guard ever so slightly to let those flurries of fists connect, killing me? It would be easier, but it's not our way.

Vipers never give up.

Vipers never stop fighting.

Vipers are winners.

Striding from my room, I ignore the others who are sitting downstairs as I slam the door behind me. They will never know how close I am to the edge. Diesel went over it a long time ago, but he learned how to live in the dark. Kenzo walks that line, and Ryder? Ryder holds it all back with pure fucking strength.

Me? I beat it down.

Again and again, no matter how much this body gets broken. It's the only way I can function. To feel that adrenaline pumping through me, releasing my fury on another person. They often don't leave the ring on their own two feet. Those people there scream my name as blood drips from my bulging muscles, and they love it.

I hate it, but it's a necessity.

It once wasn't. I was the best, even did it professionally before I realised how much money could be had in underground fighting. Now I have no other choice, I'm too brutal for professional fighting. I want my opponent to hurt, to bleed. I want their bones to break under my fists, their eyes to blacken.

I want their pain.

I paint them with the destruction of my fists.

I PUMMEL THE MAN. HE TRIES TO BLOCK, TO DUCK BEHIND HIS arms, but he can't stop me. I give him everything, handing myself over to those emotions until I'm nothing more than anger. He falls to the floor, and I follow him down.

Pinning him there, I smash my fists into his unprotected face. My knuckles crack, splitting open. My own blood coats his face, but even then I don't stop. The crowd screams, pressing closer so they can almost taste the bloodshed. They love it.

They scream my name, but it all fades to a buzz as I swing fist after fist. The man passes out, but I still keep going, his head jerking to the side with each hard punch. Someone tries to get me to stop, but I push them away. I can't stop. I can't.

I need this.

I need him to bleed.

I need the pain.

I'm yanked away from the man, his chest is barely rising, his face caved in. Turning, I snarl, punching anyone who gets too close until the ref's, and the four security guards' currently trying to stop me, faces come into view.

Chest heaving, muscles screaming and soaked in sweat, I stand in the middle of the ring with the spotlight on me. I nod to let them know I'm back, that I'm okay. It goes quiet until the ref grabs my damaged hand and lifts it into the air, shouting into the mic about me winning. I don't care.

I stand there as the crowd surges, screaming, chanting, and stomping in the basement of the old paper factory. The stands are made from what they could find, and the ring is basically a chalk drawing with ropes around it.

But some of the richest people in the city are here, as well as the poorest. Yet they are the fighters, street kids like I once was. Anyone trying to change their future, giving everything. The ref leans closer. "We have another guy, you look like you need it."

I nod, he's right, I do. Roxy's eyes keep flashing in my mind, and I need someone to beat them out. "Make it two," I snarl, as I stride from the ring and throw back some water before letting it wash across my face. Peeling back the tape from my knuckles, I assess the damage— not too bad.

A woman sidles up next to me as they pick up the guy I almost killed from the ring and toss him aside like trash. The loser gets nothing, after all. I slip the money from my winnings into my bag, not that I need it, but it doesn't hurt. The woman coughs slightly when I don't look at her, her body almost pressing to my side...another woman did that once.

Her.

I should have known then she wasn't right, but I was too fucking blind. Too trusting. Too naïve. Not anymore. Never again.

The anger comes back full force as I glance at the intruder. The dress she's wearing is too tight, pushing up her fake boobs, almost making them spill from the top. Her red hair is curled, and her face is covered in makeup to within an inch of her life.

I can't help but compare her to that firework back at our apartment. She has nothing on Roxy. "What?" I growl, done with being nice. I don't have to be here, they all know me. Know what I am.

Women ache for a taste, thinking they can handle the madness in me. The men cheer it on, wanting to watch me kill. To get their own darkness out through me. They are all wrong. They have no idea what hides in my depths.

"Want some company, baby? You're a winner, after all," she purrs, running her hand down my sweaty arm. I grab her fingers and squeeze hard, she gasps in pain, her eyes widening and fear entering those orbs as she shivers under my gaze, shrinking back.

They all do.

They all think they can handle me, but they're wrong. Even if I wanted to fuck any one of them—which I don't, not anymore—I couldn't. I would kill them.

"Do. Not. Touch. Me," I snarl, just as I hear my name announced. I push her backwards, and she falls to her ass, the people around her laughing. Turning away, I head back to the ring, ready to lose myself in the fight once again.

Maybe I'll get lucky, maybe they will be a good opponent. Maybe they will give me the pain I need, maybe they will finally kill me and end this misery...

CHAPTER FOURTEEN

ROXY

I heard the door slam not too long ago. I've been hiding in my room ever since the run-in with Garrett, trying to slow my heartbeat. The worst bit is that underneath all that fear I'm trying to hide...there's something else. Something darker that wanted him to squeeze, that wanted that anger I could see controlling him.

That wanted to see just how far I could push him...and how far he would take it.

I'm fucked up.

Pushing off the door, I stagger into the bathroom, ripping off my clothes. I didn't shower earlier. I had fallen back asleep, but with the feel of Garrett's hand still wrapped around my throat, and the smell of sweat and man coating me, I need to.

I need to wash it away, the way I felt in that moment. I wasn't scared to die, I wasn't even scared it would hurt...I was scared I would never know how it felt to feel all that power.

To get revenge.

Fuck.

Slipping into the shower, I scrub my body, ignoring my traitorous pussy, who seems way too interested in these snakes. Once I'm done, I feel slightly better, and after drying off, I find my way back into the wardrobe and slip into an old, holey, AC/DC t-shirt. One of my favourites, my comfort shirt. Then I curl up in the perfect bed. Ryder was right, they made the room so it looks like my tantrum never happened. Though I poked the mirror in the bathroom and realised it was coated so as not to shatter.

Smart man.

I want to hide in here forever, but that's not my style. I still want to be free of these men, and to do that, I need knowledge. Knowledge is power. No one else is coming to help me, and the world doesn't give a shit. It doesn't care if I'm a good person or a bad person. Fuck, I'm not even sure which I am anymore...maybe somewhere in the middle.

So, on bare feet, I slip out into the apartment, pressing my back to the wall where they can't see me as I eavesdrop. "You think he'll be okay?" Kenzo drawls, his voice distinctive with the warmth he infuses in it.

"Yes, he just needed to get it all out," Ryder replies, his tone cold.

There's a sigh and some shifting. "Do you ever wonder if it wouldn't have been kinder..."

"Stop right there," Ryder snaps. "He's our brother, his demons are our demons. He survived, we do whatever it takes to ensure that he stays that way."

"You're right," Kenzo agrees, but sounds sad. "I just wish there was something we could do. I feel useless watching him struggle."

"This is his battle, not even we can help him this time. Only he can, he must decide to keep going. He's been in limbo ever since it happened, just living. I have a feeling that having Roxy here will shake that up. Force him to face it once and for all," Ryder murmurs.

"Y-You knew that when you brought her here, didn't you?" Kenzo snaps, angry now. "You might be smart, Ryder, but sometimes you're a fucking bastard. He's our brother."

"He is!" Ryder growls. "I'm trying to save him!"

"You are trying to control everything, like always!" Kenzo yells. "For once, stop trying to be in charge, just be there for him. That's all he needs, not your fucking experiments. We aren't another one of your challenges to conquer, we are your family. I swear, Ryder, sometimes you remind me of—"

It goes quiet, and I can almost feel the drop in temperature, and when Ryder's voice comes, it's deadly, dark, and oh so cold. "Say it."

"Of Dad!" Kenzo finishes. "You do, I love you, brother, but you get more like him every day. I've spent my life fighting to not be like him, but sometimes I wonder if you don't think it's just easier to give in. Remember what happened to him, brother, don't end up like him."

Peeking around the corner, I see Kenzo disappearing upstairs. Ryder is standing in the kitchen, his head hanging as he presses his fists to the worktop there. "One, two, three, four," he murmurs. "One, two, three, four."

He repeats it again and again, until I see his body calming, once more hiding behind that ice. When he pushes away from the worktop, he straightens, once again in control. His face is cold as he buttons up his suit and heads out the front door.

I try to dart after him, to escape, but a hand clamps over my mouth and I freeze, my eyes going wide as my heart slams and my breathing picks up. A mouth meets my ear, the smell of smoke and petrol wafting to me.

Diesel.

Fuck, they all warned me to stay away from him, and now Ryder is gone, Garrett too, not that they would save me. Even Kenzo is gone. It's just me and the crazy, psychotic Viper.

"Oh, Little Bird, I caught a little bird," he murmurs, licking my ear. "Tut, tut, eavesdropping like that, naughty little bird. Do you know what they get?"

I shake my head, my gaze locked on the opposite hallway, not daring to turn in case it triggers him in some way. True fear pounds through me. This man doesn't follow the rules. He kills for fun, tortures for laughs. Wants to see me squirm, to see me suffer. I don't know what to do, how to act around him. After all, prey always recognises a predator, and Diesel?

Diesel is all predator.

Unpredictable and consuming everything in his path, like the fire he loves so much. Even now, I can smell the cigarette on his breath, his hand rough like it's covered in burns as he presses it harder to my lips, pushing it painfully into my teeth.

"Punished."

I freeze as he laughs, pulling away from me as suddenly as he came. I spin, my hand going to my heart as he strolls down the corridor, the click of his lighter loud as he flicks it open and closed.

Fuck.

I really need to stay clear of that man. Something tells me he's going to be my death. I need to escape before he decides to stop torturing me and just go for the kill.

Because right now? I'm being hunted.

Four hungry vipers are slithering closer, wrapping tighter and tighter, their dark coils shining in the light as they prepare to strike.

And I'm in the middle.

AFTER MY RUN-IN WITH DIESEL, I DECIDED TO HIDE IN MY room, not wanting to be caught alone with him again without any of the others there. They might not stop him from hurting me, but I think they would stop him from killing me.

At least at the moment.

So I did the only other thing I could—sleep. This time, I had no nightmares though, well, not of my past. Instead, they were of tattooed knuckles running up my thighs, dark eyes peering up at me, and when I jerk awake in the morning light, I'm covered in a sheen of sweat. My pussy throbs, and my thighs are soaked with my own wetness.

Groaning at my own mind losing it and betraying me in my sleep, I glare down at my pussy. "You do understand they stole us, right? As in they stole us and locked us up?" I snarl, before heaving up and heading to shower again. Stupid fucking vagina, it doesn't seem to care that they bought us.

Or that they probably plan to kill us. She's a hussy and is all like, *yes, but they are hot.* Bastards. I mean, yes, they are hot. Attractive would be an understatement, they all look like statues of Greek gods. Perfectly carved with abs that don't come from sitting around all day. They work hard to be the best at everything, and that clearly includes being the best looking.

It's not fair and has my hormones all confused. I hate them, I do. I want to kill them...but also kinda want to screw them?

Brilliant.

After washing, I brush my teeth and cleanse my face, screw those bastards. I ain't putting makeup on for them, but I do brush my hair before slipping into some tight black skinny jeans—my favourite ones with holes and tears all the way down, showing off my tattoos—and pairing them with my loose Harley vest, which I tuck in at the front. There, I'm sort of presentable in case I manage to escape.

When I open my bedroom door, I find my boots outside and, honestly, I nearly cry as I yank them on. "I missed you," I tell them, stroking the matte black material as I lace them up and tuck in my jeans. I always feel better with what Cook calls my ass kickers on.

Fuck, Cook.

I hope the bar is okay. I wonder if anyone even cares that I've disappeared?

It's not like I have anyone who'd notice, other than some staff and people who drink there all the time. They are probably more bothered that I can't pour them some drinks and have to find somewhere else to go.

Feeling stronger, I head down the corridor, déjà vu hitting me when I find them all sitting at the breakfast table. Do they do this every morning? I slip into my chair from yesterday. Garrett doesn't look at me, but I see one of his eyes is black, and when I look at his busted, blood encrusted knuckles on the table, he yanks them underneath.

His shirt is a V-neck, showing off those scars I saw yesterday. They were horrendous, he must have suffered so much pain. Endured so much. How is he alive? They looked like strips of his skin had been torn away and sewn back on, creating mottled flesh. My heart actually hurts for him.

From what I've heard, something clearly happened to him. But what? And why does that make him hate women?

I look away, not wanting to trigger him again. Ryder is reading the paper, also ignoring me, wearing the only suit he has left, which makes me smirk. He must notice because he raises his eyes before narrowing them slightly at me. "Eat, you didn't yesterday."

"Worried I'll starve to death?" I scoff.

"There are much more interesting ways to die." Diesel grins at me, sucking a sausage from his fork as he chews, leering at me.

Looking away, I watch as Kenzo fills my plate again, passing me a coffee without asking. I decide to do as Ryder orders, not because I'm being good, but because I'm actually hungry. And it can't be poisoned or they would all be dead.

I eat it so fast, my stomach actually hurts. Shit, I forgot how much starving hurts when you eat again. Sipping the coffee, I sit back in my chair, pulling my knees to my chest to try and stop the ache.

"Today, you will stay with Kenzo again," Ryder informs me, as he sips from his tiny teacup, folding the paper and placing it on the table. "Garrett, you and I need to make some visits. We'll bring you back a present, Diesel...no breaking it. Just play, a reminder."

Diesel perks up, his eyes almost blazing as he smirks. "Fuck yes."

"I mean it," Ryder warns, and Diesel rolls his eyes but nods.

"Then I need to go downtown, it seems I'm in need of more clothing." Ryder sighs, and every eye turns to me. I smirk, sipping my coffee. "I will also grab you some items, Roxxane."

"I don't need your fucking charity clothes," I snarl, sitting up.

Ryder looks me over, judgement in his eyes. "You're wearing rags, a Viper does not wear such...attire."

"Good job I'm not a fucking Viper," I snap.

His lips turn up at the corner. "No, but you are a guest. You will represent our business and family, even when you are simply in the apartment. This isn't a negotiation."

"What? Want me to take my piercings out as well?" I laugh. "Not good enough for your sanctimonious ass to rape?"

He snarls then, leaning forward. "Be careful what you say, Roxxane, very careful." Then he blinks, and he's back to being ice-cold. "No, you may keep your piercings, you do look beautiful without the makeup, by the way, but I find myself seeing it as you without war paint." He laughs.

"Good, 'cause there are some piercings that aren't so easy to take out." I shrug, and all eyes are back on me again, wondering. "You will never fucking find out."

Diesel laughs. "Don't be so sure, Little Bird."

Garrett looks away again and gets to his feet, holding himself stiffly as if he hurts. "We should get going."

"Indeed." Ryder sighs and stands, looking over at me again. "I would say behave, but I don't think you would listen. Know that Diesel will be here this morning." He almost smirks, fucker, he knows that means I'll behave so the crazy bastard won't come near me.

I take my coffee and, with one last glare at them, retreat to my room. No way am I putting myself in the path of that pyromaniac. I'll actually listen to them for once and stay away. Shit, this is getting boring though. All I'm doing is sleeping and hiding.

I thought I would be free by now.

I'm coming to believe I'll never be free again. I'll die here, at their hands.

I stay in the room as long as I can. I get so bored, I count the steps it takes to get everywhere before flopping back on the bed. It has to be hours later when I finally can't take it anymore, I've never been one to sit still. Hell, I've worked nearly every day since I was sixteen. First to pay off my dad's debt back then to Rich before he hired me on fully, then to make him proud...and then to keep my bar afloat.

I find myself missing it, not knowing how to switch off. So I open the door a crack and look out, peeking each way to make sure Diesel isn't standing right outside to pounce on me. When nothing moves, I slip into the hall, sliding my feet across the cool floor to make no sound as I head to the end of the corridor.

Once there, I look around the corner to see if the living area is empty. Kenzo is outside again, on the phone, pacing back and forth. Diesel is just heading out the front door, and I see my opportunity.

They all think I'm in my room.

My heart pounds as I rush across the space, sliding my foot into the door to stop it from closing and locking. I bite my lip to hold back my cry as it slams my foot between it and the frame, tears filling my eyes. Fuck, that hurt. I duck behind the door, peering around it, watching as Diesel waits for the elevator. His usual lighter is at his side, flicking open and closed again until the steel doors open and he gets in.

Leaning down, he lights a cigarette, the only reason he doesn't spot me as the doors start to slowly close. So fucking slowly. Glancing over my shoulder, feeling panic, I see Kenzo hanging up. Fuck, it's now or never. Slipping out the door just as the elevator slams shut, I ease the door closed.

I'm free.

I'm fucking free!

Well, of the apartment, but that's a whole other matter. I try the elevator, but there's what looks like a scanner there, and it lights up red when I try, fuck. Okay. There's a door at the end of the hallway with a fire exit sign. Hell yes! Racing to it, I slam it open, holding my breath in case an alarm sounds. When it doesn't, I relax a little.

Not too much, I still have to get out of the building. I don't know where I'll go when I'm free, it's clear I won't be able to go back to my normal life, but that's a matter for later. Racing down the steps with quick feet, I'm so excited, I almost trip and fall. Gripping the railing, I fly down them as fast as I dare until I come to another level and a door.

It's locked, so I try the next floor and the next. Down and down I go, each and every door locked with a scanner. Fuck, am I going to be trapped in their stairwell? I go past something marked for the next level, which is labelled B1. Basement maybe?

My chest is heaving, my lungs screaming at how fast I ran, and adrenaline coursing through me. Shit, I'm out of shape. There's no scanner on this door, and my eyes widen. Hell yes. I rip it open, almost crying in victory when it actually slams back. Rushing forward, I abruptly halt in my tracks, crouching behind a post next to the door which extends into the ceiling. It's a fucking parking garage. Shit, that means there are probably cameras.

Looking up, I spot them just like I thought. They seem to be rotating, so I count how long it takes to revolve before looking for an exit. There's one at the top of a ramp with a shutter. But it seems there is only a button to get out from this side. I smirk. They weren't expecting people to try and get out, or if they did, they didn't expect them to get this far.

Looking back at the cameras, I watch them sweep again before bursting from behind the pole when they turn away from the ramp. Thirty seconds, that's all I have. I race past fancy cars and bikes and empty spots, pushing myself harder.

Twenty-eight.

Fuck. Pumping my arms, I lower my head and sprint up the ramp, panting heavily.

Twenty-five.

Looking around, I slam my hand on the button. Nothing happens. Again and again, I do it.

Twenty.

Shit.

There's a slot below it for a card or a scanner. Fuck, fuck, fuck! I scream, slamming my hand into it. I was so close. My head jerks around, there has to be a door, a pedestrian exit or entrance, right?

Fifteen.

There's a booth. I'm nearly out of time, so I push the door inwards and look around for a key, a card, anything. There's a computer and a row of keys hung up at the back. Not much else. I rip open doors, kicking the chair away.

Ten.

Fuck. My hands scramble through the shit in the drawers before searching the keys on the wall.

Five.

Mercedes, Ferrari, Harley, my hands start to shake in fear that I won't find any.

Three.

No.

There's nothing here.

I'm trapped.

Two.

Fuck.

One.

I crouch just as I hit thirty, peeking over the edge of the desk to look through the glass to see the camera aimed back this way. Crouching, I wait for it to pass. That's when I notice it—a crowbar under the desk. Hell yes.

Glancing up again, I spot the camera sweeping away, and I dart from the booth. Kenzo will probably check on me soon, and if he finds me gone, he'll put this whole place into lockdown. I need to be gone before then.

Pressing the crowbar at the base of the shutter, I throw myself into it. All my weight and strength from carrying barrels of beer. But it doesn't so much as move. Screaming again, I look around. *Think, Rox, think.* The keys! Fuck, maybe I can smash my way out of here?

Running into the booth, I pick the closest one and head back into the parking area. I hit the fob button, hearing a beep, but I don't see the car. Pressing it again, I spot a silver Merc at the end lighting up. Nice, screw these Viper bastards.

They are rich, they can replace it.

Using the posts, I duck behind them when the camera comes back around. It's slow going, but I eventually make it to the car. Crouching, I open the door, a soft click echoing through the structure as I slip inside. Okay, okay.

Looking around, I find a start-stop button and press it, the car revs to life, the engine purring as the dash lights up. The fucking rich pricks. Smirking at how pissed they will be when they find out I stole one of their cars, I put it in gear and stomp on the gas. Squealing comes from the tires as I peel from the space, knocking into some other cars as I go.

Whoops, not sorry.

Racing at the shutter, I take a deep breath. *Please let this work.* With one hand on the wheel, I click my seatbelt in, knowing if it doesn't work, it's going to fucking hurt.

I force my eyes open, my heart in my throat as I race towards it. I'm near the base of the ramp when an alarm sounds, lights flashing as it gets louder. A cranking starts and my eyes widen when barriers begin to rise from the floor, cutting off the ramp.

No, no, no.

But it's too late, they are too high and I'm still barrelling towards them. Screaming, I smash onto the brakes, the car fishtailing as I try to avoid the crash. I slow down, but it's not enough, I hit the barrier. My head jerks and smashes into the window, making me groan. My neck is thrown into the seatbelt, cutting off my air supply for a moment as the airbags explode.

Fuck.

Head ringing, pain racing through me, I unlock the seatbelt with fumbling fingers and kick open the door, sliding onto the ground. Holy shit. That was so close. My heart is tripping over itself, and my stomach is rolling. Leaning on all fours, I suck in desperate breaths. When I feel more calm, I stagger to my feet.

The whole right side of the car is scratched from hitting the barrier. But it's fixable. There's a crack in the driver's side window from where my head hit it. It makes me angry, and it pours through me as I scream it all out. I was so close! So fucking close! And now, now I'm stuck here.

Where I'll die.

I don't know what comes over me, everything is too much. I'm powerless and out of control and can't help it. Scarily calm, I walk over to the crowbar I dropped and pick it up, holding it like I do my bat. I feel blood dripping down my head, but I don't care. Walking back to the car, I swing the crowbar and bring it down on the hood.

It feels good, really good, as the sound of crunching metal fills the air. The hood dents, so I do it again and again, ruining the perfect expensive toy. I smash in windows, laughing as the crash fills the air. I beat the car so good, lost in my own world. I need more, I need to get it all out.

Scrambling onto the bonnet, I bring the crowbar down repeatedly, screaming as I do. I climb to the top of the car, standing on the roof as I smash everything I can reach. My arms feel like lead, and I drop the crowbar. It hits the ground with an audible clunk as I heave in breaths, my body covered in sweat, my head aching from the hit, and my back and neck sore—but it was worth it. Seeing the destruction I wrought, I can't help but laugh.

Take that, you Viper bastards.

That's when I hear clapping. Whipping my head up, I lock eyes with Diesel and Kenzo, who are standing about ten meters away from the car, just watching me. Kenzo is rolling his dice through his fingers with a smirk on his face, while Diesel's clapping.

"I bet you she wouldn't make it." Kenzo smirks at him as Diesel stops, his face lighting up as he watches me.

His chest is bare, a few tattoos covering the golden skin, and he's ripped. Way too ripped. Shouldn't crazy people be worse looking? But no, he looks like a fallen angel. Gold hair and all, which is tied back in a ponytail. "You did, man, that was hot as hell." He nods to me and then looks at Kenzo. "Isn't she amazing?"

Just then, the door into the basement rips open and Garrett and Ryder stride in. They freeze when they see me standing on top of the ruined car with Kenzo and Diesel just watching me. Diesel whistles, winking over at me.

"Ooh, you're in trouble now, Little Bird."

Fuck.

Ryder's face is thunderous as he steps closer. His shirt is wrinkled, and his suit jacket is thrown haphazardly on. "I was pulled from a meeting to see this..." He narrows his eyes and looks to Kenzo. "Explain," he barks.

The man shrugs. "Sorry, bro, she somehow snuck out. When I realised, I searched the cameras and saw her in the basement in your car. I hit the alarm, and the barriers must have stopped her."

"Then?" Ryder prompts, gesturing to me on top of the car.

"Then she started beating the shit out of your car, screaming something about snakes and assholes," Diesel offers wistfully, almost dreamily.

I did?

Wait, Ryder's car?

Oh fuck.

The man looks back at me with cold eyes. "Get down now," he orders.

I swallow, but he must see me about to open my mouth, because he steps closer still, each movement controlled. "Now. Do not make me come up there."

I jump from the car, crunching as I land, jarring my aching head. I know he means business, especially when he grabs my arm and drags me away. I struggle in his grip, swearing, but he ignores me as he hauls me over to the elevator and smashes his hand on the scanner.

It opens, and he throws me inside. I slam into the wall, the breath knocked out of me as I turn to see him step inside before smashing his finger onto a button. We start to rise, and I watch him carefully. His eyes are dark, those emotions melting the ice there. His hands are shaking, balled into fists, and it's clear he's close to exploding.

So what do I do?

Push him.

Maybe it's because I've accepted that I'm going to die here and never be free again, and with that acceptance has come a certain bravery to see how far I can push them. It's crazy, but I can't seem to stop.

"Nice car." I smirk.

His movements are jerky, and I flinch back as he bangs his fist onto a stop button. We shudder to a halt, throwing me forward, right into him. He catches me, his hand going around my throat as he tosses me back into the elevator wall, making me cry out at the pain it causes.

"Do not push me, love," he snarls, right in my face. My heart is pounding, and he must feel it against his hand because he squeezes my throat, letting me feel all that power. The strength and emotions he hides behind the ice.

This man is deadly, a Viper, and I just poked the snake, and now he's ready to strike.

To bite.

And I'm the mouse.

But yet again, my mouth opens. "Why not?"

He leans closer, letting me see those eyes which are now on fire. Fuck, how did I ever think he was cold? He's an inferno, a wildfire. It burns everything in its path, and right now, that's me. But the thing is, I would gladly burn, and I don't even know why.

"Because I won't be gentle like Kenzo. I won't even make sure you like it like Diesel. I will tan your ass so hard that you won't be able to walk, never mind sit. Then I'll leave you in this elevator for everybody to see just how much you want us. How much you don't hate us, even if you think so. You can fool yourself, but you can't fool me, love. I will rip those barriers to shreds, piece by fucking piece. I will have you on the edge, nearly coming from my punishment alone, and leave you for everyone to see...to see how much you want it. The very people you claim to hate."

"I don't want you," I snap, tipping my head back and meeting his eyes, but my thighs clench, betraying my truth, and he no doubt notices. Ryder notices everything and uses it against me. And he's noticed something even I didn't want to. I'm attracted to them, to my kidnappers.

That's what stops me from speaking—the fact that he's right and I hate him. I hate them. I really do, but I want them so badly it's scary, and I've been trying to hide from it, taking it out on them. He smirks like he sees my battle and knows I won't fight him anymore. Stepping back, he straightens his suit, hiding behind that coolness again. His hands stop shaking as he presses the button to get us moving. "Last warning, Roxxane—do not push us. We have been kind so far, now? All bets are off, you are about to see what the Vipers are really like, and you only have yourself to blame. You're fair game now, little prey, better run." He winks. "You're a business deal, love, but now you're about to become our toy."

The door opens, and he steps out, meeting the eyes of the rest of the Vipers waiting there. Shit, how did they get up here so fast? He smirks at them, ignoring me still pressed against the wall, breathing heavily, hating him, hating myself. But at least the blood from my head has stopped.

"D, she's yours for the rest of the day. Let's show our little brat here what happens to those who betray us, who test us," Ryder orders, his icy eyes still locked on me. Only when he turns away do I start to breathe again.

Holy fuck.

I thought Ryder was ice, an unfeeling snake. I was so wrong.

Under it all is a swirling tornado of emotions barely being held in check. I glimpsed it in his eyes, felt it in his hands. He's so close to exploding and raining down destruction, I don't think he even knows how close.

The others currently don't, but I do now. He's ready to break, to snap, and when he does...who will be alive to tell the story?

CHAPTER

FIFTEEN

DIESEL

"She's yours." It repeats over and over in my head as a smile curls my lips. She steps farther back into the elevator, her eyes on me, scared. She should be. Ryder and Garrett brought me a new toy to play with, to teach him a lesson. It seems he disrespected Ryder when he was approached about not paying up.

As I step forward, Garrett's hand darts out and grips my bicep. I had just gotten started with the man when I heard the alarm, so I'm without a shirt, and he turns his lips down at that. "Don't go too hard on her."

I raise my gaze from his grip to his eyes. I would do anything for my brothers, but especially Garrett. We know each other's pain, so we are closer than the others. We are two similar souls. "Thought you didn't care."

"I don't," he snaps, dropping his arm and storming away as Kenzo laughs, watching him stomp off.

"He's right though, D. Test her, but don't break her, okay? I'm getting kind of used to the girl, so play with her, but don't kill her. I haven't had my chance to break her yet." He chuckles before he winks at my little bird and walks away, leaving me alone with her.

She gulps but tilts her head back, so filled with fear yet brave at the same time. I can't wait to peel it all back and see what lies beneath, and Ryder just gave me the go ahead. They don't know the full extent of everything I do. I get results, and that's all they care about. They let me have my fun, let me do what I need to survive.

And Little Bird?

She's going to as well.

Stepping into the elevator, I press the button to take me all the way down again. I stare at her, and feeling her fear fill up the lift makes my cock harden in my trousers. Stepping closer, I suck in her sweet scent as she presses her back to the wall. I lean down and lap at the cut on her head, reopening it so it starts to bleed again. She squeaks, and I laugh as I step back.

"This is going to be fun, Little Bird."

The door opens, and I whistle as I turn and head into the labyrinth that is my den. It's dark and warm down here, just how I like it. I glance over my shoulder to see her uselessly pressing the elevator buttons. It won't move again without my card or hand. A security measure we put in place when someone broke free of their chains and made it to the lobby, wandering around covered in blood.

That was hard to explain to the police, it's a good job we own them.

"Little Bird, don't make me come back in there and get you," I singsong, and chuckle as she jerks her head up and peers out at me.

"Fuck this, fucking crazy ass," she mutters, as she storms out, moving in my direction. "You try to kill me, and I'll feed you your own balls. Okay?"

"Later, my love, right now we have someone to deal with. We can continue the ways you wish to touch me after." I wink and turn, heading back to the room I was in before, where the man is waiting, chained to the ceiling. He's already naked and covered in blood. He jolts awake when I enter, a moan leaving his throat as tears fall down his face. "Sorry about that, you understand how hard it can be to run a business and keep your woman happy, I'm sure."

"Not your fucking woman—oh my God!" Roxy gasps as she stops at the doorway, her eyes going wide. She's horrified.

I pick up the knife I was using and point it at Declan. "This here is Declan. He not only insulted Ryder and us, but also tried to have Garrett killed." Tsking, I look back at the man. "You really are a fool."

"Wait, he tried to kill Garrett?" Roxy frowns, her eyes flashing in anger. Ah, there's the madness. Even though she tries to hide it, she's starting to like us *and* loathe us at the same time. But it's imperative she sees what betraying us looks like. What will happen to her if she tries to escape again.

She is ours now, she needs to accept it.

She can be one of us, a Viper, or she can end up like Declan.

"For all the good it did him." I snort. "So, Declan, where were we? Ah, yes, you were going to tell me how much the Triad offered you, or I was going to cut off your nipples."

"Diesel," she snaps behind me, but I ignore her.

"So, little Declan?" I prompt, pressing the blade just under his nipple. He struggles in the chains, hopelessly tugging on them, crying once again.

"Diesel," she yells, so I start to slice, making him scream.

A hand lands on my shoulder, and I whirl with a snarl. Holding the bloody knife to her throat, I back her into the wall. "Do not think you can save him, Little Bird. He dies here, but it's his choice how much pain he endures. We cannot let a threat like that stand. He tried to kill one of us. We are the Vipers, we do not die. We strike back. Get used to it, or be quiet. Like it or not, you're part of this now." Leaning down, I press the blade harder against her throat. "No one hurts us, no one. That includes you now. Do you really want to save this man's life?"

She swallows, cutting herself slightly on the blade and gasping, those lips I dream about parting. "I—"

"Would it help if I told you he raped his stepdaughter?" Her eyes fly wide, and I nod. "We do our research, Little Bird. This son of a bitch is a low life. I would still kill him if he wasn't, but I thought it might help you to know what he is—a monster. Do you know what monsters fear, Little Bird?"

"What?" she whispers shakily.

"The bigger monster," I whisper, licking her lips. "They fear me."

Leaning back, I remove the knife and let her breathe freely. Her breath whistles out unevenly from her lips as she stares at me, searching my face for answers. Answers she will only find inside herself. This is the moment. If she tries to save him, she's choosing her own fate. She will never be one of us, too weak to handle our life. And that means I'll eventually have to kill her. "Do you want to save him, Little Bird?"

She looks at the man behind me, and I see her debating her answer. If I'm lying, if he's innocent...but things like innocence doesn't exist anymore, and she needs to learn that. Everyone's a sinner in one way or another. You can cover it in roses and use excuses, but it's all the same. It could be shiny and rich, but a sinner is still a sinner in a suit. There is no black and white, only grey. Deep down, we all do things that are considered bad, even for good causes.

Me? I do them for fun.

She looks back at me. "I need to know," she whispers, and grips the knife between us. I relinquish my hold and step back, watching her, curious to see what she will do. Will she try to use it on me? That would be hot.

She steps closer to the man who sniffles. "Please, please let me go," he begs, putting on a convincing act of innocence. I'll give him that. I wonder if she cried the same way the first time he slipped into her room at night, but did it stop him? No. And it won't stop me.

She presses the knife to his chest, her hand shaking, her voice steel. "Did you rape her?"

He freezes, his eyes going to me, then back to her. "No, no, of course not," he cries, but that hesitation is enough, I see her stiffen.

She digs the knife in deeper, her hand steady now. "Do not lie to me, or I'll let him do whatever he wants until you tell him the truth."

Fuck, my cock twitches in my jeans, and I debate palming it. Watching her hold that knife...having her in my den, joining in. It's doing things to me.

"I-I—she asked for it!" he screams. "Walking around in those little undies, teasing me—"

His voice cuts off in a shriek as Roxy yells and slices down his chest. Stepping back, chest heaving, eyes hard and angry, she tosses me the knife. I catch it mid-air, making sure to grab the sharp end so it cuts my hand to match hers. "Do whatever you want to the bastard, make it hurt."

"Yes, Little Bird, whatever you want," I purr, as she hops up on a counter at the back, swinging her legs as she watches me. I step back to the man. She said make it hurt. I can do that. Continuing what I started, I flip the blade and catch it with my damaged hand, pressing it to his skin in one smooth move.

I slice off one nipple without warning and toss it away, grab my lighter, heat the blade and, as he screams, press it to his flesh. The smell of sizzling meat wafts to me before I do the same to the other one. He slumps then, passing out, so I wait for him to wake up. It's no fun when they aren't awake.

"You do this a lot."

I look over at my little bird. "It's my job."

"A killer?" she inquires, not judging, I think, just trying to understand.

Wiping my blade, I nod. "We all have our roles. It's what makes us so good—we each know our place and have our strengths."

"Will you tell me?" she asks.

"I could, it's not like you can tell anyone, but, Little Bird, what's it worth?" I purr.

She swallows. "I thought gambling and bets was Kenzo's department?"

Ah, Little Bird sees more than they think, I knew it. Heading her way, I lean against the cupboard and pin her there with my arms on either side of her. Even in this blood-soaked room, with a man hanging from chains behind me, her eyes dilate. Little Bird wants this, wants me, wants to be free, even if she doesn't realise it.

"It is, but it doesn't mean I won't make a deal with you for information. After all, I do work to get just that," I whisper, wanting to taste her more than I want to take my next breath.

Her eyes flicker between mine as she debates her next words. "Promise you won't hurt me?"

I laugh. "No, I won't ever promise that. I might hurt you, I might even kill you one day, but we both know that's where the attraction is. You're walking a blade's edge, pretty little bird, and one day, you might just slip, but wouldn't the fall be worth it?"

I can hear the hammering of her heart as her eyes drop to my lips. "Fine, what do you want in exchange?"

"Your surrender," I growl. "I know there is a wild one inside you, like me, just waiting to be set free. I noticed it in your eyes the first time I saw you. You will do anything to survive, like us. You're more like us than you can imagine. You see the darkness, and you walk that line, one foot in and one foot out. Put both feet in, Little Bird, this is your world now. Filled with bloodshed and snakes. You want something, then take it. Do whatever the fuck you want, Little Bird, because the rest of the world does."

"That's-that's what you want?" she snaps. "Me to be like you?"

"No, for you to be yourself, the one you hide, even from you. But today, today I will take something smaller. A kiss, Little Bird. Kiss me, and I'll tell you what you want to know," I murmur, watching those lips.

"You swear?" She sighs.

"Every day." I smirk.

"Fuck, okay." She jerks her head forward and kisses me, hard and quick, before pulling away. "Tell me."

"What was that?" I laugh. "A real kiss, Little Bird, like you mean it."

She snarls, getting annoyed now, her irritation overruling her fear of me. Her hand comes out and grips my shoulder, dragging me closer as she slams her lips to mine. It's hard, angry, and hateful. At my forcing her, no doubt, but she always had a choice, and she chose.

She chose me.

She tastes like sweetness and life, she's oh so fucking alive. Electricity arcs between our lips, her denial and my lust mingling with our breaths. Gripping the back of her head, I drag her closer, my hand tangling in her silky silver hair. I press my teeth to her lips until she opens enough to let me slip my tongue inside. She gasps and pushes closer, loving it even as she fights me.

Her body quivers against me, my cock so hard, I feel like I'm about to explode just from a kiss alone. She moans, a breathy little sound that goes straight to my cock. The sound seems to snap her out of it, but I refuse to let her go. I force my tongue deeper, dominating her mouth, marking her lips, bruising them. Taking what I want.

She gets angry, and starts slapping and clawing at my bare shoulders with her tiny kitten claws. She can do better. I saw her take down Garrett. She wants me to stop? Then I want to see that Roxy. Tugging her closer, I press my hardness between her legs, and she freezes before her fighting gets worse. Grinning against her mouth, I kiss her harder. "You can do better than that, Little Bird," I murmur, before biting down on her bottom lip.

She groans and slaps me. The sound is loud in the room as my head whips to the side. My eyes wild, chest heaving, and cock hard, I slowly look back at her. She's got wide eyes again, but her bruised, raw lips tip up in a smirk, one I return. "You're getting there, Little Bird. Soon, you will be free." A groan comes from behind me as the man wakes up. "Until then, ask away."

"Tell me what everyone's job is," she demands, her voice husky as her tongue slips out and tastes her lips, making me grunt.

"Don't look at me like that," I snarl.

"Like what?" she questions, tilting her head.

"Like you want to eat me, so fucking hungry," I snap.

"You taste like fire," she whispers, and then sucks in a breath. "Tell me, I paid up, now it's your turn," she retorts, angry at herself for getting into that position. For letting herself enjoy it.

Poor Little Bird has no idea how much she's going to enjoy what else is to come between us.

I've pushed her a lot today, so I step back and start talking. Today is about breaking down some of those barriers, so I'll keep pushing, keep daring, until the true Little Bird comes out to play, and won't that be brilliant?

"Kenzo is the bookie, owns the city's gambling. Horses, cards, anything you can bet on, even fights. He's the money side of things, good with numbers. Garrett used to be a fighter, so he knows a lot of tough people. He's the enforcer. He scares people, beats them up a bit to make them listen to Ryder, who's the front man. The face and the brains of the operation. They try to stop it from getting to me."

"And what are you?"

I smirk as I grab a bone saw from the table. "I'm your worst nightmare. The place you go when you're at the end. I get information by whatever means necessary. When Garrett can't scare them, Ryder can't reason with them, and Kenzo can't bribe them, then I get them. I kill our enemies, I torture those who dare defy us. I'm the reason people are scared to cross the Vipers."

"You're the assassin," she murmurs, lips still swollen from our kiss. She has never looked more beautiful.

"Yes, Little Bird, I'm the assassin, and you're my latest target." I wink before turning back to the man. "Declan, nice to have you back. Shall we continue?"

Roxy watches me the whole time. She says nothing as I rip the man to pieces, bit by bit, figuring out what makes him scream. He passes out five more times before I have my answer. Then I kill him. I douse him in petrol and set him on fire.

His screams fill the air again, the scent of blood and piss with it. I turn to look at my little bird as Declan burns to death. The flames dance across the planes of her face, lighting up her eyes and the fear and acceptance there. She has finally realised the type of people who bought her.

Finally understood she's ours. There is no way out for her. Not now. Not ever. Little Bird needs to find out how to survive amongst the Vipers, or die as our prey.

CHAPTER SIXTEEN

ROXY

Diesel's words echo through my head. Free, he wants me to give up. Accept my fate and become like them. I'll admit the kiss made me feel something—something that scared me. It was addictive, the taste of his lips lingering even now. But I can't go there. I have to remember I'm nothing more to them than a debt. A prisoner. I was bought.

No matter how much his kiss set me alight.

Or even that I could understand why he does what he does. It doesn't make it right, but there are worse people out there. Sometimes you have to fight fire with fire, and that's what he's doing. Protecting his family. I didn't even feel horror when he killed the man and set him ablaze. I expected it.

And that terrifies me. Shouldn't I care?

He was a rapist, but...but the way he died...the smell of his burnt flesh is seared into me. The screams will haunt my nightmares, and the man responsible has my panties wet. I told him to make it hurt, and he did. I need to remember to be careful of what I say, since it seems the Vipers take orders very seriously, and for some reason, Diesel listened to me.

In a way, since talking to him, I've realized something. This is like a game of chess, one I didn't even know I was playing. But I refuse to be a pawn. I'm a fucking queen and it's time I started acting like one. D was right. They all have their strengths, but that also means they have weaknesses. I will find and use them against the Vipers.

I will kill them, cut off the head of the snake.

After all, if you can't beat them up, join them and then kill them. It's time I got my hands dirty, 'cause they clearly are, and being good doesn't seem to be working for me. After Diesel stops the fire, he cleans his tools before leading me back upstairs. He lets me remain silent, lost in my thoughts. Honestly, I don't know what to say.

He casually told me he might kill me, and then the next second, he kissed me like I was air and he was a drowning man. It pisses me off. I've been kissed a lot, but never like that, never so consumingly. It set every nerve ending alive with desire, like if I didn't keep kissing him, I would die. If I didn't taste him, feel him against me...fuck.

I mean, I did feel him, it was hard not to when his cock was pressed up against me like that. Sighing, I push the thoughts away. I can't afford to let him get in my head. I need to think straight, and that means no more thoughts of the crazy man's cock.

"Ready for dinner, Little Bird?" he murmurs, flicking his lighter open and closed. I want to ask him about it, but I'm not sure I could pay the price of another question so soon. Not when the last one still has me twisted up in knots, and the more I learn about these men... the less I hate them. I can't have that.

"Starving," I reply, making him chuckle, and it's true and horrifying. The smell of that man burning...made me hungry.

Yep, I'm officially more messed up than I thought.

Diesel leads me into the apartment, and the guys are there waiting, with pizza and beer spread across the table. It surprises me, and Kenzo must see that. "We eat junk food too, now sit your pretty ass down and grab some before it's all gone." He looks me over as he speaks, but when he finds me all in one piece, he seems satisfied.

Ryder's eyes track me across the room as I plop into my seat and grab nearly a whole pizza and two beers. Ignoring his look, I scarf them down. He wanted to teach me a lesson, to control me like everything else, and it's clear he doesn't like what he can't control.

He's going to hate me.

They all watch me eat, gobsmacked, apart from Garrett, who weirdly grunts in approval. There's one last slice left, and as I reach for it, so does Diesel. He smirks at me, and I can almost see his dare to try and take it from him. So I do the only thing a girl faced with losing a slice of cheesy heaven can do. I grab my fork and stab it into his hand.

He yelps, yanking his hand back with the fork still sticking out of it as I grab the slice and take a bite, feeling smug. Everyone else is silent, watching Diesel, and when I gaze around, I realise they are all tense. I slow my chewing and look to Diesel to see what they are so worried about.

He pulls the fork from his hand and covers the holes as they bleed, his eyes slowly rolling up and meeting mine. We stare each other down for a moment before he bursts into laughter. Kenzo jumps next to me, so hard I'm surprised he doesn't fall from his seat. Sighing, he looks over at me. "Don't piss Diesel off, okay?"

"What? Why?" I ask, hiding my smile behind my slice of pizza.

Kenzo glances at Ryder, and they share a look before he brings his gaze back to me. "Just don't."

I shrug and swallow the last bite of pizza before washing it down with some beer. "We won't be here in the morning, Roxxane."

I look up at Ryder as he wipes his mouth and leans back in his chair. His shirt is unbuttoned at the top, and I swear it's the most relaxed I've ever seen him. "Huh?"

"Garrett, Diesel, and I will be gone before you even rouse. Kenzo will be here, I trust after our...demonstration, I don't need to tell you the importance of behaving." He raises his eyebrow as I narrow my eyes. "Or I will start having to lock you up again."

Fuck.

"Fine, where are you going?" I inquire.

"We have someone to deal with," he offers.

"Does that have to do with the fact someone tried to kill Garrett?" I query, and Ryder sighs, looking over at Diesel with a disapproving expression.

"Yes, the man hired was an assassin, so we are going to visit an old friend, Donald, to find out who. It's a hundred or so miles away." He shrugs.

"So why this guy...Donald?" I press.

He smirks. "He runs the assassins in this country, if anyone knows who the hitman was, it's him."

"Then what will you do?" I ask.

"To the hitman? Track him down and make an example of him," he answers, so matter-of-fact and honest, that I'm not even surprised. "Kenzo, make sure she doesn't get out this time."

"I'm not a fucking dog," I mutter.

"Then stop acting like a bitch." Ryder smirks, and my mouth drops. That motherfucker—I should have stabbed him with the fork, not Diesel. "There are new clothes in your room for you, and if you behave, I might even get you something to keep you busy."

"Well, aren't you just the best kidnappers ever?" I deadpan, and Kenzo chuckles next to me.

"Don't worry, darling, I can keep you busy." He wiggles his eyebrows at me, and I snarl, even though my heart slams in my chest.

"I have a knife as well as a fork," I warn, and he laughs, those dice running through his fingers like always.

Ryder gets to his feet, unbuttoning his shirt as he does, and my eyes widen. What the—holy fuck. He undoes the top two buttons, showcasing golden skin...covered in tattoos. When he rolls his sleeves up to his forearms, displaying large veins and muscles, I feel my mouth drop open at the tattoos covering him from the wrist up. I did not see that coming. His suit hides a lot. "I'm going to the gym, be ready to leave at three AM," he tells the others, and then strides away, leaving me there as I drool.

Get yourself together.

I snap my head around to see Kenzo smirking at me, catching me salivating over him. Shit. He leans closer. "Want to bet I know what you're thinking about right now, darling?"

I try to stab him with the knife, but he's really fast and gracefully leaps from his chair, winking at me before walking away. That leaves me with Diesel and Garrett. Nope, wait. Garrett gets up and stalks away without even a backwards glance. Okay, so Diesel and me again. I look over to see him prodding the bleeding stab wounds on his hands, his tongue caught between his teeth in concentration.

Okay then.

Maybe I'll just—I slip from the table and head back to my room while he isn't looking. Shutting the door, I spot the bags on the bed and snort. Fucking asshole, I bet he bought me fancy dresses and pant suits. That's what rich people wear, right?

Wandering around the room, I try to ignore the bags and my curiosity, but I keep looking back at them. Fuck it. Striding over, I grab the first bag and open it, pulling out the jeans inside.

I hold up the pants, my heart thundering. There are styled rips down the front and frayed edges. They are a deep black, and they feel expensive and luxurious, but look like the ones I have on today. Shaking my head, I pull open the other bags. I find some plain vests, some band t-shirts and vests, as well as some oversized dresses and shirts. All in my style, black and edgy. There are even some ripped loose pajamas in there, as well as some soft ones.

Tearing open the next bag, I find panties and bras in my size. How the hell did he know my exact size?

All that's left is a bag and a box. I opened the bag first to find two dresses. One is a silky, red, almost holographic material with spaghetti straps, which is short and tight. And really fucking nice.

The next dress is black. Its back is cut out and replaced with lace, and the front neckline is a really low V. It's hot as hell.

Overwhelmed, I open the box to find shoes. There are some new, kick ass boots as well as three pairs of heels. He thought of everything, literally everything, and it's all so...me.

I didn't expect that. Sighing, I throw myself back on the bed, unsure what to think. I frown when I feel something sharp digging into my hip. Reaching down, I extract a small bag I must have missed. When I peek inside, I spot makeup. I almost squeal as I tip it over to see the high-end brands tumbling free, all in my colours—red and purple lipsticks, dark eyeliner, and eyeshadow.

He thought of everything.

My hand catches on a small, black, velvet box at the bottom of the bag, and I pull it free, sitting up cross-legged as I flip open the jewellery box and gasp. There, nestled in the silk, are two golden snakes. They are clearly earrings with what looks like rubies for eyes, and the detail is insane. Golden scales drip across the bodies, and they're so lifelike, I can almost imagine them slithering.

What does this mean? Why did he give these to me?

I thought I was just a prisoner, a debt, so why is he going out of his way to make me comfortable—apart from today's lesson, which I guess I kind of deserved—and why are they doing this?

They stole me, I remind myself, but it feels weak, even to me. Did they? After all, they were just trying to collect their debt, it ain't their fault my dad sold me. I mean, they could have said no, or just let me be free, but I guess they have a reputation to uphold.

Fuck, am I really questioning this?

Isn't there a name for this, like Stockholm syndrome? I'm not becoming one of those girls who falls in love with her captors. Nope, not at all...but if they carry on giving me expensive makeup, I might just hate them a little less.

Maybe.

Stupid emotions, stupid hussy vagina. Rolling over, I get up and put away the clothes before kicking off my boots and jeans, and laying back on the bed in my vest and knickers.

My mind keeps going back to that kiss today. I mean, fuck, it was just a kiss, so why can't I stop thinking about it? My hand drifts up on its own, touching my still sore lips. Everything about the Vipers hurts, even their pleasure.

Smashing my hand back to the bed, I stare defiantly up at the ceiling. Okay, so maybe I can admit I want to fuck these men...maybe if they weren't talking. Yeah, I would gag them, fuck them, and leave them. Yes, that's it.

No, fuck. I can't.

I can't cross that line. It's bad enough they have taken everything away from me, but they don't care. They are smug about it, pragmatic, like they don't even see how wrong it is that they just took a person. I can't, I can't want them too. I can't give them that piece of me, no matter how much I want them.

But...what if they don't let me choose? What if they take my body like they took me?

What if they realise just how much I want them?

How much my pussy clenches when I'm even around them...like when Ryder uses that cold, dark voice or Kenzo smirks at me... Diesel's crazy yet addictive personality, or Garrett's anger.

My heart races and my thighs rub together as I imagine all that power turned on me. Okay, so I just need to relieve some tension. It's clearly been too long since I got laid, and my body has decided since they are the only men around, they'll do.

Yep, that's it. Relieve some tension, Rox, then back to planning how to escape the fucking snakes.

Alright, think of something sexy. Something other than the tattooed, powerful men in this apartment...

But my mind flicks back to Ryder rolling up his sleeves, all that power...imagining him at the gym. His body slick with sweat, his cold eyes hard as he pushes himself. To be better. Faster. Stronger.

The way his icy gaze would flicker in annoyance at himself. The way those lean fingers would grip the weights...

Slipping my hand in my panties, I groan, biting down on my lip as I find myself already wet. Dipping my finger in my cream, I circle my clit, teasing myself as I imagine it's someone else's hand. Touching me, rubbing me, making me gasp as we flick my clit.

Closing my eyes, I rock into my touch as I push up my shirt with my other hand and squeeze my breast, rolling my nipple around and imagining Ryder sucking it into his mouth. Those cold eyes locked on me as he smirks.

Biting back my moan, I dip my fingers inside my channel, slipping them in and out. Pretending it's one of their cocks, their hands. Anything. Speeding up, I chase the orgasm I can feel building. Needing to reach that peak.

My body doesn't care that I shouldn't want them.

It wants them.

It's craving them.

And in my fog of desire, it's them I see as I touch myself.

Gasping, I rock into my fingers, imagining Ryder's dark eyes as he watches me from the end of the bed. Visualising Diesel's lips crushing mine as he takes what he wants—me. Garrett is there, too, prowling around the bed, observing me for once. Kenzo's finger trails teasingly up my thigh.

Yes, fuck.

They would be hard, they would be mean.

It would be raw and filled with anger and hate, all of us not wanting it, yet needing it...

Fuck!

The orgasm rips through me out of nowhere, and I moan as I thrash in the bed, my hips lifting rapidly, fucking myself through it until I collapse, my fingers wet as satisfaction pounds through me. As does exhaustion.

I'm fucking knackered now. All this fighting, all this stress and swinging emotions has drained me. Slipping from the bed on shaky legs, I cross into the bathroom and clean up before climbing back beneath the quilt and cuddling myself into a ball.

I can do this.

I just need to keep them from finding out I'm attracted to them... or that I'm feeling fucking curious about what they would be like in bed. Yes, that's it. Keep my distance, play it cool, and earn my freedom.

Because despite the fancy gifts and the fact that they haven't hurt me, not really, I still want to be free. I still want my old life back, a life before these snakes. Before their cool eyes and harsh hands. One where people don't talk about killing someone over pizza. I mean, yeah, it probably happens at the bar, but I don't really know about it.

I've always had my foot in that inky darkness, in the underbelly of the city, but this? This is the fucking castle of it, and these four are the leaders.

The Vipers won't stop until they own everyone and everything. But that can't include me.

Not now, not ever.

Not if I want to survive.

CHAPTER SEVENTEEN

ROXY

The next morning, I learn Ryder wasn't lying, they're gone. As soon as I step out of my room, I know it—it's too quiet. Too empty. Sighing, and ignoring the fact I'm disappointed, I decide to have some breakfast. I might as well eat their food if they are keeping me prisoner.

I had taken a long bath this morning, shaving when I got bored before slipping into one of the new t-shirt dresses Ryder bought me. It has a skull and a snake wrapped around it on the front, and it's low-cut and hangs to my knees. Pairing it with my new heeled kick ass boots, which reach mid-calf, I think I look pretty good. I even put on some makeup, telling myself the whole time it was for me, to feel like myself again. Maybe if I dressed like it, I might actually be it.

But a small part of my psyche calls me a liar, accuses me of wanting to look good for them. I kill that tiny piece. Who says your inner self is right all the time? Really, she's just a snotty, stuck-up bitch.

I don't see Kenzo anywhere, but I find some breakfast left on the table for me and a warm carafe of coffee. So I sit and eat, but I find myself jumping in the quiet, expecting one of them to leap out at me. After I've finished, I sigh, already bored.

Throwing myself down on the sofa, I take the tablet and try to figure out how to turn on their TV. Why can't these people just have a normal control like everyone else? I finally get it to switch on and find the horror channel, settling in to watch the film. I wonder if they have popcorn.

That's when it hits me, I'm just sitting here. Why aren't I trying to escape? My eyes go to the door, but after yesterday, it doesn't seem like the best way to try and leave. My head still aches from smashing it into the window, and though they checked it over and it's scabbed, it's still a stark reminder. Not to mention, I don't want D to 'teach me another lesson.' I don't think I would survive it. Not right now.

Sighing, I turn my head, just as I hear footsteps behind me. I whirl around and spot Kenzo coming towards me. He doesn't have his tablet, like usual, but he's tucking his phone into his grey sweatpants.

That's not what has me staring though. No, definitely not the very impressive bulge in the joggers or the fact that those loose, low riding grey sweatpants are made purely to tease women. No, it's the fact he's shirtless.

As in I can see everything. Including the bar through his right nipple and the tribal style tattoos dotted across his shoulders. He heads to the kitchen, and I gasp at the tattoo on his back. It's a snake with red eyes, wrapped around a skull, and takes up his entire back. It's stunning artwork, not to mention the chiselled muscles underneath. "You want a drink, darling?" he calls, and I snap my eyes to his to see he's turned and is smirking at me. "Or just to drool instead?"

Asshole.

So what that he has abs carved from stone or that delicious V, a light splattering of hair leading down to his joggers and across his seriously impressive chest? Or that his shoulders are so wide that all I can imagine is raking my nails across them as he moves above me?

Pinning me to the sofa and letting me feel all those muscles...I forgot my train of thought.

Fucking joggers and their magical abilities.

At least it's more material for my spank bank.

He grabs two ice-cold waters, and I watch the droplets of condensation race down his arms. Lucky bastards. Strolling my way, he leaps over the back of the sofa in a really impressive display of strength and hands me one. I snort and take it, trying not to reveal how much his showing off is getting to me.

No, stay strong. Pussy power...that came out wrong.

I turn away to stop myself from staring at him, and try to focus on the movie, but I keep glancing at him out of the corner of my eye. His arm is stretched across the back of the sofa, his fingers almost touching me. He's leaning back with his legs spread, and his other hand is tucked into the waistband of his joggers, pushing them even lower.

Fuck.

It's like one of those thirst trap images you see online that makes you go 'dayummm.' I've definitely liked a few Instagram models' photos that don't even touch him right now. The worst bit? He knows it. There's a smirk playing around his stupid lips, and he turns, catching me staring. "Don't you want to watch the movie? Because if you want to do something else, darling, I'm down."

"Shut the fuck up," I snap, tucking my hands under my ass to stop myself from reaching out and petting his muscles. That's right. Petting them.

He chuckles and leans closer, his mouth almost at my ear. "You sure? We could wager on it..."

"You fucking gambling addict," I mutter.

"Only when you're involved. What do you say, darling? Want to play a game?" he whispers seductively.

"What would I win?" I hedge, while internally shouting at myself.

"The thing you want most..." My eyes go to his cock, and he

laughs harder. I should take this bottle of water and ram it down his charming fucking throat. But then his next words have me perking up and forgetting about making the snake deep throat a bottle. "Your freedom."

My gaze snaps to his. "You're messing with me."

"I could be, or maybe I'm just that sure I'll win." He shrugs, watching me with those dark eyes.

"So what do you win?" I ask, scared if that's my prize, then his is something worse.

He leans closer, dropping all pretense of charm. His eyes are hungry as they dip to my lips then to my body, caressing every inch of me and leaving me almost trembling with desire. "You," he rasps.

Fuck.

Fuck on a stick.

Why does my pussy clench?

"The game?" I question, and my voice is more breathless than I would like.

"Poker," he answers, and I snort.

"Hell no, you're a fucking bookie. I'm betting you're amazing at that." I roll my eyes.

He sighs, but that smirk covers his lips again. "Not the only thing I'm amazing at...but smart, darling. Fine, you pick."

I run my eyes around the apartment, trying to think of something, anything, I could win against this man, this Viper, who's right next to me, coiled to strike and eat me whole. *Bar games, think, Rox. I'm good at them.* "You got cups?"

Fuck, why is that the first game I can think of? Because he's too close, smelling like all man, and I want to taste that, to feel him, and he's distracting me.

"Yes," he replies. I nod, and he motions to the kitchen. I leap up and run into the kitchen, opening cupboards until I find what I need. Am I really going to do this? Gamble my freedom and body?

Yes.

Grabbing some beer from the fridge, I head to the table and

spread them out opposite each other. "Really?" He snorts. "Are we teenagers?"

"Scared you'll lose?" I smirk as I pour the beer.

"Nope, bring it on, darling." He grins.

I pick up the first cup, and he copies me. "First one to finish them all wins. Simple. Not easy to cheat. Three, two, one, go!" I shout, and down the cup. Wiping my mouth after, I flip it and it lands top down, he gapes at me when he finishes his. "I own a bar, *darling*," I taunt, before moving onto my next.

He swears and flips his, but it doesn't land the first time, although he gets it on the second. I carry on drinking before flipping. I'm on my third, and he's on his second, but I can't get the bastard to flip. I try again and again, watching nervously as he catches up, lands his third cup, and moves onto the fourth. Shit.

Fuck, he's winning. Desperation fills me so I cheat. I lean down and flash my tits, and he chokes on his next sip, giving me time to knock back that cup, flip it, and move on.

What's the worst that could happen? He already owns me, so if there is a chance at freedom, I have to take it. It keeps floating through my head as I drink, my eyes on him.

I down it and flip it, but we're neck and neck. On the last cup. Our eyes lock as we chug it, then he yanks down his trousers, flashing me his cock. I actually choke on my beer, and it gives him the time he needs to flip it.

I stare at him, the cup still held to my lips, beyond shocked. I lost. I lost.

He smirks and wipes his mouth. "I think I'll collect now," he murmurs, and prowls around the table towards me. His eyes are hungry, his body flexes, and his cock is hardening and pressing against his joggers. I back away, fear and desire blooming within me.

I didn't think I could lose, and if I did...I thought I could handle it. Now I don't know if I can. I want him, sure, my pussy is already wet from the thought, but Kenzo... Fuck, any of the Vipers are dangerous to more than just my body.

Like an obsession. Or a drug.

"Rematch?" I offer, keeping the table between us, but he leaps over it, landing right in front of me.

"No, fair is fair. Pay up, darling." He chuckles.

I stumble back and dart away, but he catches me, his hand sweeping out and throwing me over his shoulder. I squeal and slap at his back, but he just throws me onto the sofa where I bounce, gasping. Looking up, I push the hair from my face as I find him staring down at me. He must see my fear, because he reaches into his pocket and pulls out his dice.

"I'll give you a different game, though, guess the number. If you're right, you're safe, and if not, you have to take off an item of clothing."

"What?" I gape.

He steps closer. "Unless you just want me to rip them from your body."

Erm, yes please.

But also, fuck no at the same time.

"Fuck you," I snarl.

"That's the plan, darling. Guess." He grins.

I panic. "Seven"

He throws the dice, catching them expertly. With a wink, he shows the dice. Fuck. "Top," he demands.

"No," I snarl, but reach down and yank off my shoes, throwing them at him. They hit his chest and bounce off, making his grin grow. "You fucking bastard! Is this the only way you can get a woman?"

Even as I spit vile words at him, I can't help but pant, my legs clenching together as he watches me, his focus fully on my body. Like he can't wait to eat me, fuck me, have me. Instead of forcing me like they could have, he won fair and square.

Won me.

And my body.

But...can I pay up?

Their reach is like a venom taking root inside me. At first, you don't even realise it's there. Slowly spreading through you, changing you, moulding you, infecting you, until it's too late to be free. That's how I feel, because I hated them, still do, but now it's clouded with need.

One they forced into me, built inside me, and they know it.

I hate that.

I hate them.

Who says I can't have some fun with it? Hate sex is like nothing else, and this desire clearly isn't going away and I'm not getting free any time soon, so I might as well make the most of it...right?

That's what I tell myself anyway.

"Fine," I snarl. "Nine." I point at the dice and he rolls again.

It comes up twelve, and he smirks. "Shirt," he demands.

Ripping it over my head with a growl, I toss it at him. Why the hell did I agree to this game? I'm just in my panties and bra now, and he takes his time looking me over. I shiver under his possessive gaze, my nipples pebbling against the lace fabric, and my panties are no doubt soaking. Brilliant.

"Next guess, darling?" he murmurs, his eyes locked on my flushed chest as I clench my legs further together. With a groan, he reaches down and rearranges himself. "Fuck, you are way too beautiful."

I ignore that, because honestly, what would I say? "Thirteen," I snarl, but he's too busy staring at me still. I can almost feel the caress from his gaze. "Kenzo."

His eyes jerk up, locking with mine, and the dice go flying as he pounces. I yelp as he pins me to the sofa, ripping open my thighs and settling between them as he grinds against me. "Don't say my name like that."

"What? Kenzo?" I query in confusion, and he groans.

"Yes, like that, darling."

"It's literally your name, would you prefer I just call you asshole?" I snap, even as I arch up into him.

"Call me whatever you want, darling, as long as you don't stop me and scream it for everyone to hear." He laughs as he drops his lips to mine. I couldn't stop him, even if I wanted to, my words are caught in my throat as I grab his hair and yank him closer. He smirks against my mouth, so I bite down on his lip.

With a grunt, he wrenches away, panting hard as he glares at me. "Act like a brat, and you will get treated like one."

"Whatever, get the fuck off me," I demand. It's hard to act tough in your undies, but I think I pull it off.

He smirks again, those dark eyes locked on mine, making me weak. "Why? You like me where I am."

"No, I don't," I protest half-heartedly, my voice wavering.

He laughs, actually laughs, his whole body shaking. "Sure, so then why are your nipples hard and begging for my mouth?" he murmurs, as he rips down my bra and bares me to the room. Eyes on me, he seals his lips around one and sucks, making me moan as my eyes close and I arch up into his mouth.

Anger at my reaction flares through me, and I try to pull his head away using his hair. Laughing again, he ignores my desperate tugs and kisses down my belly, stopping at my navel piercing and circling it with his tongue before he carries on to my panties, his eyes meeting mine. "I can smell how wet you are." With his teeth, he yanks down my panties and tosses them away.

I try to close my thighs, but he shoves them open and slams them down to the sofa, exposing me to him. He groans lowly, the sound doing bad things to me as he stares at me. "You're fucking soaked. Thought you didn't want me?"

"I don't," I snarl, even as I tilt my hips, needing to be touched.

He smirks and reaches between my thighs, stroking down my lips before parting them. "What's this? A piercing?" he murmurs in shock, his finger circling my pierced hood. It was a drunken dare and hurt like hell. "That's fucking hot." He groans. "I'm so fucking close to coming in my pants, it's not even funny," he mutters, making me snigger.

He narrows his eyes and tugs on my piercing, forcing a gasp from my lips as pain flares through me, followed by pleasure. "Either get on with it or fuck off," I snarl, but it's hard to be intimidating when you're pinned beneath a man naked and wet.

Without warning, he drops to his elbows, his face right in my pussy, and licks me from clit to ass. I nearly come away from the sofa, but he bands an arm across my belly, catching on the piercing there, and holds me down.

My mind is still whirling, trying to tell me all the reasons why I should stop this, why I should push him away, why I should hate him, but when he presses two fingers inside me, that all melts away to pleasure.

My eyes slide shut as I moan, unable to look at that dark head between my legs anymore. His hands dig into the fleshy part of my thighs, holding me open for him as he lashes my clit, tugging and licking my piercing as he expertly curls his fingers inside me. He plays me like one of his games. Knowing exactly where to lick, where to touch, rub, and fuck.

I'm panting in no time with sweat coating my body, my face and chest flushed. I try to stop myself, but I can't help it, I rock against his face, needing more. He plays me like a fiddle, his fingers rubbing inside me as he keeps up that maddening pace with my clit. I reach down and flick my nipples, too turned on to care.

"You taste fucking delicious." He groans. "Too fucking good."

I shake my head, trying to stop the powerful orgasm I can feel building within me. No. No, this can't be happening. I try to push him away, but he ignores me, speeds up, and throws me crashing into that release.

It tears through me, ripping a scream from my throat as my thighs clamp his head, my pussy tightening on his fingers. It rolls through me, again and again, my chest arching up into the air as my eyes squeeze closed, until it finally stops.

Dropping onto the sofa, I let my thighs fall open, and I look down to see a grinning, messy-haired Kenzo still lying between them, his tongue lapping casually at my cunt.

He rears up, and self-hatred pours through me at the satisfied smirk curling his glistening lips. He licks his fingers clean as I watch, and I can't take it anymore. I can't believe I just let that happen or that I screamed my pleasure for everyone to hear.

He's my fucking kidnapper.

Rolling off the sofa, I storm away, and when I hear him coming after me, I move faster. My heart is racing, and my legs are still weak from him. I can't—fuck, I can't believe that happened. Or that it felt so good. I try to escape him, but he catches me in the hallway and slams me into the wall, holding me there as he leans down, his eyes angry now.

"Where the fuck do you think you're going?"

"Get the fuck off me!" I scream, kicking and struggling in his grip. He grunts and pushes me back again, trying to hold me still.

"Why?"

"I hate you," I snap desperately, and he laughs, but the sound is mean. All hints of teasing disappear in the face of my anger. But this is not all directed at him. Hell, some of it is for making me feel that way, for making me weak, but some is aimed at me.

"No, you hate that you enjoyed that, don't fucking lie, darling. You were screaming in no time, and you hate that you loved every fucking second of my tongue in your pussy."

His dirty words infuriate me, and before I know it, I've slapped him. It's loud in the silence, and I suck in a breath as his head snaps to the side. Slowly, he turns back to face me, and all hints of the usual, charming, teasing Kenzo have vanished. I can see the resemblance to Ryder now. It's the emotions, the wild, uncontrolled feelings.

He's angry.

Furious.

Well, so am I!

"You shouldn't have done that," he warns, his voice low and rough. With one hand, he keeps me pressed to the wall, while he yanks down his joggers with the other, and the sight of his hard, throbbing cock has me freezing. It's big, really fucking big. Too big.

No.

It's bad enough I let him taste me. He isn't fucking me. I channel all that rage, all that hate, and aim it towards him. All of it, from being stolen, to my dad, to these assholes, to my own emotions, I let it pour from me. Uncaring if I hurt him.

I pull back my fist and slam it into his face, then, as he's reeling backward, I do it again and again, but he catches the last one and slams my hand to the wall next to me, crushing my wrist until I cry out. He pushes his face into mine, his smirk transformed into a snarl. "You want to hate me? Fine. You will still be screaming my name when you come on my cock."

"Fuck you!" I scream into his face, lunging my head forward. It connects, and we both grunt as pain flows through my already injured head.

He grabs my other hand and slams them together above me, making me stretch up on my tiptoes, chest heaving as I kick at him. He throws off his joggers and presses his naked body against me. I hate the flare of desire that flows through me, or the fact that I want him. The fact that the sight of his pulsing cock has me wetter than I've ever been.

He strokes his length, making me watch as I pant. "I was going to be nice and wear a condom, but now?" He shakes his head and leans down, licking my lips. "You're mine, I don't have to."

Releasing his cock, he grabs my thigh and hoists me up. I snarl, fighting against his hold to hit him again. I manage to get them away from the wall slightly, clawing at his hands hard enough to draw blood, before he slams them back.

"Want to act like a fucking animal? I'll fuck you like one," he yells in my face.

Before I can retort, I'm yanked away from the wall, spun, and shoved into it once more. My hands land against it as I try to keep myself from falling, and then he's there, pressed along the length of my back, his cock nestled against my ass as his hand winds through my hair. He tugs on it, and I cry out, drawing my head back until I'm balanced with only his hand holding me up. Gripping my hip, he pulls me backwards and kicks my legs open.

"Get off me," I demand.

His hand slips between my thighs, finding me wet. "No, you fucking want this just as much as I do, darling, and I've had enough of your attitude. I'll fuck it out of you."

I struggle again, continuing to fight him, even as I push my pussy harder into his hands. I hate them. I fucking despise these Vipers.

But all this fight, all this hate, has me so needy, that when he lines his cock up at my entrance and slams inside, I scream. Not in pain. In pleasure.

He laughs as he pulls back, fighting my clinging pussy, and slams inside. "Good girl," he coos, as he licks my neck before biting my shoulder, making it hurt as he thrusts back into me, setting a hard, brutal pace.

This isn't fucking.

This is hate.

Both of us hate the fact that we want each other. I hate that they took me from my life. He hates that I'm here and have the audacity to not fall at his feet.

It flows through us, guiding us. Each slam of his hips is harsh, his hands digging into my skin as he impales me on his cock. My breasts rub against the wall, the friction making me cry out as I tighten around him.

He's so distracted with fucking me that he doesn't notice me turning. I rip my hair from his hold, leaving some strands in his grip, and his cock slips from me as I twist and punch him straight in the face. "You son of a bitch! I'm not yours!" I scream.

He grabs me and flings me to the floor, coming down on top of me. "You are," he roars as I slap at him, pushing him away before flipping over. I start to crawl away, but his hand circles my ankle and he pulls me back. I slide along the floor with a scream of anger.

Yet not once do I say no.

Because I want this.

And I hate that.

His hands are quick. They yank my hips up, and then he's there again, pulling me back onto his cock. I groan, I can't help it. He's so big, it feels amazing. He slaps my ass hard, no teasing. It isn't playful, it's a punishment. He makes it hurt, and I love it.

I cry out, pushing back to meet his rapid thrusts, the sound of our skin slapping loud as he grunts behind me. "Asshole!" I yell, even as I reach between my legs to rub my clit.

His hand gets there first and slaps me away. Leaning over me, he grips my hair once again, balling it up and using it like a leash as he arches my neck, snarling into my ear, "I didn't say you could come."

"You bastard," I cry out as he tilts my hips up further and hits that deeper spot inside me that has my eyes crossing. My breath fogs their perfect floor, my hands scrambling across it as I try to resist, but I can't.

Not when he's buried so deep within me, controlling me. Owning me.

"Admit you like it," he growls, running his teeth along my shoulder, "and I'll let you come." The fact that his voice is rough and tight makes me grin, he's not as unaffected as he thought.

"Wanker," I snap. "Fucking asshole, dick sucking motherfuck—"

His hand comes down on my ass again and again. Pain radiates through me, even as his cock drags along those nerves. I'm so close, I try to fight it, but when he reaches down and tugs on my piercing, I scream, my release shattering me.

I clamp down on his cock as I writhe beneath him. His hips stutter, then he powers into me twice more before stilling, his cum filling me. Panting, I collapse to the floor as all the fight leaves me, and he falls on top of me, his weight heavy as he pins me there.

A noise has me lifting my head, and when I see who made it, my breathing stops.

Looking up, I spot Diesel standing at the end of the corridor with a grin on his lips. "Well, well, pretty bird, that was quite a show."

Throwing back an elbow, I feel it connect with Kenzo as he

groans and rolls from me. I scramble to my feet and throw him a glare. "You fuck about as good as you fight," I snap, before tossing my hair back and, with all the dignity I have left, which is not much, I storm into my room and slam the door.

Pressing against it, my heart racing, I feel his release slip down my thighs as I hear him, both of them, laugh outside.

Fuck.

CHAPTER EIGHTEEN

DIESEL

I can't stop thinking about watching her with Kenzo. The way she screamed, the way she fought. It was breathtaking. Her beautiful, bare body writhing against the floor, filled with anger and pleasure. She hated it and loved it at the same time.

My little bird.

What she probably didn't realise was that I spilled in my jeans as she came, watching her contort in release as Kenzo pounded into her tight, slick body from behind. It did things to me. Sure, I would have preferred more blood, but it was one hell of a show.

After she stormed off, I winked at Kenzo, who laughed, and ducked into my room to clean up. You ever had jizz in your jeans? Not fun. It's almost as annoying to get out as blood. Slipping into just my boxers, I lounge on my bed. I can hear the others talking downstairs, no doubt updating Kenzo on what we found. But I was there, I don't need to hear it again.

No, what I need is my little bird. She's scared right now, even if she won't admit it, and the Vipers are circling. She's going to run again, I saw it in her eyes, and I can't let that happen.

She's mine now.

When this all started, she was just a toy, just a debt. A faceless woman I could torture for her father's sins...now she's the woman who kissed me like her life depended on it. Who looked into my eyes, who saw my darkness, my monsters hiding there, and got off on it. Even if she won't admit it. No, my little bird is more like a snake than she realises, but she's spent so much time amongst prey, she doesn't know how to be a predator.

I'm going to show her. I'm going to break her free and let all those emotions out. I'm going to make her a Viper.

She was never going to get away from us, but it's obvious to me now that this is more than that. She even has Ryder twisted up in knots, and Garrett, that poor bastard, she's bringing back all his bad memories. He hates her for that, but also wants her. I heard him jacking off last night, her name on his lips.

My little bird will either bring us closer together, or burn us. I can't wait to find out which.

So I wait for the others to go to bed, knowing Ryder will undoubtedly stay up all night in his office, trying to figure out who the hitter was. It was an insult that he managed to escape, that he almost got the drop on one of us. I can't wait to get a hold of him and show him just what the Vipers' den is like.

Once everything is quiet, I slip from my bed and pad downstairs. I walk through the dark, expecting Roxy to be trying to open the front door. But she's not, so maybe she had a turn of heart? Or maybe she's still waiting.

Heading to her room, I crack open the door and peer in. She's still, curled up on her bed in one of her old shirts. I watch her from the darkness, noting the steady rise and fall of her chest. She's asleep. No wonder she didn't try to escape yet, it seems Kenzo tired her out.

Slipping in, I shut the door gently, so as not to wake her. This is becoming a habit, watching her while she sleeps. But I'm drawn to her and need her. To rip her open and expose her insides to my flames. I can't help the compulsion.

Garrett says I have an addictive personality, probably from my junkie mother who shot up while I was still in her womb. I don't care, it means my focus is a hundred percent on my little bird. I see the things the others don't want to or can't.

Like she belongs with us, even though she hates us...but does she? If Roxy really detested us, we would be dead already, she would have slit our throats in our sleep and damn the consequences. She hasn't attacked us, even though she's angry over what happened.

No, she's wavering. She wants to hate us, feels like she has to because of how this started, but she's slowly crumbling. If it's anyone she should hate, it's her fucking father, the stupid bastard. He sold her. We simply accepted.

The best thing to happen to us is the day we walked into that bar to collect. I still remember the way she took down Garrett and tried to attack me. My cock hardens at the memory. I wonder if she'll fight me like that when we fuck.

I hope so.

Creeping across the room, I get onto the bed behind her, slipping closer until I can feel her heat. I wrap my arm around her and drag her against my chest. I've seen this in movies, but I've never tried it myself. Usually, the women I've been with are either passed out, or so scared they run away and we have to pay them to be quiet.

It loses its fun after a while—all that fear. Just once, I want someone to match me, to not burn in my fire, but be reborn in it.

I hope Roxy is that one.

Because either way, she's being plunged into it, and there is no escape for her. Not now, not ever. She knows that now, I see it in her eyes. She sighs in her sleep, snuggling closer and pressing that plump ass against my cock, making me grunt as desire pulses through me. What I wouldn't give just to rip off her panties and slam into her wet heat. To hear her scream, to paint my madness across her skin.

Sliding my hand upwards, I press it under her shirt until I feel her soft, silky skin. She's perfect. Fire and heat wrapped up in a curvy, beautiful package. I want to see her come apart for me like she did Kenzo. To feel her pussy or her ass clenching around my cock as I fuck her.

All I keep imagining is her tied up in my den, her body naked and covered in blood, the fire roaring behind her as I take her. Fuck her. She would enjoy it, my little bird, the same way she enjoyed my kiss, the same way she enjoyed me killing that man, even if she tried to shy away from it. She wanted him to pay. Needed to feel that somewhere, the world wasn't all bad, and those bastards get what they deserve.

We might be Vipers, predators, but often the men we kill are evil. Rapists, abusers, cheaters, and killers.

Our world is filled with them, and if we take down just one, and save a life, then I would dirty my soul every day, wading through the blood and bullshit. Not everything we do is about money, after all, we started when we were all lost. No family, with vengeance in our hearts. All different, but brought together by pain. By need. It shaped us, remade us until we were *this*.

And each person we tore down, each person we killed, made us lose another piece of the boys we once were. I don't care, that boy was a trusting fool who loved his junkie mother, even though she would try to sell his body for a hit. Who kept on running back, even when the state took him away. Until there was nothing to run back to.

I don't regret the path that brought me here, because it brought me to her, and I now know that was my purpose all along, all that pain, all that suffering and darkness I had to plunge into was so I could find my little bird.

She whimpers in her sleep, her body stiffening in fear. Poor Little Bird, trapped inside her own darkness. Pinching her stomach, I wake her up. I feel the moment she registers she's not alone. Her breathing stutters, her whole body tightening against me as I continue to stroke her soft stomach. So soft, so silky, I wonder if it would part for my knife like butter?

"Little Bird, Little Bird, trying so hard to fly away from us, even in her sleep," I murmur against her neck, the pounding of her pulse loud and matching mine.

"Diesel?" she whispers into the night. I don't think she realises that when she knows it's me, a breath whooshes from her and she relaxes a fraction. She's beginning to trust us, even if she doesn't see it.

"Tired, Little Bird? Not trying to escape tonight, even after you fucked Kenzo and he made you realise just how much you want us?"

She snarls and flips over, glaring at me. Smirking, I drag her closer, placing my hand on her plump arse to keep her near. "I don't want you, it was a stupid mistake...I didn't even want it."

"No? Don't lie to me, Little Bird, I saw your face. You wanted it... but let's go back...did you say no?" I ask. She doesn't get to make Kenzo feel like he took her without consent, it would wreck him. He's good like that.

She swallows hard, her eyes darting away for a moment, trying to ignore me. We can't have that. "Little Bird, answer me," I snap, pinching her ass and making her yelp.

"No, okay? I didn't say no!" she yells.

"Why?" I push.

"Because-because I wanted it." Her chest rises faster with her declaration, her eyes widening like she can't believe she admitted that.

"Good little bird, finally realising what we can all see. You yearn for us, you want us, need us," I murmur, my eyes dropping to her lips. I want to kiss her again. I wonder if she would let me.

She goes quiet, her eyes cloudy with thought before they snap back to mine. And I know, I just know she's going to try something. My little bird can't give up without a fight, she thinks it would make her weak. Nothing could be further from the truth.

Giving up and accepting us would be the strongest thing she could ever do. We're monsters, vipers, and to love a monster makes you one of the strongest people in the world. To let them into your heart, knowing they could destroy you, kill you...that's the ultimate show of strength, but she will learn that one day.

For now, I'll settle with this, being close. Holding her and her not trying to get away. It's nice, and feels right and comforting. Like coming home.

One day, that may change. One day, it may not. The only way I know how to show her my feelings is through pain. It could kill her, loving me, having me, but wouldn't that be the best declaration of love you could have?

Her tongue darts out and wets her lips, making me groan as I watch. "Don't tease me, Little Bird."

"Or what? No deals tonight?" she taunts, moving closer until she's plastered against me. Every curve pressed to my hardness.

"No deals, Little Bird, but know that tonight, I'm close to the edge. Plunge into that darkness, and you might not come back," I warn.

She tilts her head, considering me for a moment, before she leans closer, her hand brushing down my arm. "Maybe I don't want to."

I don't move when she presses her lips to mine. I let her kiss me with hard, desperate pecks as she presses closer. With an annoyed grunt, she nips my lip, hard. I snarl, then snap. I tried to hold back, but I can't.

She doesn't let me.

Gripping the back of her head, I drag her closer. Her lips part on a gasp, her hand clutching my thigh as she falls into the kiss. Sweeping my tongue into her mouth, I let her feel my need for her. How crazy she makes me. She moans, meeting me with her own desperate desire as we lose ourselves in each other.

Her hand strokes up my thigh, making me groan into her mouth as she trails it across my hard-on. In warning, I bite down on her lip, and she breaks. Her teeth crash into mine as we fight each other. Both battling for dominance. I'm so lost in her, I don't even notice her slipping her hand into my boxers where I have my knife clipped until it's pressed against my throat.

I roll us over, and her knees slip to either side of my hips as she glares down at me, knife poised, pressing to my vulnerable neck. Smirking, I tilt my head back, giving her better access as I watch her. Fuck, she's magnificent.

"I'll do it," she snarls, her pussy resting against my hard, boxer-clad cock. She's a liar. I can feel how wet she is through the thin fabric. She flicks her grey hair back, observing me like she doesn't know what to do next.

My poor, lost little bird.

"Do it, spill my blood. I'll die happily with you on top of me... fuck, you could even screw me while you're doing it. Just think how hot that would be." I groan, reaching up and gripping her hips, dragging her back and forth across my cock. Her lips part on a moan before she shakes her head and digs the knife in deeper. I feel it slice my skin, a fleck of pain zapping through me.

Grunting, I thrust up, making her bounce on me and dig the blade in deeper. She cries out, pulling the knife back as I feel my blood dripping down my throat. It's not enough, I want more. I want her to do whatever the hell she wants.

"More," I demand.

She shakes her head. "You're seriously nuts."

I smirk. "And you love it. The choice is yours, so what are you going to do, Little Bird? Kill me? You could cut off my hand to get out of this building. You would be free, I wouldn't even fight you."

"Why?" she questions, confused, the knife only resting against my skin.

"Why not? You said it, I'm crazy."

She sits there, atop me, debating whether to kill me and escape. She's smart, she's playing it all out in her head. "They would come after me, they would kill me for sure then."

"Maybe." I grin. "Or maybe you would escape them."

She swallows, staring at me. "No, I won't. I won't ever."

Ah, now she gets it.

"No, you won't. But there's your choice, Little Bird. Run for the

137

rest of your life and hope to escape them, or use that knife for something that ends with us both having a good time."

She looks at the knife, tosses it down next to me with a sigh, and rolls over, flopping onto her back beside me. "Fucking assholes, came in and ruined my goddamn life."

"Did we really?" I inquire inquisitively, not bothered if we did.

She doesn't look at me, but bites her lower lip. "I love my bar."

"Anything else? You had no real friends, no constant lovers...all you had was the bar."

She looks at me then with tears in her eyes. "Bars don't hurt you. Bars don't betray you. I loved someone, so deeply, and he left."

"He left you?" I ask, eyes narrowed at her loving someone other than me. I want to kill him. Would it be too much to hunt him down?

She snorts. "Well, in a way, but that bastard," she growls, "went and fucking died on me. The only fucking person who ever gave a shit if I ate, if I slept, and if I was alive, and he died. Not even my own dad did, and my mother didn't even know I was there, she was too drugged up to care. But Rich, he did. He took me in when I had nothing. He gave me a job, a home, and then he fucking died."

I consider her words. "He owned the bar?"

She nods. "I was already working there to pay off my dad's debt when I finally got emancipated. I was living on the streets, and he noticed. He gave me the place above the bar, paid for the furniture and everything. Gave me a job, bartender then manager."

"How did he die?" I query, prying. At least I don't need to kill him. But I'm still jealous of the love in her voice. She doesn't get to love anyone but us.

"Cancer," she whispers, tears rolling down her cheeks before she dashes them away, not letting even that weakness escape her. My brave little bird. "It was horrible, so fucking fast. By the time we found out, it was too late. The bastard went and left me the bar without telling me, told me it was my home now. Hoped it gave me a better future than him."

"I'm sorry, Little Bird." And I am. She's been through so much, survived so much, the scars painted across her body and soul. She doesn't realise she's more like us than anyone else. Maybe I should try and explain.

So even though I've never told anyone, I rip open those old wounds, the ones that poisoned me, just so she might understand. "My mother was a junkie too."

She turns her head and looks at me, her dark eyes glistening with tears. Reaching up, I wipe one away and taste it on my thumb. "She cared as long as she could use me. Drug mule, runner, even tried to sell me once. But still I loved her. I got taken away from her a lot, put into homes. But I was what they called a troubled youth. I loved her so much, she was my mother. I always ran away and went back. But it meant back to that life, the life that got me locked in juvie for a while."

Her eyes watch me intently as I turn and lay my head on my arm, my other hand reaching for her. She doesn't stop me this time as I run it up and down her thigh. "When I got out, for GBH, she was dead."

She gasps. "How?"

My lips purse as I try to push back the rage to speak. "Murdered. I figured out she owed a seller too much money, and couldn't pay it back, so he called on her. Beat her to within an inch of her life, and while she was still alive, burned down the house with her in it. I got there right after. I tried to get in, to get to her, the smoke choking me. The flames burning me." I hold up my hands, flipping them to show her the burns on my palms. "I couldn't, I could hear her screaming though. Despite all the times she had let me down, she was still my mother. For all her faults, I loved her with every fibre of my being, she was my obsession. My only family."

"Diesel," she whispers.

"I chased him down, you know? I was so angry that night, watching the flames swallow her, that I finally let go. I'd held back for so long, pushing away my anger, all the darkness writhing within me. That night I stopped fighting it, I let it consume me. I hunted him across the city."

"How old were you?" she asks.

"Seventeen. I found him, knocked him out, and dragged him to an old, abandoned warehouse. When he woke up, I made him pay. Repeatedly. I let everything out on him, and for the first time, I knew what it felt like to be free. To be me. To feel bones crack under my hands and blood spray across me, but it wasn't enough, I needed him to feel the same pain she did. So I doused him and set him on fire and watched...and guess what? It still wasn't enough. I wanted more, like that fire, I needed more. I'm fucked up, I'm crazy, I know it. Never thought I would find a place to fit in, then I found these guys and they are just as fucked up as I am, though they hide it better. We all know what it means to be lost, to be alone, Little Bird, but together? Together, we're stronger. We shed that life, like a snake sheds its skin—"

"And became the Vipers," she finishes, sighing. "Fuck, why did you tell me? It makes it harder to hate you."

"Because you really don't hate us, and you're looking for reasons not to. There's one. Yes, I'm a monster, Little Bird. I love people's pain, I love my job, I enjoy killing people and making them suffer. I love protecting my family, and I do it all for them...and now you."

"Me? You barely know me," she murmurs.

"I know enough. You are one of us now. I will protect you like them, you entered a den of vipers, Little Bird. You choose whether to remain as our prey or shed and become a predator. Choose wisely. Not everyone is invited inside, in fact, no one is. Live or die."

"But why me?" she demands. "And don't say a debt, you could have killed me and been through with it."

"Because, Little Bird, that night...the night your dad handed you over without a fight, we saw the same thing in you that's in all of us. Garrett doesn't even know why he saved you, I think. Ryder lies to himself, says it's business. Kenzo plays it like it's a game, keeping everything to his chest. But I see it. The moment your dad gave you up...you became like us. Another lost soul. Another Viper in search of a home. We all started with nothing, no one, and now look where we

140

are. A family. A broken, fucked up family, but a family nonetheless, that would kill before they let anyone take you. Think on that." Leaning down, I kiss her softly, and she sighs. "Goodnight, Little Bird. You can keep the knife, think of me every time you use it, but know if you use it on us, on my brothers, I'll have to kill you. I might even enjoy it."

With that, I slip from the bed and walk away. "Diesel?" she calls, and I stop.

"You're right, I want to hate you, but honestly, I'm hurt. Hurt my dad could give me away so easily. I shouldn't be surprised, but I guess I always wanted to see the good in him. Then you came and gave me people to aim that hate at, but I see it too. The ghosts in your eyes, they match mine...and I hate that more. Because it means..." Her words trail off, voice quiet.

"It means you're like us." I nod, looking over my shoulder at her. "A snake."

I shut the door. She won't come after me, and she won't escape tonight, I know that now, even if she doesn't. She's home, and she's finally starting to understand it.

Maybe she will still fight, but if she didn't, it wouldn't be as much fun.

I can't wait to watch her rip the others to pieces, to get into their cold hearts like she has mine. We will all burn together.

Because of one woman.

Our woman.

CHAPTER NINETEEN

RYDER

I heard about Roxxane and Kenzo. It ran through my head all night as I stared at the words on my screen. I haven't slept, how could I? My mind is whirling.

Will she destroy us? Will she be the end of us? Should I have killed her? Should I now?

All that is compounded with the answers we don't have. Even Donald didn't know who the hitter was. He suspects he was an illegal, which means forged papers to get here. But for someone to hire him, to afford those services, they're more than a disgruntled casino owner like Declan.

Sighing, my mind travels in circles as I drop my head into my hands. I have too many questions and not enough answers. My dad's words come to me, even though I hate it.

Find the answers. Do what it takes, play dirty.

He was a bastard, a shit father, and an even worse husband, but he was a hell of a business owner. The first thing I did was take all his businesses. It made sense. He's right, find answers. I'm thinking too much like a businessman. Think like a Viper.

I need to find the person who made the papers, which will lead me to a money trail. Even when they try to stop it, there's always a money trail. Then, we find the hitter before he tries to end one of us again.

With Roxxane, the Triad, and now the assassin, our plate is full. I feel like I'm losing control, and I don't know how to get it back. I saw Kenzo's face last night after he fucked her. He was lost. I've seen that expression in his eyes before. He's a dreamer, unlike me. A lover. He might have won that hand against her, but there is a whole tournament, and Roxxane doesn't even know she's playing for the highest stakes.

Not her life.

Her heart.

My brother wants it.

It means she's fair game now. Maybe that's my fault for crossing that line in the elevator, but I couldn't help myself. The issue is...do I want to play? Do I want her? My cock says yes, but my mind says no. She's trouble, we can't afford any more trouble. Someone needs to stay clear-headed where she's concerned. So no, I can't.

Standing, I make my way up the elevator to our apartment above our business. This old building was once my father's pride and joy. I relished it, took great pleasure in tearing it down and rebuilding it to our specifications. I head inside, the early morning light illuminating the living room, which is empty. I go upstairs, take a shower, and get ready for the day.

I have so much to do and no time for sleep. One issue at a time. Today, I need to find the forger. I'll put out some calls over breakfast and hope to hear back. While I wait, I'll approach the Triad again, they have been reluctant to give us an answer.

Like always, I put on my suit, ready to face the day. Appearance is important, and a suit radiates power. Before I can even open my mouth, I'm telling them I'm not someone to be fucked with.

By the time I'm dressed and downstairs, Roxxane is already in her seat with the others around her. Kenzo is smirking at her, running his eyes across her angry face. Diesel is cutting up a steak with a knife, and Garrett is glaring at the table. So, the usual.

Taking my seat, I observe them as I fill my plate and pour my tea. "We have things to do today—"

"When don't you? Do you ever take a day off?" Roxxane asks. She seems to be doing that a lot. For someone who doesn't like us or want to be here, she asks a lot of questions.

"No," I offer, before reaching over and pouring her coffee when Kenzo seems too entranced by her breasts in the low-cut shirt to do so.

Crossing my legs, I hide my own hardening cock. Does she even know what she's doing to us? Walking around in those outfits, daring us to touch. Brat.

"As I was saying," I hand her the cup and she seems surprised, "I need you to put out inquiries for a forger, he would be good, probably the best." When Kenzo doesn't answer me, I narrow my eyes. "Brother, pay attention. As lovely as Roxxane's chest is, we have business to deal with."

"Her chest is nice." Diesel nods seriously. "Though I'm an ass man, a lot more places to cut, you know?"

"Thrilling," I deadpan, as Kenzo laughs. "Forger, find one."
"I know one." Roxxanne shrugs, making us all look at her in surprise. She snorts. "I own a dive bar, remember? I know nearly every criminal in the city, plus they all like to keep me happy so I'll keep the alcohol flowing. It's the one place they don't have to worry about being arrested."

"You know a forger? One good enough to make papers for a would-be illegal assassin?" I question, arching my eyebrow.

"Yes, asshole. I was going to tell you, but now I don't think I will," she snaps, making D laugh, and even Garrett smirks.

"Fine, I'm sorry, Roxxane. That was rude." I sigh, forcing the words out through clenched teeth.

She grins, and I warn her with my eyes not to push it. "Okay, yes, I know someone like that. He's a regular, sometimes picks up clients in my bar. I've overheard him before, and he's highly recommended. I'll tell you...on one condition."

"Which is?" I drawl.

"You take me with you," she states seriously.

"No," I bark, but that wasn't what I was expecting. I was thinking money, jewels, clothes, anything. She constantly surprises me.

"Then you don't get the name. He wouldn't talk to you anyway without me there. You might be the fearsome Vipers, but he's beyond that. He's all about who you know, and you? You don't know him." She grins, knowing she has me.

"Why? Why do you want to go?" I inquire earnestly. If it's to escape, I can't do that. I would have to punish her then, and I honestly want to stay as far away from her as I can, since she already tests my control. Laying hands on her again would be a mistake.

"I'm bored in this fucking apartment. At least that way I get to do something," she reasons, as she takes a bite of her omelette and groans. "This is fucking good."

"Come on, Ry, what's the worst that can happen?" Kenzo laughs. "We'll all go, that way she can't try and escape or anything. You said we need this guy, guess that's how we get him."

Balling my fists, I count backwards in my head, trying to rein in my control. I hate rushed plans, I hate it when an unexpected, unpredictable element is thrown in.

And Roxxane? She's unpredictable.

"I'VE REACHED OUT TO THE TRIAD, AND I'M WAITING FOR AN answer. The other families deny all knowledge of the hit," I snarl.

"Then it's them." Diesel nods seriously. "Let's go kill them."

"Wait, it might not be. We don't exactly have a short list of enemies, and making a move now, hitting them, would be a mistake.

146

We're not prepared, and if we can keep them on our side, then we need to do it. Another will only pop up in their place, and I'd rather deal with the devil we know than the one we don't."

We're waiting for Roxxane to get dressed, she seemed excited. I guess being locked up in a penthouse, even with all the luxuries, is not her thing. She wants adventure, she wants stimulation. I can understand that, but it doesn't mean I'm happy to let her come with us. But if that's the only way we can get to the forger, I would be a fool to ignore that advantage.

"He's right—we wait and see, they aren't going anywhere. Let's deal with this assassin first." Garrett nods, the voice of reason among the chaos.

"Okay, oh, we should check on Roxy's bar," Diesel adds.

Sighing. I look towards the hallway to make sure she isn't spying. "I already did. There's a new bartender, someone we trust. He's opening and closing it, keeping an eye on it for her, making sure it doesn't get destroyed. All the money is being dropped into her account."

Kenzo whistles, a smirk on his lips. "Guess that means you see her as more than a debt."

"It was a simple thing, not much work, and I thought it might make her less likely to attack us."

"Uh-oh," he says. "Sure, tell yourself that, big brother, if it helps you sleep."

I narrow my eyes but don't answer as Roxxane comes down the hallway. My mouth drops open slightly. Fuck, why did I buy her new clothes? I shouldn't have bought any, then she would have to walk around naked.

The dress is a black one Garrett picked out, and it's skintight, showing off all her curves with her sexy as hell tattoos peeking through. The jacket is something that one of the guys must have snuck in. It's leather and has spikes across the shoulders, and when she turns slightly, I notice the viper on the back—smooth.

She looks hot as hell and dangerous, especially with the purple lipstick and dark makeup around her eyes—makeup I picked out. Her hair is in loose waves, and honestly, I'm speechless. She always looks beautiful, but today?

Today she looks like a Viper.

I glance at the others just in time to see Diesel leaning back on his chair, craning his neck to try and get a look at her ass. But he tips too far and goes flying with a yelp. She looks over at the crash, noticing him on the floor, and smirks. "Falling for me already, D?"

D.

She called him D.

Jealousy pours through me. She uses his nickname? I expected her to be terrified of him. We kept warning her away, but here she is, looking at him in amusement and calling him D. Standing, I draw her attention to me, trying to ignore my own foolish feelings. "Good, let's go," I order, beginning to stride away.

I stop next to her, lowering my head, unable to help myself. "You look good enough to eat."

She blinks in shock as I walk off, checking my weapons at the door as I wait for the others. She looks around at us, checking our guns and knives, and doesn't seem surprised as she tracks where we holster them. "Can I have my gun?"

"No," I almost snarl. "You don't need it, we'll look after you."

"Can I have my bat? I promise not to use it on Garrett's junk again," she offers sweetly, making him snort.

"No," he replies.

She sighs dramatically but then smiles. "One sec." With that, she dashes off to her room before coming back a minute later, tossing a knife in the air.

Where the hell did she get that?

Diesel laughs. "That's my girl. Come on, Little Bird, it's time to play." He drapes his arm across her shoulders as she tucks it into her jacket pocket and looks to me. I can't move, though, too busy staring at them—at how close their bodies are, at how comfortable they seem.

It's worse than I thought.

What am I going to do? Nothing for now, we have other things to deal with, but I need to make a decision later on—before Roxxane gets in too deep and has the power to crumble all we have worked for.

"Let's go." Ripping open the door, I stomp away, aware I'm acting irrational, so I push all those emotions down, using the time we wait for the elevator to become cold again, wrapping a layer of unfeeling ice across me. When the ding sounds and the doors open, I'm me again.

Since my car was wrecked and I'm waiting on a replacement, I decide to take the SUV. We can all fit. Garrett climbs into the driver's seat while I get in the passenger side. Kenzo and Diesel slide in and trap Roxxane into the middle seat, not that she seems to mind. She relaxes back, but threatens to stab Kenzo if he touches her thigh again.

He only laughs. Sometimes, others wonder how Kenzo fits with us, while I don't—he hides his crazy well.

"Where to?" Garrett asks in general, not looking at Roxxane, so I peer over my shoulder at her.

"Head south, go past the theater area and into the slums. Stop us at Deckly Bridge, you can't miss it. There's graffiti all over the side right next to an abandoned steel mill," she explains.

Turning forward, I pull out my phone, ignoring them all as I catch up on emails and messages. I could have our guards meet us at the location, but with all four of us, there's no point. Roxxane must be thinking along the same line. "Do you four have bodyguards? You're worth a lot of money, right?"

"We have security," I murmur distractedly. "Over seventy-five personal, spread across the city, our assets, and homes. We instructed them not to let you see them. Usually, they would be coming with us, but when all four of us go out, these three act as security. No one knows they are in charge, since I'm the face of the operation, so it makes sense I would bring security."

"Why act like security?" she inquires.

"That way, only Ryder has to worry about being the main target.

They don't care about us, we're just fodder. Means we hear more as well," Kenzo answers.

"Wow, doesn't that make you worry about having a target on your back all the time?" she asks, leaning forward as we pull from the underground parking structure.

"No, it's my job," I reply, thumbing out a response to an email before pocketing my phone. "Sit back, seatbelt on," I order.

"So, this man we're going to see?" Kenzo starts.

"Just let me do the talking, okay? He hates outsiders and is a rude bastard."

"Even to you?" he questions.

"Especially to me. It's his way of showing he likes you. Plus, if you haven't noticed, I'm a rude bitch. We get along famously." She laughs.

"Want me to kill him?" Diesel queries cheerfully.

I look back in time to see her roll her eyes and pat his chest. "No, and if I wanted him dead, I would kill him myself."

"That's hot." He nods seriously. "Can I watch?"

Rubbing my temples, I sigh loudly, knowing it's going to be a long day. Luckily, we manage to avoid a lot of traffic, and other than Diesel's loud, off key singing, they are quiet the rest of the drive. Pulling up outside the bridge, I slip from the car, checking my piece before looking around. The others flip to security mode straightaway, eyes sharp and bodies tense as they look around.

Garrett goes first, me and Roxxane behind him, and Kenzo and Diesel in the rear. You can never be too careful, after all. Placing a palm on Roxxane's back, I guide her along as we walk. "Where now?"

"Side alley, there's a steel door," she informs us seriously, obviously sensing the tension. Outside of our house, this is how we have to be, we can only relax there. The stakes are too high to let our guard down, even for one moment.

We head that way, ignoring the homeless and the needles scattered everywhere. After all, we came from these streets, we're as comfortable here as we are in penthouses and mansions, probably more so. Not that **Roxxanne** knows that.

She pushes past us and Garrett, who tries to grab her, before leaping up two stairs and hammering on the solid steel door. "Hey, asshat, it's your favourite bitch. Open up!" she hollers.

I raise my eyebrows, but a few minutes later, a latch opens in the door, revealing two bright blue eyes. "The fuck do you want, shit face?"

She pops out her hip, rolling her eyes. "To screw your brains out, obviously," she deadpans, and all of us ruffle. "Now let me in, wankstain."

I hear him chuckle before the latch slams shut and the door is ripped open. I gotta say, the guy who steps out is not what I was expecting. He's massive, as big as Garrett, with arms to crush skulls. His head is shaved and covered in tattoos, his shirt stretching across his chest. He glances at us and narrows his eyes, his voice deep and rumbling as he questions, "Who are they?"

"Friends, for now. Are you going to let us in, or am I going to have to stand here while you fuckers measure each other's cocks?" she taunts.

He sighs, a smile curling his lips as he looks down at her. She's tiny in comparison, but you wouldn't know from her attitude. "You know mine is bigger than yours, we measured last time."

"Yeah, yeah, well, you cheated, Tiny, so let me in." She pushes past him, and he follows after her. Garrett looks back at me, so I nod.

We troop inside, and as I slam the door shut behind me, I see her waiting at the bottom of some industrial stairs. The room is small, just a landing, and when I glance back, I realise there are cameras here, an automatic locking system, and a huge shotgun resting next to the door.

Satisfied we're following, she starts up the stairs. We trail behind her, my eyes locked on her peachy ass as she takes the steps two at a time. She seems to know where she's going, and when we get to the next story, she heads to the left through another door and into the warehouse.

The room is massive, and the guys split up to check it out for anyone else or hiding spots. I stand there and wait as she heads right to the sofas in the middle of the room and flops down, her legs stretched out over one. They are old and red, but she seems comfy enough.

Next to her is an impressive setup—four computer monitors all turned inward with a huge chair, which is no doubt meant for Tiny. In the back corner under the windows is a bed on the floor and a wardrobe. To the right is an armoury with guns, knives, and even a fucking rocket launcher. She wasn't kidding when she said she knew people.

Tiny steps past me and smacks her legs down as he throws himself into his chair. She sticks her tongue out at him and puts them back up. "So what's up, shit face? Heard you disappeared, family emergency?" he mocks.

She rolls her eyes. "I told them no one would believe that." I bristle, thinking we're going to have to kill this man, but she carries on regardless. "Just taking some time away from the bar, lying low."

"You in trouble?" he asks, leaning forward.

"Bitch, when ain't I?" She laughs. "Nothing I can't handle, but I do need a favour."

He sighs. "Of course you do."

"Fucker, you still owe me from last time, when we woke up on that barge. Don't whine now when you gotta pay up."

Just how close are these two? I narrow my eyes at her and head her way, perching on the arm of her sofa as the others complete their circuit of the room. Tiny keeps his eyes on them, and on the computer screens, I spot a CCTV section open to show the whole warehouse.

"Fine, what the fuck do you want?" he snaps.

She seems undisturbed by his rudeness, picking her nails with her new knife as she lounges. Why can't she be this comfortable with us? I want to smash his face in before I remember we need him. She said to let her do the talking, but I interrupt anyway. "I need to track someone who bought papers from you."

His face locks down as he swings his massive head and glares at Roxxane. "Girl, who the fuck are these guys? You been telling them shit about me?"

He reaches under his desk, so I grab my gun and lay it across my lap casually as a warning. His eyes narrow, but he stops reaching for the weapon. "The fuck you want, man?"

Roxxane sighs and sits up. "Put your fucking gun away," she snaps at me, and looks to Tiny. "A favour, like I said."

"What's it worth?"

"Free drinks for a year, on the house," she offers, and the room goes silent.

"Make it two and you got a deal." He extends his hand, and she shakes it. "Next time, don't fucking bring the assholes, stupid bitch."

He looks over my shoulder, and I follow his gaze to Diesel, who's playing with grenades in his armoury. "Don't touch my shit."

Diesel smirks and backs away, but I see him pocket a grenade, great. Turning back to Tiny, I watch him spin to face his computer. "Who are they anyway? Some sort of male harem that follows you around?"

"Exactly," Diesel calls, before flinging himself down next to Roxxane and grinning. "Her harem."

"Brave man," Tiny mutters. "Okay, who are we looking for?"

"Brave how?" Diesel grins.

"Well, last month I saw her almost cut someone's dick off with a piece of a broken glass bottle he threw at her when she broke his heart. I'm just saying, you're brave bastards." Tiny laughs.

I look at her, raise my eyebrow, and she just shrugs. "He was rude, plus that was one time...okay, maybe more than once, but honestly, people with dicks always think they know best and can act like they own you. I remind them that vaginas are stronger than dicks, as ours are inside and yours hang out...ready to be chopped off."

I cross my legs and wince for the man, even as Diesel laughs hysterically. "Feel free to cut mine off, Little Bird."

Tiny turns, looking at Roxxane. "That one ain't right in the head."

"Tell me about it." She nods, leaning forward as Diesel starts to play with her hair. "Okay, guy would have been overseas, what else?"

She looks to me then, and I clear my throat. "Male, under forty, black hair. A hitter, would have needed ways to get arms as well, namely a sniper rifle. He would have been in the life." I know he knows what I mean when his face clouds. "Not a local one, one you've never seen, expensive."

He whistles. "Better make it three years if I'm crossing that bastard."

"So you remember him?" she asks excitedly.

"Fuck yeah, dude was an asshole. Paid well though, wanted it in half the time." Tiny nods.

"Do you know who employed him or do you have any details on him?" I inquire. This is the closest we have come to not only finding the man, but the people behind him.

Tiny debates for a second before looking at Roxxane. "I want the top shelf shit, bitch," he demands, before turning to his computer and starting to type. "I run checks on everyone when they walk through that door whether they know it or not. You're right, he's German. A freelancer, no ties. Good, too, one of the best apart from that one up north and his crew."

"Donald." I nod.

"Yeah, that one. Someone was paying him a lot of fucking money, that's for sure. They really wanted you dead. He went out once to accept a call. I have the recording." He loaded it up, and we all lean in to listen.

A German accented voice comes through the speakers. "It will be done tonight, then I leave the city. I want double, you did not tell me the men you wanted killed were the men who run this town."

It goes quiet for a moment.

"I don't care about your squabble or reach for power. Double or I walk." It cuts off.

"Squabble," I murmur, it has to be the Triads. But without proof, I can't go for them immediately. I need to find the hitter. "Thank you, Tiny." I nod, standing. I hand over a wad of cash, and he whistles and looks at Roxxane.

"Your harem has deep pockets, you sure you're alright, bitch?" he asks seriously, and we all stiffen. Now would be our chance, it would be a shame to kill him, but we will if we have to. I palm my gun and notice Garret sneaking up behind the man, but I shake my head, waiting to see what she will do.

She looks at us, noticing we're waiting for her answer, ready to react. Her eyes narrow. "Nah, I'm fine. Like I said, just lying low. Take care, cock face." She gets to her feet, and I can feel the surprise written across my face.

When she steps near me, she grabs my hand holding the gun, which is concealed. "I did that to save him, don't go thinking otherwise."

I almost snort at her defence.

She's made her choice.

She's ours.

She goes to walk past us, and I step closer to Tiny, whose eyes narrow. I glance back to see her walking away, then I nod at Kenzo who crosses behind the man, his gun drawn. I draw my own again and press it to his head. He might be huge, but I have taken down bigger and more powerful men than this. "You ever call her bitch or insult her again, and I pull this trigger, do you understand me?" I murmur, my voice low and deadly.

"Ryder," Roxxane protests, but I ignore her as Garrett and Kenzo circle the man, their faces cold. They might not agree on what to do with her, but at the end of the day, she's ours.

No one insults her.

I press the muzzle harder to his head, and his hands rise, his breathing becoming heavy. "Do we understand each other?"

"Yes, fuck yes!" he yells, as Garrett cracks his knuckles.

"Good, now you won't tell anyone we were here, or I'll send the crazy bastard and the big bastard back to speak to you. I don't care if Roxxane trusts you, I don't trust anyone," I snarl.

"Got it, shit, okay, man," Tiny protests.

Pulling my gun away, I tuck it back into my holster and nod at the others. "Good, let's go."

"I can't believe you did that," Roxxane hisses, smacking my arm. Peering down at her, I stop my lips from curling into a smile. She's so brave.

"I'll do worse to protect what's mine, remember that, love," I whisper, before pressing my hand to her back and leading her from the room.

"I was wrong, they're all crazy," I hear Tiny mutter, making me smirk.

CHAPTER TWENTY

GARRETT

Taking the lead, we troop back downstairs, and I keep my hand on my gun just in case. Like always, I go through the door first, looking each way before scanning the rooftops and letting the others out.

Roxy tries to stomp away, but I circle my arm around her waist and toss her back to Ryder. Someone out there is trying to kill us, and they don't care who gets caught in the crossfire. But I refuse to let it be her. I hear her arguing before a smack sounds and she yelps.

"You spank me again, buddy, and I'll chop off your hand and give it to D." I grin at that, even as I keep my eyes peeled, scanning everything as we walk. I don't like it, it doesn't feel right.

As we cross the road, the hairs on the back of my neck rise. Clicking open my holster, I palm my gun. The others must notice, because they go quiet, and I feel them move in closer behind me, their own weapons undoubtedly drawn. Putting my back to the wall, I scan the surrounding area, and my eyes catch on a glint from the opposite alley just as they start shooting.

Grabbing Roxy, I slam her to the wall behind us and place my back to her front as I take aim and fire back. The others surround her, protecting her as they shoot. The shots are going wide, so these aren't hitters, this is sloppy and desperate. One comes way too close, though, so blowing out a breath, I narrow my eyes and fire, watching the man go down with a scream. Two more sounds of bullets finding their homes drift to us, and the shooting stops.

Breathing evenly, I scan the area for any more hitters. Roxy is grabbing onto my back, but I ignore her as I keep watch. "Garr—" She yells before pulling my second gun from the base of my spine.

I turn just in time to see her take aim and fire at a man creeping up on my left, obviously hiding and waiting for us at our car. She hits him dead between the eyes, but she fires again and again. The bullets hit him in the chest as he jerks and goes down.

I look at her, my eyebrows raised. Her eyes are round, her breathing coming in short bursts, and her face is pale, but when she looks at me, she nods and hands back the gun. I shake my head. "Keep it for now."

She blinks before a small smile curves her lips, and then she clicks on the safety and keeps it next to her leg. "Let's go," I bark. "I don't want to be caught in the open again."

"I've already texted the chief, he'll cover this up," Kenzo offers, as I grab Roxy's hand and stride past the person she killed. I open the car and push her inside before making sure the others get in. Only when they're inside and safe do I round the hood, gun still drawn, and leap into the driver's seat. Putting the gun on the console, I rev the engine and get the hell out of there.

Once we're a few blocks away, I relax my hands on the wheel but don't stop checking in case anyone followed us. How the fuck did they know we were there? Did Tiny betray her? No, he wouldn't have had enough time, which means...

"Someone followed us." Ryder sighs, obviously coming to the same conclusion.

"Yup," I snarl. "Probably from the building. They weren't professionals though. It was rushed, they took their opportunity." I smash my fists into the wheel. That was sloppy but too close, especially with Roxy there.

My eyes go to the mirror and lock on hers in the backseat. Killing someone for the first time is hard. It takes a piece of you, a piece I'm used to, but she probably isn't. She's used to dealing with bad people, but there is a difference between kicking ass with a bat and shooting someone. Her head is on Kenzo's shoulder, who drops a kiss there. Her other hand is held in Diesel's, who is playing with it as he watches her. But her eyes are locked on me. They aren't scared or even concerned. They are calm.

"You did good." I nod. "Thank you."

She saved my ass. Why? She hates us, hates that we stole her. She could have easily let me die, but instead, she took a life to save mine. She smiles softly, those lips I'm obsessed with curling up. "You're welcome. Nice gun, by the way. I'm going to call it Killer."

I snort, unable to help myself. "No one names their guns."

"Ahem," Diesel coughs.

"Okay, no one sane does." I laugh. I notice Ryder is on his phone, no doubt conversing with security at the building and the police.

"I want CCTV from around the building. Find out who they were, go to the office, and get their prints and identities from the police. I want security doubled. We're going into lock down. Someone wants us dead. Hire more men if you need to."

I leave him to it. He's good at his job. Mine is to keep us alive, but his is to make all the plans. So I focus on driving, ignoring the speed limit. No one would dare pull us over. "I'm hungry," Roxy whines.

Ryder hangs up and looks over at her. "We'll be home soon."

The fact that she doesn't question the word *home* sends something soft through me that I want to squash, but I can't seem to when she's around. "But, Ryder, I'm hungry too," Diesel complains, and then Kenzo joins in.

Ryder sighs, pinching his nose like he's getting a headache, and I can't help but laugh. This must be killing him. She's throwing all his perfect plans and control out of the window. I might dislike her because of what she represents and because I can't stop thinking about her, but Ryder? Ryder will hate her because she's his weakness.

"We could stop at Rizzo's," I suggest. "Red might know something about the hit anyway, and if anyone is waiting for us, they would expect us to head straight home to regroup." I shrug.

Ryder looks at me incredulously. "Not you too."

"I like their burgers." I grin, and he sighs, knowing he's defeated.

"Fine, we go through the back though," he warns, and I nod, checking the mirrors before changing lanes and heading to the upscale Italian place run by an ex-assassin. He's also the guy who taught me how to fight, a good, trustworthy man. Ryder doesn't trust anyone with our lives or business, and he's the only man who comes close to knowing any of it, meaning he's someone we trust with part of our lives.

I don't head to the front entrance, but around the alley out back. I get out first, checking it over before opening the back door and letting Diesel and Roxy tumble out. Staying close, knowing she's the most likely to panic in a situation, I lay my hand on her back and steer her to the back door which Ryder is opening. He lets us in first, and Diesel takes up the rear. We only relax once it slams shut.

Putting my gun away, I keep my hand on Roxy to keep her close in case anything happens. That's what I tell myself anyway. I poke my head around the kitchen door as we pass it, grinning when I spot Red barking orders. "Hey, old man, got room for us?"

He glances over, the snarl on his face transforming into a wide, crooked grin. His bald head gleams under the light, and his huge, scarred, tattooed body is encased in a chef's jacket and trousers. "Garrett, my boy! Always!" He heads my way, enclosing me in a big bear hug before pulling away and smiling at the others, then his eyes catch on Roxy and widen.

He whistles. "Well, holy hell, who's the beauty?"

Roxy smirks and pushes past me. "I'm Roxy, these assholes kidnapped me," she offers casually, and shakes his hand.

He laughs, a booming one that's familiar. "I like her, keep her," he tells me, making me roll my eyes. "Well, come on then, let's feed ya."

He guides us down the hallway, past the toilets, and to a swinging door that leads to the restaurant. Heading through, I keep Roxy between myself and the rest of the patrons, not that they would dare make a move. Half the rich people who come here don't know who Red really is. The other half do and fear him, but not as much as they fear us.

Though looking around today, it seems like most of them are assassins. You can tell by their sharp eyes and taut bodies. Never relaxing. Growing up around them makes it easy for me to recognise, but in here, it's a safe zone. No hits, no confrontation. Just a place to relax and eat.

We are led to our table at the back, sectioned off from the others behind a screen to offer us some privacy. Seeing as though we bought this place and gave it to him as a present, a request from me, he lets us eat here for free whenever we want. It helps as well that most of his customers are still in the life and he can glean information for us.

Diesel slides into the booth first and then Roxy. Kenzo goes to sit next to her, but I beat him to it, unsure why as I slip into the booth and it crinkles under my weight. Kenzo smirks, but takes the seat next to me without a word.

Roxy hesitates, unsure where to put her gun, so I lean closer in the booth. "I'll get you a holster, for now, I'll hold it, okay?" She nods and passes it over with a, "Thank you." Our fingers catch as I take the gun and desire surges through me. Ignoring it, I put the revolver in the holster and look away, my face taut.

Ryder sits, unbuttoning his jacket, and grabs the napkin and places it on his lap as he looks around. His back is to the room, another power play, even when we're relaxing. I nod to let him know I'm keeping watch. Diesel scoots closer to Roxy and leans in. "The cake here is to die for, literally, I killed someone for a slice once."

She laughs, and I wonder if she thinks he's joking. "I'll fight you for it," she retorts. Ah, so maybe not.

161

"Whatcha want, boy?" Red asks, passing a menu to Roxy, who opens it and groans.

"Fuck, I could eat everything," she mutters. Looking down, I run my eyes over her tiny, curvy body.

"And put it where, your attitude?" I snort. Her head jerks up, and her eyes narrow on me.

"I *will* get my bat on you again," she hisses, making me laugh. She smiles back, and I shake my head. I look up to see everyone gawking at me in shock.

Eyes narrowing and laughter stopping, I glare at them all as they glance between her and me. Ryder's lips tip up in a tiny smile before it disappears. Red grins at me. "Good to see you laugh again, boy."

I want to die.

"Alright, hit me, whatcha want, and I don't mean just food." He nods, grabbing a chair and spinning it around to sit on it backwards.

Ryder sighs, leaning back in his chair. "It seems we have become a target. Can you see what you can find? There's a professional after us, a German, and it seems some sloppy, second-rate hitters now."

Red's eyebrows rise. "You've been busy. Who've you pissed off now?"

"Everyone," Diesel answers with a grin, and Red releases another booming laugh.

"Alright, I'll see what I can find. You think they are connected?" he queries.

I shrug. "Could be, someone paid a lot for the German. When he didn't complete it, maybe they got annoyed and hired some local thugs."

Red nods. "Alright, now watcha wanna eat, the usual?"

"Please," Ryder replies, and Red looks to Roxy, who's threatening Diesel with a knife. Sighing, I pluck it from her hand and pass her my bigger one. "At least use this if you're going to stab him."

"Whatcha want to eat, cutie?" Red questions, and I narrow my eyes on him in warning.

"Don't even think about it, she's ours," I snap, jealousy roaring through me. Red smirks, and I know he did it on purpose, asshole.

"I'll have a double bacon cheeseburger with cheesy fries, garlic bread, and wedges." She grins at him.

He jolts back, his hand over his heart. "You sure she's yours? Can't I have her?"

Diesel's face darkens, fuck. I reach over just as he goes to throw himself across the table at the man. Laughing, Red stands up. "Alright, alright, I'll stop fucking with you and get your order in."

Pushing Diesel back, I shake my head and sip my water. That guy is going to get us killed one day, attacking an assassin like that. Hell, Diesel is an assassin in his own right, but even the bastards here stay away from him because he's too crazy.

I look over to see Roxy patting D's chest like a dog. "Good boy, I'll share my cake if you don't kill anyone all the way through dinner."

"But what if they need killing?" he asks, frowning at her.

"Then let Garrett do it," she suggests sweetly.

D sighs dramatically and slumps. "Fine, Little Bird. Only because you asked so nicely."

She leans back, looking smug as Ryder just stares at her. How the hell did she get him to do what she wants? We have been trying for years, and I have the scars to prove it. Yet one bat of those eyelashes and he's behaving like a fucking normal person.

"So, what's your next move?" she queries, playing with the straw in her water.

"We hunt them down, whoever we can find first, and give them to D." Ryder smirks, a full-fledged, nasty one. "If we can't find them, we hunt their families. Their children, their wives. We destroy their lives until they come out of hiding, then we kill them. Make an example of them, remind people what happens when you come after a Viper."

She nods like she expected that. "If you let me have a phone, I can make a few calls. Those types of people are usuals at Roxers, so someone might have heard something."

Ryder watches her curiously. "And why are you continuing to help us, love?"

She sighs. "Because it's better than dying. I'm never getting free of you fuckers, so it seems I'm along for the ride, and I really like being alive. So let me help. I ain't just a pretty face."

He watches her for a moment, contemplating her words, before passing her his phone. My eyes widen. He doesn't even let me touch his phone. It's like his bible. But he passes it over, and she thumbs in a number and waits as it rings, her fingers drumming on the table. Someone must pick up, because she smirks.

"Is that any way to greet me?" she says, and then I hear a mumble through the phone. "Yeah, yeah, I don't care how late you were up sucking dick. I need a favour."

It goes quiet, and she snorts. "Yes, sure. Okay. Right, some low lives had a shootout today near Tiny's. Can you find out who and where they are now?"

It goes quiet, and I can hear typing in the background before Roxy grins. "That's your price? Bitch, you know I ain't going out with your brother again. Last time he took me to a brothel."

She laughs and waits as we all stare... A brothel? Who is this girl?

"Yes, thanks, girl. See you around." She hangs up and looks at us, eyebrow raised. "They're gang bangers, run the Death Eaters on the south side. Small but scary bastards. If they are coming after you, they have been hired for sure, they only work for money. You can find them over at the abandoned newspaper factory near the water. They will have dogs on guard though, and there's around forty of them."

She slides the phone across the table and sips her water casually.

"And one of you has to go out on a date with her brother. Probably to a brothel."

CHAPTER
TWENTY-ONE

ROXY

Diesel laughs so hard at that he has to dab his eyes with a napkin. "I nominate Garrett." He smirks.

"Fuck off," the big guy snarls back.

Ryder ignores them all, focusing on his phone like always. I can't help but watch him, he's so graceful, so refined...so cold. Like snow. But snow is beautiful, and when it melts...it reveals all that's hidden underneath.

"Need to piss," Diesel tells us, before slipping from the booth, and not a moment later, Kenzo slides into his spot next to me.

"He'll kill you," I warn him with a shrug, leaning back and meeting Kenzo's dark eyes. He slicks his hair back, a smile curling those lips, and a flash of heat goes through me, remembering how good they felt against my pussy.

His eyes dilate like he knows what I'm thinking about. "Behave, darling."

"I am," I argue, even as my eyes drift back to his lips. We haven't spoken about what happened, but honestly, I don't think we need to.

We both had aggression we needed to get out. Hell, I still hate them... but I'm tired of fighting this need, the need to have them. To feel that power.

I know I've told myself before, but I'm not ever getting free, so why not have some fun on the way? They have a way of dragging you into their world and consuming you with it, and I find myself smack dab in the middle...and I'm loving it.

Kenzo leans closer, his finger going to my chin as he leans down, almost pressing his lips to mine. "Feeling needy, darling? 'Fraid we can't fight in here..." He licks my lips before moving away and turning my head. I let him, and my eyes clash with Ryder's cold ones. He's watching us carefully, his face empty, but below that frost, I see something.

A spark.

One he's trying to hide. Kenzo doesn't care, he runs his lips down my neck and across my thrumming pulse. My lips part on a gasp as I try to shift slightly away, but I bump into Garrett so I shift back, and Kenzo presses closer. The room is filled with chatter, laughter, and the clinking of forks on plates, but all I can hear is my own heart as he teases me.

The asshole.

His hand lands on my thigh under the table and strokes upwards along my leg, getting higher and higher as he nips my neck. Eyes still on Ryder, I shift again, trying to ignore my throbbing pussy. Licking along my neck, he starts to nibble on my ear as he parts my thighs and presses his hand to my wet knickers, the dress giving him full access.

"I can feel how wet you are," he murmurs darkly, his voice hungry. "I bet if I slipped my fingers into your tight little cunt, you would come for me, wouldn't you?"

"You wouldn't dare," I snap, trying to act tough, but as soon as the words leave my lips, I realise what I've done.

Laid down a challenge...to a man who thrives on gambling and bets.

Fuck.

Ryder's lips turn up slightly, like he knows what's going to happen. Leaning back in his chair, his phone forgotten on the table, he stares at me. No doubt noting the rise and fall of my chest, my parted lips, and the blush staining my cheeks and creeping down my neck. Arm draped across his chair, legs parted, he sits there waiting, like he's watching the fucking theater.

And I'm the act.

Kenzo pulls away for a moment, and I glance over at him in surprise. He doesn't seem like the type to back down, but then he's there, the glint of a blade flashing under the lights before it presses against my knicker-clad pussy. I freeze, barely breathing, and he laughs in my ear.

"They are in the way," he growls, before he slices them off. I gasp loudly as cool air blows across my wet center.

I watch him tuck the knife and my underwear in his pocket before his hand is stroking up my thigh again. I can't help it, I part my legs further for him, hitting Garrett's huge thigh under the table. My gaze jerks up to his to see him peering down at me. He's angry, as usual, but I also see a deep hunger there.

I want to move away, I should. He doesn't like me, or women, or to be touched. But he doesn't shift away, and neither do I. My leg presses along his as his brother's hand finally covers my heat.

Diesel arrives at the table then, dropping into Kenzo's seat. "Asshole," he mutters, and then looks at me, his eyes lighting up when he takes in my state. "Oh, what are we playing, Little Bird?"

"Yes, Little Bird, tell him," Kenzo mocks in my ear, as he strokes down my slit, up and down, up and down, teasing me.

"I—erm, nothing," I sputter, as I reach for my water and take a sip, trying to stop myself from pushing into Kenzo's touch. I've just taken a mouthful when he parts my lips and flicks my clit. Choking on the water, I slam the glass down onto the table, and he laughs in my ear as I splutter out the water and wipe my weeping eyes. This motherfucker—

A moan slips from my lips as he does it again before circling it with his thumb and pressing down, rubbing me. He licks my ear as my eyes dart between Diesel's smirking gaze and Ryder's cold one. They all watch me. I'm the center of attention as Kenzo plays me perfectly.

His friend could come back at any moment, anyone could look up and spot us. The thought only makes me wetter, and he uses my cream to sink a finger into me. Moaning, I bite down on my lip to stop myself from getting louder as I lean back in the booth, opening myself further to him, letting him sink deeper.

If you can't beat them, join them.

My eyes close as I rest my head against the booth, just feeling him. He curls his finger inside me, stroking me, his thumb still rubbing maddening circles on my clit until I'm so close. Their eyes on my body and the feel of Kenzo pressed against me is too much.

"Eyes open, darling, see what you do to them," he murmurs in my ear, and my eyes shoot open.

I look at Diesel first, the crazy bastard, who has his cock out. I groan as I watch him circle his length, uncaring about being in public. His trousers are undone, his eyes on me as Kenzo fingers me.

My mouth waters at the sight of him. He's thick, so fucking thick, and across his cock is black ink. He got his dick tattooed. It doesn't even surprise me, nor the piercing at the end—he probably got off on it. Except I can't help but wonder what it would feel like inside me, that piercing dragging along my walls...

Kenzo adds another finger, making me moan loudly as I unashamedly tilt my hips to meet the thrust of his hand. "Look at my brother, see his eyes? They're on fire, melting for you. He tries to fight it, hates that he can't control you or his reaction to you, but look."

I follow his bidding and gaze at Ryder. I meet his eyes first, and see what Kenzo is talking about—they are melting. A fire wars with ice there as his face tightens. Running my eyes across his body, I note his chest is heaving slightly, his hands are clenched into fists on his thighs, and his trousers are...stretched across his hard cock.

He wants me.

It shocks me, and I groan loudly as Kenzo speeds up his fingers, fucking me for real now. I lose myself in it, in the pleasure coursing through me at being watched, and being in the middle of all these powerful men and making them weak. Putty.

Raising my hips, I shamelessly ride his fingers, chasing release as he whispers dirty words in my ear. He bites on my earlobe. "I bet if you reach over between Garrett's legs, you'll find him hard too."

Swallowing, I glance over at the big guy, who's trying his hardest not to look at me. His face is locked in a scowl, his body tight and leaning away like he can't bear to touch me anymore. His hands... they are balled into fists, the tattoos stretching across his scarred skin, but they are shaking slightly.

My gaze slides down his wide chest to his lap, which I can spot just below the table. Kenzo is right. He's hard.

Fuck.

Kenzo chuckles in my ear. "So am I, remembering the way you writhed beneath me, how tight your cunt was around my cock, milking me. How fucking beautiful you looked under me. I bet D is recalling as well. Ryder...Ryder is imagining it, wishing he was there. Wishing he was me, feeling your wet little pussy wrapped around his fingers right now. Feeling how close you are to coming from my touch and their eyes."

Moans leave my lips unchecked, his dirty words making me hot until I want to tear off my clothes and just mount him like a fucking animal. To ride his dick right here, right now. He groans in my ear like he knows what I'm thinking, his fingers stretching me as he rubs my clit.

"I want them to see you come, to hear you moan. For everyone in here to know whom you belong to, who brings you pleasure that no one else ever will," Kenzo growls.

Panting, I shake my head, trying to fight it, but it's too late. My orgasm surges through me. As it takes hold, my eyes clash with Ryder's, and for a moment, I see the inferno raging in his gaze before my eyelids close, a low scream leaving my lips as I come.

Fireworks explode as he fucks me through it, his fingers struggling through my tight channel, his thumb rubbing over my sensitive clit, making a groan leave my lips as I try to pull away, but I'm weak and spent.

I slump backwards, panting hard, my eyes flicking open to meet Ryder's again, but he blinks and the ice is back, like I never saw what I thought I saw. Glancing over, heart slamming in my chest, I see Diesel tucking away his softened cock with a napkin balled into his hand...did he come? Christ.

Kenzo chuckles in my ear, and I shove him away. He leans back, his fingers pulling free from my soaking pussy with an audible squelch. Clenching my thighs together, I cringe at the wetness coating them.

I pant, unable to catch my breath, and my body is still shaking from aftershocks as I watch Kenzo pull his hand out, the one he fucked me with, showing them all my release across his fingers. His eyes meet mine as he raises them to his arrogant mouth and licks them clean.

Fuck.

I can't take it anymore, I need a moment to regather myself. I feel raw and exposed, and they are all still watching me.

"Can I go clean up?" I murmur.

"No," Ryder snaps.

"You will sit in your own release, knowing that's only the first of many today." Kenzo grins.

Fucking assholes.

Just then, our food arrives, and I can't meet Red's and the other server's eyes, like he knows what just happened. Shit, did he wait until I was finished to bring it over? My cheeks stain red at that. How fucking embarrassing. Even for me.

But then I gather myself. No, fuck that. I refuse to be embarrassed. This is my body, if I wanted to ride all their dicks right here, I would. Swallowing, I raise my head and meet the server's gaze. His cheeks are pink, and as soon as I meet his eyes, he drops his to the table, quickly handing out the food before running away. Red chuckles and follows after him.

"And they say we're scary, you should see you. It's fucking brilliant." Diesel grins before grabbing his burger and taking a huge bite.

I do the same, starving after the day I've had. I don't bother to eat politely. Fuck them. If they wanted a classy bird, they should have kidnapped one. I eat like me, scarfing down my food only the way a kid can who was always scared they would never have their next meal.

When I've eaten as much as I can, I lean back, guilt filling me at the garlic bread I didn't finish. Another thing I learned from starving, eat everything, because you never know when you will eat again. But I can't, I'm too full. I try to tell myself it doesn't matter, I'm not starving anymore, but it's a hard habit to break.

Ryder leans over the table and gently presses my chin up, his eyes flickering between mine like he can see my internal war. It's stupid, but panic claws at me. Will he be angry I couldn't eat it all?

He softens for a moment. "Breathe," he murmurs, before reaching down and plucking the last piece of food from my plate and eating it with his hands, which is unusual for him. When he's done, he meets my gaze and wipes his mouth, and I know.

He did it for me.

I sit back, beyond shaken from the day. Honestly, there has been too many emotions to handle. I just sit in silence as they finish eating. Glancing over at Garrett, I realise his plate is sitting in front of him untouched.

I lean closer. "Aren't you hungry?" I ask.

"Not for food," he growls, and looks down at me, his eyes dark and his lips tight with lust. I gasp, shivering under that stare. I thought he hated me.

Ryder's phone rings then, pulling me from our moment, and I glance away, escaping those eyes. Fuck, what are they doing to me? I can't zone in on Ryder's conversation, but right after, he flags down a waiter.

"Grab Red for me," he demands.

Not two minutes later, he's at our table. "We have to go, thank you for the food, what do we owe you?"

"Fuck that, you know I don't accept your fucking money, but I have some information for you." He leans closer then, meeting Ryder's gaze. "The men are local thugs, easy to deal with, but there is a bounty on your heads, my friends."

He looks to Garrett. "People are going to start coming for you, it's a lot of money."

"I see," Ryder mutters. "Not much different from normal then."

"You don't understand. They're saying once you're dead...the city will be in new hands. Better hands. They are planning on wiping out the Vipers and taking over, it's all over the streets."

My eyes widen at that. Who would be stupid enough to take on the Vipers? They own everything, everyone. They are powerful and fucking terrifying. But Ryder doesn't seem shocked, his eyes do tighten slightly though, and he nods.

"Stay safe," Red adds. "Go out the back." Then, he's gone.

"Aren't you worried?" I question as soon as he is.

Ryder smirks, but it's not a nice one, and it sends fire sparking down my spine. "Worried? No. There are always people trying to kill us, to take what we have. When you're at the top, the most powerful, they all want you to fall. We never will. It's just time to show them that again, a little lesson to remind them who this city belongs to." He shrugs and stands, buttoning his jacket before throwing money on the table, ignoring Red's words. "Let's get back, we have some things to take care of."

Diesel whoops at that. "Hell yes, it's time to play!"

Oh fuck, I don't like the sound of that. But they all seem excited at the prospect, happy to get their hands bloody. Sometimes, I forget they are murderers, killers, and snakes.

Sometimes, I don't care.

Garrett slides from the booth, and I slip across his seat. His hand comes out fast and sharp, and I flinch. He freezes and offers it to me

172

slower. I follow it up to his face and see the understanding in his eyes.

He knows.

Accepting it, I let him pull me to my feet, and he lets go straightaway, but it was a nicety I didn't expect from him.

As we leave the restaurant, my eyes catch on a woman and a man leaning close together. Her dark hair is pulled back tightly, and she's smiling—she's beautiful. The guy is blond and leaning into her, whispering in her ear, and from the grin on her lips, I would say it's something naughty. She catches me staring and nods at me as she stands.

"Where are you going, brat?" the guy calls, and she looks down at him.

"Bathroom, want to join?"

I turn away, smirking to myself. Everyone in this world is a little crazy, so what does that make me?

We had no issues on the way home, but Garrett kept making sure we were not being followed. When we got back to the high-rise, there were guards waiting at the entrance to the underground. They double checked our vehicle for explosives before standing guard behind us as we parked.

There are even two new guards at the entrance to the elevator. They stay there, though, as we ride it up to the penthouse. I can feel the tension, the anger in the bodies of the Vipers surrounding me, so for once, I stay quiet. As soon as we open the apartment door, I notice all the new guards. There are at least five in here. Shit, what do they expect to happen? They are all big, all burly, and terrifying. Their eyes are sharp, and their bodies are tense—they are obviously professionals.

"Stay away from the windows and inside the apartment. We'll be back later," Ryder informs me, as he strips off his jacket and heads upstairs. I watch from the bottom as he scans his hand and gets into that locked room. I see rows of guns from down here before it shuts behind him.

The others are equally as serious, strapping weapons on their bodies. All apart from Diesel, who is laughing to himself. His frame looks like a walking armoury, covered in guns and blades. Are they really going to try and kill them all?

Four against over twenty?

Do they have a death wish?

Ryder comes back down wearing holsters across his chest and thighs. He looks more like Kenzo now, his face cold and deadly. His body is a weapon. He steps closer to me, and I realise the others are at the door, waiting. "Behave, love."

"When do I ever?" I smirk. He turns away, but I catch his arm. "Aren't you taking any of these guys?"

Ryder looks over his shoulder at me, his lips turned up into a grin. "No, but don't worry, love, we can handle this. Just another day in the life of a Viper."

"There are over twenty of them!" I snap.

He laughs, actually laughs, and honestly, it's a terrifying sound. "Good, they might give us a better fight. They will still lose, but it will be more fun." Turning, he takes my hand and places a kiss on my knuckles. "Don't cause too much trouble, and try not to kill any of them."

"No promises," I retort with a laugh, and then he's walking away.

He looks to the guards. "She doesn't leave, and you don't touch her," he orders, before ripping open the front door. They all glance back at me, and I feel so lost, so suddenly alone without them around me. I have gotten used to their presence, and now they are leaving, maybe to their deaths.

Diesel waves at me. "See you soon, Little Bird, I'll bring you back a present."

Then, they're gone and I'm alone.

Looking around, I spot all the guards watching me. They have orders, but I'm not just sitting here twiddling my thumbs while they're out here. I have to do something, anything...I'm not worried about them, am I?

Nah, fuck that, if they die, I will too. That's the only reason I care.

"Well then, boys, what are we going to do while they're gone?" I ask.

CHAPTER

TWENTY-TWO

DIESEL

On the way to the warehouse, I strip off my shirt. It's a nice one that I don't want to get blood on. Plus, I love it when it splatters across my chest. I have visions of coming back covered in it to impress my little bird.

Ryder is silent, as always, before something goes down. Garrett is angry, his neck cracking and fingers popping as he prepares. Kenzo is also quiet, double and then triple checking his weapons. We know the odds, and for once, someone might stand a chance...well, they might think they do.

We have been fighting together longer than these punks, we know exactly how to work together. We're unstoppable, and blood will spray before the sun rises. Their blood.

From my blades and guns for their insult.
We'll remind them exactly why everyone fears us. Maybe we have gone soft recently, so a good massacre ought to take care of that. We stop a block away and get out, locking the car. Ryder has his jacket off, he means business. He palms a gun and looks at me.

"Roof." He looks to Kenzo next. "Back door." Then he tells Garrett, "Second floor."

I know he glanced over the blueprints on the way here and devised the best plan, he always does. "And you?" I smirk, knowing exactly what he plans on doing, the crazy bastard.

He grins back, a bloodthirsty one. "I'm walking through the front fucking door."

Ryder may hide behind suits, but he's just as much of an animal as we are, and he's letting himself out to play now, God help them. They thought I was bad, but they haven't seen anything yet. We split up, no other words needed. I slip down the alley with Garrett, both of us heading in the same direction. We circle the building, the water behind us. They have patrols, but they are sloppy.

Their cigarettes light up their positions, their bodies tired and eyes not sharp enough. We slip over the fence and right past them. Dogs bark, aware of our presence, but the patrols don't even check it out. Idiots. I nod at Garrett, and he presses his hands together. Taking a running jump, I let him boost me up. I grab onto the metal stairs, then drag myself up and over before looking up at the walls of the warehouse. The roof has nothing to grab onto, but there are cracks in the brick.

Grinning, I start to climb, using the fissures. I smash my feet and fingers into them, feeling my skin shred and blood slickening them, but the pain only enhances my focus. If anyone looked up right now, they would see me, but they don't, and I swing over the edge and land on silent boots.

Crawling across the tiled roof, I find a sunroof about halfway across and wait for the signal. The others will be getting into position now. The warehouse has three levels. There is the bottom floor, which is covered in pallets and crates, and in the middle are some beds and a table. Bottles of beer are spread all over, and two open fires burn in cans. The second floor has what looks like offices, the windows dirty and obscured, but light comes from inside. The third floor, just below me, is more of a walkway around the whole place with a few men patrolling.

All the old machinery must have been moved at some point. What a shame, I was hoping to kill someone with it.

I see Garrett slip through a window and crouch on the second-floor railing, his shadow blending into the rest, unless you know what you're looking for. Opening the skylight, I get ready, standing above it.

This is going to be fun.

The back and front doors blow open at the same time, guns firing, and I drop. I land right on a startled man rushing towards the sound of fighting. Slipping my arm around his throat, I lick his face. "Boo," I whisper, before snapping his neck and tossing him off the ledge.

I spot Garrett fighting two men with knives. He slashes and guts them before throwing them over too. Laughing, I palm my lighter and light up a cigarette just as a man rounds the corner. He freezes when he spots me. Clicking the lighter shut, I smirk at him and blow some smoke his way. "Run, little boy, run." I laugh.

He hesitates before coming at me with a yell. I dodge his desperate swipes with a blade and kick out. He slams back into the railing, almost going over, and with a shout, he lunges forward, right into my waiting blade.

Whistling, I yank it free and tap the bloodied end on his face. "Should've run." I grin before kicking him off, his scream drowned out by the gunfire below. Peering over, I watch Ryder move through the mass of firing bodies, walking right through it, unafraid and unaffected. He sees them coming before they even get a shot off and kills them. Calm and unmoved, his gun firing with precision. A fucking killer.

Kenzo is laughing at the other end as he rolls behind crates and jumps out at people, shooting them in the face. I spot Garrett slipping into the offices below. There are no more people up here, so I grip the railing and throw myself over. Landing on the second floor, I kick open another office door to clean them with Garrett.

A gun fires, and I duck. It's a bad, desperate shot. It hits the wood of the doorframe and explodes, splinters slicing me as I growl. Tossing my cigarette at the guy, I land on him in a flurry before he can pull the trigger again. He struggles beneath me, but I'm stronger. I turn the gun in his hands, press it to his chin, and push down on his finger, splattering his brains everywhere. My ears ring from the shot, but I get up and leave, kicking the door shut behind me before moving on to the next one.

Garrett is just going through the door, with me right behind him, and we freeze. There is a naked woman cowering on the bed. She wraps her hands around her knees as she cries. "Where?" Garret demands, the scent of sex filling the air.

She points at the door in the corner, and we grin at each other. I step closer to her. "Better leave now, darling, shit is about to hit the fan for your friends."

She nods and scrambles up, not caring about her clothes, and rushes through the door. Shaking my head, I lean against the door she indicated and knock calmly. "Come out, come out, little boy, and play with us," I call.

I hear a curse and the fumbling of shells. Rolling my eyes, I wave Garrett on. He pulls back his leg and kicks open the door. It explodes inwards, and then he's in the room, grabbing the naked guy and slamming him into the tiled bathroom wall. He smashes his fist into his face once, twice more, before dropping him in a bloody mess to the floor and looking at me. "He's yours, have fun, I'm heading down to see if they need any help."

"I'll meet you there," I grin before stepping into the man's path as he tries to crawl away, "once I've had my fun with this one." Crouching, I yank his head up by his hair. "Hello, mate, want to play with me?"

Garrett laughs as he leaves, knowing the poor bastard will be dead before long.

His eye is already sealing shut, his lip is split, and his skin is pale and clammy. "Fuck you," he yells, and spits blood right in my face. I let it drip down me without a care as my lips tug into a smile.

"No thanks, I have a little bird at home for that," I reply.

He goes to spit again, so I grab his chin and force his mouth open. Gripping his tongue, I slice it off with my knife. He screams, spraying blood as I drop his detached muscle to the floor and watch him roll around in agony.

He passes out for a moment, so I grab a cup on the side and turn on the tap, filling it before throwing the cold water across his face. He wakes up sputtering, and when he sees me, he makes a moaning noise and tries to crawl between my legs. Stomping on one of his hands until I hear his bones crack, I lean down. "You shouldn't have come for me or mine."

He whimpers and big, fat tears roll down his face as he looks into my eyes and sees his death. Taking my time, I flip him over and crouch beside him before flicking on my lighter. I press it to his skin, strike it on, and grab his head and burn out his eyes.

Now, fun fact, eyes don't just melt, they burst.

They pour down his face as I let go, and he grabs his head in a vice, a wail coming from his throat. Whistling, I put away my lighter and grab his legs, dragging him from the room. I throw some of the bedding over my shoulder as I go as an idea comes into my head.

Hoisting him up, I wrap bits of the bedding around each wrist before grabbing my knife—no need for theatrics, he can't see me, after all. I lean down and press my lips to his ear. "This is going to hurt."

I slice open his stomach and let the contents come out before kicking him over the railing.

Using the bedding, I tie him in place by his arms so he dangles over the railing. Whoever comes here to investigate will see it and word will spread. They will know it's us, and they will be scared. His intestines tumble from his stomach and drop downwards, his blood spilling too.

Whistling again, I head down the stairs at the side, stopping to admire my handiwork. Not bad for being in such a rush. Leaping down the last three rungs, I step over the bodies lying across the floor, their guns useless beside them. They never stood a chance.

When I get to the middle of the room, Ryder is sitting in a chair. His shirt is covered in blood, and his guns are on the table next to him as he leans back, sniffing at a bottle of something before tossing it away. Garrett is leaning against a crate, cleaning off his bloodied knuckles.

"I got him," Kenzo calls, before dragging over a man wearing jeans and a stained top. "Stupid idiot asked if I knew who he was. Apparently he's the leader." He tosses him at Ryder's feet, who leans down with his arms between his legs.

"Is that right? Do you know who I am?" he asks.

Fuck, I love this bit.

I giggle when Ryder slowly rolls his sleeves back, exposing his tats. "Better answer him," I yell.

"I-I know who you are," the man snarls, getting to his knees. He tries to get to his feet, but Kenzo presses his head down so he remains seated.

"Good, this makes this easier. Who hired you?" Ryder inquires casually, still rolling back his sleeves. Methodically, slowly.

"Fuck you," he snaps. Why do they all keep saying that?

Ryder smirks and stands, grabbing a blade from the table. He holds it in the air, letting it gleam in the light. "Then let us begin. I want you to know from the start what will happen to you. I offered you a way out, now there is none. I will cut off your fingers, and while you're still screaming, I will flay the flesh from your arms. Then I'll start on your feet. I will, of course, cauterise the wounds so you don't bleed out. You will talk, obviously, but understand I must make an example of you now. I will cleave your body into pieces and ship them across the city as a warning."

The man doesn't seem so brave anymore. He's sweating, and his body is shaking. "I'll tell you, God, I'll tell you everything."

Ryder sighs. "Yes, you will." He grabs the man's hand and starts to cut off his fingers.

"I'll tell you! Please!" he screams desperately as he struggles, so I step in and hold him still, watching his face as Ryder chops one finger off.

"He's going to puke," I observe calmly.

"Nah, faint," Garrett counters.

"Both," Kenzo interjects, and we all watch as Ryder starts on the next finger, carefully and coolly.

Kenzo was right, the guy pukes. I skip away to avoid it, and then he passes out, landing in his own vomit. Fuck. I hand over a hundred and so does Garrett. Ryder sits back on his heels and waits for him to wake up.

He does rouse eventually, though only after I whip out my dick and start to piss on the idiot. He chokes on it as we laugh, and Ryder starts up again. Before he gets to the second hand, the guy is sobbing like a baby and spilling everything.

Including who hired him.

The Triad.

They are trying to wipe us out.

"They-they said once you were gone, they were going to divide the city and we could have this side," he cries.

I laugh at that. "They would have killed you too, idiot. Never work with the bastards, they never keep their word."

Ryder looks pissed. "I suspect if they want a war, they are going to get one."

"So-so I can go?" the guy whimpers.

I smirk, and Ryder grins. "No, you're going to be a message, like I said. Now, please hold still and try to breathe. This will hurt."

We all sit back and watch Ryder's handiwork. I did learn from the best, after all. I might be cruel and crazy, but Ryder...he knows exactly where to cut, where to hit, where to slice to inflict the most pain. I'm pretty sure he would have made a good doctor in another life, you know, if he wasn't such a bloodthirsty bastard.

The man prays for death before it's through, and he dies in pain and alone, knowing his own mistakes are to blame. I find some boxes, and Ryder places the man's limbs in each one.

Arms.

Legs.

Hands.

Fingers.

Cock.

Head.

Laughing, we seal them up and carry them out to the car with us.

By the time we're done, it's early, and the sun is almost rising. "Let's go home." Ryder shrugs into his jacket, frowning at the bloodstains.

"Yup, I wonder what the little bird is up to."

CHAPTER

TWENTY-THREE

ROXY

"Flush, bitches!" I laugh, laying the cards on the table. "Read them and weep."

Tony groans, his big frame stuffed into the dining room chair where we are playing poker. He looks like a gorilla, but the man version. He's actually very sweet though. An ex-SAS soldier who couldn't fit back into civvy life. I've learned that a lot of the guys' security hires are the same. All men with nowhere else to go, no other place to fit or call home. My guys gave them that and a pay slip.

"Fuck, how do you keep winning?" Sam snarls, as he throws down his cards. He's skinnier than Tony, but also massive compared to me. His long, brown hair is tied back at the base of his skull.

"She has to be cheating," Dem snarls. Now him? He's an asshole. A rude fucking bastard who thinks women should be seen and not heard. It's my great pleasure to prove him wrong. Even the others seem to hate him. Pope is still patrolling the apartment and keeping watch, but the others were just sitting there, so it was getting boring.

I searched Kenzo's room until I found some cards and challenged them to a few rounds of poker while we waited for the guys. There is no way I'm sleeping until they are, so I might as well earn some money. I grab the notes and stuff them down my bra, smirking at Dem.

"You're just a sore loser, especially to a woman." I laugh, and his eyes narrow, nostrils flaring. He's a good-looking son of a bitch, it's a shame about his personality.

"Yeah, and how's it feel to be a toy?" he snaps.

I arch my eyebrow at that, leaning back as I sip my beer. "I dunno, how does it feel? You act like a walking, talking dick, so you must be a dildo."

Sam and Tony roar with laughter as I hide my smirk behind the rim of my bottle. The sun is almost rising behind us, so the guys should be back soon. I ought to put this all away before they return and get pissed at me for distracting their security.

"You fucking bitch, show me your cards," he snarls, reaching over, but I clutch them and pull them to my chest out of principle. He grabs my wrist and twists it, making me gasp as he tries to get them.

Sam and Tony get to their feet, their eyes hard. "Let her go, man."

"Not until she shows me, the cheating bitch," Dem sneers.

We're locked in a stare down when the door opens. Fuck. Our eyes slowly go to the doorway where the guys are now standing. Blood coats them from head to toe, mainly Diesel and Ryder. I even do a double take at the usual cold Viper. His sleeves are rolled back, exposing his blood-stained forearms, but under it, I spot tattoo sleeves which finish at his wrists. I was not expecting that. His jacket is thrown over his shoulder, his hair ruffled, and his perfect skin is almost completely coated in red.

They are all smiling, until their gazes land on Dem and me. Then their amusement bleeds away to pure fucking anger. Shit. I'm dead. "Hey, guys, have some fun? Did you bring me a present?" I ask, filling the silence as Tony and Sam step away. Their arms are behind their backs, their eyes once again empty as they stand before the window, leaving Dem behind, who's still gripping me, showing me and the guys exactly how much they don't like him. They don't even try to get him away before the guys react. Shit, shit, shit. Ryder steps forward, those icy eyes freezing me in place.

He's so beautiful and deadly, it almost hurts, and the anger, fuck. I want to bathe in it.

Diesel looks pissed. He circles the room to the left, and Kenzo goes to the right as Garrett slams the door and stands before it, his arms crossed and face snarling. Ryder drops his jacket on the floor and steps farther into the room, eyes on us. "What's going on here?"

"Oh, you know, just playing some poker to pass the time, kicking your men's asses." I smirk, twisting my wrist until Dem lets go. Hiding it quickly under the table, I rub at it, knowing there will be red marks, but Ryder spots the move and strides across the room.

Dem jumps, falling from his chair to avoid him, but Ryder doesn't notice. He crouches next to me, kicking the table away until he can gently grab my arm, and holds it up. For some reason, I can't look away from the blood spattering his long, lean fingers as he slowly turns my wrist, glaring at the red marks marring my flesh.

"Dude, it's fine, we were just messing around." I try to tug my arm away, but he resists. His eyes roll up to me as he leans down and kisses the irritated skin.

"No one touches what's ours. No one hurts you, love," he murmurs, before getting to his feet, his mien transforming. His body turns hard, his face blanks, and only then do I realise just how much he had been showing me. He turns his head slowly to look at Dem, who holds his hands up, fear written across every line of his face.

His eyes dart around the room, his chest heaving. "Look, man, we were just having some fun."

"He called her bitch," Tony adds helpfully.

"Ryder—" I try, getting to my feet, but then suddenly, someone is there and an arm slips around my waist, yanking me back into a chest.

"Little Bird, Little Bird, watch and learn what happens to those who cross us," Diesel whispers into my ear, his hard cock pressing against my ass. "He's a dead man walking. No one touches you, no one hurts you, no one insults you but us. You are ours," he snarls, before nipping my ear in punishment.

I'm silent, unable to look away from Ryder, who stalks Dem around the room before cornering him against a wall. "Ryder, I'm sorry! I'm sorry, it won't happen again!" Dem cries out, his voice warbling in fear. That misogynistic, strong asshole is withering under Ryder's gaze. He takes him down with no words, just a look. It's all he needs. He strikes fear in the heart of his enemies when he's in his suit.

But now? Like this? With his enemies' blood coating his body, his rage pouring from him—he's downright terrifying...and a little bit of a turn-on.

Okay, a big turn-on.

Fucked up doesn't even begin to describe me, but I gave up fighting that a long time ago. If watching a powerful man covered in blood scare the shit out of another man, while his brother holds me and whispers dirty nothings in my ear, makes me wet, so fucking what? Everyone has a kink, and the Vipers and everything they entail seems to be mine.

"You touched her?" Ryder questions, his voice quiet and deadly.

Dem freezes, his eyes wide, like an animal when faced with a predator, because that's exactly what Ryder is. "I didn't mean to," he whispers.

Diesel chuckles in my ear, rubbing his cock along my ass. "He's going to destroy him. You should have seen him earlier. It was like poetry in motion, Little Bird. So much blood, and the way he carved through flesh..." He shivers against me as he wraps his hand around my neck to stop me from moving. His thumb resting on my hammering pulse as he forces me to watch Ryder.

It's silent, just their breathing is audible, and then suddenly, Ryder strikes. He grabs Dem, who is taller and wider than him, and slams him into the coffee table. The glass cracks but doesn't shatter. Keeping a hand on his head, he grabs Dem's hand and slams it next to him, away from his body. "Hammer," Ryder demands.

A moment later, Garrett hands him one before going back to his post, but I can't look away. I can't speak. I watch with a sick satisfaction, a warmth spreading through me at what Ryder is doing. For me. It's fucked up, but no one has ever cared before. Not enough to hurt someone because they hurt me, never mind touched me.

With no warning, he brings the hammer down on Dem's hand. He screams and thrashes, but Ryder easily holds him. Dem's fingers and hand are a broken, bloody pulp before Ryder grabs the other hand, smashes it down on the table, and does the same to that one. Standing up, Ryder releases the man, holding the bloody hammer loosely in one hand.

It's then I realise I'm almost panting and rubbing myself back against Diesel, so I stop, and he chuckles in my ear. "You love it, Little Bird."

"You called her bitch?" Ryder asks, dropping the hammer to the floor. "You dare insult our princess?"

Dem quiets his screaming, blood dripping from his busted lip where he must have bitten it. I glance over at Tony and Sam to see them smirking. They knew what would happen, they have seen the Vipers in action before. A scream jerks my head back around, and I turn in time to see Ryder cutting out Dem's tongue.

I want to gag, but Diesel's grasp on my throat stops me, and the warmth pooling in my belly makes me wonder if I really care. He was an asshole, that's for sure, but does he really deserve this?

It's not my choice.

Ryder tosses the tongue away as the man screams pathetically, his ruined hands coming up to try and grip his face as blood pours from it. "Will he die?" I query, and my voice is strangely calm.

"Maybe, wouldn't that be fun? I bet it's excruciating, don't you?" Diesel whispers.

Ryder steps back, looking at the man in disgust. "Tony, Sam, take him away. I want guards outside the front door at all times while we're in here, Pope. Whenever we leave, you sweep the place for bugs and explosives, same with the cars. I want someone monitoring

CCTV at all times, no one comes and goes without a reason or a pass."

"Yes, sir," they all reply, before grabbing Dem under each arm and starting to drag him away. They don't look at me as they do, in fact, they avoid me completely. I know why now—because of Ryder and what he'll do. It's saddening, I liked them, and now I'm back to just having my Vipers to keep me company.

Not my, just Vipers, I remind myself as Diesel lets me go with a quick lick of my neck, which has me shivering and him chuckling darkly. Kenzo comes into view then, and he's smirking at me and running his eyes down my body. "Did he touch you anywhere else, darling? I could kiss it better," he offers, and the room goes quiet as they wait for my answer.

"You fucking wish," I spit, crossing my arms as I glare at them. "So I'm not even allowed to play poker now?"

"Oh, you can play, darling, with me. I might even let you win... better yet, we can play strip poker," Kenzo purrs, his tongue licking his bottom lip as he runs his heated eyes down my body.

I try to ignore the warmth that gathers between my thighs and look away, turning my glare on Ryder. "So that's it? Someone touches me, and they get their hands broken?" I snort. "Going to hunt down all my exes too?"

"That's not a bad idea," Diesel whispers, making Garrett laugh, but I ignore them as I step closer to Ryder. Angry now.

"'Cause let me tell you, they touched me all over." I grin, a dark one. "Going to kill them also? What about anyone who looks at me? You possessive fucking assholes, I'm not yours!" I almost yell.

He steps closer, his eyes cold and locked on me. "You are, you better start accepting it, love, but keep pushing me, I dare you."

I swallow and tilt my chin back. He doesn't scare me, not even after what he just did. Not because I know he won't hurt me—he would if he needed to, if I became a threat, he wouldn't hesitate—but because I know Ryder. I understand him, and everything he does is for his family. He's angry, he's cold, he's calculating, and very smart... and very fucking dangerous.

"Why? Going to break my hands too?" I challenge, stepping closer. "No, just tie me up? Keep me at your mercy? 'Cause I gotta tell you, even that crazy fucker stands more of a chance than you."

His eyebrow arches, and he goes silent. I know I've pushed him, but I can't seem to stop.

"What? Nothing to say? Big bad Ryder lost for words? Or maybe you just don't know how to act with a woman who has a brain, who you can't buy off, who isn't fucking scared of you," I snarl.

"Oh shit," I hear one of them say, but I don't look away from him, staring him down.

"Leave us," Ryder snaps, eyes on me as I stand there.

"Good luck, Little Bird." Diesel laughs as they all leave.

"Fucking traitors," I hiss, as I stare at Ryder with my hands on my hips.

"What? Going to punish me for having fun?" I inquire snottily.

"No, for letting them touch you, for distracting them," he offers calmly, as he unbuttons his shirt one button at a time. My eyes watch his deft fingers as he exposes more and more of his golden, tattooed skin. It covers every inch of him.

"I—"

"They are here to protect you. If you distract them, they can't do that," he reasons, as the shirt falls open to expose his perfectly chiselled chest, making my mouth water. He's built like a god, all perfect edges. "You let him touch you."

"How the fuck do I stop someone from touching me?" I snap, but my voice is breathless.

"You will learn. Each time someone touches you, they die. Remember that. It doesn't matter who they are, I will kill them, and you will know it's because of you."

"You cruel fucking bastard," I snarl as he steps closer.

"Yes, I am, love. Better remember that."

I stare, unable to help it. The same design as Kenzo's tattoo is on

Ryder, but it seems to start on his back and wraps around his side. The snake curves around his pec and ends above his heart. The tongue is out and so lifelike, I can imagine it flickering, those red eyes locked on me.

Ryder throws me off balance. I'm used to being the scariest one in the room, but he scares me because in this room, I'm nothing. All that money, all that power, I should hate him. But I don't. Not even a little bit. He craves my complete control, but my surrender as well. Total surrender, but I'm so used to fighting, and when he peels back all those layers of stubbornness and hate, what will he find underneath? That terrifies me, that's why I lash out. Why I push at them, poke and prod until we all explode.

"What? Is this when I'm supposed to fall to my knees and beg for forgiveness?" I laugh. "Not my style, go fuck yourself and your stupid fucking Vipers. I'm done with you all."

It was the wrong thing to say.

CHAPTER TWENTY-FOUR

RYDER

Roxxane turns to walk away, so I snap out my arm, the reaction directed by my own anger and need. How dare she? She doesn't get to walk away, she has to pay for her actions and words. Grabbing the back of her neck, I yank her around to face me and crash my lips onto hers. It wasn't planned, but I can't help myself. She isn't allowed to walk away from me. Not now. Not ever. I would kill everyone in this fucking world for her, anyone who ever dared hurt her. She doesn't get to turn her nose up at that and act like a brat. Not when there's a scarred, hard-ass survivor under-neath. She can't know the true depth of feelings I have for her, that even though I try to stay impartial, that I try to hate her, I can't.

Because I'm falling in love with her.

She freezes for a moment before melting ever so slightly, her lips fighting mine, meeting me head-on. It's hard and angry, a fight like always with her. It's a duel, a battle for dominance as I open her mouth and slip my tongue inside, tasting her sweetness. It explodes across my taste buds, the flavour of her now branded on me, and I know this was a mistake because I'll never be able to go back. Never be able to not touch her, taste her, now. I just put my family at risk, and I can't seem to care with her in my arms. All that anger, all that bravery and attitude, and she melts against me so easily. My little broken princess. She seems to realise it, and tries to push me away and starts to fight. Thrashing uselessly in my arms, she bites my lip until I taste blood, like I would ever let her go. No, she will be mine tonight. Tonight, I will satiate my lust, let all this desire for Roxxane out, and tomorrow...tomorrow I can be the Viper I need to be to protect my family. But for one night, I'll be selfish. I will damn the consequences and take what I want—her. Chuckling huskily, I pull away, ignoring my pulsing cock as it aches to be buried inside her when she fights me like that.

No, she needs to learn obedience first, to surrender to me and my control. Only then will I let us bathe in pleasure.

I feel the pounding of her pulse against my hand as it lazily wraps around her throat. Leaning down, I murmur against her lips, unable to help myself. "There is nowhere in this world you can go, nowhere you can escape us, princess." I crave her heat, her body, her mind, even her fight. She is my ever-growing weakness, a grey area blooming in my dark heart and stretching its colour across my soul until I can't help but want to be a better man for her, to be the man she deserves. But I will never be, so instead, she gets me. She will have to learn to survive it and get used to it, because I have a feeling she's going nowhere.

I wanted to punish her, maybe scare her, but I can't seem to help myself. My cock is running the show now. I'll sate my desire, then go back to keeping a cool distance. I can still control this, control her, and how I take her.

"Want to fucking bet? Let me go, and we'll see." She sniffs, but her lips are bruised from our kiss, her chest pressed against mine so hard, I can feel her stiff nipples just begging for me to play with them. I can see her need in the way her pupils are blown wide with lust as her gaze tracks down my face and back to my lips again, and in the slight tremor of her curvy body as I hold it against me. Roxxane hates that she wants me.

Feeling is mutual, love.

"Let you go?" I smirk. "Never. Now it's time for your punishment." She freezes against me, and I chuckle. "Didn't think you were getting off that easy, did you?" I push her away, and she stumbles back, suddenly looking nervous, her chest heaving and cheeks adorably tinting red.

Circling her, I pick at the long shirt dress she's wearing, the fishnets underneath letting me glimpse her pale, tattooed skin. Needing to regain some control, I push her until she's bent over. "Stay," I order, as I stand behind her.

Flicking open the button on my trousers, I slide my belt through the loops until it's free, the noise loud in the silent room, and she shivers in anticipation. I tug up her dress to expose her ass and tiny red knickers, and I have to bite my knuckles as I stare at her to stop myself from dropping the belt and going to my knees to worship her like I ache to. I want to slam my cock inside her wet heat and hear her scream for me.

Me.

Not my brothers.

But I rein in that impulse, only just, my years of careful control shaky in the face of my greatest challenge. She's wet, I can see it. Fuck. Shifting my cock in my trousers, I try to ignore the urge to just rip those taunting knickers away and thrust into her tight little pussy. No, punishment first. Then control. Only then will I have her. "Ryder, don't you fucking—"

I bring the belt down on her unprotected ass. She hisses and falls forward, but I catch her around the middle, and when she's steady again, I rub my hand across her plump silky ass, massaging in the burn before I swing the belt back and land it on her ass twice more. She cries out but stays standing, profanities and insults leaving her lips.

But she doesn't move, doesn't fight me...because she wants it. She wants my brand of control. She wants to surrender to me. She wants to be consumed by me, and I want that too.

Good girl.

Pushing aside her knickers, I feel her freeze against my fingers as I expose her to my gaze. I lick my lips and stare at her glistening lips, so wet. She smells delicious, and I bet she tastes just as good. Running my belt buckle across her center, I watch her cry out and push back, wanting more.

Laughing, I snap her underwear back in place, and when she can't see, I lap some of her juices from my belt, groaning at her taste. "So fucking wet, love. Tell me again how you hate us when you're dripping for my cock."

"Fuck you, you cocky son of a bitch—" She whimpers as I bring the belt down again. Dropping it to the floor, I bite my lip at the redness across her ass. My marks. It's hot as hell seeing her like this.

But she's had enough punishment, and so have I. If I don't have her soon, I'm going to come. I reach down and squeeze my cock. Not yet, I need her to understand who's in charge. Who owns her body, as well as her mind. She needs to give herself over to me completely, and only then will she get the pleasure she seeks. I can't let her know how affected I am.

How easily she breaks my control.

Turning away, I give myself a moment to breathe, and when all those roiling emotions are under better control, I sit down on the sofa, legs spread and arm thrown over the back as I stare at her still bent form. I run my eyes greedily down her thick, tattooed thighs and plump red ass. She's fucking glorious, the most magnificent creature I have ever seen. She shifts uncomfortably, and I take pity on her. "Stand."

She hesitates for a moment before doing as she's told, whirling to face me, making me tut. "I didn't tell you to turn, did I, princess? Shirt off," I demand.

She bristles at the order, and I narrow my eyes. "Do I need to take the belt to your plump little arse again, love? I will, and this time, it will end in pain instead of pleasure. When I give you an order, you do it. Shirt off, now. Let me look at what I own," I command.

"You don't own me, asshole, no one ever could. Not you. Not your fucking brothers. There isn't enough money in the world to buy me," she snarls, and I have a feeling she's right. It's more of a pretence now that she's ours. We all know Roxxane is not a kept woman or a toy.

She's a fucking wild card.

But she still does as she's told, because even though she fights it, she wants us too. With a snarl, she rips off her shirt, baring herself to me. I let my eyes run across her exposed skin. Her full breasts are heaving in a see-through little lace number, her rosy nipples pointy and staring at me. Her belly is curved, and her waist is tucked in, perfect to grab onto and toned, with a shining jewel pierced through her navel, begging me to trace it with my tongue. Her thighs are rounded and delicious, and I can see them wrapped around my head as I tongue fuck her cunt. Her legs are long and lean, and I can't wait to have them draped around my head either.

She is goddamn beautiful, so beautiful it hurts. All pale, silky tattooed skin, thick thighs, and attitude. A combination I didn't know I would find irresistible, but my cock jerks hard as I store every detail of her body in my memory. Every dip, curve, and scar.

She parts her legs, head tilted back as I drink her in, unashamed in her own body. No, Roxxane owns it. She doesn't strive to make it what she deems perfect, doesn't go for plastic surgery or alterations like so many in our world. She's comfortable and confident in her own skin, scars and all, and it's sexy as hell. Not to mention the tattoos painted across her skin like the finest works of art.

That's what she is. A work of art.

One I'm going to stare at for the rest of my life.

"What next, asshole? Want me to crawl to you as well?" she scoffs sarcastically.

Hiding my grin behind my hand, I rub my chin before dropping it to my lap. "Yes, actually."

"Wait, what?" she squeaks, before clearing her throat. "I mean, what the fuck?"

Leaning forward, I narrow my eyes on her, warning her not to disobey me. "Crawl to me, love." She sucks in a deep breath, debating whether or not to ignore me. Wondering what it will mean to do so, but she wants the pleasure I have to offer.

She wants me more than she hates me right now.

"Fuck," she shouts as she sinks to her knees. "I hate you." She tosses it at me like barbed wire. I just laugh, though, since she says it so often, it's becoming an inside joke now. If she didn't say it, I would start to get worried. It's better than her...than her saying she loves us. She can't do that, but this? Hate and desire? This we can do and survive.

She drops to her hands and, eyes defiant and hard, starts to crawl towards me. She doesn't even mean for it to be sexy, she's too angry for that, but the way her body sways, her tits full and almost tumbling from her bra, her arse swinging temptingly...fuck. It's so goddamn sensual, I nearly burst in my trousers.

Having her at my mercy is addictive, seeing her on her knees before me a beautiful sight. She stops when she reaches me, chest heaving in anger and lust, then leans back on her heels before she grabs my thighs and digs her nails in, making me chuckle.

Even now, she fights, even when she knows it's useless. I will have her. She will be screaming my name, those little claws slashing down my back as I fuck her for everyone to hear and see. Those men she befriended, the guards outside the door, listening to whom she belongs to.

"Take my cock out," I order, hiding my shaking hands as I watch her.

She grinds her teeth but reaches up and unzips my trousers, the hiss loud as she finds me bare and hard underneath. She gasps, her lips parting temptingly, and those dark eyes drop to my cock hungrily as she wraps her hand around it and pumps me as she pulls me out. "Tut tut, behave, princess."

I stifle my moan at the sight of my cock in her tiny pale hand, at this one little woman controlling me so easily with just one fucking touch.

She squeezes me, making me groan before I can catch it as a smirk curls her lips. "Where is the fun in that? You want to control my every action because it means you can distance yourself from it, well, fuck that. If I have to be your goddamn slave, you don't get to act the aloof asshole. You want to fuck me? Then fuck me. None of these games, none of the defences to keep me away from you. Make it hurt, make it good, I don't fucking care, but stop trying to be this cold motherfucker when I can see how badly you want this...want me."

I still at that, how the—how did she know? I search those eyes because she's smart and the same. Her bravery and toughness are an act to keep people away. To stop them from gaining control over her. To prevent them from hurting her. I see it in her gaze, she hurts them, pushes them away first so that they can never hurt her.

Not again.

"You want my control, my coldness, love. Because without it, you wouldn't survive me," I admit.

She tilts her head defiantly, squeezing my cock again and making me thrust up into her hand. "Try me," she dares. I freeze at her words, staring into her eyes as she stares right back. She doesn't know what she's asking. What she would unleash.

"You have a death wish?" I smirk to cover my unease at how quickly she's destroying my defences.

"Everyone dies, plus I could have died every minute of every day with you guys. But I haven't. I've accepted it will happen, so try me, Ryder. Show me what you're so scared of, what you don't show anyone else, and if it kills me? So fucking what. No one will miss me."

That's a fucking lie, I would. I would miss her so much, it sends a pang through my icy heart. To never hear her laugh again, to never see her challenge me, defy me...no. I would miss her.

My brothers would. They would kill me if I hurt her.

I watch her for a moment, trying to hold back. But I can't. Her touch, her words, it crushes my control. It tumbles all my carefully built walls until everything I hate surges forward. The pain, the anger, the fucking need to cause damage. To wreck everything. To destroy everything good and beautiful.

Like her. To consume and take. The traits from my father I try to fight, his very last gift. Making me exactly what I abhor. *Him.*

I grab her and lift. She gasps and places her thighs on either side of me, her head higher than mine as I grip her thighs and hold her against my hard cock, letting her feel what she does to me even though I can't speak the words. Even though I can't give her that power. Reaching up, I pinch the clasp on her bra between her ample breasts and it flicks open, her breasts tumbling out into my waiting hands. I lean down and suck one of her nipples into my mouth, groaning when she whimpers, so I suck harder, digging my teeth in slightly, unable to help myself.

Pleasure and pain go hand in hand for me.

She cries out, arching into me as I roll her other nipple between my fingers. Gasping, she tangles her fingers in my hair, gripping it and sending a spark of pain through me as she rocks against my length, taking what she wants from my body. She's unapologetic in her need and pleasure as she holds me close.

Releasing her peak with a pop, I give the other the same treatment before leaning back and watching her pant and writhe against me, her wetness soaking through her knickers. Her breasts are magnificent, I can't stop staring. Fuck, how beautiful would they look with my marks across them? Disrupting those pale globes with all that soft skin marked up for me? I resist the temptation, leaning down and grasping some of her skin between my teeth, biting until she cries out.

Releasing her flesh, I lift my head to see my teeth imprinted across her breast, so I turn my head and bite the other one, leaving my marks. She whimpers, but pulls me closer. Stroking her hip through the pain, I let go and look at my masterpiece with satisfaction. Next time, she can wear my whip lashes. I'm thinking she would love it.

"Ryder," she gasps, rocking harder against me.

I lift her and rip off those fishnets and knickers and toss them away before bringing her back down to my cock, pulling her back and forth across it. I let her coat me with her wetness. She whimpers again, her eyes dazed with pleasure as she feels every inch of me that will soon be inside her. Marking her until no other will do. Making her ours forever.

"You're going to ride me right here," I demand, leaning down and pressing my cock to her tight little entrance. My greedy little girl rocks harder, trying to sink down, but I hold her still, forcing her to look at me. She doesn't get to distance herself if I don't. She will know who's fucking her, who is in charge of giving her such pleasure she can't handle it.

As soon as those eyes meet mine, I drop her, impaling her on my cock.

We both groan. She's so fucking tight, so wet. Gripping me like a silken glove, her inner muscles stretch around me. She sways harder, instantly moving, not waiting a beat. We're both too desperate to go slow, to savour it—that will come later.

We're both scared that if we slow down enough to think about all those worries, all those factors pulling us apart and making us enemies, we'll stop this.

"Ride me, fuck yourself on my dick until you come," I order harshly, as I lean back and watch her. Her body rolls with her movements, her breasts jiggling from the force of her thrusts. My cock is buried deep inside her as she rides me, doing just what I ordered. Taking her own pleasure.

It's goddamn breathtaking to watch.

I can't help but reach out and grip her winding hips, feeling each and every movement as I fight to thrust up, to grab her and take her hard and fast, just pounding into her. No, this is about her.

Her hands come up and pinch her nipples. This isn't a show, she's enjoying herself. I can feel her wetness dripping from her pussy, coating me. Sliding her hand down her stomach, she reaches her clit and starts to rub. Moaning, her head falls back as she writhes and rubs, chasing her release.

"I'm so close," she whimpers, but I don't help her, I just watch her, and with one more flick of her fingers she comes all over my dick.

She cries out, her body seizing and shaking, her pussy clamping down on me as she rocks her hips through her release. I have to curl my fingers into fists at her hips to stop myself from moving, it's the sweetest fucking torture. Only when she slumps do I take over. Showing her exactly how much I want her. How wild she makes me.

Grabbing her hips, I lift and drop her on my dick, thrusting up and impaling her on my length. She cries out, her eyes flaring wide as she peers down at me. She's fucking stunning with her chest flushed from her release, her skin sparkling in the sunlight with her sweat. Those noises she makes driving me mad.

But I want her screams.

She's had her fun, now it's my turn. She wants me? All of me? *Buckle up, love, because you're about to get it.* Standing, still buried in her cunt, I switch positions, dropping her onto the sofa as I quickly shed my trousers. Usually, I stay dressed, but I need to feel her skin against mine. I come down above her, holding myself up, and slam back inside her tight pussy that's quickly becoming my favourite fucking thing. Her legs automatically wrap around my waist, trying to pull me back to her body, her chest arching as she takes me deeper into her wet heat.

"You're so fucking beautiful," I murmur, licking down the valley between her breasts as I thrust into her, over and over. She's so slick, I can get my full length inside, dragging it across her nerves as I reach down and rub her oversensitive clit, making it hurt just as much as I make it feel amazing.

She screams, her nails raking down my back and cutting my skin. That pain sinks into me until the last of my restraint snaps. Groaning, I let go of my control. There's no rhythm or rhyme as I fuck her with deep, powerful thrusts. Harder and harder, chasing my own release, uncaring as she fights me. Her legs pull me closer, even as she continues to thrash. Her nails slice through my flesh, and I feel it part, the blood starting to drip down my skin. It only makes me harder, my face scrunching into a snarl as I lean back on my heels and grab her thighs, dragging her arse into the air in one smooth move.

She's so perfect, too perfect. My little fighter. Watching my cock thrust in and out of her wet heat almost has me spilling. She's too easy to lose myself in, too tight, too wet, too damn beautiful it hurts, and I can't hold back, even though I want this to last.

I hit that spot deep inside that has her clawing at the sofa, her head thrashing as she fights me. "Come," I order, not recognising the sound of my own gravelly voice, needing her to find her release before I can. I'm so close, too fucking close. This never happens, I always make sure they come at least three times before I do, but with Roxxane, I can't help myself, this isn't a chore. Something to tick off my list to sate my body. I want her with every fucking fibre of my being, so much it hurts. I want to paint my seed across her chest and into my bite marks. I want to take every inch of her body with my tongue and cock, but that will come later, for now, I want it to fill her, and I can't hold back anymore.

She destroys me, and knowing she'll walk around with my cum slipping from her, everyone knowing and seeing she's mine, has me rearing up above her as my hips stutter.

"Now," I demand, as I flick her clit.

She screams her release into the quiet apartment, her pussy clenching around me so tightly, I have to fight her channel until I can't fight anymore. I roar with my own release, filling her with my seed. She whimpers as I thrust through it, my cock softening as I slip from her.

Panting, she shakes beneath me, her body spent as her eyes open and clash with mine. I'm struggling to breathe too, and my walls lie in splinters around me so she sees what I hide underneath. My blood coats my back from her nails, my cock wet with my girl's release.

"Fuck, that was hot," she purrs. "Next time, don't hold back, I want it all."

Next time?

Fuck, she's going to kill me, and I might even let her.

But her eyes are drooping, and I know she didn't sleep because she was waiting up for us. I need to look after her better.

"We need to sleep." I gather her into my arms and stumble from the sofa, my legs weak. She giggles but snuggles closer. She's too tired to fight me right now, not that she would, I think.

I should shower and get ready for the day, I have a lot to do, but I can't seem to bring myself to as I head upstairs and into my room. Laying her on the bed, I slip into the bathroom and grab a cloth, wetting it before I return to her. She doesn't even oppose me or shout as I part her thighs and clean her glistening, pink, raw sex. I can't help myself, I lean down and kiss her pussy, and she groans and kicks me away, making me laugh. Tossing the washcloth in the basket, I slide into bed and draw her into my arms.

It feels natural, right. But it's strange. I never sleep with women, never mind cuddle, but I want to. And when she drops her head onto my chest and slips into sleep with quiet, cute snores leaving her lips, I can't help but close my eyes and drift off, pulling her closer.

What is she doing to me?

I need to be careful before she destroys us all. It's my duty to protect them...but how can I when I want to burn in her flame? When her venom is racing through my veins, telling me that she's exactly where she's meant to be, and so am I. Changing me, mending me, freeing those emotions I hold back from everyone.

Tomorrow, or I guess later today, I'll put my careful walls back up and slip into a suit, changing back to the cruel leader of the Vipers, but here and now, with her sleeping against my chest, our legs entwined and fingers laced together...I let myself be weak.

For just a moment.

For her.

CHAPTER

TWENTY-FIVE

ROXY

When I wake up, warm, satisfied, and yawning, Ryder is gone. I remember him carrying me into his room, into his space and cuddling me. But he's gone, and all evidence of our time together is absent, apart from the ache between my thighs and the bite marks on my chest. Lifting the sheet, I see they're still there, red and raw. It makes me smirk.

It was fucking amazing what we did. I came so hard, I couldn't even see, and watching that ice melt into pure desire was addicting. All those walls hide such an explosive person underneath, and I have no idea how he does it. Turning over, the sheets wrapping around me like silk, I look out of the window to see the sun almost setting. Shit, did I sleep all day? Usually, I'm up after a few hours to open the bar, but I'm getting lazy being here.

Slipping from the bed, I grab one of his white shirts and do it up before sneaking downstairs. Unluckily for me, Garrett and Diesel are there. Garrett is shoving something into a bag at the table while Diesel watches. They both turn at my entrance. Diesel's smoking, his eyes running over my body. Garrett looks at what I'm wearing in disgust. Ever since the restaurant, he's distant again, almost disgusted with me...or him, I'm not sure.

"Where are you going?" I ask, knowing I have no reason to be ashamed of what I did with Ryder.

"None of your fucking business," Garrett snaps.

"To a fight. We're going to see if we can find anything else and plant a few rumours. Want to come?" Diesel questions, ignoring Garrett's snarls.

"Sure, let me get dressed." I grin.

Garrett slams his hands into the table. "She's not fucking coming, she can stay here with the guards until Kenzo and Ryder get back from work."

"Nah, that's boring, I'm coming," I offer with finality before turning and trotting away.

"Fuck's sake!" I hear him yell. Wow, someone is pissy today. Maybe he needs this fight, might help him with his anger issues.

I HAVE A QUICK WASH BEFORE GETTING READY. I SLIP INTO SOME ripped shorts and one of the new shirts they bought me, tying it so my stomach is exposed. I put on some makeup and my kickass boots and I'm ready to go. I grab my leather jacket and slide my knife into it before heading out to meet them.

Garrett takes one look at me and storms through the front door. Diesel laughs and grabs me. "This will be fun."

We ride down in the elevator in tense silence. I spot Tony and Sam at the bottom so I wave, but Diesel drags me to the car. I get in the back with Diesel and stay quiet as Garrett peels out of the garage. We drive for around twenty minutes before pulling up at another parking structure. He cuts the engine and climbs out without a word. I follow after him, the slamming of my door loud in the car park. Diesel meets me around the front of the car, while Garrett is already reaching the side door of the building with his long strides. He bangs on it twice, and it opens, music and screams pouring out.

"Who are they?" the greasy man barks, looking at me with a leer. Garrett steps into his path, blocking me from his view.

"With me."

The man snorts but steps back. "I got a slot up in ten, get ready." With that, he's gone.

Garrett glances back at me and seems to debate something before sighing. "Stay close."

I reach forward and clutch the back of his shirt. He freezes before ignoring me and winding through the crowd. The music is loud, the sound of flesh hitting flesh audible even from here. Garrett smacks and shoves people to get through, and Diesel follows to stop people from pushing me.

When we reach the front, Garrett's head cranes before he heads over to some old crates in the corner of the ring. He turns, grabs my hips, and drops me on top of one. "Stay here, do not fucking move, and shout if you need anything," he orders.

I nod, and he steps back before pulling his shirt over his head and tossing it at me. I catch it automatically, even as I drool at his chest. The scars make me wiggle uncomfortably as my pussy pulses. He's a goddamn machine, and his torso is carved for girls' wet dreams. I hold his shirt on my lap as he turns and kicks off his boots, and then he lays his weapons on my lap before, with one more narrow-eyed look at me, he heads to the ring where someone is being dragged from it, unconscious.

"I'm going to see what I can hear, stay right here. I'll have my eyes on you at all times," Diesel murmurs, before dropping a kiss on my cheek and blending in with the crowd. I look for him, but I can't spot him through the throng. However, like he said, I can feel his eyes on me, as well as others. I turn and meet their stares. They're confused as to who I am, but no one dares approach me, and honestly, I don't blame them. I walked in with Diesel and Garrett—two scary fucking bastards.

Even if they don't know who they are, they can sense the danger, so they stay clear. Garrett is up next, and they announce him as Mad Dog before a really big guy steps into the crude ring opposite him.

Then, I can't drag my eyes away from him. He needed this, I realise, to let some anger out. This isn't a game or a way to gain information. He needed to fight like he needed to breathe. His body is finally relaxing, his shoulders rolling as he cracks his neck, and a nasty smile curls his lips.

My pussy basically starts a Garrett fan club then, pom poms and all.

He waits for the other man to move first, the crowd screaming his name, but they all fade away as I watch the bunching of his back muscles, knowing he's going to move. He ducks the punch, dancing backwards on light feet, teasing his opponent.

"Hey, hot stuff, want to party?" a voice slurs in my ear.

I jerk my head around and realise I was so distracted, a man has snuck up on me. He grins, flashing crooked yellow teeth at me. His slicked back hair is greasy and unkempt, his blue eyes are lackluster, and his skin is pale and clammy. A junkie. I would recognise the signs anywhere without having to see the track marks. "Get lost," I snap, knowing Diesel will be over soon.

"Aww, come on, I can show you a good time," he mumbles, and grabs my leg—on my bare thigh. Before Diesel can kick his ass, I clutch his hand, twist it back, snap his wrist, and use it as leverage to turn him around.

"Do not fucking touch me, you piece of shit, or I'll kill you, understand?" I snarl, and push him away.

He howls but glares at me, stumbling closer, his bad wrist held against his chest. I pull back my fist and slam it into his face before grabbing Garrett's gun and clicking off the safety. Pressing it to his forehead, I meet his eyes with an ice-cold glare. I will pull this trigger without hesitation. I don't fucking care. "I'll kill you, can you see it in my eyes?" He nods, fear wafting from him. "Good, better run before I do."

He stumbles away, swearing as he pushes through the crowd that gathered to watch. I watch his progress until he's near the door, then he disappears. Turning back, I realise the fight is paused. Garrett is watching me, his eyes heated with desire and anger. He nods, and I nod back, letting him know I'm okay. A small smile curves his lips as he turns to his opponent.

The crowd starts cheering again then, but they make sure to give me space. It's strange, them being afraid of me when Garrett is in the room. But I keep the gun close in case anyone tries anything else. You can never be too careful in the underbelly of the city, and that's exactly where I am. I might be with the Vipers, but I refuse to sit here looking pretty while someone attacks me. I can handle myself, and I will kill if I need to.

I go back to watching Garrett fight, but somewhere in the crowd, I hear a male scream that makes me smile. I'm betting Diesel has found the man. What a shame. Eventually, the crowd relaxes around me, their attention back on Garrett, who's kicking fucking ass. It's hot as hell to watch, and I have to clench my thighs together, my lip caught between my teeth as I watch him. No wonder they call him Mad Dog. The crowd's whispers drift to me. I hear some saying that I'm the Vipers' girl and not to mess with me unless they want to turn up dead, which makes me laugh.

I guess they aren't wrong.

I hear other rumours, spoken out of jealousy and fear, the words murmured as they glance back at me, knowing I'm with the Vipers. I try to listen, but after I hear a few snippets of conversation about a disembowelled man and a massacre, I focus on the fight again. Garrett is a machine. Fucking art in motion. His body is a giant weapon, each hit strategically placed and filled with such power that I can see it. His style is raw and wild, his anger leaking out.

It takes him over completely until he barely sees his opponent, he just fights. Getting all that aggression out. They have to hold him back twice as they switch his challengers, but he wins each fight, and when he's done, he's sweating. His chest is heaving, his hands are covered in blood, and his face is dark. He ignores the applause and dramatics, instead leaping from the ring and heading over to me. He plucks his bag from the ground.

"Diesel?" he snaps, his face dripping sweat which I have the strangest urge to lick.

"He was listening in," I offer, just as the man in question appears next to us.

"Let's go." He nods, and Garrett storms away. The crowd parts for him as I hop down. Diesel drapes his arm around me as we follow the angry man. Everyone watches us in fear and respect, and I tilt my chin higher at that.

Diesel drives home, and Garrett ignores us the entire way, his head turned as he glares out of the window. When we get back, he prowls through the apartment and to his room, slamming the door behind him. Diesel slips away as well, and I'm caught in the hallway, unsure what to do.

For some reason, I follow Garrett, feeling like he needs me. I open his door and slip through to see him standing there, his body taut and angry, his feet bare. He whirls and glares at me. "What?"

"Are you okay? Want me to look at your hands?" I offer sweetly, softly, like you would approach a wild animal.

"Fuck off," he snarls and turns away again, as if he can't bear to look at me.

So I step into the room and slam the door. He wants a fight, then fine. "No, want to talk about it?"

"About what?" he snaps, his built shoulders tensing and drawing up, preparing to argue.

"The thing eating you up?" I press, leaning back against the wall.

He spins and rushes me, slamming me into the wall. His arms land on either side of me, caging me in as he leans closer and glares at me. "I told you to fuck off!" he roars in my face.

But his eyes are lost, wild, searching, and hurting. He's heartbroken. "Let me help," I whisper.

His eyes close for a moment. "You can't, no one can. I hate that you saw me like that..." He trails off. With a self-disgusted snarl, he rips away from me, his hands running through his hair as he starts to pace.

That's what he cares about? That I saw him lose control? Oh, my damaged Viper. "I enjoyed it. Watching you beat the shit out of those people? It was hot," I admit, unashamed that I was turned on as I observed him.

He ignores me, so I carry on, trying to pull him out of his self-hatred. "Really, it was. All that power in your body, it's sexy as hell. The way they look at you, the way they fear you...you're untouchable."

He stops, his back to me, chest heaving.

"I want you," I state, taking a shot.

He shudders, so I step around him, my eyes meeting his, knowing I'll have to take the first step with him.

"I'm wet from watching you."

"Get out before I kill you," he warns, but there is desperation in his voice, he doesn't want me to leave.

He doesn't mean it, I can see it in his face, in his eyes. He wants me to stay, he wants me to fight this for him, with him. *Help me.* I see it written across his features. I wonder if no one else has ever looked under all those layers of anger to the scared, damaged man crying out for help underneath.

His fights, his anger, all a way to protect himself.

He needs someone to push him, to rip him out of it, but it might just kill them to do so...then why am I willing to try?

He's my captor. My enemy. But I can't walk away from him.

"Nah, I don't think I will. You want this too, want me. So why not just give in?" I grin.

"What makes you think I want you when I can't even stand to look at you? When I hate you? Hmm? Tell me, baby, what makes you think you're so fucking special that I would fuck you? Or let you touch me?" he grinds out.

I revel in his anger, refusing to be intimidated and back away like everyone else. He's lashing out due to fear, due to anger. I know that, 'cause I do it myself. "Because you're hard, because you watch me when you think I don't notice, because you imagine fucking me, even if you hate it." I lay the challenge down, and he doesn't disappoint as I reach out to touch him.

With a snarl, he grabs my wandering hands before they can touch his chest and wrenches them behind my back, forcing me upright, back bowed as he leans down. Hatred and need gleams in his eyes. "Don't you ever fucking touch me, or I will kill you. You want me? You're so desperate for cock that Ryder and Kenzo ain't enough? Fine." He drags me over to the shower stall in the bathroom.

With one rough, scarred, bleeding hand, he rips off my top and shorts and tosses them away, his eyes running across my skin in disgust before he flicks on the water. He kneels down, still holding me, and grabs my boots, throwing them behind him before getting back to his feet, his hand tightening on my wrist so it hurts. Pushing me down to my knees, he ties my shirt around my hands at the base of my spine so I can't touch him. I'm unbalanced, kneeling on my heels before him as he sheds his shorts, his hard, naked body before me. Every inch is stacked with muscle. His body is deadly, a weapon he uses every day. His chest isn't ruined like he thinks, it's a masterpiece of pain and suffering. The rest of him is so stunning, I can barely breathe. His cock is hard, long, and thick, and leaking and pointing right at me. Water rushes across me, plastering my hair to my head, cooling my overheated body.

I don't care. He blocks the spray and grabs my head, forcing my mouth open before slamming his cock into it with no warning. It's not polite, not that I would expect that from him. It's cruel, a punishment for me and one for himself for wanting me.

I hold on as best as I can, just a puppet for him to use for his desire, like the outlet his fighting provides for his anger. He channels it all into me, his cock so hard and thick and long, he hits the back of my throat. I have no choice but to breathe through my nose as I roll my eyes up to his. He meets my gaze with a groan, his hips stuttering before he slams back into my mouth. Harder than before.

"Don't fucking look at me like that. Like you want this," he snaps, but I can't help it. I do. Each hard stroke of his cock in my mouth has me wiggling on the cold tile, my pussy dripping.

He takes what he wants, it's rough and hard. My lips bleed from it, his movements filled with hate and disgust...and lust. He pounds into my mouth, uncaring if he hurts me, and when his thighs clench, his abs rolling, he roars his release, shooting it down my throat. With a disgusted snarl he pushes me away, slipping from my mouth. Licking my damaged lips, I watch as he turns and, without a word, strides from the shower. His ass flexes as he pushes out of the room, the door almost ripping from the hinges in his rush to escape me.

He leaves me there, wet and bound, with tears tracing down my face and blood and cum spilling from my lips, my own wetness dripping between my thighs.

That's how Diesel finds me. He takes one look and whistles. Flicking off the water, he crouches down, his thumb rubbing at my aching lips, unconcerned about the cum. "Keep pushing, Little Bird. You're the only one who can get through to him, and if you don't, we might lose him forever." He undoes my bindings, gently lifts me into his arms, and cleans me off before taking me back to my room and tucking me in.

It's soft and sweet, and brings tears to my eyes. This crazy bastard is growing on me. Who would have thought, and what did he mean about Garrett?

I know he hates women. It's easy to see somewhere in his past, one hurt him. Badly. Did she just turn down his proposal? Is that what the ring was? No, it's something worse, I can feel it. But I doubt he will tell me. It's clear, though, Garrett is trying to hold himself back from me, but like two crashing cars, we're drawn to each other.

Who will make it out alive?

CHAPTER
TWENTY-SIX

KENZO

"Bollocks," I mutter, as we pull up outside the spa. "I forgot to say goodbye to Rox."

Ryder snorts but slips from the vehicle, and so do the guards we brought. I hop out and lean across the roof of the sports car, waiting for the SUV to arrive with the guards. "What? I heard you two last night, brother." I wiggle my eyebrows.

His lips curl into a satisfied smirk, even as he rests his arms across the car like me. "So? Unlike you, baby brother, I can separate sex and feelings."

"Uh-huh, so then why did you smack Garrett this morning for being too loud and almost waking her?" I taunt.

He rolls his eyes but loses the smirk. "She needed to sleep. I couldn't be dealing with her brattiness."

"Sure." I grin as I round the car, and we head towards the spa. "Then why did you tuck her in and kiss her goodbye when you thought no one was watching?"

He freezes, his head swivelling to glare at me. "What have I told you about spying on me?"

Laughing, I clap him on the back. "Admit it, Ry. You like her too. It's cool, I don't mind sharing, but I'm not crossing swords with you."

He sighs and puts his hand on the door. "Can we please stay focused on why we are here?"

"Right, threats, paying the enemies. I got it." I nod, and he jerks the door open, the relaxing music of the spa drifting to us as we step inside with our guards behind us. Ryder refused to leave Tony and Sam behind, in fact, he made sure they were with us. And this idiot still thinks he doesn't like her.

"We should get her some girlie shit from here to make her feel more at home," I suggest as I look around. A woman in a dress sits in the waiting room, rearranging her tits to show them off, and flashes a grin at me. I wink and lean closer. "Sorry, I'm taken, and so is he."

She slumps but grins and looks back down at her magazine. Whistling, I glance over to see Ryder glaring at me. "We're taken?" he repeats.

"Sure are! You think Rox wouldn't kill any poor girl you brought back to hurt her? If you haven't noticed, Ry, she's as nuts as we are."

He shakes his head, muttering under his breath about idiot brothers and annoying women as he strides over to the desk and raps his knuckles on the curved wood. "I need to speak to Sandra. Now," he demands, face closed and angry.

The woman behind the desk shrinks, her face paling. "I-I'm sorry, sir, Sandra is busy—"

"Take a break, Izzy," Sandra calls, as she steps from the office behind the receptionist. She's a big girl, and I mean tall. Taller than Ryder almost. Her curvy body is encased in a tight dress and heels. Her greying hair is pulled back in a taut bun, showing off her face, which is artificially lifted. Her lips are pink and way too plump to be natural. When she sees us, her eyes narrow.

She's a scary woman, enough so to make my balls shrivel, but that's why we liked her.

216

"Gentlemen, what a surprise. Please come through and stop harassing my staff," she snaps before turning and, with the clicking of her heels, striding into her office.

Leaning closer to Ryder, I smile and murmur, "I like women, but that one is fucking scary. Still not as scary as Rox though. Oh, I hid her bat in the weapons room."

He ignores me and pushes behind the desk, following her into the office. I nod to Tony, who stops at the front door. Looking around at the patrons, I grin and announce, "I'm afraid the spa is closed, please leave."

The women and men waiting start to object, so I flash my gun with a happy smile, and they soon rush for the door. Tony slams it behind them and flips the lock. Sam trails after me and stands at the office door, but I pause and let my face darken for a moment as I look between them without Ryder here. "I may not have reacted, Ryder may not have, but come close to our woman again, and it will be the last thing you do," I warn, and I watch Sam gulp as they both nod. Then, with a happy smile back in place, I pat his chest, slip in, and shut the door behind me. "Sorry about that, it seems everyone left," I comment with wide, innocent eyes as I roll my dice across my knuckles, leaning back against the wall.

Sandra glares at me, her legs crossed in her office chair, and her hands tight across her stomach as she waits for Ryder to speak. He sits on the sofa across from her, playing on his phone and making her sweat. Literally. I watch as actual sweat drips down her face and she shifts nervously.

She knows what she did, and now she's wondering if she will make it out of here alive.

Ryder keeps her waiting, and I pull out my own phone and shoot a message to Garrett to check on Rox. He sends me back a picture of her curled up on the sofa asleep next to him. His face is locked in a scowl in the picture, which makes me laugh. I forward it to Ryder whose lips turn up in a smirk before he pockets the device.

He looks up at Sandra and sighs loudly. "We haven't heard from you in a while, Sandra, which is surprising, seeing as though we own the land you are built on...so, tell me. If you aren't paying us back, where is your money going, hmm? We already know it's leaving your account."

She balks at that, probably not realising we're more than brawn. "I-I had some bills to pay and got behind," she replies, tilting her chin back, but her eyes dart around nervously.

"Don't lie to me, Sandra. I have been kind to you, and it would be a shame for me to have to stop," Ryder growls, voice cold and deadly. "You came to me with an offer, not the other way around. You needed our help, we lent you the money so you could run this place... now you're trying to break your end of the deal? Darling, it doesn't work like that."

"I'm sick of paying," she blurts before swallowing. "I-I lose half my profit to you."

"We offer less repayment interest than banks, or did you forget that? Without us, there would be no spa," Ryder drawls. "I could, of course, revert my loan, buy this place, fire all your staff, and tear it down...or I could do even worse. How's your husband, Sandra?"

"Leave Mike out of this," she almost yells, making me chuckle.

"Wish we could, darling, but Mike put himself into this. Did you know he likes to gamble?" I remark conversationally, and she looks at me in confusion. "Now don't get me wrong, it was only every now and again until I...showed him the addictive side of the city. I tried to help him." Sighing, I shake my head. "It seems he was tired of being emasculated at home. He got drunk and told everyone."

"You're lying," she snaps, so I load up the video from one of my clubs. I only show her a split second of it before pocketing it again. "So what?" she says, but I can see the hurt in her eyes.

"So it drove him to addiction, and now he owes some bad people money. If he'd come to me, I could have helped him out. But he didn't." I put my hands out in a fake placating gesture, an unkind smile tugging at my lips.

"Is-is he okay?" she asks, looking between us.

"He could be, it all depends on your choice, Sandra. I can bail him out, but of course that money would go on top of what you already owe us, or I can leave him in their hands. Now, they won't kill him for the first offence, no, just break his kneecaps. But, unfortunately, as a builder, they seem rather important, don't they?" I laugh, but it's not a nice sound, and she shivers from it.

"You fucking evil snakes," she hisses, as tears fall from her eyes, which she tries to swipe away, only smearing her makeup instead.

"No, darling, not evil, just businessmen. We gave you money, a job, we got you off the streets. We kept an eye on your husband, who would be dead now without us. Yes, we like money and we profit from our business deals...but everything is not black and white. It's filled with greys, and we just happen to run the grey area."

She turns around and slams open her drawer, scribbling a check before throwing it at Ryder. He pockets it. It's not about the money, after all, but the fucking cheek of her not repaying us after everything we did for her. The bank would have taken her spa by now. "Thanks, madame." I wink, reminding her exactly where we found her. Working in one of the Triad's clubs years ago.

She averts her gaze, sniffling hard. "I just wanted a different life," she whispers quietly, so low we aren't meant to hear.

"We know, that's why we helped you in exchange for all that information. Your debt is almost paid, Sandra, so keep your head down, and this place will be all yours before long," I offer nicely. Ryder rolls his eyes at me before getting to his feet.

"Do not make us come back, Sandra."

"And Mike?" she whispers, staring at us with huge tear tracks down her face.

I drop a quick text to the men holding him. "I paid his debt just now, he's free, but maybe keep your eye on his spending and get him some help." I play the role of the nice brother easily enough, and with a friendly wink, I turn to leave, but my eyes catch on the shelves of products.

"Oh, we need some girlie shit," I tell Sandra. She nods, tears still streaming down her face, and black mascara flowing in its wake. She's a mess.

"Take whatever you want," she whispers, looking away quickly.

"Thanks, is this face...mask good?" I question, and Ryder snorts.

"Just take everything. I'm sure Sandra here can get more stock with the money she will be getting back from the Triad. Isn't that right, Sandra?" he challenges nastily, and she hastily nods.

Grabbing a bag from the side, I dump all the stuff into it, hoping Rox likes it before throwing it over my shoulder and opening the door. Sam instantly takes the bag, his eyes still sharp, scanning our surroundings. Whistling again, I head to the door and Tony opens it but goes out first, checking everything before nodding at us.

We head back to the car, and when we're inside, I look at Ryder. "We should get her some other stuff to make her feel at home. She is staying, isn't she?"

He grips the wheel. "I don't know."

"Oh, come on, Ry, she's nothing like that bitch. She doesn't even want our money." I laugh.

"No, she wants something worse. Her freedom." He glares at me then. "She will never be happy being kept in our penthouse, she's not a kept woman. She likes to work, it's how she got by."

I nod and look away. "Then we give her a job, something, anything. Because she's not leaving us."

"We couldn't give her freedom, even if we wanted to. It would be a sign of weakness, and they have all seen her with us now. She would be dead the moment she stepped from the building." Ryder sighs and rubs his head. We both know that's the truth. By being ours, she has a target on her back, but I can't bring myself to regret that when it means I get her. "Fine, let's get her some stuff, the other bits can wait."

Firing up the Aston, he pulls into traffic with Tony and Sam behind us, and does a U-turn to take us downtown to the shopping district. "I fucking hate shopping," he growls.

Flicking on the radio, I dance along to the music. "I love it."

"How are we brothers?" he mutters.

"'Cause all the anger and madness went to you." I laugh.

He swears, and I ignore him and ring Garrett. "Hey, we're nipping to the store, need anything?"

"To be allowed to kill this fucking brat," he snaps, then yells louder, "Then don't fucking try that shit again," before coming back to the phone. "She's so annoying, you sure I can't kill her?"

"I heard that, asshole!" Roxy screams in the background. "I might not have my bat, but I'll still take you down, motherfucker."

I raise my eyebrows at that. "I thought you two had started to get along?"

He snorts but doesn't answer. Ah, okay, so she's under his skin. We can work with that. "Don't you fucking dare change that channel again," he barks.

"I'll leave you to it, have fun," I offer with a laugh before hanging up and looking over at Ryder. "She's going to have him wrapped around her finger before long."

He grins. "No doubt, she already has you."

"And D, did you hear he killed that drunken idiot at the fight?"

Ryder nods. "Sloppy, but that's Diesel for you."

He parallel parks outside a shop, ignoring the no parking lines. We wait for Tony and Sam to get out, and then they open our doors— we can't be too careful at the moment. It wouldn't be good for one of us to get shot just because we were sloppy, and with a bounty on our heads, they will all be coming out of the woodwork to try for us. We are hoping the German is one of them, which is why we are out and about.

Bait.

Heads held high and unafraid, we stroll into the shop. The greeter zeros in on us straightaway, recognising money, and his eyes light up. "Gentlemen, how may I help you?"

Ryder points at me and pulls his phone out to undoubtedly answer all the emails piling up. Wrapping my arm around his neck, I pluck his phone free and pocket it. "Oh no you don't, you stuck your dick in her too, so you have to buy her nice things to make up for your shitty attitude."

He grumbles and glares at me, pushing me away. He tries to grab his phone, but I move back, laughing. The salesman doesn't even blink, pretending he can't hear our conversation like all the best ones do. Catering to the rich and famous means you get deaf really quick or you don't last long.

"Fine, she needs more jewellery," he mumbles, making me clap my hands.

"Now you're talking. She needs more of those sexy bras, and for sure some more of those boots, they are hot as hell. Oh, we should buy her some weapons." I sigh wistfully.

He looks over at me. "And when she uses them on us?"

I shrug. "Probably only on Diesel, and he would love it, and, well, maybe Garrett, but he would just respawn like the devil he is."

"Of course, sir, if you would like to follow me. I will have my colleague Francesco escort you, sir, to the jewellery."

"Nope, we can go together, we are in no rush," I reply and wave him on. He inclines his head and leads us to the second floor and the jewellery there.

"What kind of shit do women like?" I mutter.

"Anything expensive," Ryder snaps.

"Like fuck. You think Rox cares how much we spend? She would probably just throw it back in our faces and cross those little arms and put on the cute face and be like 'I don't need your bribes, asshole,'" I mock, and his mouth drops at my girl voice.

"That was strangely accurate and a little scary. Fine, what shall we get her?" He throws his hands in the air.

"You, server guy, what should we get a woman who doesn't give a fuck about money or riches and is rocker-like?"

He ponders that for a moment. "Ah, I have some things that may work."

"Any in a snake?" Ryder queries.

222

The man doesn't even blink at the strange request. "Right this way."

He leads us to a small sitting area and then disappears. Leaning back in my chair, I look around at all the sparkling jewels around us. "Shit, I remember coming to places like this with Dad so he could show off his new trophy wife."

Ryder grunts, but I carry on, "I always hated it and the women, all they cared about was money. Yet we ended up with those types of women...well, except now with Roxxane. She really is different. Do you think it's because she genuinely doesn't know how much money we have?"

"I don't think it would matter. She was brought up on nothing, came from nothing, and she has worked for everything she has. I believe Rox likes to earn her way. She wouldn't be intimidated here, but she would also insist on paying herself."

I nod. He's right, he always is. He has a good read on people. "Did you ever think this is where we would end up?"

He glances at me then, his face cold, but I know better. My brother has the world on his shoulders, always did. Even back then, protecting me from our old man, it made him sharp, cold, and angry. "No, I thought we would either be dead or still with the bastard."

I nod solemnly. "You did what you had to, brother."

He looks away for a moment, watching the comings and goings of people. "I know." He goes quiet. "Do I remind you of him sometimes?"

I debate his question. "Yes, but you have something he never did."

"What's that?" he inquires, looking at me.

"Me." I smirk. "He had no one to drag him back down, to stop him before he went too far. You have his hunger, his smarts, and yes, his anger. But you also have a family that genuinely cares for you. We are all a bit messed up, but we know how to keep each other sane. You never have to worry about being him, I would never let you. I would kill you first," I vow, and he smiles, a genuine one, and I can almost see him as a kid, when he used to smile like that all the time before my dad beat it from him.

Just then, the man returns and arranges the jewellery before us. We pick the ones we like, not bothering to look at the prices. He promises they will be boxed and waiting for us and then leads us to the clothing area.

We sit for a while as he shows them off and coordinates outfits from what we like. Roxy might not enjoy being spoiled, only because I have a feeling no one ever has, but she has no choice anymore. I've decided we are keeping her, and that means I get to spoil her whenever I want, and she has no option but to deal with it.

She can make it up to me, show me how appreciative she is in the new underwear sets we bought her, 'cause holy hell, are they hot. I can just imagine them propping up her tits, covering her tatted skin.

Fuck, what an inappropriate time to be hard. Shifting, I rearrange myself and slide my card to the man to pay for it all. "Car out front," I answer, when he asks where to take it.

Slipping my shades from my coat and sliding them onto my face, I follow Tony and Sam outside, watching as they quickly load up the car. "We should get her a car, a fast one, she would love it."

Ryder snorts. "What part of 'she's our prisoner' don't you get?"

I look over at him then, grinning. "We both know that's a lie. From the very first moment we laid eyes on her, she was more than a prisoner."

"She doesn't need a car. We'll drive her anywhere she wants," he snaps.

I nod. "Just a thought, brother, might make her feel more free. Don't get her one yet, though, let her realise she's beyond lost in love with us first, and she'll never leave."

"Now you're acting crazy, she will never love us. We are too twisted for that, she wants us, sure, but she'd never love us," he scoffs.

"That's where you're wrong, big brother. You might be the brains of the operation, but you are wrong this time." I wink before climbing into the car.

He grumbles and follows after me. We drive uptown, taking the long routes to see if anyone tries anything. "Still nothing, we can't keep driving around, it looks suspicious," Ryder snaps, banging on the wheel. "I really thought he would take the shot with both of us here."

I tap my chin as I think, my eyes locked out the window. "Pull up here and pretend you're on a call. It's an empty area and the buildings block him from getting a shot. He would have to get close, providing a good opportunity to grab him."

"How do you even know he's waiting?" he snaps.

"Think, Ry. I know you got laid, but stop letting your dick run the show. He's here, he disappointed them once, and now he's desperate to make it up to them. That makes him sloppy, and it works for us."

He nods and takes a deep breath. "I don't like that he was gunning for you guys. It's making me angry, which is never good."

I nod. "I know, brother. You don't care when they come for you, but us? It hits your buttons. We have your back. We've got this."

He pulls into the alley like I suggested, and we wave Tony off a bit so he thinks he stands a chance, and then we wait. Ryder pretends to be on his phone, and I lean my head back, feigning being asleep, even though my eyes are cracked and my hand is on my gun, waiting.

Come on, you bastard.

The minutes drag on. Maybe I was wrong. Fuck, we need him, we need to hit the Triad and find out what he knows. Not to mention Diesel is itching to hunt the bastard down, and that would come with a body count spread across the city. No, we need to find him and hand him over to D to have some fun.

Then we'll take the bastards down who tried to harm our family.

We tried to play nice, we tried to be respectful, and this is how they repay us? Nah, it's their death warrants they signed. We will destroy them, brick by brick. It's Ryder's specialty. I already know he's working on how to crumble every one of their businesses and bank accounts to take their money. Then, he will start on their families. Only after that, when they are terrified and alone, will he turn his eyes to them.

He's a brutal bastard, the best at what he does.

Protecting those he loves.

Even when we were kids, he was the same, always the most serious. Fuck, he even used to wear suits even then. He never got a real childhood. No, he became what my dad wanted him to, to ensure I was never in the man's path. He did everything our father asked, even dirtying his hands.

I remember the night he first killed someone, he was thirteen, I was eleven. He came home, and there was something different about him. He was scared, not of Dad like usual, but of himself. He had blood on his hands and sat scrubbing at it, tears rolling down his cheeks. He told me what happened, not the full truth of course. I learned later he did it to protect me, that Dad had played on his love for me like the bastard he was. He had threatened Ryder, told him if he didn't kill the man then he would make me do it.

He didn't want me to stain my soul, so he did it. Even though it broke something in him, he did it. I held him as he cried. That was the last night I ever saw him cry or show weakness to this date. He told me he was scared that he wasn't horrified, that it felt right...that he was a monster like my father.

I promised I would never let him be. I will keep that promise. He gave up his childhood, his soul, for me. I would do anything for him. He doesn't even realise that Roxxane, as he calls her, is a part of that. He needs a weakness, someone he can share the world with, who can help him with his burden, or he's going to burn out.

And I can't lose him.

I'll protect the crying boy with the blood on his hands and she will be the key.

It started in my head the very first day after the way he looked at her like she was a challenge, a puzzle he couldn't figure out, and she wasn't scared of him like everyone else. She met him head-on, just as stubborn, just as angry at the world. Roxy will save him.

She will save us all.

And we will damn her.

I should care, but I can't seem to. Not when I get to keep her and my brother.

My eyes catch on something farther down the alley, a movement so slight, I wouldn't have seen it if I wasn't looking. "Twelve o'clock," I murmur, hardly moving my lips.

"Yes," Ryder snaps, still pretending to be on the phone.

The shadow moves along the wall and takes up residence behind a crate. I thumb out a quick text to Tony without looking, eyes on the silhouette. He fires, and we lurch forward as the car starts. Idiot, the fucking glass is bulletproof.

He tries to run, knowing we spotted him, but Tony blocks the alley at the other end, and then we're on him. Rushing from the car and leaping across the hood, I tap his shoulder, and when he turns, I punch him in the face. He doesn't go down though, he tries to hit me with his gun, but Ryder grabs him from behind and starts to choke him out, so I pluck his firearm from his hand and pistol-whip him across his temple.

He slumps in Ryder's arms, who lets him drop to the ground. "See, brother? Easy." I laugh.

Tony and Sam grab the man and drag him back to their car as we head to ours. "Diesel will be happy." Ryder grins. "And we'll get the information we need. They fucked with the wrong people."

"Vipers, brother. Even snakes fear other snakes," I agree.

CHAPTER
TWENTY-SEVEN

ROXY

I'm going to kill him.

Seriously. I'm going to kill Garrett. Garrett and I haven't spoken all morning after what happened last night. This morning, Diesel dragged me from my room, and Garrett cooked me breakfast without saying a word to me. After, they tugged me into the living room where I fell asleep on the sofa. He won't speak to me or even look in my direction.

It's driving me nuts.

So what? He hates women. And yeah, he used me, but I enjoyed it. I would have told him no or kicked his ass otherwise. I don't give a fuck, and for some reason, I want him. I need to peel away all that anger to reach that fear I saw underneath. To the man I know he is.

It seems so important, but he won't let me, instead giving me the cold shoulder. Fuck that. I've never been the type to sit idly by. I survived this long by being a fighter and never giving up, no matter how scared I was. This is no different.

Whatever is between us has morphed over the time I've been

here, and sleeping with Kenzo and Ryder has only cemented that. I want them, and I care for them—not that I'll ever tell them. The bastards would use it against me.

I can keep fighting myself all I want, or I can revel in it. Bathe in the pleasure and power they offer. I'm tired of running, tired of living day to day, and Garrett doesn't get to push me away because he's scared.

I'm terrified.

Of him, of them, and what they mean to my body and heart. But I'm still here. Still fighting. So he has to as well.

I annoy him at first, poking him, kicking him, and when he snarls at me, I smirk in triumph. He goes back to ignoring me and watching TV, so I change the channel. He grunts and yells at me, but his phone rings.

I hear him talking to someone who sounds like Kenzo, so I keep changing the channel. He gets irritated and shouts and ends the call, glaring at me. "Behave."

"Or what?" I grin. "Going to put me on my knees again?"

His eyes darken hungrily, his gaze dropping to my smirking lips in memory as he shifts on the sofa, no doubt remembering his cock there—I know I am. "That was a mistake."

"Sure, whatever you say, big guy. Hey, I was supposed to have a tattoo finished soon, can I still go?" I question.

"By who?" he counters, narrowing his eyes. At least it's a step in the right direction.

"Zeke, from Alluring Art." I shrug.

"A guy?" he snaps, his body vibrating with anger. "No."

"What? Why?" I ask, pissed now.

"No one other than us touches you," he growls, and I laugh.

"Jealous?" I smirk.

He grins again. "No, the others would kill him. Is your tattoo really worth his death?"

Diesel laughs too, as he slouches on the sofa next to me. "He's right, I would kill him, but Garrett tattoos, he can finish it for you. He did all of ours."

Garrett freezes as I perk up. "Shit, really? They're good! Will you?"

"No," he snaps, grinding his teeth as he throws a glare at a smirking Diesel.

"What? Why? I can't go to Zeke, but you won't finish it?" I yell.

His head turns slowly, eyes dark. "I'm not inking you, forget it."

"Why? 'Cause I'm a woman and you would hate to lower yourself to touching me?" I poke.

"Oh, this is going to be good, I need popcorn," Diesel mutters, but I ignore him as I stare at Garrett, not backing down now.

"Leave it," Garrett warns.

Yeah, fuck that. I'm done with his tantrums. "What's your issue? Scared of pussy, or are you just really so self-destructive and filled with hate that you can only get it up by hurting someone?"

The room is silent apart from the popping of Diesel's popcorn in the kitchen.

"Walk away, right now," he snarls, his voice low and deadly. His eyes are alight with that same wrath I saw in the ring—he's beyond angry. He's going into his fighting territory, and I'm the opponent.

The smart thing to do would be to walk away and let him calm down. Do I? No, of course not. I never said I was smart, but I do have some big ass balls. "No. So is that it, little Garrett? Was it your mummy? No, a girlfriend I bet. What did she do, cheat? Oh no, poor little Garrett, but that doesn't mean you get to treat me like shit, you big asshole. You can glare and threaten me all you want, but everyone knows the truth. You want me, and you hate yourself for it."

Life is never promised, tomorrow is never guaranteed, and I don't believe in wasting any time on what you wish you had said or done. So even though I know it's dumb, I let it all out. We can never move forward until we get over the past.

He moves quickly, probably from his boxing, grabs my throat, and drags me into the air. My feet barely touch the floor, but I don't fight his hold. I relax into it with a smirk, even as he tightens his grasp, cutting off my air supply. Those lips are curled up in hate, and his face is a snarl. Nothing but anger is guiding him. He doesn't see me, no, he sees her.

The woman who hurt him so deeply he's never recovered.

"You have a death wish? Is that it? Want me to kill you? Because I will. You might have sucked my dick, I might want you, but I will still end you," he threatens.

"Then do it, let's really end this. Kill me now, or stop using your fear as an excuse to push me away," I wheeze.

He breathes heavily, his chest heaving as he glares at me. With a grunt, he throws me back to the sofa and goes to storm away. Sucking in rapid breaths, I rise to my feet, my eyes catching on Diesel, who's sitting out of the way on the table, munching on popcorn and looking way too happy to watch the drama unfold.

Stomping after Garrett, I chase him upstairs. He slams his door, but I rip it open and follow him inside. I refuse to back down now, I'm finally getting somewhere.

He paces the floor before swinging his arm out and sweeping it across his drawers, knocking everything to the floor with a crash. Glass shatters, but he doesn't care. He swings his hand and connects it with the bag so hard it snaps and tumbles to the floor. He grabs his bed and tosses it over, and even in the midst of the destruction, it's not enough.

I can feel it.

I know that feeling, when you're so filled with hurt, with pain, it warps you. I healed mine over the years with the help of Rich, but Garrett hasn't had that chance. He bottled it all up, not wanting to show his weakness, and it's rotting him from the inside out.

It will kill him.

So even though I'm facing down death, I keep pushing. "Finished?" I drawl, leaning against the wall.

He spins, his nostrils flaring, and advances on me. He slams me back to the wall. "This feels familiar," I tease.

"Stop pushing," he growls.

"Why? I'm done tiptoeing around you. The others might, but I won't. I see the pain in your eyes, I know because I used to see it in mine. Someone hurt you, someone you trusted. Someone you loved. It changes you, it breaks you down, and in its place is a broken creature. One whose whole world crumbled. I know," I yell, "because that was me." I quiet then, breathing heavily. "It still is sometimes, I'm still running from it. Still living in fear like I'm that same little girl."

He becomes motionless, his eyes flicking between mine, so I surge forward, baring my soul even though it hurts to flay myself open for him. "I trusted him, Garrett. I loved him like a child should." Tears fill my eyes, and I hate that show of weakness, knowing he still has that power. "Every fist, every kick, or spat word broke me down. I became nothing but a survivor, living from one day to the next, and even now...even now when I'm free of him, I did the same, losing myself in booze and sex so I didn't have to face myself. Want to hear the kicker? He still managed to fuck my life over by selling me. He fucking sold me." I laugh bitterly. "As if ruining my whole fucking childhood wasn't enough, he went ahead and sold me. But you know what? I'm tired of running. I hate him. I want him to pay, but more than that, I want to be free of those claws still inside me. I don't know how to do that, but I'm trying. You have to try, Garrett, because I see it in your eyes—you're in survival mode, still fighting, living day to day, but that's no way to live. I'll stop running if you stop fighting."

He drops me and turns away. "I don't know how," he admits.

I don't touch him, I know he hates that, so instead I circle around his body to face him. "First step? Admit it to yourself. You need to heal, Garrett, or your foundations will crumble. I'm not saying you have to talk to me, but I'm here if you need to. But so are your brothers. They're out there, and they love you."

"And you?" he rasps, watching me, his eyes raw.

"Me? I don't hate you...all the time." I smirk.

"Why? Why are you trying to help me?" he asks, and it seems important.

"Honestly? I don't know. Maybe because I see myself in you. Or maybe I'm bored, maybe I'm doing it for purely selfish reasons. Either way, I'm here, and I'm not going anywhere. We have to find a way to live together. If you really do hate me, we can work out a schedule so you can avoid me, if that will help," I suggest, and then hold my breath.

He swallows, his Adam's apple bobbing and fists clenching. "I don't hate you. That's the problem, baby, don't you see that?" He shakes his head bitterly. "I don't hate you, I care way too much...but the last person I did—"

"Hurt you," I finish. "Okay, so we take this one step at a time. I'm not asking for marriage." I grin, and he laughs. "Just a truce, if we can manage it. I'll stop pushing you for a reaction, and you can stop trying to choke or kill me...okay, maybe the kill me part. Feel free to choke me any time, it's pretty hot actually."

He chuckles again, but it finishes in a groan. "You can't talk to me like that." He shakes his head. "I want you, I do, but I can't...I would kill you...I don't even know if I can be with someone like that again. You should stick to the others, to someone who can give you what you need. Not a broken fuck up."

"So try." I shrug. "Find out for real. It doesn't have to be now, but think about it. I won't lie, I find you attractive and I wouldn't kick you out of bed."

"And I thought you hated us," he scoffs.

"Oh, I still do, it's annoying as hell, but I'm trying here. Orgasms tend to lessen hate, and let's face it, we both know this is my life now. I'm just done fighting against it."

He sighs before sitting on his upturned bed and hanging his head in his hands. "Yeah, it is. We're fucked up men, we shouldn't have accepted the deal."

"Maybe, maybe not. It's in the past though, no point dwelling on it. What's done is done. I'm one of you now, and it's time I learned what that means and start acting like it. It won't be easy, I'm still pissed and might take it out on you guys, but I'll try to understand...or they can just fuck it out of me."

He groans but goes quiet for a while, so I just sit here with him. Rich taught me that it's okay to just be there, to let them know you are here if they need you. He sat outside my bedroom like that every night for a year. Every time I woke up screaming or scared, he was there, and it helped.

"Your dad...one day, you will tell us?" he whispers.

"Yes, one day." I nod.

He sighs. "Then one day I'll tell you as well, baby." He looks at me, and the word 'baby' on his lips has me shifting to ignore the heat pulsing through me. This man is capable of such destruction, such evil. Yet I want him so much. I want him to destroy me in the best way.

"Good. So where do we go from here?" I laugh.

"We-we try to get along. To stop fighting each other just because we're scared of what the other represents." He nods and looks around. "I better clean this up." He sighs and heaves to his feet.

"I'll help. I caused it, after all." He turns and offers me his hand. He's done this before, but this feels more important, like a fresh start, so I let him pull me to my feet, and this time, he doesn't let go straightaway, he smiles down at me, his touch lingering.

"Thank you."

I nod and, without a word, get started. We work together in sync, aware of where the other is. I make sure not to touch him or brush by too closely as I throw wood away and sweep the floor while he straightens the bed and hangs the bag. I pile his stuff from his drawer on the side, wincing when I find the ring. I don't ask though, I put it on top. I can feel his eyes, but he's shared enough for the day, so I carry on working like nothing happened.

When we're done, we head back downstairs. Diesel grins at us and wiggles his eyebrows as he throws a knife at cans lined up on the table. "Did you two fuck and make up? I heard a lot of crashing, but thought I would leave you to it."

235

I laugh. "The phrase is kiss and make up, crazy pants."

He frowns, suddenly serious. "Well, that's a boring way to make up."

"You know what? You're right." I grin and head his way. "Can I try?"

He holds the knife above my head. "Are you going to use it on either me or Garrett?" Not that he seems put off by the idea, more curious.

"Why? We both know you would enjoy it." I wink before punching him in the gut. He bends over, wheezing, and I pluck the blade from his hand and turn to the cans as he laughs breathlessly.

"I'm gonna marry her," he tells Garrett, but I ignore that, taking it as just another one of his crazy ramblings.

"You have to ask her, genius." Garrett chuckles.

"Nah, I'll just put a ring on her finger one day and tell her it happened," he declares earnestly.

Rolling my eyes, I toss the knife like Rich once taught me. It hits the can and knocks it off. Whooping, I turn to them with a smirk. "Remember that when you piss me off next time." Stalking around the table, I grab the knife and wander back over as they watch me in shock.

Flipping it in the air, showing off, I drop it in Diesel's hand. "Thanks, crazy."

I saunter away, their eyes still locked on me. "I think I just came," I hear Diesel say.

Garrett snorts. "You're nasty."

"You telling me you didn't just get hard?" Diesel asks loudly.

"I ain't talking about my cock with you," he replies as I giggle.

WE SPEND THE NEXT HOUR IN COMFORTABLE SILENCE, BUT I soon get bored. I need to do something. I'm so used to working that I'm at a loss without it. I use it as a distraction, but it works, and I honestly miss it. I'm not the type to sleep all day or laze around. I need to be doing something. So when Ryder and Kenzo turn back up, I get to my feet in excitement.

I watch in shock as Ryder strips off his jacket and looks around at us, but then I freeze at the blood on his shirt. We haven't discussed what happened. Yeah, we fucked, but there were feelings there. I don't know where I stand, but staring at the blood, I feel worry pool in my stomach, and I'm suddenly before him, even though I don't remember moving.

He blinks down at me, seeming confused as I finger the blood. "Are you okay? What happened?"

"It's not my blood," he assures me, his voice cold, but his face softens ever so slightly. He opens his shirt to show me his untouched chest. "See?"

I nod, relaxing and looking over at Diesel who seems way too happy. "He's going to get the information you need?"

Ryder nods as his fingers circle my hands on his chest, holding them there so I feel the thrumming of his steady heart. "Yes."

"Then I want to go with him," I declare before leaning up and quickly kissing Ryder. I'm unsure why, but it feels right. "I need something to do. I can make sure he doesn't kill him too fast," I whisper to Ryder, who seems shocked at my kissing him.

Kenzo pouts. "Aww, don't I get a kiss too?" he murmurs.

Laughing, I dart out my fist to hit him. He grabs it mid-air and yanks me against him, dipping me dramatically as he kisses me hard, solidly, until I'm moaning into his mouth, and only then does he let me up. My core pulses with molten heat from that one kiss. I stumble away, and he winks.

"Better."

"Are you sure, Roxxane?" Ryder queries, bringing me back to the conversation.

I shrug. "I've seen him at work already, and he doesn't scare me. Plus, you already said I can control him. Let me help, I'm going crazy in here."

He searches my eyes before nodding. "If he gets to be too much, come back up," he warns, pretending Diesel can't hear him.

"She'll be fine, won't you, Little Bird?" He smirks, rubbing his hands together.

"He's right, I will, see you later." I nod at them, and Diesel drags me to the elevator. I won't be coming back up, even if it gets to be too much. I need to show them I can survive their lives, and this is their lives. If I fear Diesel, he'll use it against me, and eat me up with it until I die.

No, I refuse to back down.

I know they are my future now, and I need to take control. Be part of it. Prove to them I can be an asset more than a good fuck. Honestly, my old life feels like a blur, I've become so consumed by the Vipers. I don't want to leave anymore.

I realised it a while ago, but I still fight it. I'm tired of being alone, of just surviving, struggling every day. Yes, I miss the bar, and I'll need to make sure it's still running, but truthfully, if I put aside all the bad shit, my life here isn't too bad—apart from being bored shitless. I'm hoping if I can prove myself useful, they might let me do something. My future is still uncertain. They might kill me, but as the days pass, it seems less and less likely.

They need me too.

I know it, I see it. They want me here, all apart from Garrett. Yeah, they're criminals, but half the people I know are. Yes, they can be cold, evil bastards, and this...this relationship didn't start off in the best way. But what ever does in real life? They aren't knights in shining armour, no, they are the villains in the dark, with brooding eyes and beast-like tendencies.

I never needed a knight.

I needed a body to stand with me in the dark, and these snakes? They do.

The more I learn about them, the more I realise just how alike we really are. They might have money and power, but underneath, we are all the same. Maybe that's why they seem reluctant to kill me or use me like they first wanted to.

Like recognises like.

Maybe their venom is infecting me, maybe it's Stockholm syndrome. Maybe I just don't fucking care. I've never felt so alive. They care, they notice. Their words might be harsh and their touches mean, but only because I don't think they know how to love any better than I do.

I guess we're going to learn together, because now? I'm all in. I'm walking willingly back into that den of vipers and holding out my arms to be bitten. Let's just hope it doesn't kill me.

The door opens with a ding, and Diesel looks down at me, his face transforming. He looks eager and hungry, but not for me. For pain. For bloodshed. "Ready, Little Bird? You're about to see what I'm really capable of."

"Ready." I nod, faking bravery.

He smirks as he steps out. "Good, because you won't be leaving my side until you've screamed my name." He turns and heads down the corridor.

Wait...what?

CHAPTER TWENTY-EIGHT

DIESEL

I hear her behind me. She doesn't know what she's getting into, but she had a way out and didn't take it. I've held back, trying to be good, but I'm done with that. Tonight, I'll get the information we need and take the woman who's mine.

My little bird.

I can hear the man already struggling in the chains, trying to get free. He's an assassin, so he'll be harder to break and all the more sweeter for it.

When I enter the room, he freezes, his eyes scanning me for weapons. He knows why he's here, and he knows the likelihood of him surviving is low. He's smart, I can see it in his eyes. I wonder if he'll talk first or test how far I'm willing to go.

"Let's begin, shall we?" I grin, and I hear my little bird enter the room, but she won't be just watching this time, no, she'll be helping.

She wants to be one of us? Then this is how it'll happen.

"Little Bird, hand me the large knife," I instruct.

I hear her hesitate, and I look over at her. "Now, Little Bird."

She searches my blue eyes before sucking in a breath, grabbing the knife from the tray, and passing it over to me. Smirking, I lean down and kiss her hand. "Good girl." I turn back to the guy and step closer. I know all his weapons have been removed, but you can never be too careful.

I make a few quick slices and rid him of his clothes until he's hanging from my hooks naked—his shoulders have to be hurting by now. Roxy gasps, no doubt at his extensive scarring. He is an assassin, after all. "Now, is there anything you would like to tell me before I start?"

Please say no.

He purses his lips, his eyes darting to Roxy before he spits at me. Laughing, I flip the knife in the air. "Thank fuck. This is going to be fun."

I toss it again, straight at him. He braces himself as it embeds in his shoulder. The only sound he releases is a hiss between his clenched teeth. "Little Bird, Little Bird, they always break so easily... but I don't think this one will."

"Is that a good thing?" she asks, and I feel her hand on my back.

I glance over at her and grin, and she swallows at the sight. "A very good thing," I purr, and she hands over a scalpel without me even asking. Ah, now she's getting into it.

Turning back to the man, I let him see the madness that lurks deep within me, the fire they started in me as a child that not even I can control.

Stepping closer, I stare into the assassin's eyes as I drag the sharp edge of the blade across his skin, cutting through thick scar tissue until he hisses again, his eyes squinting. I do it again across his chest and arms before grabbing the knife in his shoulder and twisting. "Now, anything to say? How about we start simply—who do you work for?"

"Santa," he sneers, making me laugh, so I dig the blade in deeper, watching the blood drip from the wound.

"As an assassin, I'm betting your trigger finger is important, correct?" I muse out loud.

He swallows, his Adam's apple bobbing, and I suddenly yank the knife out, forcing a scream from his throat. The sound is sweet to my ears and makes me hard like nothing else can...other than my little bird.

Turning, I grab the saw, reach up, and start in on his finger, whistling to myself. He shouts and jerks, trying to fight. Blood squirts across the shackles and his hand until I hit the bone. Swearing, I work the blade harder. "Stupid saw, it's so hard to find a good bone cutting one that doesn't blunt too easily," I tell him conversationally. "You wouldn't believe the amount of times I've had to replace it." I sigh as I rip his finger off and toss it away. Dropping the saw to the floor, I grab my lighter and, grinning inches away from his face, press it to the wound to stop him from bleeding.

He screams again, and as the scent of burning flesh hits me, I groan. Flicking the lighter shut, I step back with a nod, looking him over. "Shall we try again?"

"Fuck you." He spits at me, snot dripping from his nose and saliva dribbling down his chin.

"Very well." Grabbing the scalpel again, I begin to stab and slice, my movements random and chaotic so he can't brace.

But his screams ring in my ears, echoing around me, drawing up other screams from the past, mixing with the scent of burnt flesh. I cut faster and faster, stabbing.

I keep slashing with screams, laughing in between. I can't stop. Fire flickers around me, my mother's shrieks ringing in my head until a hand pierces the flames. Coming straight to me.

"D, look at me," the voice demands. It's low, sultry.

Familiar.

"Little Bird?" I murmur, freezing.

She grabs my hand and the blade. Panting, I blink, and the room comes back into focus. She's standing before the bloodied, gagging man. Her hand is gripping the blade, cutting her own skin to stop me from using it again. When she sees me back, she smiles. "You left me."

"Never," I murmur, looking into those eyes.

"You can't kill him, not yet, you haven't got your information," she cautions.

"You weren't trying to save him?" I inquire with a frown, a sudden burst of jealousy pouring through me. How dare he? She's mine!

She leans into the blade to draw my gaze back to her, and only then do I realise I had started growling like an animal. She gasps in pain, her eyes dilating as her blood drips down the knife's edge and across my hand, making me groan. "No. Trying to help you," she whispers, her voice pained.

Covering her hand, I dig the blade in deeper, and she whimpers but lets me. I groan and pull her hand away, tossing the blade before pulling her into my arms. Her hands come up to my face, framing it. I can feel her blood on her hand, coating my cheeks, and my cock jerks at the sensation as she desperately reaches up, but she's small.

Grinning, I lift her from the floor until our lips meet. It's a raw, painfilled kiss, and brings me back from the brink like nothing else can. Replacing the impression of flames licking at my skin with her softness. The taste of smoke with her sweetness. The sound of my mum's screams with her moan which I swallow.

Pulling away, I place her feet back down on the floor, and she wobbles slightly, unbalanced, so I hold her up.

"I need to sit down," she murmurs, panting.

"My face is available," I retort, and a laugh tumbles from her swollen lips.

Grinning, I carry her over to the toolbox and sit her upon it. I unpeel her curled in, injured fist, and I take a look at the cut—it's not too deep. Leaning down, eyes on hers, I kiss it, her blood coating my mouth. I straighten and lick my lips, tasting the metallic tang of her, and she shifts, licking her own lips.

Oh yes, my little bird likes me feral. Mean. A beast.

Mad.

Feeling more like myself and in control, I turn back to the man and smile. "Sorry about that. Now, do you have anything to say?"

He pants heavily, his head drooping. "The Triad, they hired me." Each word is rough, his voice undoubtedly damaged from the screams.

Gripping his hair, I lift his head and turn to grin at him. "Very good, but how?"

"How the fuck do you think?" he snaps, making me frown and him swallow. "Through acquaintances."

"I thought they were struggling financially?" I ponder with a frown.

He shakes his head desperately. "No, it's all a lie. Covering their true earnings. They have been dealing in other cities to earn back some money, they knew they would need it to come after you."

"And how do you know this?" I ask casually.

"I do my research." He laughs bitterly. "Clearly not good enough, I picked the wrong side."

I grin then. "That you did."

He turns his head and spits some blood on the ground. "I guess we better continue?" he suggests, seeming tired, so I tut.

"Oh, don't give up so easily. You were so strong at the beginning," I comment, as I look over at my tools. "How about a nice bit of water-boarding to wake you back up?"

He scoffs, "What? Nothing new? I'm disappointed, I have to say. The great Diesel, using old techniques. I thought you were more creative."

I freeze. Oh, he wants to play this game? Fine. Grabbing my toy, I turn around with a smirk. "Something new? How about this? I made it myself. Took a few concepts from other devices of course." I shrug as I step closer.

His bravado drops for a moment. "Yeah? What does it do?"

"This." I smirk as I push the channel onto his cock and click the lock. He freezes, barely breathing, but when nothing happens, he relaxes. I watch his face until he realises it's slowly clamping down on his cock. His eyes bug out as the tube closes, compressing tighter and tighter, and when he starts to scream, I know it's cutting into the skin of his dick. "Hmm, how's that for new?"

I step back and lean between Roxy's legs as I watch the man scream. She drapes her arms across me, relaxing against my back as her chin props on my shoulder. "Does hurting people get you hard?" she questions randomly, making me blink before I smile.

Turning, I grab her hand and press it to my cock. "What do you think?"

She tilts her head, her lips caught between her teeth as I release her hand, but she doesn't move it away, no, she rubs me through my trousers, making me grunt. Leaning into her, fists on either side of her thighs, I lick her lips. "Do not tease, Little Bird, unless you want me to fuck you right here."

She sucks in a breath. "Would you like to hurt me?"

"Yes," I admit without shame. "I want to carve up your skin, watch the blood drip as I pound into you."

She sucks in a shaky breath, her hand pressing harder against me. "Would I survive it?"

"Would you care?"

She shakes her head. "Maybe, but I seem to want to find out."

I grin. "I knew you would, Little Bird, you are so brave. Thinking you can control me...stop me before I kill you. Tell me, can you turn that bloodlust into just lust?"

She leans into me, biting down on my lip. "I want to try."

A particularly loud scream comes from behind me. "Hold those thoughts, I don't want him dying just yet."

It's hard to pull away from her exploring hand, but I do. I spin and flick off the clamp and pull it from his cock, wincing for him when I see the bloody, cut up mess. "Dayum, hope you didn't want kids." I laugh. "I'll give you a moment to get yourself together. I just have a few more questions, and then we're done."

Tossing my contraption to the side, I turn and lock my gaze back on Roxy as he passes out behind me. I prowl towards her, and she smiles, not the least bit afraid. Maybe I was wrong, maybe she isn't a bird. Maybe she's a snake.

Like me.

She watches me with desire in her eyes. My little bird is freeing herself from her cage with every day, every action. I want it. Her freedom, her pleasure, her pain. I should be focused on the assassin, but with her here, all I can think about is bending her over that toolbox and slamming into her pussy, watching her cunt take my cock as bloodshed and torture surround us.

She licks her lips like she knows what I'm thinking. "Are you going to fuck me?" she inquires nonchalantly. I circle around her, trailing my fingers across her shoulders and hair as I take in a lungful of the sweet scent that is Roxy. It settles into my bones, making my cock jerk, and the only way it could get better would be with her blood.

"I'm thinking about it," I reply.

"In front of him, or will you kill him first?" she asks, arching to give me better access.

Stopping behind her, I push her hair to the side, and she stills as I lick and kiss along her neck, feeling her pounding pulse against my lips. She's so fragile and so strong at the same time. "I think I'll kill him first, then, with his blood still on my hands, I'll rip this dress from your body and fuck you, leaving handprints across this perfect pale skin."

She gasps and shivers, leaning against me. Little dirty bird, she loves it. Humming, I nibble on her neck before biting down. She gasps in pain but pushes into my teeth, daring me to go further. I know what she's doing, testing her control on me and challenging herself.

She thinks if she can take me, have me, she can survive this world. We'll see.

"And what if I use some of my toys on you, Little Bird? Would you still come so prettily with my knife in your skin and my cock in your pussy?" She moans, her hand reaching back and circling my head, dragging me closer as she rocks on the toolbox.

Running my hands across her shoulders and down, I cup her heaving breasts and squeeze, hard, making her whimper. "I saw you take Kenzo's cock. You liked the fight, the pain, but how much pain can you handle?" I whisper against her skin.

"All of it," she replies, as I trace down her stomach and to her pussy before cupping it, letting her rock against me as I nip and lick at her neck.

"I guess we will see. The others won't save you now. You came down here, and you won't be leaving until I'm satisfied with your cum on my dick and your blood on my hands. Brave little birdy, walking right into the Viper's den," I murmur, as the assassin starts to wake up.

Pressing my hand harder against her soaking cunt, I roll my eyes up to meet his as he blinks and lifts his head. He meets my gaze, and his eyes widen in fear as I play with my girl. Tracing back up her body, I caress her breasts before biting her neck hard, making her scream. Laughing, I pull away. "He's awake, Little Bird, so you will have to wait for me to play with you. Feel free to play with yourself while you wait, though, as long as you don't come and he doesn't see an inch of your skin."

He closes his eyes. "I didn't see anything," he rushes out, as I stalk around her.

"No, you didn't," I growl possessively. "Can you smell her arousal?" I suck in a deep breath. "I can. She likes watching me work, likes the blood. The pain. My dirty little bird."

He shakes his head, purposely trying not to breathe, but his breathing stutters, and he inhales. Darting forward, I cover his mouth and nose and get into his face. "You do not get to smell her," I snarl, and his eyes widen as he attempts not to take another breath.

We watch each other as he struggles, no doubt his lungs are closing. "D, be nice," she calls from behind me.

Laughing, I pull away, and he sucks in a deep breath and coughs. "Say thank you to my little bird for letting you live."

He coughs again, his eyes watering as he raises his gaze and looks at her. "Thank you, Little Bird."

I freeze, and she swears. "Did you just call her 'Little Bird'?"

He swings his eyes to me and realises his mistake. "No-no, I was just—"

"D," she murmurs, but I ignore her as I get into his face.

"Choose your words carefully. Is there anything else you can tell me?" I ask, holding back for now, trying to do my job, even though I want to rip him to pieces.

"They have hired others, kids, to kill you. They won't stop until you're dead, and they have someone who knows things about you," he rushes out.

"A mole?" I demand.

He shakes his head harder. "No-no, some of the intel was old, I'm guessing an ex-employee."

I slap his face lightly. "You did good."

I'm beyond pissed someone we gave a job to has betrayed us. I'll have to tell Ryder and let him search through them. We tend to monitor old employees to make sure they don't need anything, but this? This is betrayal.

Turning away, I smirk at my little bird as I palm my small knife from my waist. She gasps as I spin and slice his neck. His eyes widen in shock, and he sputters as blood squirts and pumps from the wound. He can't stop it, and I put my face directly in his as he dies, seeing the light dim from his eyes. "She is mine. Mine!" I roar.

I watch him die, and then, still feeling that need roaring through me, I turn to face my woman. She's watching me with fear and desire warring in her eyes as I step closer. Good, she should fear me. I could burn her as easily as she could consume me.

She knows I'm dangerous, knows that maybe being in my arms means her death, but she steps forward willingly. We are just two people who found each other in this dark, brutal world. She's fucked up, but I am too. Together, we could be something amazing, or we could explode.

I want to find out.

I won't be her saviour, I'll be her sinner.

But she's okay with that—more than okay as she presses herself against my chest and tilts her head back to grin up at me. I can hear the blood dripping to the floor behind me, but she ignores him as much as I do. We have been dancing around these flames since she first got here, and it's time for us to ignite.

"Diesel." The way she says my name sends a pulse of lust straight to my already hard cock. Her lips are parted in desire, the crests of her breasts almost tumbling from her top as she breathes heavily.

"Little Bird," I reply, lowering my head slowly, giving her a chance to pull back. I wouldn't let her escape, but it would set the tone for how this is going to end. Does she want a fight like with Kenzo, or does she want to surrender to me and the pain and pleasure I wield?

She meets me halfway. I tangle my fingers in her hair and drag her closer, forcing her onto her toes as I kiss her. She calls to that feral part in me, beckons it out to cover her skin in it. "Please," she begs against my lips.

It's her plea that does it, and she knows it. Her eyes are alight with mischief, my little bird knows exactly what to say to play this game. She's willing to do anything to get what she wants, and right now, that's me.

Deep inside of her.

Her cheeks are flushed with desire, and her eyes sparkling. Even down here in the basement, she shines like a jewel. Her hand trails down my chest, and I let her. She deftly unfastens my jeans and frees my cock, her eyes dropping to it.

She takes in the tattoo on my dick and the flames that lead up across my hips, and licks her lips. "Flames?"

"A reminder of how easily we can all fall," I murmur.

She nods in understanding as she circles my length before

flicking my piercing on the end. Growling, having had enough of her playing, I grab her hands and drag them over her head until she's stretched. "That's not how it's going to be, Little Bird."

"No?" she challenges with a grin flirting on her lips.

"You want soft, go to the others, you come here, and you get pain. But you already know that, Little Bird. You came here to punish yourself with me, for wanting us, for giving in. I will gladly oblige."

Her knees buckle so I hold her up—no, this won't work. I need my hands free.

Keeping her hands in mine, I trap them under my arm as I quickly undo the ties on the assassin's chains and toss his corpse into a corner. I drag her behind the pool of his spilled blood, and I chain her one hand at a time, forcing the chains down until they circle her wrists and she can barely touch the floor. I make sure to wrench her shoulders back until she gasps, the pain constant and unsparing. Keeping her on edge.

Pleasure is just another form of torture, and I am a master.

Her eyes are wide, her chest heaving as she watches me. She wants this, she entered this place willingly. Now I'm going to take her, again and again, until I'm satisfied, and if she survives it, then she is one of us.

Using the same small knife I wielded to slit the man's throat, I slice down her top, cutting it off her. It falls away to reveal her breasts, which are tumbling from a see-through, black lace bra. I make sure to carefully remove her boots, knowing she's fond of them. When her creamy skin is exposed to me, I wipe the blade and disinfect it, needing it to be clean for what I have planned.

She watches me with a gulp, eyes wild. Her blush stains her chest now as I trace my eyes down her tattoos and curves. She is delicious, all temptation. Thick thighs, tattoos, and a crazy attitude that has me rock-hard all the time.

"I'm going to run this knife across your skin, not cutting, not yet, just dragging. Leaving delicious pink marks for my mouth to follow," I tell her, letting the blade catch in the light and glisten.

Stepping closer, I brush my lips against hers. "Right to your sweet little wet pussy that I can smell." As I talk, I slice downwards, cutting off her bra. Tossing it away, I slide the knife edge between the skin of her hip and the string of her thong, making her still as I slash upwards quickly. I toss that away as well. She's fucking stunning. Her skin is marred by some scars and ink—she's mouth-watering.

Addictive.

My favourite new obsession.

"Then do it, stop talking," she snaps.

"Or maybe I'm just not done playing with you? Maybe I'm waiting to see that fire in your eyes." Grinning, I step around her, trailing my finger across her plump ass and around her hip to her stomach, stopping at her belly ring. Eyes locked on hers, I tug on it. She stays quiet at first until I pull harder, then a whimper escapes her, making me groan. And there it is, that fire. "There, that's better," I murmur.

"Asshole," she spits, trying to lean back, the chains rattling.

I lunge forward, pressing the knife to her neck where, not minutes before, I had slit a man's throat. She swallows and tilts her head back, and when her eyes meet mine, she presses into the blade, testing me. Seeing how far I'll go. When it breaks the skin and her blood touches the blade, I pull away, and she laughs.

"So not to kill me then? Then why not fuck me?" she taunts, and spreads her creamy thighs, flashing me her glistening pussy and trying to get me to rush.

Tutting, I trace the blade down the valley of her breasts before circling around her nipples. I make that loop repeatedly, pressing harder each time. "You can't rush me, Little Bird. I've been imagining all the ways I could fuck you, hurt you, and make you bleed and scream since I saw you."

Raising the blade, I smirk at the pink marks I have left behind, and like I promised, I lower my head and follow the path with my tongue. She gasps, arching forward to try and press a nipple into my mouth. Greedy little bird.

Lifting my head once again, I trace my blade from her breasts to her stomach and around her navel before dropping to my knees and following that path. Rolling my eyes up, I flick my tongue across her belly jewel, and her head falls forward, her eyes meeting mine. Her lip is trapped between her teeth as she shivers from my touch.

Rolling my tongue around her piercing, I pull on it a bit, making her moan before turning my head and biting down on her hip without warning. Her moan turns into a scream as she jerks in the chains, swinging away slightly, so I grab her hip and dig my teeth in deeper before releasing her skin and kissing it better. Licking and biting my way up her body, ignoring my aching cock, I trace the knife across her nipple. She moans at the dangerous edge of the knife across one of her most sensitive areas and tilts into it, so I do it again and again, before licking over the path. She moans my name again, my little bird trying to tempt me.

So, in punishment, I slash out quickly with the knife, drawing two thin cuts across the crests of her breasts. Leaning back, I watch the blood well in the slices as she whimpers, "D, please."

Eyes locked on hers, I lick along the cuts, prodding the edges with my tongue until she grunts in pain but shivers in pleasure. "Did you know, Little Bird, an edge of pain can enhance your pleasure? Now, normal people like just a little, while others can handle a lot...I wonder how much you can tolerate?"

Licking up her neck, I stop at her lips. "We're going to find out, keep pressing forward until your screams of agony mix with your shrieks of bliss." She nips at my lips, making me grin. "What shall we start with, Little Bird? I can carry on with the knife... I have visions of it against your pierced clit as my tongue fucks your channel... Or maybe your tight little ass filled with my cock?"

She gasps, jerking against me. "Knife," she whispers breathlessly.

"Very well." Dropping to my knees, I spread her creamy thighs to expose her pussy to the room. She's so wet, it's dripping down her thighs, and when I part her lips and lap her pierced clit, she presses closer. I would die happily with my face buried in her pussy, tasting her on my tongue.

Running the knife up both thighs, leaving a stinging trail, I circle it around her pussy before wetting the blade with her cream. I lean back and meet those eyes, letting her watch as I lick the sharp edge clean of her juices. "Mmm, delicious."

Her eyes close for a moment before blinking open. "Well, you going to fuck me or just sit and talk?"

Gripping her thigh, I dig my nails in as I press the flat of the blade against her clit, hard, holding it there as I dip my tongue inside her channel. She groans my name, jerking in the chains and pressing closer. But it's not enough for me or her. Pulling away, I lick her clit and remove the knife before flipping it until the thick black handle is pressed to her entrance. Her eyes widen, and her breath stutters before she nods, pushing against it to try and take it into her body.

"This is the knife I killed him with. Did you see how prettily he died, choking on his own blood?" I murmur, as I press it into her before pulling it out and then pressing it back in an inch further.

"The blade easily slit open his skin, all that blood, the blood you're standing in..." I trail off, licking my lips to keep the taste of her pussy in my mouth. "Next time, I'll make you watch. I'll fuck you with the blade to your throat as they die in front of us." With that, I slam the handle inside her.

She screams from both pain and pleasure, and I chuckle before twisting the handle, the ribbed grip of it making her hips jerk forward as she tries to take more.

"Yes, more," she screams, as I pull the knife free from her clinging body before slamming it back in, fucking her with it. She chants my name and words of encouragement as I watch the flush creep down her body, her thighs shaking as she reaches that peak. She's so close, her head dangling back in bliss, her eyes closed and face slack.

So close.

I yank the blade free, and her eyes snap open. "What the fuck?" she screams.

Chuckling again, I lick the handle of the blade clean as she watches, chest heaving. "You don't get to come yet. You're going to ride that edge, again and again, until it's so painful for you that you beg to come."

"You fucking prick," she snarls before she swings in the chains, kicking out at me. I grab her ankle mid-air and hold it to my lips as I scrape my teeth across the arch of her foot, making her gasp.

"That wasn't nice, Little Bird," I murmur, before dropping her leg and getting to my feet. Stepping away, I slowly pull off my trousers and she groans, her eyes dragging along my body, her thighs clenching together.

Grabbing a wooden pole I sometimes use to bind their arms, I trail it between her breasts and down to her pussy, giving it a light smack before walking around to her back. Her hair trails along her shoulders, and I push it away as I lay a kiss on her neck. "You want punishment? You got it."

I bring the stick down on her back in quick succession, repeatedly. She writhes and screams. I don't go gently, and as I pull away, I notice the welts across her skin, decorating it so prettily. "So beautiful, watching your skin mark up for me. Knowing you will have to walk around with them, the others wondering what I did to you... I wonder, Little Bird, do they know how twisted you really are?" I whisper against her skin. "Because, right now, I know if I reach between those silky thighs, you'll be gushing from the pain. Do they know you like it as much as I do?"

She shakes her head, whimpers leaving her lips.

"Didn't think so. Big, tough Roxy, putty in my hands. Surrendering everything to me." Bringing the pole down again, I watch it darken her skin. "Only to us. Everyone else gets the bitch, we get the softness..."

"Fuck you," she whispers, almost groggily.

Laughing, I slap the pole across her ass, making her swing forward with a cry. "Not yet, Little Bird. I want to see what else you can take."

"Everything. Anything. You think you can hurt me? You can't. I've had so much worse done to me. So bring it, all your twisted desires, do it. I can handle it. I can handle you," she snarls, her voice strong despite her naked, yielding body.

"I guess we'll see." I smirk, wondering if she actually can. Others have tried, thinking they could tame me. The guys have thrown women at me, and I have broken every single one. Will my bird be the same?

Not once did I want them as much as I do her. She sets me alight, while they didn't even cause a spark. It's a bad thing for her, she has to take the brunt of my obsession, but we can't move forward unless she does. Unless I know she can survive the madness that hides within, or I could accidentally kill her and the others would be pissed.

Dropping the pole, I grab her neck in a vice. I won't play nice anymore. I was trying to hold back, because I care for her, but she keeps on poking...

Now she gets the flames.

She gasps and arches back, rubbing her sore ass against my hard cock. Making sure to cut off her air supply, I grab my cock and kick open her thighs, slamming it inside her. She jolts from the force, unable to make a noise as I pull out and slam back in. The chains clang loudly. I keep her on the edge, forcing her body to its very limits of what she can take.

Her pussy clenches around me, her wetness letting me slam easily in and out of her body. She trembles again as I tighten my hands, and she starts to tug at the chain as I take the life from her before she suddenly stops and relaxes back into me. Good girl, don't fight it. I let up the pressure a bit, and she sucks in a breath, pushing herself back to meet my thrusts at the same time.

Leaning down, I grab the blade again. As I sink deep into her core, I trace my blade across the swell of her breasts. She moans loudly, unafraid as she lets me do whatever I want with her body.

She might fight Kenzo, she might talk trash and be the bravest person I've ever met, but down here, with me, she lets go of that built-up control, her walls crumbling around her as I take her like an animal.

I slice between her breasts, down the valley between, and feel the blood flowing from the cut. Rubbing my hand in it, I press into the cut and make her scream in pain. Chuckling breathlessly, I trace that blood-covered hand down her stomach to her pussy and flick her pierced clit until she's back on that precipice.

Then I stop, stilling, with my cock inside her body and my finger on her clit. She whimpers, trying to push back to get leverage to come. Bringing the knife back around, I dip the handle in her cream, coating it nice and good before slipping my cock from her clenching pussy. Grabbing her hips, I tilt her further back and part her cheeks. "Tell me, Little Bird, have you had anything back here before?"

I hear her gulp loudly. "Yes," she whispers.

"Did you enjoy it?" I ask, genuinely curious, not that it will change what I'm about to do.

She shivers in my hold, trembling. "Yes."

Chuckling, I press the handle of the knife to her hole. I manage to work it in an inch then back out again. It's slow going until the handle of the small blade sits in her ass. Stepping back, I look at the sight— the red welts on her ass, a knife sticking from it, her cream coating her thighs. Fuck. I almost come from the sight alone. Grabbing my phone, I take a quick picture and send it to the guys, letting them know what they are missing before tossing it away and taking her hips again.

"Diesel," she starts, as I line up with her pussy, the blade pressing to the fleshy skin above my hip. "You'll hurt—"

With a roar, I slam back inside her, impaling myself on the knife. It slices through my skin, and it's a good job I know where to cut so it's not fatal, but it hurts like a son of a bitch. The pain surges through me, meeting the flames in my stomach and balls. I take it out on her, fucking her harder, faster, the knife slicing in and out of my body as she screams. Blood drips down from the wound onto our joined bodies, making the passage even slicker. I can't move much, I don't want to shred my insides even though the knife is small and just going below the skin.

She whimpers, her pussy clenching and wanting more, and I do as well. So even though I love the pain and the blood now coating our bodies and hands, I grab the knife between us, moving it away to give me room.

I twist the knife, causing her to groan and me to grunt in pain before I yank myself back and pull the knife free, tossing it away as I fuck her.

Blood runs freely from my wound, and I know if I leave it too long I'll pass out. It needs to be stitched up at some point, but for now, I'll survive. "You're going to have to stitch me."

"What—" She moans, barely able to talk.

"Once we're done, stitch me or I might die," I tease, but she gasps, thinking I mean it. Laughing, I grab her hips and slam into her again and again as I rub my blood-covered finger over her clit. My balls are drawing up, pleasure and pain roaring through me.

I'm too close, I want this to last forever and would happily die here, but I need to come. To see it dripping from her bloody, wet cunt. "Come," I demand, and she screams as I yank on her clit piercing, her pussy clenching around me as she does. I grunt as I slam into her and still, filling her with my cum.

Panting, I lean against her, the chains swinging loudly before, with a groan, I slip free from her body. I reach up and wince at the pain that movement causes on my damaged skin as I free her and catch her before she falls. Even though it hurts, and I'm feeling a bit weak from the blood loss, I cradle her in my arms and head over to the crate, setting her down. Her eyes are still closed, her body shivering in aftershocks.

She survived it.

Brushing hair from her face, I kiss her gently. "Little Bird, Little Bird, I knew you would be the one. You will never escape us now, you are mine. Forever. Bound tighter than any ring or marriage ever could. You try to leave, and I will hunt you down."

She grins, and I lean next to her with a groan. "Feel like stitching me, Little Bird? I hope your fingers are steady."

She blinks open her eyes and locks onto the wound in shock, gasping. "Fuck, okay, yeah, I can stitch. I've had to do it a few times on myself. I learned quickly. You got a kit?"

Laughing, I point at the kit in the corner that I have stashed here just in case they try to bleed out. It's coming in useful now. She stumbles from the crate and, on bare feet, pads over and grabs it, her blood-covered ass shaking enticingly. Closing my eyes, I wait for her.

I feel her close and open them again to find her kneeling at my feet, the pack open as she grabs what she needs. She cleans the wound, making me hiss, even as my cock hardens at the pain. She smirks and ignores it as she starts to stitch the cut together again. "It's not too bad, just a bleeder is all. You crazy bastard."

Once she's done, she sits back, laughing at my hard cock. "Well, that was fun." She falls onto her side and rests against me. Leaning down, I stroke her hair. "Mmm," she hums, just relaxing. "I'm not helping you get rid of the body though. I think you broke me, I need sleep and food."

Grinning, I kiss her, ignoring the pull of the stitches. "Next time. I'll get you upstairs, I'm sure Kenzo will take care of you all sweetly."

She glances up and pouts at me. "Especially if I make that face, I bet I could even make Ryder run me a bath."

I laugh. "Evil little thing, you know exactly how tightly they are wrapped around your little finger."

She doesn't look the least bit ashamed. "More like my pussy."

"That too." I nod seriously, waiting for my strength to return before I move. "Next time, Little Bird, I will think of something even more daring."

She groans at that. "I can't wait, but seriously, I need to bathe, I'm hella sticky."

"In a bit." I nod and slide to the floor, pulling her into my arms, liking the thought of her covered in my blood and cum.

"Is your name really Diesel?" she inquires, curling into me, blood and sweat coating her body. It's such a beautiful sight along with my marks.

"No," I reply, and she lifts her head to peer at me. "What's it worth to you, Little Bird?"

She kisses me, hungry and hard, before pulling away as I groan. I drop my head to the floor. "Good God, you're trying to kill me. No, my real name is Kace. I took Diesel after that night. Kace died in that fire with my mum, and I was born."

She searches my eyes before laying a gentle kiss on my lips. "I don't know about anyone else, but I like Diesel. Even if he is a bit crazy and tends to watch me sleep."

I laugh and pull her closer. "You haven't seen anything yet, Little Bird, you are mine now. I can't decide if I want to go on a murder spree or fuck you."

CHAPTER TWENTY-NINE

ROXY

After a bit, Diesel gathers me to his chest and, not worrying about clothes, strides down the corridor—even with his wound, which is self-inflicted, so I don't have much sympathy—and heads to the elevator. What we just did was...fucking amazing.

I feel refreshed, which is strange, like he helped me get out all that pain inside of me. Every inch of agony he inflicted broke down the walls holding my own, until my anger and fear was nothing but feeling for him, surrendering everything to him. He's right—with others I'm different, but down here, I got to be just what I needed.

They all offer me a different escape, Diesel's just happens to be twisted and bloody and filled with pain. Other people would scream at what we did, and shrink away, but it was all consensual and ended in pleasure, so I don't give a fuck. Maybe it's the rest of the world that's crazy, not us...

Then again, maybe we're just too insane to see how not crazy everyone else is. I don't know why, in these Vipers' arms, I'm not only discovering myself, but I'm finally shaking those walls I've had in place my entire life.

A woman can be strong and weak.

Beautiful and scarred.

Scared and brave.

Smart and sexy.

They teach me that, and I find myself standing taller with their support. I am who I am, I shouldn't make excuses for it. Even at the bar, I felt the need to be 'Roxy the Hitter,' that dark, angry bartender. I was never allowed to be weak. Even when I needed to be. Here, I can be.

Fuck, it doesn't mean I'll stop giving them shit, fighting everything, punching people, or being a general bitch. But just maybe, maybe I can trust them with everything else the world doesn't see.

When the door to the elevator opens, he manages to unlock the apartment door with one hand, and when we walk in, we freeze. They are all there, sitting on the sofa waiting. Kenzo runs his eyes across me, and when he sees me in one piece, he winks. Garrett snorts, but I see respect in his eyes before he looks away. Ryder nods, but his lips twitch slightly.

"I got some information," Diesel starts, his tone serious before he grins. "Roxy is a screamer. I can inform her dad now."

Ryder laughs, the sound carefree for once. "I could have told you that."

Men.

"But I did get some from the assassin as well," Diesel offers, and Ryder sobers.

"I'll find out from Ryder, let me take care of Roxy while you share what you learned." Kenzo smirks and sweeps down, grabbing me, and I yelp as he chuckles and ambles away. Peering down at me, he grins softly. "I can't believe you survived him. You are bloody fierce, woman. You know what that means though, right?"

"What?" I ask, cuddling into his hold. I should demand to be put down so I can walk...but I seriously can't be bothered.

"You have only challenged him to find new ways to make it hurt." He laughs. "It's a good job he likes you, there is a whole lot of pain in your future."

I groan, "Fuck, he's crazy," but even as I say it, I smile.

"He's not the only one." Kenzo laughs, looking at me pointedly before kicking open his door and sweeping through the room. Holding me on his lap, he starts the bath and fills it with something to make it bubble before pulling me closer.

We sit in silence as the bath fills, and I relax into his arms. I should question why I don't care about sharing my body with him and his brother, or why he doesn't care...but honestly, I've done worse, and I refuse to be ashamed of that. For them, I think it's because they went into this knowing they had to share 'the debt.'

I'm so lost in my own thoughts, I don't even realise the bath is full until Kenzo squeezes me. "In you go."

He dunks me into the water, making me shout when I surface and glare at him.

"I love it when you scream my name."

"I didn't," I sputter.

"No? Let me rectify that." He winks, making me grin, what a cheesy bastard. He groans, his hand over his heart. "Fuck, you're way too fucking cute. If you weren't relaxing, I would give you an orgasm right now."

I splash him and float in the huge tub, my whole body aching and my pussy and ass sore, but it was worth it. He steps back and pushes his hair away from his face before shedding his shirt and trousers. Naked, he lets me drink in his body, my tender pussy fluttering at the masterpiece that is Kenzo, but neither of us act on the attraction, even though his cock is hard.

He slips into the bath and pulls me into his arms, holding me from behind as I float with his knees on either side of me. He lathers up his hands and starts to wash me carefully. "Why are you so nice to me? When I first got here, the others hated me, even though they brought me here, but you were still nice."

He hums. "I saw in your eyes, like I said, the same ghosts we carry. Honestly, we needed someone to come here and shake us up. We were just functioning, barely a family anymore. The business and money were taking its toll, and we were all becoming cold—Ryder too serious, Diesel too wild, Garrett too angry and withdrawn..."

"And you?" I prompt, as he cleans my pussy, making me gasp.

"Too wandering. I kept going further and further, but you bring me home, Roxy. You bring us all back and remind us why we started this. Love and family," he whispers before kissing my shoulder. "Never stop being you, even when you're angry. You push them to be more, you question things they had stopped questioning, yet you don't blink at death. You can play with Diesel but talk shop with Ryder. You don't understand how rare that is."

I sigh. "I'm not rare, I'm just as messed up as you guys."

"Exactly." He laughs. "You meet our messed up with your own. You are this tiny little thing, yet you can take us down and give us shit. It's fucking hot. Even when you tell us you hate us."

"I do hate you," I mutter.

"Sure." He chuckles. "Just don't make Diesel angry, okay?"

"Wait," I sputter, yelping as I try to turn and almost drown, so I give up. "This hasn't been Diesel angry?"

He laughs, pulling me closer and holding me up. "Nope. You don't want to see it—it's fucking terrifying, and I don't think even you could bring him back."

We just sit in the water, and I almost fall asleep, it's so relaxing. He kisses me and drains the tub, helping me out.

I'm so drowsy and tired from the warm water, I don't even protest when Kenzo dries me off, carries me into the other room, and sits me on the bed.

Kenzo slathers me in cream to help with the welts before kissing each one better, then he pulls me into his arms, bending his body

264

around me until his knees are bent in with mine and we're curled together. I fall asleep like that, but it must only be for a short time, because when I wake, I barely feel rested, but I can at least function now.

"I'll let you get dressed. We have a surprise for you, come out when you're ready," he murmurs, kissing my cheek before slipping from bed. Flipping onto my back, I yawn and stretch, wincing at the soreness between my legs and on my back. Even after Kenzo looked after it, they still hurt, but oh well.

Surprise? I wonder what it is. It's what gets me moving, and I pad over to my clothes, throwing on Kenzo's discarded shirt and nothing else before heading to find out. It better be good. Like food or a gun.

I PRETTY MUCH HAVE TO WADDLE TO THE LIVING ROOM, WHICH is honestly not attractive, but whatever. When I get there, Kenzo looks really excited, and even Ryder isn't on his phone. Garrett offers me a small smile, a truce, and Diesel is, well, Diesel is bouncing up and down on the sofa, waiting.

"I need coffee," I grumble, and point at Diesel. "Coffee, now."

All three jerk their heads to Diesel and jump forward like they expect him to explode or something, but he simply laughs and rolls over the back of the sofa. "Sure thing, Little Bird."

I look at the others to see Ryder smirking. "I would say we need to do what you do to get him to behave, but...well, we all saw what he did to you, and I can't say I'm too interested."

Rolling my eyes, I throw myself down in his spot. "I bet I could make you," I taunt, and he laughs.

"Probably, but still, wield your new power over him carefully," he warns, and leans closer. "Don't take advantage." He's teasing, but there is a hint of caution there.

"I'm not going to make him my own personal assassin, or you

265

guys would be fucked, I just want coffee...and food...maybe orgasms." I shrug.

Ryder grins at me, flashing white teeth. "I'm sure I can help with that," he murmurs seductively, his eyes glancing down at my lips and tits, which are pressing against Kenzo's white shirt and leaving nothing to the imagination. I gulp loudly, clenching my aching thighs together. My pussy literally took a beating, but it still throbs at his words. Hooker.

He grins, swiping his finger over my exposed collarbone, making me shiver, but all he does is push a strand of hair behind my ear before looking away.

Dear fucking God, these guys are not good for my pussy. All they have to do is look at me with those mean eyes, and I melt.

Diesel slips in behind me on the sofa, jostling me forward as his legs go to either side of me. His chest is still bare, and my sewing work is hidden behind white gauze. He wraps an arm around my waist and drags me back until I'm locked between his thighs. With his other hand, he offers me a steaming cup of coffee.

Groaning, I take it and burn my mouth as I take a sip—worth it. My stomach growls then, and he laughs as he kisses my cheek. "Presents first, food after."

"Presents?" I perk up. "Is it a new bat?"

Garrett laughs.

"Told you," Kenzo grumbles, and hands some money over to him, which he pockets before winking at me. Dayum, this truce thing is really working.

"No, no bats, I'm afraid, darling," Kenzo tells me, leaning forward to meet my gaze. "We wanted to show you that we can be more than...well, mobsters. This is all for you. Whatever you don't like, we can take back, and we can get whatever you need." He scrubs the back of his head. "I know we started off...awkwardly, but your happiness is important to us."

I look over at the bags and boxes on the table I didn't notice

before. There are so many, they spill onto the floor. What the—
"When did you even get all this?"

"Earlier, Ryder and I went shopping." Kenzo laughs.

I look at Ryder, who only sighs. "He made me."

"You don't have to buy me shit," I grumble. It chafes me, I like to buy my own way in life...this feels like I'll owe them something after.

Ryder leans over, uncaring that I'm wrapped in Diesel's embrace, and grabs my chin hard, making me look at him. "No strings, no expectations. This is just something nice, and I know that's hard to understand, I still struggle, but we did it because we care. Accept that, love."

Fuck, how did he know?

Because Ryder knows everything, and he's made it his business to learn everything about me. That fucking man. He smirks like he knows my thoughts and leans down, licking my lips before humming. "Mmm, coffee."

He pulls away, leaving me breathless and slightly wet. Asshole. *Okay, no strings. Normal people can accept gifts. You can do this.* "Seriously, I hope you didn't spend a lot," I murmur, and my eyes widen when I spot the Cartier box.

Diesel laughs when I try to run away, wrapping his legs around me until I have a psychotic human koala draped around me, keeping me still. Ryder plucks the coffee from my hand before I spill it and, with his eyes on me as I struggle, places those lips where mine were and downs it.

"Motherfucker," I hiss. "You owe me more coffee."

"I'll make it up to you." He winks and grabs a box, a small one, and thrusts it at me. He suddenly seems nervous, which isn't a word I would normally use to describe Ryder. "Here, this is one I picked."

Unable to escape, I sigh and accept the box, flipping over the lid. Inside, nestled in silk, is a necklace. It's fucking stunning. It's a thick golden coil, a choker, with a snake head at one end and the tail at the other. Scales cover the gold surface, and the eyes are bright red rubies. It's breathtaking, and no doubt expensive.

Two parts of me chafe—one that expects strings to come with this, and the other that wants to be mad. I'm not something they can buy with jewels. I don't want their fucking money.

Kenzo leans forward. "Darling, accept this. We plan to spoil you a lot."

"Why?" I demand, clutching the box, angry now.

He shrugs. "Because we can, because we all know where you came from and most of us came from there too. You should have nice things, you should be spoiled with jewels and gifts that hardly compare to your beauty. Get used to it, it's happening."

"But—" I start, but Ryder narrows his eyes.

"Just say thank you, we don't want anything in return...well, maybe don't kick Garrett in the family jewels again."

"The money—"

"We have a fucking ton, more than we could ever fucking need, so accept the damn gifts or you'll hurt their feelings. The stupid assholes never do anything for someone else, so don't turn this around now," Garrett snaps.

Well shit.

Sighing, I gather my courage, knowing this is my issue to deal with. I decided to go all in with them, to give up fighting every little thing. This is my issue with money and presents, not theirs. Garrett's right. "I'm sorry," I whisper, before looking at Ryder and Kenzo who appear deflated. Ryder is grinding his teeth. "Thank you, I've never had a present before, and I guess I didn't know how to respond."

"Never?" Garrett rumbles.

I shake my head, reaching out and stroking the snake. "Never, we didn't celebrate any holidays or my birthday as a kid, so as an adult?" I shrug. "It never happened."

"Fucking assholes," Garrett grumbles, as Diesel pulls me closer.

"When is your birthday?" Kenzo demands.

"Erm, May, I think." I sigh, and Ryder looks at me quizzically. "They never told me exactly."

His eyes narrow, his fists clenching. "I will find out."

268

Diesel kisses me again. "I never had presents before these guys either, but look at them, look how happy they are, you've given them a purpose. They have all this money and no one to spend it on, so let them spoil you, Little Bird. It's as much for them as it is for you. Their father used his money like a weapon, another thing to hoard. So this? This is good for them, showing them it can do something other than make you powerful."

He's right. Kenzo is smiling widely, and even Ryder is relaxed and seems happy. "It's beautiful. I'm seeing a pattern though." I laugh, and Kenzo reaches out and passes me another two boxes.

Carefully shutting the necklace's box, I look around for a place to put it when Ryder's hand curls over mine and extracts it, his sad, dark eyes meeting mine. "Thank you," he whispers, and I follow his gaze to Kenzo. There's a story there, that's for sure, but not one for right now.

I nod, and he passes me the next two. I open them cautiously, not even shocked at the jewels inside—just how rich are these guys? In one box is a belly charm with a dangling gold snake, which makes me laugh. In the other is a ring that has me gasping. It's black and large, set in a gold setting that has fangs gripping the jewel.

"They are—" I shake my head. "Amazing," I whisper.

"I guess this makes up for all the birthday, Christmas, and everything else you ever missed." Diesel laughs.

"Not yet, that will take at least three more hauls," Kenzo adds with a grin.

Fuck, three?

"Give her the next one," Kenzo insists excitedly, and before I get the chance to gape at the jewellery, they are taking them away and a new box is placed in my hand.

I open it carefully, almost shaking my head at the bauble inside, another ring, like the first, but red this time. There are four more pieces of jewellery, climbing snake earrings, an ankle bracelet, and a headpiece. I feel overwhelmed, and they must realise it, because

Ryder calls a break for coffee. I snuggle back into Diesel's arms, letting him hold me as I try to process all of this.

It feels like a dream.

Kenzo shifts closer while Ryder is gone and grabs my hand. "I'm sorry if this is too much, I just wanted to spoil you," he offers, and seems suddenly gloomy, so I remember Ryder's look and force a smile to my face.

"It is a lot, honestly, and it feels like it's happening to someone else, but thank you, it means so much to me," I tell him, and then, being brave, I lean forward and kiss him. He moans against my lips, and as I pull back, he seems to perk up. He glances over at Garrett before sliding to the floor and sorting through the remaining boxes and bags.

Ryder returns and passes me a mug, which I blow on this time, waiting for it to cool. He sits next to me, close enough to whisper so no one else—well, apart from my koala—can hear.

"My father never bought my mum a present, not once. If he ever got us something, it was because he expected something in return, it always came with strings. Kenzo used to love Christmas, opening the presents from our mum, but my father would tally up each one in his head. You could see it hurt our mother, she was so quiet, a frail, weak woman, even if she loved us greatly. Eventually, Christmas stopped, but Kenzo used to find a way to get her a present every year. He earned his own money and would buy her something, sneaking it to her when my dad wasn't looking. He thought it would help make her happy, it was how he showed her he loved her. Right until she died."

I look at him, searching his eyes. He said it coldly, like it didn't happen to him too. Is that ice hiding his true feelings again? I think so, so I reach out and run my finger across his jaw. "That must have been hard on both of you, how did she die?"

He sucks in a breath, that ice melting slightly. "She killed herself, we came home from school one day to find her hanging in the hall-way. I managed to stop Kenzo before he saw—"

"But you did," I whisper.

270

He nods. "Kenzo was young, I got him outside and then...then I tried to save her. I heaved and pulled, trying to get her back over the balcony, but I was so small back then. I couldn't do it, I couldn't save her."

"Ry," I whisper, "It wasn't your job to save her. You were a kid."

He shakes his head. "It was my job to protect them both, and I failed. I won't fail ever again."

I nod, now understanding why he is the way he is. "Thank you for telling me."

He shrugs, that ice coming back as he tries to move away, to distance himself, a coping mechanism, so I grab his hand and link it with mine, not letting go as Kenzo excitedly hands me a small bag. Laughing, I open it with one hand, refusing to release Ryder's. He needs to feel this, to be here, to not lock it away and sit back, protecting us, but to enjoy this like Kenzo. He went through the same upbringing, and when he told that story, I felt his pain and how much he wished he could show his mother he loved her. He doesn't get to back away now, I will melt that ice one bit at a time.

Inside the bag is a new top. The following gifts are a lot of new clothes, and when there are no more boxes or bags, I sigh in relief. As amazing as it was, I'm still struggling to accept it, but I'll deal with that.

I'm juggling the bags one-handed with Ryder's hand still in mine. Fuck this. I clasp his hand tighter and press it to my breast. "There," I mutter, as I manage to put down the bags with two hands.

When I look up, they are all staring at me. "What?" I ask, and suddenly they all roar with laughter.

"Assholes," I grumble, as Ryder squeezes my breast.

I look to him to see those cold eyes sparkling and his grin wide and unrestrained. "Never change, love."

"Shut up. Now feed me, you kidnappers, I'm hungry."

Ryder leans closer, grabs the back of my head, and kisses my fore-head, lingering there. "Of course," he murmurs, before getting up and heading to the kitchen. Kenzo sweeps down, kisses me hard, and follows after him.

I'm left with Diesel and Garrett, and suddenly, Garrett looks uncomfortable, but he throws a box at me without looking. "Here."

"What's this? Did we miss one?" I inquire, confused.

"It's from me," he mutters, rubbing at his head.

I grin. "From you?"

"It's an essential, I still hate you," he snaps, making me laugh.

"Don't worry, I hate you too." I nod, and he smirks at me for a moment.

"Open it," he demands.

I do as I'm told, and a huge grin covers my face. It's a gun, better than my old shitty one. No, this one is fancy, and carved into the slide are the words "Vipers' girl." "There is no ammo in it at the moment." He coughs.

"Didn't want me to kill you?" I grin. "Accidentally, of course!" I flutter my lashes at him, and he barks out a laugh.

"I need to make sure you know how to properly shoot it. I'll take you later." He nods, and I perk up.

"Hell yes! Will you teach me some of your fancy fighting moves too?" I grin.

"No," he snaps, frowning. "You might use them on me."

"Or I might use them on D." I grin, and Diesel shivers.

"Please do, Little Bird," he murmurs.

"You two are messed up." Garrett rolls his eyes, but there's a smile on his lips.

Vipers' girl indeed.

Ryder and Kenzo feed me enough to have me lying on the sofa, unable to move, and I end up napping there with my feet in Ryder's lap as he strokes my toes, his other hand on his phone. My head is in Kenzo's lap, and Diesel is lying on the floor next to me, his hand reaching up to grab mine. Garrett sits on the other sofa, but he doesn't leave, which is a plus. When I wake up, everyone but Garrett is gone.

Stretching, I yawn and look around. "Shit, how long was I out?"

Garrett glances up from the blade he's sharpening and puts it away, leaning back as he watches me. "A few hours, you needed it." He gets to his feet and stretches, his shirt riding up to expose his abs, and I can't help but stare.

He catches my ogling and must think I'm staring at his scars, because he shuts down, his eyes darkening. "You ready to try your new gun?" he offers, but he seems distant now.

"Sure." I get up and slip my shoes on. "Do we need to drive there?"

He grunts and heads of out the front door, so I follow after him, my new gun in tow. He heads to the elevator, not speaking to me the whole way down, and I know I need to rectify this shit before he goes back to hating me fully, but as I go to talk, the elevator door opens and he strides out.

Sighing, I follow him, but I freeze when he leads me into what looks like a fucking shooting range. What the hell? What else are they hiding in this building?

"You have your own shooting range?" I scoff.

He shrugs as he sets up. "We have everything we need in the building—a gym, a restaurant, a shop. It's a self-sufficient tank."

I move his way, and he drops earmuffs on my head. "Have you ever shot a gun before?"

I nod. "Once or twice, Rich taught me, but...well, nowhere like this. We shot in the forest."

"Rich?" he echoes, peering down at me.

"He owned Roxers," I inform him, and then look away. "He—my dad owed him some money, and I got a job there to clear his debt, but, well, I loved it, and Rich took me under his wing. When I left home, I had nowhere to go, so he gave me a home, a place to stay. He helped me. Rich was a good man."

"What happened?" he asks softly.

I gulp and stare at the gun. "He died." I suck in a breath and look at him. "So, how do I do this?"

He shows me how to stand and the proper way to hold the gun

before letting me fire off a few shots. He corrects my stance a few times before allowing me to continue firing until I'm grinning again. Stopping, I flick on the safety and take off my earmuffs, looking at him as he stands next to me. He avoids my gaze though. Apart from talking about Rich, he still seems pissed about the staring.

Alright then, guess it's up to me to fix this. No way am I letting our truce break over a misunderstanding.

"You going to glare all night or fucking talk to me?" I snap, cocking out my hip.

He grinds his teeth but ignores me. "Dude, get some balls. What's wrong?"

He snarls, "Sorry my scars disgust you, fucking princess. Time to go back upstairs."

Pressing the gun to his chin, I narrow my eyes. "I don't give a fuck what you think about your scars, Garrett, but you will listen to me. I love them, they make me feel better about mine. Each one was earned, and it shows you survived something most others wouldn't. When I see them, I'm reminded how strong you are, and honestly, they don't detract from your hotness, but add to it. I was staring earlier at your fucking abs, okay? Wondering if it would be weird if I licked them."

He freezes, his eyes wide. "What?"

"You saw what you wanted to see in my eyes—disgust, because it would make it easier to keep pushing me away." I sigh. "We have a truce, Garrett, so if you're mad at me, just talk to me, okay?"

"Did you love him?" he inquires, throwing me off. I must look as confused as I feel because he clarifies, "Rich."

"I did, not the way you're thinking, but like a father. It seems older men don't really do it for me. I prefer snarky assholes who kidnap me." I grin.

He smirks then, pressing closer to the gun, our bodies almost touching, and it sends a spike of heat through me. I want Garrett, I even told him that, and he clearly wants me, but something is stopping him, holding him back. Knowing it's a stupid move, I open my mouth. "What happened to your chest?"

He freezes, his eyes darkening and body hardening. He asked me, and I told him about myself, so why can't he trust me just a little? He pulls away and turns. "Put the gun away, we'll go back before the others get home."

"So that's it? I get some snarled words, I bare my pain to you, and all I get is locked out?" I snap. "You don't get to do that to me, I'm not asking for anything but the past."

He snarls and spins around, his body heaving. He looks massive right now. "You're asking too much!" he yells. "My pain is my own. I didn't ask for yours, nor do I want it. You might have the others, but you will never have me."

"Fuck you!" I shout. "You can't try to cut down people's walls and get into their heart without showing yours, that's not how it fucking works, you asshole!"

"Who said I wanted in your heart?" he murmurs, leaning his head down, his voice cruel. "I don't even want in your knickers. You're trying to mistake lust for love, *love*," he mocks. "As soon as they're bored of you, they will toss you aside like all the others."

I jerk back at that...is he right? "Fine, they might. I can manage on my own, but until then, I'm here. I'm one of you—"

"You will never be one of us. Just because you open your legs, it doesn't make you our equal," he roars, and I actually fall back from the venom in his tone. This ain't Garrett anymore, this is a wild animal lashing out at everyone and everything because he's scared, scared I was getting too close. Scared to get hurt. "You are nothing more than a debt."

"I hate you," I hiss.

"I hate you too," he snarls, and without another word, he storms off, leaving me there wondering if everything he said is true.

I stare after him before turning and grabbing the earmuffs, taking my anger out on the target. I fire again and again until I'm panting and filled with more questions than answers. Leaning against the wood partition, I hang my head. I shouldn't have pushed him, he wasn't ready...but the shit he said...

Is he right?

"Don't you dare let him get in your head. Garrett is many things —a fighter, a killer, and yes, an asshole—but he's not right. Not this time," Ryder murmurs, and I feel him press against my back. He heard all that? I didn't even hear him come in. "He's scared, love, scared that you are one of us, that you fit so easily...scared what that means to him, and he lashes out. He didn't mean what he said, and you know you are more than a quick lay."

"Do I?" I ask, brave since I'm not looking into those icy eyes.

"Yes," he snaps, gripping my hips and turning me. His chest presses to mine as he backs me into the wall and traps me there, lowering his head until he's in my face. "You think we let just anyone into our home? Into our lives? Trust them with our secrets? There have been women, but we have never, not ever, let them inside our circle. You? You're right in the middle of it, Roxxane. If I wanted a quick lay, I would go out and get one, but I don't."

"Then what do you want?" I query.

"You, and all the attitude that comes with you. Even when you hate us, even when you attack us." He smirks. "Even when you're a brat, I want you, princess, so don't let him make you question that. Keep pushing, you're going to have to be stronger than you have ever been to get through to him."

"Why do you want me to?" I question, searching his eyes.

"Because I'm realising it's all of us or none of us. I know Garrett wants you, wants what we're building, but he doesn't know how. His past is blinding him to what's right in front of him. Rip open that wound, drag him out kicking and screaming, and make him yours the same way you have everyone else."

"Like you?" I ask, our lips almost touching.

"Like me." He grins against my mouth. "Don't think you can start ordering me around though, love, or I'll remind you exactly what happens." His eyes heat, and I shiver. He chuckles and pulls me closer, kissing me softly. "Come on, let's head back before D gets worried and hunts you down. He's worse than a rabid dog."

Laughing, I follow after him, feeling better. He's right. I've let Garrett hide long enough. I might be a debt, but this debt? She conquered the Vipers, she survived Diesel, she won Kenzo, and she sure as fuck ordered Ryder around.

He will be mine.

CHAPTER

THIRTY

RYDER

I t's my turn to stay home with Roxxane. I don't think she will try to escape anymore, but I don't feel right leaving her alone while the Triad is clearly wanting to kill us. Plus, I have some research to do. Diesel is out hunting down paid thugs with Garrett, reminding them who we are. We might not be able to get to the Triad yet, but we can cut off their supply until they become desperate.

Kenzo is with his guards, checking in on the rest of our businesses to make sure they don't feel like they can't trust us anymore. I am, of course, responding to legitimate business emails and skype conferences. It's hard to run an empire. We still have to do actual business in the city, and for that, we're technically an investor and architecture company with many different sections that need overseeing. Not to mention the board who needs constant updating—it gets exhausting.

I keep my eyes on updates from the guys as well, so before I know it, it's almost midday and I haven't seen Roxy at all. Is she okay? I pull myself away from the screen and head out to find her.

I find her sitting outside near the pool in some lace knickers and a bra, her hair pulled back and face tipped up to the sun. Fuck, did we not buy her any swimming wear? I make a mental note, even as I run my eyes across her curvy body. Turning away and ignoring my cock, I go to the kitchen and make her a coffee and me a tea. By the time I'm done, she's heading inside in a long shirt, making me frown. I wonder if I could convince her to walk around naked.

Not that I would get any work done then. In fact, I should be preparing for another meeting, researching the new manager...fuck. She smiles at me and heads over, hopping onto a stool opposite me, the loose shirt gaping and showing me breasts glistening with pool water. I watch the droplets, pondering if I could get away with licking them clean.

She clears her throat, and my eyes run up her throat to meet her gaze, which is laughing at me. "Morning, Kenzo said you were working, so I didn't want to disturb you."

Passing her the coffee, I lean back against the counter, mentally counting to stop myself from throwing her on the counter and fucking her. *Work, Ryder. You have work to do, you have that meeting, you also need to check in on her dad, make sure Kenzo is okay and that Diesel isn't—*

"Do you ever relax?" she asks, tilting her head as she watches me. "I can see your mind working every minute of every day. Do you ever just stop?"

Arching my eyebrow, I sip my tea. "No, I don't have time."

She snorts. "Find time. If you're not careful, you will think yourself into an early grave. Life is so amazing, Ryder, look around you. Look at where you are, what you have at your feet, do you ever enjoy it or just keep on climbing higher? When will it ever be enough?" Her eyes search mine knowingly.

"It isn't about the money, it's about keeping my family safe. Giving Diesel a place where he can be himself, and providing Garrett with a home to retreat to and be protected," I murmur.

"And Kenzo?" she prompts.

"He needs a family, people to care for and love." I shrug.

"And you?" she presses with a smile.

"Me?" I repeat.

"Yes, Ry, you. What do you need?" she inquires.

I hesitate, and she smiles wider. "I don't think you have ever thought about that, have you? Too busy being the best, and giving them everything they ever wanted and needed, that you never thought about what you wanted."

"I want them, my brothers. I want their happiness and safety." I shrug.

She nods. "I know. I gotta ask, though, how did you meet them?"

"Kenzo is my brother. We met Garrett at one of his fights when he was a professional, we stayed in contact, and when he went underground to earn more money, we started working with him. We ran into Diesel one night when he was chasing someone. He was working as a hired assassin back then, the thing he was good at, but I could see how lost he was in his eyes. It brought us all together. We had the money, our father's money, and we had plans. Plans that needed more than us, and we just found them one day and became family. Been inseparable ever since," I explain.

She sips her coffee, moaning, and I shift to adjust my hard cock. "Is Viper your real last name?"

I laugh then, I can't help it. "No, we took it after my father died. We never wanted his name nor to have any of our success resting on his surname. We took Viper, because when you back a snake into a corner, they are more dangerous than anything. We had all been backed into those corners. By family. By grief. By money. We were all vipers...and now you are too."

"Me?" she scoffs, shifting, making her shirt gape further.

"You were backed into a corner and came out stronger. This might not be the life you imagined, but you're making it work, you're using what you have. You are smart and strong, you're a Viper," I insist, leaning towards her, pressing my knuckles to the counter.

She perks up then, almost laughing. "It's sure as shit better than my father's name, the rat bastard."

"Didn't you change yours to Rich's last name, the man who owned the bar?" I ask, genuinely curious, since there is only so much you can learn online and from rumours.

"Always researching, huh? Yeah, I did, I did it for his birthday, though it worked for me as well. A final cutoff from my family who did nothing but hurt me. But not him." She seems sad now, so I reach across and cover her hand. She stares down at it, probably unused to comfort, but she doesn't pull away. "I suppose you know he died?"

I nod, and she sighs.

"He was a good man, a very good man. He did some bad things in his past, but that never bothered me. My father has a clean record, always seen as charming to others, yet he was a monster. Rich was seen as a monster, but he cared for me more than anyone ever had. He helped me study and finish school, start a life, and have a job and a roof over my head where I could sleep without wondering..."

"Wondering?" I prompt.

"Wondering if I would be woken up by mean hands." She shrugs, unashamed.

"He beat you." I already knew this. "My father did too."

I don't know why I'm telling her this, other than the pain in her eyes as they level on me—the embarrassment and anger there calls to me. It makes me want to tell her, to help her understand that we aren't so different. I need something stronger for this talk, though, so I turn around and pour us both two fingers of scotch and pass it over. I toss mine back and lean against the worktop, steadying myself by gripping the counter hard. She waits patiently, rolling the glass around in her hands.

"He was a bastard, but I'm guessing you know that by now. He was rich, powerful, and charming. Everyone loved him or wanted to be him. He made his millions by tearing down weaker people and stepping on them. But at home? He was even worse, he was fucking evil. He hated us, especially Kenzo. He thought him weak because he loved, because he laughed. I had to protect my brother. I know he hit him sometimes when I couldn't save him, but for the most part, I took

282

every blow, every whip, every beating. I stepped between him and my mother, not that it made her love us more. Kenzo always hoped she would take us and leave him, but I knew better. She was weak, which is horrible to say because I did love her, but she was weak. She needed his money to survive, and she would never leave him out of fear. Not even to protect us."

"Ryder—" She shakes her head, and I smile sadly.

"It is okay, Roxxane. It's in the past. I'm telling you this because I want you to know it doesn't matter where you come from—from the dumps or skyscrapers—evil is still evil. We might have bled onto marble floors, but we still bled, and if I could go back, I would do it all again. I would take every thrashing stoically."

"Why?" she queries, frowning.

I look around. "To be here with my family. I paid a high price, but now it's all worth it. I'm surrounded by the best brothers, even when I forget sometimes, lost in the numbers and business. I have everything I always wanted."

"Always?" she mumbles, and I regard her then.

"Always," I whisper, meaning her as well. The love of a good woman, one strong enough to survive us, to survive me and the monster my father created in me. Placing the teacup aside, I feel the desire to reach for her, but I don't know how. I'm not as loving as Kenzo, I've never even had a relationship. My father ruined it for me with the way he treated my mother...I think the only reason I'm letting Roxxane so close is because I have no choice.

She started as a business deal, one I couldn't avoid, and now I can't get her out of my head or my cold heart.

But she gathers that bravery again, slips from the stool, and marches around the counter, only stopping when she's in my arms. I wrap them tightly around her, wondering how I'll get her to stay here forever. All thoughts of business fade from my mind as those grinning eyes peer up at me.

How such a small person can hold such strength astounds me. She could have let her abuse and her father break her, she could have stopped fighting. She could have stopped even when we stole her, given in and withered away. Instead, she thrives. Diesel is right—Roxxane lives for danger, for stress and dark times. It's when she is most herself. I wonder if she knows that. It's probably why she decided to run Roxers, to feel that hit every night.

The one Diesel finds in flames, Kenzo in gambling, Garrett in fighting...and me in deals, in winning and manipulating people. But I'm the one being manipulated here, and I don't think she even realises it.

Reaching up, I cup her face, searching those eyes that hold me prisoner. If only my enemies knew that to get us all, to kill us...all they would need to do was take her. Hurt her. It would destroy us.

When the Vipers do something, we do it hard, and Roxxane? She hasn't been here but a week, yet she is already intertwined with us, so essential to our lives. She has changed us, made us love, and made us angry. Yet here, with her in my arms, is where I finally take a deep breath, my hand shaking against her cheek in fear. What if I am too like my father?

What if I hurt her?

"You are the only one who ever gets to see my hands shake, love," I murmur, and she smirks.

"Good, don't let them see it." She nods, playing the game as well as we. "And no, I don't think you will hurt me."

I blink in astonishment, and she laughs. "You're not the only one who can read people, asshole."

I laugh then, and she leans into my hand. "You are not your father. I see that worry. You're so scared you will become him that you haven't noticed you aren't being yourself either. Stop fighting it, that inferno inside. Use it. The anger he made, I have the same kind. We are two different sides of a coin. You tried to bury it, I let it build me. Neither is right or wrong, but I know, Ryder, I know you will never hurt me, not physically. I know it. You might with words, you might try to push me away or pretend you don't want me for the same reason I do, but no, you will never hurt me."

"How do you know?" I question, truly wondering. I don't even know myself. Doesn't my control, my need for her utter submission, mean one day I might take it too far and hurt her?

"Because we have both seen what that does to people, and the idea of doing it to someone else would never cross our minds. Plus, I would never let you. I might not be as strong as you guys or have the money, but I'm a fighter like you said. Survived that way. You will never hurt me because I will never let you. I would kill you, kick your fucking asses if you tried. Diesel might cut my skin or fill me with pain, but it's my choice. I want that, and I refuse to be ashamed by it. But I always want Kenzo's smile and soft teasing...and your ice and fire."

"And Garrett?" I have to ask. She's right, she's too strong, not like my mother, she would never let us hurt her. She would kill us first. That thought settles me, and I actually sink into her and relax.

"I want him too," she admits. "I even told him that, but we're taking it slow. I won't ask what happened again. He'll tell me when he's ready, and I hope one day, we can work through it."

"That sounds like the words of someone who plans on staying," I tease, and she sighs.

"Do I have a choice?" She winks, but I sense real truth in those words, and it makes me harden.

Does she?

Would I—we, let her go, even if she didn't come back? What I told her was true, she started as a deal, one we planned to use and dispose of. But she's here now, in us, one of us...but how can she truly be one of us if it isn't her choice? We all chose this life...but she was forced into it.

The very same way that I was by my father.

"Ryder," she starts, and I wait, but she bites her lip, probably realising the same thing—there is nothing she can say that wouldn't be a lie. Yes, she wants us, but how much? Is it because she's making the most of a bad situation, or does she actually want us?

"I better get back to work," I murmur, before leaning down and kissing her softly, wishing I knew. I pull away and turn, feeling her staring after me, and I stop at the door. "Your birthday is May seventh, you were born at eight fifty-five am," I offer, and she sucks in a breath.

"Thank you, Ryder."

I nod and leave, unable to stay any longer, my thoughts spiralling with worry. I need to speak to my brothers. We have a choice to make. We can keep her, force her to stay, and she might not even hate us for it. But she will never love us, not like we want. How can you love someone who takes away your freedom?

I don't know, but I also don't know if we could let her walk away now. Not just because of what she saw and knows, but because the others are attached.

I'm attached.

In the afternoon, I lose myself in work, trying to avoid the questions swirling around my head, until Garrett rings me. Picking up the phone, I hit the green button and lean back in my chair.

"Speak."

"Well, we have cleared the city. The only people who will be taking the bounty are out of towners or people hired directly by the Triad," Garrett rumbles into the phone.

"Good, did we figure out anything about the leak?" I inquire, and Diesel snorts.

"He won't let me play with them," he whines, making me grin.

"We're going to head out again tomorrow and get back on it. We cleared a few names. Simply threatening their families and their lives was enough, they didn't betray us."

"But someone did," I snap, and then sigh, drumming my fingers on the table as I think. "It has to be someone who worked here, they wouldn't know anything otherwise, keep looking."

"Sure," Garrett grunts, and then it goes quiet, but he doesn't hang up. My eyebrow arches in surprise, Garrett isn't usually chatty.

"What's up?" I ask, and I hear rumbling down the phone before he sighs loudly.

"Diesel would like to know if...if Roxy is okay?" he queries, sounding pained. I smile, but manage to hold back my laugh. I'm betting it's more than just Diesel, but I'll let him use D as an excuse.

"She was fine last time I checked, though I think she's bored. You were right, we will need to give her a job at some point."

"You don't sound sure," Garrett observes.

"Tonight, when you all get back, we need to talk," is all I say before hanging up. I can't decide anything without them, that's not how it works. We all say yes, or we don't do it.

And this is about Roxy's freedom.

I'm unsure if Diesel would even let her go at this point, but I have to know. Dropping my phone onto the desk, I loosen my tie and close my eyes for a moment. There's always so much to do. Is Roxxane right? Do I not know how to relax?

I hear a creak as the door opens, but don't open my eyes. It's her. I know it. Anyone else would knock, too scared not to, only my girl would be brazen enough to stroll into my office—which she somehow found. She must have bribed one of the guards again.

"Yes?" I ask, and she laughs. When I open my eyes, she's lounging on the chair opposite my desk.

"I'm bored, can I help?" she requests, her bare feet waggling. She is in nothing but that shirt still.

"You want to help?" I question, arching a brow.

She sits up and stands, and I watch her carefully as she rounds the desk. She kicks back my chair and hops up on the desk right in front of me, kicking her legs as she grins. "Yup, so who needs killing?"

"We do more than that." I laugh. "We actually run businesses, invest in people, build buildings, and renovate struggling areas. We run homeless shelters and soup kitchens, we help with charities..."

She waves that away. "I get it, you have your fingers in everything."

"Not everything...yet," I murmur, running my eyes across her parted thighs, which allow me to see her knickers.

"Smooth," she teases.

Narrowing my eyes on her, I point at the floor. "On your knees, love."

She smirks and sinks down without question. Roxxane might like to be in control, but with me, she loves it when I control her. In fact, I'm betting if I reached into those little knickers, she would be soaked. "Shirt off," I order, leaning back and watching her. My cock hardens in my trousers as she rips it off and throws it away. Her breasts are bare except for that little scrap of lace. "Off," I command.

"This?" she purrs silkily, before caressing the swells of her breasts.

"Now," I demand.

Grinning, she unclasps the bra before slowly sliding the straps down each arm, holding it against her until I clench my fists, and then, with a laugh, she pulls it free, baring her magnificent breasts to me, her nipples turning into stiff peaks as I watch.

Her hands reach my thighs and stroke upward, coming dangerously close to my cock, which is pressing tightly against my trousers. "Free me," I demand.

She teases me again, knowing she will get into trouble for it, she wants it. Her hand strokes across my cock, not doing as she was told. "Now," I snap. "Then you will suck me for not doing as you were ordered fast enough."

"Yes, sir," she murmurs, before freeing my cock and taking it into her hand.

Silver hair tumbles over her shoulder, which she tosses away expertly, as those dark eyes meet mine as she closes her mouth around the head of my cock and hums. Groaning, I watch her as she lashes her tongue over my slit, digging for my pre-cum before pulling back, her hand wrapped around my base, squeezing. She licks her lips. "Delicious."

Grabbing her hair, I tug her closer without a word, and she swallows me down, taking me nearly all the way before pulling back and then rolling her eyes to mine once again before consuming me whole.

I grunt loudly, jerking in her mouth as I reach the back of her throat. Fuck, fuck, fuck. She pulls away, dragging her teeth along the underside of my cock before slipping back down, bobbing until I'm almost spilling in her mouth.

My phone rings, making me groan, and she pulls from my cock with a smirk, licking her lips teasingly. "Answer it," she purrs, voice hoarse. "Let's see that icy control now, *love*."

She waits, and I grind my teeth but reach for my phone, not looking as I hit answer, my eyes on her. "Hell—" I cut off in a gasp as she swallows me again.

"Mr. Viper? Sorry, is this a bad time?" a scared, weaselly voice asks.

"Who is this?" I snap, thrusting up to meet her mouth, trying to contain my desire as that ice melts away. I reach for my control, counting in my head, but I don't reach four because she hums again.

Fuck.

"Mr. Viper, are you still there?"

"What the fuck do you want?" I snarl, making her giggle, so I yank harder on her hair, taking over as I slam into her mouth again and again.

"I have the numbers you were wanting from the new club, which you asked for," he rushes out in a squeak.

Club...oh, right.

"It seems like a good investment, but I would like to ensure the owner is capable of paying back the loan, so I was hoping I could look into their information," he blurts, probably not wanting to annoy me. I am known for being an asshole, and they don't call me a beast behind my back for nothing. They all fear me, I'm not known for being polite.

Biting back my groan, I try to keep my voice even. "I agree, let's pursue that."

I don't hear his reply, because Roxxane does something with her tongue that has me arching into her mouth and growling loudly. "I have to go. Get me those numbers." I hang up, throwing my phone away as I glare down at her.

She pulls her mouth from my cock and wipes it with one finger, looking smug. "Problem?"

Grunting, I grab her and pull her up. Freeing my tie as she watches, I jerk her hands behind her back until her chest is arched out, and she gasps in pain. I tie them at the base of her spine, kissing her hard and tasting myself on her lips before ripping away and spinning her around. I tear away her knickers, leaving her bare, even though I'm still in my suit, minus the tie, which I will never be able to wear without getting hard again.

She laughs as I kick open her legs and force the top of her body down onto the desk. "I wonder if you could concentrate on work now," she teases breathlessly, as I palm my cock and run it down her crack to her soaking pussy. She moans loudly, pushing back to try and take me, so I reach up and wind my hand through her hair, yanking her head up painfully.

"I could fuck you, making you come again and again and still run this empire, love," I snarl, even as I press the head of my cock to her pussy. When she goes to answer me, no doubt with a teasing remark, I slam into her, making her scream.

When I still, she pants, leaning heavily on the desk. "Really? I don't think you could, poor little Ryder...his cock taking over."

"Behave," I growl, smacking her ass as she moans and clenches around my cock.

"Why would I when your punishments are so good?" she whimpers, pushing back to meet my brutal thrusts, the sound of our skin slapping together loud in this room. My control is shattered to pieces.

Slamming into her, I twist my hips as I reach between her legs and flick her slick clit, making her scream my name. "Yes, fuck," she groans, pushing back harder, taking all of me, her tight cunt so wet.

I grunt again, trying to slow down, to stop the release I can feel building. I want this to last, to see her explode around my cock only when I say so, but she doesn't let me. She pushes back desperately, making me jerk and ram into her with hard, feral thrusts.

My phone rings and it's Garrett so, grinning, I pick it up, smacking her ass. "Quiet, unless you want them to know," I mock, not telling her who it is as I continue to drive into her with one hand gripping her hip as I answer the call, and hold my phone to my ear with the other.

I'm almost panting now, but I try to concentrate on what he's saying and not the clinging pussy wrapped around my cock, the way sweat drops down her spine to her bound hands, or how fucking beautiful she looks bent over my desk, taking me like a good girl.

"Speak."

"We have covered half the list, but Diesel is threatening to burn my balls unless I bring him home to see Roxy, so we're on our way." He sighs.

Laughing, I put it on speaker and lay it on her back as I drive into her. Little breathy moans escape her lips as she tries to stay quiet. "She's here," is all I say as I reach between her legs again and rub her clit relentlessly. My own release is building, my balls drawing up, pulled from the very base of my spine as I try to hold back. My thrusts stutter, becoming jerky and desperate now.

"Roxy?" Garrett asks, and then I hear a yelp and another voice, no doubt we are on speaker now, even better.

"Little Bird, what mischief are you up to?" Diesel questions.

"Goddamn it, my nose, you asshole," Garrett snarls.

Grunting, I bite my fist to stay quiet, but I shouldn't have cared, because with one last thrust, and one flick of my finger, she comes with a scream, her body writhing beneath me, her pussy clenching so tight, I can't help but come myself. I spill into her as I still, panting and containing my own yell.

291

She drops to the desk, breathing heavily as I quietly chuckle, still locked in her tight channel. The phone is quiet for a moment until a laugh comes through. "Oh, I see what mischief! Did you come for him like a good little bird?"

Garrett groans. "Did you actually just put us on speaker so we could hear her scream?"

Laughing, I sit back on my chair, pulling her with me, keeping her impaled on my already hardening cock with the phone held in my other hand as I stroke her trembling side. "Yes, she was being punished." I shrug, making her laugh.

"Didn't seem like a punishment to me. Hey, crazy man," she greets Diesel. "Hey, angry man."

They both laugh. "We won't rush back then. We'll bring in some food, you'll need it," Diesel offers before they hang up. I toss the phone away then, her slick back pressed to my chest as she wiggles, making us both moan. Gripping her hips, I force her to still as I press my forehead to her sweaty shoulder. "Be still."

I'm hard, wanting to fuck her again. Christ, will this ever lessen? This fucking desire for her? How can one woman control my emotions so much and force me to lose control with just a smile and a few words?

"That was amazing. Ready for round two?" she asks, and lifts herself before dropping down on my cock.

Fuck.

"Always," I snap, helping her ride me, watching my cock slip in and out of her wet hole, her ass pressed to my hips. She rolls her hips enticingly, and I reach around and grab one of her breasts, tweaking her nipple and forcing a moan from her throat.

"That was just your first orgasm. Let's try for three, shall we?" I murmur, as I stroke down her belly to her clit and flick it again.

She comes three more times. Twice on my cock and once in my mouth. By the time we're done, we are both boneless and covered in a sheen of sweat. "Let's shower before they get back," I suggest, and she sighs, snuggling closer.

"I can't walk, so carry me," she demands.

"Still ordering me around, princess?" I tease.

"Still pretending it doesn't work?" she taunts, as she nuzzles into my chest.

I lift her, and she wraps her legs around my waist as I carry her from my office and to my room where we shower together. Only when I'm dressing do I realise I left my phone on the desk. I freeze. Me? Leaving my phone? Unheard of. But as I'm about to go back and get it, she grabs my hand and leads me downstairs to where the others are waiting.

I soon forget about it again. It's my first night off...ever.

I like it. Especially with her perched on my knee, sharing my food, a beer in one hand, and a smile on my face as Diesel tells his stories for the day, making her laugh along with us.

It's nice.

It's home.

CHAPTER

THIRTY-ONE

ROXY

It's early when I wake up, I don't know why. Flipping onto my back, I sigh. I'm so used to waking up in the afternoon, that even though it's only ten am, I feel like a whole new person. Getting up, I don a dress, not bothering with shoes, but I do stop as I pass the mirror before going back and adding the earrings and the rings Ryder bought me.

They look good and cause me to smile as I head outside, already hearing them arguing at the breakfast table. It's a habit now, eating with them, and it's probably why I woke up. How my life has changed. When I sit down, they all give me a smile before doing a double-take at the jewellery. Ryder looks smug, Kenzo grins at me softly, Garrett just grunts his approval, and Diesel leans forward.

"Yes, one of us, one of us!" he chants, banging his knife and fork on the table, making me laugh. "Oh, you wanna see something?" he asks me, wiggling his eyebrows.

"I don't know...do I? If it's your cock, babe, I've seen it, and as nice as it is, I would rather just eat the sausage on my plate," I quip, as

I accept the mug from Ryder with a gentle smile at him. His lips quirk up at that, bigger than normal. Maybe that ice is finally cracking.

"No...that will be later. Once you see this, you are bound to jump me." He laughs as he gets to his feet. I look over just in time to see him rip off his shirt.

"D, your abs are nice—" I start, but freeze at the new ink on his chest. I don't even get distracted by the muscular torso of the crazy man like normal. He stands there proudly, puffing up, with that insane smile on his lips, while all I can do is gawk.

There, on his chest, right over his heart, is a bird.

The bird sits on his pec, perched on a coiled viper. They both look so lifelike, I ache to touch them to see if they're real. The bird is standing there, so brave and unafraid of the snake, its beak held high, and the snake? It's wrapped around it, not restraining it...keeping it.

Me and him.

The crazy bastard got a tattoo of us over his heart.

"Like it, Little Bird?" he asks, and he suddenly seems nervous.

I glance around, and Garrett widens his eyes, jerking his head towards Diesel to prompt me. Swallowing, I look back at D and lick my lips. "I'm guessing that's me...and you?"

"Course." He grins. "My little bird, right over my heart."

"I—" I swallow again. "I love it."

And I do. It's magnificent, clearly Garrett's work again, but what does it mean? A small part of me knows, and fear and excitement fill me. Does Diesel...love me?

To be loved by him would be both dangerous and an adventure. It might kill me, it might consume me, but I would die smiling. Except he can't love me. Can he? And is that how he sees me? Standing so strong, capturing them?

"It's beautiful," I murmur, and he rounds the table, crouching before me.

"So are you, Little Bird." He winks before leaning in and kissing me hard, not seeming to realise I'm frozen. He pulls back, looking

296

way too happy. "I told you, you're ours, Little Bird, and you're never getting away from us. This is just to show people. You wear our marks, we wear yours."

My eyes widen at that. Did everyone else get this too? The thought overwhelms me. "Just D," Garrett comments, like he knows my thoughts, and I deflate. Thank fuck. D is crazy, and his emotions are different than everyone else's. He wants me, he takes me. He loves me and hurts me. It's simple for him. For the others to get it would be another reason why, and I don't know if I'm ready for that.

But Diesel?

It doesn't matter if I don't say it back or if I'm unsure how I feel, he knows. He always does. He kisses me again, and this time I return it. He laughs, happy as he returns to his seat, but I'm quiet the whole meal. I can feel Ryder's eyes on me the entire time.

Is this my life now?

Falling in love with the Vipers? Lust and accepting my new life is one thing...but can I really love them? We started out rough, and part of me still hates them.

Somewhere along the line, did the 'hate yous' really start to mean something else? I don't know, and that scares me. Ryder is terrified I'll destroy his family...what if he's right?

But what if I don't? What if I find happiness here? I suck in a breath, deciding I have to try. I might be afraid to love someone... more than some*one*, but I don't want to give this up yet, so I won't let them know just how hard it is for me to love, or how messed up I am that when people say they love me, I wait for the pain to come. Because it always does.

Those who love us have the opportunity to hurt us the worst, and in my experience, they always do.

AFTER BREAKFAST, I RUSH TO MY ROOM TO HAVE A MOMENT TO myself. I end up falling asleep, and when I wake up, I feel better. I can't let this freak me out.

I can hide away, cut this off, and let it control me...and maybe lose the guys—the best thing to ever happen to me

Or I keep living, despite the fear, and keep accepting them. I know my choice, so I put on my warpaint, feeling better, stronger with my makeup on. My eyes are lined and dark, my lips are a deep red like blood, and I add the necklace they bought me, the choker, before slipping into another dress. It's a black one with lace sleeves that gape. It's a bit dressy, clinging to my body, but it makes me feel good. Lastly, I do my hair, straightening it.

I head out, but only Kenzo is there, his hair slicked back, wearing a white shirt with the sleeves rolled back to expose his thick forearms, a grey waistcoat, and trousers. He looks amazing. When he looks up with a soft smile and sees me, his mouth falls open, making me feel sexy, so I strut over to him and, being brave, straddle his lap. His tablet falls to the side forgotten as he grips my ass and drags me closer.

"You look good enough to eat, darling," he growls.

"That a promise?" I grin down at him, slicking my hand through his hair so some of it falls to the side.

He groans. "I wish, I have to go soon."

"Where to?" I ask, feeling his hard cock pressing against me.

His eyes are dark with lust. "A game," he murmurs. "There is someone who will be playing that I need information on."

"About the hits?" I press.

He shakes his head. "About the leak. An old player of mine, someone who used to run bets for me."

I perk up. "Can I go?"

"You want to go?" he queries slowly, and I snort.

"Hell yes, I'm bored as fuck, let me help. Plus, booze, gambling, and you? Sounds like fun."

He groans, licking his lips. "That's ridiculously hot." He runs his eyes down my body, making me shiver. "You can come, but just know that your dress will be on my floor before the end of the night. You're my winnings."

Leaning down, I kiss him softly. "Promises, promises," I murmur, as I get up and saunter away, stopping at the door to glance back at him. His eyes are closed, lips pursed. "Coming?"

He scrambles to his feet, smirking at me as he straightens his waistcoat and grabs his phone before pocketing it. His hand twists his dice as he heads over, draping an arm around my shoulder. "Can't wait, darling."

We head downstairs, his hand stroking down my back to my ass in the elevator. I grin as the door opens, and he guides me out, under his arm, and over to a red Ferrari. He opens the door, and I slip in, watching as he rounds the hood and slides into the driver's seat. He winks over at me. "Hold on," he warns, and the engine revs as he peels from the spot.

I scream in ecstasy as we break free of the building and race out into the streets. It's getting dark now, the city coming to life as he weaves through traffic. We leave the city and head onto an open stretch of road. With one hand on the wheel, the other on the stick shift, he speeds up before reaching over and laying his hand on my bare thigh, squeezing it as he drives.

My hair blows back, my heart hammers from the speed, and a grin curves my lips. This is amazing. I open my legs farther for him, and his hand slips higher, stopping when his thumb brushes my pussy, just staying there as he steers. The way he handles the machine, and how fast we are going, still climbing, turns me on.

Why is that so hot?

It takes barely any time before we turn and head down a private driveway on the wealthiest side of town. "Why don't you guys have a house here?" I ask.

"We do. We hate it." He grins over at me as we pull up at a black, ornate fence with a crest on the front. "We hate rich people, stuffy bastards."

"You are a rich person." I laugh.

"True, and aren't I a stuffy bastard?"

The gate cranks open, and he speeds through it, driving down a lit cobbled lane to a circular driveway with a fountain in the middle, situated before a giant mansion. He pulls up right outside the door and throws his keys at the valet there as he gets out, rounding to open my door for me. He offers me his hand, and I accept it, then he helps me up and wraps his arm around my waist as we head up the steps to the entrance.

The door is opened for us. Music pours out, and when we step inside, my mouth almost drops. Fuck, this is a how the other half lives. Chandeliers hang everywhere, with old-style, gold framed art hanging on every wall alongside family portraits. Two curving stair-cases lead up to the first floor from the lobby we're in.

Music and laughter and the clinking of glasses reaches us. Women walk around in tight dresses and jewels, decked to the nines on the arms of men in suits. It all screams money, and I'm sure as shit out of place. But Kenzo doesn't care, he leans down to murmur, "Fake it, baby, they all are, all of them hiding their own, dark little secrets. See the one with the moustache?"

I nod as the man in question walks past. "He's sleeping with his stepdaughter, the one laughing in the giant group of rich douches. He's going broke. It's all a game, darling, a dangerous one, but a game nonetheless. Here, they use words, not fists, but it's still the same. You know how to play, so do I. They aren't better than us, no, they are nothing. Just pawns, all wanting power and money, doing anything for it." He kisses my neck and straightens as a man heads over to greet us. He doesn't even look at me as he shakes Kenzo's hand.

"Good to see you. You owe me a hand later to try and earn back my money." He feigns a laugh.

"Of course." Kenzo grins, but it's a mask, I can see it. "Please allow me to introduce my date, Roxy."

The man finally looks at me, running his eyes up and down my body, his own beady ones heating. "Nice to meet you...Roxy," he greets, taking my hand and kissing the back of it.

"I wish I could say the same, but since you didn't introduce yourself before staring at my breasts, I can't exactly meet you, can I?" I smirk.

He laughs and seems more interested now, perking up like he, himself, was playing a game. "Of course not. I apologise, I am used to the dumb arm candy who only care about the colour of your credit card. I am Stefan, it is a pleasure, Roxy." He nods, seeming respectful now.

"Sorry, but we have others to meet, money to take," Kenzo remarks, and pulls me away with Stefan watching after us. "Charming men already, darling?" he murmurs to me. "Be careful, baby, they are all snakes here."

"None as much as you," I offer, looking up at him as we stop in a doorway. "And yet, I am on your arm, asshole."

"You love it." He winks as two drinks are delivered to us. He passes me the scotch and downs the champagne before passing it back to the server. "Another scotch for me."

I almost laugh that he knew I wouldn't drink that bubbly shit as I sip the drink, letting the warmth wash through me as I survey the room. Tables are set up around the space, like a casino but in a mansion, and there is a bar and tables. It's impressive and filled with the city's rich and powerful, all gambling their money away.

The same money they steal from the poor.

"Who runs this? You?"

"No, the gentleman we are here to see. He is past city limits, which is why I don't own him, plus he's an old acquaintance," Kenzo answers quietly, smiling and nodding to people as they pass.

"Not a friend?" I inquire, scanning the crowd.

"I don't have friends, darling. I have brothers and you," he offers distractedly, before pulling me through the crowd. "There he is. Don't hold back on my account, these rich pricks could do with your attitude, baby, so shake them up and call them on their shit. Fuck knows I do."

"Yet they love you," I comment, as I see them all greeting him.

"They love my money and the power I hold. They don't know how to take you, but you're with me, so they will laugh with you and they won't fight back. Do as you wish, be as mean as you want, be you."

Well, he gave me permission. He will regret that.

We stop at a full table, and suddenly, a seat becomes available at his presence. Kenzo sits and pulls me into his lap. There are four men, the dealer a female in a short cocktail dress. "Danny." Kenzo nods at the man opposite us.

He's a ginger with a thick beard, piercing blue eyes, and pale skin in a half unbuttoned shirt. He looks menacing as he watches us. "Kenzo, don't remember inviting you."

"When does that ever stop me?" He laughs as he squeezes me tighter.

Danny's eyes go to me, taking me in and flicking away in disinterest. Fucker. "I don't know, baby, he looks like nothing to me," I remark, leaning into Kenzo who kisses my shoulder, his hand stroking my thigh under the table as he accepts his cards.

Danny looks back at me, his eyes alight with annoyance, nostrils flaring. "What did you say, girl?"

"I am a woman, not a girl," I retort, and then turn away, ignoring him. "I don't think he's the one we need."

Danny narrows his eyes on me. I can feel it as I caress Kenzo's shoulder while he plays a hand. "We can find someone else, the money is good enough."

Kenzo smirks when he wins, and a new hand is dealt. Another man at the table glares at me, and I glare back. "Problem, asshole? Need a Viagra to get it up, or just a flash of my tits?"

He recoils in shock, and I laugh. "Don't worry, your wife won't care, she'll be just as disgusted in her pearls as you are to have your boring ass vanilla sex while dust escapes your old bones."

He sputters, and Kenzo laughs, but doesn't stop me. I look around at the other man, he's middle-aged and a little chubby. "Let me guess, daddy's money? You spend it on whores, which is why you're scratching your balls. Too many STIs, am I right?"

Danny laughs loudly as the other two leave the table. It's just Kenzo and him now. "I like her, where did you find her?"

"Nowhere you would go." Kenzo smirks as he lays down his cards and takes his winnings, making Danny swear as they deal another hand. "I need information."

"Nice for you." Danny snorts.

"He's a pussy." I laugh. "Would rather play with cards than real money."

Kenzo slips his hand higher, uncaring about the others, and cups my pussy. I groan into his ear as I nip the lobe, his focus on his cards and winning, even as he caresses me, and I let him. My pussy pulses and aches, wanting him. Seeing this side of him, the control, the power...it's doing things to me.

I'm wet as hell.

He must feel it, because he groans, making me grin as I lick his ear again. "I'm imagining you fucking me in front of all these old, rich bastards, and showing them what being alive is really like," I purr into his ear.

He swears and loses the next hand, which causes Danny to laugh. "Info, you say? Fine, whatcha want?"

But Kenzo stands, pulling me with him. "Later," he barks.

He drags me up and, gripping my hand, winks at Danny, making me wonder what he's playing at, but he drags me from the room, seeming desperate. He ignores everyone who's trying to speak to him, his eyes darting around until he yanks open a door and pushes me inside. I go flying into the wall, grunting. It's a cleaning cupboard. I turn to watch him as he shuts the door and flicks the lock before he turns to me. His eyes are dark and hungry.

"I'm going to fuck you, darling. Better scream loudly so they can hear you, and you can really shock these old, rich bastards." He smirks as he steps closer. "You shouldn't tease me, darling."

"Who said I was teasing?" I grin, grabbing my dress and pulling it higher, exposing my knickers. "Well, are you going to fuck me?"

He undoes his belt and pulls down his zipper as his eyes run over me. Then, he moves fast. Too much pent-up desire, too much need. Last time, I fought him, but this time, I don't. I want this, him. I want his cock inside me, in the mansion surrounded by the rich fuckers I always hated.

I want them to hear what he does to me, to know they might own money and people, but they will never have what we do. Realness. Raw fucking desire and need. Another person.

He slams me into the wall and hoists me up. "This is going to be hard and fast, you fucking tease."

I groan, tilting my head back as he pushes my underwear aside, lines up with my wet pussy, and slams into me. I scream then, from pain but also pleasure. He doesn't stop, he pulls back and thrusts into me as I wrap my legs around his waist.

The door handle jiggles, and I laugh and he chuckles. "Busy fucking my girl, be out soon," he calls, before slamming into me again.

"They probably had a heart attack." I groan, my eyes slipping closed.

"Probably. Wouldn't that be great?" he mutters, as he licks down the valley of my breasts.

I dig my heels into his ass, urging him on. His hand presses to the wall, the other on my hip as he fucks me. He groans my name. The way he said it, the syllables rolling from his lips while his thick cock drives into me, spearing me, sends a spike of desire through me. He's panting, our hearts hammering in unison as he shoves me into the wall from the force of his thrusts.

Hands digging into his shoulder, I yank him closer, my release rushing through, drawn by his hands and cock. He bites down on my chest, and I scream my release. It rushes through me while I shake and shiver, and he grunts into my chest as I feel his release fill me.

Holy fuck.

Both of us are breathing heavily as we lean against the wall, my legs weak and still wrapped around him. He lifts his head, his eyes dark and smirking. "Wonder if they heard that, or do we need to go again?"

"I don't know," I say breathlessly. "Maybe again?"

He grins wickedly and pulls from my clinging body. My legs hit the floor, they are weak and almost buckle, but then he's there, holding me up with a hand around my waist as he kneels at my feet, his face burying in my pussy.

Moaning, I throw one leg over his shoulder, but he grabs the other and tosses it there too, lifting me effortlessly as he laps at my clit, uncaring about his release slipping from me.

He licks me from top to bottom, dipping into my pussy before focusing on my pierced clit, playing with it, tasting me. I force myself closer, almost suffocating him with my pussy as my thighs clamp around him.

He doesn't care, his hands grip me tighter, like he can't get enough of me. His tongue expertly presses and licks where I need him to. The door handle rattles again, but we both ignore it.

"Yes," I groan, my head dropping back. "Kenzo, please," I beg.

I need to come again so badly, my stomach clenches as lava flows through my veins from his talented mouth. He groans against my pussy, the sound vibrating through me as he tugs on my piercing. "God, yes," I yell, dragging him closer, reaching down to grip his hair as I roll my hips, desperately fucking his mouth.

It's building, I can feel it. I'm so close to the edge that when he yanks on my piercing again, it sends me over with a scream. He licks me through it with gentle, lapping strokes against my oversensitive clit as I pant and relax into the wall, my stomach still clenching and my thighs shaking around him.

He helps me stand, lowering my feet to the floor. He's still kneeling, his chin and mouth covered in my release as he smirks up at me.

"Open the door, ya fucking prick, I got that info for you," Danny

305

yells, as Kenzo wipes his mouth and, with a wink at me, stuffs himself back into his trousers, does himself up, and checks that I'm okay before opening the door.

"You alright, mate? Need something?" Kenzo questions, blocking Danny's view of me as I straighten myself and steady my breathing.

"You wanna know who betrayed you, right?" Danny snaps, voice low.

"Did I? I don't know..." Kenzo grins.

"Shut the fuck up, you know I couldn't talk out there. Going to let me in?" He barges past Kenzo, rolling his eyes at me. "It stinks of sex in here."

"Does it?" I grin. "Must have been the card game, really got me going." I wink.

Kenzo shuts the door, leaning against it, and grins over at me. "What can I say, I can't help myself around her."

"Yeah, yeah, I don't fucking care about you getting your dick wet. I can't be seen talking to you, they will kill me. You want the info or not?" Danny snarls, spinning away from me to stare at Kenzo's face, which has darkened and turned serious.

"What do you know?" Kenzo demands.

"Enough to know being your friend is dangerous right now, even the rich pricks here know it, but they fear you more. Someone knows everything, man, and it ain't an employee. They know details no one else does. It's outdated, but it's there," Danny grumbles. "If I were you, I would look at your past and stay low."

"Why?" Kenzo demands.

"'Cause there's a hit coming, and I don't think you will survive it. If you do, we'll play again, maybe bring your girl so I can win some more." Danny nods, and Kenzo nods back with a calm smile.

"Thanks, man."

Kenzo lets him out and shuts the door. "That's it? You are very calm."

He laughs. "Darling, we already know there's a hit, there always is, we live with that continuously. I have four guards here, blending with the crowds. Nobody is hurting you," he growls, his eyes darkening again, "but us."

"Romantic," I tease, as I straighten my dress. "So, are we leaving now?"

"The night is young, let's go win some money." Kenzo winks, grabs my hand, and twines our fingers together. When we open the door, a man is passing, and his face reddens when he sees us, no doubt having heard what we were doing as he ducks and rushes away, making us both laugh.

This should be fun, and it's been way too long since I've been out. Time to enjoy the rich life and take all their money. Did I mention I like to gamble?

Whoops, I guess I forgot to tell Kenzo.

CHAPTER

THIRTY-TWO

KENZO

My girl is a natural, she dazzles the room. Not just with her quick wit and smart mouth, but she drains the rich old pricks dry. She takes their money with a cheeky smile and a dirty word. They don't know what to make of her, she holds nothing back. She's rude, she's loud, and she's fucking perfect.

She cleans the table at poker, and sits in her chair like a fucking queen, her legs crossed and flashing long, lean limbs that were wrapped around my head not too long ago. Knowing she has no knickers on leaves me in a constant state of arousal, not to mention how fucking good she is. A girl after my own heart.

She knows when to fold and when to bluff.

It's hot as hell. Our snakes gleam in her ears and on her neck, marking her as ours. I split my attention between her and the crowd, looking for threats. Normally, I wouldn't care, I would enjoy a good fight, but with her with me, nobody is getting close enough for that.

Nobody touches her.

She wins another hand and winks over at me, sending desire right to my cock. "Looks like these rich bastards really like to part with their money. I gotta say, I expected them to be better at this shit, seeing as they wanna keep their money to stay rich." She laughs, and the other women laugh with her. "What are you laughing at, Karen? We all know you lie on your back for those jewels." She snorts at a youngish woman, who's with the old, wrinkly bastard glaring at my girl.

The woman gasps, looking shocked, her mouth opening and closing, but she's not denying it. Everyone knows she's a gold digger, though I don't actually think her name is Karen. "You play as good as you fuck," I tell my girl, and the men hear, looking uncomfortable while I smirk.

"So do you." She grins. "If they do also, I feel sorry for their wives. That's clearly not why they married them."

I laugh so hard I almost cry. God, this is amazing. Roxy was never going to blend in here. She's got a brain, she's too opinionated, and she doesn't stay quiet, but her mouth? Fuck, I love it. She doesn't give a shit that these are the most influential people in the city. She acts the same around them as she does us and the patrons in her bar.

It's refreshing and so fucking alluring.

She stands. "I'm bored, they are too easy." She looks at me. "How about one-on-one." Her eyes run down my body. "Give me a real challenge, you're a rich prick, after all. What do you have to lose?"

Laughing, I toss back my drink and stand. "You're on, darling. What's your price?"

"Everything." She grins. "I win, I get everything, I get you." It reminds me of when we first played, and that's the point. Fuck.

"And I if win?" I murmur, pressing against her, uncaring about the disgusted eyes aimed our way for breaking social protocol. Fuck their judgement.

"You get me," she murmurs seductively.

"Oh, darling, I already have you, but you're on." I lead her to a private table and get started on showing her why everyone hates betting against me.

I win.

It pisses her off, but she accepts it as we stand again and make our way around the room. I purposely steer her to people I hate and introduce them to see what she will say. It's my favourite new game, I never know what will come out her mouth. When we approach people, they actually try to back away, not out of fear like normal, but out of disgust for what my 'trash-mouthed whore' will say.

The man who said that might currently be knocked out in the toilet, my handiwork. "Darling, this is Mayor Brentworth," I inform her, introducing her to him and his wife.

"It is nice to meet you, Roxy. I hear you're making a real stir." The mayor laughs.

"Maybe, or maybe you rich people aren't used to hearing the truth. I know you ain't. When was the last time you looked past your skyscrapers to the people sleeping rough, your people? Next time you bet ten grand on a game, think of what it would do for those in need, hmmm?" she offers, angry now.

Ah, my little viper. Always trying to save people.

He whitens like a sheet, even though his wife laughs. "I like her. I've been telling him he needs to invest more money in the outskirts, and less in these rich men."

Roxy blinks as a slow grin stretches across her face. "I like you." She nods, looking back at the mayor as she adds, "She's smart, you should listen to her once in a while, Mayor, and maybe less people would hate you." She tosses back her drink and turns to me. "I'm bored, wanna leave?"

Smirking, I circle an arm around her waist. "Hell yes, let's get out of here. I can fuck you on a bed of the money you won." Her eyes light up as I hear those around us gasp, making me laugh harder as I lean into her. "Never change, baby, tonight is the most fun I've had in a long time."

"Shocking old men?" She grins.

"No, laughing while I work. This life...I sometimes hate the money side of it and the people it brings around like vultures.

Tonight...tonight I got to be me and have fun, thank you," I drawl, as I lead her from the room.

When we get outside, the valet runs to get our car, and it's just her and me. She leans into my chest. "Thank you for bringing me. I had fun, it was nice to get out, to be helpful, and it wasn't hard to insult those fuckers for you. I don't like the way they were looking down at you."

I snort. "I come from old money, darling, but they know it's blood money. They have and always will look down on us. We gave up trying to fit in years ago."

"So? They don't get to look down on you, not while I'm around." She grins as the car pulls up.

I can't speak, so I just kiss her. She was trying to protect us, to fight for us in her own way, and I can't help but love her for that. Our very own little hitter.

A Viper like us.

I get her in the car before speeding away, but at the end of the drive I stop and look at her. "Tired?"

She shakes her head, leaning back in the seat and watching me. "Not even close, why?"

"Want to see where I really go? Where I am myself?" I ask.

She nods with a confused smile, and I pull away.

SHE LIVES IN THE MOMENT. ROXY WAS NEVER MADE FOR THAT life, she was just waiting until we found her. I'm only sorry it took so long. She belongs in our world, she shook it up and made us realise we were losing ourselves.

With her, I'm myself.

With her, I'm happy.

And now I'm going to take her to the one place I never take anyone. No riches, no clubs, or games. Just a place I go to escape it all sometimes, a place I don't even tell Ryder I visit. It would make me sentimental, but it helps me too.

We drive through the city, but leave the music and lights behind. I know she's wondering where we're going, but I can't bring myself to speak, even as we pull up at the cemetery. She gets out, and I silently take her hand and unlock the gate. I can feel her staring at me, but I walk with her silently down the path, finding the grave I want near the back. It's away from others, with a huge angel reaching into the sky and a bench before it. I sit, and so does Roxy, her hand still in mine, her shoulder pressing against me as she undoubtedly reads the stone.

My mother's.

"She wasn't a bad woman, she loved us deeply. I think Ryder forgets that sometimes. He did pay for this, though, to look after her in death. I come here a lot to speak to her, to feel close to her. To never forget where we come from and the strength of love and bonds," I whisper into the dark.

"Kenzo," she whispers, pressing closer.

"She would have loved you, you know?" I grin. I used to find sadness here, but not now. I find it peaceful, my escape. I miss her, I always will, but she wasn't made for this world. Too soft, too loving, too caring. My father destroyed it all. I will never let Ryder become that. He protects us, and I keep him humble...well, I try.

"You think?" she queries, seeming surprised. "I'm not exactly...on your level, babe."

I snort. "She came from the streets. I guess I never told you that. She ran away from her father at fifteen after he raped her one too many times. She told me once when I was upset about my father, and I didn't understand why she stayed." She presses closer still, as if her presence can ward off the bad memories.

"He found her on the streets, saw her beauty. He lavished her with money and gifts at first, protecting her like no one else ever had. That's why she stayed at first, darling, to be safe. Then, she remained because of

313

us. She might have been weak, but she was also strong, so strong, because she stayed in a monster's lair to protect us, to love us, even when it led to her death," I whisper. Roxy sighs, and when I look over, there are tears in her eyes. "Roxy, she was strong, and so are you. But you're stronger, so much stronger, and you are smart, savvy, beautiful, and kind, yet you also know how to hold your own. You're mean, you're angry, and so fucking amazing. If you want, this can be your spot, too, when it all gets to be too much. When you hate them, when you're mad, you can come here. I'll always bring you, even if you don't wanna talk to me."

I look back at the grave then, but she reaches out, cups my cheek, and turns my head. I lean my forehead against hers. "Thank you, Kenzo," she whispers, before kissing me tenderly. "I can feel how much she loved you and you her. She was so lucky for that and so were you."

"I know." I grin softly.

"Tell me about her?" she requests, and kisses me again before leaning her head on my shoulder. There, under the moon, I tell her stories of my mother. Ones I have never spoken. Ryder doesn't want to hear them, they hurt him. He won't admit it, but he never forgave her for leaving him, for not saving us. I did. So it's nice to share them with someone.

With my girl who laughs with me, and when I finally cry, holds me. Wrapping me in her arms and stroking my hair, she rains kisses down on my head. "I'm falling in love with you, darling," I murmur, and she freezes.

"Don't, love has a way of changing to hate," she whispers fearfully, and I lift my head. It's my turn to hold her.

"We started with hate, baby, I don't think it's going to go the other way for us. Love can hurt, I know that." I look to the grave pointedly. "But it also gave me those stories, which I treasure to this day. Anyway, it's not something you can stop, Rox." I grin widely. "It's happening, so get on board." I wink, making her laugh.

"Idiot."

"Ahh, it's better than asshole, which is what you usually call me."

"Oh, you're still that too," she whispers, as I kiss her again. "I'm scared," she admits.

"I know, so are we. But you have never been one to let fear stop you, and neither have we."

She nods, and we go back to sitting side by side, lost in our own thoughts, our bodies tangled together under the night sky. I should return home, the others will be worried, but I want to steal one more moment with just her and me. Because tonight, I have seen more of the real Roxy, of the person she tries to hide, the one her father tried to beat out of her, than I have since she came to me.

Us.

Every time I find another piece of this woman, I fall harder. The question is, will she love me back?

CHAPTER
THIRTY-THREE

GARRETT

We all heard Kenzo and Roxy return. I peeked over the balcony to see him kiss her deeply at her door before telling her to get some sleep. He'd been grinning wide, happier than I've ever seen him. He didn't even notice me staring as he went into his room.

Lovesick fool.

Rolling my eyes, I slam my door and lie in bed, my arm tucked under my head but, like always, I'm unable to sleep. When I do, it's always to memories, *those* memories. Is it not bad enough I see the physical scars from it? I have to relive it every fucking night.

Closing my eyes, I force myself to sleep, I have no choice, but like I expected, the nightmare takes hold.

I can smell my own blood. It coats the air, as do my screams. I held strong at first, but as more and more of my skin was carved away from my body while she laughed, I couldn't stop it. They flowed from me, my screams of agony.

She grins down at me madly, those blue eyes I once loved dark

317

with greed and lust. Lust for my pain, my death. She thinks it will get her what she desires. I want to give in, to fall into that light warmth calling to me, but I fight it. I need to get free, to kill her before the others find her. They will torture her, they will make it hurt...and despite it all, part of me still loves her.

Even now, as her blade flashes in the light as it comes back down on my chest, slicing through more of my muscle, flaying it away, I care for her.

Struggling in the chains, I fight her while she giggles. "Oh, Garrett, always the fighter until the end. I love that about you, you know? Seeing the pain you caused, all that blood on your body as you fought them." She groans, grinding on me and making me gag. "But I was wrong. You're weak, fucking pathetic. Just a dumb rich guy, not like me at all." The ring on her finger I gave her a few hours ago shines in the light as she holds up the knife coated with my blood.

It was supposed to be the happiest night of my life. The others left to give us space so I could propose, and now here we are. I'm dying.

I can feel it—too much blood loss.

Is that what she wants? Fucking anger stokes within me, one I feel during fights, the one that keeps me alive. It roars through my veins as I glare at her. I clamp my lips shut and refuse to let another noise escape, but she doesn't like that. With a yell, she stabs and slashes. Pain like no other courses through my bound body...

I jolt awake with a start, something's wrong. I feel it then, a chain on my arm. With a roar, I grab it and twist, throwing the person next to me before I pin them there. Fury and fear flow through me, blinding me. I wrap my hands blindly around their throat until a small voice reaches me in my haze.

"Garrett?"

Blinking, I stare down at Roxy. "Rox?" I murmur in confusion. I swallow and notice my hand on her throat and sit back, moving away from her quickly. The dream still lingers, making me feel raw and angry.

She sits up, seeming unafraid, even though I almost just killed her again. My body is heaving, my chest hurting from the dream. She can't be here, not right now, but she doesn't seem to fucking care, as usual. "Are you okay? I heard you yelling and came to check on you..."

"I'm fine, get out," I snap, holding back the rage inside me that wants to break free and punish her, even though it's not her fault.

She frowns. "Garrett, are you—"

"Get. Out," I snarl.

She freezes, watching me. "Is this about why you hate women... the woman who did that to your chest?"

It's my turn to freeze then. "How?"

"It's not hard to figure out. I don't know who she was or what happened, but I'm guessing it was a woman who did that to you." She smiles sadly. "I'm sorry, Garrett, no wonder you hate women."

"You know nothing, get out." I look away in shame.

"Then tell me," she pleads, reaching for me, but she stops short of touching me. "I'll understand, I could help. What happened?" she implores. I grind my teeth, and she sighs, letting her hand drop to the bed between us. "I just want to help, Garrett, I swear I won't hurt you. I just want...well, you. However I can get you, even as a friend."

"Don't you see I'm ruined?" I scream. I know the others heard me, but they don't try to stop me or save her. Fools. She sighs, looking annoyed.

"Where? Where are you ruined?" she snaps, obviously sick of being kind. "Your chest? It's hot, get the fuck over it, you have a few scars." She snorts.

"A few?" I roar, and get into her face, pointing at the melted tissue across my torso. "It's a fucking horrendous mess that makes me feel sick to even look at. How could you ever expect me to think you find this attractive?"

"You don't get to tell me who I find attractive," she counters with a growl, angry herself. "I love your scars the way I love my own. They actually made me feel close to you before anyone else. Someone with those scars knows pain, like me. So yes, I like them, yes, I want you so fucking badly it's stupid, so badly I touch myself to the thought of you, even when you're mean and hateful. You don't get to tell me what I want because you're fucking scared!" she yells, and then breathes heavily as we stare at each other.

"Of course I'm scared, I'm fucking terrified," I shout, slamming my hand into my chest. "She ruined me, my body, my mind, and fuck, Rox, how can you want that? How could you want me to touch you when I'm such an asshole? When I might kill you?"

"What's a little danger?" She grins. "I've been with Diesel, dude, you aren't worse than him."

I go quiet then, unsure what to say.

"They didn't tell you what happened?" I ask lowly.

"No, it's your story to tell," she replies quietly, not angry anymore. Fuck, we're messing this truce thing up. "Are you okay?"

Scrubbing my face, I sit, pressing my back to the wall, and she sits with me. "Yes, no," I mutter, unable to look at her. "I've had night-mares ever since, but they've been worse recently."

"I'm sorry," she murmurs, and I nod. We sit in silence and she sighs. "I'll leave, I didn't mean—"

"Don't leave," I snap straightaway, and I feel her whirling around to gape at me.

But I don't know what to say or do. I'm so fucking rusty at this shit, and I don't know what will trigger me. How can I reach for her when I know I might hurt her? Isn't me wanting her selfish? But I do. I want her.

I've wanted to kiss the shit out of her every time we argue, wanted to throw her to the bed and fuck her. But I can't.

She slides closer, but I still can't bear to look at her. She laughs quietly, and then the next thing I know she throws her leg over my lap and she's before me, hovering above my hips. "This okay?" she inquires.

All I can do is nod mutely, and she smiles down at me. "Garrett, you noticed before any of them that I flinch when someone moves too fast. You know why, right? I'm betting you have worked it out or they have told you."

"Your dad." I nod, wishing I killed the bastard when I had the chance.

"My dad." She nods and smiles bitterly. "The first time I had sex after..." She swallows. "It was hard, it was my first time, it was supposed to be amazing, but we were drunk, and all I kept seeing every time he grabbed me was my dad. It was over quickly, and I cried and walked home. It got better, I learned to block it out. I got good at it, at handling my reactions. It took a lot of years, fuck, I still flinch now. I still have nightmares, it doesn't just go away—trauma sticks with you every day of your life. But we have a choice whether to let it control or destroy us. I decided neither, because that way he wins. That sounds stupid and conceited, like I just simply decided one day, but I did. I was tired of being afraid, so even now when shit terrifies me, when I get flashbacks or nightmares or react wrongly...I choose how to deal with it. Me. No one else, because they can't understand how I'm feeling in the moment. No one else can. Healing isn't easy, sweetheart. In some ways, it's worse than the actual...abuse, and you will have setbacks and get disheartened, but it's worth the try. Other-wise, you're still caught in those memories, still fighting for survival..."

"I'm tired of fighting," I admit, and she grins.

"Me too. So if I do shit wrong, if I trigger you or anything, speak. Let me know. Let us know how we can help in any way, because they want to. Your brothers, they are reaching for you, trying to under-stand how they can protect you. Help you. As am I. You have to decide whether you can let us."

"I need to do this alone," I mutter.

"I know, but we're here," she whispers, "and sometimes that's enough, or maybe I'm just half asleep and rambling."

I chuckle, and she grins.

"Want to watch a movie or something?"

"No, I really fucking don't," I snap, and her face drops. As she's about to shift away, I dart my hand out, slower than I normally would so she can see it coming, tangle it in her hair, and yank her to me. She gasps as I slam my lips to hers. I freeze at first, unused to contact, but when she starts to move against me with a moan, I can't help but grunt and kiss her.

She whimpers into my mouth as I sweep my tongue between her lips and tangle it with hers. The kiss is desperate and raw, filled with a need so strong, I can't help but imagine her lips around my cock. But then she drops onto my lap, obviously tired of holding herself up, and I freeze.

I wonder if she can taste the fear on my lips, fear that this will disappear and become just another dream, and I'll go back to wanting her from afar. Craving her with desolation running through my mind.

The pressure of her on me, above me.

Fuck.

I don't even remember moving, but when I blink, she's pinned on the bed beneath me and I'm snarling at her. Horrified at myself, I scramble away. "Fuck, sorry, fuck."

I can't bear to look at her, but her hand lands lightly on my shoulder, unafraid even after I tried to hurt her yet again. "It's okay, was it the kissing or me being on you?"

"Fuck, Rox, why does it matter?" I snap, as I scrub my face. "You being on me," I whisper sadly. "She-she was on top when she did this." I gesture at my chest. "I was tied down, unable to move or escape."

"And me being on you—" She sighs. "Fuck, I'm sorry, Garret."

"Yeah, me too, I'm fucked up," I growl.

She goes quiet then, and I turn to her, suddenly angry with myself—with my past, with women, with my own fucking need that I can't goddamn sate. "I'm fucking sick of this shit, of being fucking hard and unable to touch you. I want to fuck you so badly it hurts. I wake up coming on my own goddamn stomach imagining you beneath me, me pounding into you. Those screams you give the others in my ears." I shake my head, slamming my fist into my chest.

"I want you so fucking badly. How can you sit there so calmly?" I almost yell.

Chest heaving, I stare at her as she sits up and crosses her legs, her eyes going faraway. "In your dreams, am I below you?" she asks.

"What the fuck does that matter?" I snarl, my hand circling her throat, squeezing as I bring her closer, but she doesn't fight it.

"I'm just thinking. If you really want this, like I do, why don't we try me below you? Hell, you could even tie me down!" She shrugs.

I revolt at that, and she smiles. "Babe, I like to be tied, don't stress. If you tie my hands, I can't reach you, I can't touch you, and you might feel more in control. Like when you tied my hands when you fucked my mouth."

I growl at that, and her eyes darken, dropping to my cock with desire. "Only this time, you fuck me for real, like we both want."

"Roxy—" I start, and she grins.

"I bet Diesel has chains." She wiggles her eyebrows. "Whatcha think, big guy, wanna give it a go?"

My eyes trail down her body. "I'll try anything if I get to fuck you."

She laughs then. "That's the spirit."

She goes to get up, but I keep her there, slowly leaning in and kissing her, to prove to her and myself I can. She moans into my mouth as I squeeze her throat before letting her go. She gets up with a snigger, and I smack her ass, making her laugh harder as she slips from the room. Two minutes later, I hear a yelp and then Diesel laughing.

Eyebrow arched, I watch her come back to my room and shut the door, chains in hands and face flushed. "I thought I would try and scare him in his sleep like he does me, it didn't work."

I laugh. "What did he do?"

"Slapped me with his cock." I gawk and then burst into laughter. She grins but props her hand on her hip. "Seriously, Garrett, whose first thought is to slap an intruder with their cock?" She throws her hands in the air.

"He probably knew it was you, also, it would certainly stop me if I was trying to kill or rob him." I grin.

"Men." She shakes her head and comes closer before stopping hesitantly. "Do you need me to chain myself to the bed, or I can get Diesel so you don't have to." She looks down at the chains. I do as well, waiting for them to set me off, but they don't

"No, I think I'm okay, she-she used a rusted chain from outside, that was—"

"An actual restraint." She nods, understanding. She reaches out and drops them into my hand and waits. I do too, but when nothing happens, I narrow my eyes at her.

"On the bed, face up, now," I snarl, my desire taking hold. If this works...

Fuck. I can finally have her.

See her screaming beneath me while I fuck her tight little pussy.

Her eyes flash like she knows my thoughts. Stepping back, she sheds the tiny shorts and top she was sleeping in, leaving her naked, and all I can do is stare. She's stunning, all soft creamy skin coated in scars and tattoos, thick thighs, full breasts, and a snake gleaming in her belly button.

I almost come there and then.

"Bed. Now," I order, making her grin. She saunters closer and climbs onto the bed, swaying her ass at me as she climbs to the head-board, making me groan and reach out to run my hand across a peachy cheek. For another day, I always was an ass man.

She wiggles her ass again, so I bring the chain down across it lightly, causing her to gasp and jerk. She tumbles forward and flips, her hair spread across my pillow and her eyes blown with lust. She parts her thighs unashamedly to show me her pink, glistening pussy as she lifts her hands above her head and presses them together. Her breasts jiggle with the movement, drawing my gaze. Crawling closer, I kiss each one as I reach for her hands, locking them in place around my headboard with the chains before sucking one of her nipples into my mouth.

She moans loudly, arching into my touch as I pop it free and do the same to the other before sitting back and looking at the pink peaks. Her chest rises and falls quickly, her face flushed, the blush creeping down her throat to her chest as I just sit back and stare at her. I can't remember ever seeing anything as beautiful before.

My hands are scarred and blood-stained, her flesh too perfect to touch, but I will. I'll dirty her with them, with the very hands I kill people with, because I can't not.

Gripping her legs, I pull them farther apart so I can look at her pussy, memorising it. My lips tingle with the need to taste her, to see if she is as sweet as she looks, so opposed to her usual attitude. "Did you forget how to do it? Dick in hole," she taunts, making me growl and dig my hands in deeper.

"Watch your mouth."

"Or what? Will you fuck it again?" She grins, lifting her hips enticingly. "Is that a promise?" she whispers hoarsely.

Motherfucker.

I want to go slow, to take my time, to savour her, but I need her too much. Since the moment I met her and she kicked me in the nuts, I've wanted her. My very own little fighter.

"Ryder is right, you're a fucking brat," I snarl as I crawl above her, resting my hands on either side of her head. "A foul-mouthed, dirty little brat."

"You love it." She grins. "So does he. He made me scream even as he called me that," she teases.

Gripping her throat, I narrow my eyes on her. She doesn't struggle, just smirks at me, her legs wrapping around my waist to try and drag me closer. "You are mine."

"Possessive," she murmurs. "Put your dick where your mouth is... in fact, put your mouth there too."

"So fucking needy," I mutter, as I squeeze her throat again, making her moan.

"Enough talking, fuck me already, Viper," she growls, jerking in the chains to try and get closer.

Sitting back on my heels, I shed my boxers I was sleeping in, and her eyes run across my scarred, tattooed body. She moans wantonly, tilting her hips. She wants me. Scars and all.

It breaks that last bit of hesitation. Roxy isn't that good of an actor, she has no time for bullshit or lies. She wants me.

Ripping open her thighs, I drag her ass down, stretching her arms above her as she presses her feet on my ruined pecs, her knees bending. I grip her hips meanly with one hand and circle my cock with the other. "Hard and fast, baby, you're going to be screaming my name."

"Want to bet?" She laughs.

Narrowing my eyes, I line my cock up at her entrance. I'm big, probably bigger than the others, so despite the fact she's soaked, I go slowly, not wanting to hurt her. I slip in an inch before pulling back and working in another, but she gets sick of waiting, and with a determined grin, slams herself onto my cock.

She screams noisily, and I groan, my eyes closing.

Fuck, fuck, fuck.

She feels too good, too tight, too wet. I'm not going to last, it's been too long. Even now, my spine almost bows from the sensation. When her screams taper off into a whimper, I open my eyes and press a hand into the mattress, pulling out slowly before pushing back in.

She gasps and presses down to take more of me, and we quickly find a rhythm. It's slow at first, but becomes fast and hard. Neither of us are able to control ourselves until I'm just slamming into her, stretching her cunt around my cock. She thrashes in the chains, yanking on them so hard, the headboard creaks.

"Garrett, God, more," she demands, her legs bending wider, deepening my angle.

Gritting my teeth, I fuck her harder, losing control. It's tempting fate, I could snap and kill her, I could hurt her, but neither one of us cares. We're too lost in the need surging through us. I couldn't stop even if I tried, I'm too far gone.

Lost in her.

She screams my name when I lean down and bite her nipple

before sucking it better, her chest arching into my mouth before I straighten and, with a growl, flip her. Her hands twist in the chains, no doubt painfully as I drag her ass into the air and slam into her pussy, grabbing her hips to tug her back.

Moaning, she pushes back to meet my thrusts again and again, her pussy pulsing around me. She's close, I can feel it, but I am too. I want this to last, to be buried in her all night, but I can't fight it. My balls are drawing up, my stomach is clenching. Reaching between us, I rub her clit. "Now," I snarl.

She whimpers, shaking her head as I impale her repeatedly, and then, with a roar, I come, my hips stuttering, my back bowing from the force of it. She screams loudly, shaking beneath me as she comes, clenching around my cock, only drawing my own release out until it seems to go on forever.

Eventually, it stops, and I collapse forward, half on her and half on the bed. Holy fuck. "Round one," I mutter, making her laugh before she whimpers.

"That was one? Fuck."

"That was just to take the edge off," I mumble, before kissing her shoulder and rolling off her. She flips onto her back as we lie tangled together, relearning how to breathe.

Once my breathing has steadied, I look over at her with a huge smile. I did it, I let her touch me. "Thank you, baby," I murmur.

Swallowing, she turns and grins at me. "You can make it up to me in orgasms, please."

Laughing, I roll back onto her, and she giggles, which soon turns into a moan as I kiss her.

CHAPTER THIRTY-FOUR

ROXY

"Diesel, what the fuck, man?" I hear Garrett mutter.

""Well, someone kept us all awake all night, so I figured if I came and cock-blocked I could sleep," Diesel murmurs. Groaning, I bury my head further into the pillow.

Wait, Diesel?

My eyes flare open, and I roll onto my back to see him grinning down at me, Garrett still on my other side. "You know, you have an issue with watching me sleep. It's creepy, dude."

His grin widens. "That isn't all I do when you sleep."

I blink. "It's too fucking early for your crazy," I grumble as I stretch, and then wince when my body protests. My thighs are sore and so is my pussy, both well and truly used. Garrett doesn't exactly have a small cock, and all the sex I've been having has taken its toll.

"Diesel, my pussy hurts," I complain, and he and Garrett laugh.

"Good."

"Assholes, both of you," I snap. "Don't even care that you and your big cocks have hurt my little vaj-jay-jay."

"Uh-uh, didn't you want it each and every time and beg for it?" He smirks.

I narrow my eyes. "I don't like you anymore."

"You liked me before?" He perks up.

"Crazy bastard," I mutter. "I'm going to find Kenzo. He'll care and look after me."

They both laugh. "Probably, soppy bastard."

I go to move, but Garrett hooks an arm around my waist, drags me back to his side, and closes his eyes. Diesel snuggles closer behind me, his cock hard against my naked ass. "Don't even fucking think about it. You bring your little snake near me, and I'll cut it off," I snarl, as I close my eyes again.

He chuckles in my ear. "Little snake? Do I need to remind you how big it is?"

Garrett growls, "Shut the fuck up and sleep."

"He started it," I mutter, and wiggle closer to Garrett and away from Diesel, but two seconds later, he's plastered against my back again, like a fucking Viper sandwich.

"I hate you all," I grouse, and Diesel bites my shoulder, making me yelp.

Somehow along the way, my 'I hate yous' have started to mean something else, but I'm too tired to think on that, so I fall back asleep between my Vipers, and when I wake up, they're still there.

"Don't you have work?" I ask as I stretch again.

Garrett's eyes flicker open, watching me as I do, his gaze heating, and I glare at him. "No, bad Viper," I snap, smacking his nose. Diesel laughs while Garrett snorts and flips onto his back, stretching himself.

"Not today, it's Kenzo's and Ryder's turn," Diesel answers, as he pulls me back until I end up lying across his chest, my back to his front. Weirdo.

He hugs me like a teddy, and I try to wiggle free, but I stop when he groans. Dirty bastard. "So what are we doing today?" I inquire, hopeful it's something fun.

"We can't leave here, they took most of the guards. Sorry, Little Bird. We can find something to do though," he offers, so I roll from him and the bed, landing on my knees and getting to my feet.

"Nope, I'm going to shower." I turn and glare at them. "Alone, no dick time, go make me food and coffee."

As I turn and strut away, I hear Garrett laugh. "She was a lot less demanding when she hated us."

"I still hate you," I call, as I flip him off over my shoulder. "I just like your dicks!"

After I've showered and feel more human, still on a self-imposed dick ban, which is harder than it sounds with two horny, hot as hell men around, I find them in the kitchen. They are busy cooking, but Garrett hands me a mug and turns back to carry on, but he hesitates before spinning on his heel, leaning over the counter, and kissing me hard.

My pussy actually clenches as he pulls away, grinning to himself. Fuck, ban? Maybe I should rethink that. He winks like he can hear my thoughts, and Diesel laughs. "Cure his dick, and now he's fucking Sir Charming."

"You're just jealous." Garrett snorts and Diesel narrows his eyes.

"Oh yeah? You call that a kiss?"

Oh fuck.

I try to get away, but he leaps over the island and grabs me, dipping me as he kisses me hard, his hands twining in my hair. It's over quickly, and he helps me stand as I pant. Screw the dick ban.

They can fuck me right here and now if they want.

He laughs and saunters away, asshole. "That's a kiss," he tells Garrett.

"I hate you both," I mutter, as I sip my coffee. "Fucking Vipers, more like fucking children."

They both laugh and ignore me. Finally, the food is ready and we sit at the island today, but I miss us all eating together. It twinges in me, but I push it away, knowing they are busy. They have a lot to do, it makes sense they can't do that every day.

After I've finished eating, I sit back. "So what now?"

"I could tattoo you," Garrett suggests, and I freeze.

"Really?" I grin, perking up.

He shrugs. "If you want. Didn't you say you had one that needed to be finished?"

Diesel grins. "Fuck yes, let's do that."

"Why are you so happy?" I snort.

He grins, running his eyes down my body. "I remember our conversation, don't you, Little Bird?"

I frown for a moment before it clicks. I gulp, fuck, I do. He found out I got wet during tattoos, that I enjoyed the pain...maybe this isn't a good idea.

"What conversation?" Garrett queries, confused.

"Nothing!" I blurt, as Diesel laughs.

"You'll find out. Go on, get your shit, I'll get it set up down here," Diesel tells him, as he downs some coffee.

They both rush off and leave me in the kitchen. Fuck, I didn't think this through. Hot as hell Garrett tattooing me while Diesel watches?

This dick ban is going out the window, I can feel it. Stupid vagina and its dick obsession.

I'M LYING ON ONE OF THE SUN LOUNGERS FROM OUTSIDE, WHICH we pulled into the living room, in just my knickers and a crop top. My outside leg is exposed, with me positioned on my side, so he can look at the existing tattoo while I explain what I want. "I can do free hand if you trust me," he murmurs.

"No dicks," I snap, as he cleans the area. I'm shaved at least, so there's no need for that.

He smirks but doesn't respond. Diesel is behind me, his eyes locked on my ass. The dirty bastard. He's watching for me to get all hot and bothered so he can tattle to Garrett.

"What about a snake?" he asks, and I freeze. He looks up. "You can say no, but I could put a viper in there."

"Just do it." Diesel grins.

The fact that he asks makes me sigh. Diesel's right, they could have just done it. After all, they still class me as theirs. But the idea of having a viper on me is actually appealing. I imagine their eyes lighting up when they see it, and Ryder's and Kenzo's reactions...hell yes. Plus, it doesn't mean anything, right? It's just a snake, nothing else. "Sure." I shrug. "I trust you." And I mean it, I do. Garrett would never hurt me. He's an enforcer for a living, but in here? His home? He's a protector.

I lay my head on my arm as the buzz of the needle starts, and he draws closer, one hand braced on my thigh as the other presses the needle to my skin. He does a tiny line then stops and watches me, clearly expecting me to wimp out. "Babe, I'm covered in tattoos," I remind him, and he smirks, starting back up again.

I watch him for the first part. The concentration on his face and the way he bites down on his lip is adorable. He seems relaxed, which is a first, comfortable. Is this what he does to escape? Like Kenzo's mother's grave and Diesel's torture? Maybe, either way, I'm happy to help, and as the pain sinks into my bones with the humming of the needle, I try not to shift or give any indication that it's getting to me.

Because, fuck, it is. Having him so close to my pussy, his scarred, tattooed knuckle touching my skin as he inks me? It's hot as hell. Those same hands, capable of such death and destruction, are creating beautiful artwork on my skin, mixing with the pain. Yeah, I'm wet.

I'm betting Diesel knows as well, but Garrett seems oblivious as I shift awkwardly to try and relieve the pressure on my pussy. I close my eyes and imagine anything else, but with each swipe of the cloth and each buzz of the needle, I'm aware of how close he is. How near his hand is to my pussy. Of the pleasure he can bring, even now as it hurts. I bite my lip to stop my gasp from escaping, restraining myself from tilting my hips as my pussy clenches, my knickers dampening with need.

"Okay there, Little Bird?" Diesel questions, and I can hear the amusement and desire in his tone. The asshole is probably getting a kick out of this. Wait, of course he is—this is torture for me, he would love that. I'm surprised he's not bloody stroking his cock, though Garrett might hit him if he did.

"Fine," I reply breathlessly.

The buzzing stops, and Garrett lifts his head, frowning at me. "You sure?" he asks, obviously thinking I'm in pain.

Fuck me.

"Yes, Little Bird, you sure?" Diesel laughs.

Garrett seems confused, and I sigh. "Dude, I'm fine, Diesel is just teasing me because I like the pain of tattoos."

Garrett frowns harder, watching me, and then it seems to click, and his eyes widen and his mouth drops open, making me grin. "I bet you don't get that with this lot, do you?" I tease.

He actually blushes, which causes me to laugh harder. "I don't—fuck, baby," he rasps, looking from my face back to my tattoo. "Now I'm going to be hard while I try to do this."

"Well then, we're both struggling." I snigger.

He takes a deep breath, but then groans again. "Fuck," I hear him mutter, and then the buzzing starts up. I stop trying to hide my reaction, because honestly, watching him struggle is fun.

When he covers a particularly sore patch, a moan slips free, and he swears, his head whipping up as he glares at me while Diesel laughs. "I swear to God, you do that again, and I'll screw the tattoo and just fuck you instead."

"Nope, tattoo first, big guy," I counter, as he moves my leg around to get another angle and starts again, but every now and then, his gaze drifts up to my eyes, and when he turns to dip the needle in the ink, he stares at me knowingly.

Diesel shuffles closer, and his breath wafts over my ear as the buzzing begins. I don't look at the tattoo, wanting it to be a surprise when it's all done. "I wonder if he will let you come after, or if you will by the time he finishes," he whispers loudly, so Garrett can hear. "I think he's imagining all the ways he can fuck you on this chair. I know I am, Little Bird."

"Diesel," Garrett snaps, before sighing as he stops again. "Behave, both of you."

We both laugh, and Diesel strokes up my arm and around to my chest, cupping my unbound breast through my shirt. I didn't bother to put a bra on, sometimes your tatas just have to go free. But that means he grabs my bare breast, tweaks my nipple, and makes me moan again. Garrett swears. Licking my ear, Diesel chuckles as he twists and flicks it until I jerk in the chair and Garrett snaps away. "Fuck," he growls. "I've only been at it two hours, and I have at least another thirty minutes to go."

"Thirty minutes?" I laugh, as Diesel plucks and twists my nipples. "Yeah, I won't last that long."

Garrett appears pained as he watches Diesel touch me, his hand still on my thigh as he tries to calm himself enough to return to inking me. "I have an idea, Little Bird." Diesel grins and then looks to Garrett. "I can keep her distracted. She can sit on my cock while you finish up."

"How will that fucking help? You think I can work with her moaning and screaming?" he growls.

Diesel laughs. "Not fucking, not moving, just being inside her, teasing her. Torturing her." Garrett's eyes darken at that. "And when you're done, I'll make her scream for you."

Fuck me. Literally.

Someone better fuck me right now.

My eyes nearly roll back into my head at the idea as I arch my chest into his hand, wanting that so badly. "You can fuck my mouth," I offer Garrett, and he snaps.

He rips off his gloves and storms away. Two minutes later, he's back and glaring at us. "This is going to be the longest half hour of my life," he mutters. "Fine, while I wash my hands, do it."

I suck in a breath, my body trembling at the thought. Diesel wants to torture me, have his cock in me while Garrett tattoos my flesh. This will be pure fucking hell, and I can't wait. While Garrett stomps away, Diesel uses his knife to cut off my knickers before sliding in behind me on the chair. I have to inch forward, so I'm nearly falling off. He lifts my leg and drapes it over his, his cock against my soaked pussy.

"Fuck, Little Bird, you're drenched," he mumbles, as he reaches around me, dips a finger in my wetness, and smears it on my clit, rubbing it. Just as I'm moaning, writhing in his hold, he slams his cock into my sore pussy, making me scream. He stills and kisses along my shoulder as I settle. His arm wraps around me, keeping me immobile as he stays there, buried to the hilt, almost falling from the chair.

"Ready," he calls.

Oh fuck.

Garrett comes back, and when he sees me, his fists clench, his dark eyes focusing on where Diesel is buried balls deep in my pussy. He sucks in a breath, his eyes closing for a moment before he snaps on his gloves and sits down, rolling closer.

"Okay," he mutters, and grabs my leg, pulling it over his lap. "There, that's better...at least I can't fucking see your pussy anymore," he grumbles, making Diesel laugh and me moan as he jiggles me on his cock.

When we settle down, Garrett begins tattooing, and I try to stay still and quiet to let him concentrate, but Diesel shifts every now and again, a slight move that drags over my interior nerves, mixing with the pain, and I whimper.

"Pretty little bird," Diesel murmurs in my ear. "You should feel how wet she is," he tells Garrett.

I narrow my eyes and reach back to slap him, but he grabs my hand and drags it up my body to cup my own breast. "She's fucking soaked, and every time you hit a particularly painful patch—oh yeah, like that—she squeezes my cock."

Garrett grunts, his hand clenching on my leg before he sucks in a deep breath. "Shut the fuck up, or I'll draw a dick."

Diesel laughs, so do I. "I don't think he would, Little Bird. He would have to look at it then when he fucked you."

I try to hold in my giggle and then my moan as he presses in deeper. Garrett drags over a sore patch, and then again, and I realise he's doing it on purpose, the asshole. I glare down at him and his eyes rise for a moment, those lips curled into a smirk. "Bloody wanker," I hiss.

"Don't worry, D, I'm nearly done, then I'll fuck her mouth so she can't insult us anymore," Garrett comments, as he lowers his head again.

"Nah, she does that when she's turned on." Diesel chuckles.

"Really?" Garrett mumbles. "That true, baby? 'Cause you insult me a lot."

"Fuck off, both of—agh." Diesel bites down on my shoulder, making me clench on his cock. I try not to move and close my eyes to stop myself from rocking back into him, needing more friction, needing to come. He's right—this is torture.

The desire is muddling my brain, my whole body alight with it, and if Garrett doesn't finish soon, I'm going to say to hell with the tattoo and drag him up my body. I keep still like that for another fifteen minutes, the longest fifteen minutes of my life. Then, a kiss comes on my thigh, farther down. "All done, baby."

I feel him cleaning it as I open my eyes, and I go to lift my head to look, but he rips off his gloves and throws his needle away as his dark gaze locks on my mouth. "Look later. You can thank me now. Mouth open, you fucking tease."

"I want to see—" I start, but then he's there. He unbuckles his jeans swiftly and pulls his big cock free. It's hard and dripping at the tip, and he presses it to my mouth, tapping my lips with it.

"And I want you to shut the fuck up and suck my dick so D can finally fuck you. I spent two hours with my head nearly in your pussy, staring at your fucking wet cunt and imagining my dick in there. Then another thirty minutes of seeing D's cock actually inside you and you moaning above me. So. Open. Up. Now," he growls, his fingers threading in my hair and yanking my head forward roughly.

Eyes narrowing, I do as I'm told. He shoves his cock into my mouth, almost making me choke. He grabs my chin and forces my lips closed around him while Diesel grips my thigh and starts to move in slow, measured thrusts, which have me reaching out and clutching Garrett's thigh. He groans, and I roll my eyes up to meet his dark, desire-filled orbs as I suck him down.

Moaning around his cock, I dig my nails into his thigh, and he doesn't freak out. Maybe because I'm restrained by Diesel, who's licking and biting my neck, his hand dragging down my stomach to flick and tug at my clit piercing. The pain from that and my tattoo on my thigh flows through me, meeting that fire of pleasure low in my stomach.

This has been brewing for the last few hours, and now I'm wild with it, just a ball of desire. Needing more, needing everything. Needing the pleasure they can give me. Keeping my eyes open and locked on him, even though they want to close, I suck him down deeper. I feel spit dripping down my chin, but I don't care. I push my ass back against Diesel, moaning around Garrett's cock as he slams in and out of me.

Garrett groans, his head dropping back as he starts to thrust into my mouth in quick, hard jabs as he chases his orgasm. Sucking him down, I bob my head, faster and faster, in time with Diesels thrusts, all of us locked in this loop of pleasure. Diesel groans dirty words in my ear, spurring me on, his fingers teasing and flicking my clit until I scream around Garrett's cock, my orgasm rushing through me. I try to pull back, but his hand in my hair keeps me there, and he takes over.

Using my mouth, abusing it with hard thrusts which have him down my throat, he yells as his hips stutter before his seed fills my mouth. I have no choice but to swallow it, and only then do his fingers untangle from my hair.

Panting hard, my lips and cheeks hurting, I open my eyes to find him smirking down at me before he stumbles back into his chair. "My turn," Diesel rumbles in my ear.

I yelp as I'm flipped and turned until I'm perched on his lap. Diesel is on his back beneath me with my ass towards his face as he lifts and drops me on his cock. I reach out desperately and grip either side of the chair as I roll my hips, that same pleasure building back up again.

Garrett watches me, watches me fuck and ride his brother. Grabbing my nipple, I twist and pluck it as I bounce on his dick, his thrusts mean and hard, unrelenting. "Fuck." He groans. "Little Bird, I'm so close, make yourself come, now," he demands.

Whimpering, I reach down and rub my oversensitive clit as he thrusts up so hard, I almost fall forward, but it does the trick. It rushes through me, pulled from every nerve until I can't think or breathe. Pleasure rolls through me again and again as I clamp down on his cock.

He groans loudly and stills, keeping me locked on his cock as he comes. I tremble and shake, unable to help it, my pussy still pulsing, my stomach clenching and heart slamming in my ribcage. Holy hell.

He finally releases my hips and lifts me from his cock before pulling me back to his chest. I lie there, breathing heavily, and look over at Garrett to see him watching me with soft, dark eyes. He nods, then disappears for a moment. He returns with a bottle of water, which I gratefully sip as he cleans me up, softly and without a word, before handing me a large mirror. "Take a look, baby."

I lift my heavy head as he holds the mirror, and I tilt down until I can see the tattoo. When I do, I gasp. It's fucking beautiful, sore and bleeding a little bit, but absolutely amazing. It's delicate, unlike their thick, heavy tattoos. Roses climb down my thigh with sharp thorns, dripping mandalas and beads, and curving around the stem of a rose is a tiny viper, its eyes peeking from the leaves. It's stunning and so lifelike, its shading making it look like it's alive.

"I love it," I whisper, and meet his eyes. "You're so talented. Thank you, Garrett."

He shrugs and wipes it for me before leaning down and kissing my lips. "You're welcome, baby," he murmurs softly, and tries to pull away, but I grab the back of his head and keep him there, showing him with my kiss how much it means. When I pull away, he's grinning.

"Ever thought about being a tattoo artist?" I ask curiously.

"Nah, my dad was, though, before he got himself killed by one of the families that used to run this town before us. I guess I just like how it reminds me of him, fighting was always my thing," he explains, as he sits down again.

"You enjoy it?" I query, snuggling into Diesel's chest.

"I used to." He sighs. "A lot. Now? Now, it's a release for me, of emotions, and one of the only places where I don't have to worry about holding back. I can just hurt people, and that's okay."

Diesel snorts. "He used to be a professional boxer, and he was fucking good too, had some titles behind him."

"Really?" I ask, eyes wide.

Garrett nods. "Was always too...restricting for me. I prefer fighting without rules. I like to hurt people, baby, always have, always will."

I grin. "So? You don't think I like it when I use my bat on people? Or when I kicked you in the balls?"

He laughs and so does Diesel. "I'm never going to live that down."

"Nope, sorry, big guy." I sigh and rest my head on Diesel. "Did they find who betrayed you?"

"Not yet, but we will, Little Bird, and when we do..." He groans. "The things I will do to them and then you."

I shiver from the promise in his tone, and he laughs, slapping my thigh. "So what do you want to do now, Little Bird?"

I debate my options. "I want to see you work, not torturing. I saw Kenzo in his role...but what do you guys do every day?"

Garrett snorts. "It changes. We don't tend to be in the boardrooms, that's Kenzo and Ryder. We run the bars and casinos, and gather information on the streets and from vendors."

"We could take her to The Lounge," Diesel suggests.

Garrett raises an eyebrow. "The strip joint? Why?"

I perk up at that. "'Cause she wants to see us doing business, and we need to check in anyway, make sure that old Cherry bitch hasn't been talking."

Garrett looks at me, and I grin. "Naked women in glitter? I'm there."

He blinks in astonishment, making me laugh. "Babe, you forget I run a dive bar, and just because I don't like the salad doesn't mean I can't appreciate the aesthetic."

"Salad," Diesel wheezes, and then we all burst into laughter. When we get a hold of ourselves, he slaps me again. "Go get dressed. Wear something so I can see your new ink, Little Bird, and we'll take you."

———

AFTER A WHORE'S WASH—NOT WANTING TO EXPOSE MY TATTOO to the shower—and straightening my hair, I put on makeup and my viper jewellery before looking over my new clothes. Deciding on the black number Ryder bought me, I slip into it and some heels, looking in the mirror to make sure it shows off my ink, which it does. I freeze then, staring at myself.

I don't look like me, but at the same time, I do. This Roxy is better dressed, surrounded by colours, but it's the smile on my face that shocks me. When was the last time I just smiled? I actually can't remember...am I happy here?

What does that mean?

I don't want to leave, I know that, but I'm still...mad. I want my freedom, I want my own life and the right to choose, but I'm still... fucking happy. Because of them. My door opens just then, and Diesel comes in. He wraps himself around me from behind, his head resting on my shoulder, his blond hair loose and those baby blues alight with happiness.

He's in a leather jacket, tight, black ripped jeans, and no shirt. His golden chest glistens, his new tattoo proudly displayed, and his abs catch my eye for a moment. We look good together, light and dark, all golden skin and golden hair for him, all pale skin and silver hair for me.

"So perfect, Little Bird," he murmurs, kissing my neck as he meets my eyes in the mirror. "You're perfect. Always. Come on, you want to see what the Vipers get up to? You want to see who we are when we're out there, and we want to show you off. To let them know you're our girl."

"Vipers' girl?" I smirk, and he grins against my skin.

"Forever," he murmurs.

"You ready?" Garrett yells from down the corridor.

Diesel takes my hand and leads me from the room before rushing back in, then he stops me in the corridor and gets to his knees. Looking up at me, he grabs the edge of my dress and pulls it up slowly, revealing my thighs. Pulling something black from his pocket, he wraps it around my not freshly inked thigh and slips my blade into it, the one he gave me. "There." He kisses my thigh and pulls down my dress before taking my hand again.

We meet Garrett in the hallway. He's busy looking at his phone, but I can't help but gasp at the sight of him. These men are too dangerously good-looking. His hair is slicked back, and he's scowling, which only adds to the appeal. His thick, tall frame is encased in all black, his tattoos peeking out, his hands big and scarred.

When he realises I'm there, he pockets the phone and goes to smile before his eyes drop to the dress, and he groans instead. "I'm going to have to punch some people."

"Won't it be great?" Diesel laughs, twirling me across the floor until I stumble into Garrett's chest, who catches me and holds me close. His big hands go to my ass and yank me closer as he massages my cheeks, his head tilting down to murmur against my lips.

"I will kill anyone who looks at you wrong. Stay by our sides, but show no fear, baby. This might be the Vipers' den, but out there? It's a fucking hornet's nest." He kisses me before ripping open the door and heading out first. Diesel takes my hand, but his other is on a knife at his side.

"Garrett has to keep his hands free for his guns," he explains, and I nod.

Heading down to the garage, we take one of the bigger, still sporty, Audis. Garrett doesn't let Diesel drive, and when I question it, he shakes his head. "Trust me."

Diesel snorts but gets into the back while I climb into the passenger seat. "I wouldn't have killed us with my little bird here."

"Sure," Garrett scoffs as he fires up the car and pulls up the barriers, which begin to rise. "Buckle up, baby."

I do as I'm told, and as we race into the city, I look at the buildings and people going past. We're in the rich part of town with designers, boutiques, sports cars everywhere, and women and men in no rush to get anywhere. Everything screams money. I feel less at home here than out on the street, so when we pass into the darker side of town, I actually relax. I know how to live here, to survive, but on the glittering streets lined with blood and money? Not so much.

We don't head near my bar, but we're on the other side, just past all the big banks and money places, which makes sense. We pull up right outside, and Garrett gets out first and rounds the car, keeping me from getting out as he looks around. Only when he's happy does he open the door for me. Diesel takes my hand again and leads me to the club with Garrett behind us, watching our backs.

From the outside, it looks like what you would expect for a strip club—big, tacky neon sign, and dark, blacked out windows. I love it. Diesel doesn't pay or even glance at the man at the door, just opens it and pulls me in.

Instantly, it's dark, and the sensual music hits me, as does the scent of cigars, booze, and sweat. The wood floor in the hallway leads down to two, big double doors, which we open before slipping into the main area of the club.

The bar is behind us to the right, with the stage area taking up most of the room. There are floating platforms and cages in the air, and a VIP area upstairs. There are curtained off booths around each wall, which I have to squint to see. Everything is dark and moody with coloured lights. Poles are everywhere and small tables surround the stages.

It's definitely a dive, so I feel right at home. There are neon signs across the walls—cherries, lips, you name it, they have it. The floor is a sticky wood, and my heels cling to as we walk. It's busy, even at this time of day, with men in suits and leathers sitting around, and a few women too. Cocktail waitresses in slinky outfits wander through the crowd with trays, and there are two women behind the bar as well. A dancer is currently on stage in a jewelled bikini as she swings around the pole and writhes to the music. I tilt my head. "She's good." I nod, and Diesel smirks.

"You're a strange one, Little Bird, I love it," he murmurs, leaning down so I can hear him over the music.

"Hey, I took pole dancing, that shit is hard. These women are fucking athletes, and trying to get that glitter out? Not easy," I scoff.

Just then, a woman approaches, and she smiles nervously at us, her eyes flickering between the guys. "Cherry is in back, honeys, want me to grab her? She's in a meeting."

"No, it's fine, we can wait," Garrett tells her, and then takes a table near one of the walls so he can see everyone. His hand is on his lap where his gun is resting, and his eyes are sharp, scanning every-thing. Diesel, on the other hand, grabs a chair and yanks me into his lap as we watch the woman on stage.

"Want a dance while you're waiting?" the nervous waitress asks, clearly knowing who they are.

"No," Garrett snarls.

"Sorry, I brought my own." Diesel laughs.

The waitress scurries away as fast as she can, and I spot the others

344

in the bar glancing back at us nervously. Some clearly know who we are, because they get up and leave, while the others stay. They might not know who Diesel and Garrett are, but they can sense what they are, even if they don't know them personally.

Killers.

Rich.

Powerful.

The mood dampens as men straighten and sober up.

Every eye is on us, even if it's quick glances so they don't get caught. Drinks are dropped off instantly, we are checked on every second, and waited on hand and foot. This is the reaction the Vipers get from people—fear and awe. Like royalty.

"I'm going to the bathroom," I murmur to Diesel as I get up. Garrett catches my hand and narrows his eyes on me, communicating without a word. "It's right there, big guy, you can see into the door from here. I'll be right back." I lean down and kiss him, and I can tell I've surprised him when he lets go of my hand.

"Be quick, baby, or I'll come after you," he growls, as I pull back.

I wave that away and stroll through the crowd to the toilet, feeling every eye on me, all of them wondering who and what I am to the Vipers. I slip into the bathroom and do my business before washing my hands.

I open the door and the music hits me again. Just as I'm stepping back into the main club, a man blocks my path. He's big, double my height, wearing an ill-fitting suit and a fake watch on his wrist. He's trying to look richer than he is, unlike my guys, who don't even flaunt their wealth.

The man's eyes are glazed, so he's high or drunk or maybe both, as he stumbles over to me. "Hey, darlin', here's fifty for a blowy." He throws the cash at me.

Snorting, I roll my eyes before kicking out and slamming my heel into his crotch. He goes down with a squeal, dropping to his knees and wheezing.

"What the fuck, bitch?" he yells, as Garrett comes up behind him.

Pulling back my fist, I punched him in the face. "Finders keepers, honey." I laugh as I pocket the notes and step over his prone, whimpering form.

"Stupid slut," he snaps, and Garrett hears it, but so do I.

Nobody gets to insult me. Spinning, I grab my knife from my thigh and yank his greasy hair back, holding the blade to his throat. "You ever insult me again, and it will be the last thing you do. Is that understood, shit for brains?" I snap.

He freezes, the scent of alcohol wrapping around me, and I feel his body tremble.

"When I let go, you're going to apologise. You will say, 'I'm sorry, almighty Roxy, I'm a meat-headed idiot with a small cock,' and then you will pay for all our drinks tonight, won't you?"

He nods, and I laugh as I slide my blade away and step back in case he tries anything. He stumbles to his feet and turns, his face pale as he looks at me.

"Say it." I grin, tapping the blade on my thigh.

"I-I'm sorry, almighty Roxy, I'm a meat-headed idiot with a small cock—" He stumbles, his eyes flaring in panic.

"You will pay for all our drinks," I prompt, and he nods rapidly.

"All your drinks, so sorry," he calls again, as I turn with a grin to see Garrett smirking at me.

"Baby, where were you even keeping that blade?" he asks, his eyes dark with hunger as he runs his gaze down my body and my extremely tight dress. Grabbing his hand, I drag it up my thigh until he feels the sheath. He groans, his eyes closing for a moment. "Shit, Rox."

I pull away, giggling. "Don't hurt him, I took care of it." Keeping his hand in mine, I tug him back to the table, where Diesel is watching me with a grin.

"Little Bird, that was so hot," he murmurs, running his eyes to my knife. "You're using that on me later."

346

Laughing, I drop into his lap, knowing Garrett needs to keep his hands free. We watch the next girl as another bottle is dropped at our table. It's champagne. I pop the cork and take a swig, toasting the guy I threatened at the corner table with it. He nods and looks away in fear.

Just then, a bouncer stops at our table. He takes a look at me and snorts. "Get backstage, girl." He turns to my guys. "She's ready to see you, follow me."

Diesel stiffens against me. Oh fuck. I throw myself harder against him before he can kill this idiot, but then Garrett's there in a flash. He's so quick, I didn't even see him get up. His fists move rapidly, and then the bouncer is on his knees, his nose and lip bleeding, both busted, and Garrett is standing over him angrily.

"What did you say about her?" he snarls, his voice low and rumbling.

I watch the bouncer's gaze widen as he realises he royally fucked up. He tries to look over at me, but Garrett steps into his path, blocking his view. "Do not look at her, ever."

"I'm sorry, sir, I thought she was a dancer. I'm really fucking sorry," the man rushes out. A minute ago, he was a big, burly fucker who even I would have hesitated to take down. Now he looks like a scared, little boy when faced with Garrett. "Please, please, I'm so sorry," he begs.

"You insulted her," Garrett grinds out, and he smashes his fist into the guy's face again.

I sip my champagne while I watch. He kinda deserved it, plus Diesel is still trying to get up, and if he joins in, the guy will die, which wouldn't be good.

The bouncer falls to his stomach, and he tries to crawl away, but Garrett is there, pressing his boots to the guy's hand and stomping down. The bouncer's scream rings out loudly. The music cuts out, and the whole club freezes. Garrett doesn't care, they're untouchable.

"You insulted her," he snarls again, as he stomps on his other hand before kicking him. "Get up."

Shit. The bouncer stumbles to his feet, his hands held against his chest and tears tracking down his face. "I'm sorry, I'm so sorry, please," he beseeches with snot dripping from his nose.

Alright, he's had his fun. I get up and, grabbing my knife, I press it to Diesel's throat for a second. "Do not fucking move, or I swear I'll never play with you again."

He pouts but nods, taking the champagne from me as I slide my knife away and turn to Garrett just as he's cocking back his fist again. I can see the fury vibrating through his body. He won't stop, like when he's in the ring, but we came here for a reason, not to beat up idiots.

I lay my hand on his back, and he stills, his head swinging to look at me with those dark eyes. "Let it go, big guy," I murmur.

Just then, a female voice sounds near us. "What the fuck is happening here?"

We all turn to see the person it came from. She's a tall woman, over six feet, with giant breasts. Seriously, what the fuck? They are huge and escaping her tight pink dress, which clings to her thick stomach and thighs. Her hair is red and puffed up like back in high school. Her lips are red, her eyes brown, and her face is covered in heavy makeup. She narrows her eyes but seems to hesitate when looking at both Vipers before she shakes it off.

This woman has big balls. I'll give her that. She tosses her hair over her shoulder. "Cher, what are you doing to my staff?"

Garrett straightens and glares at the man once more. "Go, before I change my mind."

The bouncer doesn't hesitate, he runs away quickly, and Diesel gets to his feet. They stand on either side of me. Her eyes run across them in more than a clinical sense, which makes me bristle, before they land on me. She purses her lips like she doesn't like what she sees and tosses her hair again. "Nice to see you two, come back to my office."

Wow, that bitch just ignored me. How fucking rude.

Diesel leans in closer. "Want me to kill her? Or hold her and you can?"

Laughing, I push him away, but he wraps his arm around me and follows after her as Garrett trails behind us again, always in protection mode. The woman leads us down a corridor next to the bar and into a door at the end which opens to an office. She perches on the desk, parting her thighs so we can all see up her dress.

Diesel guides me over to the sofa, leaning against the back wall, and yanks me down next to him. His hand plays with my hair while Garrett shuts the door and stands against it, his arms crossed. Laughing and still ignoring me, she walks over to him, shaking her hips and ass.

She reaches out to touch him, and I leap up, grabbing it before it can drag down his chest. Tightening my hand around her fingers, I narrow my eyes as she gasps in pain. "Do not touch him," I warn, knowing he hates it, and yes, I'm a little bit jealous.

I push her away, and she shakes it off with a nervous giggle as she sits back on the desk. I tug Garrett to the sofa and drag him down next to me until I'm bracketed between them again. He leans in and kisses my cheek. "Thank you, baby," he murmurs quietly.

"So, to what do I owe the pleasure of your visit? I'm guessing since Ryder isn't here, it's not about the business?" she asks with a grin, her legs still parted. She drags her hand up her thigh to try and draw their eyes, but they don't even twitch, which settles me.

"Yes," Garrett snaps, obviously tired of her already. It makes sense, since she's a woman using her sexuality and she almost touched him. He probably hates her. Diesel is too busy playing with my hair to notice, but he does snort at her actions.

Her hand trails along her ample chest, trying again to draw their gazes as she leans forward to spill more of her breasts. "What kind of business?" she murmurs suggestively, her voice low.

That's when I realise she wields her body like a weapon, using her sexuality to distract. She isn't the biggest or the strongest, but she's survived this long by knowing how to play men and play the game. I respect her for that, and when I recognise it, I relax. "Cherry, we aren't here to hurt you, you can lose the act."

Her eyes flare and then harden as she drops her hand from her chest, the real Cherry coming out, even her face slackens. Suddenly, she looks a lot older. "Thank you." She grins, giving me a friendly smile. "Sorry, it's a habit."

"I bet. I do the same, usually with my tough ass bitch routine and my bat." I shrug.

"I like you, so why are you here?" she queries, only looking at me now, which makes me tilt my head curiously. "Come on, they're rich and powerful, but they're not in charge here, you are. So why are you here?"

I'm in charge? I wait for them to correct her, but they don't, so I sit up taller. Fine, we are playing this game. "We need to know if anyone here would betray us. If anyone has been asking questions or acting suspicious."

She purses her lips again. "How would I know?"

"Don't play dumb, Cherry, it doesn't suit you. You're too smart for that. You make it your business to know, and your girls? I saw them collecting information like they collect money. People talk freely around them. We just need to know if you heard anything. It would mean a great deal to the Vipers, to us, and you would certainly be owed a favour."

I'm taking liberties here, but the guys don't stop me. Let's hope Ryder doesn't kill me after.

She smiles, a full genuine one. "Shit, you're good. Okay, fine. Yes, I know information. I know about the hits on you guys, but I'm not stupid enough to be involved, I know your power. You will always win, as for the betrayal?" She sighs and sits behind her desk. "I've heard there's a silent player feeding information, but I can't figure out who. I've been trying so I could sell you the information. I had a few of the Triad's men in here the other day, and I put my best girls on them, but all we got was it's an old friend. I heard they are coming back after a run next week. I can let you know when they are here if you wish...and you could speak to them." She grins. "I could, of course, provide a private room for that...conversation."

"I would appreciate that." I quickly write down my number. "Text me, and we'll be here. In the meantime, if you find out anything, we'll gladly reimburse you for your time and effort." Standing, I reach out and shake her hand, making her laugh.

"Girl, I've heard of you. Roxy, isn't it? Rich's daughter?" she asks knowingly, and I smirk. If she knew me, why did she give me all that shit? She must see the question in my eyes. "I had to make sure you were the girl he spoke about. Gave no shit, did whatever and whoever she wanted. Wasn't afraid of anything. Fearless. Brave and too fucking smart."

"Checking up on me?"

She laughs then, fully belly laughs. "A girl joining the Vipers? One I've heard has their utmost, undivided attention and loyalty? A lot of girls have tried, so yeah, I was interested. Rich was an old friend though, a good man." She frowns. "I'm sorry about his death, the old bastard deserved better."

I nod. "He did, he was one of the only good men I ever met. Took me in as a snot-nosed kid full of attitude."

"Yeah, how did that turn out?" She smirks.

"I got a bigger attitude." I wink. "And the skills to back it up."

She grins then. "No doubt. He was the one who got me out of an abusive relationship when he found me crying in the toilet of Roxers." She smiles sadly. "I owe that man my life. I never got to pay him back, so keep your money, Roxy. That debt now passes to you, and I will help you in any way I can. For Rich." She nods.

I nod back. "Thank you, and feel free to bring your girls to Roxers anytime, free drinks." I wink. "Fuck knows we could use the...appeal they'll bring." I laugh and turn to leave. At the door, I pause and look back at her. "You're good at the game, Cherry, just make sure it doesn't get you killed, it would be a fucking shame."

Swinging the door open, I slip out, Diesel and Garrett following

351

behind me. Garret leans down. "That was fucking beautifully done, baby."

"Wait until we tell Ryder." Diesel whoops. "I knew my Little Bird was going to be the shit."

I shake my head with a laugh. We head through the club, winding through the tables, but just before we get to the door, we're stopped. There's a man there, one who was with the drunk guy from before, and he looks enraged. "Fucking whore, spending all his money. Can't afford it yourself?"

Oh shit.

I feel the two men tense behind me, but the stupid fuck carries on. "You leave my brother alone. You got a problem, we'll be in booth three. You can suck us off for that money you want."

Welp, this stupid motherfucker is dead, and there ain't no way I'm helping him.

"What did you just say?" Diesel growls, his face closing down. He slowly turns to the man. "You called my girl a whore?"

Where's the popcorn when you need it?

He sheds his jacket, tossing it at me, and pulls back his hair, tying it at the base of his neck in a bobble. His chest glistens under the strobe lights as he prowls around the man, who now looks like he regrets his words.

"D—" I start, but he ignores me.

The swagger in the smooth way he walks has me licking my lips. He truly is fucking stunning, dangerous, dark, crazy, and fucking beautiful. He pulls his knife and holds it up for the man to see. "You didn't think I would hear you insult our girl?"

Yeah, this guy is dead. I watch the stupid fuck who still looks like he might take Diesel on. It's all false bravado of course, anyone can see how dangerous Diesel is. He's a match waiting to be struck, and this guy? He fucking struck it.

"Run while you can, you daft sod," I advise, but he spits in my direction. Well, I tried.

Instead, I grab a shot from the closest table and toss it back, leaning into Garrett to watch my crazy man at work. "This should be fun."

"Baby, nothing is ever boring with you around." He laughs, even though I feel him scanning the crowd in case anyone decides to get stupid and jump us or D.

"Fuck you," the guy snarls. "You think you're tough 'cause you're here with your whore?" The guy laughs again, making me wince. Damn, this is going to be bad. "You are nothing, just two idiots being led around by your dicks by the same, low-rent whore."

Diesel is done talking. He strikes with the precision of a man used to killing, who knows exactly where to hit. He's unafraid and bold. His knife catches the man across the face, and the idiot stumbles back with a pained yell. His hand comes up to block Diesel's next slice, which gets him across the chest, splitting his shirt and skin and spilling blood. But Diesel is a man possessed. He doesn't torture or tease like normal. He spins and slices, enraged, his face locked in anger and death. His eyes hard.

He cuts the man's wrists and the back of his knees, making him drop to the floor with a pained shriek. Everyone is watching, unsure whether or not to help as Diesel blows back his gold locks and steps behind the man. With narrowed, enraged eyes, he grabs his hair and yanks his head back. "That whore" —he spits the word— "tried to save you. Remember that when you're in your coffin." Diesel slices his neck from left to right, and it splits open like a gaping, bloody smile. Effortlessly, D tosses him to the floor to choke on his own blood, which is pouring from his wound.

Stepping over his body, Diesel prowls towards me, not stopping until he's pressed to my front, and he hands me the knife like a present. "Want me to cut off his balls for you, Little Bird?"

Laughing, I take the knife and lay a kiss on his lips. "No, babe, that's fine. Let's go, I'm tired."

He grins and pulls away, grabbing his jacket and tossing it over his shoulder. His other arm slides around my waist, taking me from Garrett. "Let's go home."

I look around. "I bet the police are coming."

There are people on their phones, folks crying, and girls scream-ing, and then Cherry storms through their midst—calm, collected, and in control. She takes in the man then us and nods.

"I got this, go," Cherry tells us, before turning to the clients and girls. "You saw fucking nothing! Now get back to work! Rick, pour free drinks for everyone!"

Nodding in gratitude, though I don't think the guys would have much issue with the police, we leave while we can. They might have some sway, but I'm betting they would have to answer some questions and that wouldn't be good with the violent mood they are both in.

Not to mention it would annoy Ryder. My first trip out with the terrible twosome, and we get arrested? Yeah, I would be punished all night...

On second thought...I should go back and get arrested.

CHAPTER
THIRTY-FIVE

RYDER

Gripping my hair, I drop my head into my hands. "Five, four, three, two, one," I murmur, chanting it over and over until I feel more in control. We have too much to do. *I have too much to do.*

I still need to find out who's betraying us before it gets us killed, and I need to deal with the Triad as well as run our legitimate business. I'm exhausted, my eyes stinging and body tiring, but I have to keep going. I can't stop until I save my family.

I have to protect them, even if it kills me. Nothing else matters. "Five, four, three, two, one," I whisper again, as I hear the front door open and the telltale giggle of Roxxane. Shoving my hair back, I straighten and return to checking the bank transfers from ex-employees. It would be the first sign they were betraying us. I could get Kenzo to look into it, but he's tired and needs sleep.

I've set up at the table, not wanting to be in my office all night. I have papers in piles all over and my two laptops open, my phone and tablet also scrolling through information. There is too much for me to handle, but I have to. I don't glance up when I hear them stop laughing. I hear a few whispers, the sound of retreating footsteps, and then a clearing of a throat.

Sighing, I don't look up. "Garrett, I'm fine, I'll sleep once—"

"Sorry, I'm better looking than him," Roxxane teases.

My head jerks up, and I frown. "Sorry, I thought—" Scrubbing my face, I smile softly. "Sorry, love. Did you have a good night?"

She looks over the papers and me, and nods. "I'll make coffee."

I hold up my mug. "I have—ah, I seem to have drunk it."

Laughing, she leans over and drops a peck on my lips. "I got this, okay? Let me look after you while you look after us."

I blink in astonishment, but then she's gone. I hear her in the kitchen arguing with the cupboards, trying to get them to open, which makes me smirk as I glance back at the bank records I was looking at—H. Fedred, it's definitely not him. His bank is almost overdrawn, his bills taking all his incoming money from his job, which I tracked to make sure it's legitimate. He used to be a security guard, front desk I think, he was a good man.

Grabbing my phone, I transfer him a couple thousand to help before loading up the next bank transfers list that Kenzo got me. He worked all day on collecting this information. I don't ask how, I don't care, but it's a big help. I've got guards I trust checking current security, but I agree, this is someone who worked for us before. They don't have up-to-date information.

Roxxane returns, and she places a mug next to me, her hand on my shoulder as she leans in close. I can't help but relax back into her warmth for a moment, seeking the comfort of her body, even though I don't deserve it. Why can't I find out who is betraying us? Leaning forward, I get back to work, pulling away from her.

I need to find out who is double-crossing us. I have to.

"Let me help," she offers.

"I'm fine, go get some sleep," I tell her distractedly, and then my chair is suddenly yanked back, and she's dropping into my lap. I automatically grab her and make sure she doesn't fall, blinking at her incredulously.

Her face is hard, her eyes narrowed. "I wasn't asking, now let me help or I'm going to annoy you all night. You're tired and stressed. I know you think you have to solve everything, that the weight rests solely on your shoulders, but you have to lean on someone eventually, Ry. Please, let me help," she says softly, as she reaches out and cups my face. I can't help but lean into her, and she grins. "It doesn't make you weak, you are still our leader, still in charge, but even the best leaders need help every now and again."

"Roxxanne." I sigh. "Are you sure?"

She nods, leaning down and kissing me. "Now, boss man, tell me what to do, and if I'm a good employee, you can reward me later."

Laughing, I help her up as she takes the chair opposite me, kicking off her shoes and getting comfortable. I can't help but smile, she is so cute. And not going anywhere. If I don't let her help, fuck knows what she'll do. It sends a burst of relief through me as I think it over. Logically, it would mean this would work faster, and therefore might help us track them before they can hit us again. I push the tablet over to her. "We are checking bank records for anything suspicious. If you find something, flag it for me. Any recurring large payments over a thousand and up to probably a mill." I nod, thinking it over. "Better safe than sorry, then we can work down that list. Oh, also flag anyone who is struggling financially," I add as an afterthought, and feel her staring at me, so I look over at her again. "What, love?"

"You're going to send them money if they're struggling?" she inquires, a grin appearing on her lips as I frown. "Big, bad Vipers, who knew you were such softies?"

"Softies?" I snort. "Don't tell anyone."

"Or you'll kill me," she teases, as she starts to scroll through the log. "Threat's a little old now, babe."

"You know, I think we have been too easy on you, love. You're far too cocky." I grin as I flick through the information.

"Uh-uh, babe, I was cocky before you met me, you don't get credit for my wit and mouth." She grins, her eyes on the tablet. "Now, get to work, I want my reward when we find this bastard."

Sipping the coffee she made, I lose myself in bank statements, answering the occasional email as I go. We work mainly in silence, but she fills my coffee a few times before going back to work. After a couple of hours, I lean back and stretch. "Anything?"

She looks up and places the tablet down next to a list she has. "A few, three to be exact, but I still have four names to check. What about you?"

"I have four to examine in depth and seven names left." I sigh, rubbing my eyes. It's the middle of the night, but I can't stop now. "Let's get through these last ones, and then I'll make us some food."

She smirks at that. "It better be good food."

Laughing, I quickly scan through the remaining names. She's done before me, of course, and I notice her looking over the list with a frown, so when I'm done, I grab it and cross a few names off. "Some of these still do odd jobs for us, hence the transfers." That leaves us with ten names between us. "Okay, I'll get Kenzo to check these out tomorrow, maybe wire them and put tails on them. You hungry, love?"

"Starving." She groans as she gets up and stretches, making my eyes drag down her delicious body. She grabs our mugs as I stand and roll back my sleeves.

"Homemade pasta?" I ask, and she stops.

"You cook? Make homemade pasta?" she murmurs, and I smirk.

"I do."

"Fucking assholes, is there anything you lot can't do?" she grumbles as we head to the kitchen again. She hops up on the island to watch as I grab the ingredients I need.

But her words stick with me. There's something I've been thinking about, running around in circles in my mind. The only way I will ever know for sure is to ask her so, leaning back against the worktop, I narrow my eyes on her and settle in. "Roxxane?"

She tilts her head. "Uh-oh, am I in trouble? Is it about the guy I beat up?"

I blink in shock. "You beat someone up again? What—never mind, we can come back to that. I need to ask you something."

"Sure, what's up?" she inquires casually.

"Do you want to be here?"

She freezes, her eyes widening.

"I mean it. I know...I know we didn't give you a choice. But now, it seems like you are almost happy. I see the way you are with my brothers, I have to know, I have to know if you're going to try and escape again, or if you could ever stay and be happy with them?"

"And if I say no?" she asks slowly.

"I-I need to protect them, love, even from their own feelings. This is getting more serious than I could have ever imagined. Tell me the truth, Roxxane, do you want to stay? With us?" I hold my breath, waiting for the answer, because the truth is...I want her too.

She is the best debt I ever collected, and the most important business deal.

But for her, did she accept the inevitable? Are we just a decision to give up fighting? If it comes down to her or my brothers, would I choose wisely? Could I even choose anymore? For all my intentions at keeping her at bay, the little minx has got behind my armour, and now, even my own heart is on the line.

Held in this woman's grasp.

She has the power to destroy us all. Does she know it?

She seems to be thinking, debating her answer. "Love, look at me. Are you happy? Do you still want your freedom...or do you want us?"

"Are those my only two choices?" she queries, and then glances away for a moment, the light of the city arcing across her heartbreakingly beautiful face. "I don't know. If you asked me a week ago, I would have taken my freedom...but you've gotten under my skin. You've got your venom in me, and in this last week, I have felt more alive than I ever have. D keeps telling me I belong, Garrett is finally letting me in, and Kenzo is so sweet and shared his past with me...

and you. You, Ryder, are giving me a chance to be part of a real family..."

"But?" I prompt, my hands digging into the granite as fear surges through me. I hate fear, it makes us weak. She makes me weak.

"But...how can I be completely happy as a captive? Don't you want me to choose you? To not need you, but want you? I've lived my own life, I have my own place, my own business. I earn my own money and pay my bills and buy the shit I want. I'm not rich, but I'm comfortable. I learned to change bulbs, to mow the fucking grass, to change a goddamn tire. To build furniture, to travel and be alone. In all that, I learned I didn't need a man to be with me, to do things for me, I could do it for myself. Nothing is too difficult, you can always find a way. But that means, when I'm with someone...when I choose someone, it's because I want them. Not because I need them for something, because I have to be with them, but because I *can* be with them. Don't you want that?"

It's my greatest fear and what I knew from the start. Why I tried to stay away. Roxxane wants to be free. From us. To leave...but would she come back? She's asking for that choice, and who am I to keep that from her? If I truly care for her, surely I should let her choose us. But what if she doesn't? D will never let her go, it would break Kenzo's heart, and Garrett—fuck, he's finally letting someone in again, trying to heal.

She would kill us all, and break everything we have worked so hard for.

But the other option is that she will slowly begin to hate us again when the glamour and kindness isn't enough, when we aren't enough to stop that hate, the hate from having her own choices taken away. After all, isn't that what her father did? She despises the man. Are we any better than him?

We aren't good men, we're criminals, but for her? Could we do something good, just this once?

I turn around and start making the food, debating my answer.

"Ry?" she whispers. "I don't want to hurt anyone, I really don't.

At first I did, I hated you all, and I think a part of me probably still does, but I also care. D told me something which makes sense now. If I really hated you, I would have killed you that first night, and he's right. I'm strong, I know that, I could have killed you, I had plenty of opportunity. But I didn't want to, I didn't want to earn my freedom that way. But like D's name for me, I am a bird, I need my wings. I need my freedom. It was taken from me as a child, I lived in constant fear and hatred so strong it warped me, and when I was free? I could be me, I found who I was. I don't want to lose that again. I don't want to hate you." Her words end on a whisper, and I shiver.

"I don't want you to either," I tell her, "but I don't know how to let you go."

"I know." She sighs before her arms wrap around me from behind. "I'm your worst nightmare, Ryder Viper, something you never saw coming. Something you can't control."

I grip her hands to my stomach as I lean into her. She's right. But she's also the best thing to happen to us. She's filled with such life, such capability for laughter and joy. She brings out the best in us and accepts the worst. Could I love her?

And if I do...

Can I really deny her?

Could I bear for her to actually hate us in the future? Like my mother hated my father?

"Maybe I'm more like him than I want to admit." I sigh.

"Like who?" she questions.

"My father. I know you know some about him, but he was a bastard, love. A true bastard. He moulded me to be like him, but what if I am? What if all that moulding, all those lessons, made me into the very thing I fucking hate? Kenzo sees it, so do you. I am capable of such destruction, such vile acts, yet I excuse it with the need to save my family. Yet here you are, my prisoner, and I don't want to let you go. I want you to ourselves, to lock you away in here so no other can ever have you. Just like he did to my mother. Am I doomed to repeat his mistakes?"

She's quiet for a moment. "Am I doomed to repeat my father's actions?" she counters. "To be a person so weak and cruel? I don't know, I could be. But I think the fact we are worried about it shows that we won't, because we don't want to be, because we are aware. Yes you can be cruel, cold, and manipulative. I can be mean, a bitch, and cruel too. But that doesn't make us them. It makes us, us. Stop fighting who you are, Ryder, stop fearing who you might find if you do. You never know, you might even discover you love yourself." She pulls away then, and I let her go, because I have to.

I could keep her here with me, but that might kill the part of her I love. The strong, crazy, unpredictable Viper, because that's what she is—one of us. There is no use denying it, I knew it when I first saw her. Which is why I was so afraid. Because if she is one of us...what happens when she leaves?

I've done some evil shit in my life. I've stepped on people. I've killed them. I've destroyed their lives and families and businesses without a blink. My hands are covered in more blood than she could ever imagine. All for them. My family.

So what will I do for her?

Everything.

It comes to me easily. I would do anything. Everything. I would burn this whole fucking city to the ground and find her in the cinders. I would kill, I would steal, I would lie. But what about letting her go?

Can I do that?

To everyone else, we are the villains, we are the evil in this city. Men immersed in power and money. We are the ones they fear, whom they hide away from. Yet she doesn't, she basks in it. What if I kept her? Here, forever? Would that really be so bad?

I'm turning to grab the pasta cutter when something hits me in the face. Coughing, I swipe away the white powder and spin to see Roxxane laughing, holding a bag of flour in her hand. She smirks at me, the one that makes me want to do bad things to her. One smile, and it pushes away all my demons that are longing to be free.

"Run," I snap.

She giggles and backs away.

"Run, love," I warn, as I prowl around the island towards her. Laughing harder, she tries to escape, but I grab her, capture her again, and yank her to me. "You should have run faster," I murmur in her ear.

"Maybe I wanted to be caught." She laughs as she wiggles, trying to break free.

Grabbing the eggs from the side, I crack one open right over her hair. She screams and lurches away. Watching it drip down her face, I can't help but laugh. Her nostrils flare, her eyes narrowed. "Oh, you're dead. Now it's your turn to fucking run!"

She grabs the butter on the side and throws it at me. Ducking, I chuckle as I grab some pasta and lob it at her. She screams and chases me with some milk, making me laugh as I swerve and avoid her. She turns to snatch something else, and I wrap my arms around her waist from behind. "Truce," I cry out with a chuckle as she kicks and laughs.

Stilling, she giggles and leans back into me. I turn her in my arms and grin down at her as I brush away a scraggly strand of egg-covered hair. She smiles up at me, her dark eyes shining with happiness. How did she do that?

She set me free from my demons without even trying. Never has this home had such laughter or happiness. It echoes around these silent, miserable walls, filling it with life. Filling it with her.

Flour covers my face, I have food in my hair and on my clothing, and I'm smiling so large, I don't remember the last time I kissed her. A desperate, clinging kiss. A goodbye, because I know now. I have to let her go.

Even if she doesn't come back to us.

Because Roxxane was never meant to be locked away. She is meant to be free, wild, and uncontrolled. Even now, with laughter on our lips and happiness coating her expression, I know she's pondering if she would really be here if she had a choice.

She's too strong, too fucking strong for this.

If she chooses this life, I could accept it, but she didn't, she had no choice, and I have to give her that. Even if it ruins my family.

Even if it means the end of the Vipers.

I have to let her go.

CHAPTER
THIRTY-SIX

ROXY

I slept in Ryder's arms again last night, after we had showered of course. At least he stopped working for a little bit, even if the conversation did turn dark. So when I wake up and he's gone, I'm not surprised to find a note on his pillow.

See you soon. Behave.

Asshole. With a smirk, I slip into one of his shirts and then freeze, recalling our conversation last night. Was he really contemplating letting me go? I don't know, but if he does...will I leave? I've gotten used to living here, and I really do care for them...they make me feel alive, they make me happy, but can happiness, can love, really happen when I had no choice?

I don't know, but I doubt it will bother them. They made a choice, and they will stick to it. I already decided to stop fighting and just start living, so even though I miss my old life, I push it away.

When I get downstairs, it's just Diesel and Garrett. I slip into my chair, and Garrett passes me a coffee, our fingers lingering. "So, where's dumb and dumber?" I smirk.

Garrett snorts, but Diesel doesn't even look at me. "Going through that list."

I nod and lean closer to Diesel. "Hey, hot stuff, guess that means it's you and me again." I wiggle my eyebrows at him. He grinds his teeth and storms off, leaving me staring after him. "Erm, care to explain?" I ask Garrett.

I turn back to see him watching me sadly before he wipes his face clear of emotion. "It's nothing, just a bad night, don't worry about it. So what do you want to do today?"

"Erm, anything," I answer distractedly, as I look in the direction where Diesel disappeared to. "Is this him angry?"

Garrett actually laughs. "Hell no, you'll know when you see him angry, baby. He will be okay. Now, today..."

I nod as he talks, but my mind keeps going back to Diesel. What's wrong with my crazy Viper? And how do I make it right? I never thought I would miss his brand of crazy, but as the morning drags on, I hate it. I want my crazy, batshit Diesel back, so I enlist Garrett's help. He sets up as I go to find him.

I find him lying on my bed, staring at the ceiling. Leaping onto it, I crawl up his body and press my face to his. "Your little bird is being naughty, want to help?" I grin.

He blinks, his arms wrapping around me. "Like you need my help," he mutters, but his voice is off, his blue eyes not as brilliant as usual.

"Uh-uh, come on, crazy pants, or I'll have all the fun, and then who will punish me?" I wink and grab his hands, yanking him up.

He sighs but lets me, and when he's on his feet, I throw myself at him. He has no choice but to catch me as I wrap my legs around his waist and bite his lip, making him groan. "Play with me," I murmur.

His hands clench my ass and hold me tighter. "Little Bird," he growls, and I've never been more relieved. Biting his lip until I taste blood, I yank myself away and tumble to the floor before I get up and run.

I hear him laugh as I race down the corridor. "I'm going to get you, Little Bird!" he calls. Once, that would have terrified me, but now it just sends desire spiking through me while I laugh.

I make it to the living room and leap onto Garrett's back, who's bent over and sorting the chair. He grunts, reaches out, and grabs my legs to keep me there as he straightens just as Diesel slides into the room with a smirk. "Hiding, my little bird?" he coos and prowls closer, making me laugh in Garrett's ear.

"Uh-uh, she bribed me into one of her plans." He shrugs and then laughs as he tosses me at Diesel. I yelp as I fly through the air, but Diesel catches me with a grunt, knocking the breath from my lungs for a moment as he wraps me in his arms.

"So what's your evil scheme, Little Bird?" Diesel grins down at me.

"We're going to tattoo Garrett." I smirk.

He laughs. "How the fuck did you manage to convince him of that?"

"Easy." I snort as I get down and wink at him. "I have a vagina he wants to fuck. You going to help me or what?"

"She also threatened to beat up my balls again," Garrett calls.

I nod seriously. "That too, this time with a frying pan, seeing as though I still don't have my bat."

Diesel laughs. "You gotta stop beating people up, Little Bird. It's easier to just kill them."

I wave that away. "Killing spree later, dick tattoos now."

"No fucking dicks," Garrett yells, and I turn around and narrow my eyes.

"I will do a dick if I want to do a dick," I snap.

He glares and goes toe-to-toe with me. "No. Fucking. Dicks. If I so much as see a goddamn dick on my skin, I will..."

"Will what?" I prompt sweetly, trailing my hand down his chest to his dick and cupping it. "Well?"

"Fair is fair," he growls. "I will draw one on your face."

"You wouldn't dare," I seethe.

"Try me." He smirks.

"I liked you better when you just grunted. Fine, no dicks, sit down," I demand, letting go of his hard cock and stomping around him while he laughs.

But then an idea hits me, and I beckon D closer as we debate what to draw. I lean in and whisper in his ear so Garrett can't hear. "We're going to sneak a dick in it, in the design space, he will never know."

"He's going to murder you, I'm in." He laughs.

"He could try." I grin as I snap on the gloves and wiggle my finger. "Probing time, baby, bend over."

Diesel does so, wiggling his ass at me and making Garrett groan. "Children," he calls, and we look over as I spank Diesel. "No ass play before tattoos."

"After?" I ask seriously, and he throws his hand over his eyes.

"This is a fucking terrible idea, and they call him crazy, she's just as bad," he mutters to himself.

I sit on the chair and roll closer, debating where to tattoo. He doesn't have much room. "What about your ass?" I murmur, looking him over again.

"You are not tattooing my ass," he snaps, and I huff.

"Where else? Your cock? I ain't touching your big ass toes." I shiver in disgust.

He looks down, searching for room. "Shit, baby, please not my ass."

I look him over again. "Ass or cock, your choice."

He narrows his eyes, and I grin.

"Bend over, boy."

"No vagina is worth this," he snarls, as he unfastens his jeans and yanks them off, leaving him in little black boxers, his thick thighs covered in tattoos as he desperately hunts for some room. He doesn't find any and stares at me with wide eyes. "Fuck."

Grinning, I twirl my finger at him, and he grudgingly turns and lies face down. I tug down his boxers and reveal his peachy fucking ass, but then I freeze. "Are you okay?" I ask lowly, remembering.

He stills but nods, then he turns his head until he can see me. "I'm okay, I can see you."

I nod and grin again. "Diesel, razor."

He hands me one, and I clean his cheek before I start to shave it. "Can't say I ever thought I would be shaving my boyfriend's ass," I mutter, making Diesel laugh.

Garrett groans. "I'm never going to live this down. No Barbie or some weird shit, baby, or I'll do something worse to you."

"Fine." I pout as I look at his pale skin. What to do? I grab the needle and, like he showed me earlier, line it up with his skin. I do a tiny heart and then glance up to see him breathing heavily, his eyes closed tight, so I roll back. "Done!"

He opens his eyes and looks at me. "Baby, it's okay."

Leaning down, I kiss him softly. "Turn over, I can do your chest," I suggest, knowing if we stop it will kill him.

He nods and pulls up his pants and flips over. I wipe the area just next to his belly where there is some space, some scarring too. "You sure?" I query softly.

He grits his teeth. "I got this, do it."

"Let me know if you need me to stop," I order, and he nods. Diesel slides in and helps me, and we start the tattoo. I hope he likes it. Honestly, I'm scared he won't, but it's too late now. I only do a small patch, and I'm nowhere near as good as Garrett, but I'm okay. I used to love drawing, so it's not too much harder. Okay, that's a lie, but still.

When it's done, Diesel adds detail and shading as I grip Garrett's shaking hand and lean into his face, grinning at him. "It's totally a dick, will you punish me again?" I grin, and he laughs.

"You fucking bet, baby." He keeps his eyes locked on me, and I babble, distracting him until Diesel is done.

369

"I'm so fucking proud of you," I murmur against his lips. He grips my head and groans.

"I trust you, baby."

It floors me.

I can't speak as he pulls away and checks out his new tattoo. I'm frozen in place. He trusts me. I hear his gasp.

"Holy fuck, Roxy."

I turn and stare at it through the mirror, worried he hates it. What started as a joke actually means something now. He trusted me enough to touch him... Fuck, what was I thinking? It's some of his skin peeled away where the scar is, and underneath it are moving snake coils, like his skin was flayed away to reveal the viper underneath. Diesel's details make it look so much better, and there's no dick. I figured Garrett was too brave for that shit.

He turns, his eyes wide and shocked. "Baby—"

I shrug. "She might have cut you up, Garrett, but underneath all that skin is a viper, a predator, stronger than ever."

He storms towards me, and I hold my breath, but he tugs me against him and kisses me hard, desperately, lovingly, before leaning his forehead against mine. "I fucking love it."

"Yeah?" I ask.

He nods, but then narrows his eyes teasingly. "What did you draw on my ass?"

I pull away and point at Diesel. "He did it!" I yell, before starting to run.

I hear him pulling down his pants. "Roxy!" he shouts while I laugh.

Garrett catches me, though, and scoops up my legs and holds me to his chest. "A heart? Really?"

"It's cute." I grin, and he snorts as he brings me back to the living room. "What trouble can we get up to now?" I question, wiggling my brows.

It turns out we could get into a lot of trouble. I seem to have started a prank war among the Vipers, but these criminals don't fill water balloons with flour or hide fake snakes somewhere. No, they play it for fucking real. It's crazy, and I can't help but laugh as we mess with Kenzo's car. We decided to spray paint it, which I'm betting is worth millions. I draw dicks on it, because why not, and so does Diesel. Garrett helps, and we all giggle like kids as we do it.

For Ryder, we head to his office which is below the apartment. Diesel suggests a grenade under his chair, but we luckily manage to veto that idea. I really want to ask where he got the grenade, but honestly, it doesn't even surprise me. Instead, we do something equally as crazy.

We buy a brothel in his name.

All communications are sent to his email, and within a few minutes, he calls us. "What the fuck is happening? Have I been hacked, or did you get bored and buy a fucking...what the fuck is this shit, Garrett? Slippery Hole? What the fuck?"

I can't stop laughing, and he must hear it. "Love, if you did this, why are they asking me if I want a test run? My preferences are...a fucking golden shower by men? Jesus, Roxxane." But I can hear the smile in his voice. "You want war, love? You got it." He hangs up.

Oh shit.

I'm so dead.

We all wait in the garage downstairs for Kenzo to get back, and he pulls in driving a car I've never seen before. It's black, a matte black, which is hot as hell. It's sleek, low riding, and a sports car, but honestly, I haven't got a clue what kind. Ryder pulls in behind him, and we leap out as they slide from their vehicles, all standing around Kenzo's car.

He comes towards us and then freezes when he sees the new paint. "You fucking didn't," he snarls.

"Us? We wouldn't dare." I bat my lashes as his eyes catch the graphic diagram of him and a stick figure.

"Darling, this car cost more than a goddamn city," he grouses. "And to think I was going to give you your own car..."

"Wait, what?" I gasp, rushing around, but he shakes his head, holding up the keys. "That sexy as fuck machine is mine?" Normally, I would be pissed at them for buying something so expensive, but...it really is fucking sexy.

"Was going to be, but I don't think you deserve it. Do you, brother?" he asks.

Ryder snorts. "I'm still getting emails about slip and slides of urine. I told her to behave, so I say no."

"But it's so pretty," I whisper, peeking around him and gaping at the car. "Is it really for me?"

He drops the keys into my hand, but I just stand there, and his face softens. "It's a car, darling, not a fucking kidney transplant. It's just money, go." He shoves me towards it, but fuck. How much did this cost? Not that I should be surprised, these idiots don't know the concept of moderation.

I step closer, but I don't want to even touch it. It's so goddamn pretty...what does it mean? Is this Ryder's way of giving me some freedom?

"Get in the fucking car, baby," Garrett orders, so I roll my eyes and open the door, slipping into the black bucket seats, which are leather and fucking comfy as shit. The dash is covered in gadgets and lights up with bright purple LED lights.

"It's yours," Ryder calls. "Why don't you take it for a spin?"

Diesel whoops and gets into the passenger seat, grinning over at me. "Gun it, Little Bird!"

"No crashing!" Ryder shouts, as I start the engine with a purr.

"Damn, I think I'm sexually attracted to this car," I mutter, as I shut my door and drive to the barrier, which lifts. I pull out onto the road, going slow and being extra careful, this car is too pretty to ding up, but Diesel snorts.

"Fucking gun it, Little Bird, life is too short to go slow."

So I do.

I laugh as we race through the city, and only on the way back do I realise I was out, I was free. Yes, I had Diesel, but I could have kicked him out. I didn't even think about it. What does that mean? I'm quiet as we drive back and pull into the garage where the others are still waiting. They are arguing, but it stops when we pull up and I slip out.

"I love it," I tell them, but I'm also confused, and Ryder must notice.

"Come on, love, I need your help with some more paperwork."

Looking back at the car, I nod and follow after him. I lose myself in the work, trying not to question why I didn't escape. That night, I feign being sick and go to my room, spending the night alone for the first time in a while, and none of them come to me.

Loneliness settles in, and I can barely sleep. I stare out of the window, wondering what I have become.

Do I want to stay?

I don't know, I really don't, and that scares me. It's so easy to get lost in their lives, but I don't want to lose myself. Not again. I have to be me, and they encourage that, especially Diesel, but...but what if I can't be myself here?

Fuck knows I don't blend with their rich friends, but does that matter?

When the sun comes up, I have no more answers than when it set. I'm confused and feeling like shit. They do all these nice things for me, they buy shit for me and give me everything I could ever want.

But is it enough?

What if what I need can't be bought?

But has to be given?

CHAPTER
THIRTY-SEVEN

KENZO

Ｎone of us slept.

Diesel stormed off after the decision was made, fuck knows what to do, but I know there will be a bloody path through the city, and I don't know if he will come back. Garrett leaves as well, to fight, no doubt. For someone who wanted her gone since the moment she arrived, he was reluctant, angry even, at the mention of letting her go.

Because he loves her like I do.

But I love her enough to let her go. To give her what she needs. I thought the car might help, but when she got back, I could see the truth in her eyes. It will never be enough. We will never be enough, not without her freedom.

I heard her the other night with Ryder, and he hasn't been the same since, so when he called the meeting after she slipped off to bed, it wasn't a surprise. I was ready. They call me a romantic, soft, and maybe I am, but Ryder? He's logical, and it's the only reason I think the others listened.

Roxy is free from us.

We are letting her go.

And I'm praying to whoever the fuck listens she'll come back because, for once in my life, I'm happy. I have everything I need, something money could never buy—someone to walk this life with. It just so happens that someone is also for my brothers as well, which makes sense. No one would ever come between us.

The same brilliant, strong, fierce, angry, smart, and sexy woman.

She's our heart. Our softness. Our reason, in such a short amount of time. But for her? We are her captors.

I wait for her to wake up, my heart in my throat and my stomach in knots. Will she be happy? Sad? Fuck. Ryder sits with me. Two brothers, side by side, ready to face another problem together. It feels like when we were kids, waiting to confront our father, waiting for the hurt to come. Ryder retreats into that ice like always, but I can't. I feel it all.

Pain.

It's in every breath I take. If she leaves, what will become of us? Diesel and Garrett have already left. If she isn't here, will they come back?

We can go on without her, we will survive, like always, but we are tamed snakes now, and without her, it will all be for nothing.

I fell in love with her slowly. The first time she smiled at me. The first time I made her laugh, our first kiss, our first time together. When she fell asleep in my arms and held my hand at my mother's grave. When she confided in me, trusted me. When she stopped flinching, when she started reaching for me. Trusted me.

I fell a little more each time until, before I knew it, I was completely in love with her. I'm hers, but she's not mine.

Not fully. Her heart still reaches out to the city. To her old life. To her freedom beyond these walls. Nothing will replace that, no gift or love. She needs to be free.

And I need her to not hate me.

I couldn't bear it.

I couldn't stand hate in those eyes once again. Love means pain, I know that, but this pain? It might just wreck me this time. I survived loss before with my mother, but this feels so much worse.

She's awake early. I hear her moving around, and I can't help but smile. She's like us, always ready to face the day, dressed and made up, only letting her guard down around us. Ryder is frozen next to me, but I see his hands curled into fists under the table, so I do something I haven't done since we were kids—I reach over and grip one. "Whatever happens, you will never lose me," I tell him without looking. It's something I should have said a long time ago. I know his fears. That he thinks he will become our father. "You will never be him. This is the right thing to do, brother."

"I know, but it feels so wrong," he whispers brokenly.

"I know," I whisper back, throat clogged. "But her life is not ours to take. It never was. She was never a debt, never a business deal, she was always our destiny, but sometimes it comes at the wrong time."

"What do we do now?" he queries, and I turn my head to meet his lost eyes. In his suit and those dark eyes, I see the kid he once was, the one who lost his mum too young, who lost his innocence at the hands of a cruel father. The man who always knows what to do is lost right now, same as me. Our perfect life and plan are broken because of one woman.

His greatest fear realised.

"We keep living, like always. One breath after another. Let me protect you this time, brother, let me do this," I tell him, being the strong one for once. He needs it. He needs to lean on people, even if he doesn't know it. Roxy taught me that.

I hear her door open, and her feet coming our way. He clenches my hand tightly and cools his expression, and we both turn to see her as she enters. There are bags under her eyes, and she's tired. She probably didn't sleep either. She glances between us, and Ryder stands.

"I won't repeat my father's life, love," Ryder snarls. "I couldn't bear you hating me, everyone else? Fine, but not you. Not ever."

Then he leaves, letting me deal with it like I said I would. He's not running away, he's not hiding, he's learning that sometimes it's okay to let others help.

"Ry?" she calls, as he storms upstairs, but he freezes, his hand on the bannister.

"I love you with all the broken, blood-stained pieces of me," he murmurs, and then he's gone. She gasps, stumbling back, and looks at me in shock.

I stand and step towards her, but I can't close the distance between us. If I do, I might hold her and never let her go. I need Ryder's cool confidence now, and I need Garrett's strength and Diesel's conviction. I need them all, and they are here, all of them, in my heart. With her.

"Roxy, I need you to listen for once and keep that pretty mouth of yours shut until I'm done. You're the love of my life, darling. Someone I didn't even know I was searching for all these years. But you're here, and I love you more than words, which is why I'm giving you these keys. I know you can never love me the way I love you when you're not free. I'm hoping, I'm fucking hoping, that even though you can leave, that you're free, and I promise you are. We won't chase you, we won't hunt you. You are truly free...I'm hoping that you will still want to stay. With us. Love us, Roxy. I know I'm not asking for something easy or simple, I'm asking for everything, but I can't not. You're our heart, Rox, our living, beating heart. The piece we were missing from our family. You turned our world upside down. We aren't good men, we aren't soft or loving, we are hard and our hands are stained with blood. But I swear, I swear if you stay, you will never want for anything, and no one will ever hurt you again...well, apart from us."

I smirk, and tears fill her eyes as she stares at me, speechless.

"We will love you effortlessly, always, even when it's hard or hurts, when we are hateful and dark, even when we scare everyone else but you." I step closer and pass her the keys to her car. "So I'm here, begging you not to leave, even though you can. I will lose all sense of dignity and pride for you. I'll do what they can't." I swallow, the words hard as I look into those eyes I know better than my own. "Stay, be ours. Keep Ryder sane, melt that ice and give him the love he never had but deserved. Love Garrett, even though he struggles to love himself. Love Diesel, even though it might kill you...and love me, even though I don't deserve it. Be my greatest win."

She blinks and glances away for a second, so I turn her to face me, my hand lingering on her cheek.

"I have no gifts, no jewels or expensive clothes or...or anything to offer. Just me and my heart." I smash my fist into my chest. "The one my father tried to carve out of me. It's broken, damaged, and dark like the rest of us, but it's yours. Along with my gun and my loyalty. Forever. Stay, darling, please stay."

She swallows, not letting those tears fall, she's too strong, our girl. "I'm really free?" she asks.

I nod. "Free, you can go back to your life, if that's what you want."

She stares wordlessly into my eyes. My heart is slamming against my chest so loudly, she must hear it. My legs feel weak, my stomach torn, and when she steps back, letting my hand drop from her face, it all breaks.

My chest cracks open, my stomach drops, and my legs nearly buckle. I watch her silently turn and run to the door. She rips it open, hesitates, and for a moment, I have hope, hope that she will stay, but then she's gone, the doorframe empty.

I fall to my knees, my heart splintering into a million pieces as I watch the empty space where she stood. My home is cold and empty. I'm alone.

And I just had my heart broken.

She left.

She left us.

A noise has my head jerking up to the balcony. I see Ryder's retreating form, and then hear his door slam. She broke more than one heart today, but we will keep our promise.

Her freedom.

But-but what if I can't?

Because as the seconds tick by, it gets harder and harder to breathe the farther I know she gets away from us. What if, without her, there is no us?

What if I can't let her go?

What if I'm not strong enough?

What if I'm too much of a Viper to release our prey?

CHAPTER
THIRTY-EIGHT

ROXY

My heart is hammering and my lungs ache, but I outrun it. I grip the keys so hard, they cut into my hand, even that pain doesn't register. It doesn't compete with the sick feeling in my stomach or my screaming heart.

He begged.

He laid it all out for me and asked me to stay.

And I left.

I run faster, throwing myself down the stairs until I reach the garage. I put my hand on the scanner and it flashes green, letting me through. With hurried steps, I reach my car and throw myself into the driver's seat, but with nowhere else to run to, it all hits me.

The pain in his voice. The love in his eyes. The desperation I saw in the set of his shoulders. They have given me everything I ever wanted since they first walked into my bar...but what if what I want has changed? What if this snake has shed her skin and became something new?

No, don't let them get to you.

This is what you wanted, I remind myself. I grip the wheel and turn on the engine. I'm free. I'm not theirs anymore.

But sitting in the car, I can't move. My old life is filled with ghosts, an empty, lonely shell. Do I really want to go back to that? Is there anything to even go back to?

The Vipers aren't a walk away situation, they are for life. If I choose them, I'm choosing them forever and everything their life entails.

Because somewhere along the way, 'I hate you' became our 'I love yous.'

I do, I hate them so much, it scares me. That's really why I'm walking away, but I can't let fear hold me back. Not with so much on the line. Not with four hearts. It's simple. I want them, they want me.

Freedom, family, work, none of it matters. Only them.

The Vipers.

My Vipers.

I'm their girl.

So why am I running? Because I'm scared, that's why. Scared how much I want them, how much they have consumed me. How right I feel in their arms, in their life. The cold, controlling alpha. The damaged enforcer with a heart of gold. The romantic, charming gambler. The insane killer with an obsessive heart.

What does that make me?

Their captive?

No, not anymore. It makes me theirs, a Viper. It makes this home.

As soon as I realise it, I know. I know I didn't want to leave, haven't for a long time. That fight and hate was aimed at myself, because I knew if I didn't, if I gave in, I would have seen the truth all along. From the first kiss, wink, and smile. I was theirs.

But you can't take and not give.

They took me, but they gave me themselves.

And I just ruined that. I refuse to be like Ryder and Kenzo's parents. I refuse to be the bitch who ruined Garrett. I refuse to be the mother who never loved Diesel. I refuse to repeat the past.

This is our future, they are my future. I turn off the engine, and when it doesn't feel wrong, I know this is the right decision. I'm staying with them. With their lifestyle and all that includes—enemies, blood, riches, parties, snakes, and liars. All of it. Slipping from the car, heart hammering, I turn to run back to them and freeze when I spot Kenzo there.

He's standing behind the car, his eyes filled with tears, his chest heaving, body shaking, like me. Both of us are fighting, but what I told Garrett is true, I'm done fighting.

He steps closer, and this time I don't retreat. "I lied," he croaks. "I will follow you always. I'll hunt you across this world. Even if you hate me, us, for it. I will drag you back kicking and screaming. Hit me, slap me, fight me. I don't care, the pain is worth it to have you with me, darling. I love you too much to let you go. I'm too fucking selfish to let the best thing to ever happen to us walk away. You're ours."

I rush to him, and he meets me halfway, lifting me instantly. Our lips meet here in the parking garage. Pulling back, he grips my hair harshly, his eyes sharp and cruel. "Don't you ever fucking walk away from me again, darling."

"Don't fucking let me," I snap, and slap him as I smirk.

He groans, his head jerking back around, and he kisses me hard. He starts walking backwards to the elevator, but stops and slams me into the concrete wall, making me gasp at the pain. His eyes are brutal, and I fucking love it. "You aren't getting away from us now, Roxy."

"Good." I smirk. "Is that a promise?"

He grunts when we hear the garage open, and I look over his shoulder to see Garrett storming in on his bike. He rips off his helmet, and when he sees me, he prowls over, his eyes angry and body taut with anger. He gets right up to us, uncaring about the position we're in. "You're not fucking leaving."

"Thought you hated me," I tease.

"I do," he snarls, his hand wrapping around my throat as he gets in my face, unbothered about Kenzo. "But you don't get to leave."

"I hate you," I snap, and he smirks.

"I hate you too, baby."

Kenzo pulls me away. "Upstairs, now," he demands, and rushes us into the elevator. Garrett stabs his finger on the button, his dark eyes on me, and I know whatever they're planning will hurt. In the best fucking way.

He watches me the entire ride up, and when the doors open, a wild-looking Diesel is there. He stops when he sees me, his eyes narrowing. "Little Bird, Little Bird, trying to escape?"

"Nah, just wanted to be punished." I grin.

He smirks, his eyes running across me hungrily. "That can be arranged."

Kenzo refuses to let me go as we leave the elevator, but Diesel manages to get close. "You thought I would let you leave? I told you, you're mine, they would have to kill me to stop me from coming after you."

I melt at that. Once, it would have scared me. The first time I saw him, I thought him mad, he still is—fucking batshit. But he's my batshit. And when he whispers threatening, dirty things like that, I can't help but wiggle, wanting more.

Guess I'm crazy too.

I have to be to love four Vipers.

The door is still open, and Kenzo storms through it, dropping me to my feet in the living room and standing in front of me, arms crossed and angry. "Strip. Now."

"What, no dice this time?" I taunt, even as my pussy clenches at the order. Where's Ryder?

Diesel prowls around me, and Garrett watches me from the sofa, legs spread and eyes hungry. But they are still angry, angry that I almost left. I am too. The best way to solve that? Fuck it out.

"Better strip, Little Bird," Diesel growls.

So, rolling my eyes, I rip off my crop top, and kick off my boots and shorts until I stand bare before them. I feel confident in my skin, so I don't bother hiding. I run my hand down the valley of my breasts, feeling powerful when three sets of eyes watch the movement and masculine groans fill the room.

Yes, the Vipers might bite.

But I do too.

And they are mine.

"What's—" Ryder snarls, and I look up to see him frozen at the top of the floating stairs. "Roxxane?"

I wink up at him. "Coming to play?" I'm nervous, but I try not to show it. I'm betting he knows I left, but I'm back. Does he still want me?

He watches me, noting every fucking inch of skin, every movement, every flicker of my eyes, like always. Analysing it, using it like a weapon. "It depends, love, plan on leaving again?" he snaps cruelly.

"It depends, *love*, plan on giving me some orgasms?" I mock.

His eyes narrow, and his fists clench as he strolls down the stairs, not stopping until he stands before me, the others closing in behind him. Me versus four angry, horny Vipers. Seems like fair odds, in fact, they could probably do with more men.

He grips my chin hard, his eyes cruel and mean. Icy. "Don't mock me, love. Just because you think you can handle us doesn't mean you can. So fucking prove it."

He's testing me, pushing to see if he can keep me away, always trying to protect their hearts. Well, fuck that. "Fine," I retort, even in the face of his dark malice. In his demons.

I won't say he will never hurt me. He might. He might even kill me one day, but his love is fucking worth it. They are fucking worth it. I can't say it's too much of a hardship to prove it. So I drop to my knees like a good little girl and flick open his trousers, shoving my hand inside. "Are you all going to stand there and watch, or get in on the action?"

They hesitate for a moment, locking my eyes on Ryder, I lick his hard cock, reminding him how good we were together. He thinks I can't handle them? I'll fuck them all and prove him wrong. They are my family, my Vipers, and you don't love a Viper without loving the pain.

He grips the nape of my neck and yanks me away, throwing me backwards. I tumble onto my back, panting, a smirk curving my lips when I see he isn't as unmoved as he would like to pretend. His eyes narrow dangerously. "Diesel, remind Roxxane whom she belongs to."

"Oh, Roxxane, I'm in trouble," I mock, as Diesel comes up behind me. He yanks my head back and presses a knife to my throat before running it down the valley of my breasts, cutting away my bra and dragging it down to my belly button, the scratch of the blade making me moan.

Kenzo gets to his knees and kisses up my thigh, so at odds with Diesel's harsh, mean hands. His mouth reaches my pussy and closes over it through my knickers, tasting my wetness.

Groaning, I arch up into him and the blade, cutting myself. Blood trickles from my tiny cut down my belly, making Diesel grunt behind me, his hand tightening on my hair. "Dirty little bird."

"Orgasms," I demand breathlessly, pushing my pussy into Kenzo's mouth.

Diesel laughs. "Let me," he murmurs to Kenzo, as he drags the blade lower and, with one smooth, expert flick, slides away the lace to bare me to them all. Eyes open, chest heaving, I glance up at Ryder and Garrett.

Ryder is icy still, his eyes locked on me, watching my every reaction. Garrett's hands are balled into fists as he paces, his eyes focused on me too, hungry and angry at the same time.

"Don't let her come yet," Ryder orders, as he sits down on the sofa and watches us. Fucking asshole.

I narrow my eyes on him, and he smirks like he knows my thoughts. "Garrett, do you think if Diesel held her head with his cock in her mouth, and Kenzo restrained her hands, you could fuck her pussy?"

Garrett looks at me seriously, and I freeze, even as Diesel runs the knife up and around one of my nipples, and Kenzo's tongue laps at my pussy with teasing little strokes like I'm his favourite dessert, making me whimper and want more.

"Yes." He nods.

"Good. Brother, get her nice and wet for him, then you get her hands until he's done," he commands. The fucking ass is trying to control everything, like normal. I'll let him for now, because it will help Garrett, but after? All bets are off.

Kenzo does as he's told, those eyes rolling up to meet mine as he seals his lips around my clit and sucks, his fingers sliding into my wet heat. Diesel presses the cold, steel blade to my oversensitive nipple, keeping it there as I rock into Kenzo's mouth.

It doesn't take long for me to build up to my release, but like the fuckers they are, just as I'm about to come, Kenzo pulls away. Groaning, I close my eyes, swearing until my head is turned and a cock is shoved in my mouth. I choke for a second, a piercing dragging along my tongue as my eyes flicker open to meet Diesel's gaze. Kenzo binds my hands, and two rough palms trace up my thighs and push them farther open. I want to turn to look, but I can't, Diesel is controlling my head, and he isn't going easy. He fucks my mouth hard, punishing me for leaving. Tears fall from my eyes at the force, my throat constricting as I try to breathe through my nose and the panic. Only when I relax do I feel Garrett line up at my pussy.

He rubs his huge cock along my wetness before slamming inside me, making me scream and choke around Diesel's cock, who, in punishment, slices across my breast with the knife. Blood wells, I feel it, and the sudden pain has me clenching around Garrett, making him groan as he fights my tight pussy.

"Fuck, baby," he groans, his hands clasping my thighs harder as he drags me farther down, my body stretching between them as they take their punishments out on me.

Garrett fucks me hard and fast, dirty and raw. His cock drags along those nerves that have me groaning around Diesel's cock. His blue eyes are locked on me crazily as he presses his finger to the wound on my breast and flicks and rips at the edges, the pain mixing with pleasure. "Little dirty bird," he groans, his cocking jerking in my mouth as he pulls his finger away to show me my blood on his hand. He pulls his cock from my mouth, and I pant as I watch him wrap his bloody hand around it, stroking along his wet length with his eyes still locked on me. Then, he presses the tip to my lips. "Suck me down, dirty bird, and taste yourself on me. See how prettily you bleed for my blade. If the others weren't here, I can't guarantee you would survive me with the way I'm feeling today," he growls.

Garrett catches my attention, flicking my clit until I scream, my mouth opening, and Diesel thrusts inside. The taste of copper and man explodes in my mouth as I groan and suck him harder.

"Don't let her come," Ryder orders, and I tremble from the force growing inside me. "You don't get a reward for walking away, Roxxane. You will take their cocks and cum like a good girl, and only when we're finished will we decide if you get a release or not."

Diesel smirks down at me, rolling his hips and thrusting into my mouth until I just have to hold on. Garrett pounds into me, so big it's on the edge of pain. I feel his nails digging into my skin, almost cutting. "Fuck, baby," he growls. I feel his hips stutter, and then he groans, bursting inside me before pulling out. That bastard!

Diesel laughs and grabs my head harder, slamming me onto his cock and pushing right down my throat until his eyes close and, with a groan, he comes too. His abs clench as he pants, then he pulls away and falls back with a satisfied smile on his face.

"You fucking assholes," I rasp, my voice raw as I swallow and lick my lips. Kenzo chuckles and releases my hands. My body aches, and my pussy clenches again and again, so close to coming yet so far away.

They've had their fun, now it's my turn.

I sit up, not even wincing when I feel Garrett's cum slipping from me. I turn my head and meet Ryder's gaze. He's in control here, but he forgets I don't take orders well.

"You don't get to control everything, Ry," I murmur, as I crawl towards him. He watches me approach, his lips parting and eyes melting. I crawl up his legs and slide onto his lap, grabbing his cock and lining up before dropping down on him. He groans, grabbing my hips to still me, to control my movements, but I won't let him. I want to come, I want to come on his cock, and I take what I want. I rock, lifting and dropping, his brother's cum helping me. It's a wild, uncontrolled ride until he swears and finally lets go.

Kenzo moves closer, and I turn my head, opening my mouth to him. He slips inside, his brother buried in my pussy and his other two brothers spent and watching.

I'm so goddamn close to coming that when Ryder leans forward and sucks my nipple into his mouth and I grind down on his cock, I come with a scream around his brother's cock. They don't let me pull away though, Ryder's hands tighten and move me harder, fucking me now. Kenzo slams in and out of my mouth, their eyes on me as they take what they want. I shake and tremble between them, barely over my release even as another builds.

"Fucking hell, Little Bird, you should see yourself. A cock in your mouth and one in your pussy, blood on you, a fucking masterpiece," Diesel calls from behind me, and my eyes shut at the words as I clench around Ryder.

"Eyes open, love," Ryder snaps. "You will watch us fuck you and fill you with our cum. Every goddamn time you try to get away from us, we'll remind you exactly whom you belong to. This body?" He groans. "Is ours. This pussy? Ours. Never fucking forget that."

Kenzo is panting, his eyes wild as he stares at me. "Darling —fuck."

I reach up and roll Kenzo's balls in my hand while I ride Ryder's cock. Kenzo swears, his eyes closing as if in pain. "I'm so fucking close, Rox. God, stop—"

But I bloody won't.

I almost lost this.

Lost them.

Because of pride and fear.

I suck him harder and squeeze his balls. He yells and jerks, thrusting into my mouth before suddenly pulling out, his hand wrapping around his cock as he watches me. My mouth is sore, my lips swollen, and he glares at me. "We'll all mark you," he snarls, and pumps his cock twice more before coming, his cum spraying across my breasts. He groans, and when his eyes open again, he sees his cum on me and he grunts. "Fuck, that's hot."

Running my finger through the mess, I suck my finger into my mouth as I turn and look into Ryder's eyes. He was letting me finish with his brother before all my attention was brought back to him. Then, he reminds me why I love his punishments, his pain and fire.

Why I love him.

He flips me, bending me over the sofa, my head dangling as he gets to his knees behind me and slams into my pussy. One hand tangles in my hair and yanks my head back as he bites my neck, his cock hard and thick, dragging along those nerves that have me almost screaming and my eyes crossing from the pleasure.

"Don't you ever fucking leave us again," he demands, voice wild.

"Never," I pant, pushing back to meet his thrusts.

"Say it again," he orders, as he pounds into me.

"Never, never, never," I chant, as he controls my body. I can feel him losing his restraint as he pushes his finger into my ass, sending me tumbling over that edge. I come with a scream. I can barely feel my body, my eyes darkening, and when I come to, I'm leaning into the sofa with his weight on me and a wetness between my thighs that tells me he came.

He licks my neck again. "We are nowhere near done. When the sun comes up, you won't even be able to walk after what we have planned for you. For daring to leave. We are Vipers, love. We bite, and we never stop hunting."

He slips from my pussy, and I tumble to the sofa, boneless and sticky but beyond satisfied. My pussy aches, but like he promised, he isn't done with me.

Kenzo cleans my pussy with soft strokes of a cloth before he tosses it away and his fingers take over, stroking my raw pussy. I try to protest, but he's slow and gentle, and before I know it, I'm tilting into his fingers again.

He slips two inside me and strokes until I'm panting and rolling my hips up, only then does he drag my legs to the end of the sofa and bury his face there. Licking and lapping me, soothing me with his tongue.

"How does she taste, brother?" Ryder murmurs, and I turn my head to see him watching us. They all are, and they are all hard again. Dear God.

Garrett groans, licking his lips as he steps closer, making me pant harder. "Like fucking heaven," Kenzo groans, his hands grabbing me greedily as he consumes me, faster and faster.

"Kenzo," I whimper, arching up when Diesel's blade suddenly nicks my skin, making me jerk and turn my head to see him behind the sofa, leaning over to touch me.

"She moans so sweetly, doesn't she?" Diesel laughs. "You should hear her scream as you carve her skin."

My eyes close at that, I can't take it, and when Diesel squeezes my throat, cutting off my air supply, and Kenzo curls his tongue around my piercing, I come with a scream, all of them watching me as I writhe in pleasure.

"I want her ass," Diesel tells the others, and Kenzo kisses each thigh and rolls me over. I can't even talk, never mind argue, and when I feel Diesel's rough, calloused hands stroking up my thighs, I whimper, burying my head in the sofa.

Oh God, I can't.

"D," I whisper, but he hears me, and his teeth suddenly dig into my thigh, making me scream.

"Ours," he snaps. "I'll have you however I fucking want, Little Bird. It will hurt, and you will love it all."

Torture.

This is him torturing me tonight for daring to leave him. They all are, but when it comes with some of the best orgasms of my life, how can I protest? So even though I'm exhausted, my body tired and sated, I don't object when he drags my ass into the air.

"I love you, Little Bird. You're the gasoline to my fire. I never would have let you go, and the others wouldn't have either. They are idiots if they thought they could," he murmurs, as he pulls apart my cheeks and licks down my ass. "Ready for round two?"

Oh shit.

CHAPTER THIRTY-NINE

RYDER

R oxy turns up for breakfast with a big yawn. The shirt she's wearing is see-through, and she has no knickers or a bra on. I almost drop my cup, I'm staring that hard. She smirks when she catches me and winks before plopping into her seat and putting her legs on my lap. Rolling my eyes, I cup her toes as I go back to reading the updates on my phone.

She slept for almost a day after our reunion, as Diesel is calling it. Her body is still sore, so I don't push it, even though I want to bend her over the table and fuck her. We put her through hell that night, her blood covering the living room, she paid her penance with orgasms for trying to leave us. And she loved every goddamn minute, even though, when we were finally done with her and held her as she fell asleep, she said she hated us. She's such a goddamn liar.

"Diesel, care to explain why we now have another yacht?" I ask, looking up to see him leaning back with a smirk while Garrett groans.

"I told you he would find out, D." He laughs.

D shrugs. "Well, you see, I was walking along, minding my own

393

business, when I saw a yacht called Roxy. Now, of course no one other than us could own a boat named after our girl, so I offered them lots of money to buy it." He shrugs as Roxy laughs, cupping the mug of coffee Kenzo hands her.

"You're forgetting the part where he said no, so you beat the shit out of him with a frying pan and told him the boat was yours now and to call you Captain Crazy," Garrett adds as he eats.

It's silent for a moment, then we all roar with laughter as Diesel grins. He glances over at Roxy and winks. "You can just call me crazy, Little Bird."

"We already have a yacht." I sigh when I can control my laughter.

"Well, now we have two, we can race them." Diesel laughs, flipping his lighter open and shut.

I'm about to try and explain why we won't be doing that when my phone rings, interrupting me. Answering it, I massage Roxxane's cold toes, but freeze at the words that come down the line.

"There's been an explosion."

I sit up, my body rigid, as all hints of anything but the Viper disappear. "Where?"

"The old house." Tony sighs.

"Any hurt or dead?"

I can feel the others staring, so I hold up my finger to tell them to wait.

"No, it was empty. Fire and police are here, but we know them, so they are going to say it's a gas explosion and will be gone soon."

"Thanks, Tony, keep me updated," I snarl.

"Oh, and boss? We found motorbike tracks leading onto the dirt road behind the house, four of them." He hangs up.

Bikes.

Triad.

Those fucking idiots. I'm going to kill them for this. This isn't just a sly dig at our power, this is an all-out act of war. We could have dismissed the assassination attempt as youthful enthusiasm and still got them in line, but this?

394

This marks their deaths.

Slamming the phone down, I look to the others who are ready, their bodies vibrating with tension, knowing something has happened. "They blew up the old house."

"Triad," Garrett growls, his hands clenched into fists, and I incline my head.

"They found bike tracks out back. Police and fire will rule it as a gas explosion." I grind my teeth, and I can feel Roxy frowning at us.

"The old house?" she asks, but I'm too infuriated to answer, too busy counting mentally to even speak. To not explode and rain down fucking hell across this city that dares cross us.

"Our father's house. We lived there after his death for a while as we built this," Kenzo tells her, but even his voice is tight.

To hit that house, our house, they are trying to provoke a reaction. If we don't retaliate, we'll be seen as weak, like we are scared of them, which we aren't. Their family might have used to run this town, but now they are nothing but relics.

Relics can be forgotten.

"What's our move?" Kenzo questions. No one is eating now.

"We get them back, of fucking course, and we kill them all," Diesel snarls, stabbing his knife into the table, his face twisted in anger.

"No, not yet. We show them we can easily get to them. We prove our power, we make them fear us like everyone else. Then, we destroy them," I outline, as I calmly put my teacup down and straighten my suit.

"I'll get the rocket launcher," Diesel adds.

"No, they own a restaurant, don't they? Their parents ran it for many years and lived above it, get me the address. Also, get me the address of all three brothers. It's a Sunday, so they will be at home having a family day." I start to grin, and Kenzo mirrors it.

"I'll make the calls. I like where you are going with this, big brother."

Picking up my own phone, I stand. "I want police at all three doors, arrest them on any charges, show them up, let them know it's from us, and shut down that restaurant, repossess it, it's ours now."

"What are you going to do?" Roxy inquires curiously, not seeming upset in any way.

"I'm going to check the papers for all of their family members and employees. Any who are here illegally will be deported immediately. We are going to take them down, this is war."

She stands then. "Let me help."

The others are rushing off on their phones, but I hold my call and stare at her. "You want to help?"

She nods, a sly grin covering her lips. "You think you're the only one who can? I have an idea. Do you trust me?"

I stare at her, and she steps closer. "Ryder, do you trust me?"

The words echo around me as I nod my head in affirmation. She grins wider than before, kissing my cheek. "Good, because shit is about to get real."

She strolls away while I stare at her retreating form, wondering if I should be more worried about her than Diesel and his launcher, but I don't have long to debate. If I want this done today, I need to make calls and fast.

By the time I'm off the phone, it's hours later, and Roxy comes back looking way too pleased with herself with Garrett on her heels. "It is all done, now we sit back and watch."

"And what did you do, love?" I ask, calmer now.

She drops into my lap, smirking at me, and leans in. "Watch and learn, baby." She kisses me and stands again, whistling as she heads to the living room and flicks on the TV to the news.

I follow after her, leaning against the back of the sofa, and watch above her head as it mentions raids in the city—no doubt on their homes and restaurant, which makes me smirk—but then it flips to a new news report, and my mouth drops open.

It's focused on their import business, the Triad's. "Turn it up," I demand, and the TV booms through the room, making Diesel and Kenzo appear.

The news reporter explains a whistle-blower has verified the business has been stealing from the city and importing drugs, with informants, which they call local dealers, confirming they are their suppliers.

I turn off the TV and glance over at Roxy, who's examining her nails with a grin on her face. "Love…"

"How the bloody hell did you do that?" Kenzo gawks. He looks at me in shock. "Did you know?"

I shake my head, and Roxy turns and stares at us. "You aren't the only ones with friends. The one who reported their business? He comes in all the time to complain about his wife, loves bourbon, and owed me a favour." She shrugs. "I did promise him a job here though, seeing as though he's lost his now. It probably won't stick for long, but it will shut them down for a while and drag their name through the mud."

"The dealers?" I ask with a frown, while Diesel laughs maniacally.

"Oh, Wheels and Timmy? Yeah, good boys, lived with them for a while on the streets. They had cops breathing down their necks anyway, so this helped throw them off and to their suppliers." She wiggles her brows. "I promised they wouldn't be arrested, and if they did, we would get them out. Problem?"

I just stare at her, unsure what to say.

"Holy shit, darling, that's fucking incredible. I swear I'm way too goddamn hard right now." Kenzo laughs.

Garrett even grins. "Baby, you are definitely one of us, you cruel bitch."

She winks at him as Diesel swoops in and kisses her hard. "Told you, Viper through and through."

They all look at me as I just stare at her, and she tilts her head with a grin. "Your plan was better, but attacking from every angle will keep them running and give you time to take them down." She shrugs.

"Love." I shake my head and crook my finger at her. She slides closer, and I cup her chin, her eyes blown a little with desire, those lips parting. "You're a genius," I murmur, as I lean down and brush her hair behind her ear. "Keep doing things like this, and we might start to think you don't hate us at all, that you even like us," I tease.

She snorts and pulls from my grip, throwing her hair over her shoulder. "Don't get cocky, I was bored and this was fun, that's all. I still hate you."

I smirk at her, running my eyes down her body. "Is that right? Still sticking to that old lie?"

Diesel sidles up behind her, smirking now too. "Little Bird, I don't think you hate us at all."

She narrows her eyes and then spins, smashing her knee into his junk. He falls to the floor laughing, even as he winces and covers his cock. The idiot loves it. She grabs his hair and tugs his head up, staring down at him like a fucking queen. "Don't go annoying me, we both know that will only end up with you bleeding again."

She looks over at us then, not afraid even in the least, hoping we will push her, get her all riled up. "Anyone else want a reminder?" She zones in on Garrett. "Want to go for round two?"

He grins at her. "You couldn't handle me, baby. Remember what happened the first time?"

"When you had to ice your cock?" she retorts sweetly, and he booms out a laugh.

My phone rings, and I answer it as she threatens Kenzo next, a smile on my lips. "It's done. It won't hold for long, but it's long enough to send a message. You were right about those papers though. We're on our way to secure ten employees and five family members."

"Good." I hang up and look back at her. "Stop teasing them, love, we have work to do."

She strides past Kenzo, who leans in. "You love us, admit it."

She socks him right in the face, and he falls back to the chair, laughing even as blood pours from his nose. Shaking out her hand, she storms up to me, her eyes alight. "If I had my fucking gun..."

"Yes, well, that's why you don't get weapons, you have a tendency to use them." I smirk as I wrap an arm around her. "Come on, you're coming with me to a meeting. We'll give those poor bastards a break from you beating them up."

She huffs but lets me lead her away, and when we get to the door, I hear Diesel declare, "I'm going to marry that woman."

She struggles in my arms. "Let me stab the bastard—"

Laughing, I toss her over my shoulder. "Behave, or I'll let him play with you. God knows he might even marry you without telling you."

She freezes then. "Fucking animals. Stupid motherfucking snakes." I smack her ass, and she yelps.

"Unless you want me to fuck you in the middle of a board meeting, enough with the language, brat."

When we're in the elevator, I drop her to her feet, and she glares at me—such a fucking fighter, our girl. Doesn't mean I've forgiven her for walking out, but it's a start. "What's the meeting?" She looks down at the see-through shirt then and at me.

"With the board. We are expanding. It's boring stuff now that we have a few days to deal with the Triad and put a solid plan in effect, but we still have to run our everyday business. Prove their attack didn't affect us." I shrug.

"And I'm coming half naked why?" She sighs, crossing her arms. I don't tell her it just presses her nipples tighter to the material and makes my mouth water.

"Because I hate them and get bored. With you there, I might enjoy it."

"Ryder, you can see my vagina," she points out.

Running my eyes down her form, I smirk. "Can you? What a shame, might rouse the old bastards enough to get stuff done."

"Uh-huh, or give them a heart attack?"

Leaning closer, I cage her in. "Own it, love, you do everything else. If you're good, I might even let you beat Diesel up later."

"Like you could stop me. We both know that crazy bastard will be waiting." She smirks but tosses her hair over her shoulder before eying me. "Fine, give me your jacket."

I do as I'm told and she slips it on, rolling back the too long arms. She doesn't bother buttoning it, but it covers her chest enough that you can't see her breasts, to my disappointment, and she looks some-what dressed. What a shame.

"I am telling you, no one will notice." I roll my shoulders back as we stop.

"Yeah, how?" she scoffs.

I smirk and wrap my arm around her shoulders as it opens onto the top floor we use for meetings. There are a few staff members up here, but as soon as we exit the elevator, they quickly look away. "Because they wouldn't dare look at you," I murmur, as I stride to the conference room. They are all there, ten men and three women, sitting around the table waiting for me. I stroll in and take the seat at the head of the room. Roxy drags a chair close and sits next to me, her legs going up and onto the table, bare.

I grab the file and flip through it. "Anyone who even so much as looks at Roxxane will be fired on the spot," I warn casually. I hear uncomfortable shifting and a quick cough, but when I look up all eyes are very purposely locked on me. "Begin."

"Sir, our sales have increased over the last quarter, and since our profit has doubled with pharmaceuticals, we are looking to buy out our competitor and expand that way," one of the females starts, Rechel.

"Do it." I nod. "Next."

A plump man next to her coughs nervously, his face red. "I—we have managed to get the permits we need to build the new tower—" He keeps glancing at Roxxanne, and I hold up my hand as I glance down at the report.

"You're fired," I tell him without looking up from the numbers.

400

"W—sir, what?" he sputters, his face red and mottled.

"You looked at my woman, you are fired. I want you gone in the next hour." I look to the woman next to him. "You, tell me what he was incapable of sharing."

"The permits are secured, we begin building at the end of the month," she rushes out instantly.

"Good. What is your position?" I query, as the man storms from the room.

"I was his vice CEO." She tilts her head back proudly.

"Not anymore, welcome aboard, CEO, make them aware you will need his wage and benefits immediately." I nod and move on. We go around the room with no more issues, and Roxxane watches it all until we get to the last man.

"We have secured properties across the city for your new venture into the catering and bar business."

I nod. "Good, that will all be going through Roxxane here. She's in charge."

I feel her staring at me and wink over at her. "Roxers is included in that. You may do whatever you wish, make them profitable, I'm sure—" I look over at the man, and he grins.

"Ried."

"Ried here can help you with whatever you need."

He looks at her then, and I watch him carefully, but he keeps his eyes locked on her face. "It's a pleasure to work with you. I've seen Roxers, and it has a rustic appeal everyone is searching for now. I believe, with your vision and knowledge, we will have some amazing establishments."

Her eyes widen as she looks him over. "You're too clean, kid. Lose the tie and then we can talk." I chuckle, unable to help myself, and she leans in closer. "Also, you ever get drunk? You look way too young."

He nods nervously as he loses the tie. "Once or twice. I've been busy with university—"

"Good. First things first, go get trashed. You want to run a bar?

You gotta know what sells, what they want. Go find it out," she directs effortlessly. She might not realise it, but Roxxane is a natural born leader. She has all the requirements and doesn't scare easily, she will be an added bonus to our company.

"Dismissed," I call, and they all talk among themselves as they quickly collect their bags and folders and go to leave, but Ried hesitates, looking at Roxxane again.

"Ma'am—"

"Fuck, don't call me that, it's Roxy."

He grins then, relaxing. "Roxy, would it be possible if I could present some ideas as well?"

She smiles at him. "Hell yes. I haven't got a clue, kid, so you're my go-to man."

He seems to puff up at that and finally leaves.

"Roxers?" she asks, her eyebrow arched.

"It's your bar." I shrug. "Now you can do whatever the fuck you want...start a franchise, I don't care, make your own money. Want to build a casino? Do it. Want a whole goddamn island? Just ask."

She shakes her head, and I lean over, covering her mouth. "Our money is yours now, plus I invested some of your own from Roxers' profits and you have more than you think. Get used to it, love."

"I gotta admit, that was hot as hell watching you." She laughs, leaning closer as I relax back in my chair. Grabbing her, I drop her onto my lap, and she rests back against the table, my suit jacket parting to show her rosy, perky nipples peeking through the shirt.

"Was it?" I press, my hands stroking up her thighs.

She nods, letting me push up the shirt. "Fuck yes, all in charge and in control. You should see how scared they were of you, it's mental. So, all this business before dinner, what now?"

"Now? I'm going to fuck you on this table, Miss CEO, and then we're going to take down the Triad." I smirk.

She laughs as I push up the shirt until it bunches under her breasts. "Sounds good, get to work."

CHAPTER

FORTY

ROXY

"D is in his den. Go see what he's up to, will you?" Kenzo requests.

"Why me? I'm comfy." I moan as I curl into his chest as we relax on the sofa while Ryder cooks.

"'Cause if I go, he won't listen, but if you do, he will." He smirks and then pushes me away. I tumble from the sofa with a swat, huffing as I turn on my heel and storm off. I rip open the front door and head to the elevator. The whole building's scanners and security knows me now, so I can leave or go where I want. I ride down to the basement where D plays, and when the door slides open, I hear the screams from here.

I march down the corridor and lean against the doorway as he taunts the man he has in chains. "Who is he?" I call over the screams.

D turns with a wide grin on his face, his chest sweaty and bare, covered in blood. "A threat. Little Bird, come play!"

I grin but stay where I am. "Nope, this is all you."

"Please, please fucking help me, he's crazy!" the man yells, lunging in the chains, and D frowns and turns to him.

"It's rude to interrupt a conversation," he admonishes, and quickly stabs him before looking back at me. "Sorry, Little Bird, he has no manners. Everything okay?"

"Came to see what you were doing, I miss you." I smirk, and within a second, he's on me. He grabs me and tosses me to the wall, his lips crashing onto mine. He tastes like fire and blood, and I can't help but groan.

"Hold that thought," he mutters, as the man continues to scream. Panting and leaning against the wall, I watch as Diesel turns, grabs a fucking meat pulveriser, and smashes it through the man's open mouth. With a turn, and what I can only describe as a ninja kick, he smashes it through his skull.

It stops the screaming, but it also seems to kill the man, and D frowns. "Shit, well, I guess you're my plaything now," he murmurs as he turns, his attention locked on me.

He heads my way and hoists me onto the toolbox again. We seem to end up in this position a lot. I'm still wearing the see-through shirt, but I put on knickers, not that it makes a difference with these men. He pulls his gun from his side and presses it to my head. The breath catches in my throat, even as my pussy clenches. Ryder and I were interrupted earlier. He almost shot the man, but he had work to do, so I haven't orgasmed in like...twenty-four hours, which is just annoying.

"Little Bird, Little Bird, would you die for us?" he murmurs.

I smile. "Would I need to?"

He pulls the trigger, and I don't even flinch, don't even blink. He laughs and presses it to his head. "I would die for you." He pulls the trigger again, an empty click sounds, and he grins. "Whoops forgot the bullets. Oh well, it can still come in handy."

He presses it to my mouth, and I open up. D slips it inside, and I lick around the metal before he pulls it free, wet with my saliva. Running it down my chin, he rips open my shirt until I'm bare to him, his hands covered in blood, yet I'm already wet. I crave his brand of madness, I want it all.

With him, I'm free.

Nothing will ever shock him, scare him. I could never do something that would disgust him or make him fear me. He would love it, revel in it, and worship me.

Gasping at the cool metal of the gun running across my chest and down my belly, I watch him press it into my knickers. Parting my legs, I roll my hips into the metal. He rubs it back and forth across my pussy, wetting it before pressing the barrel to my entrance, and leans closer. "If I fuck you with my gun, will you come for me?"

"You know I will." I moan as he pushes the barrel inside me slightly, the foreignness of it making me jerk and moan louder. "D, please, Ryder already teased me before we got interrupted, do you want to play or not?"

"With you? Always, Little Bird." He groans before ripping away my knickers, his eyes locked on the gun at my pussy. Gliding it back up, he presses it to my clit as he yanks down his trousers and wets his cock in my cream. "Always so fucking wet."

"Fuck me already," I snarl.

He grins. "You have a filthy mouth, I'm going to fuck that later."

Without warning, he slams inside me, and I let loose a scream that has him laughing. He wastes no time. We don't make love, we fuck hard and fast like always.

Wrapping my legs around his hips, I lean up and kiss him hard, the stubble across his jaw scraping against me as we desperately fight for release. He keeps the gun pressed against me, a constant threat, a reminder of his power. The hard metal rubs against my piercing almost painfully, yet I can't help but twist my hips to increase my pleasure.

"More," I demand.

With a grunt, he picks me up and slams me back down, his cock filling me again and again. The gun held against my hip as he controls me. His bloody, sweaty chest rubs across mine, his blood-soaked hand gripping my hip meanly.

Reaching down, I grab the gun and twist his hand until he releases it. I turn it around and run it across his chest and to his mouth. "Suck," I demand with a grin.

He laughs, stilling as he wraps his lips around the barrel and licks it clean of my wetness. I pull the trigger and he groans, his eyes fluttering shut as he jerks in my pussy. He grabs the gun and hoists it to his forehead and presses into the muzzle. "Do it, shoot me," he breathes as he fucks me.

I pull the trigger, again and again, and he groans loudly, his face slack in bliss. When I reach between us with my other hand and yank on his nipple hard enough to make him grunt, he stills, his orgasm ripping through him suddenly. He fills me up, panting as he leans into the gun. I laugh, feeling weirdly accomplished. I managed to turn the tables and get him to come. But then his eyes flicker open, and he narrows them on me.

"I wasn't done playing, Little Bird," he snaps, yanking the gun from my hand, my wrist aching from the abruptness. He pulls from my pussy and presses the gun against my entrance. "I was going to let you come on my cock, but now you're going to do it on my gun."

I gasp, unable to help it. The cool metal feels so strange as he presses it inside me, my pussy slick from my cream and his cum, helping it slide. He fucks me with it in shallow, slow thrusts before giving a few hard ones, keeping me on edge, never knowing which will come. The shape of the barrel makes me groan, and my eyes flicker closed.

This is so wrong, so fucking deadly.

There is a goddamn gun in my pussy, and I'm almost coming just from the thought.

He presses his forehead to mine as he fucks me with it, stretching me around the weapon as he shoves it deeper. "What if I loaded it, Little Bird?"

I shiver, clenching around the metal, and he grins, licking my lips.

"You dirty little bird. I wonder...I wonder what other weapons you would let me fuck you with."

Oh God.

I'm so close, I can feel it building and building. I try to hold back, wanting this to last, but he doesn't let me. He bites my chin as his thumb rubs my clit, the gun slamming inside of me and making me scream as I come around it. He pulls it out a little and slowly pushes it back in, guiding me through the release before pulling the gun free.

I collapse backwards, unable to move as he holds up the glistening gun, meets my gaze, and licks along the barrel, tasting me. "Fuck, this might be my new favourite gun, knowing it's been in your pussy. Every time I use it to kill, every time blood covers it, I'll think of you screaming your release with it buried in your sweet cunt."

Well, fucking shit. What can you say to that?

He laughs and pockets it before turning away and cleaning up, giving me time to recover.

When we get back upstairs, I can feel the tension. They are all wondering what will come next, how the Triad will react and retaliate. This is more than a gang conflict, this is two families going to war. The city is their battle ground, filled with blood and money, and it's only big enough for one of them.

My Vipers.

Because they don't plan on losing, they will do anything to win, I will help them. This is my life now. They are my life. I chose this, I want this, and honestly...it feels right. It's bad, but the excitement of it all has me happier than ever, and I finally feel alive. They did this. Made me into the woman I usually hide away. They pulled back the curtain and let me shine, unafraid of what they would find.

"They were freed three hours ago. I wonder what they are planning," Kenzo mutters, his eyes on his tablet.

"Something big, we embarrassed them." Ryder grins.

"It's happening, our safe house downtown just went dark," Garrett snarls, as they all get to their feet.

It's time to go to war.

CHAPTER

FORTY-ONE

GARRETT

We wait until the next morning and then split up. Ryder is going to check all the businesses, Kenzo the illegal side of things, and Diesel will hit the streets and find out anything he can while I inspect the safe houses. We all take guards with us and are armed to the nines with weapons. Before we depart, we make Roxy promise to stay inside just for today and leave some guards behind.

They will be looking for payback, and grabbing one of us won't be easy, but we still have to be careful. I ignore my fury at how close they got to us. The hits came way too fast, they never planned to make a peace. They have been building this up to take us down. We let their families live, and this is how they repay us?

I'm going to kill them all.

Taking the armoured car, we drive to the safe house that was hit last night. I had Tony and a few others go straight over after it happened, but I need to see it for myself as well. First, the old house, then this. How the fuck are they getting this information? Ryder is stressed as well—he wants the rat and he wants them now.

I can't wait to see what Diesel will do to them when we find them.

The ride to the safe house doesn't take long. We keep them running for any of our employees or even us if the need calls for it. We also have five escape plans—six now, thanks to Roxy. When you're the most powerful people in the city, you sure as shit have a target on your back and gotta know when to run.

But this isn't one of those times.

This? This is just another fucking lesson to assholes who think we're weak, who think we're nothing more than Ryder's daddy's money.

We pull up outside the safe house. I let them get out first, even though it chafes me, and with my hand on my gun, I slip out after them as they rap their knuckles on my door. I keep my eyes peeled, looking everywhere at once, checking doorways, other cars, rooftops, and windows. You can never be too careful, and with Roxy expecting me home, I find myself wanting to live.

The safe house itself is a tiny bungalow tucked between two other bungalows on the suburban side of the city. It's small and unassuming, just how we like it. We have a whole hotel of tiny houses spread across the city—you can never be too careful, after all.

The guys go before me as we head down the old, cracked driveway and past the overgrown garden to the yellow peeling front door. The handle is broken, the lock too, and I tap their shoulders to let them know I'm behind them. They go in first, and I draw my gun, even though Tony has already been here. It could be a trap. We sweep into the house and split up to check it out. The one bedroom and bathroom are clear, the living room and kitchen too. Holstering my gun, I frown as I look around. The place is trashed with things ripped from walls, dents and cracks in the plaster, and furniture turned upside down. It appears like they were looking for something, but we don't keep anything at safe houses, so this is all a threat.

A reminder they are there and angry.

That they can get to us. Curling my fists into my sides, I stomp through the mess, kicking aside the broken sofa. "Check on all the other safe houses, I want a report back. Find whoever the fuck is betraying us!" I snap.

Grabbing my phone, I dial Ryder. "Speak," he snarls, obviously having as much fun as me.

"It's trashed, they fucking knew exactly where to go. We need to find the fucking bastard who is giving them this information," I growl, smashing my fist into the wall.

"I fucking know that, I'm trying. Go check out the other houses," he orders, before hanging up. I pocket my phone. He's stressed as well, we can all feel it. Before, it wouldn't have mattered, it would have been fun, a game to destroy them, but now we have Roxy to think about, and we don't want her caught in the crossfire. My phone vibrates as I'm slipping it into my front jeans pocket, so I yank it out and read the message.

Kenzo: No luck here.

Fuck.

Putting it back, I circle my fingers at the guys. "Let's move out. We're checking all the houses until we find someone, and when we do, we're going to fucking kill them."

They nod, and we rush off to search the next safe house.

FIVE SAFE HOUSES LATER, AND I'M PISSED. THREE HAVE BEEN hit, but there's no sign of whoever did it, or whoever told them about it, because we all know it's the Triad, a revenge hit. Maybe they were hoping they would find someone at one of them, I'm not sure. Either way, I want to smash someone's face in.

I have to hold back the urge, my body vibrating with tension and anger, the feeling I get when I'm winding up to fight. Breathing through it, I try and tamp it down for as long as I can. Suddenly, my phone rings, and I answer it without looking.

"What?" I snarl into it, as we head to the next safe house.

"How fucking rude! I was going to be nice for once, but..." She laughs—Roxy. I relax instantly at the sound of her voice, a smile coming to my lips.

"You okay, baby?" I ask, my voice softer now. I see the two men in the front shifting, so I glare at their backs, and they hunch.

"Yeah, you, big guy? I got worried when I hadn't heard from any of you." She sniffs.

"You're bored, aren't you?" I chuckle.

"Out of my fucking mind." She groans dramatically, making me laugh harder.

"Haven't got up to any trouble yet?" I query, staring out of the window. All my tension seems to float away for a moment as I imagine her guards chasing her with pale faces, trying to keep up with whatever trouble she's up to.

"Psh, not yet, but it's only...nine in the morning." She laughs, the sound heading straight to my cock and hardening it. "Though I did order us some new chains to play with." Her voice goes low and sultry.

Fuck me.

I groan, closing my eyes for a minute. "Baby, I'm in a car with three other guys, you can't say shit like that."

"Why? You wanna chain them up too?" she teases.

"Behave," I snarl.

She scoffs, "When the fuck do I ever behave? Now hurry your big ass up and get home, I'm fucking bored, and who knows what I'll do."

She hangs up, snickering. I pocket my phone again, but I feel calmer now. More relaxed and in control. I feel the guys looking at me, so I turn my head and narrow my eyes. "Do not even think about her, look at her, or go near her, or I will fucking smash your faces in."

They all turn away instantly, and I smirk, even as Tony

chuckles from the front. The next safe house is an apartment above a coffee shop, so after we check it and find it trashed, I decide to take a break. I didn't eat this morning, and I find myself missing our usual breakfast dates. When I hated her, or at least tried to, they were the only real times I could be around her without the others catching on to my desire. I could stare at her without them noticing.

Sighing, I head inside. One of my guards stays in the car, another stands outside the shop, and the third sits and waits, his eyes scanning everyone. But I do it anyway, it's a habit, and that's when I see her.

Her.

Here, staring right back at me.

She has on a hood, hiding half of her face, but it's her. I would recognise her anywhere. Her lips are turned up in a knowing smirk, her one cornflower blue eye locked on me. I used to stare into her eyes for hours, wondering if she was my forever, and now she's here.

My whole body freezes, my chest and muscles burning as fear and fury pour through me. "Sir?" the woman behind the counter calls in confusion. I'm at the front of the queue, it's my turn, but I can't look away from her.

Daphne.

The bitch who tried to kill me, who stripped the skin from my chest. My ex-girlfriend. She's sitting in the corner with an untouched mug before her, watching me the same fucking way she used to. An expression I didn't realise was so cold and calculating, the greedy cunt, until it was too late. Until she had her blade in my chest, carving me to pieces while she laughed.

When I woke in the private hospital, the guys were there. They knew where she had run to, she had never gotten far enough to escape us. No place would ever be far enough. I didn't ask, I just told them to take care of it. To make it hurt.

To make her suffer for what she did.

Because when I peeled those bandages away, I gagged at the sight of my own chest, and I couldn't let the nurses help me wash it. Diesel

413

had to. I couldn't stand their hands on me, and when one tried, I snapped her wrist. This woman tried to kill me, ruin me.

Even managed it for many years. Only now, with Roxy, am I finally starting to live again, yet she's here, staring at me like nothing happened.

How is she alive?

"Sir?" comes again, but I turn away and storm right up to her. I want to ring her neck, to snap it, but that would be too fast. How did she survive whatever the guys did? It had to be bad, they assured me she was dead.

How is she fucking alive?

And why do my hands shake? I hide them behind my back as I tower over her table. She tries to play it cool, her hand reaching for her mug, but I see the tremble in them, the fear in her eye. Unlike Roxy, she was always slightly scared of me for what I could do. She was disgusted at my fighting, yet the cold fucking bitch had no issue with *my* blood.

Cunt.

My gaze catches on her wrist as her hoodie pulls up with her movement, revealing mottled, burnt flesh. She gasps and yanks her hand under the table, her one eye narrowing on me.

"Gar," she breathes. "You look good...almost fully healed." She smirks.

"How are you alive?" I seethe, holding myself back from attacking her. It wouldn't do us any good, but fuck, it's hard. I want to snap every bone in her traitorous body. To make her feel the pain I felt, and not just at her betrayal.

"It wasn't easy." She shrugs. "But I had things to survive for."

"Like a fucking cockroach you can't get rid of," I snarl, and she laughs, the annoying, high-pitched tittering sound that used to make Diesel threaten to stab her. That should have been warning enough. They didn't like her, but I was blind.

I even protected her from him, let her pull me away from my brothers when she was scared of them. I hurt them, not that they will ever say it. I know that's why Ryder is so panicked about Roxy, because I couldn't just walk away from them for her.

I would do anything she asked.

I used to think Daphne would be it for me, that we would settle down and get married. It seemed like the right thing to do, since she was expecting it, dropping hints. Even though I wasn't sure, I got the ring anyway. How was I ever this fucking blind?

She is cold, cunning, and a gold-digging cunt.

Roxy is so alive, so full of laughter, and if I ever tried to give her money, she would throw it in my face. Her hate, her anger matches mine, her scars mirroring my own. She is my world now, and it only shows me how desperate for love I was to not only fuck this woman, but propose.

"Gar, I remember when you didn't want to get rid of me," she purrs falsely.

"Don't fucking call me that," I growl. "Why are you here? In my city? You had to know I would find out and fucking kill you."

I sense people staring now, fucking let them. Let them watch as I wipe this cunt from the face of the planet, let them fear me, I don't care what they think. There are only five people I care about, and they would stand behind me, fuck, they would hand me the blade.

"I hear you have a new little toy, she's cute. Does she know your penchant for pain? Or how you like to fuck hard and fast..." Her eyes drop hungrily to my chest, and I slam my fists onto the table. "I bet she doesn't. I wonder, can she even bear to look at your chest?"

My lungs are heaving, and I can almost feel the blade carving into me again, flaying me open. Darkness circles me, my demons growing and demanding to be let free. "Answer me now."

She grins and leans back, and I get sick of the games. I grab the hood and yank it back. My eyes widen as she quickly stands, pulling it over her head. But she's not fast enough. I saw what she was trying to hide.

Half of her face is gone, melted—no hair, no eye, and her skin looks like dripping wax. No doubt Diesel's handiwork. It makes me grin, and it's not a nice one. "Oh, poor little Daphne, can't use your looks to get your way anymore? It's not like you have any other moves, you stupid cunt. Why are you here?" I sneer for the last time.

I'm a string pulled too tight, ready to snap, faced with the woman I once cared for, the one who almost took everything, and I find myself craving her death. I feel like Diesel, wanting to bathe in it, to watch her blood cover my skin and then storm back to my girl and fuck her with it across my body.

"I have unfinished business, Garrett. With you and your fucking Vipers," she snarls, and pushes closer until she invades my space. I don't move back, even as my head roars at me, my hands itching to grab her and kill her. "You will pay for what you did. I'm going to be there to watch you fall," she whispers as she leans closer, her red tipped nails running down my chest.

I stiffen at that, my head blurring with anger, and I'm moving before I know it. Grabbing her wrist, I thrust her away, and she hits the wall hard, laughing. I'm on her in a moment, my hand wrapping around her throat. Her eye widens in fear. For all her bravado, she's afraid.

Deathly afraid. Of me. Of us. Of what we will do to her.

She isn't pulling the strings, she's a puppet...for who? The Triad? Is it possible we have more than one enemy coming at us? No, they have to be working together. They were looking for a weakness, a way to get to us, and they thought they had it with her.

But she was never really one of us. She never stayed in our home, never saw our business. She saw what we wanted her to, nothing more. I squeeze tighter, not even using my full strength to hold her in place. I let her see it in my eyes, how easily I could kill her, end her, and no one would care.

No one could stop me.

But it would be too quick.

The noise of the shop around us comes back. People are screaming, and I hear them on the phone when a tap comes at my shoulder. Turning with a snarl, I throw her to the floor and meet my guard's eyes. "Unless you want to spend hours talking to the police, we need to leave. If you want her taken or dead, say the word, we'll organise it and call Ryder to clean up."

He doesn't question who she is, doesn't even blink as he says it. I look back at her, but she's scrambling to her feet and straightening her hoodie. She blows me a kiss. "Be seeing you soon, Garrett, and say hello to your girlfriend for me." Then she's gone, rushing into the scrambling crowd and blending.

"No, follow her though," I snap.

He rushes off, and I stomp through the shop, the patrons falling as they try to get out of my way. Their faces are pale and scared as I rip open the coffee shop door and head outside.

I grab my phone to dial Ryder and tell him I know who the mole is, but when I dip my hand into my pocket, it's gone. I have a flash of her sidling close to me, her hand stroking down my chest...I was so panicked, so angry, I didn't even think anything of it when I shoved her away.

Fuck.

She has my phone.

CHAPTER FORTY-TWO

ROXY

I'm fucking bored. The only reason I don't leave is because they asked so sweetly. They were not demanding or authoritative, they genuinely needed me to stay. So I do.

I never said I would behave, just that I would stay. They should have known better. I do some work. Ryder left me with the contracts and information for the bars he wants to buy or build, so I flip through them, noting which will be good and discarding those that won't be. He also included Roxers' earnings and his investments with the money. It's doing good, more than fucking good. Ryder has an eye for money and investments—the profit has tripled.

I have money.

More than I know what to do with or need.

He knew it would keep me busy for a while, the sneaky bastard, and it does, I'm excited to do something I love. Something good. I make a plan to only hire ex-cons and runaways. People who need it. They will get a good wage, and we can build some accommodations, give them a second chance at life. Like Rich gave me. That's what I'm going to call it, the Rich Fund.

For him...the man who saved my life, the opportunity to create the fund given to me by the men who love me.

Who knew this is where I would end up? Not me when I slept under a bridge, freezing and starving.

After I make a plan on that, I find an old Polaroid camera tucked away in Kenzo's room, and I take dirty pictures for them and hide them under their pillows, giggling the whole time. Next, I decide to try and break into their armoury, because honestly, I want my bat back. My eyes go back to the gunroom. It has a hand scanner, I wonder if I could open it. They added my prints to the building, surely that would include that? Unless it's on a different system.

Deciding to try it, I head upstairs and press my hand to the screen, but it flashes red. Motherfucker. Now that I'm thinking about it, I want to know what's inside. I need to. Mischievous urges fill me, the same ones that led to me ripping Ryder's clothes and trashing his car, to leaving dirty pictures under their pillows, to buying that present which is on the way...

Fuck it.

I wonder... Sneaking downstairs, I grab a knife and head back to the door, trying to jimmy the lock, but it doesn't work. "Hey, buff security dude?" I call, hanging over the balcony. "I need your body."

He looks up from the window he was guarding and pales, stumbling away, his hands out as if to ward me off. "Please, please no, they will kill me. I—a...you're very beautiful, but, fuck, don't tell them I said that," he begs, his eyes wide.

Laughing, I wave him up. "Not in that way, dude. I got four cocks, you think I need more? I won't tell them if you throw yourself into this door for me."

He glances at the door and shakes his head. "Hell no, they will murder me."

"Nah they won't, I won't let them. I'll tell them I did it. Come on, big dude, help a sister out," I plead.

He looks to the others before sighing and coming upstairs, where he eyes the door. "You want me to break it down?"

"I could try, be all woman hear me roar, or I could be super smart and let a big, tough guy like you do it for me," I offer sweetly, and he snorts.

"You're more manipulative than them, I see why they love you," he comments offhandedly, before pulling back his foot and kicking open the door. It smashes inwards, the lock dropping to the floor. "I never did that, you didn't see it." He huffs before wandering downstairs.

My phone vibrates, and I check to see it's Ryder. I've been texting them all morning. Diesel's last message was a picture of his face covered in blood with the caption, "You're sitting on this later," but this is a video call now. With a grumble, I head into his bedroom and flop on his bed, not wanting him to know what I'm up to yet.

I answer and angle the phone to see my face. He's in a car, the phone held to his face so I can see just a peek of his suit. His hair is slicked back and his eyes are cold, but when they lock on me, they seem to melt a little. Even through the phone, I can feel his power, his all-consuming interest, and it has me shivering in need. Ryder Viper is a fucking weapon...to my vagina.

"Love, what are you up to?" he asks straightaway, his deep, husky voice having me clenching my thighs together, and then a naughty thought comes to mind.

Smirking at him, I angle the camera down and run my hand over my chest to cup my breasts before trailing down my stomach. He groans as I start to drag my dress up to reveal my thighs. "Love, are you on my bed?"

"Yes." I laugh. "And I'm bored and horny," I tell him, as I flash him my thong, parting my thighs as I let him watch me cup myself.

He groans and then snaps something off camera. I hear a squeal then a door. "What was that?" I laugh, tilting the camera back to see those icy eyes demanding and tight.

"I was not going to let them overhear you," he snarls, as though it's obvious, his tongue darting out and licking his bottom lip. "Show me again, love, touch yourself."

"Oh, feeling naughty?" I laugh.

"Now, don't make me ask again, Roxxane," he orders.

"Or what?" I grin, trailing my hand up my thigh and showing him. "You are too far to do anything..."

He grunts. "Open your thighs, dip your fingers in, and show me how wet you are."

Teasing him, I run my fingers across my pussy, pushing aside my thong. "If you were here, you could see for yourself."

"Don't fucking tempt me, love, Roxxane, do as you're told," he demands.

Gasping, I push my thong further aside, exposing myself to him, and I hear his answering groan. "So fucking wet," he mumbles. "Touch yourself, let me watch."

Arching up, I dip my fingers inside myself where he can see before circling my clit, wishing it was him. "Make yourself come, love. Let me watch. Then, if you're good, when I get back, I'll spend all night between your thighs eating your fucking pussy like a starving man."

Imagining it, I rub faster, dipping my fingers inside myself again and fucking my pussy as he watches. I'm aware there are security guards downstairs, but I don't care. "Yeah? No punishment?" I challenge breathlessly.

"Oh, love, there will always be a punishment, because you don't know how to behave. You will come at least five times before you take my cock into that sweet little pussy. I'll make my brothers watch while you scream and beg for me, fighting me even as you give in."

His dirty words have me moaning loudly as I spread my thighs wider and speed up, rolling and thrusting into my fingers, reaching for that release I can feel approaching, needing it. "That's it, baby girl, fuck yourself for me, take your own pleasure. Let me see those fingers inside that greedy little pussy."

My pussy is still a little sore from last night, but I don't care, the pain only adds to it, heightening the pleasure coursing through me.

Whimpering, I angle the camera further down, and he groans. "Are you touching yourself?" I gasp.

He groans. "Like a fucking teenager. We're in a bloody parking garage with my guards right outside, and I'm fucking my hand, wishing it was your cunt."

I can just imagine it. "Show me," I beg.

I look at the screen, watching as he tilts it down. His suit is perfectly in place apart from his exposed cock. It's in his hand, which is squeezing and stroking. The sight of his big, scarred hands wrapped around it have me almost screaming there and then as I come, writhing in the sheets as I almost lose my grip on the phone. "Let me watch," he demands. "Don't you fucking dare drop that phone."

Whimpering, I clench around my fingers again, my pussy pulsing before I pull them free of my clinging muscles, soaked with my release. Lifting the camera up, I meet his wide, lust-filled eyes with my own and suck my fingers into my mouth, licking them clean. He grunts loudly, his eyes shutting for just a moment before they're open and on me again. That ice is gone, and in its place is the volcano, the violence he hides underneath. "Fucking hell, love. I'll be home in two hours. Two fucking hours, and then that pussy is mine."

"Yeah?" I grin, pulling my fingers free. "You'll have to catch me first, I plan on being very bad in the meantime."

"One fucking hour," he snarls.

Laughing, I hang up and slip from the bed, my heart slowing down. I clean up in his bathroom before going back out to the armoury. I'm not ashamed if they heard me downstairs, let them. If Ryder was here, I would have fucked him in front of them with no regrets. When it comes to my Vipers, I'm helpless to resist.

Okay, I made a dare to be bad. So it's a good job we broke into this room. I can almost imagine the punishment now, and I can't fucking wait. They have been too nice recently, and I crave their cruelty. Their power.

Sauntering into the armoury, I whistle as I take it in. This isn't a goddamn room, it's a fucking arsenal. Complete with weapons covering every wall and table, and rows upon rows of guns, swords, knives, grenades...and fucking missiles. Jesus. There is body armour and black cargos in the corner.

"Goddamn, it's like I'm dating John Wick," I mutter, as I look around. "I wonder if I could get one of them to role play being him." I sigh as I trail my fingers across the weapons.

I bet Kenzo would, and with that dark hair, he could fit the role. Diesel is a little too crazy to be Keanu. Garrett would just tell me to fuck off, but then fuck me. Ryder would smirk and demand I give him something in return.

Bastards.

Even as I think that, though, I smile. I find my bat at the back of the room and grip it lovingly, raining kisses across the smooth wood. "I missed you too, baby, so much. I will never let them take you again. We'll be back to kicking ass soon," I promise lovingly.

Just then, my phone goes off. I'm torn between hugging my bat and answering, but when it buzzes again, I place my bat down and yank it out of my pocket...yes, that's right, bitches, my dress has pockets. Ain't anything better. You can hide snacks and weapons so easily.

Mardyfucker: I need your help, meet me at Hotel Mors.

I reread the text with a frown. If Garrett needs me, it must be serious. Peeking over the balcony, I look at the security dudes. I'm not stupid enough to go without them, he would get mardy. "Yo, big dudes, we're rolling out."

"Miss, we have been told for you to stay—" One of them starts.

I hold up my phone. "Garrett texted me, he needs our help, come on, autobots, unite!" I call, making one of them snort.

One of them pulls out their phone as I head downstairs. "Ryder isn't answering. Okay, we go, but at the first sight of any trouble, we're out of there. I don't want to be killed because of this," he mutters.

"You got it, big dude, and thanks to your body, I now have some new toys to take." I grin, holding up the guns.

He winces. "They're going to murder me."

"Nah, okay, maybe, but they would make it quick." I shrug as I strap on my weapons like a badass.

Female John Wick.

Lady Wick...nah, that sucks, I'll come up with a kickass name on the way.

CHAPTER

FORTY-THREE

ROXY

This is probably a bad idea, but I'm aching to get out, to help them. I'm not the sitting on the sidelines type, so I jump at the chance. I do, however, bring the security guys as backup and let them call some of the shots to let them think they are in charge. It's cute how flustered they get when I don't listen.

I'm also strapped with weapons, guns, and knives, some I've stolen. I almost snigger at that. I can't carry my bat discreetly, so I leave her behind. I do pull on the closest pair of heels though, not wanting to waste time finding my boots, and then we're on the move.

The hotel is downtown, and we get caught in some traffic on the way. They continue to try and ring Ryder, but he doesn't answer, which is not surprising, considering he was going into a meeting. We pull up outside, and they frown at it. "I don't like this," one of the mutters.

I sigh, looking around. "Maybe you're right. I don't see him anywhere, and no way am I walking my ass into a random building from a text. I'm not fucking stupid."

I try to ring him, but it goes to voicemail. Shit, what if something is wrong? "What do you want—" I get cut off by bullets.

"Down!" one of them screams.

I throw myself on the backseat, shielding my head as more bullets fly and glass shatters. I feel it sprinkle over my back, and then it all stops. Pushing myself up, I stare into the front, gasping when I find my guards dead with bullets in their heads. Fuck. Grabbing my gun, I debate getting into the footwell, but if someone rips open the door, I'll be a sitting duck. I crawl across the backseat, open the door, and slip out, using the car for cover. Searching my pockets for my phone, I swear when I come up empty. It must have fallen out, but it's too late to go back for it. I raise the gun, flick off the safety, and wait.

I can hear an engine, but it's quiet, and then boots. Peeking under the car, I see four pairs heading straight for me. Fuck. This wasn't random, this was planned, and someone got a hold of Garrett's phone to lure me here. *Fucking stupid, Roxy!* I hope he's okay, but I don't have time to worry about him. I need to worry about myself and get my ass out of here.

I wait until they open the door before I make a break for it, heading to an alley at the side of the hotel. I run as fast as I can, pumping my arms, my old days running from the police as a rough sleeper coming back to me.

Fuck, fuck.

I hear boots behind me, followed by their yells. I round the alley and almost scream. There's a fucking fence at the end. Fuck this. I refuse to go down without a fight. Ducking behind a bin, I wait. One of them runs right past me, and I slip out, firing as I go. He crumples easily, and I look back to see three more men in fucking bike helmets coming at me. Taking off again, I aim straight for the fence.

I got this. I throw myself at it and start to climb. I slip, cutting my fingers, but I harness the pain with a growl and drag myself up. A shot goes wide, and I flinch, but carry on going as they shout.

"Don't fucking shoot, we need her alive!"

Well, that's something at least.

Throwing my leg over the top, I yell as a hand grabs my ankle. I look down into the helmet and use the gun like a bat, smashing it across the visor. It shatters, and he tumbles from the fence to the alley below. Using the distraction, I heave myself over the top and land on my knees, forcing myself quickly to my feet, my heels catching in a fucking hole. I don't have time to stop, however, because they're coming. I can hear the clink of the fence as they climb it.

My breathing is loud as I push into a sprint, but I can still hear them behind me, their boots loud. Hell fucking no. I'm not going down like this, not now, not ever. I didn't survive all this shit to die in a goddamn alley.

"Stop!" comes the yell.

I snort, like that will work. I pump my arms harder. The alley breaks up ahead into what looks like a parking lot. From there, I can run into the road, lose them in traffic, and get away. But they are too close, my heels slowing me down. An arm grabs me.

Not bothering to scream, knowing no one will help me, I stomp on his foot and kick back. He falls away, and I turn, firing as I go. He goes down hard, and remembering my stance, I lock my arms and fire at the other two, but they duck behind more bins. The slide locks back, empty, and I curse, knowing I don't have any other bullets with me. I have knives, but they will have to be close for that.

I drop the gun and take off again. I can hear them catching up, they are too fast. I won't have a chance to get to the road, so I turn into the parking lot and duck behind a car, breathing heavily as I try to stay quiet while I crouch. Reaching down, I palm two blades.

If they thought I was going to be an easy target, they have another thing coming. Someone will have heard the shots and the police will be here soon. I just have to take down these two assholes and get free and back to the guys.

"Go that way!" one of them screams. They're splitting up, which makes it easier for me. I crouch walk to the boot of the car and peer around it. One of them is heading the other way, but one is looking around and under cars, growing closer to me.

Steadying my breathing, I hold tight, waiting for the right moment to pounce. I only have one shot at this. They are bigger and have weapons. I don't have my bat or familiar surroundings, so I need to make this quick.

Come on, motherfucker, just a bit closer. Tightening my hand on the blade, I wait for him to round the back of the car, his head turned slightly away. Then, I strike, fast and low. He doesn't even get his gun up before the blade is in his leg. He drops with a scream as I yank it out and, with a war cry, land on his chest and stab him again and again.

When he stops jerking, I grab his gun and turn to get the other guy, but I'm too slow. Too fucking slow. I see the butt of the pistol coming just seconds before it hits me in the face, and then everything is dark.

GODDAMN, THE BACK OF MY HEAD HURTS. I LIE STILL AS I FEEL something moving. Oh wait, that's me, I'm moving. What the fuck happened?

The text.

The attack.

I keep my breathing even, like I used to when I was a kid and hoped my dad wouldn't realise I was awake. My head is pounding, and my face feels sore, that bitch better not have broken my nose with his gun. How goddamn rude. Ignoring the pain, something I learned years ago, I focus on where we are. There's a hard but soft seat beneath me, and I'm leaning against something cold and vibrating. There's a purr beneath me, and the sound of horns surrounding us.

We are in a car.

I crack open one eye, noting I'm propped against the window in the backseat. I daren't turn my head, but I can feel someone next to me, someone big. I can also see two men in the front—one driving and one in the passenger seat. The radio is on low, an upbeat pop song pounding through the speakers to match the pounding of my head.

Okay, three guys.

I've taken more than that, and I don't mean sexually...though that's true now, I guess. Three big guys, packing no doubt, but I have the advantage. They want me alive, I want them dead.

My hand is trapped awkwardly between my body and the car door, so shifting slightly, I pull it free. I freeze when I feel the guy in front glance over to check on me. Only when he turns back do I move again, slowly, so as not to draw attention. I run my hand down my thigh—shit, they took my weapons.

I'm betting all of them, the handsy bastards. Diesel is going to be pissed. It doesn't even cross my mind that Garrett was in on this. If he wanted me dead, he would have killed me. No, someone got to him, I just hope he's okay.

Okay, no weapons. *Think, Roxy.* Fuck, my head hurts. This is the worst hangover ever, and I didn't even get the buzz of the alcohol and bad regrets to make it worth my while. Moving my legs slightly to get into a more comfortable position, I freeze. I have my heels. My fucking heels.

The bitches are sharp...I wonder...

We're slowing down, and I know we must be running out of time. God knows how long I've been out for. It's now or never. The worst that will happen is I end up getting knocked out again...right?

I shift again until I can reach down and grab a heel, then I pull it off and hold still, taking a deep breath. *Now or never, Rox.*

Flopping my head to the side, I open my eyes and lock them onto the guy opposite me who's staring out the window. He turns his head, undoubtedly feeling my movement, so I burst into action. I hear a yell, but I ignore it, praying they need me alive more than they want to shoot me.

I stab using the heel, my hand gripping the shoe. I drive it into his chest and neck, and as he turns his head to look at me with wide eyes,

I drive it into his eye. It sticks from the socket as he screams. The car whips from side to side.

"Grab her," I hear them yelling from the front.

Reaching across the guy who's trying to pull the heel free, I grab his gun and knife and unclick his seat belt. I kick open his door and push him out. He screams as he hits the pavement, and I blow him a kiss before spinning to see the two men in the front.

The one in the passenger seat swears as he tries to get a needle ready while reaching back for me. Fuck that. I fumble with the gun and accidentally pull the trigger, gazing with wide eyes as the man in the front seat screams as it hits his leg.

"Oops, sorry," I offer, as I grab his head and, using the knife, slice it across his throat. I don't give myself time to think on what I'm doing. I'm in survival mode, it's me or them. In this life I now live, blood was bound to cover my hands. You either get dirty or you die.

Only the driver is left now. He swears as he pulls his gun, done with me, one hand on the wheel. Looking out the front window, I see we're on a dual carriageway, and it's busy, which helps, because we have to go slow. Probably thirty miles per hour. Shit, this is going to hurt.

Grabbing the gun, I point it at his head and fire. He slumps forward, the ringing loud in my ears from the shot going off in such close proximity. Groaning, I slide between the seats and clutch the wheel, leaning over his body to try and swerve us around the other cars, but I can't get the angle right. We catch the end of a van, and it spins us. Screaming, I hold on as we spin and spin, my stomach revolting, and then we stop.

It's all quiet for a moment as I fall into the backseat until it's not. A car hits us from the side and plows us into the middle barrier. We hit it and flip. It happens in mere seconds, but it feels like a lifetime as I roll around in the car. I manage to grab the seat, and when we finally land on the roof, I drop onto it with a crunch.

Groaning, I look down at my body. Holy fucking shit.

I'm okay! Fucking hell, that was goddamn lucky. The back door is warped and won't open, so I kick at it, bracing myself on the roof and giving it all my strength. After the fourth kick, it opens, and I crawl out onto the broken glass of the road, cutting my hands and arms. Staggering to my feet, I lean against the car. This side of the road isn't that busy, and the people who are passing are gawking at me. One even stops. But I can't hear anything.

My ears are ringing, my body is in agony, and my head is pounding so hard, I have to turn and vomit. Fuck, I'm worse than I thought. Stumbling forward, away from the car in case it explodes or some shit, I walk into the lanes, but my body is done. I can't help but fall to my knees. Whether it be shock or injury, I don't know, but it refuses to listen, and my vision is swimming.

Move, Roxy, move!

But I can't.

Panic winds through me, pushing back some of the numbness that's threatening to swallow me whole, but it's not enough. A noise catches my attention through the haze, and I turn my head. Two black cars have stopped near our wrecked one. Men pour from it, heading straight to me.

There are more than I'll ever be able to handle, but that doesn't mean I'm going down without a fight. I stumble to my feet, my fingers numb as I grab a piece of broken glass, the closest thing I have to a weapon. "Bring it, assholes!" I don't know if I scream it out loud or in my head, but they do.

They come right for me.

I try to stab with the glass, but it's slow, my body too goddamn sluggish. They knock my arm away, and my fingers spasm, making me drop the glass. I kick, I punch, but it's like my movements are listless, too slow to make contact, and there are too goddamn many of them.

This is going to hurt a lot. I know it. So I brace for it, waiting for the pain, but it's a quick one, barely a pinch, and when I turn my head, I see the needle they are pulling away. The bastards cheated.

At least they didn't hit me in the face again.

CHAPTER
FORTY-FOUR

RYDER

"We should look at the numbers and compare them—" I zone out of the meeting, wondering what Roxy is up to. I promised her one hour, but it's been an hour and a half. I'll have to find a way to make it up to her. I almost smirk, thinking of all the ways I could, each of them involving her naked and coming beneath my tongue.

My phone vibrates for the hundredth time, so I turn my chair and discreetly check it. This meeting is important, and if it goes well, we're expanding into other cities, both legitimately and otherwise.

Unknown: Roxy is gone.
Unknown: They got her, Ry.

Two texts, two fucking texts, and they destroy my world. Fury like I've never felt before flows through me. That ice I have cultivated around me for so long cracks, and the lava flows through, burning everything in its path.

They took my girl?

Our girl?

I stand, ignoring the questions fired at me, and storm from the conference room, my phone already to my ear. "Tell me everything," I snap. I listen as Garrett explains, his voice tight and angry. I hear Diesel in the background screaming at someone, and then gunfire.

"We followed the trail of bodies to a car park and saw the tire tracks. They must have grabbed her there." He goes quiet for a moment as I leap down the stairs of the building, taking them two at a time. "Ry, fuck, she put up a real fight, there are bodies everywhere."

"Garrett," Diesel snarls, and there's a moment of silence before Garrett swears.

"What?" I demand.

"Watch what I'm sending you," he growls.

I pull my phone away and stop on the stairs, my hand gripping the railing as the video loads. I watch it once, then twice. That pit in my stomach grows, those demons escaping until I'm nothing but a man possessed.

They hurt her.

I watch her crawl from the wreck of the car, the CCTV from the highway zooming in on her. She stumbles away with blood dripping from her head, her hands, and her arms. She only has one shoe on, and her face is pale, her eyes fuzzy as she falls to her knees. I watch again as they come at her, she still fights, trying to take them down. That's my fucking girl, a fighter to the end, but she doesn't see the needle coming.

I watch her fall, and this time, they catch her and carry her back to the cars. Then, they are gone. Breathing heavily, my muscles shaking with the need to kill people, I put the phone to my ear. "Track the cars."

"Diesel's new friend is already on it." He pulls the phone away from his mouth. "D, he can't work if you keep stabbing him," he snaps, and then comes back. "I can't get a hold of Kenzo, he gets no signal in the basement of Diamonds. Get him?"

"On it," I snarl, and the line goes quiet. "Garrett, we kill them."

"Too fucking right," he retorts. "Anyone who touched her dies horrifically, and the Triad? We are going to fucking burn them alive for taking our girl."

I hang up and send a message to my driver and the guards downstairs, so when I make it into the lobby, they are there. The car is idling outside, and I get in quickly. "Diamonds, now," I demand.

First things first, get my brother. Then they are dead men.

They feared my father, but they should fear me more. Roxxanne is mine, she owns us, and they took the one thing we will do anything to protect. They kicked the goddamn vipers' nest, so now they get the fangs. This city will run with blood before tonight, and when I find them, I will make them scream for every finger they ever put on her.

I dial a number for their restaurant, knowing they will get it. They will understand. "You took something of mine, something precious." There is no use denying it, they already know what they have, it's the only thing keeping her alive right now. "I'm going to let the streets run red with your people's blood until I get her back, and then? I'm going to kill you all. Starting with your families, your wives, your sons and daughters, even your parents. Only then, when everything is burning and destroyed around you, will I kill you. You fucked with the wrong family." After I leave the message I hang up.

One, two, three, four, five.

I repeat it again and again, trying to stay calm, but I can't. It doesn't work. Fuck the calm. All I can see is Roxy, the smile on her face before it fades to that blank, scared look she had on the highway.

The city is about to go to war.

And before the sun rises tomorrow, only one family will be left.

Ours.

We pull up outside Diamonds, and I wait as they get Kenzo. He slips into the car next to me, frowning. "What's wrong?" he asks straightaway, pulling out his phone before I stop him.

"She's gone." My voice is empty, not reflecting the inferno burning inside me. How can I sound that calm when I'm this fucking angry...and scared? Scared I will lose her. Scared that the best thing that has ever happened to me will be gone before I can even tell her. Scared to lose my love.

"What?" he questions, scowling and looking at me over.

"Roxxane, they took her," I rasp.

He freezes, his head jerking down to look at his phone as he scrolls through the messages. "What?" he gasps. "No." He shakes his head as we pull away from the curb.

"Yes, they did."

He turns to me then, his eyes outraged, his lips curled into a snarl. "How can you be so fucking calm?" he screams, and then throws himself at me. He always did wear his emotions on his sleeve. I capture his head in my hands, pressing my forehead to his as he struggles and swears.

"Brother, look at me," I whisper, but he's still fighting, so I grip him harder. "Look at me!" I command, my hands shaking against his skin. He stops fighting then, staring at me. His eyes are lost, scared, like mine. "We will get her back, I promise you that," I whisper. "I'm not calm, I'm anything but, yet I have to hold it together. For you, for her. Now more than ever, she needs us, and we need to handle this, we need to find them. Breaking down will not help, not now. We need to use every goddamn ounce of our power and intellect."

"You promise?" he begs, searching my eyes like he used to when I was a child and he was scared, when I swore to protect him. I do the same now, protect him, it's my job. Because, honestly, I don't know if we will get to her in time, and that makes me feel so sick, I want to throw up everywhere, knowing what they will do to her.

Every minute counts, but if he needs my lies to function, then he can have them.

"I promise, we will get her back, and then we'll kill every last one of them," I vow.

His eyes shutter for a moment, those long lashes concealing him from me as a shaky breath leaves his lips. When they open again, they are hard, cold, like mine. It saddens me, but I understand. "I can't lose her," he admits, his voice making my heart ache. I wish I could shield him from this. I wish I could keep this from him like everything else.

"I know. We won't. I need you, she needs you," I tell him, and he nods.

"We kill them all," he agrees, deadly calm. He's feeling the type of tranquillity where you feel too much and you become numb. He's nothing more than the Viper now.

A cold-blooded snake striking out.

In those eyes, I see myself and I see our future, because if we lose her—the thought even hurts—there will be no coming back. We will cease to exist as we do now. All laugher and love will be gone until nothing, nothing is left but our venom.

He moves away, and I let him, hiding my shaking hands from him. He needs my strength, not my weakness. Because that's what she is, our weakness, but they don't know she is also our heart, our strength, our reason we fight now.

"What's our first move?" he asks, his voice dead.

I stare out of the window, a cruel smile curling my lips. "We hunt them across the city, starting at the bottom. Get your gun, it's about to get bloody."

CHAPTER
FORTY-FIVE

DIESEL

"Y ou need to calm down, you have already killed four
people," Garrett snaps, but despite his words, his hands are
clenched and his body is vibrating with lethal intent. I'm
not the only one struggling with our girl going missing.

My little bird.
Mine.
And they took her.
I will paint this town red. I will kill everyone in it and wear
their skin to find her. She's mine!

"They had it coming." I shrug, wiping the blood from my hands.
"That last guy?" he scoffs, and I look over at him with a smile
which he winces at. "D..." He sighs. "He only asked what he could do
to help."

"I didn't like his attitude." I sniff, and I feel him staring at me.
"We'll get her back, D, but ya gotta hold on, okay?"
"We will get her back." I nod calmly and then look at him again,

grinning. "I'm going to rip their hearts from their chests and give them to her."

"That's...the spirit." He sniggers. "Fucking idiots don't know what they have unleashed."

"You are one to talk." I grin wider. "Why did you beat the shit out of the security guard at the apartment?"

He scowls then. "He let them go. Idiot."

"He's in ICU," I point out cheerfully, but inside, a fire is burning. Like always, it flays me from the inside, but these flames are growing higher than before without my little bird to help control them. They scream for blood, for death, and I'm twitchier than normal. I don't know what is right and wrong...even for me.

Garrett is right, I'm already carving a bloody path through the city, but I don't care. When I was hunting my mum's killer, the bodies piled up, and I never even loved her that much. Little Bird? She's my world. My goddamn black beating heart is hers and she is mine.

Mine.

And they took her.

The carnage will be unimaginable. They will call me a serial killer. They will all fear me, but I don't care, as long as she's back in my arms before the night is through. When I saw the bodies of her guards in the car and her blood on the backseat...fuck.

Panic like I have never felt before poured through me. No one gets to hurt her, to hear her screams, but me.

She fought, of course she did. She's a fighter, a Viper. She killed them and would have slain them all if she could have. But she couldn't, so I will for her. I will place their bodies at her feet for hurting her. And after...

After she will have to survive me.

Because I am unleashed.

WE MEET RYDER AND KENZO AT THE WAREHOUSE. THEY HAVE been busy as well. The scent of the ocean wafts to us, which is just behind the dock. The shops are not too far away, but inside the warehouse is an entirely different world. Our security is swarming the place, all of us are together.

All of us are furious.

All of us are seeking blood.

On their knees before my brothers are eight men, who no doubt work for the Triad. I don't ask how they found them so quickly, I don't care. I can already feel their screams, their bones breaking in my hands. I ache for their pain, to sate the monster inside me until I get my hands on the bastards who took her. But Ryder stops me as he steps forward and eyes them with disgust.

"The Triad took something of ours, and we won't stop until we get it back. Anyone with any information is to come forward now. You all know something, you work for them." He waits, and the men all shift nervously, not wanting to betray their employers. Ryder loses his patience.

Usually, he would let Garrett or me do the dirty work, not that he's afraid of blood, but it paints him as the cautious leader. But now? He pulls his gun and suddenly fires, shooting the man at the very left in the head without even blinking, his face cold. The men on their knees shy away, some screaming, some crying. "I will kill you one by one until I get what I want to know, and if none of you know it? I will start on another lot, I don't need you alive. I will kill all of you. So I will ask again, any information?"

"Oh God," one of them sobs, and Ryder shoots him next.

Six left.

I prowl around them, taunting them, kicking them, needing to feel their pain, needing to make them hurt.

Crouching behind one, I stroke his sweaty hair. "I would tell him. I might be crazy, but he's worse," I murmur to him, as I look up at Ryder and Kenzo. Ordinarily, Kenzo would be smiling, playing the good guy and hiding the Viper underneath.

He might be soft and romantic for Roxy, but only for her.

And she isn't here.

The Viper is unleashed in him. His face is dark, thunderous with anger, his suit is stripped off, and his dice move rapidly through his fingers as he shakes with the need to do something. Anything. I know, 'cause I feel it too. Garrett is the same, storming around the warehouse on his phone, no doubt searching for anything, anyone we can use.

"Please," he whimpers, shaking with fear, sweat pouring down him. "I know nothing, I'm just a delivery—" I snap his neck and stand as Ryder frowns at me, but he knows better than to try and stop me. Especially with her on the line, my little bird.

Just the thought of her has me turning and grabbing the closest man. I roar into his face, screaming into it. He screams back, trying to get away, but it's no use. I need blood. I need pain.

Now.

Everything's a blur, but when I come to, I'm heaving and my body is shaking with adrenaline. I lift my hands and notice they are covered in blood, as are my arms. I can feel it dripping down my face, and at my feet is the mauled corpse of the man. He's a bloody mess.

I glare at the others, and they scream, one even pisses himself, the smell filling the air as I prowl closer. "D, enough," Ryder snarls.

I scowl at him, but he narrows his eyes. Garrett steps closer to me, watching in case he needs to restrain me. It wouldn't be the first time he tried. Until my little bird came, I did my own thing. Only doing as ordered when it suited me.

But then she wrapped me around her little finger. One smile, one punch, and I was hers. Her animal. Her killer.

"Diesel!" he roars, and I slink away, not far though.

"Anyone?" Someone shifts, and Ryder sighs, aiming again, and the man screams.

"Wait, wait! I know something!" he begs.

Ryder pauses, stepping closer and pressing the gun to his head while I laugh. "Tell us, better tell us." I grin.

"They have taken one of your safe houses, that's where they are keeping her, that's all I know, I swear. I overheard it!" he sobs.

Garrett snarls and punches a cement support, which must hurt. "Fuck, we have loads of them, which fucking one?"

"We need to find Daphne and ask her."

Garrett turns and, without a word, shoots all the men as he converges on me. "How is she alive?" He towers above me, but I've never feared him.

"I don't know." I shrug, I really don't. "I played with her for a bit before I burned her in a building. She was tied down."

"Fuck," he snaps. "She's helping them, we need to get her."

"Roxy first, she's all that matters," Ryder reminds us, and we all look at him. "We need to know which safe house, call everyone in. Find it."

Kenzo doesn't speak, just turns away and stomps to the car waiting for us. I look at the bodies. "We should send a message," I murmur.

Ryder nods. "Do it. I want this city turning on them. Let them know anyone who's helping them is now our enemy and will die like the rats they are. Hunt the bastards down, make it rain."

I grin then. "Are you letting me loose?"

He stares at me as he holsters his gun. "Go fucking wild. Make them come to our door, begging for forgiveness, while I find the safe house. Garrett, go with him, you need to release some tension. I will warn the police to stay out of our way," he orders, before looking at the car Kenzo went into. "I'll find the house with Kenzo, we will have it before dawn. Be ready to move."

I glance at Garrett then, and even he looks worried. "D—" He starts.

"You heard him." I laugh. "Let's play."

"Oh fuck," he mumbles. "This should be good."

For you, Little Bird, I'm coming for you.

CHAPTER
FORTY-SIX

GARRETT

I watch D play with the man. My own hands are caked in blood, and the pain of my knuckles breaking has long since passed. Ryder gave us permission, and we didn't need to be told twice.

I let it all out—the aggression, the hatred. All my emotions pour into the city like a disease, leaving bodies behind. They should have never challenged us...and taking Roxy? Dumb fucking move.

We might have let them off easy before. Now? Now they will die with our names on their lips.

I shy away from thinking about her, because when I do, I can't control what happens, and right now, this guy is D's, but the idea of her in pain...of her scared... alone, fills me with such fury, I have to kill something, anything.

We promised to protect her always.

And look what happened. I will never forgive myself for it, or for the fact it was my own fucking fault. If I wasn't so consumed by my hatred for Daphne and the shock of seeing her alive, I might have noticed her using me to get my phone, to lure my girl, but I didn't until it was too late, and now this. I am to blame.

She came for me.

And now I will come for her, always. I will save her, and then I will damn her, making her mine forever. If there's one thing I've learned since I found out she was gone, it's that I can't live without her. Not anymore.

She worked her way under my armour, under my ruined skin to the fighter, the warped killer beneath, and she loved him and made him love her. She is my reason to breathe now, to fight my demons every goddamn day. D laughs, bringing me back from my morose thoughts.

The man is crawling with tears pouring from his eyes. His legs are broken in millions of places, dragging uselessly behind him. The blood trail he's leaving almost makes me laugh. He pulls himself away while D laughs harder, holding the hammer he used to break his legs in his hand.

"Where is she?" he screams, and then brings the hammer down on his back. I watch, letting him get it all out. He dies shrieking in pain with no information for us. So we move on to the next one.

But before we can, I get a call back from Cherry. She owed Roxy, and she mentioned Triad members before, so I told her to put in some work. "What?" I answer, snarling.

"They're dead, all three men that come here. They didn't know much, but they mentioned something about the men you assigned to trail the ex—they're dead." Fuck, that's why we can't get a hold of them, and it leaves us with another dead end.

"Thanks, Cherry, want me to send clean up?" I inquire, trying to play nice.

"No, we got this, you just get her back," she demands, as she hangs up.

We jump on our bikes and speed away, pushing it as we wind dangerously through traffic. I need that adrenaline, that high, and the wind to carry me away for just a moment, but when we end up outside the next building, a convenience store, it's all back.

I have to get it out before it twists me and there is no coming back. Yanking off my helmet, I swing my leg over and look at D. "This one is mine," I growl.

He nods but follows me in, and I head straight up to the counter. The man there glances up from his newspaper, and his face pales when he spots me. He stumbles away as D starts wrecking the shop behind me, throwing shit everywhere, getting his own feelings out.

"Oh God!" He grabs a bat from under the counter and tries to strike me. I catch it mid-air and wrench it from his hands, snapping it over my knee before grabbing him by the collar of his shirt and dragging him over the counter. He screams and jerks as I throw him onto the floor. He starts to scramble to his feet, so I bring my boot down on his back, grinding him to the ground, but it's not enough.

It will never be enough until she's back in my arms.

"You know why we're here," I growl.

"Oh God, please, please, no, I worked for them years ago—"

I snort. "Once a hitter, always a hitter." I stomp on his back before picking him up, holding him effortlessly in the air. He strikes out with a knife he got from somewhere, and I frown down at the small weapon sticking from my side before glaring up at him.

His anger drains away as I smile. I smash my fist into his face repeatedly before throwing him onto the counter and continuing the assault. I can't stop. All that anger pours from me, my knuckles cracking as his face splits open, and it's still not enough.

My demon calls for more until a noise draws my attention. Jerking my head up, my chest heaving, I meet the eyes of the man hiding in the back room. We stare at each other for a moment before the owner tries to grab the knife in my side again.

I go back to pummelling in his face as he tries to block, tries to fight back, but I'm too strong for him.

I'm beating the shit out of him as D laughs. "Oh, they have Mars,

I love Mars ice cream," he calls, and when I look over, he's sitting on the freezer, munching on an ice cream.

Just then, when I'm not looking, the man breaks free from the back room and runs past me. "D, stop him," I snarl.

He sighs but his leg goes out, tripping the man before he goes back to eating his ice cream, his legs swinging back and forth happily like a fucking child.

The man against the counter isn't moving now, so I turn to the man on the floor who groans. Grabbing his head, I drag him to his feet and lean down to get in his face. "Warn them, tell them we are coming, let them know this city will run red with the blood of anyone who ever helped them, worked for them, or knows them. They will all die, because of them." I let go and move away.

The young man turns to look at me before taking a step back like he doesn't believe me. "Go!" I shout.

He turns and dashes away. Yanking the knife from my side, I throw it at him, hitting his shoulder. He screams as he falls. "Better go faster before I change my mind!" I call, and he gets to his feet, gripping his bleeding shoulder, and disappears, blood trailing after him.

D groans. "Let me hunt him, look at that pretty trail."

"No, you can get the next one," I snarl, as I turn back to the other man who is immobile. Grinning, I turn back to D. "We're done here, that felt good."

He nods, licking another ice cream before he offers me one. Snorting, I take it and rip it open, swallowing it whole while he watches. "And they say I'm nuts," he mutters, before flinging his arm around me. "Where to, big guy? The clothes shop or the market?"

"Market," I snap.

"Market it is." He laughs and then chucks the wrapper away. A woman with grey hair walks past, and he grabs her. He turns her, his hand on her throat, and I watch her scream and kick. His face is dark, needy. "Little—" He realises it isn't Roxy and tosses her away. She falls to her knees with a whimper, takes one look at us, and gets the fuck out of here. I clap him on the shoulder as he glares after her. "Soon, brother, soon, just hold on."

"Let's go kill some fuckers," he growls.

CHAPTER FORTY-SEVEN

KENZO

I can feel Ryder's eyes on me, sense his concern for me, but I can't speak to reassure him because I'm not okay. I'm furious at Roxy, at the Triad, and at myself. I should never have left her. This should never have happened. We promised to protect her, and now she's in the hands of our enemies and they are doing God knows what to her.

She's a survivor, a fighter, but she shouldn't have to be. Spinning, I slam my fist into the wall, watching with sick satisfaction as it cracks open the plaster. Pulling it free, I shake off the pain and turn to Ryder, who has stopped talking to gape over at me. When he meets my eyes, he sighs and turns back. "I want everyone on this. Go."

Tony rushes off, and Ryder glances back at me. "We are getting her back, hold on, little brother."

"But what if she can't," I growl, pacing now, my hand bleeding and dripping onto the floor as I go, ruining it. I don't care.

"She will," he insists.

"How do you know?" I yell.

He steps into my path, blocking me with his own anger. "Kenzo, Roxxane is stronger than any of us. She's been through hell already, she can survive this. If anyone can, she can, and right now, we need to trust in that. To trust in her. Just like she will be trusting us to come and get her. I can't do that with you losing your shit!" he shouts, and then pants as he stares at me. "I need you, I—" He looks away then. "I'm struggling too. I need your help, Kenzo, to get her back. Nothing can go wrong. We can rain down fucking hell on them once we have her, but until then, we have to keep it together. For her."

I stare at my brother, lost for words. In his eyes, I see the truth, the fear there, the anger...the need. He needs us now, more than ever, and so does she. He's right, I can't lose it now, not when we're so close. I just wish I was with Garrett and D, letting off some steam.

He sucks in a breath, and I know he's counting because, when it's over, he seems calmer. I wish I could do that. "Calls are already coming in from people who worked for them years ago begging for peace, giving us anything we want if we don't kill them. The city knows, and they are turning their backs on them."

"That's good." I nod. "Which safe house though?"

"Garrett checked a lot the other day, they couldn't have captured it since then, so it has to be one of the ones he didn't check," he murmurs, thinking out loud. It's his turn to pace. He's lost the jacket and tie and stripped off his shirt. He looks so much like our father it's scary, apart from the tattoos. Father would never have sullied his body with ink, said it was the mark of the poor. "It has to be, but which one? They would need space, they would need no neighbours." I let him think, knowing he's onto something, knowing he will get there.

He always does. He's the fucking brains. If anyone can solve it, it's him. I'm trusting him, Roxy is trusting him. All that burden is on his shoulders, but as always, Ryder thrives in it. "Space...space, lots of space. Fuck, of course!" He turns to me, his eyes lit up. "The old hotel. We never go there, and it's in a rundown neighbourhood with hardly any neighbours. The police never get to that side of town because of the gangs. It's the perfect fucking spot."

"Shit," I whisper. "You're right, it would be the last place we looked." Mainly because it was once our father's, and although we couldn't bring ourselves to tear it down, it's well known we all hate it. Ryder wanted to see it rot and destroy itself, and now they've taken our girl there.

To the place where this all started.

The place our father died...at our hands.

He stills, no doubt reliving that night. I can feel the memories reaching for me as well, trying to get their claws in my skin. Flashes of blood, Ryder's pale and panicked face as he tells me to run...

I shake it off, not wanting to go back down that alley. I refuse to live in the past, and what we did, we did to survive. The old man fucking deserved it, and Ryder might live with the burden of being the one who pulled the trigger, but I was the one screaming for him to do it.

And now we're heading back there.

"Call them back. We hit it at dark. No survivors," Ryder snarls, before he turns away. I lay my hand on his shoulder.

"There is no room for ghosts tonight, brother. What happened then is in the past and best forgotten. She needs you to be at your very best tonight. Don't let him win again," I console, before I pull out my phone and dial Garrett and Diesel.

I know Ryder struggles every day with the sins of his past, with the shit he did to keep me safe. I wish I could take that from him, but I can't, and that night...that night, he committed the ultimate crime to save his family. To save us.

It's one of the many reasons I will never leave him, never betray him, never turn away, even when he's cold. Because underneath that ice is the boy who took the gun from my shaking hands when I was scared, who followed me into our father's hotel when I planned to kill him...

And pulled the trigger when I couldn't.

"Anything?" Garrett snarls, as I hear what sounds like a chainsaw in the background.

"Come home, we know where she is," I tell him, before hanging up.

The Vipers are coiling, ready to strike. Nothing of the Triad will remain after this.

Hold on, darling, we are coming.

CHAPTER

FORTY-EIGHT

ROXY

Motherfucking shit balls.

My head aches, my body hurts, and there is a weird ringing in my ears. My mouth feels fuzzy, and my eyes refuse to open. Where the hell am I? What happened? I rack my brain, searching past the fog clinging to it and ignoring the splintering pain. It's important, I know it...

Fuck.

The crash.

Shit, they got me...so where am I? My head feels like blood is pooling in it, like when you lie upside down for too long. My ears still ring, but I can hear past that and my slamming heart to the dripping surrounding me—like water slowly hitting tile, again and again. Other than that, all I can hear is the rustle of wind seemingly far away...then silence.

Okay. Calm the fuck down, Rox. First things first, open your fucking eyes and find out where you are. Then we escape and kill these motherfuckers.

I'm going to make those bitches cry for their mommies...just as soon as I can open my eyes.

I don't let the panic settle in or give it a hold on me, it won't do anything. This is life or death, and I need to get out of here before they come back. I know it will only mean torture until they are done with me, and then I will end up with a bullet in my head. I refuse to die that way. I'll die as I lived, with a beer in my hand and riding a dick.

I manage to finally pry my eyes open. They swim with tears, and I have to blink several times to clear them. When I do, I frown in confusion, trying to understand what I'm seeing.

Am I upside down?

My hair is trailing below me, touching the floor and soaking up the blood from a rapidly growing puddle there. The floor is carpeted, a dirty white colour. Lifting my head with an audible groan, I take a look around the rest of the room. The carpet trails to cement farther out into the space, the walls painted an off white. There's what looks like a boiler to the right, and the rest of the room is almost empty apart from nudie mags taped to the wall in the corner with an old wooden chair angled next to it.

She's got nice tits.

Shit, focus, Rox.

There is an off, damp smell in the room, and it's musty like it's been closed up for a while. I can't spot any windows anywhere either. Fuck. Lifting my head higher, my back straining, I glance up at the ceiling to see I am, in fact, chained to it, dangling there like fucking meat in a butcher's shop. I twist my hands, which are tied behind me, and notice my lips are sore like they were duct taped. The fuckers.

No wonder my head is rushing, all the blood is draining to it, and I'm starting to feel lightheaded. My body is weak, and I have no choice but to drop my head down, forcing my frame to swing precariously. I swear if I fall right now, I'm going to be pissed, but the chain holds even as it creaks.

Okay, so I'm tied upside down...ideas? Ugh, my brain hurts.

Then I remember the knife I had at my spine. I strain my hands, trying to feel if it's there, my shoulders aching with the movement, but it's gone. They took it. Okay, so no weapons either. I could keep swinging, try and break the beam I'm hanging from. The only issue is I might crack my head on the floor or the ceiling might come down, which doesn't seem like a good idea.

I'm betting by now the guys know I'm gone. They will be pissed, and Diesel will be infuriated, but I can't wait for them to come save me. I need to get my own ass out of here. Then I hear boots coming my way. My breathing picks up, my heart racing as I swallow back my bile.

Okay, whatever they do, I can handle it.

A lock clicks, the door opens, and three men step into the room. The door slams shut behind them with a loud snap. I'm locked in with them. Brilliant. I should play it cool, play it smart, but as always, my mouth runs away with me.

"Evening, arseholes, is this a new kink? 'Cause I gotta admit, it's not doing it for me. I'm wet, but honestly, I think I peed myself a little, so I wouldn't take that as a point for you."

They don't respond, but the one in the middle steps forward. He's wearing a black suit with the top buttons undone. His short black hair is swept to the side, and his brown eyes are tight and angry. His lips are pursed, and I spot the number 'three' starting on his neck and stretching onto his shoulder. The other two are clearly goons. The one on the left has a shaved head. His body is bulky, encased in black jeans and a black t-shirt. I spot at least three guns on him, and he looks more like brawn than brains. The one on the right has a purple mohawk, a piercing through his left eyebrow and nose, and even one on his lip. His eyes are blue and a little wild as he grins at me. His body is lanky and covered in tattoos, and he has no shirt on, just some leather pants.

"Do they chafe you? I got the worst chafe from them, you know? Especially when you start sweating a lot, and in leather that's all the time, am I right?" I ask him.

He grins wider. "Baby powder."

"Huh," I say seriously. "I'll have to try that, thanks."

"Enough!" the man in the suit barks, drawing my gaze back to him.

"What? I was just getting started. You should know I once talked my way out of a ticket...okay, three times, but who's counting? Then there was that time I was in a Mexican jail and I—"

Fuck.

My head snaps around, and I swing from the slap he delivered. My cheek stings, but I laugh as he catches my swaying body and stills me, turning me to face him. "Damn, that's fun, do it again, see how far you can swing me!"

He backhands me again, and this time I twirl, it sends bile rushing up my throat, and I hold it until I face them again, and then spew it on them. It sprays across his shoes and trousers, and I laugh as some of it drops down my cheek. "Damn, that was fun." I cough.

He yells, stepping back and looking at his once shiny shoes in disgust. The mohawk guy laughs, and I wink at him. "I thought you would like that."

"Shut her up," the man in charge snarls, as he lifts his foot, glaring down at it.

The other man, Baldie, steps forward and slams the base of his gun into my stomach. My breath leaves me in a grunt, and I swing back and forth, pain splintering through my gut. He does it over and over until I can barely breathe, never mind talk. I feel my ribs crack, shit. So every breath I take hurts, causing pain to flow through me.

But I've had worse, so once I can breathe again, I let out a pained chuckle. "That was good. Got to admit, though, my boy is a torture master, and he's a lot more inventive. Where are the toys? The fear? Come on, you guys can do better."

"Oh, that will come later." Mohawk grins in a good boy type of way.

"Roxxane, look at me," the suit guy demands. So I do, and he steps closer, grabbing my shoulder and holding me still as he tilts his head down to meet my eyes. "I'm giving you a chance to tell us everything. We know you don't want to be there with them, they stole you, but we can help you. Just tell us what we need to know to kill them, and then you will be free."

"Yeah...see, I'd believe that more if you didn't have me hanging like a pig. You should start with that before the chasing and the drugs, but your information is out of date, babes, I'm a fucking Viper." I lunge my head forward, smashing mine into his.

Headbutts are not fun.

Headbutts hurt, kids.

He stumbles back with a howl, his nose busted as pain flares through my head. "Damn, dude, you got a thick skull," I groan, closing my eyes for a second.

When I open them again, he's cupping his bleeding nose, his eyes furious. "Andrew, she's yours. Get me everything I need to know then kill her," he orders, before turning and ripping open the door.

Baldie follows and it clicks shut, the lock sliding into place. Andrew, the mohawk guy, steps forward, cracking his knuckles as he grins at me. "This will be fun."

I sigh. "Andrew, really? I was expecting some cool name. Does your mummy even know you're here? Do you need a permit?"

He grins wider, and then his fist comes at my face and everything goes black.

WHEN I WAKE UP, I'M TIED TO A WOODEN CHAIR. GROANING, I stare down at my hands, each one bound to the chair arms, my legs are restrained too. Fuckers. The barbed wire they used to tie me digs into my wrists and ankles as I shuffle in the chair, trying to break free.

Well, that's new. Stilling, I lift my head, saliva and blood dripping down my chin. There's a marching band in my skull, my shoulders and back are killing me from hanging upside down, and my lungs are tight and my ribs creak with each breath.

Andrew isn't here, probably somewhere jerking himself off, so I close my eyes for a moment, breathing through the pain. Those minutes fade as my mind drifts. It's funny how when the end is coming, you start to think about the beginning.

My life has never been easy, but I gotta admit, I didn't think it would end here. Of all the ways I thought I would die, this was never one of them. That's the thing, though, life doesn't owe you a goddamn fucking thing.

It doesn't owe you life, you have to fight for it to endure and survive. And I did.

It's filled with moments, of winding paths and unexpected turns. Each person that comes into your life offers you a new world, a new place and feelings, not always good, and from each one, we have the opportunity to learn. Whether we accept those lessons is on us. From my dad, I learned to accept pain, to under-stand how strong my body is, even when it's broken repeatedly, and from that, I know I can survive this. Each person has taught me something.

Love, love is enduring. Love is blind. Love is messy and so perfect, we search our entire lives for it, even when we think we aren't. I guess I wasn't either, but I found it anyway in the form of four criminals. Their hearts as dark as their souls.

The thing is, I never tried to fight them, not really. I guess a part of me recognised them, and even though my mind was muddled with betrayal and anger, deep down, we clicked like pieces of a puzzle slot-ting together.

Diesel saw that before any of us. The rest of us lived in ignorance, unwilling to bend and break. Not him, he ripped open those walls inside me, refusing to hide from the truth. Some might call him crazy, but maybe he's just enlightened...and, okay, a little crazy.

Kenzo...fuck, Kenzo. It will kill him if I die. He already lost his mum, and he's got such a caring heart, even if you don't always see it. When he loves, he loves hard. He's all in.

Ryder will blame himself. He thinks it's his job to protect everyone, to see everything coming, but he's only human. It won't stop him from hating himself however.

Garrett is so close to the edge anyway, this might push him over. My scarred enforcer will become lost in his demons until it gets him killed.

So no, I can't die here, because it might break them, make them weak, and let the Triad kill them. I refuse to be the reason they die. I refuse to die myself.

As soon as I realise that, calm settles in my bones. I'm not fucking dying here. If I'm going to die, it will be surrounded by my men with a gun in my hand and a smile on my face. I need to tell them I love them.

The door opens, and Andrew strolls in, followed by Baldie. Shit, okay, it's torture time. I've survived worse, I can survive this. I keep telling myself that as I tilt my head back and offer them a smile. "Hello, boys, my safe word is bubbles, by the way."

"You won't need a safe word," Baldie jokes.

"I bet you say that to all the girls, probably why you don't get past the first date." I grin.

Mohawk, Andrew, laughs. "She's not wrong."

Baldie steps towards me and slams the gun into my stomach, making me puff out a breath. When I can finally breathe again, I grin. "Damn, boy, don't you know how to play? You gotta start soft, get them all warmed up for you. You don't just slam your piece in hoping for the best." I look over at Andrew. "Who's the newb? Do you bring him around like one of those women with chihuahuas in their purses?"

He bursts out laughing and glances over at Baldie, whose whole head is turning red. I watch with sick fascination as it crawls along his shiny head. "Do you wax that? Like, do you buff it too, like polishing floors? 'Cause it's hella shiny—"

This time, he smashes the gun into my aching shoulder. A grunt escapes my lips from the sudden blast of pain, and I try to curl into it to protect it. I learned when I was young that eventually, everyone screams, it might spur them on, but honestly, people only don't scream in the movies. Oh, a knife in your gut? Let me just stay silent, it doesn't work that way. But there are two ways you can play it—you can let them destroy you, break you down, or you can use it against them.

Flip the narrative, be unexpected.

That's what I do. When I can breathe without crying, I wink at him. "Is your nob bald too?"

He slams his gun into my other shoulder, and I feel a crack, goddamn bitch. "Motherfucking bald bitch," I snarl. "That ain't no way to treat a lady."

"You ain't no fucking lady, you whore, you're a dead woman walking."

It goes silent then, and I look over at Andrew. "This is super awkward, 'cause I'm not walking. Do you think he gets all his lines from bad action movies?"

This time Andrew stops him. "Franny, enough," he snaps. "She's mine, you're here for muscle."

I hold in my laughter for as long as I can, which is all of thirty seconds, then I laugh so hard, a bit of pee comes out. "Oh my God, your name is Franny? Holy shit, no wonder you've got anger issues, poor Franny!" I howl.

Baldie growls and comes towards me, but Andrew slides in front of him and, for a moment, I see why he's the torturer. Anger flickers across his face, and he seems to grow larger. Baldie, aka Franny, backs down, swearing as he turns away, and then Andrew relaxes, slouching again and grinning like he hasn't got a care in the world.

But I've seen it now, what he hides underneath. The true Andrew, he likes pain, he likes it to hurt, this should be...fucking horrible.

Andrew turns and shrugs. "Behave, he might kill you."

"Yeah, that ain't gonna work. People have been telling me to behave since I was a kid, and look where I am." I shrug in an 'aww

464

shucks' type way as he heads over to a tray and sets out his equipment. "So tell me, how long have you been doing this?"

"Oh, a few years," he replies, as he picks up a scalpel.

"Get a lot of customers?" I inquire calmly.

He steps before me with a cruel smile. "You're a strange one, do you know that? Never mind, they all bleed red."

"How freaked would you be if my blood came out blue now?" I laugh, but it turns into a groan. I grind my teeth as he slashes across my face, a light cut, but enough that I feel blood drip down my cheek. "Motherfucker, that's the goddamn money maker, kid."

"Apologies." He nods and drags the blade down my arm. "Is that better?"

"Much, thanks. Don't fuck up my tats, though, or Garrett will be pissed, and last time he had to tattoo me...well, let's just say it was a happy ending all around."

Andrew grins. "Of course." He starts to slice the knife across the top of my feet, and I let out a little scream which has Baldie laughing.

"Hey, Franny, you think your mum called you that because of your giant vagina?" I call breathlessly.

Andrew steps it up a notch then. When he slices across my stomach, I have no time for talking, all I can do for the next however long is breathe and scream. When he moves back, my head hangs as I struggle to hold in my tears, so being the crazy bitch I am, I twist my wrist in the barbed wire, cutting it so the pain pushes back the waterworks.

They can have my screams, nothing else.

When I'm more me, I raise my head and spit blood at Baldie and laugh. "That was fun, what's next?"

"Tell me how to get into their apartment?" Andrew questions. Ah, so they don't know that much.

"I don't know, they like to blindfold me, the kinky bastards." I grin.

He stabs me again, and I groan but breathe through it, the agony surging inside me now. Shit, shit, shit. *Do not fucking pass out, Roxy.*

465

When I feel like I'm not going to, I smile at him, my lips feeling a bit numb. "Can I call a friend for the answer?"

He sighs and wipes the blade. "Come on, Roxy, it would be a shame to waste such a woman. Tell me what I need to know. Tell me everything about the Vipers."

"Yeah, I'm gonna hard pass on that one. No passing go, no collecting your money, bitch, those fuckers are insane."

He crouches and grabs my knees, peering up at me. "More scared of them than me?"

"Hell fucking yes. Did you not hear me? They are insane, and they like me! Imagine what they do to people they don't like..." I grin wider then. "Imagine what they will do to you for touching me. Last time, they broke the guy's hands and ripped out his tongue...I wonder, will you scream?"

I watch as he lifts the knife covered in blood. It reminds me of Diesel, and weirdly, my pussy clenches...like, really, ho? Now is not the time.

Yeah, I've successfully pissed Andrew off.

He backhands me, and my head snaps to the side as blood fills my mouth. Spitting it out, I turn back around with a laugh, grinning widely at him, blood undoubtedly covering my teeth and lips if his disgusted sneer is anything to go by. "You call this torture? My foreplay is harder. Come on, you can do better," I taunt.

"Tell me!" he roars in my face, impatient now that he's realising how hard it will be to break me.

Licking my lips, I look between his eyes. There's no way I'm betraying my guys. They tell you under torture to reveal information that's not important and is close to the truth, but no way am I risking that. Diesel would murder me, love or not. I know it's going to bring a world of pain, but I can take it.

I can survive it.

Sucking in a deep breath, I nod seriously, my whole body aching, blood dripping down my curves, and agony ripping through my veins. "Okay, okay, I'll tell you..."

They both wait expectantly as I try to make myself look meek and broken, even letting tears fill my eyes, real ones from the hurt. Sucking in another painful breath, my ribs protesting, I belt out, "And I will always love you..." Andrew flinches from how loud I sing.

He backhands me again, cutting me off mid-song, so I spit the blood out and spin back to him. "No? Not feeling it? What about some Metallica? No, what about Tay-Tay? You look like a secret Swifty fan!"

Baldie steps forward, aiming his gun at me. "Make her talk," he demands. "We don't have long before they come for her."

I grin at that. "Franny, they already are, and you're so fucked. Now where was I? Oh, Tay-Tay—" I start to sing and, with a growl, he rips open the door and storms off. "Wait!" I call. "We were having so much fun, Franny! I didn't even get to my originals yet!"

Andrew sighs as if he's disappointed in me. "Roxy, this could have been so easy. You could have died quickly."

"Yeah, I never liked the easy option. What can I say? I like them hard." I grin at him.

He rips off that calm mask now, though, and I know I've got a world of pain coming. Let's hope I can survive this shit, because my Vipers are coming, I know that, and if they find me dead...the city wouldn't survive their wrath.

The time passes slowly, excruciatingly slowly, like the pain flowing through me all over my body. He's masochistic, not as good as D, but it still does the trick. My screams ring out around us, and tears finally fall, covering my cheeks. Blood pools beneath me, my fingers slippery with it. He pulls some toenails, breaks some toes. He snaps my finger. He stabs, slices, and cuts. He covers my head in a bag and pours water across it until I can't breathe, until I think I might drown, and when he rips it free, water flows from my mouth to my chest, my lungs burning from the icy liquid.

"Thanks, I was thirsty," I croak.

He's trying his hardest. His job and life are on the line if he doesn't get the information, but here's the thing...I would die before I betrayed them, before I betrayed anyone who gave me a chance, who was kind to me...and my Vipers?

They love me.

And, weirdly enough, I fucking love them too.

So if I die here, alone in a goddamn nasty room, then so be it. I've been flirting with death since I was a kid, and dying for the people you love seems like a good way to go.

Andrew can't change that. He can break my body over and over again, he can make me scream and cry, he can make me beg for death, but not one word about my men will pass my lips. I think he's beginning to realise that when he sits back and watches me.

"I have to admire your loyalty." He sighs. "Irritating, but impressive. Tell me, did they really buy you?"

I nod, wetting my lips.

"So, why the loyalty?" he asks curiously.

"'Cause we started off badly, but now they are my everything." I shrug. "You know how it is, let's face it, every romantic story is fucked up in some way. *Romeo and Juliet*? They were fucking kids, and they died. Don't even get me started on that atonement, Jesus, I cried like a baby. Loyalty is earned, not bought."

"And they earned it?" he queries.

I don't answer, and he nods. "I have to update my boss, think on that." He stands and leaves, and I watch him go, the slam of the door and click of the lock loud in the dank room.

Have they earned it? His question reverberates in my head.

There is no question we are all messed up and our love is weird... but loyalty? Yes, they earned it, and they will continue to, because I know they will do anything to protect me. Save me. Give me anything I need.

When no one else did, they saw past the attitude and scars, and kept going until they got to me.

I'm not a child or stupid. I know if I betray them they will kill me, even if they love me, but that's not why I don't do it. It's because I couldn't stand to hurt them that way, even to save my own life, and if that isn't love, I don't know what is.

Sometimes in life, you meet people worth dying for, and they are usually the same people who are also worth living for. But you can't always have both. If all I can offer them now is my silence and death, I'll do it.

I just wish I could take some of these fuckers down with me.

My men might be criminals and deal in death and power, but when it comes down to it, all they really want is love. A family. I refuse to break that.

They might be my strength, but I'm their weakness.

Just then, an explosion sounds above me, and the whole building rocks as dust falls from the ceiling. I smirk, knowing exactly who it is.

I don't need no fucking hero to come save me, I can save myself, yet not once did I doubt they would help me, help me save myself, and I was right.

For once, someone didn't let me down.

And I refuse to disappoint them.

It's time to get free and meet my boys, then we are killing all these motherfuckers.

Okay, Roxy, time to rock this shit. As more explosions and gunshots go off upstairs, I look around before an idea comes to mind. It's a stupid fucking idea, but it's better than nothing. So, rocking from side to side, I build up momentum.

The chair starts to wobble, rocking with me, the creak loud in the room, but it's drowned out by the fight going on. I swing harder and, with a yelp, the chair falls to the side. Crashing to the floor, I groan as I bang my head, but the chair explodes. I roll onto my back and moan, lying there for a moment. I landed on my left shoulder, which isn't working. Shit, I think I dislocated it.

Fuck me, John Wick made that shit look easy. He lied, it hurts like a son of bitch, worse than that first cock in the ass.

Sitting up, I notice the chair pieces are still attached to my arms and legs by the wire. Shit. Smashing my wrist into the floor, I manage to get the wood free and then unwrap each wire before doing the same to my ankles. I'm only able to use one hand, since my other arm is hanging funny. I whimper as I peel the barbs away, watching the blood gushing from my ankles and hands. The bitches.

It's slow going, really slow going, and when I'm done, I'm panting and drenched in sweat. Now to get the door open. Pushing up to stand on unsteady bare feet, I hold my arm across my chest protectively, wincing at the pain racing through me.

Here's another dumb idea.

"Yo, Franny, you out there?" I scream. "Franny, I'm free, better come get me!"

The door clicks and opens, revealing Franny. When he sees me, he growls and comes at me. Here goes nothing...

I pretend to fall, grabbing the bottom of the chair arm in my good hand, before I leap up as he gets closer and smash it into his stupid face again and again with a scream. He howls and lurches back, trying to block me, his gun dropping to the floor.

I keep smashing until he's on the ground. Panting, I grab the gun in my other hand and press it to his head. His eyes widen, blood flowing down his face. "Bye, Franny, been nice knowing you." I pull the trigger. Clutching the gun closer, I groan as I step towards the door.

God, I want a nap.

CHAPTER

FORTY-NINE

RYDER

Sitting in the car down the road from the hotel, I check my guns and weapons as we survey it. "They will be keeping her somewhere safe, probably below the actual hotel. They will be heavily manned, but I don't expect the whole Triad to be here—it's too dangerous having them all in one place. It's going to get messy. Stay close, check your corners, and watch each other's back. We move from room to room until we get her," I order, strapping my vest on. It will protect me a bit, but a bullet to the head will still take me down, so we need to be smart.

Even as rage flows through me, I need to get to my girl.

Diesel puts on his bright purple fanny pack, complete with a sparkly unicorn on the front. I don't question it, because we honestly don't have time for his crazy. Garrett has a shotgun fastened to his chest and a fucking grenade launcher on his back—after all, he will be going in first. Kenzo is heavily armed too.

We're going to be outnumbered, but where's the fun if you're not?

"Let's go. We go in loud, don't hold back, and remember what we are fighting for," I snarl, as I snap the clip into place.

"Oooh, I know this one! For my little bird!" Diesel grins.

"Are you okay?" Garrett asks. "Not mentally, we all know that, but—"

"Oh, I stabbed myself with some adrenaline. Let's go!" he cries.

Laughing, I slip from the car, and then we go silent. We move in formation towards the hotel. We have the advantage, we know the layout, and we know the passages and ways to get around quickly. They don't.

Plus, we are fighting for our girl, nothing will stop us.

We run across the road, the night cloaking us, and I put my back to the wall next to the front door, the chain that once locked it lying forgotten on the pavement. Garrett puts his back to the other side, and I nod, counting down on my fingers. He palms the grenade launcher and, with a burst of movement, I rip open the door. He goes in, ducking and firing before pulling back out as explosions rock the building.

Shouts follow, and we all file in through the smoke, breaking apart to take each side of the large foyer. I duck behind a post, and Garrett does the same while Diesel flies over an old sofa as bullets fire at him. Kenzo slips behind the front desk. I peek around to see bodies on the floor, but from the stairs and up above, they're firing what sounds like submachine guns, the bullets spraying everything as wood and sofa bits fly everywhere, the roar loud.

Then it goes silent, and we all move at the same time. Stooping down, I take aim, choosing the top floor since I'm the best shot. I trust my brothers to deal with the others. I drop two men before ducking back behind the pillar as they start firing again, their shouts echoing. Looking to Garrett, I nod. He palms the grenade launcher again, and I cover him, darting out and firing randomly as he lines up and shoots.

We both hide behind our cover as the explosions sound again, and then it's silent. He slings the grenade launcher behind him and grabs the shotgun. I nod, and we break from our cover. There are only two guys left in here, and they are coming down to meet us. Diesel flies at one with a roar, slicing and ripping him to pieces. Kenzo takes the other, sliding over the desk and sneaking up behind him, shooting him in the head.

"We go down. Garrett, you take the back," I instruct, as we head past the staircase to the stairs that lead to the basement. No doubt they are waiting, so I tear open the door and toss a smoke bomb down there, waiting until I hear the yells and coughs, then I sneak down. Kenzo's hand clutches my shoulder, Diesel is behind him, and Garrett is taking up the rear, watching our backs.

Ducking at the bottom of the stairs, I peer around the corner to see three men, all coughing and whining, looking around wildly.

"Where are they?"

"Fucking find them!" they scream.

Steadying my breathing, I pick off all three before swinging my rifle behind my back and grabbing my pistol and knife. Kenzo taps me, and I nod, then he slips past me and into the space, his gun drawn as he leans down and checks them, ensuring they are dead. When he nods, we break into the room. There are two doors, both cupboards, and we investigate them. The only way out is farther down through a narrow corridor.

It could be a trap. It's a risk we have to take.

"Diesel." I nod, and he slips down the passageway. If it's a trap, only one of us dies. It's the rule.

He moves on silent feet, a machete in one hand and a pistol in the other. When he reaches the intersection, he presses to the wall before rolling around one corner and aiming at the other end. When nothing happens, he waves us on. We follow, and once we get to the junction, I frown. *Which fucking way, Ryder, think.*

We hear a yell to the left, a very familiar yell.

We all share a look before Garrett tries to break into a sprint, but I hold him back with one hand. "They could be using her as bait, fucking think."

I move faster now, drawn by her. If they are hurting her, I will fucking kill them and rip them to pieces. The hallway goes on for a while, and there is no one here. It opens into a large room at the end with other doors leading off. I know because Kenzo and I used to play hide and seek down here while Dad was working.

"Okay, Kenzo and I have eyes up top. Garrett and Diesel, left and right." I nod as Garrett moves to the other side of the hall and nods at me, ready to go in first.

Always ready to die for us...and now her.

Our protector, our enforcer.

But this time, I hesitate to give the order, hating the unknown of that room. We usually have a plan, this is fucked and rushed, but he grunts and nods at me again. "I got this," he mutters, before breaking free without my orders and stepping into the room. Swearing, I follow after him, the others close behind.

Someone fires, and I duck behind a barrel, peering above it to see at least eight men waiting for us at the other end of the room. They hide behind an overturned table, beer and cards scattered across the floor. They heard us coming.

"Diesel," I hiss. "Is it time to open the fucking fanny pack yet?"

He laughs. "Nope! This is easy, give me cover," he whispers, before sneaking into the shadows of the room. To draw their eyes, we quickly fire, making sure they are concentrating on us and not the crazy bastard now climbing across the pipes in the ceiling like some kind of monkey.

I keep my eyes on him, switching between firing and watching him. He crouches when he's near them, and then, without a word, he drops down behind the table right behind them. "Boo!" he screams, and I rise to my feet, firing as I walk, the others doing the same.

Diesel takes two down, but we hear him yell before he shouts louder. "You bastard!"

Oh shit.

We take the rest down, but when we round the table, he's punching the shit out of a man. "Shoot me? Bitch, you motherfucking ass dick, bitch, I'll eat your fucking heart—"

"D?" I call, and he glances up, blood dripping from his ear where the guy obviously got a shot off. "I think he's dead," I point out dryly.

He looks down at the man and, with a snort, drops the body before wiping his face on his arm, smearing blood across it. "Where were we?" he asks, as he picks up his machete and tosses it. "Ah, yes, rescuing my little bird."

"You good?" I query.

He nods and wipes his face again as he steps over the bodies and joins us at the only corridor, which leads to the boiler room. We hear another yell, and we break into a sprint, knowing she's down there.

The door at the end of the hallway is open, and we aim for it.

We round the door and just stare. Our girl is smashing the butt of the gun into what used to be a face, and when she hears us, she tosses her hair back, straightens, and smirks. "Hey, boys, good timing. Hope I didn't miss all the fun!"

Blood covers almost all of her, one arm is held oddly at her side, a gun is clutched loosely in her hand, and her body is shivering, but she has never looked so goddamn beautiful. Striding across the room, I grab her and crash my lips to hers. She moans and presses against my body before wincing and pulling away. Breathing heavily, I look down at her, noting every wound and her arm. "What happened?"

"Dislocated, I think, when I smashed the chair to get free." She sighs. "Don't try it, it's not fun."

Laughing, Diesel grabs her from behind. "Little Bird, Little Bird."

Kenzo pulls her from his arms and kisses the top of her head, pushing her hair back. "Darling, you scared the shit out of me," he whispers raggedly.

Garrett plucks her from his grip and presses his forehead to hers, searching her eyes. "Don't you ever try that shit again," he snaps, before kissing her. She pulls away with a laugh.

"I missed you all too," she murmurs.

Diesel prowls around the room, his face cold and angry, his emotions altering so quickly. I nod at Garrett, who takes the door to make sure no one is sneaking up on us. "You left," he snarls.

She looks over at him and rolls her eyes. "Someone sort out my fucking arm, it's pissing me off."

I nod and grasp it softly. I hold it out straight while I meet her gaze. "This is going to hurt, love."

"Fucking do it," she snaps, and I do, popping it back into place. She yelps and punches me, I let her. Chuckling, I kiss her hand better when she shakes it out. "Stupid hard head."

"You left!" Diesel screams, and we all look over at him. Shit, he's exploding.

"Oh fuck," Kenzo whispers, and points his gun at him. I hold up my hand to stop him.

"D, calm down," I order, but he ignores me, shaking his head as he smashes his hands into it.

"Left! She left!" he roars.

"Oh yeah, 'cause it's my fault for getting kidnapped—" She starts, but doesn't get to finish. Diesel is there, kissing her hard, tasting her blood, before he bites her injured lip. "You are in a whole lot of fucking shit when we get home, Little Bird."

"I can't fucking wait," she murmurs against his lips while he laughs, but then, suddenly, his hand darts out, circles her neck, and squeezes, not playing. I keep my eye on him in case he actually tries to kill her. He releases it and drags his hand down her front and digs his fingers into a wound, making it bleed more, but she groans and presses closer, even as he's hurting her.

"I'm so fucking angry at you," he growls.

"Yeah? You can fuck it out of me later." She laughs, pressing against him, unafraid, but he pulls away and paces again, his sparkly fanny pack bouncing with the movement.

She doesn't even question it, used to his brand of crazy.

"You try shit like this again, and I'll make you wish they had killed you," he warns as he stops, his hands clenched, and I share a look with Roxy.

Garrett sighs. "I told you not to piss him off, baby."

She throws her hands in the air. "Next time I'll tell them not to kidnap me, okay?"

Kenzo sniggers, and she glares at him. "Don't you fucking laugh." She turns back to D. "Calm down, babe, just think of all the people upstairs you get to kill."

It seems to settle him marginally, but he's still pissed, and I press against her back. "You're about to see why we warned you not to piss him off," I murmur, and she shivers against me as she leans back into my chest.

"I can't wait..." She sighs. "Thank you for coming for me, I didn't doubt it for a moment, but...thank you."

"Always, darling," Kenzo offers, as he steps in front of her. "How many times do we have to tell you that you are one of us?"

I hear boots upstairs and step back, readying myself for what's to come. We don't have time for a proper reunion, we have some enemies to kill, and then we need to get our girl checked out. The list goes on and on, so I straighten and square my shoulders.

"They will be waiting for us upstairs. Ready to give them hell?"

She snorts. "Always."

"D, go first. Love, you stay in the middle of us. Kill anyone who isn't a Viper. No prisoners," I order, and they all nod, wearing matching, bloodthirsty grins on their faces.

Ready to kill them all with our girl at our side.

CHAPTER

FIFTY

GARRETT

I'm happy, but there's no time for reunions. We need to get out of here, then I'm going to show her exactly how much I missed her. I can still taste her lips on mine and feel her body against me. I wish I could slam her into a wall and fuck her , right here, work out my frustrations and regrets, but I can't.

She's depending on me, they all are. I focus on what's coming next, not the woman walking in front of me, her ass swaying temptingly as I hold the shotgun. She glances over her shoulder at me and winks when she catches me checking out her ass. "Later, big guy, killing time now."

I smirk at that as we stop at the end of the hallway, D checking out the room. Leaning closer, loving her shiver as I press into her, I murmur in her ear, "Who says you'll survive later? You have four angry boyfriends to deal with."

She laughs quietly. "I can handle you four."

I nip her ear and she yelps. "Dude," she protests.

"I'm a Viper, baby, biting is our thing, and I plan on biting and licking you all over later while you fuck my brothers."

"You know, there is nothing hotter than a man knowing how to use a weapon," she calls, watching us with our guns.

"She's talking about our dicks!" Diesel retorts, as he pops around the corner. "Clear, they must be upstairs."

"I'm surprised you haven't asked about the fanny pack," I scoff to her.

She looks at me with a grin. "On the list of weird, crazy shit Diesel does, that's pretty low, plus he looks cute."

D snorts, and she sighs. "Fine, you look hot as hell. I can barely keep my hands to myself. The sparkling unicorn really brings out the crazy in your eyes," she deadpans.

"Better, now let's go." He grins as he leads us back across the room. Roxy doesn't even blink at the bodies as we troop up the stairs and stop there, knowing they have to be waiting for us.

"We go out blazing, don't hold anything back," Ryder orders. He looks over at Roxy then. "Stay close to one of us and kill all of them."

She holds her gun closer at that. "Got it, babe, let's go. I'm getting hungry."

"You can eat my dick later, darling." Kenzo grins, and honestly, it's nice to see him joking again. For a minute there, I thought we lost him.

D grabs the handle and looks back at us. "Three, two, one, go!" he calls, as he breaks open the door and rushes out. We follow after him, aiming around, but no one is here. Stepping up next to Roxy, I watch her back as we sweep the room. Ryder nods at the stairs, and I go first, Roxy behind me as we reach the first level.

There are two ways to go, so I glance back at Ryder and gesture to Kenzo. He nods, and Kenzo breaks off and goes with me. I look to Roxy then. "Go with them, baby, and watch their backs for me. I'll see you soon." I turn away, but she grabs me, and her lips crash into mine. Groaning, I kiss her back before she pulls away and turns, gun in hand, and follows after Ryder with D trailing in her wake.

480

I watch her go, my heart slamming in my chest. I'm going to marry that girl one day and make her mine forever. Until then, I need to clean this shit show up and get her home. Kenzo walks behind me, his back to mine as we begin to sweep the corridor. They have to be here, and I'm betting there's at least one Triad member.

They have a rule, they are never all together, but they would have wanted information, so one would have been here. We find him, get what he knows, and then we hunt the others down. Destroying their worlds.

Then we make her the center of ours.

I open a bedroom door and sweep it before moving on. Kenzo takes the left side, and I take the right, before we go upstairs again. We get halfway up when shots come down at us. Slamming against the wall, I take aim and fire back, but the angle is wrong. Cocking the shotgun, I rush up the stairs, firing as I go around the corner, taking the man by surprise. There's one next to him, and he slashes out with a knife. I smash the gun across his face, and he falls back to the wall, then I fire at him. No point being discreet. Looking around, I reload.

Kenzo moves past me on the third floor, but ducks back when a bullet hits where he just was. "Five, end of the corridor and moving down."

I step up behind him and nod at him, ready. We both kneel and fire around the corner. Yells of pain come and the shooting stops. At least three of them are dead, one is crawling to his gun, and one is struggling to breathe, his hand covering his bleeding chest.

Kenzo slips down the corridor, stomps on the crawling man's back, and blows his brains out as I snap the neck of the man leaning against the wall. After checking the others, we move on. We have to be getting close to where the Triad is waiting, and they must be rapidly losing numbers.

"Last door is shut," Kenzo murmurs, and I look up to see he's right. All the others are missing or open, so we head down there.

I kick open the door and rush the man taking aim, slicing easily

481

across his neck as I glance around. "Fuck, they are like rats," I mutter, as I meet Kenzo out in the hallway.

"You're not wrong, looks like the roof." Kenzo sighs, noticing the propped open door leading to stairs that go up.

"Fuck," I grumble, and slip through it.

At the top of the stairs is a metal door, and we have no idea what's behind it. I look to Kenzo who grins, loading his gun again. "One more time, brother. Let's kill them and get our girl out of here."

Grinning back at him, I grip the handle and count down silently, then rip it open as we both pour onto the roof.

It's teeming with them. The fucking bastards were just waiting for us—a last stand. One catches my shoulder with a bullet, so I throw myself to the side and duck behind an air vent while Kenzo manages to shield himself with a post.

Knowing Kenzo can handle himself, I lean around the vent and try to pick them off. I manage to drop a few before they get smart and just continue firing. It keeps me so distracted, I don't notice the men suddenly at the door to the roof until it's too late.

One manages to grab me, and I have to roll, stopping in the open doorway before rolling again as a barrage of bullets follow me. A pained yell sounds nearby as I stumble to my feet.

My head whips around, and I spot the knife glistening with blood protruding from Kenzo's stomach as he tumbles to the floor. I notice the man creeping up on him, and I know there is one coming for me, but it's not a choice.

My family comes first.

I take aim and fire at the man sneaking up to kill him.

"Garrett!" Kenzo screams in warning, but I turn too late, already knowing that when I took aim, it was him or me.

As my eyes are closing from the hit, I watch Kenzo try to get to me before being knocked out himself. At least they didn't just kill us here...

CHAPTER
FIFTY-ONE

DIESEL

Following after Little Bird, I try to contain myself. My hands itch to rip her open and put her back together again for daring to get kidnapped, for daring to leave us. Anger is pouring through me, lighting the inferno inside me until I'm a ticking time bomb.

So, when we open the first door and interrupt a man beating another with a bat tied to a chair, I lose it. Pushing past Ryder and Little Bird, I rush in. I hear him warn her to leave me to it, but then everything blurs. Just my demons and me.

Grabbing the bat from his hands, I turn it on him, letting my demons out to play. My arms strain from the force of my swings. The room is quiet except for his screaming and my...laughing.

Huh, that's me.

When it's over, I look up. My whole body is covered in blood, my eyes are dark and crazy, but Little Bird pushes free of Ryder's hold and walks towards me unafraid. Pressing up on her toes, she kisses me softly. "He's dead, come on, babe."

She plucks the bat from my hand and leans it against her shoulder as she walks past Ryder, both of us staring after her. "I love her," I state seriously, and Ryder laughs.

"You fucking better. Nobody else is putting up with your crazy ass."

We both turn and follow her, checking each door as we go, but all the other bedrooms are empty. The blood starts to dry on my skin and gets itchy, but I ignore it, my eyes locked on my little bird. Even at my darkest, she loves me, isn't afraid of me.

It might kill her one day...

But fuck, I'm too selfish to care. She's mine. I'm going to stick a goddamn ring on her finger so the whole world knows. I might even carve my name into her skin. I bet she would like that...especially if I fucked her at the same time—

"D," Ryder murmurs, and looks over me. "You're thinking out loud."

I blink and look from him to Roxy to see her grinning. "Carving, huh? Save it for later."

She's walking while she's talking, and that's when we hear a distinctive click. Fuck. She turns just as I see it fly towards us through the air. "Grenade!" Ryder screams, reaching for it to protect her, but I watch in awe as she tightens her hold on the bat and, like a total fucking badass, swings, hitting the grenade.

We all watch open-mouthed as it flies back to where it came from, exploding as it hits the stairs, throwing us backwards.

I make sure to grab her when I land above her, shielding her. Her laughter reaches me through the ringing in my ears, and when I glance over my shoulder to make sure no one is firing or coming at us, I gape down into her grinning face. "That was awesome," she declares.

Grinning, I lean down and kiss her. "And hot as hell. Keep that bat, we're playing with it later."

"Kinky." She nods as I push to my feet and grab one of her hands, with Ryder grasping the other, and we pull her to her feet. He quickly checks her over before nodding and handing her the bat.

"Come on, let's keep moving," he mutters, his shoulders covered in dust and soot.

We pick our way up the stairs, avoiding the destroyed railing and corpses there. When we reach the landing, it opens into a large sitting room, and Ryder seems to freeze for a moment. "Ry?" Little Bird asks, laying a hand on his back.

He shivers under her touch and swings his haunted eyes to her. "One day, I will tell you why this room is the place where this all started, but not right now," he vows, and then seems to push it back, straightening. "I'm betting someone in charge is in there. It's a big room with an overlooking balcony office."

Roxy grips her bat tighter. "Let's do this."

I nod, and he grips his gun. "Let's."

We burst into the room, having mere seconds to read the space. There are at least ten men in here, all packing and waiting for us. I spot an Asian man in a suit on the balcony, and when he sees us, he ducks. "Fire!" he screams.

Oh shit. Throwing myself at Little Bird, I tackle her behind a side table as Ryder throws himself behind a bar. They fire at us in a hail of never-ending bullets, and Roxy flinches, curling down lower as I grin at her.

"Isn't this fun? I gotta admit, I'm hard, this is totally our foreplay for the day."

Laughing, she slaps me. "Focus, think with your other head."

"Oh, I am, he's thinking about fucking your ass," I mutter, as I lean around the table and throw my knife, not watching where it lands, but I hear the plunk as it embeds in its target and a gun stops firing. "Or your pussy...or mouth, honestly, I'm not fussy as long as I get to do it with blood still covering me."

"You're crazy." She laughs, but when she says it, she makes it sound like a good thing.

Grabbing another knife, I toss that as well, but I miss, and Ryder glares over at me. "Open the fucking fanny pack!" he screams.

Roxy laughs. "What's in it?"

Leaning back on my knees, I unzip it and show her the grenades inside. "Do you always keep your grenades there?" she inquires, the firing still going on around us.

"Not always, sometimes I keep knives or tacos in it," I murmur as I palm one.

"Tacos?" she echoes.

"I get hungry when I fight." I shrug and pull the pin, tossing one, and then cover her.

It explodes moments later, the blast followed by a scream, so I throw two more, the bangs loud. I don't wait, I leap to my feet and sprint around the table to see all of the men down, some dead, some just knocked unconscious from the blast. Zipping up my pack, I grab my lighter and quickly ignite one of their coats as I step over them, whistling as I do.

"He's wearing a fucking fanny pack," one of them wheezes.

"I think it's hot." Roxy shrugs as she spins the bat in her hand and hits him on the twirl, knocking him out.

"Crazy bitch." Another man reaches for a gun, so with one grenade still left, I shove it in his mouth and pull the pin before diving at both Roxy and Ryder. We make it behind a table as it explodes, raining gore all over.

"That was fun!" I yell, as I leap to my feet, and they slowly get up and check on the rest.

Ryder takes care of the others while Roxy looks around for the stairs to go up. "Over there," Ryder calls, and leads her over.

Fuck that. "Stairs are for pussies!" I shout, as I leap onto the sofa and then grab the chandelier above. Swinging my legs back and forth, I manage to rock towards the balcony, gripping the edge at the last second and swinging myself over to meet the panicked eyes of the Asian man.

"Hey, man, stairs suck, am I right?" I remark, as I punch him in the face and disarm him, throwing the gun over the balcony as I wait for the others. He goes down hard, but quickly gets to his feet. By then, Roxy and Ryder are up here.

The man with the three tattooed on his neck looks at Roxy and spits. "You stupid whore, aren't you dead yet?"

"Nah, sorry, I live to disappoint," she offers, as Ryder lashes out, stabbing him in the stomach. It's not a killing blow, though, but he does fall backwards, blood flowing from the wound.

Just then, we hear a yell, and we look around to see a man with a mohawk running at us with a chainsaw from the other side of the balcony. Roxy thrusts out her leg, tripping him, and I give him a helping hand over the edge of it. We all look over as he falls with a scream and lands on the table below, impaling himself on a decorative statue there.

Looking back at number three, I grin. "I would give him an eight out of ten for his landing."

"You think you're so smart? Better check your people again, I'm betting you're missing one." He laughs, and Ryder steps closer.

"Who?"

"That enforcer of yours?" Number three chuckles, gripping his bleeding stomach harder as he falls to his ass. "We made a promise, and he will help us keep it..."

"Where is he?" Roxy yells, pressing her bat to his chin.

"He'll already be dead anyway." He chuckles weakly. "You're all fucking dead," he sneers. I go to raise my knife, but Roxy beats me to it.

With a savage yell, she brings the bat down on him, again and again, caving in his head as his laughter cuts off into a choking noise. But she doesn't stop there, she keeps swinging, over and over like a woman possessed until she can no more. The bat drops to the floor with a clank, and she stands there panting with blood on her hands and arms, spatters of it across her face.

Pushing back her hair, she licks her lips and straightens, looking over at me and Ryder, who are just staring at her in shock. "What?" she snarks.

"Nothing, Little Bird...just, fuck, that was hot." I nod, then look at Ryder. "If she wasn't ours, I would totally stalk her, hack her cameras, watch her through the windows, the whole nine yards."

"Well, aren't I a lucky bastard?" She huffs. "I get to live under the same roof as you, so now you just get to stalk me to the bathroom."

Flicking open my lighter, I grab a cigarette and talk around it. "Exactly, you really are beautiful when you shower."

She blinks and looks at Ryder. "I would ask if he was serious, but I don't need to."

"Children," he snaps. "Let's find Garrett. He's probably lying to spook us, but I would rather be safe than sorry."

The mood sobers instantly. "Garrett. No one takes that big fucker, it would be like trying to carry an elephant."

As Roxy slips past me, she pats my chest. "I'll tell him that."

CHAPTER
FIFTY-TWO

ROXY

We quickly make our way back through the hotel looking for Kenzo and Garrett, and a bad feeling starts in my gut as we go down the corridor they traversed and to an open metal door at the end. Heading up, we step out onto a roof where there are bodies littered everywhere, but no Kenzo or Garrett.

But then I hear it.

A grunt.

Following it, I drop to my knees behind an old section of piping to see Kenzo there with blood dripping from his chest. His face is pale, and his eyes are barely open. Gripping his hand tight, I gesture the others over. "Babe, what happened?"

He groans and looks at Ryder. "They got Garrett, they wanted him all along. I couldn't stop them, I'm sorry."

Ryder smashes his fist into the pipe, but I wipe Kenzo's sweaty forehead and kiss him softly, seeing the distress and pain carved there. "Shush, it's okay, we can get him back." Lifting his hand from the wound, I spot the blood there. "We need to get him to a doctor."

D leans down and inspects it before slapping him. "Stay awake. Okay, this is going to hurt." He grabs him, hoists him over his shoulder, and casually stands, not like he's got a Kenzo backpack on. "Let's go, Little Bird."

Ryder is on the phone as we head down through the hotel, and when we get into the car, I slip into the back, and D places Kenzo along the back seat between my thighs. I hold him there, stroking his hair and kissing his head.

"Missed you, darling." He sighs, his eyes on me as he reaches up with bloody hands and grips my own, tangling our fingers together.

"I missed you too," I admit. "Those suckers knew nothing about how to kidnap a woman, honestly."

He laughs at that, the sound tapering off in a groan as we speed through the city. "They have no finesse, that's why," he wheezes out. "You gotta trick them into loving you, duh."

"I was going to ask something stupid like, does it hurt?" I snort as I lean down and kiss his head. "Don't you fucking die on me, you hear me, asshole?"

"Got it, beautiful, no dying, but you can play nurse and kiss all this better later." He winks.

"Even dying, you're a total flirt," I scoff, though panic winds through me at the blood he's losing. I look up and meet Ryder's eyes, who's staring back at his brother in alarm. Kenzo reaches out and grabs his hand, squeezing it.

"I'll be fine, brother, don't worry about me. Deal with Garrett, okay?"

Ryder sucks in a breath but hesitates. "I'm sorry you had to go back there," he offers lightly.

"Me too. When this is over, we're burning that place down." Kenzo grins, turning his head to meet Ryder's gaze. "No more ghosts, no more bad memories, just us, okay?"

Ryder nods and glances at me. "Take care of him."

"Always," I reply, as I look back at Kenzo. "You're going to be alright, you're too fucking stubborn to die on us."

"Yeah?" he whispers.

"Yeah." I nod. "Wanna bet on it?"

He groans. "God, I fucking love you."

"The winner gets to trash Ry's new car," I murmur, making D laugh.

"If I win, you have to marry us, that way you can never leave." He grins.

"Fuck, you always play the high stakes," I mutter. "Just 'cause you're dying doesn't mean you get to ask for weird shit."

"Course it does," he whispers, but his face is paler now. Fear blasts through me as I lean down and press my lips to his. "Don't fucking die, and I'll marry you all, I'll even wear a fucking dress and everything."

"Deal," he mumbles.

"We're here, doctor is waiting," Ryder announces, as we skid into the parking garage. My door is ripped open, and I tumble out into D's arms as two burly security men grab Kenzo and carry him away. I watch him go with fear in my heart and my hands covered in his fresh blood. My fear turns into anger as I look at Ryder.

"We need to find Garrett, then we kill these fucking assholes. No one takes what is mine," I snap, as the elevator closes after Kenzo. There is nothing else I can do for him, and I refuse to let Garrett suffer. That man has been tortured enough, I don't want any more nightmares for him.

"I don't know where to find another one of the Triad. Go clean up. We'll search the city and get the information however we have to. D, where are you going?"

I look over my shoulder to see D getting into a car. "I'll find out where the Triad is, you be ready."

I don't ask how, I don't care. We need that information. Ryder twines his fingers with mine, and his free hand comes up as he swipes his thumb across my lips. "Kenzo will be okay, my brother is a fighter, but right now, Garrett needs us...stay with me, love."

Licking his thumb, I nod. "We need more weapons."

"Let's go get some then," he murmurs, as he leans down and kisses me softly.

I don't clean up, but I do change my knickers and dress, 'cause fighting in wet panties is no fun. The blood dries on my hands and face, and I leave it. Let them see it, let them die by my hands covered in my lover's blood.

I slip into the red dress Ryder bought me so long ago, then I add my earrings and necklace. Let them all see that I'm a Viper. That they fucked with the wrong family.

When I meet Ryder in the living room, he's watching Kenzo, who's now sleeping. The doctor managed to stop the bleeding and has stitched him up, but he's having a blood transfusion now and needs to rest.

Leaning down over his prone form, I kiss his still lips. "Be home soon, be good."

I turn away and head out of the front door. Kenzo is safe, but Garrett isn't, and every minute that passes is a minute he could be being tortured or killed. I refuse to let that happen. These are my men.

My family.

No one hurts them but me.

No one gets to make their lives a living hell but me. It's time the Triad realised that they fucked with more than just the boys—they fucked with a goddamn ruthless bitch.

When we get to the parking garage, D is waiting there. "I know where one of them is, get in." I slip into the back and Ryder gets into the front, and D skids from the garage, making Ryder grunt.

"We need to get there in one piece, brother," he snaps.

"Yeah, yeah, I won't kill you." D laughs as he turns the corner so fast that the wheel actually comes off the road, so I click on my seat belt. As we straighten out, something bangs behind me, making me jump.

Staring at the boot at my back, I frown as it comes again, then I hear the definitive sound of muffled screaming. "Erm, is there someone tied up in the boot?"

"Duh, where else do you keep them?" He laughs.

"Okay, D, why is there a man in the trunk...and how long has he been in there?" I ask as I grab on to the 'oh shit' handle when we almost crash.

"I grabbed him while you changed into that sexy as hell dress." He winks over at me. "I'll rip that off you later by the way."

"Eyes on the road," Ryder barks.

D laughs and looks back, avoiding running over someone walking across the street. "He was the one who told me where he is, he's his driver, I got lucky."

"So where are they?" I query.

"One of the them is where this all started—their restaurant. I figure we go there, I scare and torture him, get the information and free Garrett, then hunt the other rat bastard down, and then an orgy." He leans out of the window as he swerves around someone. "You drive like a fucking snail!"

I glance back and notice it's a police car, but I have way too much information to deal with to focus on that. Ryder sighs. "Yes, we are finishing it tonight. They should have known better than to come against us. Now their family will be wiped from the map."

"Are there a lot of families in the city?" I inquire, trying to pass the time and not think about what's happening to Garrett.

"There was once, but now there are only three in this whole area. Us, the Triad, and the Petrov family, the Russians. They keep to themselves, though, and own the city down the road, but the Triad has always been greedy and unwilling to do the work to build an empire. Instead, they are like rats trying to feed on others."

We pull up outside a restaurant, and Ryder looks at me. "Stay close, don't let them see your weakness or how worried you are for

Garrett. They will use it. This is a game, love, we have to play it well."

"I don't like fucking games," I mutter, and he smiles nastily.

"I know, but I'm the best at them. I will get him back with you on my arm. Are you ready?" I nod, and he leans back and kisses me softly. "Just be you. I'm trusting you in there more than I ever have with the others, princess."

He's trusting me.

I tilt my head back. I won't let him down. I slip from the car, and he comes around and takes my arm, leading me to the restaurant like we are here for a nice meal and not to start a war. When we slip through the front wooden door and into a dark, candlelit restaurant, I let all weakness go. Garrett needs me, Kenzo needs me, they all need me. Now is the time to step up.

Ryder passes the host stand, ignoring the man in the suit there, and rounds it into a Chinese restaurant before leading me up a curved staircase. We step into an open restaurant, which is up top and looking over the area below, with white cloth covered tables. Along the back wall are floor-to-ceiling windows showing the city all lit up in its glory. The walls are a deep black with red and orange accents in paintings, tapestries, and prints. The ceiling is covered in hanging lanterns. It's dark and moody, and I love it. If it weren't for the men who own it, I would want to eat here, looking out at the city and watching it all go by with Ryder's hand on my thigh, Kenzo's fingers slipping into my knickers in front of everyone, and the food forgotten before us...

Ryder tugs me after him as he winds through the tables to a raised area at the back, where a circular table sits, slightly hidden, behind a white letter covered screen. I don't look at anyone specifically. The restaurant is empty except for the men in suits, hired muscle, all watching our progress, yet Ryder is unafraid. As is Diesel behind me.

Three versus at least fifteen men, that's how many we can see, yet they don't let any concern show. In fact, they stroll through the room like they own it, the power flowing off them in waves, and then I

494

realise what it means to be a Viper. Even surrounded and in an enemy's nest, we are still the big bad.

The baddest motherfuckers in the city.

Even in the face of loss, even in the face of death, we own this shit. I raise my head and add confidence to my walk. I'm a fucking Viper, it's time I start acting like it. We take what we want, we do what we want.

There is a lone man sitting at the table with his side towards us. He picks a napkin up and wipes his mouth as he sits back and waits for us to reach him. His short hair is pushed back, and he looks similar to the Asian man from the hotel. He has a number two tattooed on his neck as well. Is this like fucking Thing One and Thing Two?

Uncaring that he didn't invite us to join him, Ryder pulls out a chair for me, and I sit. He pushes it back in, but not too much so I can access my weapons and move quickly. He sits next to me, legs parted, hand close to his gun, even as he leans back like he has no worries in the world. His face is cold and empty, that usual control in place. I envy that, I don't have that kind of bluff, so I'm going to own being a mean, cruel bitch.

Relaxing back in my chair, I tilt my head and let my eyes run across him. "I don't know, number three had more of an air of power about him...you look like a little bitch." I grin as his eyes narrow and flicker to Ryder.

"You came here unannounced to insult me?" he snaps, but there is a quiver in his voice. This isn't in their plan, he doesn't know what's happening or what to do.

"Of course not, but you can understand Roxxane's anger. You did, after all, kidnap and torture her." Ryder's face tightens at the words, his anger flaring, so I lean over and lick his ear, my eyes on number two.

"Stay cold, baby, you can let it all out on me later," I murmur, and he groans.

"She tends to hold a grudge. I know that from personal experience."

He laughs. "But no, we are not here to talk. We both know the time for talking has passed. Your family has signed their death warrants, and now you have a simple choice of how quickly you die." He grins.

The men in the room rustle, and one in particular steps closer, his gun drawn. Diesel shifts behind me, protecting my back. Straightening in my seat, I wink at number two. "He's right, I do hold a grudge. I'm very fucking good at it. Ask my men. Oh wait...you have one of them." Wagging my finger, I lean into the table, flaunting my breasts as I take his wine glass and sip it, watching him before leaning back in my chair. His eyes flicker to the blood still on my skin, and he swallows. "So where is he?"

Ryder doesn't stiffen at me taking over for him, no, he relaxes more, he's too emotional to act the part right now. I don't have to be composed, I'm the scorned girlfriend, so I can be as crazy as I want, and I plan to be. They took what is mine.

They hurt me.

They hurt my family.

Number two licks his lips nervously before he smiles. "Probably being cut open as we speak."

I freeze and carefully, calmly place the wine glass on the table. "I will ask once more, and you should know that every person who has ever hurt me has a tendency to wind up dead...and you know the man behind me, right?" I relax back into D, who bends down and kisses me, making me moan as he flicks his tongue across my lips, tasting the wine there. "He's a master of torture, and I learned from the best, so one more time before I get mad. Where is Garrett?"

Diesel's hand circles my throat possessively and drags my head back again, kissing me hard and biting my lip until I taste my own blood before he releases me. Licking my lips, the blood undoubtedly dripping, I look to number two. "I'm waiting," I purr.

"Go fuck yourself, you stupid bitch. You will all be dead when this is through, and no one will remember you and your fucked up family," he snarls.

I blink, letting his words drop into the silence for two seconds before I jump into motion. Yanking out Ryder's gun, I point it at the man closest to him and fire, hitting him square between the eyes as I push back from the table and stand. Yells go up, then guns are drawn and firing as I let off four more shots, killing four more guards before giving the weapon to Ryder and storming around the table. Trusting them to protect me. I hear Diesel laughing and others screaming as I meet number two head-on. He's tangled in the tablecloth as he gawks at what's happening.

He thought he was untouchable, but he's wrong. No one is untouchable but us. Everyone can die, I will kill them all to get my man back. No one fucks with what's mine, my damaged lover.

I kick back the chair, and it crashes to the floor with a loud thump. Stepping over him, I press my foot to his throat to stop his struggling, my heel pressing against his soft flesh. He gulps, his hands going out to the side in a gesture of peace, his scared eyes locked on me. He's finally realising his family is dead. Everything they did to win, every law and rule they broke, and everyone they bribed or killed was for nothing. All because they got greedy and took something that wasn't theirs.

"Where is he?" I snarl.

The firing stops, but I don't look away as Diesel rounds the table, crouches next to number two, and looks up at me with blood on his face. "That was fucking beautiful. You are wearing those heels later," he murmurs, as Ryder steps up next to me and stares down at number two.

"We warned you, where is he?" he growls.

I hear a rustle at the stairs and Diesel, without looking, pulls his gun and fires. I hear a grunt and then the distinctive sound of someone falling down the stairs.

"Sorry about your brother, he was a real prick though." I smirk, leaning forward like I'm sharing a secret. "He talked like a little bitch at the end of my bat." Number two sputters, and I laugh. "Don't ever fuck with a Viper. Just because I have a pussy doesn't make me weak. You fucked with the wrong family."

He narrows his eyes, but he sees the truth in my gaze and deflates. "Please don't kill my wife, she's innocent in this."

I don't speak, but I dig my heel in deeper. "Did you afford us those same niceties?" Ryder snaps.

He closes his eyes for a moment before opening them and looking at me. "He's being held at our family's home, 478 Rosewater. The mansion on the hill overlooking the city."

"Security?" I ask, and I can feel Ryder's surprised and appreciative gaze.

"Over thirty men, the last of us, my brother will be there too...and her," he sputters as I jab in deeper.

"Her?"

"Daphne, his ex, she was working with us," he wheezes. "Came to us wanting revenge. We made a deal to kill you all, but she could do whatever she wanted with him. She's been supplying us information."

"Fucking knew it," Ryder snarls.

"I should have tortured her more." Diesel grins. "I won't make that mistake again."

I look to Ryder then. "Why did she betray him in the first place?"

The man under my heel struggles, so I push harder, and he starts to pant. "Why?"

He looks at me sadly. "For money and power. She was offered both by a rival, she thought they would own the city, but she was wrong. It almost killed him, they paid her to do just that, but he survived. We hunted her down, and Diesel killed her, or so we thought."

"Now she has him," I hiss. "She's going to finish what she started," I whisper in shock. "Ryder, we have to get him now."

He nods and is already on the phone, so I glare back down at number two. "Anything else?"

He shakes his head, his eyes wide, so I grab my gun, the one

Garrett got me, and I shoot him in the face. It explodes, and I close my eyes as brain and gore hits me and Diesel. Some even gets on Ryder, but he doesn't blink at it.

Stepping away, I rip off my heels, and with a cry, drive them into his chest before standing and brushing my hair back. "Let's go get him," I demand, as I turn and pick my way over the bodies. I feel my men behind me.

What started as a business deal has now become my life. There's an old quote, 'Throw me to the wolves, and I will come back leading the pack.' I was thrown to the Vipers, and now they are mine.

Never underestimate a woman, because those seen as weak have a lot less to lose than those with everything.

I'm used to being the underdog, but no longer. No, I'm a fucking viper queen, their girl, and I'm going to tell the whole city tonight after I get my man back and we kill the Triad for good. No one will ever come for us again, let this be their final warning.

We own this city.

We own them.

CHAPTER FIFTY-THREE

GARRETT

I know instantly something is wrong, the bed under me is too soft to be my own. The smell is wrong, not to mention my arms are straining and my legs are in an uncomfortable angle. My head is fucking killing me, like I took one too many hits to it. I don't let on to anyone who is watching, my breathing remains the same, even as my anger chases away the haziness moving sluggishly through my blood.

The hotel.

The roof...Kenzo.

Fuck, I hope he's okay. If anyone can survive a stab wound, If anyone can survive a stab wound, it's that slippery bastard, but right now, I'm in trouble too. They came at me, it was a fucking trap, they wanted me, but why?

I twist my hands experimentally and find my wrists are bound, ankles too. I'm spread eagle, the cool air hitting me, then making me shiver. I try to push back the panic at being tied up again, flashes of the past sneaking into my mind. The room smells clean, like mint and bleach, but the bed feels unmade and mussed.

Where the fuck did they take me?

I'm going to fucking kill them all. I had plans, like to remind Roxy that she was mine and not to get her ass kidnapped...then I went and got my ass taken.

I don't understand why they singled me out. The smarter move would have been to take Ryder or, hell, even Diesel so that he wouldn't hunt them. No, this feels personal. Just as I think that, I hear a door open nearby. Keeping my eyes closed and my breathing even, I wait as I hear soft footsteps, muffled by carpeting, heading my way.

Her perfume hits me first. Even now, she still wears that same piss stinking Chanel, and I know why me. *Her.* She wanted me. It was probably her condition for working with them, the stupid cunt. I feel her long nail next, running down my chest, and I realise I'm naked, bound, and helpless to her once again.

Ain't life a fucking bitch.

I survived this once, I can again, but I refuse to be that same, shocked, betrayed boy. I'm a goddamn Viper.

My eyes open and meet hers as she grins down at me, her face half burnt away. Finally, the rot inside of her shows on the outside. "You look fucking awful," I sneer.

She frowns and narrows her eyes, digging her long nails into my chest. "And you look better? Poor, little damaged Garrett. I wonder, can you even still get it up for a woman, or does she have to be cutting you up?"

"So you're working with the Triad? How many cocks did you have to suck to get them to even pay attention to you?" I taunt nastily.

She snarls and digs her hand in deeper, cutting my skin, but I don't even react, which she hates. "None, they want you gone. We made a deal so I could have you. Right now, your little whore and brothers are being killed."

"Doubtful," I scoff. "You can never kill them, especially Rox, that bitch is too stubborn to die."

At her name, Daphne snarls and drags her nails down my ruined chest, making me grunt in pain as she draws blood. "Yeah? Then she will live long enough to get your broken, bloody body back. You die tonight like you should have back then, but that doesn't mean we can't have some fun first." She flutters her lashes, her half-melted face pulling in what I'm guessing is supposed to be a seductive expression. Jesus, how did I used to fuck this woman?

"No, thanks, would rather stick my dick in a chainsaw, it would be more fun than your rank cunt." I laugh.

She stabs her nails into my stomach, making me crunch inwards as I swear at her. Laughing, she pulls back and licks my blood from her nails, causing me to gag. "You're fucked up in the head."

"True, but I'm tired of talking. How about we recreate some old times?" She plucks a knife from the side and lets it shine in the light, showing me. "This is the very same knife I used on you last time. I kept it as a memento, but then you had to go and survive, didn't you?"

I don't reply, just grinding my jaw as I stop the flashes from coming back to me, of waking up in the hospital with tubes down my throat while I panicked. I refuse to let her see how much she's affecting me, how the terror is flooding my system. I refuse to give her any more power over me than she already has.

Climbing up onto the bed next to me, she glides the knife down my face, but I twist away. She snarls and grabs my chin, pulling me back around, her lips crashing onto mine. Her taste makes me gag as I rip away and headbutt her for touching me. She falls away with a cry, but then she's back in an instant, the knife held to my cock, her lip busted and bleeding, which makes me grin.

"I wonder, does your little Roxy know how you used to like to hurt me? That it got you off? That you liked watching me with others?" she whispers.

I can't help but smirk. "It was the only way I could come with you. I didn't even know that was messed up until her. I like to hurt her too, but she fucking loves it, she comes on my fingers and tongue from the pain while she also fucks my brothers."

I throw it in her face, knowing she always wanted them as well, the power and money she would get from being their girl. But they hated her, could smell her fear and see the truth before even I could. She digs the knife into my thigh near my cock, and I freeze as she snarls, "She's fucking dead anyway!" she screams, before sucking in deep breaths. "And soon you will be too, and I'll be the queen, I'll have money and power."

I snort. "You're fucking delusional. Once they are done with you, they will kill you. They can't sell you, you're too fucking ugly for that trade. Nah, they will make it quick. You are nothing. Just a withered, old, gold-digging bitch. You will never be anything more."

With a shriek, she swings her legs over me and starts stabbing. Screams get trapped in my throat as I thrash to try and dislodge her, my blood covering her blade and splashing her hands and arms as she screeches wildly.

Fuck!

I can't die here, I can't...

CHAPTER FIFTY-FOUR

We speed towards the house. Tony, Sam, and the others are behind us in another car. I'm not waiting for them. She will kill him, but she will make it hurt. It's time this bitch dies. I'm tired of her ghost hurting him.

Only I get to do that.

The farther we head from the city, the quieter the roads get. Diesel passes over more weapons they had in the car, and his fanny pack is back on, but this time, it has a happy, fiery sun. Seriously, does he collect them or something?

I'm going to need to investigate that shit as soon as we get back, because it's so weird seeing this big, bad, crazy, beautiful man...with a sparkling fanny pack. It's also weirdly hot. I don't ask what's in it this time though.

"Diesel, you go left, I go right. The others are going through the backdoor. Love?" Ryder glances over at me as he drives, his hand grabbing mine for a second and squeezing. "I need you to get my brother out. He will be somewhere on the second floor."

I suck in a breath, knowing he's trusting me to do that, but I nod and grip the bat between my legs tighter. "That bitch is mine."

He grins and looks back at the road. It's long and winding as we head through the hill to the lit up mansion on top. From here I can see the glass balconies surrounding the white, two-story building. It's a nice fucking house, too bad it will be gone by the end of tonight.

We pull up behind the gate and get out, all the guards strapped to the teeth. But when another car pulls up, we all point our guns and wait, the headlights blinding us slightly until the driver's side door opens and Kenzo tumbles out.

He grins at us. "Didn't think you could leave me behind, did you?" He laughs as he walks towards us. His chest is covered in a vest, but he's leaning slightly to one side.

"No, go home, brother," Ryder barks. "You are hurt."

He rolls his eyes as he reaches us, kissing me hard. "Hey, darling. Didn't think I would let you have all the fun, did you?"

"Kenzo—" Ryder starts, but Kenzo snarls at him.

"He's my brother too. I'm here, I'm not going home, and neither would you. We do this together. Every minute we waste, he could be dying, so for once, just shut the fuck up and listen to me," Kenzo snaps before softening. "I'll be fine, the doc gave me something for the pain that will keep my muscles lose and won't tear my stitches until I do something stupid."

"Fuck!" Ryder yells, but turns to look at the house, knowing he's right. "Fine, but you stick close to me," he demands.

"Got it, brother." Kenzo looks down at me and winks. "Don't think I've forgotten our bet. Doc said you even cried, how cute. I knew you loved me."

"I did not fucking cry, there was dust. I still hate your guts," I snarl, even as I lift up on my tiptoes and kiss him hard. "Do not do anything stupid."

I turn to Ryder and grab his shirt and drag him to me, kissing him too. He groans into my mouth as I pull away panting, then I'm spun and dipped, and Diesel kisses me. "Later, Little Bird," he promises, as he lets me up.

My heart is hammering and arousal flows through me, but now is not the time. I have a man to rescue, and I'm going to call him Princess Garrett for the rest of our days. He can call me his white knight.

I'm still in my dress, but Ryder fastens a vest over me, his vest, without a word, and then we head towards the gate. We don't sneak through or buzz, Diesel blows the fucker up, laughing to himself the whole time. I swear, I get why people are terrified of him, but when I look at him, all I want to do is ride that crazy train.

Literally ride him.

But like he said, later.

It does the trick though. Guards stream from the house, and we pick them off as we advance down the driveway, me behind a line of men, playing it smart. The front door is open, the blood of the now deceased guards lining the steps as we head into the hallway. I take a quick glance around. It's a nice house, all white walls and marble floors, with a grand staircase on the left, art on the walls, and big, decorative chandeliers. It screams money, and you can see the Asian accents dotted around here and there. It really is beautiful, what a shame.

I wait for the guys to break up, and Ryder looks back at me and nods. I press my bat to my shoulder, holding my gun in my other hand as I suck in a deep breath, and as the bullets fly, I run to the stairs. I have no time to waste, they could kill him if they hear us coming. I can't let that happen, they are all expecting it from me, he's expecting it.

They only die if I kill them.

I take the stairs two at a time, ducking when an explosion goes off, until I'm standing on the landing. It opens into a living room, and there is only one hallway off of it. He has to be down there. Hurrying across the living room, I press against the wall as a shot comes from the hallway, aimed right at me. Fucking bastard.

Gripping my gun, I duck around the corner and fire. I hear someone cry out, but the hallway is almost too dark to see down. Rushing down it, I almost stumble over the man clutching his arm. Taking him by surprise, I swing the bat, bringing it down on his leg. I hear the crunch as it gives in, so I swing back again, hitting it from the other direction, and he crumples to the floor, his leg bent in two places. He's passed out, but I can't let him sneak up on me, so I grab his gun and shoot him before moving on.

Come on, Garrett, where the fuck are you?

The gun fire from below seems to get quieter and quieter the longer I wind down the hallway until I'm alone. Fuck, when this is through, I need to go on a vacation and ride lots of dick...and have orgasms. Lots and a lots of orgasms.

I want to feel like I'm dying from them. Stupid Vipers and their stupid enemies getting in the way of my dick plans. There's a door to the left and, remembering what I saw in films, I put my back to the wall and hum the *Mission: Impossible* theme song. I swing it open and jump in. It's empty, and it feels kinda anticlimactic, but I slip out and to the next door. There are only three. This one opens into an empty bathroom, so I suck in a breath and approach the one at the end.

This has to be it.

Is he behind this door? Fuck, let him be okay. I ain't the praying type, but right now, I'm praying to anyone who will listen, God and Satan, 'cause let's face it, if anyone is gonna have our backs, it's probably my dude Satan.

Reaching out, I grab the silver handle and steady myself for whatever I might find on the other side. When I swing it open, I have a split second to take in the room, and when I do, my anger surges through me again.

This fucking bitch.

She is poised over him, straddling his lap, his body bare and covered in blood from various wounds. His hands and feet are chained, and she has a knife aimed at his slick, bloody chest.

His face is twisted in a terrified snarl, his eyes wild and wide. I can feel his anger, pain, and terror from here, and see the ghosts circling him. In that split second, I hate her more than I have ever hated anyone.

Not because he used to love her and she betrayed him, but because of the pain I know he will have to live with again after this. The hate fills me, my movements jerky, and I must make a noise because she starts to turn towards me.

I've never wanted to hurt someone so much before, to feel them bleed, to hear their screams and know they are suffering as much as they made him. But for her, it's an expectation. I get it now. Why Diesel does it, why Garrett fights. I need that too.

I need this bitch to suffer.

Striding across the room as her head lifts, I watch as her eyes widen and her mouth drops open. I swing my bat, gaining momentum until I'm next to her, and then I smash it across her face.

She flies from the bed, and I scramble after her, landing above her on the carpet. She screams, grabbing for her fallen knife, and I drop the bat, smashing my fists into her face again and again.

"He's fucking mine, you cock sucking, son of a bitch, psychotic cunt." I can hear words leaving my mouth, but all I see is the horror and pain twisting Garrett's face, the knife covered in his blood, the grin on her lips.

Blood bubbles from her lips as she gasps and struggles beneath me. "Wait!" she calls, her voice choked, but I can't hear her. All I see is the blood on her, Garrett's blood. More words tumble from my lips as I smash my fists into her face over and over. I feel my knuckles crack, my own blood joining hers and Garrett's, but the pain of it only adds to my hate.

I can't stop.

Her nose breaks, the sound loud, and her lips burst like ripe fruit. Her head thrashes from side to side with my blows. Her face is caving in, her eye dulling as I kill her. It's still not enough, it will never be enough. When I physically can't hit anymore, I drop my hands to her chest, panting heavily and looking at the bloody pulp which was once a woman.

My own hands are slick with her blood, and I know some is Garrett's. With a pained scream, I bring my fist back and smash it into her face again, my arms sore and aching like I'm lifting weights.

Breathing rapidly, I fall to the side and crawl along the floor to the bed before I stumble back to my feet. Ignoring her unmoving, bloody body, I rush over to Garrett, who is thrashing and yelling in the chains. His eyes are wild, his chest heaving, his blood covering the bed.

He can't see me.

He's seeing her, lost in his own memories and panic. Fuck.

But I have to try, I have to get him to see me, so I climb up next to him and yank on the chains, trying to free him, knowing better than to touch him right now, but she must have the key. He stops moving, and I look down into those eyes, those damaged, pained eyes, and I can't help it. Tears slip down my cheeks as I cup his face with blood-stained hands. "I'm here, big guy, she can't hurt you again," I whisper, before choking on a sob. I slide my hands back into the chains, slipping with my blood-covered, clumsy fingers, but I manage to finally undo one.

It was a mistake.

I don't see him coming, and he doesn't see me—no, he sees her. His hand darts out and circles my throat, squeezing hard, cutting off my air supply. My eyes widen as my hand comes up to claw at his before I stop myself, that won't help. Instead, I relax into his touch, even as my lungs scream for air.

See me, big guy, please, feel me. See me. Come back to me.

I beg him wordlessly as I relax into his touch, my eyes fluttering shut as everything starts to go dark. If I die here, at his hands, then so be it. But I know that will kill him, more than she ever could, so I fight, hanging on as long as I can, having hope that he isn't too far gone.

That he can chase those demons away and come back to me.

Please, come back to me.

"Baby?" he croaks, his words pained, and my eyes snap open.

His mouth drops open, his eyes blinking rapidly, and I know it's him. He looks down at his hand and yells, jerking it away. I fall forward, weak, sucking in desperate breaths. I hear him tugging on his chains, no doubt to get to me. "I'm okay, I'm okay," I croak, and I feel him freeze next to me.

"Baby, God, I'm sorry. Fuck, God, I'm so sorry—" I lift my head, hearing the pain in his voice and seeing the tears in his eyes. "I couldn't see you, I couldn't, I swear, I thought it was her, I thought it was her," he sobs, big racking ones that shake his entire body, and no matter how tired, how weak I'm feeling, I drag my ass over to him and lay against his chest, pressing my forehead to his as I cup his cheeks and wipe away his tears.

"I know, shush, I'm here. I'm sorry I didn't get here quicker, but she will never hurt you again, I promise. God, babe, I'm sorry," I whisper, my own tears dropping onto his face.

Just two broken souls meeting in a blood-stained bedroom, both lost until we are in each other's arms. His pain is mine, and right now, I wish I could take it all away. Drain it from him. I want my cruel, mean asshole back, the one afraid of nothing, but right now, he needs to be weak.

He needs me to hold him while he's vulnerable so he can be that man again, so he can find his way back. So even though I know we need to move, I hold him, kissing across his face. "It's okay, I'm here, she's gone." I just keep repeating it.

"Baby?" he croaks eventually, and I look back at those eyes. "I hate you," he whispers, a small smile covering his trembling lips.

"I hate you too," I whisper, as I lean down and kiss him softly. "We better get going, big guy, that okay?"

He nods and sucks in a breath, seeming to regain control of himself a bit. "Yeah, are the others here?" he asks, clearing his throat.

"Downstairs," I say, as I sit up and undo his other hand before crawling down the bed and unfastening his feet. Once he's free, he tries to sit up but collapses back, no doubt from blood loss and shock. I help prop him up. "Take your time."

"Where is she?" he snarls, and I point over the edge of the bed.

"Dead, sorry, I couldn't help myself." I shrug, knowing he probably wanted to do the honours.

"Good," he snaps, and sucks in a breath, scooting to the edge of the bed. I get to my feet, holding my arms out in case he falls as he grabs the bed and hoists himself up, wincing in agony.

"We just gotta get downstairs, big guy, then we're going home," I assure him, and he looks at me and gives me a fucking heartbreaking smile.

"Wherever you are is home," he whispers.

"Yeah, you've lost too much blood, you'll hate yourself for that later," I tease. "But don't worry, I'll remind you that you said that when you're calling me a brat again."

He snorts and then groans in pain, his arm covering his chest. He has small knife marks and puncture wounds everywhere, too many to count, which is probably why there's so much blood. He's also naked, so I hurry away until I find some sweats and then kneel at his feet. "Use my head, let me help you," I offer, as I hold them there.

He grips my hair, lifting one foot after the other, as I tug the sweats on before I get to my knees and pull them all the way up, covering him. I can't ask if she hurt him that way, not yet, but if he wants to talk about it, I'm here. I won't pressure him. I'm just so fucking glad he's alive.

Getting to my feet, I wrap his arm around my shoulders, and we lumber from the room. He manages to hold some of his weight, but the farther we walk, the harder he's leaning into me. It's slow going, and when we hit the stairs, I can't hear any more fighting. Each step is agony for him, and I have to grit my teeth at the pressure on my body.

By the time we reach the bottom, we're both panting and covered in sweat. I manoeuvre him around the bodies, making sure none are my guys. I spot Sam in the corner and freeze for a second. His eyes are empty and unseeing, his face pale, his gun on the floor next to him like he dropped it, and there's a hole in his chest.

Swallowing hard, I turn away, knowing I need to get Garrett free. The guys will meet me out there, I know it. They have to. We head through the front door and up the driveway, each step slower than the last, until I'm grunting, holding nearly all his weight. "Come on, big guy, stay fucking with me, okay? Not much farther."

"Love you, baby," he slurs, and I look up to see his face is pale and way too much blood is dripping from his chest.

"Oh no you fucking don't, hold on!" I demand, and he snorts again.

"So bossy," he murmurs.

"You know it, so fucking listen to me for once, you wanker." I drag him as far as I can, just passing the gate, when I hear a noise and glance back.

As I hold Garrett against me, I see Ryder striding towards us. He slips his head under Garrett's other shoulder and helps me. Kenzo isn't far behind, but he's holding his stomach and wincing, otherwise he seems okay.

"Where's D?" I ask in concern, just as I see him stroll from the house with a cigarette in his mouth. He waves at me casually before flicking it back at the house and running towards us.

It takes all of three seconds.

The house explodes.

CHAPTER FIFTY-FIVE

DIESEL

Garrett is in a bad way. He's pale and losing a lot of blood. We manage to get him into the back seat. We leave Tony to clean up and bring number one, as his tattoos indicated, back home to us. All that matters right now is our family.

Our broken family. Kenzo is hurt. Garrett is dying...he can't fucking die.

I can't lose him.

Panic surges through me until I smash my head into the dashboard to silence it. Ryder glances over, grim-faced, as he starts the car and backs away. "Can't die, die, no die, can't die." I don't even know I'm talking until a slap lands across my head.

"He's not fucking dying, you hear me? So shut the fuck up, D!" she screams, and I look back to see the tears in her eyes. Her dress is torn and covered in blood, and the terror in her eyes is because, despite her yell, she's worried he will.

"Little Bird," I whisper, trying to help her, but Garrett groans just then, and she turns back to him.

"I'm here, big guy, I'm here," she whispers, and his eyes open slightly.

"Sorry, baby," he murmurs.

"No, don't you fucking apologise. Just stay with me, okay?" she demands, and he snorts and then screams in agony, the sound filling the car and causing Ryder to smash the gas pedal. I jolt in my seat as Kenzo grips Garrett's head tight to stop him from moving.

He settles down, but seems mostly passed out. As each mile ticks by, more panic fills me as I glance from the road to him.

Looking in the back seat, I watch our girl hold the dress to his chest to staunch the bleeding, her face locked in a determined snarl. My own panic winds through me, but I can't help but admire her. She leans down into his face and slaps him. "You do not fucking leave me, you hear me? If anyone is going to kill your stubborn ass, it's going to be me, so fucking fight!"

His eyes open again, his lips kicking up. "D told us you liked us."

"Shut the fuck up." She laughs, the sound choked from tears. "I still hate you fuckers."

His eyes close again, and she leans down. "Please, please don't leave me, everyone leaves me, please, not you too." Her ragged plea fills the car, and tears well in my eyes as I watch her.

If I could do anything, I would. If I could save him or her from this, I would, but I'm useless, and it kills me. His hand is hanging from the seat, so I reach back and squeeze it. "Hold on, brother," I order. "Who else will stop me from doing crazy shit if not you?"

"Or stop Ryder from being such a wanker." Kenzo laughs, the sound weak.

"Or Rox from killing everyone," Ryder adds.

"Yeah, you bastards need me," Garrett mumbles, making us all laugh.

"We do, big guy, I need you, okay? Please, just hang on," she begs, kissing him softly.

"The doctor is still there. I told him not to leave in case one of us got hurt," Kenzo informs us. "We just gotta make it there."

The next few miles pass silently, only broken by the jagged, wet breathing of Garrett and the whispered words of my little bird to him. They seem to do the trick, though, since when we get into the garage, he's still with us. We can't go to the hospital, they ask too many questions. No, here is better. We rush him upstairs, but he refuses to let go of Roxy's hand, even when we lay him on the table and the doctor starts to treat him.

"Please, I need room," he tells her, and she steps back, but Garrett jerks upright.

"Roxy!" he screams wildly, so she rushes to his side, soothing him as he settles back onto the table.

"I need to sedate him," the doctor mutters, and before Garrett can protest, he does just that. We all watch with fear in our hearts at losing our brother. Our shoulders brush together as our woman holds him and the doctor works.

It takes hours until the exhausted man steps back and nods. "If he makes it through the night, he will live."

Garrett is still knocked out, and at this point, Little Bird looks exhausted, her body swaying, though I don't think she knows it. Her face is pale and lost. She looks so small, so quiet for our Roxy. I don't like it.

I can't help him, my brother, but I can help our girl. I look to Ryder and jerk my head at Rox. He nods as he helps Kenzo sit as the doctor looks at his stitches. Leaving them to it, I head her way.

Blood covers her hands, my brother's blood, her lover's blood. Her face is pale and shocked, and she's not moving or speaking, so I gently lift her and cradle her in my arms. I take her to the bathroom, not wanting to be far in case he wakes up and starts fighting again when he doesn't see her, but she needs looking after too.

She doesn't fight me or speak, and that tells me everything I need to know. I run the sink and quickly, but gently, clean her hands, wincing at the split knuckles before washing her arms and face. She leans into my touch, her eyes closing as tears track down her cheeks. "We almost lost him, we almost lost them both."

"But we didn't, Little Bird," I murmur softly. "We didn't, thanks to you, and now it's our turn to look after you."

She lifts her head, her eyes finally connecting with mine. "D?" she whispers.

"Yes, Little Bird?"

"Tell me something, anything, to keep my mind busy," she whispers so brokenly, I want to stab everyone. No one hurts her, no one makes her cry, not even my own brother. When Garrett survives and is better, I'm going to kick his ass.

"I never knew my real father. I liked to pretend the man she dated for most of my childhood was him. But then he left, just like everyone else. I tried to find the real man once," I admit, sharing something I've never told anyone.

"Did you find him?" she asks, seemingly more alive now.

"No, probably some boring as hell accountant somewhere, could you imagine?" I tease, and she giggles slightly. "I know, I know, tell anyone and I'll kill you, Little Bird."

"I love you," she whispers, leaning her head into mine.

"I love you too, Little Bird," I reply.

We sit like that for a while, just staring into each other's eyes, letting her rest, relax, and process, while I stay by her side. Her eyes search mine, and I stroke her, her thighs, her hair, her hands, every little piece of her until she curls into me. "Can I see him?"

Lifting her into my arms, I take her back into the living room and drag a chair closer before I sit and perch her on my lap. The doctor looks her over and binds her broken toes and fingers, cleans the cuts, and stitches one that needs it. She has cracked ribs as well, but there isn't much he can do for that apart from giving her pain relievers, which she accepts. Her head is also bumped, and he warns she might have a concussion.

After he's done, I move us closer to Garrett. She reaches out to him and twines her fingers with his. His head is turned this way, and his eyes are closed. It's the most peaceful I have ever seen him.

"He loves you," I whisper to her. "More than anything in this world. He never feared losing or dying before, not until you."

She trembles against me, and Ryder and Kenzo drag chairs on either side of us. And that's how we sit, all night, with our eyes on our brother, who's fighting for his life, our woman between us.

When the sun rises, Ryder makes coffee, silently passing Little Bird one before sitting back down. "He'll be okay," she whispers.

"How do you know?" Ryder asks, weariness in his voice.

"Because he's a Viper. Vipers don't die," she states. It's the same thing we have said for years, and it's like something clicks into place. How easily she slipped into our lives and became the center of our world. It will never be easy—fuck, I'm glad it won't be, easy is boring —but having her in my arms makes all the blood, all the pain and power games, worth it.

And when Garrett groans and opens his eyes, clashing with Roxy's gaze, it's clear that without her...we are nothing. What started as a business deal has grown into something much more than we could have ever imagined. A life. A home.

Love.

The very things none of us knew we needed, including Little Bird, but now we have them together, and we are never letting that go. Or her.

I would chase her to the ends of this earth and drag her back, kicking and screaming...actually, that would be fun.

"The fuck you all look so morbid for," Garrett rasps, then coughs.

We all share a look before bursting into laughter.

Vipers never die.

Vipers never fall...unless it's for a tattooed, foul-mouthed bar owner.

CHAPTER FIFTY-SIX

KENZO

"She's finally asleep," I tell them, watching our girl. We moved Garrett to his room early this morning, and Roxy followed after he freaked out and punched D when he couldn't see her. Now they are curled up together, snoring. Good, they need sleep. I do too, so even though it pains me, I let Ryder and Diesel sort out the arrangements for funerals of the men we lost, including Roxy's friend Sam.

I also let them deal with the rest of the Triad. I have more important things to do, like hold my girl. Sometimes being the boss's brother and also being injured has its advantages. As they grumble and get off to work, I slip into bed with Garrett and Roxy, pushing up against her back and burying my face into her neck and hair.

"Fuck you doing?" she mutters, making me chuckle.

"I gotta heal, darling, your body helps," I tease.

"Fucking cheese ball," she mutters, even as she wiggles closer to me, causing me to groan. "I'm injured, not dead, don't tempt me with that fucking ass."

She laughs, and Garrett groans. "Shut the fuck up, or I'll throw you out."

"Me?" Roxy giggles, and he growls and drags her closer, even as he moans in pain.

"No, that fucking idiot. I don't have enough blood left for a hard-on, so shut up." We both laugh, and I snuggle closer again, just smelling my girl. I can smell hints of blood and sweat, but underneath it is all her.

"Shush, injured people trying to sleep," I mutter.

They laugh, making Garrett groan. "I fucking hate being injured."

"Me too." I sigh.

"I could kiss it all better," she offers, and we both turn rigid against her.

"I love being injured," I correct, and Garrett nods silently.

"My new favourite thing. I think I'll let D hurt me every now and again," he mutters.

"Men." She sighs. "Now shut the fuck up. I'm tired after saving your asses. By the way, you all owe me lots and lots of orgasms for that shit show of the last few days."

Grinning, I kiss her neck, making her shiver in need, even as she yawns. "Anything you say, darling."

"So bossy," Garrett mutters.

"Assholes," she snaps, and then sighs. "Hate you."

"Hate you too," Garrett replies.

"Hate you more," I add, and she snorts but snuggles closer, both of them going quiet as they drift off. Who knew this is where we would end up? I thought our lives were perfect until Roxy came along and showed me just how empty and meaningless they were.

No, I can't imagine them any other way without her in the middle. It might be strange, and others might never understand it, but we have never been one to follow the rules. We make our own, and Roxy? Roxy is ours.

Forever.

RYDER

WHILE MY BROTHERS AND GIRL ARE RESTING, I MAKE arrangements. I sort the funerals, and I reimburse their families, making sure they never have to worry. I contact clean-up and the police. I release a statement, acting saddened by the tragic massacre that took place in our city. I play the good leader.

And businessman.

Then, I strip off my suit and head down to the basement and to D. He has the third and final member of the Triad strung up in chains. He has already been busy keeping the man occupied, of course, until I enter.

"How awful it must feel knowing your whole family is dead." I sigh as I step into the room, grinning as I meet his scared, angry eyes. "Don't worry, you will soon join them."

"You fucking snakes," he spits, his accent pronounced more than normal.

"Very true." I grin as I strip off my shirt and step towards him. Diesel laughs.

"Oh, you're in trouble now," he taunts, circling him as I step before the man. "You should have never come for my family, you should have rolled over and accepted the deal. You're a fool."

"I thought it would be easy," he whispers, defeated, the man has nothing else to live for. I've taken everything he loves.

"You thought wrong. Never back a Viper into a corner, we always strike back harder," I tell him, as I pick up a screwdriver and hold it to the light. "I have to make an example of you. Your brothers, I'm afraid, were all disposed of, but I still have you."

He swallows and tilts his head back, his eyes tired, his age bearing down on him now. "We were never going to win, were we?"

I smirk at that. "No, never."

He nods. "Will you kill our families?"

523

"Maybe." I shrug. I don't tell him I've already had them deported and set up wherever they wanted to go with new identities and money to live out their lives. I don't kill innocents unless I have to. They didn't know, and their blood ties are severed. I feel repaid, and the threat is gone, so they are safe from us. Unless they ever come at us again. They have been warned to never speak our names or step foot in this country.

I have a feeling we will never see or hear from them again.

"Let's begin, shall we?" I ask, and he nods, his spirit broken, his honour gone. He failed—they lost and we won. Now it's time to show everyone what happens to traitors, so they think twice about coming at us.

No one will hurt my family again, I will ensure it. Spill the blood now, save it later down the line. Especially now that Roxxane is here, my protective instincts are higher than ever. It's going to be harder to protect her because she's unpredictable and wild, but when I saw her tonight...when she truly became one of us, it was magnificent.

Poetry in motion.

She was not just a Viper tonight, she was the Viper.

She was ours.

And we protect what is ours. Always.

I start at his feet, working my way up his body. Diesel has to help. We break his ankles, toes, kneecaps, ribs, fingers, and nose. Then we skin him alive, which is harder than it sounds. The number one we cut from the rest to be kept as a show of strength, and when we're done, we are both covered in blood and he's dead.

It's over, my family is safe...for now.

We still have a few other matters to deal with, but they can wait for now...for a few days at least. For once, I'm taking some time off to spend with my brothers and my love. I'm going to relax and enjoy their company, something I haven't done for years.

We are going to heal. Together.

CHAPTER FIFTY-SEVEN

ROXY

Washing blood away is harder than it sounds. I woke up a few hours later, hot and sticky and way too itchy from the blood in places it shouldn't be, despite how hard Diesel had tried to remove it, not to mention my hair is now red and not silver. So leaving Garrett and Kenzo to cuddle, I head to my old room to shower. I'm only in my bra and knickers, so I drop them to the floor, knowing I will never wear them again, and step into my bathroom.

It's strange how it all started in this room. When I woke up here, I thought it was going to be the end of my life, that this was where I would finally die. Now? It's my home, and I have never felt more alive or loved, even when it hurts or it's scary.

It's strange how things turn out.

Flicking on the water, I step into the spray, shivering when it's cold and waiting for it to warm up. I close my eyes, still tired, but also too wound up to sleep. My dreams are haunted from not reaching Garrett in time, and I see snippets of him dying under that blade while I'm screaming and trying to get to him, waking me over and over.

I jump when an arm slides around my throat from behind. When the scent of fire and smoke reaches me, I relax back into it with a smile as steam starts to fill the room. "Hey, hot stuff."

"Hello, Little Bird," he murmurs, licking my ear. "I've been busy, and now I need you."

Turning in his embrace, I see the blood covering his naked body. I don't ask whose, but there is something about a naked Diesel coated in blood that has my pussy clenching. His blond hair is sticky and matted with it, his lips tipped up in that cocky, crazy smile.

Maybe it's the fact that I almost lost them. Maybe it's the fact that I need to feel alive, to feel them in my arms. Replace that blood on my hands with their skin and love. Or maybe I'm just fucked up and constantly want to screw their brains out. But I fling myself at him, and he catches me with a laugh, his hands going to my arse and squeezing as he walks us backwards until my back hits the wall, hard. I gasp as my breath is pushed from me, my ribs still weak, as he smashes his lips to mine.

I taste cigarettes and blood on his lips and groan, searching for more as our tongues tangle. Our bodies become slippery with the spray cascading down on us, washing us free of our sins for just a moment.

I can't even begin to tell him how much it meant to me when he looked after me last night. He was so soft and sweet. Yes, Diesel might be crazy, he might be obsessive and blood crazed, but he's loving. He's kind and passionate, and when you become his, you become his for life.

He moans into my mouth as his fingers snake between our bodies, slip down my wet pussy, and dip inside me with a quick, hard thrust. "So fucking wet, Little Bird," he murmurs against my lips.

"Always," I reply, rubbing against his hand. "Going to fuck me or tease?"

He growls, leaning down to bite my neck hard, making me whimper, even as I clench around his fingers, the pain and pleasure chasing away all the uncertainness, fear, anger, and helplessness from the last two days.

Diesel always knows how to make me feel alive.

"Fuck me," I snarl against his lips.

Chuckling, he pulls his fingers free, drops me to the slippery floor, and quickly turns me, smashing my injured cheek into the tiles as I groan from the pain. He rubs his hard cock along my arse, licking and biting my ear. "Do you remember our first time?"

I nod breathlessly as I eagerly part my legs, letting him rub his cock along my pussy.

"I remember the first time I saw you. So beautiful, so dangerous. I fell a little bit in love with you that day, when those big, fierce eyes locked on me. I haven't stopped thinking about you ever since. You're my fucking obsession, Little Bird. Always will be," he growls, as he lines up and slams into me, making me scream in both pain and pleasure.

He presses me hard against the wall, his hand on my neck to keep me there. "This will be quick and fast. It's been too long. Later, I'm going to fill your ass with my cum as they watch, but for now...now I get you all to myself."

Pressing my hands against the wall, blood dripping from our bodies and mingling by our feet at the drain, I moan his name. He tugs my head back with his hand in my hair, his cock slipping in and out of me, harder and faster as my hands splay across the tiles.

"D, please," I beg.

He snarls and slams in and out of me with no rhythm. I'm helpless against him as he drags my pleasure from me. "I love you so fucking much, Little Bird, you are my everything. I would kill anyone for you. I would do anything for you. I would crawl on my fucking knees to be at your side."

I whimper at his words, the pleasure building inside me, drawn from my very toes. I'm desperate, pushing back into his hands and cock, needing to come so badly. My head is going dizzy, my eyes closing and ears ringing, and I know it's just going to explode out of me at any minute.

"I fucking love you," he roars, his other hand reaching around and grabbing my pussy in a possessive, hard grip that has me slipping over the edge.

I scream my release, helplessly fighting it, clenching around him, my hips moving and voice cracking as I shake and writhe. I feel his head meet my back as he pants, his cum slipping from my pussy as I breathe heavily against the shower wall.

He presses his body along the length of mine until there isn't an inch of space between us, both of us shivering from aftershocks. His voice comes out gravelly and low. "I knew you had it in you, Little Bird, to become ours...to become a Viper. Now look at you—our very own fucking queen."

Queen.

It has a nice ring to it.

Life with them will never be boring.

GARRETT IS HEALING SLOWLY, AS IS KENZO. THEY ARE BIG babies, though, and I have to tell them to man the fuck up and stop moping after two days. Ryder has taken some time off work, and honestly, it's nice to have him around. Diesel disappears for a whole day, but when he comes back, he vows never to leave my side again.

And then he gives me a hand.

In a box.

Honestly...it's romantic as fuck. Turns out it was the mohawk—Andrew—guy's hand. What a softie.

Though I don't really know what to do to preserve a hand, so I leave that up to Diesel. I even catch him high-fiving Garrett with it once, to which the big guy punches him in the face and knocks him out cold. When he comes around, he's laughing his head off.

Crazy bastard.

Ryder returns to work, but he's started doing it from the dining room table. I hear a lot of swearing on the other end of the phone. Turns out, he's destroying everything that is left of the Triad.

One day, when I'm feeling annoying, I prop myself on his lap while he's on a call—okay, so I'm hoping for a repeat of the office incident, but it doesn't happen. He seems nervous suddenly and holds me closer. His nose goes to my neck, and he sucks in a breath before he straightens and starts the call.

It's a woman's voice on the other end, a husky one that even has me wiggling, not that Ryder seems to notice. No, there is respect on his face for this woman, whoever she is. Jealousy shoots through me, and he must notice, because he drags up my shirt and grips my bare pussy under the table. Just holds it. All possessive like.

Yeah, it kinda helps.

Though I want to take a bat to the sexy phone voice woman.

"Mr. Viper, how lovely to hear from you. I understand you had a little trouble recently—"

Ryder smiles, a mean one. "Nothing I couldn't handle."

"Of course." She laughs, it's a smoky sound. "We, too, had a small issue with them, but they seemed to have focused all their efforts on you. You can rest assured we have no quarrel with you or your city, we have our own to deal with."

I look at him at that. Who is this? "I never asked, did I?"

She laughs again. "Let's not play games, we are too smart for that. I know why you're ringing, and yes, we are still allies. You have your city, us Petrovs have ours."

Ryder relaxes a bit, and I realise he was worried he was going to have to go to war with the Russian family he told me about. "That's good, please let me know if I can help your...quarrel, in any way."

"Your kindness is appreciated. I hear you have found yourself a woman finally. Do I need to buy a dress for a wedding?"

I freeze, my eyes wide. Wedding? Oh fuck no! I try to run, but Ryder chuckles and wraps his arm around me tighter, obviously knowing what my reaction would be. "In the future, yes, she is very...slippery."

Slippery? Oh, I'll give this bastard slippery. Yanking my elbow back, I drive it into his stomach, and he gasps and releases me. Standing, I narrow my eyes on him. "Slippery? I wouldn't marry you fuckers even if you held a gun to my head," I hiss, before storming away.

I hear their laughter trailing after me. "I like her, bring her to visit. Goodbye, Mr. Viper."

"Roxxane," I hear him call after me, his voice cool and demanding. Ah shit, I'm going to pay for that. Looking over my shoulder, I see him stripping off his shirt, those eyes locked on me and heating fast.

Shit, shit, shit.

I do the only thing I can—run.

He laughs as he chases me. I should have known he will always catch me...and when he does, well, I'm screaming for good reasons, not bad.

CHAPTER FIFTY-EIGHT

DIESEL

"I'm sorry, I'm sorry, but I swear I didn't know what they were going to—" I cut off his words by grabbing the needle and putting his head in a vice-like hold.

Tears fall from his eyes as he struggles in the chair, his arms and legs tied to it with barbed wire, like they did to my girl. "Shush, don't move or I could mess this up," I snap, as I start to thread it through his lips.

He moves and screams, but when I step back, it doesn't look too bad. Even stitching, not too far apart, and his mouth is effectively sewn shut. His eyes bug from his head, blood dripping down his chin as I hop on his desk and swing my legs.

Ryder is destroying the Triad's business, and I'm cleaning up our beloved city. Anyone who ever wanted to stand against us, who ever worked with the Triad or made threats, they die. We can't risk one of them getting ideas and coming for Roxy. Not again.

"They were your sons, you knew." I snort.

Oh yes, Triad's daddy, all the way over in China. I hopped on our

jet while Roxy was sleeping and came straight to his corporate building. He knew, his sons never made a move without his approval.

"Unfortunately, we don't have a lot of time. I have to be back on
the plane before the authorities catch me. I would have preferred to
play more—" My phone rings, and I look to see it's Little Bird. "Hold
one moment, the old lady, you know how it is."

Answering, I put it on speaker as I hop from the desk and circle
their dad. "Little Bird?" I murmur.

"Where are you?" she asks, her voice sharp.

"Missing me?" I tease, as I grab his head, rip it to the side, and
tear off his ear. He tries to scream, the muffled sound filtering down
the phone.

"Ahhh." She laughs. "Sorry, didn't know you were working."

"I always have time for you, you know that," I murmur, as I do the
same to the other and toss the bloody appendages on the desk.
"What's wrong, Little Bird?"

"I'm bored, and Garrett and Kenzo are sleeping, and Ryder is off
somewhere. I wanted to play." Her voice drops an octave, making me
shiver and my cock turn hard.

"Torture Garrett for a while, I'll be back as soon as I can," I
promise.

She sighs. "Fine," she mumbles, then seems to perk up. "Gar-
rettttttt, Diesel said you had to play with me." Her voice is sweet as
sugar, but it makes me laugh.

I hear him swear and then grunt as she laughs. "Bye, D, see you
soon!"

Holding the man in the chair, I hold my phone to one ear as I
lead him over to the bay of windows. "Bye, Little Bird, be bad."
Hanging up, I pocket the phone as I press my face to his, looking at
our reflection in the window.

"Women, am I right? Can't live without them, can't kill without
them." I nod seriously. "Now, I want you to say hi to your sons for
me." I laugh as I straighten, and my phone rings again. Sighing, I
answer it.

"What did you tell her?" Garrett roars.

"To play, why?" I query, looking at my blood-stained nails.

He groans as if in pain. "D, she's wearing chains as lingerie, I'm supposed to be on bed rest."

Laughing, I wink at their dad. "Then be on bed rest...with her in the bed with you. Gotta go, bye!"

Putting my phone away, I grin down at the Triad's daddy. "Sorry, mate, duty calls. I'll have a nice flight if you do." I laugh as I pull back my leg and kick.

I watch as he rolls towards the glass before flying through it, the pane shattering around him. Leaning through the broken window, I watch from the fortieth story as he falls to the concrete below with a splat. Now that was fun.

Laughing, I wipe the table for prints and, whistling to myself, take the stairs back down. I have a plane to catch, my little bird needs me, and now that the city is clean...she is all I have to focus on.

I hope she's ready.

RYDER

I KNOW I SHOULD BE CELEBRATING, EXCEPT I CAN'T HELP BUT blame myself. With the emotions Roxxanne has unlocked in me... for her, it comes with guilt. If we hadn't taken her, she would have never been tortured and almost killed. She's still limping, her toes, ribs, and fingers hurting her when she thinks we don't notice. I've been making sure she takes her pain relievers, but she got hurt because of me.

Not to mention my brothers, who even now are still healing. They almost died because I wasn't smart enough to see this coming. My father was right, I will never be good enough to lead.

Knocking back the scotch, I turn to the windows around the conference room. I don't know why I came here, only that it felt right. I'm too dark, too angry and confused to be with anyone tonight, even my love. She would try to save me from it, and I can't have that. My failures are mine, and I have to learn from them.

I need to do better in the future to keep them all safe. I need to see the looming threats to protect them. Which is why I hired more guards and the treaty with the Petrovs is officially in effect. It took a lot of negotiating, but they are a good, strong family to have our backs.

It might keep my family safe. I knew this life might kill us all when I entered it, I welcome it gladly, but now with Roxxane here, I wonder if I made the right decision. She would be just as happy living in a shitty apartment and working at the bar every night, she doesn't need money or power.

Just us.

As if summoned by my dark, turbulent thoughts, I spot her in the reflection in the window. Turning, I meet her gaze. She's framed in the doorway, wearing nothing but one of our shirts. "Go to bed, love, it's late," I tell her, but my voice is trembling, so I turn away, my hands shaking again. Why does she have this effect on me?

I never worried like this before. Never second-guessed my every decision, wondering if she would agree if it was right. Fuck, I even keep going through my past and everything I have done, all the demons that hide there, pondering if she would be disgusted by the man she shares her bed with if she knew.

"Come with me," she murmurs.

"Not tonight, love."

I hear her sigh before her arms wrap around me from behind. "You don't have to suffer alone, Ry. I'm here, your brothers are here. I know the weight you carry, trying to save us all, but that isn't your job, okay? I don't need you to save me. I need you to stand with me, to lean on me so I can lean on you. You don't always have to be perfect, cold, and calculating. It's okay to break every now and again, but don't do it alone."

I don't reply, and she kicks my chair around and gets in my face, her own contorted in anger now. "Fucking talk to me, Ryder. Don't shut me out. Don't be that asshole, or I swear you will lose me. You want to protect us? Fine, you want to wallow in self-pity? Fine, but do not dare freeze me out, not now, not ever."

With a roar, I'm up and in her face in an instant, my hand around her neck. "No? Would you rather I took it out on you? Hit you? Hurt you? Because that's what will happen if you keep pushing, **Roxxanne**. I am him, after all." I push her away in disgust, not at her but at me, knowing if I don't, I could actually hurt her. His blood runs through my veins, and it was a day like this where he used to take it out on my mum.

I feel it too.

The need to forget, to hurt someone so I feel stronger, less out of control. To control her and her actions so that all these...these fucking emotions and turmoil goes away again. I'm a monster like him.

And it's my biggest fear that I would hurt her, because I love her.

And my love? It comes with barbs.

CHAPTER

FIFTY-NINE

ROXY

"**Y**ou want to hurt me? Fine, do it if it helps. I can take it," I snap, sick of this bullshit. Just when I think I'm getting close, he pulls away again, only offering me the pieces of him he wants to, shielding the others. I'm done with it.

He slams his hands onto the window, his head pressing to the glass. "Get out," he orders.

"No," I reply calmly, crossing my arms. "Not until you get all this shit out in the open. You're worried about hurting me? Because of your father? Right? Or maybe you're just blaming yourself for everything that's happened." I snort when he flinches. "I know you, Ryder, probably better than you think. You will run through every goddamn detail, blaming yourself, thinking you could have prevented it, but, baby? Sometimes shit just happens, and guess what? I don't blame you, and your brothers don't either. Because of you, we are alive and together. Shit happens, Ryder, you have to deal with it and move on. If you get trapped in the past, you will never be free of its ghosts."

He's quiet for a moment, and I think I've pushed him too far, but when his voice comes out, it's small and scared. "It's my job to protect you all."

Dropping my arms, I head over and press my head against his back, wrapping my arms about his trembling body. "Yes, and no. It's our job to protect each other. We all knew what we were getting into, Ryder. This life isn't easy. If it was, everyone would do it, but stop trying to take all the weight for yourself. A Viper needs balance, you need your brothers and me."

He turns, and I'm pushed back. His eyes are wild, his mouth is pursed in a snarl, his body is shaking, and his fists are clenched. He looks magnificent and fucking terrifying. "And when I can't? What if I let you all help me? What if I let it all out and I'm just like him?" he screams.

"Like your father?" I ask.

He looks away, jaw grinding. "He was a bastard, Roxxane, a true fucking bastard. He-he hurt my mother and me and Kenzo." He shakes his head, seeming to deflate as he watches me. "What if I hurt you?"

"Then I'll kill you." I laugh, and he glares at me. "Ry, you can't hurt me unless I let you. I'm sorry, but I'm not your mother, I'm a fighter. I survived my father, I survived D and Garrett, I can survive your demons. I would never let you hurt me more than I wanted to, and neither would the others. You are so scared of being him, you're stopping yourself from being you."

He swallows, his eyes searching mine. "I killed him."

I blink at that. "Okay?"

He laughs, a self-deprecating sound. "You're not even surprised."

"That you killed a man who hurt your mother and brother?" I snort. "No, Ryder, I'm not surprised. I wish you had done it sooner."

He grins, but it soon deflates, and he sits back down, his body heavy as if he's tired. "Kenzo tried to," he admits, his voice laced with pain and guilt. How long has he been holding onto this? "I'd killed before, my father made me, shaping me into his enforcer. I did it to protect Kenzo, because I knew if I didn't, then he would make my brother. But I couldn't protect him forever, and even though I tried to shield him from that life, he walked into it anyway to save me from my dad. He saw what it was doing to me and hated it. He took my gun one night when I was asleep, went to the hotel—"

"The hotel? Where I was?" I question, as I plop into his lap. He needs to talk, but he needs me there too. He wraps his arms around me gratefully, his head pressing to mine.

"One in the same, love, it's ours, I wanted it to rot." He kisses me then softly, so softly. "He went there to kill him, to save me. But when he got to my father, he couldn't do it. He's a lover, and the first time you pull the trigger is hard, love, and on our own father? Impossible for Kenzo. He saw the good in everyone and loved them, even when they didn't deserve it, still does."

"Hey," I protest, and he smiles.

"Not you, Roxxane. If anyone in this world deserves love, it's you and him, but Garrett, D, and me? Not so much."

I shake my head, but he covers my mouth. "Let me talk, okay? I woke up, and when I saw my gun was missing, I knew. He had been acting weird all day, and I just knew, love. I've never been so scared. I knew my dad would kill him, and by the time I got there, Kenzo was bleeding, on death's door. I took the gun from him—"

"You killed him," I mumble against his hand.

"I killed him, shot him in the head, then unloaded the clip on him." He winces then. "And I felt nothing, nothing, love. Not even joy, it was just something that needed to be done. I helped Kenzo up, and we just stood over him. All our lives, he had been a tyrant, such a big, strong man. All that power and money, and in the end, all it did was sign his death warrant. He looked so weak, so small. It was easy to do, kill, easier to take over his business and destroy it. It was when I was in my element, destroying things, while Kenzo was the builder." He sucks in a breath, and I push closer, offering him comfort as he unloads all the weight pulling him down.

"He pulled this family together. I think he did it for me, to try and keep me anchored because he saw it too—my ability to destroy, my potential to be worse than my father, and he was trying to stop it, and it worked, love, for so long. It grounded me, but then you came—" He shakes his head again, his eyes lighting up and his lips curling. "Like a fucking hurricane. You shook up my world. I knew you would when I saw you, but I just couldn't walk away. There's an innocence to you. I know you've seen the shit life has to offer, but you still smile, still laugh. I craved it, wanted to make it mine and...and destroy it. But I didn't count on your fucking will. You wrapped me—us, around your fingers so easily. I would do anything for you, love, be anything you needed, and that terrified me because that same power, those same demons who made my dad him are in me, and you have to deal with them all. Because I can't let you go, not ever."

My heart cracks at his words. Ryder, God, my poor Ryder. So worried all the time. No wonder that ice is there, it keeps him and everyone around him safe from the fire within. D uses it, Kenzo blocks it, Garret unleashes it, but Ry? Ry lives in it.

"That makes me a bastard, I know, but when you are in my arms, I feel invincible. I feel so fucking strong, like I could do anything. You make me like that. You make me stronger, and because of that, you have to deal with the consequences..."

Pushing his hand away, I kiss him hard. "And I'll gladly take them. Ryder, you're stronger than you know, so fucking strong. Why do you think I stayed? Even when I first came, I didn't really try to escape and never really knew why. Maybe it's because I knew this was where I belonged. In your arms. So you have demons? Baby, they match mine. We can do this together, but no more icing us out. We are family. They won't judge you, just like you don't judge them. It's time to let go, Ryder, let the ghosts die with that hotel, because you have so much more to live for now. And I will remind you every fucking day if you need me to. I will take it all, every bit of anger and destruction. Paint it across my skin, I'll wear it gladly. I'm yours, Ryder, and you're mine."

He searches my eyes. "Promise?"

It's a child's word on a man's lips, a man who lost everything for so long. Who was never taught love or kindness. We are learning together. Words might not always be loving, no, sometimes they are downright venomous. Poison on our lips like fire pouring from our souls, but they are always true. "Promise," I whisper.

He groans, closing his eyes for a moment. "I fucking love you, Roxxane, even when you're being a brat."

I can't help but laugh at that. "Don't worry, I still hate you."

He grins, his eyes flaring open as he circles my neck with his hand, those long, elegant, scarred fingers anchoring me to him. "Is that right?" he murmurs, his gaze flashing dangerously, and it's a testament to how fucked up I am that my pussy clenches at that one look. "I bet I can make you scream 'I love you' for everyone to hear."

"Doubt it, buddy." I snort, even as I lean into him, ripping my hand down his shirt. The buttons pop off, leaving his chest bare for my hungry gaze, his collage of tattoos almost blinding me. He's a work of art, and he fucking knows it.

A goddamn painting in motion. His soul is as dark as his ink, and his eyes are as cold as the society he swims in, yet I crave him. His brand of pain and love. I ache whenever I look at him. He's too fucking much, yet he's all mine.

He can be cruel and callous. His hands and tongue a weapon. He can take me down, break me and destroy me as easily as he can have me screaming in pleasure. It's a double-edged sword with each of the Viper boys. They love as deeply as they hate.

They hurt as much as they breathe, and I am in the middle of all of that, with all of their eyes and attention on me. If I'm not careful, they could kill me as easily as they love me. I stole their hearts, and they stole mine.

They keep it safe in their blood-soaked palms, and when Ryder strokes his hands down to my arse and squeezes, I moan wantonly. Such pain, such death they leave in their paths. These hands belong to killers.

Sinners.

Vipers.

But I want them all the same. I want their bite, I want their particular brand of venom coursing through my veins, remaking me into their girl. Every touch, every look is a balm into the soul of a girl who was never loved properly.

One day, it might consume us all and we might explode. But what a beautiful death it would be.

"Ry," I beg, dragging my nails down his chest, cutting his skin and leaving my mark, giving as good as I get. They love me because of this, because I am capable of the same blood and destruction, hate and torment, because they live in the shadows and so do I.

"Scared, love?" he murmurs, almost pressing his lips to mine. His breath is minty with a hint of scotch, wafting over me as I wiggle on his lap, feeling his cock harden against me.

"Of you? Never. Of not getting an orgasm any time soon? Abso-fucking-lutely," I deadpan.

"Well, we can't have that, can we?" He grins and stands, holding me against him before dropping me onto the glass table. His hands grab my thighs and shove them open before he twists his hand in the front of the shirt and tugs, snapping the buttons until it falls open and I'm bare before him.

His eyes run down my body, his tongue darting out to wet his lips. "Every fucking time I forget how beautiful you are." His hands drift up my thighs, his knuckles catching on the edge of my pussy, making me groan. "Every goddamn time, love, you take my breath away."

"Prove it," I demand, spreading my legs farther. His eyes drop to my pussy, and he groans as he falls to his knees.

Having the great Ryder, the lead fucking Viper on his knees looking so hungry, like he could devour me whole, is heady. The power makes me smirk as I reach down and grab his head as he trails his tongue along my thighs, teasing me, punishing me.

"I might get Garrett to tattoo 'Ryder's Property' above this pussy."

"Not fucking likely, unless I get to tattoo 'Roxy's Property' on your cock," I snap, making him chuckle and blow warm air over my needy pussy. I shiver. "Enough talking."

"Do you give the orders here, love?" he challenges, nipping my thigh in punishment. "Because I can easily fuck this tight little pussy, fill you with my cum, and leave you behind, needy as hell without release."

"You bastard," I hiss.

"That's right, love, and I'm your bastard, so lay the fuck on your back and let me stare at my property for as long as I goddamn please. You will get my cock when I tell you, you get my cock," he growls, digging his teeth into my skin. I jolt as I drop my head to the glass and close my eyes in pain.

I'm so wet, it's embarrassing, needing him inside me, my empty pussy pulsing and clamping on air. Feeling his dark, hungry gaze on my pussy isn't helping. I actually jump when his fingers touch me, parting my lips before his tongue touches my clit, circling it, then tracing it down my center and dipping inside me, lapping at my cream hungrily. My hands tighten in his hair as I push myself against his face, grinding onto his tongue as my eyes flutter closed. My heart pounds and body slicks with sweat.

"Ry, God, please," I implore, as he removes his tongue and lifts his head, those dark eyes meeting mine as he licks his lips.

"You taste like fucking heaven." He groans before his head drops back to my pussy and he stops teasing.

His eyes roll up to meet mine over my body as he wraps his lips around my piercing and sucks, making me come off the table with a moan. Releasing it, he laps at my pussy like it's his favourite fucking dessert. His fingers circle my hole playfully before dipping in and out barely an inch. I cant my hips, trying to get more friction, needing to come so badly it's my only goal.

I'm mindless, aching for pleasure as I press closer. Words leave my lips, threats, promises, all making him laugh and tease me more until I finally stop and just relax, letting him do whatever he wants to me.

Then he shows me just how much he was teasing.

His fingers slip into my pussy, stretching me, my breathing loud in the silent room as he plays my body like a fucking violin. His hands skate up my stomach and grab my breasts, hard, squeezing them as he licks and flicks my piercing, tugging it. The pain and pleasure mix together. His wet fingers circle my nipples before tracing back down my body and slipping inside me.

They scissor, rubbing my inner walls as he focuses all his attention on my clit. Each flick of his tongue and glide of his fingers has me rocking into his mouth. "Ryder!" I scream, as his teeth clamp down on my clit.

It throws me over the edge, ecstasy washing through me as I jerk beneath him, my orgasm taking me by surprise and making me cry out. He licks me through it before crawling up my body and lapping my cream from my nipples. Panting heavily, I open my eyes to meet his dark ones. His chin and lips are coated in my release, and he looks fucking feral. I love it.

"That was just a start, love," he murmurs, his teeth catching on my nipple as I shiver beneath him. "I just wanted you to realise that you belong to me, and only when you behave, do you get what you need."

I can't speak, my mouth is dry and my tongue is too numb to move, and he chuckles, the rat bastard. He flips me over and drags me to the edge of the table, stripping my shirt until I'm naked. His hands trace down my back before his mouth follows the path, his teeth digging into my ass cheek, making me groan.

"Diesel told me he fucked your ass with a knife, is that true?" he murmurs.

I refuse to be ashamed. "Yes."

"Good, because I'm going to fuck your ass. Be a good girl, and I'll make you come more times than you can count. Be a brat, and I'll make it hurt, and while you're crying, I'll make you come, make you love the agony."

Goddamn, why is that so hot?

His hands stroke along my ass before he slaps both cheeks, making me jerk and yelp. He laughs and rubs in the sting before he presses his cock to my pussy. He slides it back and forth across me before slowly pushing inside. He only thrusts two times. I'm just starting to push back and meet his thrusts, when he pulls out and leaves me empty.

"Goddamn it, Ry," I grumble, panting as I press my face to the table and my ass into his hands.

"Just getting my cock nice and wet for your plump little ass," he growls.

My eyes flicker closed at that as I pant, my hips rolling instinctively. I can't help it, I need him so badly. He spanks me again, twice before rubbing in that sting. I moan loudly, unable to help myself. He makes me so weak.

Makes me surrender completely.

When I relax, he licks my ass. "Good girl, love, that's it, relax and take my big cock." He presses the head to my ass, and I relax as he pushes in. He's thick and big, and I can't help but bite my lip as he slips past my muscles. "Good girl, look how pretty you are," he praises, as he pulls back and thrusts in, working his cock into my ass an inch at a time.

When he's buried deep, he massages my cheeks. "Such a fucking good girl, look at you."

Goddamn, I want to snap at his condensing words, but with his cock in my ass, I can't really complain. He chuckles like he knows my thoughts and slowly starts to move, fucking me gently. Softly.

Holding back like normal.

Trying to protect me.

I know he needs more, he needs pain and hurt as well as control, but Ryder loves me, fears hurting me. I need to break him. "What's the matter, Ry? Going soft on me?" I taunt. His hands dig into my hips as he slams into me harder, but it's still not enough. "Oooh, please, Ry, don't hurt me," I mock.

I glance over my shoulder at him. "Your brother fucks harder, need me to teach you how?"

His eyes narrow as I smirk at him. "What's wrong, Ry?" I lick my lips and push back, taking him deeper. "No quick come back? No demands or orders? Gotta say, I'm disappointed...you promised to hurt me. Guess it was all talk, alpha," I gibe.

That breaks him. He slams inside of me so hard and fast, it does hurt, making me cry out. His hand darts out and wraps around my throat, squeezing as he leans down and bites my ear. "You want it to hurt? You want me to stop looking after you?"

He's clutching my throat so hard, I can't breathe.

"Fine, you think you can take it, love? Prove it." He pulls out of me and lets go of my throat. Yanking me up, he spins me so fast, my head whirls and I stumble.

He doesn't care, he drags me over to the window and smashes me into the glass. A sharp pain goes through my injured ribs, and when he grabs my hands and slams them to the window above me, my injured shoulder and finger twinges. The pain melts through me, turning to pleasure, my cream dripping down my thighs.

His hands go to my hips, and he jerks me back, palming my ass as he pushes back inside me again with quick, hard thrusts, not gentle now. He forces his cock into my ass over and over until I'm being pounded against the glass.

But it's not enough for him.

His hand strokes down my side, those elegant fingers tracing my ribs, and then he squeezes, squeezes the still aching, healing ribs until I scream in pain, shuddering around him. It makes him groan as he fills me with his cock. "Fuck, love, you scream so sweetly. No wonder D loves it."

I can't help it, the pain fades to pleasure, especially when he reaches around and rubs my clit, driving me back to that peak again, even as my body protests the fucking.

But suddenly, he pulls out again, leaving me cold and shivering against the glass as I wobble on unsteady feet. My ass is sore, my ribs hurt, and my pussy throbs like a heartbeat, dripping my cream as I slowly come back from the edge of release. Turning my head, I watch as he strides over to the table in the corner, his fingers running over the objects there. "I wonder, Roxy, just how far are you willing to go?" He looks over at me, dragging his eyes down my body. "Just how far can I push you? Hurt you?"

He grabs a bottle of fancy water from the side, and I freeze, wide-eyed, as he comes back to me, kicking open my legs and pressing it to my pussy. "Thought you could handle it, love?" he taunts, as he slams it inside me. I scream at the burst of pain followed by a whimper as he grips my hips and pushes back into my ass. The bottle and his cock stretch me so much, it borders on agony. He keeps me there, riding that fine line as he starts to move.

He keeps the bottle still, my pussy clamping around it as he slams in and out of my ass, making me ride the object. It feels so fucking wrong, so goddamn dirty, but good. I'm so full, I can't even think, barely breathe.

"Ry, God," I cry out, feeling the bottle slip farther inside me with each punishing thrust of his cock in my ass.

"If they look up, they can see you, love, see you getting fucked, knowing you belong to us as you scream into the night," he snarls into my ear, biting down afterwards and making me jerk back onto his cock.

"Fuck, fuck, fuck, please, Ryder," I beg, shaking my head. It's too much. The sensations are overwhelming me, the cool glass against the front of my body at odds with the heat of his body behind me. The round bottle fills me, stretching me, and makes my ass that much tighter for his huge cock. Every movement is pain and pleasure. I want to stop it, yet I can't get enough.

He's making me ride that edge. The edge he always rides.

But I meant what I said, he could never hurt me. Even now, even when his hands dent my hips, his cock forces my ass to stretch around him, and the bottle he shoved inside me makes me wince. I still want it.

Want more.

Want everything.

When his strong, sure fingers wrap around my throat, anchoring me as he pounds into me, I lose it. My eyes close, stars bursting behind them. I can't hear over my own heartbeat, and between one thrust and the next, I explode.

He snarls into my ear as he reaches down and, as I'm in the throes of release, yanks the bottle from my pussy and slams it back in. One orgasm tumbles into the next, pulled from me on his command. He fucks me through them, keeping me on that edge until he can't take it anymore.

He slams into me, grinding down as he does, filling my ass to the hilt as he groans. I feel him explode inside me, my pussy aching now as he slowly extracts the bottle and tosses it away.

I feel raw, sore, and used.

And oh so fucking satisfied. A smile curls my lips, even as I slump into the glass, breathing heavily. He presses along my back, wrapping an arm around my middle as he helps me stand, both of us sweaty and trembling with aftershocks.

"Christ, Roxy," he groans, licking and kissing my cheek. "How did I get so lucky?"

"Sometimes you gotta steal a few girls before you meet the right one," I tease, voice low and husky from my screams.

He chuckles breathlessly and groans when it jerks him inside me. "Love, I steal things every fucking day, I'm a goddamn mobster, but you? You're the best thing I ever stole, and I plan on showing you that for the rest of our lives, until you get bored with us and try to kill us."

"Try?" I taunt. "Bitch, please, we both know there would be no try."

He laughs again. "Admit it, love, we stole your heart."

"Nah, you stole my pussy." I laugh, even as I melt back against him. "Orgasms are the way to a woman's heart though..."

"Well, I better get to work," he murmurs.

CHAPTER

SIXTY

GARRETT

"You sure you're okay, baby?" I ask, and she licks her lips and nods.

I was sent in here to check on her. We are all dressed and ready, but everyone can wait until she's ready to go. We only told her yesterday that today would be Sam's funeral. She liked him, and we knew this would be hard for her, but it's important we go. Her black dress is modest and falls just below her knees, her leather boots leading up to meet the hem. Her makeup is kept to a minimum, but her necklace, which she never takes off, is the only colour. She looks fucking beautiful without even trying.

And sad.

She liked Sam, she had become friends with him even, though we threatened him. And now he's dead, and his funeral is today. I know she's struggling and she feels guilty, blaming herself and missing him. She needs comfort right now, and I'm not the best choice for that, but she has no one else here right now, so me it is.

Wrapping my arms around her, I drag her back to my chest as I look at her in the mirror. "You've got this, baby, all eyes will be on us today, but you can do this. We will be right there. Just hold it together for a little longer, and you can break all you need to later, I promise."

"I don't care about the eyes, I care about his family," she snaps, and then sighs. "Sorry."

"Don't ever be sorry for caring," I murmur, and kiss her cheek. "But we need to go, baby."

"I know," she whispers, and then shakes herself. "Okay."

She slips on some shades before turning and placing her hand in mine. I lead her out and down to the cars, where everyone is waiting. Tony is there to drive us in the limo, and everyone is wearing black suits. The scene is morbid.

Roxy drags me over to Tony, not letting go of my hand like it's a lifeline. He smiles down at her sadly, and she returns it. "Are you okay?" she asks him.

Our selfless Viper. She might be a cruel bitch sometimes, but she has a heart of fucking gold when it comes to people she cares for.

"He was a good friend, but he loved what he did." He sighs. "Doesn't mean I won't miss the kid."

Roxy nods. "I'm sorry, Tony, I really am. Take as much time off as you need, and we will be here for you," she offers, without questioning the fact that she just ordered our staff around. It makes me smirk and Ryder laughs before coughing to cover it up.

Tony smiles at her. "Yes, Miss Roxy, thank you. But I would rather be here protecting you."

Goddamn this man, now we can't kill him and he knows it.

Roxy nods and leans up to kiss his cheek, but freezes and looks at us, her eyes narrowed. "You kill him, and I chop off your dicks." She kisses him before letting me pull her off to the limo.

Ryder grabs her throat and drags her closer as Diesel presses to her back. "One-time exception, love."

Diesel sniffs her neck. "I'll still kill him," he threatens.

It makes her laugh and glance back at him. "No, you won't, because it would hurt me, and unless it's physical pain, you hate it."

550

Diesel snarls and pulls away. "Bloody little bird, too smart for her own good."

It makes her smile though, and that is what we all wanted. Kenzo leans down and kisses her softly. "I won't let them, darling. Come on, it's time, and then we can come back and eat pizza and drink beer." He straightens and winces in pain, making her sigh.

I, myself, don't let the pain show, even though each step tugs on my stitches and makes me want to punch someone, but she knows because she walks slower than normal, and when I slip stiffly into the limo, she smiles and kisses me. Fuck, I'd get tortured every goddamn day if this is the result.

The drive to the church doesn't take long. Roxy sits between us, quiet for once, and when we pull up to the busy car park and see the cameras there, she winces. They might not have known Sam, but they knew we were coming, as are some of the most powerful people in the city. It's almost a celebrity funeral.

As soon as our door opens, they are there, firing questions and taking pictures. It's not the first time. We manage to avoid the press frequently, but being the bachelors of the city, as they call us, it happens every now and again. I know Ryder and Kenzo had to deal with it for their mother's funeral too.

But we know how to handle it.

Ryder takes Roxy's hand. We already decided to present her with him to the press to keep her safe and the questions at bay. He slips out and wraps an arm around her, ignoring the cameras as I push through, with Diesel and Kenzo behind them, to part the crowd. We walk quickly, but not too fast, to the church, only relaxing when the door shuts.

Heading down the aisle, we take one of the front pews, and I glance over to see Sam's widow alone on the other side. Tears slowly roll down her cheeks, and her eyes are faraway. Her hands are clenched together in her lap, trying to hold it together. Roxy follows my gaze and sucks in a breath before getting to her feet.

I grab for her, but she sidesteps my hand and, ignoring the people staring, she covers the distance and sits next to Sam's widow, silently taking her hand and holding it. The woman glances over in shock, but Roxy doesn't talk or prod, just sits there for her.

We nod at Tony, and he goes and sits on the woman's other side. I hate that Roxy is so far away, but I know why she did it—so Sam's wife wouldn't be alone. I can't protest or drag her back though, because the ceremony starts.

It's a good one as far as funerals go, and when we are directed to the cemetery nearby, Roxy finally heads over to us and leans into Ryder's side. He kisses her cheek and follows everyone out of the church, where the cameras are still waiting, photographing everything, the bright bulbs flashing and making me growl. I once smashed their cameras, I'm tempted to now, but I can't. This isn't about us.

Not today.

So I endure it, but I stick close to Roxy just in case. We circle around her, creating a protective bubble as we head through the grass and old stones. While we walk across the grass, Roxy finally speaks. "I was alone at Rich's funeral, no one should go through that alone," she whispers.

We say nothing, but we press closer, hating that she was alone when she needed us. If only we found her sooner, but she's right, we can't change the past, only how we act in the future, and Roxy will never be alone again.

We all stand in the wind around the grave as the coffin is lowered into it. When it's over and people start to disappear, Roxy leans down and throws some dirt on the wood. "I'm sorry," she whispers, her voice choked.

"Baby," I murmur.

She stands and looks over at us, tears in her eyes and anger vibrating from her body. There is nothing we can do to help, and I hate that. I feel fucking useless. My fists clench at my sides with the need to hurt, to destroy, and help. But she needs softness, kindness right now, and I don't know how to offer that.

She doesn't care that we have no softness. She reaches for us anyway.

There, with cameras and the eyes of the city on us, she reaches for all of us. We all share a look. We are not embarrassed by our relationship, and anyone who has anything to say can die, but we didn't want her reputation ruined. We are helpless, however, when it comes to her. So Diesel presses to her side, and I hold her hand as Ryder presses against her back. Kenzo grips her other hand.

With her in the middle of us all, I hear gasps and whispers, but we don't care. This isn't about us today, but a man who gave his life to save ours. A true fucking hero.

CHAPTER
SIXTY-ONE

KENZO

R oxy is quiet today, and these idiots don't know how to act. Ryder offered money to the widow. Garrett offered to hurt someone. Diesel offered to kill someone. They all look flabbergasted when it didn't work. Shaking my head, I sweep Roxy into my arms and lay down on the sofa, gripping her tightly.

"It's okay, darling, we are here," I whisper to her, and she buries her head in my chest, twists her hands in my shirt, and cries.

I hold her through it, stroking her back and kissing her head, telling her we are here, that we love her, that I'm sorry. Her tears do funny things to my heart though, making it ache. They affect the others as well. Garrett mumbles about going to fight. Ryder seems helpless and stares at me in pain. Diesel growls and storms away, probably to kill someone.

But she doesn't need that right now, she just needs to feel, so I let her, and when she finally lifts her head, I brush her tears away and press kisses to her face. "I love you, darling."

"I love you too," she whispers, her voice thick before lowering her head again.

That's how she falls asleep in my arms, and I look to Ryder, who watches her with his face contorted in pain. "You knew what to do," he murmurs lowly, so as not to wake her.

I nod, and he sighs, scrubbing his face. "I didn't."

"You don't have to know how to do everything, she needs us all," I whisper, and he nods and gets to his feet.

"I'm going to work. I'll check in on her bar and everything. Let me know if she needs anything." He walks away then, almost running.

These idiots. When faced with tears, they turn into scared little boys. I don't tell her about the breaking stories and gossip spreading about us all. Everyone wants to know about the woman who tamed the Vipers. The picture of her between us at the funeral is being spread everywhere. Ryder put protections in place, of course, and keeps her identity a secret so they can't dig up her past and hurt her.

But every eye is on us now. Everyone wants to be her.

But all we want is her.

Our Roxy.

"KENZO?" SHE WHISPERS, HALF ASLEEP.

Shifting, I pull her closer. "Hey, darling." She blinks her eyes open and looks up at me.

"Sorry, didn't mean to cry all over you." She sighs.

"Cry all over me anytime, Rox." I grin. "It's an excuse to keep you close."

She snorts and rolls over, so I flip onto my side and hold her in my arms as she absentmindedly traces her finger across my chest. "I guess it brought it all back. I kept seeing Rich—" She hiccups, and I hold her tighter. "It's easy sometimes to not think about it, to just keep busy so I don't have to, but I couldn't today—"

556

"That's okay, darling, you're allowed to miss him. You are allowed to hurt, you loved him," I soothe, and then deciding now is the time, I pull the picture from my pocket and hand it over. "I thought this might be important, I took it the day we took you."

She grabs the photo and stares down at it, tears filling her eyes again, even as she smiles. "He was a fucking hard man, so gruff and snappy, but God, I miss that. I miss his 'hey, girl, get yo ass over here.' He would pretend he didn't care, but whenever I needed him, he was there. Never judging, just understanding."

"He sounds like an amazing man. I wish I could have met him."

She nods, brushing her hand over the photo. "Thank you for bringing it."

"Always. Tell me more about him?" I request.

She sighs and looks at me. "He would have hated you guys, probably would have tried to kill you. I remember this one time I brought a guy back—"

I listen to story after story about the first man she ever loved, and I can't help but fall more in love with her. She loves so deeply, cares so deeply, and I owe that man everything. Without him, I might have lost Roxy before I even knew her. For that, he has my respect and loyalty, and I will ensure he is never forgotten.

For her.

"I have an idea," I tell her later on, when we're just watching the sunset through the windows. I know she's been thinking about starting a fund in his name, but maybe...just maybe... "Why don't you name your new bars after him?"

She shuffles back further against me where we sit on the balcony. "You think Ryder would let me?"

"They are yours, darling, not his, name them whatever you want. It was just an idea," I offer, wrapping her tighter in my arms.

"That's a good idea. He would like that," she whispers, and I press my face to her head.

"Kenzo?" she murmurs.

"Yeah, darling?"

"I still fucking hate you all, and I want my bat back," she snaps.

I can't help but laugh, and she joins in, and when we stand up and she pushes me into the pool, I come up sputtering but smiling. She's going to be okay.

Roxxane is a fighter, but she will never have to do it alone again.

CHAPTER SIXTY-TWO

DIESEL

"What do you think?" Ryder asks, sweeping his hand out to encompass the house.

"It's...homey." I never pictured myself in a home like this, but now that we are starting our family properly, it makes sense. "The massive bed in her room is a nice touch." I snort, flicking open my lighter and lighting a fag.

He smirks. "I figured you'd like that, almost as much as the basement."

I perk up at that. "Basement?"

"Basement." He nods. "To turn into yours and Roxy's dungeon. Do whatever the fuck you want down there to each other, but work stays at the apartment building."

"Fucking deal," I murmur around the cigarette. "Goddamn, I can't wait. Think of all the toys I could fill it with."

The house itself is a fucking safe house. It's massive, with barri-ers, fencing, and guards ready to patrol. It has an armoury, bullet proof windows, and escape tunnels. It's a goddamn fortress, just what we need. It's also black.

Like our fucking souls.

All black, the outside, and even most of the inside. Roxy will love it. I don't even ask when Ryder had the time to start on this project. It's clear he's had this house renovated to his specifications, the sneaky bastard. But he's right—our apartment is nice, but it's not a home.

This is.

With Little Bird.

I can't wait to show it to her and play in our new dungeon, I'll have to get her a housewarming gift...whips are good for that right? I must say it out loud, because Ryder laughs and claps me on the shoulder.

"It's a good job she loves you, D, because you are one crazy bastard."

I blow smoke in his face for that. "Yup, but Little Bird wouldn't have me any other way."

"I'm thinking we could be in as soon as the end of the month. I'm going to need help, but with Roxy busy working on her bars, this should be easy enough to do. Garrett is already working with security specialists to secure it, and I've set up a home office so I can be around more."

"What about Kenzo?" I inquire, trailing my hand across the black and gold marble kitchen counter.

"He's aware. I wanted him to have the home he always wanted as well. This was the place he used to want when we were kids. He's happy to work from home as much as he can, which is why the garage is so big—for his toys," he informs me.

"A home." I sigh and look at him. "Gotta admit, never thought I would have another one."

"Me either," he replies, looking around. "But it feels right."

I nod. "It does, as long as you get a maid or some shit. Blood will be hard to get off these floors."

"They will be fine." He purses his lips, looking at the tile.

I grab my blade, slice my hand, and let it drip onto the floor. "Clean it up and let's see."

"Fucking hell, D!" he snaps, and looks around for something to clean the blood with. Blowing out more smoke, I watch him rip off his jacket and drop it onto the blood and start cleaning while my hand drips more and more on the tiles. "Fucking wanker, carry on, and I'll ruin your little bird's surprise for you."

"Surprise?" I ask, freezing.

He smirks then stands, holding his jacket away from him with a disgusted sneer. "Yes, surprise, asshole. Try me."

I wrap my hand, wondering what Little Bird is up to. Fuck, I hope it involves pain and her pussy. I've been missing our little sessions, but I wanted to give her time to heal after what happened.

ROXY

"I'm going for a nap, want to join me?" I ask the room in general.

"A nap?" Garrett snorts. "What am I, eighty? Don't think I don't know Ryder is making you look after us."

Propping my hands on my hips, I glare at them both. "Fine, then let's cut the shit. Get your fine asses upstairs and rest. You need to heal, and the longer it takes, the longer you will have to sit around acting like fucking weak bitches."

His mouth drops open, and I grin sweetly.

"And the longer you'll have to go without sex."

That gets them moving. Kenzo scoops me up into his arms, and they take the steps two at a time, heading to his room. He throws me onto the bed where I bounce as they quickly strip. My mouth drops open at all the skin and muscles, but they don't give me time to drool as they climb into bed, Kenzo on one side and Garrett on the other.

561

They both try to pull me into their arms, and it starts a tug-of-war with me in the middle.

"I'm not a fucking toy, stop tugging at me like you do your cock," I snarl, as I slip under the quilt and press my front to Garrett's chest. I feel Kenzo press against my back, their legs and arms wrapping around me.

"If your cock so much as touches me, I'm out," Garrett growls.

"Got it, no crossing swords," Kenzo teases, making me giggle as I close my eyes.

"Sleep, now," I demand.

"So fucking bossy, darling. All you need is the suit, and then you're Ryder."

I snort at that. "Nah, I'm smarter than him...don't tell him that though, he'll cane my ass."

Garrett grins and snuggles closer. "And you would love it, baby."

"Too fucking right, now sleep so I can have wet dreams about canes and cock."

They both groan but quiet down, even as I feel Kenzo's hard cock pressing against my ass. I wiggle back and push into it. He groans and nips my shoulder. "Behave."

I huff. "I am, that was a mistake."

"Uh-huh, you big tease."

I mumble something about them both being wankstains, but I do eventually manage to sleep. When I wake up, I'm hot and bothered with two very hard cocks pressed against me and wandering hands gripping my legs and sliding back and forth.

"You're cheating," I mutter sleepily.

"The nap worked, I'm healed," Garrett declares, stroking higher and pushing up the shirt I'm wearing.

"Me too, all healed," Kenzo agrees, kissing across my shoulder. "So fucking healed."

"Uh-uh, we could tear your stitches," I protest, but not too strongly because, shit, I'm wet as hell and already aching for them. Their harsh hands and teasing lips are getting me all wound up. I almost lost them both, and since then, we haven't been together. I'm craving their bodies as reassurance that they are really here, really alive, and don't plan on dying on me.

"Nurse, I require you to heal me." Kenzo grins against my skin as Garrett caresses over my knickers.

Shit.

"Me too," Garrett murmurs. "I've heard the best form of treatment is with orgasms."

I huff and try to wiggle free, but they clamp their legs around me to stop me from moving away. My hussy vagina is on team sex too, basically holding up a sign saying 'screw me.'

"Healing," I blurt. "Rest."

But they ignore me, the stupid wankstains and their stupid, seductive penises. Peni? What's the plural of penis? Oh, who the fuck cares.

"Fuck it," I mutter, and Kenzo breathes out a laugh.

"Thank fuck." He flips me and grabs my head, yanking my lips to his as Garrett kisses down my shoulder and slips down my thighs to part them before throwing one over Kenzo's leg.

I rip myself away and roll to the end of the bed, raising to my knees to stare at them. They turn over and grin at me. Garrett's arm goes behind his head, his chest muscles stretching enticingly as I run my eyes down his torso before looking to Kenzo, who's watching me hungrily, his chest bare too. They look like two fucking Greek gods, all dark eyes and muscles, and they both watch me, waiting for me to make a move.

Two predators observing and waiting, but they should know I'm the bigger one, and I have them exactly where I want them. Wanting me, waiting for me to make a move. A viper's game of who strikes first.

I'm Roxxane fucking Viper. They don't say how or when. I do.

Gripping the bottom of my shirt, I smirk at them. "You want this off?"

They both nod, and Garrett releases a rumbling groan as his eyes drop to my thighs and back up my body again, making me shiver with desire. From one fucking look. It isn't fair, the power these men have over me, but then again, I have the same power over them.

They are poised and ready to strike, all coiled muscles and power, but they watch and wait, listening to me. Bending to my will. "Then you will do as you're told."

Kenzo grins as he leisurely leans back, those charming lips curling in his arrogant smirk, his eyes glittering with respect and need. "Do tell, darling."

I debate how this is going to work. Garrett is the most hurt, but he won't be able to be beneath me. I flicker my gaze to him, and we share a small smile, silently asking if he can handle this. I don't want to hurt him further, but his eyes darken and greedily drop to my body. "I want Garrett in my pussy," I murmur, my heartbeat kicking up a notch in excitement. "And you in my mouth." I look back at Kenzo as I crawl closer on the bed, poising above his lap.

His mouth parts slightly, his eyes widening, and he seems unsure on what to say for once, making me smirk as I blow air across him. "That a problem, darling?"

Garrett groans, his hand reaching out and pinching my side. "Be nice."

"Oh, I am. If I was being mean, I would sit here telling you all the things I want you to do, like Kenzo filling my mouth with his cum until I have no choice but to swallow while you fuck me and hard and fast, your thick cock filling my pussy until I'm screaming." I glance over and wink. "See? Nice."

His eyes narrow on me, and he slaps my side. "Better get to it then, baby. Open that pretty mouth and be real nice to Kenzo," he orders, as he gets to his knees and moves around me until I can't see him anymore.

I shiver in anticipation, but when he doesn't touch me, I glance back at Kenzo and pull down his boxers, his hard cock springing free as he watches me hungrily, desperately. "Is that what you want?" I purr. "For me to be nice?"

He swallows hard, his Adam's apple bobbing with the movement as he watches me, entranced. Grabbing his hand, I pull it up and, as he watches, suck his finger into my mouth, wrapping my lips around it and lashing it with my tongue. He groans, and I jump as Garrett smacks my ass, hard as hell. It surprises me so much I let Kenzo's finger fall from my mouth as I jerk forward. The sudden pain almost causes me to yelp until his big, rough hand starts to massage in the sting, making me moan and push back.

"Baby, I said nice."

Kenzo digs his fingers into my hair, the long, lean digits working through the tangles until he anchors at the base, wrapping it around his fist and dragging me closer. "You heard him, darling."

He tugs me down but lets me choose what I want to do, which is always him. Encircling my hand around the base of his hard cock, I roll my eyes up to his as I suck the mushroom head into my mouth. He groans, his hips lifting and forcing his cock in deeper. Garrett's hand strokes down my spine and back up where he presses my head down until my ass is in the air.

Swallowing Kenzo fully, I bob up and down but stop when he starts slow, measured thrusts into my mouth, trying to make this last. I let him for now. Just staring into those eyes as I feel Garrett behind me, his big hands spanning my hips before they slide down and drag my thighs open.

"She's fucking drenched, brother," he growls, as his hand dips to my pussy and parts my lips, stroking me lovingly. "So fucking wet, but we are going to need more for you to take my big fat cock, baby."

Shit, his dirty words almost have my mouth popping off Kenzo's cock, but he grunts and drags me back down again, using my hair to move me how he wants until I have no control.

Garrett ignores my struggles and dips his finger inside me before adding another and stretching me. He curls them and strokes along my walls and the nerves there, which has me bucking. Pleasure pounds through me, and my body is almost shaking as he teases. My pulse thumps, I am that turned on, imagining him behind me, watching me suck his brother's cock as he strokes me.

Fuck.

I moan around Kenzo, and he grunts, twisting his hand in my hair until a splash of pain sparks through me, which makes me clamp around Garrett's fingers. He chuckles, the bastard, and pulls them free, stroking back up to rub my clit, fast and hard. I push back, my pussy clamping on air, desperate to be filled, but he doesn't. He ignores me and just keeps rubbing my clit until, suddenly, my release hits me out of nowhere.

Blowing through my body like one of Diesel's bombs. I whimper around Kenzo's cock, making him groan as his hips stutter for a moment before speeding up, pushing faster into my mouth until I have to hold on, even as I shake from the aftershocks. But I have no time to calm down, because Garrett's cock is there, the thick mushroom head pressing to my entrance as he strokes my side lovingly.

"So fucking beautiful, baby. Out of all the fights I've been in, I've never been happier than to win the one for you," he rasps, which makes my heart skip a beat. How can he say such things when I can't respond? In fact, that's probably why he did it, the bastard.

He laughs like he can feel me insulting him and, gripping my hips, he yanks me back, impaling me on a few inches of his cock before pulling out and working his way back in. "Fuck, she's so goddamn tight," he growls through clenched teeth, making Kenzo groan beneath me, his cock jumping in my mouth as he desperately rolls his hips.

"Fuck, fuck, fuck," he pants. "Her mouth is too fucking much, man, and those eyes." He flutters his open and locks them on me, groaning loudly. "I can see your hunger in them, just how much you like sucking my cock, darling. You kill me, I'm helpless even now, when I'm trying to make this last, to keep your mouth on me as long as I can."

Popping free of his cock, I drag my teeth down his length before licking back up. "Why?" I murmur, voice hoarse. "I already said I want you fucking my mouth and shooting down my throat," I purr, as I lick the head, tasting his pre-cum, which makes me groan. My eyelids flutter closed, and I lick my lips, opening my eyes before rolling them back to him as Garrett pushes in another inch, pushing me forward, Kenzo's cock hitting my lips.

He drags me closer with my hair, and his eyes turn wild, desperate. I open my mouth like a good girl and swallow him as Garrett finally bottoms out in my pussy and stills. His thick cock stretches me to the point of pain, and yet he doesn't move, but I need him to. He has to, because him just filling me like this—fuck. I push back, and he smacks my ass again, not a soft love tap, no, he fucking tans my ass so hard, I cry out around Kenzo.

"Behave, baby. I know that's hard for you, but if you don't, I'm going to fuck you and spray my cum in your pussy without letting you come again," he growls.

"Bastard," I mumble around Kenzo's cock, making him groan and narrow his eyes.

"Don't do that." He grunts, his thrusts stopping as he throws his other arm over his eyes. "Fuck her, Garrett, because I'm not going to last much longer."

"You hear that, baby? Is he close? Is his cock filling your mean little mouth?" Garrett asks, as he pulls out and slams back in, forcing me to take Kenzo's cock deeper, all the way down my throat, which makes Kenzo yell and jerk.

Garrett laughs, pulling out and slamming inside, each thrust pushing me back and forth on Kenzo's cock like he's controlling us both. My eyes widen and water as he hits the back of my throat over and over, but I don't gag. I'm stuck between them, my other hand ripping into the bedding and fisting it as I take what they give me. Garrett's smooth strokes slowly rebuild that fire inside me, stoking it with each twist and roll of his hips.

Kenzo's moans fill the room, and he finally gives up trying to hold back. He moves his arm, his eyes heated and locked on me, his hand painfully tugging my hair, but it's oh so fucking good. Kenzo is wild beneath me now, his hips lifting desperately, fucking my mouth hard and fast. Saliva drips from my lips, my cheeks ache, and my hand squeezes the base of his cock until he's grunting. His eyes slip shut, and his mouth is wide open. His amazing chest is covered in sweat, and his abs clench as he tries to hold back.

Garrett grunts, his thrusts speeding up until he's just fucking me hard and fast, the way only my enforcer ever can. No games, just raw fucking. Nothing held back. He owns my body, not questioning whether I'm enjoying it, since he makes me. His thick cock fills me and drives me to my limits again and again. I push back to meet him, panting around Kenzo's cock.

"Darling, fuck, God, I'm going to—" Kenzo warns, his cock swelling in my mouth. I swallow him, locking my lips around his base and hum. He yells and jerks in my mouth, shooting his load down my throat before he collapses back onto the bed, his muscles shaking as he releases his hand from my hair and strokes along my cheek with shaking fingers. "Fuck me, I love you so fucking much it's unreal."

Yeah, I don't answer that shit. It's a bit awkward to have a lovey-dovey moment with another man's cock still pounding away in your pussy, not that he cares. He smiles with smug satisfaction and slips from my mouth.

Swallowing, I wipe my lips as I laugh breathlessly, and that's when Garrett decides to show me he was just playing. His hand wraps around my throat, and he drags me to my knees, my back hitting his chest. Kenzo reaches out lazily and traps my hands in front of my stomach until I'm helpless but to take the hard pounding thrusts he slams into me.

Again and again.

"Fucking love being inside you," he growls in my ear. The dirty, guttural words having me crying out as I push back as much as I can to take him, the new angle hitting a spot inside me that has my eyes nearly crossing. "I swear you are enough to make a goddamn priest sin, baby. This hot little body drives me wild, until you're all I think about. Fuck, I even dream of your hot little cunt, of you bouncing on my cock, and I wake up hard and wanting."

His words undo me. I squeeze his cock as my eyes close, it's too much. Too fucking much. That spark is an inferno now, burning for him, for all of them. And each stroke of his thick cock inside me drives me higher and higher to that brink. My pleasure is his to control, and my damaged enforcer is giving me everything I always wanted.

Him.

"Fuck, baby, I can feel your pussy clamping down on me like a fucking vice. You like it when I talk dirty? You like it when I treat you like the bitch you are? When I fuck all this hate out of me?" I whimper in response, and his hand squeezes tighter, his thrusts jiggling my breasts, and Kenzo groans at the sight, his tongue running along his bottom lip.

"I think you love it, love when I'm a dick to you. It gets you wet as hell, you love the fight, the game, until one of us finally gives in and breaks. Tell me, baby, who's going to break first?" he murmurs, his tongue tracing my ear as he tries to slow his thrusts, but I slam myself back, taking him deeper, and he groans, his hand flexing on my neck. He has so much goddamn power. It's the same hand that kills men with a snap, which is covered in so much blood, he will never be clean.

"You," I grind out, making him grunt as I purposely squeeze around his cock.

With a snarl he releases my neck and pushes my face into the bed, his hands gripping my hips so hard, I know it will bruise as he hammers into me. It's on the edge of pain and it mixes with the pleasure until I'm shaking, just holding on as he proves just how much he hates me.

"I hate you, I hate you." I feel it chanting from my lips as I push back, meeting his wild thrusts.

He grunts and slaps my ass again and again, until with one last thrust, he slaps his hand over my pussy, catching my clit and sending me tumbling over the edge with a scream. I come so hard, I almost pass out, my vision dimmed, and when I come to, I'm shivering and shaking, my pussy dripping as I pant loudly. He drags me up again, stroking my neck lovingly as he kisses my throat.

Relaxing back into him, I let him hold me up as I turn into nothing but a satisfied mass of sweating flesh. He chuckles into my ear, which makes me clench around him, and in turn, causes him to groan and still. "Goddamn it, baby, you wreck me."

"I fucking hate you," I murmur, my eyes closed.

"I hate you too, baby." He smacks my hip, and I fall forward again as he releases me, his cock slipping free. We both tumble to the mattress next to Kenzo, who turns and pulls me into his arms, his cock hard once again, but we both ignore it.

We all fall into an exhausted heap, our bodies slick with sweat, and I notice Kenzo's wound is leaking blood, but he disregards it and snuggles closer. I want to check on Garrett's too, but he's behind me, and if the hard way he's holding me is any indication, it shows he has no inclination to move any time soon.

Morons.

Ryder is going to kill us.

But in my defense...how am I supposed to resist them? They have abs, for fuck's sake. Those little dents of happiness are my weakness, and seriously, would any girl turn down orgasms from their powerful, tatted, muscly—wait, I forgot my train of thought.

Ah, fuck it.

"I fucking love naps." Garrett huffs, making us all laugh.

"Naps are my new favourite thing," Kenzo states. "I think I need some more healing." He wiggles his eyebrows, making me smack his chest.

"Yeah, well, so does my pussy, so shut your mouth and let's actually nap," I order, and they both chuckle.

"So cute when she orders us around," Garrett mumbles, pressing closer to my back. "Baby, you think you control us?"

"I don't think, I know I do, now shut up and let me sleep," I demand, closing my eyes, and like I thought they would, they stay quiet.

Yeah, I control these bastards, they just don't realise it.

CHAPTER

SIXTY-THREE

ROXY

After our little nap, I wake up before the other two and leave them to heal. I text Ryder, mentioning he might need the doctor to check up on them, and then I fall into an exhausted slumber in my own room. I must have slept the rest of the day and night away, because when I wake up, it's sunny again, so it's clearly morning.

I guess the last week has taken its toll, but I feel full of energy today, and when I stretch and hit something hard, I don't even scream, I just flip over, grab the knife from under my pillow, and have it at his neck in no time.

Diesel barely opens one eye, but a smile curls his lips. "Morning to you too, Little Bird," he murmurs, before grasping me and dragging me back to his chest.

"D!" I gush, snuggling closer. I missed the crazy bastard. He was gone all day yesterday, busy working he said.

"Told you I would be free today. You've been busy," he mumbles, stroking down my back even as I hold the blade to his throat.

"What can I say, I get bored," I tease, making him laugh before he groans.

"We better get up, it's breakfast time, and I'm starving. If no one feeds me soon, I might eat you," he warns darkly, then chuckles.

"Anytime, babe, any fucking time." Sitting up, I slip from his chest with the knife still in hand and stroll naked to the shower. I hear his groan behind me.

"Not fair, Little Bird," I hear him call as I laugh and shut the door.

After I've showered and dressed in a shirt, I head out to find them all at the table like normal. Honestly, I've missed these breakfast meets. It's the only time we're usually all together, and with Ryder going back to work and Diesel off and busy, it's not been the same. I slip into my seat. Ryder pours me a coffee, and Kenzo fills my plate, his hand landing on my thigh under the table after, stroking it casually as I yank up my other leg and lay it on Ryder's lap.

His hand drops to it and massages as he sips from his teacup. The sight of him doing that still drives me mad for some reason. Every day, I watch him drink from it like a goddamn ritual, like he has mesmerised me.

He catches me staring and winks, and his eyes seem...warmer today. Has he been melting more and more around us and I haven't even noticed? Hell, he doesn't even have his phone on him.

"Morning, love," he murmurs, and leans over and kisses me ever so softly, tasting the coffee on my lips before he goes back to sipping his tea. "Okay, D, update."

"Triad daddy is dead, rolled right through a window, whoops, and yesterday, I made sure there were no others hiding in the city." He grins, flipping open his lighter and lighting a cigarette before snapping it closed. His feet come up and land on the table as he crosses his legs, still smoking.

"Garrett, how are you feeling?"

Garrett shrugs and finishes his mouthful before leaning back.

"Fine, the doc redressed the wounds." He winks at me then, making me giggle.

"Kenzo?" Ryder asks.

Kenzo leans into me, still stroking my thigh. "Healing and fine. You can thank Roxy here for our set back."

"Uh-uh." I shake my head. "It was all you fuckers. There I was, innocently napping—"

"With your ass pushing against my cock," Kenzo interjects, but I ignore him.

"And you decided to have a quick sausage party." I grab a sausage on my plate and gesture through my fingers with it to explain, making even Ryder snort.

That's when I realise this is their version of a check in—sometimes about business, sometimes family. This is how they stay together, because they listen. It's adorable really, but I don't say that out loud, 'cause four men would hunt me and prove it wasn't, in fact, adorable.

Dropping it, I look to the man in question. "Ryder?"

"Yes?" He sounds confused.

"No, I mean check in, how are you?" I snort.

He blinks, and that's when I realise no one has ever asked him before. "Erm, fine, I have an open day today." He wipes his mouth and puts his teacup down. "Which reminds me, we need to discuss something."

My stomach sinks, and I look around to see all their faces darken. "Going to try and kill me?" I query casually. Honestly, I wouldn't put it past them if they thought they had to.

"Not today," Diesel responds, toasting me with his cigarette.

"We need to talk, love," Ryder repeats seriously, making me suck in a breath. Something is wrong, it has to be...but how does it involve me?

I haven't beat anyone up today, so it's not that.

575

RYDER

I sit her down on the sofa and crouch before her, holding her hand in mine. Kenzo and Diesel bracket either side of her, and Garrett stands behind her, protecting her back like always. "Love, we have been thinking." I share a look with the others, who nod their encouragement. "Your father—"

She narrows her eyes at the reminder, and I smile sadly and cover her lips with my hand before she can start shouting, telling us she hates us again.

"Your father, Roxy, he needs to pay for what he did to you, both in the past and recently. We might have accepted the deal, but now that we-we—"

"Love you," Kenzo inserts confidently.

"Yes, love you." I nod. "It means we can't let an insult like that stand to our girl. Now, I know you hate him and he's responsible for heinous things in your past—trust me, love, I understand that—which is why I want to know if you want us to deal with it." I release her lips, and she licks them, looking between us.

"You mean kill him? You would do that?"

"Baby, when are you going to realise there isn't anything we wouldn't do for you?" Garrett snorts.

"I-I don't know if I can face him, it's been years," she admits, and Diesel presses closer.

"I know, love, which is why I want you to let us do it for you," I reassure her, but I know before she's even decided she would never let us. This is her monster to slay, and as much as I wish we could do it for her, he's hers to deal with. Our Roxxane would never make another deal with her issues, no, she's too strong for that, and it only makes me love her more.

"No, no, you're right. It's been a long time coming. I guess I just —" She shakes her head. "Honestly, I forgot about him for a bit, but you're right, he will never stop," she agrees sadly, and meets my eyes.

Hers are shaded with ghosts, but as strong as always. "Yes, I want to be there."

"Just be there?" Diesel questions. "Because if you don't want to deal with him, you know I will, Little Bird."

She smiles, but it's an evil one, like the one she used to give us all the time. "No, he's my father, my responsibility. I want you there, though, this has been a long time coming and seeing him again—"

"Will bring back memories." I nod, understanding that myself. "We have your back, always, you are our family now. Not his, never his. He will never hurt you again."

She nods, reaching for Diesel's and Kenzo's hands. Garrett lays his on her shoulder, and I grip her knees as she sucks in a breath. "I guess I always knew...knew he never loved me. This needs to happen. He will always think he can control me, use me, and that also extends to you now. I can't let him. It's time he paid for his sins."

She raises her eyes, and there's no weakness there now. Just a fucking Viper flashing in those dark depths. "He dies today."

So be it.

CHAPTER SIXTY-FOUR

ROXY

The drive there is quiet, as my men are letting me prepare for what's to come. They are right, he is a threat, not just to me, but to them now as well. They are my family, he never was. He might be my blood, but all that means is that he was my beginning, not my middle or end.

Blood doesn't always mean family. Sometimes you find your family in friends, in father- and mother-like figures...or in lovers. I look around and smile, thinking sometimes you find that when you're least expecting it. Our family might be messed up, hateful, powerful, and rich...but when we are together, we're happy. We are safe, and that's all that matters.

Now it's my turn to keep my family safe, to protect the men who would protect me against anything, who would hunt me and anyone who hurt me or us across this world and never stop.

My father—no, I need to stop calling him that—Rob is nothing more than a threat, and to a Viper, a threat is easy to deal with. We kill them.

His blood might have saved him from me once, when I chose to run instead of fight, but he signed his death warrant when he decided he couldn't leave me be. Now a darkness fills me, one he created, a killer he made with his fists, with his cruel words and abuse.

A fighter.

A survivor.

I survived him once, but he won't survive me ever again.

I'm a motherfucking Viper, and he is nothing. Just a dead man walking.

We pull up outside the house. The sun is shining, and it warms me through the tinted window as I stare at the rundown house that once felt like a prison to me. How I used to crave Rob's love, or even for just his eyes to move along, to not see me. I left here as a child, and now I'm coming back as a woman.

"Ready, love?" Ryder asks, breaking into my thoughts.

I swing my head around to see them all staring at me, all offering me their strength. I nod and slip from the car, the slamming of the doors loud in the derelict neighbourhood as they follow after me.

We stand outside.

Ryder in a suit, Kenzo too. Garrett in his leather, and Diesel in his jeans and wife beater, but they scream money, and I guess I do now as well. My body is encased in ripped jeans, kick ass boots, and a designer shirt.

I came from nothing, just like my men, and now I own this town. With them.

Walking up the path is like taking a trip down memory lane, as flashes of the night I ran away crowd my memory. It was night, they were asleep, and I was so scared to be caught, my meagre possessions stuffed into a plastic shopping bag. I had fallen, scraped my knees and hands, and had to bite my lip to stop from crying out so they wouldn't hear. I looked back at the house, the curtains shut and windows dark.

Just like now.

I reach the door and, sucking in a breath, I raise my hand and rap my knuckles on the worn wood. We wait silently, but no one answers, so I knock louder and hear shuffling inside.

"Yeah, yeah, if this is those bible cunts again—" He slurs and rips open the door, freezing when his eyes land on the men and then me, a sneer curling his lips. His dark eyes, the same as mine, are filled with annoyance.

"The fuck you want? You bought her, I don't want her back," he snaps, and tries to shut the door. I slam my boot in the way and then push it open, causing him to stumble back, even as he starts to yell.

"The fuck do you want? I covered the debt, and I don't owe you bastards—" Ryder shoves him into a chair.

"Sit down and shut up for once," he snarls, before stepping away and leaning against the wall, rolling back his sleeves.

Garrett shuts the door and stands before it, his arms crossed. Diesel wanders around the room, giggling and flicking open his lighter repeatedly. Kenzo stays close to me in case I need him. I'm frozen on the spot though, looking around.

It's smaller than I remember, smellier too. I guess pain warps your memories. In my head, this was hell, and when I have nightmares about it, it all seems so much...more. I guess facing it now is making me realise I have been building this place up in my head, and now that I'm standing here, I'm not afraid.

My eyes return to the man who caused me so much misery. His shirt is dirty, stained, and ripped in places. His beard and hair are unkempt, his eyes blurry from whatever he was drinking or shooting up. His body is almost wasting away, lanky and skinny now, smaller than I remember too. His face is gaunt, his eyes sunken in, and his hair is thinning and greasy.

I can't believe I used to be so terrified of this man. Walking around the couch, I drop onto the edge of the stained cushion and stare at him. "Hi, Dad, how have you been?"

He snorts and turns his head to spit on the carpet, making me purse my lips in disgust. "The fuck you want? We had a deal."

"Oh, yes, me for your debt. I mean, really, Rob, still using me as your punching bag because you're not adult enough to deal with your own issues?" I laugh bitterly.

He narrows his eyes on me, but looks to Ryder. "Better control your cunt before I remind her who's still the man of this house."

"Not you by the looks of it," I snap, bringing his eyes back to me. "They won't help you, they are here to help me."

"The fuck you talking about, girlie?" he sneers, leaning forward and sniffing hard, wiping at his stained mouth.

"The fuck I mean is I'm one of them now, and they don't take well to anything or anyone being able to hurt us. Like you, Rob, you just keep coming back. I could have walked away if you had let me go when I ran, but you didn't, you sold me. You inserted yourself back in my life again. Yes, it worked out well for me, but I can't have that happening again. All it would take is the wrong person to come knocking, and you would fold like a cheap fucking suit and the rat you are. I will not let you put us in danger," I snap.

"Fine, whatever you say, what will it take to make you go away again?" He sighs, not getting it. I shake my head at him and wag my finger.

"Nothing you can afford," I taunt.

He just laughs and leans back, his body seeming incapable of holding him up. I watch him then, really watch him, and realise just what a broken man he is. He has nothing or no one but the bar booze he drinks. He's getting older and will probably die soon from all the abuse he has put his body through.

I can't do it, I can't kill him. Not because I still fear him or love him, but because he's nothing. He's pathetic, he's a ghost, and killing him won't bring my mother back or stop the nightmares. It won't change my past, and I wouldn't want it to. So I stand up, ready to leave. I got what I needed here—closure. My past is dead and forgotten like this house, and I will leave the ashes where they lie.

Buried.

"I have money!" he yells, staring at me. "Take the money, girl, and we can be a family again!"

582

I cringe at the word on his lips, and my men step closer.

"I don't want to be part of your family, I have my own," I reply coolly.

"Do as you're fucking told and listen to your daddy," he barks, puffing up like he used to back then, but now he just looks pathetic.

"Don't worry, she does, and she will be calling me daddy later." Diesel smirks even as I gag and glare at him.

"No I fucking won't."

My dad laughs bitterly, and I glance back at him. "Yeah, least ya finally turned out good for something, right, girl? A whore for money."

It goes silent for a moment as the world holds its breath before my men burst into action, all rushing him. I watch them grab him, but a coldness flows through me, an anger...an anger to hurt the man who hurt me.

"Stop," I order calmly, and they do, all looking back at me. "Drop him."

Again, they do, and step back, their eyes on me as I stop before my wheezing father, his face red as he falls to the floor. Crouching there, I tilt my head as I watch him. I used to fear this man so much, he haunted my every step, but now my Vipers do, replacing him. How can I fear this-this broken man, when I have seen the evil the world has to offer and the snakes that fill my bed?

He is weak.

He is pathetic.

This place is nothing but a house, and he is nothing but a man.

Me? I'm a fucking snake, baby.

"I used to be so fucking scared of you," I admit, those ghosts and phantom fears rising within me. "I used to fear the dark because it was when you hurt me, but then I faced those demons. I looked into the dark and embraced my fear because hurt comes both day and night. The monsters don't wait for the sun to set, this isn't a goddamn fairy tale. This is life and monsters...monsters are everywhere. But they are human. Flesh and blood like me and you. I hated you for so long, your control over me even after I left. But I'm finally moving on, and to do that, to move on from you, I have to forgive you. To yank those claws free, to let the pain and the fear go. To forgive the dark and myself for hating you for so long and holding onto that until it warped me." He blinks hard in confusion. "I see it now—how weak you are. Your own fear is in your eyes, fear of yourself. Of what you are...of what you have become, but, Daddy? You should fear what you created more."

"What the fuck—"

I shake my head and slap him, shutting him up. "I'm talking, and you will fucking listen!" I yell. "I was ready to walk away, to leave you here to rot, but now? Now I won't. You will never hurt my family or me again.

"Maybe it would make me a better person, a stronger person, to walk away, but fuck knows I don't care. I don't care that I want to kill you, and what that means for me and my soul, because these men? They love me for it, and I'm tired of fighting myself. I am who I am. Born out of blood and pain, I'm a fucking Viper."

"You are nothing, just a cheap whore sleeping her way to the top, and when they don't want you anymore, they will throw you away." He chuckles.

"Nah, they won't." I laugh. "We are family, we are the thing people fear in the dark now. All of us are born from necessity, from people like you. They slayed their pasts, and now it's time for me to do the same. So any last words, Father?"

"Fuck you," he snarls, throwing himself at me.

I move, my hand already cupping the blade at my hip. He blinks in astonishment as I stare at him from inches away, my knife buried in his chin, piercing it from underneath and spearing into his mouth as blood bubbles at his lips. His eyes dart from side to side in fear. "Not very inventive last words, but they will do," I murmur. "Don't ever fuck with the Vipers."

I pull the blade free and quickly slice it across his throat. Blood sprays me as his jugular is cut, covering my face and chest until I have to blink the droplets from my lashes. I can taste it on my lips, but I still don't move as I stare into his eyes.

His hands come up to cover his neck, but Diesel is there and slaps them away quickly, laughing as we all watch the man, my father, finally meet the end he deserves.

Maybe I should have walked away, been a good person, and let him live.

But I never claimed to be a good fucking person.

It takes longer than I would have expected, and when he finally stills, his chest unmoving, his eyes are still open...but empty. Like me. Because I feel nothing. I thought I would, but I don't. This was just another job to do, to take care of.

Diesel leans into my view, his hand tracing down my cheek and coming away covered in blood. "I love you, Little Bird, it's over."

I nod, and he leans in, uncaring of the blood, and presses his lips to mine as I feel the others move closer, always there, always protecting me.

Sometimes you don't need to find a hero, it's enough to find someone who will stand with you in the dark and not be afraid of blood and death. No, sometimes you don't need a hero...you need a criminal, a villain.

"Let's go home, love," Ryder murmurs, as his hand lands on my shoulder and squeezes.

Yes, home.

With my men, my family.

My Vipers.

CHAPTER SIXTY-FIVE

DIESEL

Two weeks have passed since Roxy killed her dad. We dealt with the aftermath of course, calling in clean-up and our police buddies so they would never know what really happened. Just another junkie dying in the slums. That's how they spin it.

He can never hurt her again.

If she hadn't killed him, I would have for what he did to her. He deserved worse, but it was her justice to give, and she did so beautifully... I could taste his blood on her lips when I kissed her. Can still hear her screams as Ryder and I washed her clean in the shower and filled up that emptiness we saw in her eyes with pleasure.

I haven't seen much of Little Bird today, not since breakfast, and now it's almost the middle of the night. I've been busy at the house, getting our new dungeon ready, but I'm starting to think she's suspecting something, because she hasn't replied to my messages all day. So instead of pulling a long night to finish the dungeon, I head home intent on finding her after Ryder texts me.

When I reach the penthouse, though, the door is open and everything is black. Narrowing my eyes, I rush inside, fear pounding through me. "Little Bird?" I yell. "Roxy!"

No one answers. Grabbing my phone, I dial Ryder as I stride through the room searching for answers, only to stop at a note on the table just as Ryder answers. He chuckles. "Have fun, D, try not to kill her." He hangs up while I'm still staring at the note.

Fancy a hunt? Find me if you can. I'm yours if you catch me.

Signed with a drawing of a little bird.

My cock hardens instantly as I toss my phone away and rip off my shirt so I'm just in my jeans and boots. She wants to play? About fucking time. I'll find her, and just like she said, she will be mine. I'll have her screaming for more, even as I carve open her skin.

My favourite fucking game—her.

"Little Bird, Little Bird," I call, tilting my head to listen. "You want to play?" I prowl around the dark living room, grinning as I check every place to hide. "You should have said so, because I want to play with you." She's clearly not here, so I head down the hallway to her room, not that she really sleeps there anymore.

"When I find you—" I suck in a breath, moaning at the images crowding my head. "I am going to make you wish you had just asked."

My voice is the only sound as I slip into her room. There's a bulge under the quilt, and I yank it back, laughing when I spot the pillows shaped like a person. I check the bathroom and wardrobe too, but they are all empty, so I head back out to the hallway, running my finger across the wall as I hunt.

"Little Bird!" I call. "Come out, come out, wherever you are! You know you want my cock...and hands...and pain."

I hear movement upstairs, so I race through the living room and take the stairs two at a time until I'm on the landing, and then I look around. "Little Bird," I coo, "don't make this worse for yourself. The longer it takes, the more I will make it hurt."

I hear a scuffle again, so I turn to Ryder's room and quickly check it before emerging into the hall again. "Did you organise this just for me, Little Bird?" I yell, as I head over to investigate my room and the others. "Have you been wet all day, waiting for me, imagining what will happen when I find you? Which I will."

The rooms are empty, and I'm annoyed, so I storm back down the corridor, my cock jerking in my pants at the anticipation of what I will do to her when I find her. Her skin bruises so easily, her blood covering my hands and cock...fuck.

I'm so distracted that I just walk back and forth, calling out to her.

I'm slipping back past the armoury, which we don't bother to lock anymore, when the door suddenly opens and something hard and metal presses to my chin, tilting it up. In the dark, I can barely make her out, but I can see enough. My little bird is holding a bat right under my chin as she smirks at me, wearing nothing but her skin. The skin I ache to touch, taste, and make bleed.

"Thought you were hiding?" I murmur.

"I got tired of hiding, it's not my style. I realise I would rather hunt you." She grins.

I surprise her when I grab the bat and jerk it to me. She gasps and falls into my chest as I throw the weapon away, grabbing her neck and slamming her into the wall. I press my front against her back as my hands rove across her skin, squeezing her plump ass and nipping her side before I reach around to tweak her nipples. She moans, even as she struggles.

"Little Bird," I murmur, biting her ear. "Kept me waiting for what is mine, and I have no toys with me." I tut. "I guess I'll have to improvise."

"Yeah? I said you had to catch me first." She laughs, and then her elbow comes back, hitting me right in the gut. I let her go as I double over wheezing, and she rams her knee into my face before taking off.

Laughing, I straighten and feel the blood running from my nose. *Oh, it's on, Little Bird.*

I fly down the stairs after her, catching her around the waist and throwing her into the living room. She smashes down on the coffee table with a groan, but rolls free and gets back to her feet, still grinning at me. "That all you got? The great Diesel can't even catch his own woman?" she taunts.

She tries to rush past me, but I bend down and throw her over my shoulder, ignoring her struggles as I stride over to the table and lay her on it. "Stay," I snap, as I move away, quickly rushing upstairs to get my rope. Of course when I return, she's moved and is standing beside the table glaring at me, even as her lips quirk.

Running the rope through my hands, I lick my lips as I feign left around the table, making her run right, which I do too before grabbing her again and throwing her back on the table. She kicks and struggles, but I get both legs tied down and then each hand, slamming them to the shiny surface and looping the rope around each corner until she is trussed up for me.

She glares up at me as I prowl around the table, trailing my hand across her body and making her shiver again. "And I thought you wanted to play," I mutter.

"I did, but not to be hogtied to the fucking dining table," she growls. Eyebrow arched, I trail my hand up her parted thighs and over her wet pussy. I glide my hand over her pussy again, eliciting a gasp, before caressing up and across her arm and stomach, making her huff in annoyance.

Ensuring the ropes tied to each leg of the table are tight, I flick open my lighter as she watches, her chest heaving and her blood staining the table, which only makes me harder and her wetter. I can see her cream dripping from her pussy, down her thighs, and to the table below as she watches me, tugging on the ropes as I tut. "Should have been a good little bird, I might have let you come right now if you had."

"Fuck me," she demands.

Laughing, I grab two candles and light them before leaning close to her face. "When I want to, I will, but for now, I want to play."

Holding up the candles, I let her watch as they melt. "Ever felt hot wax dripping on you, Little Bird?" Her eyes widen in understanding before darkening in hunger. "Ah, you have. Do you like it? What about all over your body?"

Tipping the candle, the flame flickering, I hold it above her chest as I smirk at her. The wax slowly drips and lands on her collarbones, making her hiss before it turns into a moan. "That's what I thought, Little Bird," I coo, as I grab the other candle and, holding them both, tip them right over her chest. As it burns, I drizzle them down between her breasts to her stomach, wax dripping onto her skin as she whimpers and tugs on the ropes.

"Little Bird, Little Bird, how prettily you melt for me." I laugh as I hold a candle over each breast.

She shakes her head, but I tip anyway, and it lands on her exposed breasts. She gasps loudly as I purposely direct someone of it to land on her nipple. She lets out a yelp, even as her hips lift. Letting the wax cool on her skin, I trace my hand down her body and cup her soaking pussy again. "I knew you would love it, Little Bird, and look." Using my other hand, I flick off some of the hardened wax to the pink skin underneath. "It marks you up so pretty."

"You bastard," she spits, even she pushes into my hand holding her cunt possessively.

"Little Bird, watch your mouth, or I'll fill it and it won't be with my cock."

She drops her head back to the table, her body shaking slightly as I trace my tongue up her belly and kiss the jewel there before pulling out my knife, letting her see. She stills, even as she shivers in desire, her eyes blown wide, her lips open on a pant. I lower the blade and use the pointed edge to flick off the hardened wax, slowly and methodically, until her chest and stomach are clear again, except for the pink marks left behind that have me reaching into my jeans and squeezing my cock.

"Going to keep making promises?" she challenges, taunting me even as she lies bound and surrendering to whatever I want to do to her.

"Little Bird, you knew what I would do when I caught you. Torturing you is my favourite hobby. You wanted this, so be a good girl and let me play." I laugh.

She huffs but doesn't protest as I drag the knife down her throat and stop above her heart. "Would you fight me right now?" I ask curiously, as I dig the tip in enough to break the skin. A drop of blood forms where my blade meets her flesh. "Would you try to stop me?"

"No," she replies instantly, arching up and pressing the blade deeper as she groans. "I would let you."

"You would, wouldn't you?" I whisper, as I lift my head and press my forehead to hers. "You would let me kill you."

"I would." She nods, licking my lips. "I would die with a smile on my face."

My demons are crowding closer, wrapping around me in their madness, making my hand slip lower and dig the blade in deeper until she gasps in pain. Tears form in her eyes, but she still doesn't fight. No, she brings me back from the brink.

"But you don't want to kill me, D, you don't want my death, that would be too easy. You want my life, forever, to torture me and play with me for the rest of our days. Ending it now would be too quick. You don't deal in just pain, but pleasure too, and right now, baby, it's just pain," she admits.

I blink and look at the blade in shock and toss it away. "Little Bird, Little Bird, always trying to save me."

"Nah, not save you, burn with you," she murmurs, before lifting her head and slamming her lips to mine as her chest bleeds between us. On her lips, I taste her desperation and hunger...but also her love. For me.

Her damaged Viper, her crazy bastard. The man she pulls from the flames of his own mind again and again without thought for the way it burns her. I want to show her how much that means. This started out as our game and turned into something real.

Something life and death, because I could easily kill her without meaning to and she knows it. Yet she doesn't care, she wants me anyway, moaning into my mouth and nipping at my lips to try to urge me on.

"D, please," she begs, surrendering to me even further, not taking, just asking.

How could I deny her anything?

I have been hers since that first day, yet she never demands with me, never orders me. Just asks, pleads, begs. Licking her lips, I trail my mouth down her chin and neck to the wound, and circle around the blood dripping there right above her heart, knowing it will probably scar.

"Anything you ask for, anything, Little Bird, it's yours. This world is yours if you want it, I will make them bow at your feet," I murmur, as I trail lower and crawl down her body until I'm above her pussy. "I'd make them bleed for you, make them scream, make them die for you," I vow, as I lick her pussy, groaning at the sweet taste of my girl. She's my fucking obsession, my weakness, and my strength in the sweetest goddamn package.

She groans, tilting her hips as much as she can to push her wet cunt to my face. Tracing over her lower lips, I part her further and dip two fingers inside her, watching her hole clench around them, her clit engorged and begging for my lips and teeth. Her piercing shines in the light, matching the one in my cock.

She cries out as I twist my fingers and wrap my lips around her clit and suck, her hips bucking as she gushes around my digits. Digging my teeth into her vulnerable flesh, I add pain to her pleasure until she screams, coming so quickly I almost come myself.

So fucking perfect, that's what she is.

Perfection.

Licking up her release, I pull my fingers free and clean them with my tongue, unable to get enough of her sweetness. It's even better than her blood. I dip them back in for more, and she cries my name, twisting in her bindings. "Diesel!"

Rearing above her, unable to help myself, I lean down and snap the rope on one of her legs. She quickly wraps it around my waist, trying to pull me to her as I hover over her body, holding myself up with a palm next to her head. Her back arches, rubbing her blood and tits across my chest until I can't take it anymore.

Grabbing her hips, I line up and slam inside of her, making her scream for me again. Her hands twist in the bindings, gripping them as I fuck her hard and fast. Nothing is between us.

This is us.

This is the life, even with death wrapping around us.

Her head tilts back, and I drag my teeth down her neck as I slam into her harder and faster with each thrust, unable to hold back when it comes to my Little Bird. Pleasure rocks through me, almost bowing my spine at how fucking tight and wet she is. The feel of her wrapped around my cock like a vice. Her softness pressing to my hardness. Her blood marking me.

Fuck.

She urges me on. "Yes, God, yes, baby, more. Fuck, make it hurt!" she screams, as I punish her with my thrusts. Reaching down, I press my thumb to the wound as I make sure I hit that spot inside her that has her screaming again in no time, coming around my cock so prettily.

Her eyes are shut, her face is lax in pleasure, and her mouth is bruised and parted as she shakes and tries to breathe beneath me. But I'm not done yet. Snapping the binding on her other ankle, I pull free of her clinging, pulsing pussy and flip her quickly, dragging her ass into the air.

Her arms stretch out above her, her face turned and pressed to the table as she struggles to breathe. Her back is dotted with small cuts and oozing blood. Her ass is red and so fucking beautiful, and I'm going to fuck it.

Pushing her legs closer to her body, I watch her part them willingly as I spread her ass cheeks. I lean down and run my tongue around her hole before sliding down to her pussy and back up again. She whimpers and pushes against my tongue.

"Oh fuck, that's so goddamn wrong." She laughs. "Don't fucking stop."

I have no plans to as I tongue her ass until she's pushing back again, my fingers digging into her plump cheeks. I keep her against my face until I can't take it anymore. Kneeling on the table behind her, I run my finger down her crack to her pussy and slip it inside, stroking her before pulling it free and circling it around her other hole. My dick is still dripping from her cunt, and I grasp it, pressing it to her ass.

"You liked my knife in your ass, but you are going to love my cock more, Little Bird, and I might even leave you here tied up and bleeding, my cum dripping from it until the others come back."

"Fuck, fuck, fuck," is all she says, pushing back and making me laugh.

Seeing the thick head of my cock pressed to her ass has me nearly coming, so I take it slow, pushing in past the ring of muscles as she relaxes for me. "Good girl," I coo, stroking her side as I pop past them and work myself in an inch before pulling back and pressing in again, getting farther with each thrust until, finally, I'm balls deep in her ass.

Leaning over her back, I lick down her spine, the blood from her cuts filling my mouth, and I catch on a piece of glass still in her skin and cut my tongue. Groaning, I jerk her back harder, impaling her on my cock as she cries out. Blood drips from my mouth onto her pale skin, and I trace it back up and down her, leaving a blood trail as the pain of the cut has me twitching in her ass.

But she's bored of me not moving, she pushes against me, forcing me deeper. Grunting, I sit back, her thick hips filling my hands as I drive into her ass before pulling out. I don't go slow now. No, I fuck her, like the dirty little girl she is.

She's fucking tight, so goddamn tight, it's almost impossible to fuck her, and she's moaning loudly now, almost screaming. "Like my piercing in your arse, Little Bird?" I tease, my own voice low and gravelly as I hold back my own release, edging it, almost painfully so.

"God, I feel so full," she murmurs.

"Next time, I'll get Kenzo to fuck your pussy at the same time, and then you will be very full, Little Bird," I snap, making her scream as I watch my cock going in and out of her ass, the sight undoing me.

"So fucking hot," I mutter. A tingling starts at the base of my spine and flows through me, pulling at me, demanding I let go. I can't hold it back. It's too strong, her blood, pussy, and ass dragging it from me.

"Oh, God, Little Bird, I'm so fucking close." I groan, unable to pull my eyes away from my cock moving in and out of her ass faster and faster.

She whimpers, her pussy pulsing again, and I know she's close. Leaning down, I bite her ass, digging my teeth in painfully, and she screams her release, her ass clenching on me until I can't pull out anymore and the vice has me exploding.

It seems to flow through me again and again, pulling everything from me, filling her repeatedly, spurting in her ass until I'm finally spent. Pulling my teeth free, I see the bleeding indentation there and smirk. I slowly slide from her ass, whispering soothing words as I flop down next to her and pant.

I try to relearn how to breathe as my heart slams in my chest, so loud it's all I can hear, my legs weak. When I feel like I can stand, I stumble from the table and into the kitchen, cleansing my cock before taking some towels back, cleaning up Little Bird, and tossing them in the bin. Climbing back on the table, I undo her hands and drag her into my arms. Blood and cum cover us, but fuck, I can't move again, even if I wanted to.

"I love you, Little Bird," I whisper against her lips. "I'm so glad you punched me in the face that day."

She laughs. "Me too. I love you too, you crazy bastard."

Kissing her softly, I pull away after a moment. "I can't wait to hunt you for the rest of my life."

She laughs at that, and I join her, even though I'm serious, but seeing her face light up, her lips bruised from my kisses and body filled with my marks...I have never been happier.

For a boy who lost everything to a man who lived in fire and blood, Little Bird is my freedom. My second chance. My love.

CHAPTER

SIXTY-SIX

GARRETT

Standing above Roxy as she sleeps, I can't help but stare. She's too beautiful. Her silver hair is thrown over Kenzo's pillow, one arm under it and one over it, her back bare and exposed from where she must have kicked the covers down during the night. I can't help myself, I drag them farther down until I can see her peachy ass and long, lean thighs, smirking at the healing teeth marks on her ass from D. I had almost kicked his ass when we got back that night and saw the marks on her, but she just laughed. The wound on her chest is still healing though, and the doctor thinks it might scar, much to D's amusement.

Tracing my hand down her side and over her ass, I almost groan. How did I ever think she was anything like that cunt? She is fucking amazing, all soft skin and tattoos, but she has a mean streak in her, my little fighter, and when I get her all riled up...it's amazing.

The doc has finally given me the go ahead to return to fighting, but only part time and on the condition I only do one a night. No more killing myself in the ring, not that I need to now with Roxy here. I just don't have the urge anymore. Oh to fight, I sure do, and to hurt others, that will always be with me, but I don't want to die.

Instead, I want to take her with me, have her watch me. Last time when I'd won, she had looked at me with such lust, such dark, hungry eyes, but I had been too lost in my own anger and self-hatred to act on it. Not anymore. I'm going to take her on a date to a fight, and she will love it.

"Just going to stare?" she asks, not even opening her eyes. I smirk, wondering how long she's been awake and knowing I've just been staring at her like a weirdo, but she doesn't care. She flips over, hair mussed and eyes blinking open, face bare from makeup. The sun streams in, the low afternoon light kissing her tanned skin and catching on the jewel in her belly, our snake.

She stretches leisurely, her body rolling and tightening with the movement, making my mouth dry and cock hard, but I have other plans than to bend her over and fuck her right now. "Napping?" I growl, crossing my arms.

She peers up at me, that taunting smile curling those lips I'm obsessed with. "With Kenzo, he convinced me."

I snort, I bet he did. We can't keep our hands off her. Even during meetings, Ryder has kicked everyone out four times this week alone, and he has her screaming in no time.

Slapping her thigh, I lean down and kiss her, loving that I can now. "Get showered and dressed, and then meet me downstairs."

She pouts as I pull away. "Where are we going?"

"Out," I snap.

"It's a date, isn't it?" She laughs.

"No, it's fucking not," I snarl as I stomp off, but a smile curves my lips.

"It is!" she calls loudly. "Knew you liked me!"

I chuckle and head downstairs, finding Diesel lying on the dining room table with a weird, vacant, dreamy look on his face. "D, you okay?" Then I notice his hand is in his pants. "Dude, what the fuck? We eat there!"

He blinks and carries on wanking as he meets my eyes. "I'm remembering the other night." He sighs. "It was so good."

"This is so fucked up. Don't stare into my eyes, that's so weird!" I snarl, as I stride away, shaking my head and texting Ryder to buy a new dining table. No way can I eat there now. I hear him groan behind me.

"I'm finished now if you wanna talk, man!" he calls after me, laughing.

Crazy bastard.

I wait in the kitchen, purposely not staring at him. Roxy comes down about an hour later, washed and dressed. We have all started keeping some of her clothes in our rooms for that very reason...well, Diesel actually stole all of her clothes and put them in his room, so we had to take them back first.

She's in some tiny, black ripped shorts that cup her peachy ass and have me almost drooling, a loose, ripped cropped shirt with a snake nestled in the middle, and fishnets covering her long, lean legs and ending at her favourite boots. Her hair is up in a messy bun, wisps of silvery strands escaping. Her lips are painted red, and her eyes are lined dark.

She looks like a fucking goddess.

I rush to her before Diesel can and wrap my arm around her, steering her to the door as I hear him flip from the table. "Play with me, Little Bird!"

"You already played with yourself!" I shoot back, as she chuckles and grabs her leather jacket from the cupboard on the way out.

When we are in the elevator, I slip my hand in her back pocket, squeezing her ass, and she presses to my side, knowing that's okay now as we watch the numbers drop. "So where we heading on this date?"

"It's not a date," I grumble, and she laughs.

"Totally a date, but okay, keep it a surprise." She huffs as the door opens into the garage. I lead her to my bike and hand her a helmet. She slips it over her head as I swing on and pat the seat behind me.

She climbs on easily and wraps her arms tightly around my lower stomach, her head turned as I rev the engine and head out into the city.

Her hands sneak lower and lower until they press against my hard cock. The fucking tease. So I speed up and take the corners faster as the sun finally sets and the night spills through the city, bringing all the sinners and criminals out.

Like us.

I find the old gym it's at tonight and park around back in case we need to leave quickly. She swings off and waits as I do the same, and I store our helmets before I take her hand and lead her to the metal door at the back. I bang on it and Sheehan appears, grinning when he sees me. "Wondered if you'd died or some shit, lad. Come on, I got two men—"

"One, you get him for one fight so pick his opponent wisely, probably the biggest bastard in here," Roxy drawls, grinning at Sheehan who laughs and nods.

"I got just the fellow," he tells her, as he disappears back inside.

"Biggest dude?" I snort.

She laughs and turns around to look at me, my hand still in hers and stretching out between us. "Wouldn't be a fair fight otherwise, gotta give them a chance." She winks, running her eyes down me. "You're still gonna kick his ass, big guy, but this way, you can get your aggression out for longer, and if he's not enough?" She leans closer. "You can get it out inside of me." Then she laughs and turns, walking into the gym.

Groaning, I follow after her. The crowd is already parting for her, not just me, they all know who she is now. A Viper. They both fear and respect her. Rumours easily spread of the bloodthirsty woman we love, and I notice more than one pale face staring at her.

I smirk at that. It seems she's now as famous as we are. I lead her to the chairs in the corner where two rich pricks are sitting. "Move," I snarl.

They turn to argue, but when they see us, they rush to their feet and scamper away. She throws herself into one, her legs outstretched on the other as I strip off my shirt and hand it to her, my gun and knives also, which she holds on her lap, her eyes running down my chest hungrily. Once, that would have made me angry, but now it makes me hot and hard, which isn't good going into a fight.

Leaning down, I kiss her in front of everyone, staking claim. "Be good, baby, shoot first and ask questions later."

She laughs and pushes me away, smirking. I turn to the ring, which is an actual ring today. All traces of amusement and desire leave me with each step I take, and when I duck under the ropes and step onto the padded mats, I'm ready. Anger and hatred fill me, my fists clenching at my sides. Cracking my neck, I pace around my corner waiting for the fight to start.

They announce the other guy, but I don't even look until I hear the bell. Like always, the crowd and everyone fades as I turn to see the big bastard coming towards me. He's mean looking, clearly Russian, and used to fighting.

But that won't help him.

I hear my girl cheering for me as I lose myself in the fight, in the swinging of fists, the ducking, the pain and blood. When I'm dragged away, I'm still fighting and they can't stop me, darkness covering my vision, but then she's there before me.

Her hand is on my heaving, sweating chest, freezing me. I blink and stare down at her, ignoring the four men trying to control me, yet this one woman stops me effortlessly. She grins, her eyes dark, hungry, and impressed. "That was hot, big guy, but he's out, wanna fight? Fight me," she purrs.

I ignore the chanting crowd and toss her over my shoulder before leaping from the ring. I grab my stuff and stride through the throng until I find a door at the back marked 'locker rooms.' Shoving it open, I kick it shut and lock it behind us. It's dull in here, only one light flickers, but it's still working.

The lockers are covered in graffiti and some hang brokenly, the wooden benches damaged. The showers at the back are filthy. I find the closest bare wall and slam her against it as I drop my gun and knives at our feet for easy access in case anyone gets stupid.

She grins, wiggling. "Was that a yes, big guy?"

I drag her arms up and hold her wrists in my hand above her head as I reach between us, flick open her shorts, and drag them down. She steps out of them, and I yank her legs around my waist, ripping a hole in the fish nets over her thong-covered pussy and pushing those aside, then I slam inside her. We are both too wound up from the fight, and it's a quick, dirty fuck.

She screams, her pussy clenching around me, wet as hell like I knew she would be. "Dirty fucking girl, you get all wet watching me?"

She moans, her eyes unfocused, her hair messed up from my hands, and her lipstick smudged from my lips, it's no doubt all over my lips and chin too. Good. It looks like blood smeared across her, making me grunt. She's all clean and put together, and I'm a sweaty, bleeding mess. My knuckles are split and bruising from the fight, but it only makes her want me more.

"Hell yes, you're like a machine...all that power, fuck, I kept imagining it aimed at me, you fucking me like that," she cries out, squeezing my cock so hard, I groan. Her legs wrap tighter around my waist until there is no space between us, her breathing coming out fast and faster as I pound into her, each move slamming her back into the wall.

"Fuck, Garrett, yes. God, yes!" she screams, her eyes closing as she tilts her hips to meet my thrusts. I'm so close already, all riled up from the fight and her, and she's the same. I can feel her tightening around me, her release impending until, suddenly, she screams.

Her nails dig into my hands as she clamps around my cock. Groaning, I fight her tight muscles, but only two thrusts later, I follow her, spilling inside of her. Her eyes flicker open and meet mine as we just stare at each other in the dingy locker room.

She grins suddenly and then starts to laugh, and I join in,

pressing my sweaty forehead to her chest as I suck in breaths. "Well, that was a great date."

"Not a date," I growl, even as I smile.

"Sure, big guy, there was entertainment and it ended in sex—it was a date." She laughs, making me groan as she clamps around my softening cock. Slipping free, I stuff myself back in my jeans and help her into her shorts before someone comes in and finds us. "It was just missing food."

"You want food?" I snort.

"Hell yes, burgers. Sex always makes me hungry." She grins, taking my hand after I have my shirt and weapons back on.

"Done. Come on then, baby, let's feed you before you get annoyed and shoot someone."

CHAPTER SIXTY-SEVEN

ROXY

"Darling?" I perk up and look over from the contracts and job applications for the new bars I'm in charge of to see Kenzo. He's dressed up in a purple silk shirt, his hair is swept back, his black jacket is unbuttoned, and his dice are rolling across his knuckles. His lips curl into a grin as he leans closer. "Want to go for a drive?"

"Always." I smile, leaping over the sofa and dropping a kiss on his lips. "Let me grab some shoes, any dress code?" I peer down at the loose shirt I'm lounging around in.

"One of those sexy as hell dresses." He smirks.

"Yeah? Going somewhere nice?" I laugh.

"No, I just love those dresses and having easy access." He winks, and I flip him the bird as I head down the hallway to my room.

I quickly slip into a dark purple, spaghetti strap satin dress and some heels before adding some lipstick and fluffing my hair. When I'm done, he's waiting in the living room on his phone, but when he sees me, he pockets it and whistles. "In fact, let's not go out." He

607

starts towards me with a hungry expression, making me laugh and push him away.

"Later," I promise.

He crowds behind me, kissing my neck. "Later, you will have your legs around my head and you'll be screaming my name," he vows, before taking my hand and, ignoring my breathy moan, leading me down in the elevator. When we get to the garage, I figure he's driving, so I head to his car, but he tugs me over to mine instead.

"You're driving, darling." He smirks and tosses me the keys.

I squeal and slip inside. I haven't had a lot of time to drive the car they bought me, and I have to admit, I've been wanting to take it out and see how fast it can really go. I rev the engine as he gets in, and he laughs. "Head to Chinatown."

I nod and pull from the garage, peeling away as soon as I can, laughing as the car purrs and bursts with speed. "Holy fucking shit, I love this." When I glance over, I spot Kenzo watching me with a loving smile, so I wink and grab his hand and place it on my thigh as I change gears. He chuckles and strokes across my bare skin as I weave in and out of traffic.

Usually, I would be worried about a speeding fine, but honestly, the guys never get one. I don't ask how, but I'm guessing that extends to me now. He points out shortcuts and directions when I need them, until we pull up behind a bar. Slipping out of the car, I meet him around front, where he takes my hand and leads me to a door at the back.

He opens it without knocking and guides me down some steps to another metal door. This time he has to knock, and a sliding slot opens and eyes peer out. When they see us, it quickly slams shut and the door is ripped open, revealing a tall, skinny, beautiful Chinese woman. She bows to Kenzo and steps back, admitting us.

The room is smoky and dark with low level lighting all around, giving it a cosy feel. It's one big room and looks like how I imagined a casino would...just a back-door version. There are men in suits dotted around all the tables and at the bar. Women are here too, and I even spot one in a suit, which makes me grin. The servers move through the crowd with trays and dispense drinks.

Music and laughter fill the room, and it makes my shoulders settle. I much prefer this over the rich bastard's house we went to. This feels like here, we can be anything. We get a few looks, but everyone seems respectful and actually leaves us to it.

Kenzo slips his hand down my back to my ass and leads me through the tables to a booth at the back, which is cordoned off by a golden rope. It's darker back here, and after we slide in, drinks instantly appear. He nods as he scans the crowd, grasping the tumbler and taking a sip as I lean into his side.

"Is this one of yours?" I finally ask, and he turns to me, his arm going around the back of my shoulders, his legs crossing as he peers down at me where I'm lounging next to him.

"It is, one of the very first actually. I used to come here to gamble when we initially started buying up the city. I doubled our money every night, and eventually, I earned so much that the owner got suspicious and he pulled me aside. He taught me everything he knew once he realised who I was. I guess he always knew what we would become, and he wanted to retire. He gifted me this place." He runs his eyes around it. "It's my favourite, the very first place I found my talent."

"Gambling," I tease.

"Strategy," he murmurs, looking back at me. "It's all about strategy and reading people, darling, just like I read you that first day and every day since."

Laughing, I take a sip of my drink and look around again. I get it, it's like Roxers. This is where he's comfortable and happy, where he found his future. When I look back, though, he's staring at me. "You're the best bet I ever won, darling," he murmurs, his fingers tracing my shoulder. "And this is now your empire too."

"Yeah?" I grin, leaning in. "What if I decided I didn't like the way some of your clients looked at me...could I kill them?"

He snorts. "Darling, you could do whatever the fuck you wanted in this city and get away with it. Everyone knows who you are now, and no one, no fucking one, no cops, no judges, gangsters, or criminals, would dare question you. You're our girl, it comes with privileges."

"What other kind?" I query, trailing my hand down his chest to cover his cock and squeeze until he groans. His eyes flash dangerously. "What if I yanked up my dress and decided to ride you right here and now?"

He licks his lips, those dark eyes tracing my own lips hungrily as he watches me like I'm the only one in the room. "Then I would say what are you waiting for? This city is yours, and so am I."

I feel someone close to the table, but I don't turn my head and neither does Kenzo. No, we make them wait. I'm beginning to realise what this power offers me. If they want our attention, they will wait there silently for hours, not daring to disturb us until we are ready to speak to them. The power is heady, we are fucking untouchable.

Leaning in, I lick Kenzo's lips. "Why don't you prove it to me? You say you're mine...but that makes me yours, darling." I kiss him hard and fast before pulling back and looking at the man waiting, his eyes dropped to the floor out of respect.

"What?" I snap.

He swallows hard and shifts, but still doesn't raise his eyes. "So sorry to disturb you, sir and madam. We have a problem, and since you're here, I figured you would want to deal with it."

"What kind?" I question, leaning back.

"Erm, someone has been stealing all night," he answers quickly, making Kenzo snort.

"Idiot." He laughs.

"Yup." I grin, and watching the guy, I turn to Kenzo. "We can't have that, can we?" I purr.

"Call the guys, let's have some fun," Kenzo orders, downing his drink. "Tie him up in the kitchen and make him wait," he instructs the man, who nods and rushes off to do just that.

Laughing, I send out a group text, and we wait, both of us teasing each other as we watch the room. The man returns to guard our booth and wait for further instructions as we flirt.

The Vipers will never settle down, this is their world, and right now, I'm all the way in. He's right, this is going to be fun. I'm going to see my guys in action again, and we all know how wet that gets me.

Not twenty minutes later, they stroll into the club, and every eye turns to them including mine. The power they hold, it flows from them, it's addictive. Even if it was my first time seeing them, I would see that authority surrounding them in the way they hold their heads up, their eyes flickering across the room and dismissing what they see until they land on me—all three sets hungry.

All three mine.

I'm a lucky fucking bitch.

Ryder is in a suit and looks as perfect as always—cold eyes and too perfect face and body, untouchable. Except for me, I can touch him all I want. Which sounds dirty...but I guess it's true. His lips kick up in a familiar, arrogant smirk as he moves through the crowd like a snake, all smooth, coiled tension and power. I see the flash of a gun at his hip, and it makes me lick my lips as my eyes flick to Diesel next to him.

He has on his leather jacket and nothing underneath, showing his built chest and framing the bird and snake over his heart perfectly. There's a knife sticking up from his black jeans with rips down the front. He has a cigarette held between his lips, his blue eyes grinning as he watches me. His blond hair is pulled back behind his head, making the sharp angles of his beautiful face stand out. I can't help but wink as I look to Garrett next. God, when I first saw this man...I thought he was a fucking giant.

I'm right. He's huge. Towering over everyone here. His body screams danger, killer. The tattoos covering every inch of his skin are like intricate works of art, and with him wearing all black and weapons, he looks like an assassin. His hair is pushed back, his piercings shining, and his stern gaze scanning the crowd for threats until they land on me. He smiles, making the rest of the room disappear.

Yes, I'm a lucky fucking bitch. All three are gods, untouchable Vipers, and all mine.

Kenzo licks my ear. "Ready, darling?"

It's time to play.

Slipping from the booth as the others reach me, I let them run their eyes across the dress. Diesel drops to his knees and kisses my hand dramatically. "Goddamn, Little Bird, please tell me you called so we can fuck."

Laughing, I lean down and kiss him. "Later, baby."

Ryder kisses me softly before nodding at Kenzo. Garrett nods but hesitates, so I slip past Diesel and press into his chest, letting him decide. He lowers his head slowly, and I kiss him softly. "Hey, baby," he murmurs.

"Hey, big guy," I whisper, before pulling away reluctantly. I grab my drink and toss it back. "Someone is stealing from us. He's tied up in the back. I figured we could have some fun with him," I offer, and then turn back to the man who tied him up and is currently patiently waiting. "Lead the way."

He nods and hurries away, checking that we are following every few steps. All eyes are on us now, all scared, but they are safe for now. I keep my head held high as I stroll behind the man. Ryder's hand lands on my back as he leans in. "Like a true fucking viper queen," he murmurs, making me grin as the man opens a door and leads us through a hallway to swinging doors.

He pushes through and holds them for me, my heels clacking as the floor turns to tile. I step in and glance around. It looks like a rundown kitchen with most of the appliances pulled out apart from the counters, and in the middle under a swinging old light is a man tied to a metal chair. He's struggling as we enter, with two men in black watching him from each wall. When they see us, they straighten. The man's eyes widen as we fill the room, and he tries to talk, but his lips are covered in duct tape.

"Leave," I demand, and the guards quickly and quietly do just that, leaving just us Vipers.

Strolling closer, I run my fingers up his tied arm and across his shoulder until I'm behind him, then I lean down and whisper loudly, "Did you really think you could steal from us?"

The guys watch me, their eyes hard and angry, all apart from Diesel, who looks like he can't decide between fucking me or killing this guy. Probably both if he had his way. Instead, he hops up on a counter and swings his legs, smoking as he watches me.

"Did you think you could dupe the snakes?" I whisper, and lick his ear, my eyes on my guys as I do. I feel the man shiver, but it's from fear, not lust. "No one takes what is ours. You are going to wish you were dead before we're through."

I straighten and trail my hand down his other shoulder, circling him as he struggles, his muffled voice coming from behind the tape. Dropping myself into his lap, I press my finger to his lips over the tape. "Shush, I didn't say you could talk," I snap, and lean in, balancing on his lap, but then there's a hand in my hair, yanking my head back as I grin. The man stops struggling, stilling, his face pale and eyes wide and scared.

"Do not fucking touch him, darling," comes a low, deadly voice next to my head as lips meet my cheek. "Or I will have to kill him before we have our fun."

Grinning, I wink at the man. "Possessive."

He swallows, so I quickly grab the duct tape and rip it free. When he screams, I punch him, snapping his head to the side. "I said not to talk," I snarl, before getting up and turning to Kenzo. I run my hand down to his cock and cup it, feeling him hard and heavy against my palm. "Then I will just have to direct from the side, Viper."

His eyes darken, and then he grabs my hand in a mean grip and squeezes, making me pant as his lips quirk up. He grabs my hips suddenly, and holding me up effortlessly, he plops me down on the counter next to Diesel, pushing his way between my thighs. "Tell us what you want us to do to him, darling, and we will, let's not get your pretty dress dirty."

He kisses me and steps back as I feel my hand picked up, and when I turn my head, Diesel is licking at the blood on my knuckles, making me laugh. He winks and guides my hand to his hard cock as he leans in. "Watching you work is hot as hell, Little Bird. We are going to have to do this more often."

"It's a date," I promise, as I turn back to see Garrett stripping from his shirt and cracking his knuckles. Ryder comes over and leans next to me, straightening the cuff links on his suit as he watches the man. Kenzo is standing next to him, his body vibrating with anger. Diesel kisses my cheek and hops down, stripping from his leather jacket and laying it on my lap as he rolls his shoulders and starts to prowl towards the man.

"So, love, what do you want us to do to him?" Ryder looks over at me, handing me his control.

Vipers' fucking girl.

CHAPTER SIXTY-EIGHT

KENZO

He touched my girl. It doesn't matter that she started it, he's dying here. But first, h e will pay for stealing from me, from us. Right in my fucking house. He trembles from fear as he watches all three of us, but we don't touch him, waiting for Ryder or Roxy to give the orders.

"Boys," she calls, her husky, velvety voice heading straight to my already hard cock. Seeing her take charge like that...seeing just how deep she is in our family, our fucking queen, has me wanting to rip up that dress like she teased and sink into her quivering wet pussy. But that can wait for now, business first.

We all turn to her, and the man in the chair peers around us to her as well, knowing she is in charge of his fate. "Have some fun, won't you?" She grins, leaning into Ryder and propping her chin on his shoulder like he's her leaning post and not the most terrifying man in the city. "I want him to bleed."

Diesel blows her a kiss. "That we can do, Little Bird."

I wink and turn back as Garrett steps up and smashes his fist into his face again and again, until the guy's eye is ballooning shut, his nose is broken, and his lips are bleeding, then he steps back and lets Diesel have a go. All of us try to impress Roxy.

When I glance over my shoulder, she's watching us with hungry eyes. Ryder is still propping her up with his hand on her thigh, stroking circles as she parts her legs as I watch, making me groan and turn back.

I knew the guys were busy tonight. Ryder was meeting with security for the new house, Diesel was finishing up the basement, and Garrett was sorting out the new gyms he's buying, but as soon as she called, they came running. It almost makes me laugh as I watch the man cry.

"Please, please," he blubbers, looking around to Roxy. "I will give it back, all the money!"

"Is that right?" she queries, and hops to her feet, strolling over and pressing her back to Diesel's front, who starts kissing along her neck and shoulder as she talks. "But a little birdy told me you already spent it...is that true?"

He swallows and mumbles something, so I drive my fist into his face. "When she speaks, you answer."

He cries out but nods. "I had to pay some people back, but if you give me time I can—"

She snorts and waves it away. "Blah blah, you took our money, I think we'll take it out of your flesh instead."

She looks at me. "Kenzo, what do you think?"

I smile and nod. "Seems equivalent. Tell me how much you stole again?" I ask him, and he cries out but answers.

"Forty thousand," he whispers.

"Seems fair. If you can survive forty minutes of torture, you can walk free." I nod, and she laughs.

"Beginning now," she purrs, and steps back. Ryder wraps his arms around her and drags her against his chest as we circle him like vultures. "Good luck."

Garrett starts first. We keep him on the edge of unconsciousness, not letting him pass out, and when Garrett steps back, it's my turn. Rolling my dice over my fingers, I watch him. "Call a number."

He shakes his head, still crying, and I tut. "Call a number. If it's right, you get your freedom."

"And if it's wrong?" he whimpers, making me grin widely.

"Well then, I would have to take my winnings of course," I remark nicely, and he cries louder until Garrett smacks the back of his head. "Guess."

He screams the numbers as I throw the dice in the air and catch them in my closed hand. Staring at him, I open my palm to reveal the two dice. "Oops, wrong," I announce, making him struggle in the chair again. I drive my fist into his stomach in rapid succession. Just because I don't always fight doesn't mean I don't know how, after all.

He pants as I step back, his head falling forward as he tries to curl in on himself. "Again," I demand.

"Fourteen," he wheezes.

I toss the dice and laugh again. "Nope, wrong, and I thought you were good at bets." I tut as I grab his fingers on his left hand and quickly break three. "Again."

"Please, please, God, no, please," he sobs.

"Again!" I roar, as I toss the dice.

"Nine," he whispers.

"Wrong." I grin, grabbing my knife from my ankle, and I stab it into both knees before pulling it free, wiping it clean on his shirt, and slipping it back in the holster.

"My turn," Diesel murmurs, and I grin, knowing he's been waiting patiently, but he's tired of waiting now. I pocket my dice and lean down to the man's face.

"Should have guessed right. D is going to make you wish you were dead," I promise, as I step back and he bleeds and cries.

I hear Roxy before she's pressed against my back as we watch Diesel work. "Ryder has this...want to go for a drive?" she purrs, and when I turn, she's grinning and stepping back farther, her eyes trailing over my body. "I might even let you collect your winnings, darling." She turns and, with a wave at the others, disappears out of the swinging doors.

Ryder claps me on the shoulder where I'm just staring after her. "Better get her before I do, brother," he teases as he takes over for her. I nod and rush after her, hunting her through the club. She's waiting at the door for me, and I grab her hand and drag her outside as she laughs. She swings the keys in her other hand and goes to open the door, but I slam her into it and kiss her hard.

She moans into my mouth, her leg hitching up against mine as our tongues tangle. Panting, I pull back. "Better drive fast, darling, or I might just fuck you in your car."

She groans at that, her eyes widening with need as I chuckle. Pulling her away from the door, I open it for her, and she slips in as I shut it gently before rushing around to get in as she revs the engine. Taking my advice, she races away from the club. Both of us are feeling it, the need always sparking between us.

I might have been the first to have Roxy, but I will never be the last. I'm okay with that, as long as she keeps looking at me the way she is now. Her eyes flicker over to me, full of lust and need, her body trembling slightly for what she knows is to come.

"Faster," I demand, reaching out, tracing my palm up her thigh and pushing her dress up. She groans and yanks the wheel to the side. I barely look outside as we suddenly stop, realising we are in a car park of some kind. She pulls to the back under some trees where the lights don't work. It's empty and quiet, out of the way. She clearly can't wait either.

She turns her head, and as soon as our eyes meet, the need bursts. Reaching out, I clasp the back of her head and drag her close. Our lips clash in a flurry of teeth and tongues. Her hand traces down my chest, trying to rip open my shirt as I chuckle breathlessly and pull back, but there isn't much room in the car, and she groans in frustration.

I get out and round the car, opening her door as her head turns to me in confusion. "Out, darling."

She slips out, and I push her against the side of the car, dragging my hand up her dress and cupping her pussy through the fabric as I kiss her again. She moans into my mouth, pushing into my hand as I slip past her thong and stroke her pussy. She is wet as hell, no doubt from watching us work, our dirty little girl. She bites my lip in punishment, making me laugh as I slip two fingers inside her, but she doesn't want my fingers.

"Cock, now," she demands, so I slip my fingers free and trace the wetness over her lips before licking it off.

"You aren't in charge anymore, darling. Get your beautiful ass up on that bonnet and spread your legs," I order, as I pull away and undo my belt before yanking down my zipper as she watches, her lips parted and body shaking slightly. "Now," I snap.

She huffs but pushes away from the car to the bonnet, trying to slide onto it, but she's small and it's slippery, so I grab her hips and help her up, pressing a hand to her chest and pushing her to lie back. Her grey hair spreads across the matte surface, her breasts almost tumbling from the dress as her chest heaves. Keeping her up with one hand, I snap off her thong and stuff it in my pocket as I strum along her pussy again. "I've been imagining fucking you over your car since I bought it for you," I admit.

"Well, we wouldn't want to let those fantasies go to waste, would we?" she murmurs, arching up as she traces a hand down her chest, cups her breasts through her dress, and pushes her pussy into my hand again. "What are you waiting for, a fucking bet? Here's one, make me scream so everyone hears, and I will suck your cock every day this week. If you don't, you have to get my name tattooed on your ass."

Groaning, I lean down and kiss her. "Deal, darling."

She drops her head back, her eyes on me as she pants. I drag my finger up her pussy and circle her clit before flicking it as she watches me. She groans, her eyes sliding closed as her hips tilt, rolling into my touch. I keep up the incessant touches until she's almost coming, and then I pull away, making her snarl.

"Thought you wanted my cock, darling?" I tease, as I wrap my hand around myself and press against her pussy, dragging myself back and forth across her wet heat until she's crying out again, becoming putty in my hands.

"Oh, for fuck's sake, Kenzo, if you don't—" I slam inside her, and her threat cuts off with a low moan as she writhes in my hands, her tight pussy clamping around me as the moon shines down on us.

Thrumming her clit fast and hard, I pull out and slam back in, jostling her with the pounding. Her hands stretch out on either side of the car as she lifts her hips to meet my thrusts. It's fast as hell, a quick fuck, knowing we could be found at any time, making it all that much hotter.

My heart thuds against my chest as I curve over her and grip her neck tightly, fucking her. She takes it all like a good girl, her thighs coming up and wrapping around my waist to keep me to her as her tight pussy constricts around me. She is so close already.

"Goddamn, Roxy, how are you this fucking perfect? Even when you're fighting me, you make it so easy to love you, to want you," I murmur, licking along her chin to her chest as I kiss over her heart. "To need you. I only ever feel alive when I'm inside you."

She cries out, her chest arching as she tightens around me, making me groan. I hold back my release as I fight her pussy, slamming inside her. Our panting and the slap of our bodies is loud in the quiet night.

"Kenzo!" she cries, her eyes opening and clashing with mine right as I slip my hand between our bodies and flick her clit, needing to see her come. She screams loudly, her hands coming up to dig into my shoulders as she leverages herself against me, slamming down on me and grinding until I can't hold back anymore.

The release roars through me, pulled from every cell by her tight little pussy and screams. It explodes out of me, spilling inside of her as I bury myself to the hilt, making her feel every fucking inch.

When it's done, I drop my head as her legs tremble around my waist, but I stay locked there. We just hold each other, knowing we should move but not wanting to pull away. Roxy wasn't given to us to make us better men—no, she was given to us to make us fight harder, to have something to love and come home to. To kill for. To die for.

She gave us purpose again.

A family.

And one day, we might get married and have kids, or maybe fucking not. I'm a jealous bastard, and sharing her attention with kids...yeah, Diesel would probably flip too. Either way, we are together forever now. Nothing or no one could ever come between us.

"I love you, darling." I search her eyes, the stars shining above us, but none compare to the one in my arms. "So much."

"I love you too, but I love your cock more." She laughs.

CHAPTER

SIXTY-NINE

RYDER

"So opening is in a month, we will set a date later. I have already reached out to local food and wine magazines, as well as a few large influencers online to help get exposure. Marketing is handling the social media aspect, and I have a manager in place. The building is complete, and they are decorating right now while the staff learns the ropes. I kept it as authentic to a dive bar as possible, but with upscale aspects and amazing food, all in the style of bar food, burgers, and wings..."

She trails off as I look over the notes. She's nervous as hell. I can hear it in her voice. Some of this might be her money, but she already mentioned she has no illusions that we didn't give her this opportunity to be more than she ever thought she could be, to grow her business and give back to this city...and to the man who saved her—Rich. It's an apt name, and I have commissioned his photograph to be blown up and added over the bar.

A surprise for her when it opens.

Leaning back in my chair, I steeple my fingers as she shifts nervously in hers opposite my desk. It's not often that I see Roxy nervous. It's cute, but she shouldn't be. She has become a businesswoman so easily. She has a good eye for staff and great ideas, and with our help and the assistance of her people, she will go far. I have no doubt her collection of bars will take off. Their mix of rustic, dive charm and upscale cocktails and food, and the dark black and moody ambiance is perfect.

"I love it," I tell her, and she smiles suddenly, relaxing. "I really do, love. It's amazing, and your numbers look good. Your online presence so far is astounding. It's going to be incredible." She sighs and gathers the papers back into her file. "He would be so proud of you."

She freezes, her eyes filling as she blinks and looks up at me. "You think?" she asks quietly.

I nod and lean over the desk, taking her hand in mine. "I have no doubt. You have become an amazing woman, Roxxane. So strong, so sure, and this will be no different."

She smiles, a sad one. "I hope so. One of the last times I saw him, he told me he was always hoping I would make something of myself, that I could go far if I tried...if I stopped letting my fear hold me back. He had a way of seeing through me. That's why he left me the bar, to help me along, a push...I just hope he can see me finally listening."

I squeeze her hand and tug her closer. She gets up and rounds the desk as I pull her into my arms. She cuddles into me, her head on my chest as I stroke up her back. "He would be so proud, and so am I. No one could ever stop you, Roxxane, not when you set your mind to it. This is only the beginning, love."

She sighs and leans up, kissing me softly. "God, sometimes you're too perfect to be true." A glint of mischief lights up her eyes as she reaches up and musses my hair, making me snort. "There, that's better."

"You heard from Garrett?" I inquire, as I reach for my phone and scroll through the emails and messages. There are none from my brothers, so I drop it again and focus on the woman in my arms.

She hums. "He sent me a dick pic about an hour ago." I blink, and she laughs. "I asked him to. He's still out, sorting the gyms he wants to buy and figuring out how to get the kids off the streets and in there so they can get jobs."

I nod. "It's a good plan, gives them an opportunity if they want to take it, and some training to protect themselves."

"Yep, you are all giant softies really." She laughs, making me narrow my eyes on her, and she giggles. "I won't tell anyone, your secret's safe."

"We are not softies," I snap.

She raises her eyebrow and leans up, straddling my lap and leaning back into the desk as she looks at me. "Really? Buying gyms and homeless shelters to help those who are suffering? What about the money you send every month to the charities in the city? Or the house you bought to turn into a safe haven for lost kids?"

I narrow my eyes further, my ice melting as she grins at me. "Babe, admit it, you are all softies."

"I'll give you soft," I snap, picking her up and dropping her on my desk. Her pupils blow at that as she laughs. "I have something very fucking hard."

"I bet," she teases. "What's the matter, Ry? Big bad Ryder the softie," she purrs.

"Softie?" I taunt, as I rip off her knickers, toss them aside, yank open her thighs, and drag her to the end of the desk as I lean back in my chair. "I think you forget who I am, Roxxane."

"Ooo, Roxxane, I'm in trouble now." She laughs.

"You are, love. Touch yourself, let me watch, but you do not get to come, understand me?" I order, getting comfortable in my chair as she watches.

"What?" she scoffs. "How about you just fucking touch me?"

"How about you do as you're told, or I will punish you and you will not enjoy it," I snap.

"You sure about that?" she teases, but trails her hand up her thigh and pushes up her dress to show me her glistening pussy. "You know

I like you mean." She rubs her clit and traces back down and circles her hole. "Cruel," she adds, as she slips a finger inside herself. "Hateful."

Grunting, I watch entranced. "Another finger," I demand, controlling her even now, knowing she loves it when I do.

She does as she's told, a moan leaving her lips as she slowly pulls them out and pushes them back in, her other hand dragging up her thigh to rub at her clit desperately. "Eyes on me," I bark.

She flickers them up to mine as she fucks herself on her fingers, her hips rising to meet her touch as she rubs and fucks. Her breathing is speeding up, her cheeks flushing, the blush crawling down her chest, and I know she's close. "Stop," I command.

She carries on for a moment, and I narrow my eyes.

"Stop now."

She whimpers but pulls her fingers free and, watching me, licks them clean. My cock jerks in my pants, pushing painfully against the zipper as I watch her. Fuck.

"Dress off," I order, unzipping my pants as she watches. She pulls it off and tosses it away, her breasts unbound and bouncing with the movement, the globes begging for my mouth, but I resist for now. "Lie down, pull your knees to your chest, and hold them there."

She does, wrapping her hands around her shins and holding herself open for me. I run my eyes down her dripping pussy, licking my lips as I stand and push down my trousers, circling my length as I step closer. "You will stay like that or I'll stop, understood?"

"Yes," she moans. "Please, Ry."

Stroking along her pussy, I dip a finger inside and twist, making her cry out before I extract it and press my cock there instead, letting her feel my hardness. She tries to push down to take me, but I pull back, and she stills again, panting on my desk. My very own Viper at my mercy.

When she behaves, I press my cock against her entrance again, and in one smooth move, bury myself inside her to the hilt, the tilt of her hips making her cry out as she clenches around me. Always so fucking tight and wet. "Goddamn, love, you feel so good. Look at that pretty pink pussy taking me like a good girl."

I watch her pussy swallow my cock as I thrust in and out of her. Her fingers turn white with how hard she's holding back from touching me, trying to be a good girl for once.

"Ryder, fuck," she moans.

"So goddamn beautiful. Every time I'm in here, now all I see is you bent over my desk, it makes it very hard to work," I growl, running my finger around her clit until she's gasping and moaning loudly. "So goddamn hard, like my cock whenever I even think of you."

"Please," she begs, and I tap her leg.

"Stay still, princess," I demand, as I drive into her again and again, rubbing her clit until she screams, coming around me. Only then do I let her drop her legs. I flip her over, bend her over my desk, and fuck her for real.

She gives as good as she gets, pushing back to meet my thrusts, her hair wrapped in my fist as I bite and lick her neck where her pulse hammers against her skin. "You fucking undo me," I mutter.

"Show me, show me how much," she demands, her voice hoarse and body covered in a thin sheen of sweat as I lick her neck again and drive into her with wild abandon. That ice I once held onto so tightly is just a puddle of water with her, my walls down.

We are just a man and a woman in love.

Just two Vipers locked together.

"I love you," she pants, and I groan.

"Say it again," I demand. I never tire of hearing it, especially from her lips. She only ever seems to say it when I break her down.

"I love you, love you, love you," she chants, as she meets my brutal thrusts. "Love you!" she screams, as I slam into her once more and still, melting, my balls emptying inside her as she comes as well.

We collapse to the desk, me still inside her, and when she starts to push back again, my softening cock begins to harden. "Goddamn it, love."

"Better get to work, Mr. Viper," she purrs, making me chuckle.

"Every goddamn day," I promise, as I start to move again with shallow, little thrusts that she rocks to meet. "I love you, Roxxane, my weakness, my love."

CHAPTER

SEVENTY

ROXY

I watch them interact as I sip my coffee. It's our morning routine now, and I love it. They know it, so they always make sure they are here every morning. Garrett laughs at something Diesel says, and Ryder shakes his head as Kenzo smirks.

If I look closely, I can see the change in them since the first time I sat in this very chair—hell, I can see the change in myself...all thanks to them.

"We have something to show you, love," Ryder tells me, startling me from my thoughts.

"Yeah?" I ask, and down my coffee. "Something good?"

"Something amazing," Kenzo corrects, just as I'm about to ask if it's their cocks, and smacks my thigh. "Go get ready."

I dress quickly, feeling excited, and they blindfold me when we get in the car.

"Kinky," I mutter, making them laugh. We drive for a while, and I try to remember the turns, but I get bored and distracted when someone starts stroking my thigh, the bastards. When we finally stop,

I'm wound up and annoyed. The doors open, and then a hand grabs mine and pulls me from the car to what feels like gravel under my feet. They step behind me. "Ready, baby?" It's Garrett.

"Yes, fucking show me, you assholes," I snap, making them laugh again as the blindfold is removed.

I stare in confusion at the house before me...well, it's more like a fucking mansion. It's black. A fucking black mansion. I glance around at the trees shading it from view. There is a garage to the left, one that's massive. The double doors are open, and I frown harder. It's stunning, absolutely stunning, and honestly, I've never seen a black house before, whoever it belongs to is a fucking genius.

"What-what is this?" I query, confused.

"Our home. We are a family now, and we need more than an apartment. This is for us to start our future right. It's safe and we have security and no one knows where this is..." Ryder trails off nervously, so Kenzo steps up and carries on for him.

"It's for you, darling, to show you we're in this forever. This is our home."

"Our future," Diesel adds, and then winks. "It even has a basement for us to play in."

"A gym," Garrett murmurs.

"An office for us both," Ryder inserts.

"Ours?" I whisper, looking back at it before I squeal. "Can I go in?"

They nod and laugh, and I rush through the doors like a child, just gawking. It's beautiful. The walls are a deep grey, and the floors are a dark white and black gold marble. The stairs are split into two and curved up. It's modern like the apartment, but I can feel the difference, the warmth and rightness of being here. It looks huge, and I can't wait to explore. I never imagined a home for myself because it wasn't an option I had, but now that I'm here...I can't help but think it's perfect.

It just needs the finishing touches, like lots of skulls everywhere... not real ones, though I wouldn't put it past Diesel.

Ryder grabs my hand and links our fingers, leading me through a door to the left and into a living room with a huge TV, five leather sofas, a low coffee table, and a rug. Dark mahogany bookcases line the back of the room. It screams money, but also looks cosy and very me...us.

"Is this really ours?" I whisper.

He nods. "It's not all finished, we wanted you to pick out some furniture, but there are ten bedrooms and nine baths, a pool out back, a gym, a garage, two offices, a library, a game room, a basement, and so much more. It's home, love, however you want to make it that."

"Home," I murmur, as arms wrap around me from behind.

"Our home," Kenzo whispers excitedly. "An opportunity to be nothing like our father. It will be filled with laughter and, hell, probably bloodshed, but I can't wait, can you?" he offers wistfully.

I swallow as I look around again. I can feel them all watching me for a reaction. This couldn't have been easy to do, but now that I'm here, they are right, it feels like home. I love the apartment, but it would be nice to have more space. I almost snort at that. Jesus, when did an apartment not become enough for me?

To think I was once a girl living in a flat situated above a bar. It feels like a fairy tale, only these boys aren't the heroes. They are the villains...even in the bedroom.

It only makes me love them more.

With them next to me, I turn and take in their eyes. "You keep saying you don't want to be like your father." I look to Kenzo and Ryder. "Your mother." I look to Diesel. "Your anger and hate." I look at Garrett then. "But the question isn't who you don't want to be, but who you do want to be. I think you've finally decided," I whisper, tears in my eyes. "And so have I. I want to be yours."

When you find love, you hold on hard. It's a fragile little thing, and once it's gone, it leaves a hole and memories, we all know that. Ones you wish you could relive, but from every love, you learn something. Something important.

From my mother, I learned to be strong.

From my father, I learned to embrace pain.

From Rich, I learned to love while it lasts and that endings aren't always a bad thing.

From my Vipers, I learned love is unconditional and can come at the strangest of times and places.

And from myself? I learned it's okay to love yourself. Even the darkest parts of you. No matter the shape, size, or weirdness you came with. Embrace your scars and never be ashamed to be who you are, because there is only one of you.

And if you don't love you, how can anyone else?

I am imperfectly perfect. I am a lover and a fighter. I am strong and weak. I can be cruel and a killer, but also kind and a healer. I am all of those things, and loving my weaknesses means I can embrace my strengths and be just whom I want to be.

With their arms around me and our new house over our heads, I have hope. Hope for a better future, and hope that, for the first time, the darkness might just be a good thing.

I am theirs.

They are mine.

And it's time to start our lives together.

EPILOGUE

ROXY
Six months later...

"**W**here are we going?" I ask for the eighth time. I had been busy setting up the last bits in the fifteenth Rich's bar. That's right, fifteenth—they were a hit. Taking off so rapidly I didn't even know what to do. I guess now I'm also rich. Not that the guys care, they still spoil me like they are making up for a lifetime of neglect.

I let them of course.

The last six months have been a whirlwind. We moved into our house a couple of months back, and it's not quite finished yet, but it's fucking close. I love it, waking up every day there and having break-fast with my men. Ryder is still super busy with work and running the city. Garrett has three new gyms now, and spends most of his days helping underprivileged and street kids get new opportunities and find ways out of their difficult lives.

Diesel...well, Diesel is Diesel. He spends his days inventing new torturing toys for me and anyone who crosses us. We will never go legit with me, after all. There is just so much fun and money had to be bad.

Kenzo opened his twentieth casino the other week, and there was a big grand opening where we were pictured shaking hands and kissing. Fuck, it even went international in advertising. If anyone ever knew what we truly were... I almost laugh, making Kenzo look over and wink at me.

Which brings me to today. They kidnapped me from the bar and dragged me to the car. "I swear to fucking God, you assholes, I will still kick your asses. Where are we going?" I snap again, as we pull up into an underground parking lot. They all seem excited. Diesel is nearly bouncing in his seat, and as soon as we stop, he's out and dragging me after him.

The others laugh as we head up some stairs, and when it turns into marble floors, I frown. We head to an office at the back. It's late, so I'm surprised when we open the door to see an old, grey-haired man in judge's clothes sitting behind this desk.

He doesn't seem surprised to see us. "Seriously, what the fuck is going on?" I growl. "You guys in trouble again?" I snort.

"Nah, you are, Little Bird," Diesel murmurs in my ear as he spanks me, making me yelp and move away, right into Kenzo's arms, who kisses me.

"You better tell her," Ryder warns, and Garrett laughs.

"Tell me now," I order.

"We are getting married!" Diesel cries out, and grins at me widely while I just blink at him.

"What the actual fuck?" I yell, throwing my hands in their air. "You're supposed to ask—a ring a—" I sputter.

"This isn't legal," the judge whines, and I throw him a glare.

"Stay the fuck out of this," I snap, even as I turn back to them.

"You heard him, it's not fucking legal," I snarl. They have been asking me for months, but I refuse to marry just one of them, it would

634

create jealousy...it seems my men have decided to break the rules once more—all of them marrying me while I officially take their last name.

Ryder rounds the desk and pulls the judge out, and I gawk as I realise he's tied to his chair...they kidnapped a fucking judge. Diesel presses a gun to his head, still grinning madly. "It's legal if we say it is." He giggles. "Now marry us."

I can't help but laugh. They saw a problem and found a way to fix it...an illegal way, of course, but it makes me melt inside as I look between them. "You crazy bastards, I hate you."

"Hate you too, love. What do you say? Want to get married, to be an official Viper?"

"Bitch, please, we already know I am." I snort. "Fuck it, let's get married."

"That's the spirit!" Diesel laughs, and Ryder steps forward and drops to his knee with a box in his hand. Garrett kneels next to him, a box in his hand as well, and with a wink at the judge, Diesel does the same. I blink and laugh as Kenzo drops down as well, all four on their knees, all holding boxes.

"Tell me there aren't four rings." I groan, even as I grin so wide my face hurts.

"Of course!" Diesel grins and opens his to reveal a beautiful orange stone set in a band etched in flames.

Kenzo opens his, and I laugh at the red stone with carved dice on the side of the ring.

"Baby," Garrett murmurs, drawing my gaze, and he open the box to reveal the ring from Daphne. "This was always yours, I just gave it away by mistake."

Ryder clears his throat as tears fill my eyes, and he opens his box to reveal a traditional, cold-looking, huge diamond. "Roxxane Viper, will you be ours?"

"Forever!" I laugh as they jump to their feet and circle me. "I still hate you," I mutter, making them all chuckle. We turn to the judge, and he sighs but seems to smile anyway.

"Well, you are all clearly crazy, but fuck it, whatever. Do you—"

The ceremony is quick, thanks to D, who tells him to hurry it up because he wants to put me in a white dress and cover it in our blood. Ryder kisses me first, sealing the deal before passing me to his brother who dips me, making me laugh. Garrett grips my cheeks, no words needed, as he looks into my eyes and kisses me so softly, like I'm made of glass.

Diesel? Diesel slashes his hand and then mine, making me gasp, and presses our bleeding palms together as he kisses me. "Forever, Little Bird."

I pull back and look between them all, having to smile.

I've got the rest of my life to make them pay for it. I can't wait, and judging by the expressions on their faces, neither can they.

I've learned a lot since I met them.

Like that life is not guaranteed, it's made up of thousands of tiny moments that span a lifetime. Choices, actions, each and every one leads us down different paths. My path, my choice, led me to them. Four men who saw past my skin and armour, past my smart mouth and anger, to the woman underneath. The beautifully flawed survivor, because that is who I am.

A survivor.

A warrior.

A queen.

A Viper.

I am all of those and so much more. When my path took me down the darkest of roads, I found the strength to go on at the very blackest of times. When I knew my parents didn't love me, when they broke my heart, I went on. When I was alone for the first time, when fear was my constant...I chose to go on.

Or when I held the hand of the first man I ever loved, the man who helped save me, as he died, I chose to fight. As I watched regret and wishes fill his tear-soaked eyes as his frail hand clutched mine, his voice raspy and skin grey...I chose to go on. But from that moment, I learned a lesson that lives with me always. Death comes for all of us, and until it does, we have to do our fucking best to live. To live our lives to the fullest, to never regret. To love so deeply it could fill an ocean, to not let fear stop you from being who you want to be.

Because if you don't, if you let fear win, regret will eat you up and it will be all you have at the end.

I refuse to be that person, I refuse to regret my life or who I am. So I choose them every goddamn day that I wake up. Four flawed, scarred, powerful men. Even when it's hard, even when the world is against us, I choose them every time, over and over, and they choose me. My heart is theirs, and theirs are mine.

We aren't perfect. We are criminals, gamblers, fighters, business-people, and assassins.

But these four criminals? They are my happiness.

They are my life.

They are my home, and wherever our path leads us now, we do it together.

Just five Vipers entwined in a den.

Until the end.

ABOUT THE AUTHOR

K.A Knight is an indie author trying to get all of the stories and characters out of her head. She loves reading and devours every book she can get her hands on, she also has a worrying caffeine addiction.

She leads her double life in a sleepy English town, where she spends her days writing like a crazy person.

Read more at K.A Knight's website
http://www.katieknightauthor.com
Join her Facebook Reader Group.
https://www.facebook.com/groups/KatiesKnights
Sign up for exclusive content and my newsletter
http://eepurl.com/drLLoj

 facebook.com/KatieKnightAuthor

twitter.com/K_AKnight

instagram.com/katieknightauthor

bookbub.com/authors/k-a-knight

ALSO BY K.A KNIGHT

THEIR CHAMPION SERIES

- The Wasteland
- The Summit
- The Cities

- The Forgotten
- The Lost

DAWNBREAKER SERIES

- Voyage to Ayama
- Dreaming of Ayama

THE LOST COVEN SERIES

- Aurora's Coven
- Aurora's Betrayal

HER MONSTERS SERIES

- Rage
- Hate

THE FALLEN GODS SERIES

- PrettyPainful
- *Pretty Bloody (Coming soon!)*
- *PrettyStormy (Coming soon!)*

STANDALONES

- Scarlett Limerence
- Nadia's Salvation
- The Standby
- Den of Vipers
- *Divers Heart* (*Coming Soon!*)

CO-AUTHOR PROJECTS

- Circus Save Me
- Taming The Ringmaster
- https://books2read.com/DTvolumeone (contains One Night Only and Circus Saves Christmas)
- The Wild Interview
- The Wild Tour
- The Hero Complex
- Shipwreck Souls
- The Horror Emporium
- Capturing Carmen
- Stealing Shiloh
- *Harboring Harlow* (*Coming soon!*)